Alan J. O'Reilly

Desired Haven

Llumina Press

By the Same Author:

Sound of Battle

Requests for permission to make copies of any part of this work should be mailed to Permissions Department, Llumina Press, PO Box 772246, Coral Springs, FL 33077-2246

ISBN: 1-59526-365-9

Printed in the United States of America by Llumina Press

Library of Congress Control Number: 2006922124

Desired Haven

One

At Rest

Grandma Colleen died yesterday. She went peacefully, in her sleep. We are deeply saddened of course, especially insofar as she appeared to be in good health. In truth, she'd never known bad health and she was still beautiful. Though her luxuriant auburn hair had long since faded to white, those green eyes hadn't lost their sparkle and her mind was as sharp as a razor.

Nevertheless, Grandpa's death last year undoubtedly contributed largely to her passing, so in a way, we half expected it. When husband and wife have been as close as they were for well-nigh sixty years, parting by death is hard on the survivor and though she put on a brave face, Grandma never really came to terms with her loss.

The rest of the family are making the arrangements and that has enabled me to start on the account that I always promised Grandma and Grandpa I would write. Better late than never. I hope they would have agreed I'll have told it like it was. It's something for which we should always be grateful. What is more, they did our country a great service at a time when understandably most of their generation simply wanted to get back to normal after the six-year-long ordeal of the 1939-45 War.

Uncle Bill and Aunt Annie[1] will be coming down for the funeral, likewise Uncle Jim and Aunt Jeannie[1] from Cumbria. They're not related to us but we've called them that for as long as I can remember because they've always been like family. It's quite a way for them but as Uncle Bill says: "You can always go the extra mile." He should know; he and Uncle Jim were World War Two paratroopers. They have made quite an impression on me ever since I was a young lad, along with my granddads, now sadly both deceased, so much so that I did a short service commission in the army when I left university about five years ago. I'll always be grateful for the way they taught me how to stand and be counted as a Bible believer in that environment. Not easy but like Uncle Jim said: "That's what makes it worthwhile."

We hope our other grandma can come too but it depends on what her GP says. As one of Grandma Colleen's dearest friends, she very much wants to be there.

Aunt Annie was especially upset because she and Grandma Colleen went back over sixty years, to when they both started nursing at the General on Teesside, at the outbreak of the war. In fact, Aunt Annie had a frightening experience there during the Blitz[1] that relates to this narrative, so without further delay, I'd better start putting things in context.

For that, we've got to go back to the spring of 1945, to a British Casualty Clearing Station in the shadow of the frowning, jungle-clad Pegu Yomas range in Burma and a night of torrential rain, during the height of the monsoon.

Two

Monsoon

The two slim young women in Jungle Green protective dress and trench mackintoshes sprinted across the vehicle park that was fast turning into a patch of mire beneath the downpour, their boots splashing through puddles. One of them pushed aside the flap at the entrance to their mess tent and held it open for her companion, who hastened inside. The other girl quickly followed.

"Chuckin' it down," she exclaimed, letting drop the canvas and taking hold of the towel her friend held out to her "Thanks, Coll, I reckon Noah'd be on edge out there. At least the tents don't leak." She doffed her raincoat and began dabbing at her blonde locks with the towel.

"Met report said an early monsoon, Trish," said the other girl. She took off her mac and pressed a towel against her shock of auburn hair. "Brew's up, nevertheless," she added brightly. "Woody's a gem, best orderly in Fourteenth Army."

A couple of minutes later they were seated at the trestle table in the centre of the floor space, sipping the well-sugared concoction from enamel mugs, by the flickering glare of a paraffin lamp.

"Be a long night, Coll," murmured the blonde-haired Trish.

"Yeah, better top up the urn for Robbie and Gwen," said Colleen, with reference to their two QA colleagues, who were assisting in theatre. She arose from the table, tipped a couple of pints of water into the container, adjusted the paraffin burner and resumed her seat.

Casualties had been streaming back for days on end from the battles that raged further south as Allied infantry and armour advanced doggedly towards Rangoon, against fanatical, indeed suicidal, Japanese resistance. The wounded were a typical Fourteenth Army conglomeration, sturdy little Ghurkas, tall, bearded Sikhs, all manner of Indians from dark-skinned Madrassis to lighter-skinned Pathans plus the English, Welsh, Ulster and Scots contingents of the all-British battalions. Sodden, shocked, filthy, shivering, lacerated by bullet and shrapnel, they were stretchered into Resus in their blood-soaked JGs to be cleaned up, plasma-transfused, injected and resuscitated for emergency theatre. Many needed additional treatment for suppurating jungle sores, malaria or dysentery.

The strained whispers of those that could speak unfolded litanies of horror with which the Sisters were all too familiar.

"It's like all the devils in hell, Sister, a Banzai. Blow half of 'em to bits, rest'll keep comin' 'til you have to use the bayonet."

"You hear the odd random shot, Sister. They're firin' from the trees, want you to shoot back, give away your position, so they can stonk the daylights out of you."

"Japs'll crawl up close at night, Sister. Call out like our own blokes; 'Help me, I'm wounded.' We fell for it in the Arakan and got cut up pretty bad. Can never drop your guard or the slit-eyed rascals'll be all over you."

"It's OK, Sister, I know the leg's got to come off. Could be a lot worse – they'll never send me back there now, thank God."

Colleen and Trish had been on their feet for most of the last day and night. The occasional hiatus like this one was heaven sent, after which they'd return to Resus and rejoin the orderlies on duty, including one invaluable Indian OR per shift who could interpret for his Urdu-speaking countrymen. Colleen and Trish's QA companions had been similarly stretched and were due for a much-needed rest as soon as they'd finished in theatre.

Rain drummed heavily on the canvas roof, cascading in rivulets into the drainage ditch adjacent to the tent. The air inside was well-nigh stifling and both girls sat with sleeves rolled up and shirts partially unbuttoned, elbows resting on the tabletop. They could hear the thudding of artillery, its flashes adding to the spasms of forked lightning that lit up the vehicle park. Rolling thunderclaps mingled with the roar of the guns.

"Should be OK, the ones for theatre," said Trish.

"Hell for them coming up here in the ambulances, though, on a night like this," her friend said, taking another sip of tea. "Roads must be quagmires in parts. When's the next lot due?"

"Any minute, I reckon," said Trish. "Uh-oh, do you hear what I hear?" she added, inclining her head.

The sound of tyres squelching through mud caught their attention and they set aside their mugs. Almost at the same time, a male voice called urgently from outside.

"Sister Calder! Sister McGrath! Next convoy's here!"

"Dear old Woody," said Colleen. She rose to her feet, adjusted her clothing and reached for her mackintosh.

"Always on the ball," said Trish, also getting up.

Grandma Colleen little knew that one of the casualties in the approaching convoy would have a significant impact on her life, and on that of her friend Trish Calder. How he came to be there must now be told, by reference to events that began the previous afternoon, during another deluge of rain.

"Mr Calvert!"

A rangy young subaltern hastened from the assembly area in response to the summons relayed by an OR and knelt by the stretcher. He stared down at the waxen face of his company commander, whose voice came hoarsely through mud-stained lips flecked with bloodied foam. The major had been shot during the action at the crossroads. All the company officers apart from Calvert had suffered wounds in the encounter, necessitating evacuation.

This left Sergeant-Major Warwick as Calvert's second-in-command.

In addition, the company's remaining two sergeants were on secondment elsewhere in the battalion to provide much-needed experienced leadership. The CO was of necessity gambling on the relative strength of battle-seasoned corporals and ORs amongst Calvert's men but it left the company's command structure seriously stretched.

The OC was understandably perturbed.

Also kneeling beside the major, a worried-looking Royal Army Medical Corpsman kept a watchful eye on the drip bottle mounted above the casualty, striving to keep the rain off the major's face by holding out a gas cape above his head.

"You shouldn't try to talk, sir," the RAMC man advised. He glanced toward a nearby jeep with a stretcher carrier mounted. The OC had refused a place in an ambulance. "Give it to one of my boys," he'd said.

"The hell with that," gasped the major. "Listen, Calvert, you know the drill, you've got to press on at all costs." The OC stopped abruptly, coughing up blood coloured mucus. The expression on the RAMC orderly's face grew more anxious.

"Yes, sir," said Calvert. "We'll sweep the houses either side for snipers and MGs. Sappers'll go forward with us to deal with booby traps. MMG and mortar teams will follow."

The OC nodded, his breathing laboured.

"Good lad," he wheezed. "Don't forget, Nips'll blow themselves up with you if they can."

The officer coughed again, turned his head to one side and spat blood.

"Right, sir," said Calvert.

The major was citing well-established facts but it was typical of his paternal concern for "the lads" that he should reiterate them to his junior commander.

"We really ought to get you aboard, sir," the RAMC man urged.

"OK, OK," the major grunted testily, blinking away raindrops that evaded the cape. "It's all yours, Digger. Good luck."

"Yes, sir. Thank you, sir."

They shook hands, and the medics hoisted their charge aboard the jeep. It trundled away into the splashing gloom. Lieutenant Matt Calvert, formerly of the Ninth Australian Division, AIF, now on secondment to a British infantry battalion battling for the crucial railhead town fifty miles north of Rangoon, jogged back to his formation, raindrops spilling from his bush hat.

He stopped beside a waterlogged ditch by the road that led into the residential area of the town's northern sector. Two figures were crouching in the ditch, Sergeant-Major Warwick and Private Grafton, Calvert's batman and acting signaller, carrying the Number Eighteen set. Calvert stepped in next to them and hunched down.

"Tanks still bogged, Sergeant-Major?" he asked.

"According to the latest from Battalion, sir," said Warwick. He glanced at Grafton, who nodded.

"Won't be with us 'til well after sunup, sir," he said.

"We go in anyway," Calvert informed them. "We'll leapfrog through each property in turn, winkle out the Nips as we go, sappers with the leading sections. You take this side, Sergeant-Major. I'll take the other. Follow me."

Rickety dwellings mounted on thick bamboo stilts were dimly visible in the enveloping downpour. There the main body of the foe would be lying in wait. Calvert was acutely conscious that the remainder of the company had to press on before the Japanese launched a counter-attack. Small arms fire clattered continuously from right and left of their positions and from further south where other assaulting battalions were trying to wrest the railway station from enemy hands. Reports of grenade bursts sounded persistently amid the gunfire. Flares pop-popped repeatedly, lazily shedding their phosphorescent glare in the darkening skies.

"Yes, sir," Warwick and Grafton said in turn. They each held rifles at the ready.

Calvert sped at a crouching run to the opposite verge where a forward platoon waited apprehensively in the drenching rain amid dripping palm fronds. Warwick ran to the head of a platoon on the other side of the road. Grafton accompanied Calvert.

"Move out," said Matt to the corporal in command of the leading section.

He waved the signal to Warwick, who acknowledged it and relayed the order to his parallel formation.

Matt crept towards the nearest dwelling, Lee Enfield carbine raised. His sections advanced in open order, REs in support, the men's boots squelching in soggy turf. Sub-units filed off to check the surrounds, mindful of trip wires and telltale signs of disturbed earth concealing mines.

At Calvert's order, Grafton hurled a couple of flares in amongst the wooden stilts on which the house stood. The illumination showed nothing significant. The house appeared deserted.

"Thought so," grated Calvert.

"They're there somewhere, sir," said Grafton anxiously.

"Surrounds clear, sir," said the corporal, hastening up.

"OK, Corporal," said Calvert. "Grenades. Then follow me, Gruffie."

The NCO summoned a couple of his ORs. At his command, they lobbed Mills Bombs through the open window spaces. The explosions ripped and flashed through the interior, shearing the front door off its hinges.

Covered by a half-section, Calvert and Grafton dashed up onto the front veranda. Reaching the front door aperture, Matt tossed in another flare. As Grafton covered him, he leapt inside, sweeping his weapon across the room lit by the blaze. It too was empty, even of furnishings. With battle imminent, the town's citizens had fled, taking what belongings they could.

"Check out the rest, Corporal," Calvert ordered his point section commander, who'd caught up with him.

Followed by Grafton, Calvert vaulted out of the nearest window and dropped onto the soft earth below.

"All clear, sir," whispered the NCO to Calvert after his men had gone through the entire house. He jumped down from a rear side window.

At that instant, a fusillade of rifle and machine gun bullets slashed splinters from the house's timbered supports and snapped spitefully overhead, interspersed by tracer. Calvert's men immediately returned fire. Across the road, another similar outburst indicated that Sergeant-Major Warwick's force had likewise encountered opposition. Grenades thrown by the defenders in the next house detonated in violent yellow spasms, obscuring their fire positions but not soon enough.

"Second window from back," yelled Calvert, his voice mingling with others shouting the same warning. "MG fire rear corner ground level!"

Calvert's right-hand section was enfilading the Japanese position when suddenly the enemy survivors debouched from their positions and charged screaming like banshees, brandishing rifles with bayonets fixed. Caught in a withering crossfire, most of the enemy were quickly silenced. A few blundered in amongst Calvert's men but were summarily dealt with, shot, clubbed or bayoneted to death.

"Sergeant-Major, casualties?" shouted Calvert, venturing to the verge.

"None, sir, enemy accounted for," Warwick's calm north-country voice called back.

The company pushed on doggedly as darkness closed in. Time and again, the sappers had to deal with obstacles placed adroitly in the line of advance, to which explosive charges had been wired. Split bamboo stakes also barred the way, razor sharp and steeped in human excrement to infect any gashes sustained. The REs used plastic explosive or Bangalore Torpedoes to clear a path through the menaces, punctuating the advance with further deafening bursts and lurid flashes to add to the flares and flashes of White Phosphorus grenades thrown forward to pinpoint the defenders. The fetid smoke of battle hung over the scene, though the pelting rain doused any fires.

Through it all, the young Australian led from the front, as he had done at El Alamein and in New Guinea and ever since he'd joined the battalion in February, in time for the crossing of the Irrawaddy River and the subsequent capture of Meiktila, vital to the subjugation of Mandalay. Here in Burma, the dour determination of infantrymen from the old country had elicited Matt's deepest admiration.

Nevertheless, concealed snipers exacted a price and the RAMC men were busy attending to the victims. Individual defenders tried to inflict widespread casualties by rushing out and blowing themselves to pieces with satchel charges attached to their bodies, as the major had warned. Oftentimes, unlike their colleagues who'd died in the first encounter, they sprinted forward silently, hard to detect in the soaking gloom. All the shouts were in English.

"Seven Section, Jap bombers ten o'clock, open fire!"

"Nine Section, Jap bomber front gate, get him!"

"Medic! Corporal Howard's down, medic!"

Calvert was growing increasingly apprehensive. He sensed the enemy were gathering strength for a counterattack. In the lee of a derelict outhouse on the corner of a wide intersection, he conferred again with Warwick.

"We'll have to hold the line here, Sergeant-Major," he said grimly.

Warwick nodded sagely.

"I'll get the lads organised, sir. We'll be ready."

"Right, Sergeant-Major. I'll inform Battalion."

"Seems like the other companies are held up as well, sir," said Warwick.

To left and right, the bickering of small arms fire and the 'crump' of grenades continued incessantly but had not advanced in the last hour. Calvert nodded. His second-in-command hastened off to oversee the defence.

"Check where the MMGs and mortars are, Gruffie," Matt ordered his batman.

Medium machine gun and mortar sections from Support Company were following up from the crossroads. They supported each company from flank positions taken up as the enemy were pushed back. Infantry sections from the reserve company in turn protected the mortar and machine gun teams. It was a precarious and difficult business in the dark but the teams were past masters of their craft and by means of aerial photographs minutely studied before the attack, those allocated to Matt's company had sited themselves to cover the entire thoroughfare in front of Calvert's sector.

Grafton reported a minute or so later.

"MGs and mortars in position, sir."

"Tell them to watch for the Verey," said Calvert. "Then they can range on the intersection."

Calvert and Grafton crept to the front yard of the house, where Bren gunners and riflemen were frantically digging in.

Warwick returned to confirm that the perimeter was established.

Matt fired the Verey.

Its pop and whoosh heralded the green glare lighting up the intersection. Red tracer from the Vickers mediums streaked along the thoroughfare. Mortar bombs crashed down after them. Showers of mud flew up and splashed to earth.

"They've got the range, Gruffie," said Calvert. Grafton radioed the information.

"They'll try and overrun us, Sergeant Major," Matt said to Warwick. "Drive a wedge between the flank companies and split the battalion in two."

"We'll hold 'em, sir," Warwick assured him, then jogged back to his HQ on the other side of the road, now a channel of liquid mud.

Thatched bungalows on the far side of the intersection loomed threateningly out of the dark, lit by lightning flashes from the rainstorm that continued unabated.

Matt sensed that the enemy were close by, many, many of them, hidden in the shadow of the bungalows. Right and left of him, lying beneath clumps of shrubbery in shallow fire trenches hastily scraped in the sodden earth, his men waited, poised behind their weapons.

Suddenly, the darkness to their front *moved*.

Calvert instantly fired off another flare. Warwick did so almost the same second. The double glare illuminated a bizarre scene. Like ragged devils from the nether world, their Oriental foe surged forward en masse, again *silently*, their split-toed shoes making virtually no sound as they converged on both arms of Calvert's defence line.

The Verey lights were the signal to open fire. Bombs fired from mortars with sights on their lowest setting exploded with thunderous flashes in amongst the attackers, hurling up dismembered body parts, some flopping onto the ground near Matt's HQ. Enfilading MMG bursts etched with tracer tore into the onrushing Japanese. Calvert's men poured hundreds of rounds from rifles, SMGs and Brens into the assaulting waves at virtually point-blank range. The roar of concerted battle was transcended only by the screams of its victims. All across the intersection, they lay mutilated by the maelstrom of jagged, searing, tearing metal.

Yet incredibly, some Japanese staggered on to close with their antagonists in amongst the house gardens and bungalow grounds, wielding rifle, bayonet, pistol and Samurai sword. The alert defenders quickly dispatched most of the frenzied interlopers.

But not all.

"To your right, sir!"

Half-crouched, intent on cohesion of the perimeter to his direct front, where the foe was pressing hardest, Calvert glanced in the direction indicated by Grafton's desperate shout, drowned in the bark of Gruffie's Lee-Enfield. A Jap officer fell prone, dropping his uplifted sword but in that instant Calvert heard the harsh crack of a pistol shot that sent his batman sprawling, clutching a bloodied laceration where the round had fractured the collarbone. He saw the terrifying Dervish-like figure lunging at him and fired into it. The figure lurched backwards but Calvert was horrified at the sight of an object that tumbled from the dead Jap's other hand.

Shouting "Grenade!" he flung himself face down, to be bludgeoned by the pile-driver force of the explosion that slammed him into unconsciousness.

Perhaps the Great Enemy had an inkling of what lay ahead. Even as the ambulance convey wended its way northwards to Grandma's CCS, bearing amongst its passengers the wounded Matt Calvert and his faithful batman, the adversary was exploiting someone else to serve his purposes – while Providence was about to furnish a second individual to thwart them. Some of what follows is conjecture, but the events happened as Grandma described them.

INA Subahdar Ranjeev Kapoor surveyed the encampment from beneath the dripping scrub on the jungle fringe. He smiled, confident that his luck was about to change. After deserting the Japanese HQ, where he had served as a liaison officer, he'd existed for weeks by scrounging for rations from unburied corpses of his countrymen and their allies, pilfering from Burmese villages, digging up edible roots with his bayonet until it had fractured at the hilt on a concealed rock. He was thus weaponless, having that day lost his carbine crossing a swollen *chaung* when the current almost swept him off his feet.

But now he was gazing at a fully equipped British Field Hospital, or CCS as they called it. The cursed British! They always had the best of everything and they still ruled over his country. So much for allies, he reflected bitterly, even if the Japanese had won, he knew now they would have been even more ruthless masters. They despised the INA.

Nevertheless, these English swine could at least fulfil the gnawing pangs in his stomach. The enemy had thrust a deep, narrow salient on this side of the Yomas but though it was near the battlefront, they obviously believed this area to be secure because only minimal guards were posted and he'd easily eluded patrols. Moreover, he'd even seen women amongst the CCS personnel, nursing Sisters, no doubt, pale-skinned, willowy creatures, tall, with light-brown, blonde or reddish hair, typically English, and dressed in the same clothing as the men, a custom that his family would have considered grossly immoral. Subahdar Kapoor's lips twitched with distaste. With considerable chagrin, he knew he could simply walk out with his hands above his head and have his every need attended to as a prisoner of war. But that would be an insult to his ancestors. The enemy's air force had dropped thousands of leaflets promising care and protection for all members of the Japanese, Indian National and Burmese National Armies who surrendered to the advancing British-Indian Fourteenth Army but he'd had only one use for the copies he'd found.

He had identified the messing area and field kitchen, with a storage tent adjacent to them, stocked with victuals. All were located well within the camp perimeter, away from the sentries, who patrolled the outskirts and vehicle entrances. Glancing up at the heavily overcast sky, Kapoor knew that the monsoon must burst upon them soon, earlier than anticipated but that would help conceal him. He would wait until well after dark, then make his move.

Several hours later the monsoon had broken and, drenched to the skin, Subahdar Kapoor succeeded in creeping unseen inside the storage tent. It was only yards from the field kitchen where two cooks were preparing a late meal, probably for patients recovering from their operations. Kapoor had seen most of the medical personnel assembling by shifts in their mess tents earlier and he knew these British formations ran like clockwork. Intent on their labour, the cooks' backs were turned to him and the glare of their lamps filtered into the storage tent. Good! That would aid his mission. Moreover, several ration boxes had been broached for the meals and some were still half full. Excellent! The cooks would reseal them later but for now Subahdar Kapoor could help himself.

He quickly filled his pockets with tubes of condensed milk and packets of dried fruits, pressed cereals and dehydrated vegetables. He had an American water canteen with its form-fitting container in which to soak them.

Stealthily he made his exit and headed for the jungle fringe. The he paused. Suppose the tents that housed the personnel contained valuables? These he could trade with local villagers for more food.

He slipped into one of the nearer tents. Two camp beds, shrouded in mosquito netting, stood side-by-side on a floor of water-proofing with a gap of a few feet between them. The absent occupants were two of the nursing Sisters. He sensed that immediately. Groping in the darkness, he disturbed a small book at the head of one bed. He discovered another copy at the head of the other and straightaway realised what they were.

"These women must worship the Christian God," he whispered, picking up one of the Bibles. "Should I worship You, God of the Christians? My own gods have failed."

But he was more intent on his immediate quest. He dropped the Book and turned his attention to the tin trunks that he could feel in the dark behind the beds.

"Dressers," he said to himself, smirking. "These Englishwomen have turned their trunks into dressers. They all want to look like Hollywood whores."

He deftly rummaged through the items atop the trunks, seizing upon combs, steel mirrors, brooches, compacts, lipstick containers and other manicure items. These too he stuffed into his pockets.

Someone was coming!

He slithered under one of the beds. A nursing Sister entered, removed her coat and sat on the end of the other bed, uttering a sigh. He reflected it was the first female voice he had heard in a long time. She rubbed her head with a towel, then took off her boots and short puttees. He had a chance to escape, if she fell asleep quickly and her companion delayed her return.

But then, she paused, swiftly replaced her boots, stood up and backed toward the entrance. Involuntarily, he gasped in dismay.

"Orderly!" he heard her call. He had to escape, now or never!

Kapoor scrambled out from beneath the bed, rising nimbly to his feet.

The girl screamed.

"Stupid cow!" he snarled and lunged at her throat. He'd have to throttle her. His lean fingers were already fastening around her neck. He sensed the touch of her delicate skin.

A savage blow to his chin, followed by a sickening thrust in the groin blocked his attack.

"Bitch!" he hissed. He lunged at her again but she had fallen through the tent entrance, still screaming.

Abruptly another form confronted him, leaping over the Sister. Too late Subahdar Kapoor glimpsed the muzzle. A blinding flash...

"Well, you're back with us again."

Calvert stirred at the sound of the gentle female voice. He'd woken up beneath a mosquito net in a darkened tent, realising that he was warm, relatively dry and lying on his right side in a camp bed. The whole of his left side, from his head to his waist, ached from what seemed to be a thousand sword cuts. A drip bottle was suspended by a cord above his left arm, connected via rubber tubing to a syringe inserted into the limb, fastened with sticking plaster at the point of entry. This spot ached, too.

He looked up at the speaker, who had pulled the net back and saw an English nursing Sister, the first he'd seen since he had gone down to the hospital at Alexandria from El Alamein.

An orderly in a floppy bush jacket stood beside the Sister holding a hurricane lamp and in its muted glow the young nursing officer looked lithe and slender, clad in JGs, with blonde hair cut short above her collar. The loveliness of her face matched that of her voice and she bestowed on Calvert the most engaging smile. With calm efficiency, she took his pulse, checked his drip, placed a small thermometer between his lips, recorded his temperature and carefully examined the wad of dressing wrapped about him for any fresh bleeding. It hurt to turn his head.

"I'm Sister Calder," she said softly. "I was with the MO when you were brought into theatre. He took some grenade fragments out of you, but you're going to be fine, even if you feel a bit sore. I sewed you up[2]."

"You're a dab hand with a needle, Sister," Calvert managed to whisper. "Feels like I've been crocheted, well and truly." His throat was also sore.

The Sister laughed demurely, a beautiful sound.

"Your batman, Private Grafton, has been asking about you," she said. "I'll tell him you've come round."

"Is Gruffie OK, Sister?" Calvert asked anxiously.

"He is," she said. "Collarbone fracture with the GSW but they'll heal."

Trish explained briefly where Calvert was.

"You're the first Australian we've seen here," she added, sounding intrigued.

"It's a long story, Sister," he said. "Only too happy to tell you."

"I'll come see you again in a bit," she said before moving on to the patient in the next bed. "Lance Corporal Wood here'll get you a cup of tea and sort out any other needs."

Please hurry back, Sister, Calvert said to himself. "And I bet every bloke on the ward thinks the same," he whispered.

Nursing Officers Gwen Lewis and Robyn Gray pushed through the tent flap, took off their mackintoshes and joined their companions at the ward's admin desk.

"Bad as last year's monsoon," said Gwen. "Worse than winter in Llangollen."

Colleen smiled at the way Welsh Gwen pronounced it "Thlangothlen."

"All Norwich'd be awash in no time at this rate," remarked Robyn, who was from East Anglia. "Any more convoys due?" She began towelling down her fair hair.

"Not 'til first light," said Colleen.

"Any more cases need special attention?" Gwen asked, patting her light brown hair with a towel.

"Some more abdominals and head fractures, a few more amputees and facials, I'm afraid," said Trish. "But they're stable."

"We'll try and get some food into whoever we can," Robyn suggested.

Trish nodded. "Lots of them are still coming in like scarecrows, what with being on half rations for weeks, poor lads," she said.

"We've got an Australian over there," said Colleen. She inclined her head in Calvert's direction. "I think my oppo[3] fancies him."

Colleen winked at Robyn and Gwen, who turned enquiring glances on Sister Calder, seated at the desk.

"You minx, Coll," whispered Trish, laughing softly. "All I said was I lived in Banbury and my dad's a vicar."

"An Australian? What's he doing here? Is he air force?" asked Robyn. She washed her hands in a bowl of hot water supplied by the orderlies and dried them on a fresh towel. Her husband, also from East Anglia, was a Flight Lieutenant with 221 Group RAF. Trish shook her head.

"On secondment to one of our battalions," she explained. "Said he wanted to go up to Oxford to do a Master's after the war. On our common Anglo-Saxon heritage."

"Curiouser and curiouser. You must have really got talking," said Gwen, also carrying out the preparatory ablutions.

"Only while I was changing some of his dressings," said Trish nonchalantly. "Anyway, I've given him a shot of morphine and he's asleep now."

Robyn and Gwen went over the rest of the patient details with their companions and departed for their rounds. Colleen reached for her mac.

"Should be able to get in a couple of hours before sunup," she said with a yawn. "You coming, Trish?"

"In a minute," said Trish. She glanced at the papers spread before her next to the flickering lamp. "I'll just tidy this up."

"OK," said Colleen. "See you in a bit, then."

Colleen stepped out of the tent into the warm, teeming rain and trudged toward the quarters she shared with Trish, head bent under the mac's hood, her arms folded across her chest. This time, she didn't run.

"I'm too knackered," she said.

Lance Corporal Wood and a couple of his fellow orderlies had adjourned to the ORs Mess for a quick brew before turning in. Taking off his bush hat and gas cape, Wood removed his bush jacket and placed it over the back of a chair at the end of a trestle table close by the tent flap. Sitting down, he reached into a pocket in the jacket for his cigarettes. An ex-collier from Tyneside, his wiry physique was taut with sinewy muscle beneath his string vest but more noticeable was the forty-five calibre Webley revolver inserted into a cutaway shoulder holster strapped to his chest.

"Keep tellin' you, Woody," one of his mates admonished him while pouring compo tea into the mugs set out on the table. "You oughta stash that cannon. We ain't in a box you know[4]."

"Can't leave the lassies without protection, man," protested the doughty pitman as he lit a cigarette. "Never hear the end of it from the missus."

"Reckon lassies'd *want* protection if they knew an armed and dangerous Geordie lunatic was on wards with 'em everyday," said Woody's other mate, who was squeezing sweetened condensed milk into the tea. He passed a mug to each of his companions.

"Ah, champion, thanks, Donny, man," said Woody "Gives it some body, that."

"And *you'd* never hear the end of it from the CO," the first speaker warned. "He'd have you in the glasshouse 'til kingdom come."

Woody's thin face creased in a grin. They'd had this conversation several times. The banter flew back and forth as they sipped their brew.

"He's not going to find out, is he?" Wood said confidently. "He never comes in here."

"He'll find out if you use it."

"Aye, but then I'd be a hero, man, Mentioned in Dispatches, me."

"Mentioned in close arrest, more like, if Army Regs are owt to go by."

"I didn't join the army, man, I joined the Durhams."

"So you keep telling us," said Woody's other mate. He stared into his half empty mug, then looked up, puzzled at the sound.

"What was that?" he asked. "Hey, Woody!"

But Lance Corporal Wood had already shot out through the tent flap, his chair having thumped noisily onto the floor in his wake. His discarded cigarette rolled off the tabletop.

Still poring over the patient records, Trish was startled by the sound of a cry, unmistakably from a woman.

"My God, Colleen!" she exclaimed, leaping up. More cries of distress arose.

Trish dashed out through the tent flap, heedless of the soaking deluge, to be greeted by the sudden report of a pistol shot.

Colleen entered the darkened tent, took off her mac, pushed the mosquito netting back and sank down onto her camp bed with a sigh. She reached for a towel on the end of the bed, dried her face and hair, then leant over to unfasten her puttees[5] and unlace her boots. Removing these and unwrapping the cotton rags she preferred instead of socks, she felt her feet and ankles for leeches. These bloodsuckers could crawl in through an eyelet and glut themselves until they were bloated like putrid black grapes, squashed and messy when you removed a boot. You had to use a glowing cigarette end to get the little beggars off, or salt. Even Wellie boots weren't entirely proof against them but she found these too cumbersome.

Thankfully, for once her flesh was free of the loathsome parasites and Colleen began unbuttoning her shirt.

Then she paused, the hairs of her scalp prickling. Something was in the tent, she was sure.

Clammy beads of perspiration broke out on her forehead. Was it a rat, or a snake, flooded out of its lair, a cobra, maybe? The girls had seen several of these beasts, ugly brutes that could rear up waist high, hissing with bared fangs and hoods spread. Some of them could actually spit venom at your eyes.

Then she noticed the smell of male sweat.

It hadn't registered at first, because it was so familiar. Her daily environment usually reeked of blood, sweat, pus and other bodily secretions besides iodoform, anaesthetic and insect repellent.

Thoughts tumbled through her brain. There's a man in here! Where? Is he armed? Her keen ears caught a faint sound, like – a breath?

Colleen quickly replaced her boots, cautiously stood up and edged back towards the tent flap.

"Orderly!" she called anxiously. "Woody!"

In that instant a ragged form slithered out from under Trish's bed, scrabbling like a giant spider.

"Woody!" Colleen screamed again.

With a guttural exclamation the form sprang at her throat.

In terror she felt his fingers fastening on her skin.

With great presence of mind, Colleen rammed the heel of her hand under the attacker's jaw and brought her knee sharply up into his groin.

He faltered, snarling with fury, but went for her again as she lost balance and fell heavily through the tent flap, soaked almost instantly, still yelling for Woody.

A booted figure sprinted out of the rain-pelted gloom and leapt over her.

Colleen saw a flash and heard an ear-splitting crack as Lance Corporal Wood's revolver discharged full into her assailant's face. It erupted in a spray of blood and brain.

Then her rescuer was helping her up. She could smell cordite smoke.

"It's all right, Sister," he said gently. "It's all right now."

She leant on his arm, sobbing.

Other personnel were converging on the scene from all sides, Trish among them. A couple of ORs ventured into the tent. Colleen couldn't hear what they said above the throbbing in her temples. She was shaking and Trish put an arm around her. Lance Corporal Wood quickly conveyed them both to the QAs' mess tent.

"Get the CO!" he called back over his shoulder. "Sister McGrath's all right, but she's had a shock."

Inside the mess tent, he promptly poured her a tot of rum and passed it to her.

"Here, Sister," he said. "I'll get a brew on."

"Thanks Woody, please do," said Trish. "Any chance you could get hold of a blanket?"

She checked Colleen for any injury, then sat beside her at the mess table, again putting an arm around her distraught friend's shoulders.

"Aye, Sister, right away, I'll get a couple, you've both had a soaking," he said, turning up the burner for the urn. "Will I get you some dry clothes?"

"That's OK, I'll sort it but thanks, Woody," said Trish with a smile.

She turned her gaze back to Colleen, who was holding the mug containing the rum with trembling hand. She swallowed the scorching liquid, teeth still chattering with shock.

"Thanks again, Woody," said Colleen.

She was struggling to keep her voice steady and trying to smile. Before Wood departed to fetch the blankets, he proffered her a steaming mug of richly sugared compo tea. She took it gratefully.

Hastening out through the tent flap, Wood almost collided with the CO, who'd hurried over from his HQ in response to the urgent summons. The officer stared wide-eyed at the butt of the Webley showing conspicuously in Wood's shoulder holster. The lance corporal snapped to attention.

"Just getting a couple of blankets for the Sisters, sir," he explained. "Seems a Jiff deserter invaded the ladies' tent for a spot of loot but I've accounted for him and I'll forward a full report first thing, sir."

"Thank you, Corporal, please do," said the CO. "How did you know he was a Jiff?"

"Caught a glimpse in the muzzle flash, sir. Lads'll have his dog tags by now."

"Right, then, Corporal, carry on, I'll see to Sister McGrath."

"Yes, sir," said Wood. Smartly, he stepped outside.

The CO carried out his own examination to confirm Colleen hadn't been injured.

"Heard the shot," he said. "Sent my batman to investigate and he bumped into Wood's mate."

Wood returned with the blankets and then discreetly retired.

"You've done extremely well, Sister," said the CO. "I'll leave you with Sister Calder for now. You can doss down here for the rest of the night while your place gets fumigated. I'll send in some more bedding and post a double guard. See you after sunup."

"There'll be no action taken against Lance-Corporal Wood, will there, sir?" Colleen asked anxiously. "I know he's not supposed to be armed inside the perimeter."

The CO shook his head vigorously. "No, of course not," he assured her. "Just as well he was. Explains why he always wears that floppy jacket that's about two sizes too big for him, cunning Geordie beggar. Pity about the dengue, the Durhams lost a good man."

"Our gain, sir," said Trish warmly.

"Hmm," the CO murmured. "Maybe I ought to get him retransferred. Can't be anything wrong with his joints now, the way he must've legged it over to here."

Lance Corporal Wood had been medically downgraded after a severe bout of dengue fever and transferred from the DLI to the RAMC.

"Please, not right away, sir," said Colleen in a trembling voice, though again she forced a smile. "He's my Sir Galahad just now."

"Well, perhaps not," said the CO. "I'll tell Sisters Gray and Lewis you're OK. They're desperate to know, as are the patients. Good night, ladies."

"Good night, sir," they both said. "And thanks again."

The CO left and Colleen continued to sip her tea, as Trish adjusted the blanket around her friend's shoulders.

"How do you feel now, love?" she asked. "You sure did well to fend him off."

"OK," said Colleen, her voice still shaking a little. "Yes, thank the Lord. Not every day you get to tangle with a marauding Jap. Dear old Woody, deserves another stripe."

"Amen to that, but seems it wasn't a Jap, actually," said Trish. She topped up Colleen's drink from the compo container.

"No?"

"No, INA apparently. I'm pretty sure Woody said 'a Jiff' when he was talking to the CO. Though you couldn't have known in the dark."

"Yeah, I was a bit *non compos mentis* at that point. Must be lots of 'em fending for themselves out there, now their army's breaking up. Why do you reckon he was in our tent? I'd have thought he'd have headed for the cook shack"

Colleen took a long draft of tea. The hot brew slid fierily down her throat but she was glad of its sedative effect.

"Seems he'd already been there," said Trish. "I overhead one of the lads say his pockets were full of nosh. After our stuff to barter with, most likely. Agile chap, to hide under my bed like he did."

"Thieving sod."

"Not half. We'll all be looking under our beds from now on," said Trish. She helped herself to a mug of tea.

"Sisters?" said a voice from outside the tent. "We've got your bedding here."

"Thanks, lads," Trish called. "You can bring it in."

"You better turn in, Coll, you look knackered," she advised, after the orderlies had departed. "I'll get some dry clothes for us when you're tucked up."

Colleen nodded and thanked her.

"You know," she said, trying to sound light-hearted. "Thank God I tumbled to that gyppo when I did. Another minute and I'd've been down to bra and pants. Imagine me traipsing round the camp in that gear."

"A tad embarrassing," said Trish, laughing. "Boys would've enjoyed it, though."

Then instinctively she put her arm around her friend's shoulders once more, a moment before Colleen lowered her head to her chest and started sobbing again.

It wasn't the last time the Enemy tried to cancel out Grandma - and by Enemy, I don't mean anything human. He had good reason for attempting to do so. And Grandma would need abundance of grace to survive.

Three

Naples

Providence had dramatically intervened on Grandma Colleen's behalf during the night of the monsoon. We must now look at how she had been brought to that point of crisis – and why the Great Enemy made such a desperate attempt on her life.

Colleen's odyssey to the CCS beside the Yomas began the previous summer when she boarded an armed merchant cruiser at Liverpool docks bound for the Italian theatre of operations. The Normandy invasion had consumed vast resources of RAMC manpower and the British Eighth Army, battling doggedly through the Apennines, was critically short of nurses.

Paradoxically, even though it had received a share of convalescents from Normandy, Sister McGrath's hospital unit, at Ormskirk, seemed to have been otherwise forgotten, in the way such things happen in wartime. Colleen and three of her friends therefore volunteered for Italy.

"Beats forever lining up in head squares and starched frocks for forces newspaper photographs," declared June Taylor, the eldest and most senior of the four. Tall, with richly dark-brown hair and blue eyes, she was of striking appearance and commanding presence. A diplomat's daughter from St Albans, she'd joined the QAs by forfeiting promotion to Sister, a considerable sacrifice about which her family hadn't altogether approved.

"And filling in forms or falling in for inspections," added Marjorie Hopgood, a cheerful Londoner with whom Colleen shared a cabin. Margie, or 'Hoppy' as she was usually known, was a pretty brunette who enjoyed swimming, tennis, volleyball, cycling, dancing and bending the rules. She and Colleen got on famously.

After almost a fortnight of plunging through heaving Atlantic rollers that occasioned considerable discomfort for many of its passengers, including Sister McGrath, the converted liner at last steamed in sight of the Rock of Gibraltar. Its ancient promontory arose sentinel-like from the vast expanse of indigo ocean one afternoon a little before sunset. The convoy sailed through the straits past the Rock and continued on in sight of the North African coast, heading for Algiers.

It arrived during the second day from Gibraltar. June, Colleen, Marjorie and Olivia Dale, the fourth member of the quartet, known as 'Dollie,' stood leaning on the top deck railing, gazing over the clustered roofs of the town as the liner eased towards its berth.

"Bet you're glad of calm seas for once, Coll, your tummy especially," said Margie with a pert grin.

"Especially after puking my guts up into the lav for most of the trip," Colleen answered, her lips twisting with distaste.

Now at least she could join her companions for mess, without fear of having to rush off to the head. She'd subsisted mostly on hard tack biscuits and compo tea, made from the pressed cubes of powdered milk, sugar and tea concentrate, as a consequence of which she reckoned she'd lost about half a stone in weight.

"And you do look a bit peaky, dear," her friends had agreed.

The anti sea-sick pills, with which they'd been issued, had only been marginally effective but at least she'd managed to maintain her dignity during the boat drills, clambering abroad the squat little craft while encumbered with tin hat and Mae West. She was glad, too, that she'd been able to do her stints of duty in the ship's hospital, to assist the AMC's permanent medical staff. With hundreds of troops on board en route for Italy, it was inevitable that medical crises of one kind or another could arise in the course of the voyage, such as an attack of acute appendicitis or gastric complaints stemming from the poor diet the soldiers had to endure. Nursing officers, quartered in their own separate and well-guarded part of the vessel, ate better, though until recently Colleen hadn't been able to enjoy much of the available cuisine.

"You were supposed to use the vomit bags, of course," said June airily. "Just as well we didn't grass on you to the chief steward."

"I didn't trust those things," Colleen retorted. "And I could never find one in a hurry. Carrying 'em around for emergencies only brought them on."

"Poor lass," said Dollie. "We thought you'd pop your clogs any tick of the clock. We'd already decided how to divvy up your trunk."

Slender and elegant, Dollie always seemed able to keep her blonde hair well-groomed, much to the envy of her friends. She was from Hertfordshire and her dad was a clergyman.

"Thanks, Dollie, good to know who your mates are," said Colleen in mock indignation.

They were sweltering in their khaki protective dress under a cloudless sky. Heat waves shimmered from the jumble of old dwellings known as the Kasbah and from the white-fronted colonial buildings of the new city, situated among scant cork oaks beneath the imposing cathedral of Notre Dame d'Afrique. Scummy water lapped lazily against the ship's sides and the anchors fell seawards with resounding splashes. Open-decked lighters with native crews began chugging towards the vessel. On shore, vehicles loading or unloading stores queued along the waterfront roadway. A couple of sombre British men-o-war rode at anchor not far from where the liner had tied up.

"Take a good look, girls," said June. "It's all you'll see until we head back this way."

"Don't think I want to see any more," said Colleen, wrinkling her nose at the smell of crowded humanity that wafted across the harbour.

The liner stopped only to resupply the local garrison and take aboard some more kit-laden infantry reinforcements for the Eighth Army.

"Wonder if we'll be taking care of any of them," Dollie remarked.

"Certain to be some like them, Dollie," said June sagely.

A couple of days later, the grey merchantman hove in sight of Naples, during the late afternoon. Masts and funnels of sunken ships in the harbour told of the devastation wrought during the battle for the city the previous year, together with the grim sight of bombed-out dockside buildings. However, the panoramic vista of the magnificent bay in the setting sun with Vesuvius louring over the city was breathtaking, a vast plume of brownish haze issuing from the wide cone shape of the volcano's crater.

"Hope it doesn't blow off again while we're here," Hoppy declared when they ventured to the railing again to view their destination.

Vesuvius had erupted in March. Towering pillars of volcanic ash had blanketed the town. Though darkness was falling when their transport wound through dingy streets up from the harbour, the girls could easily discern the gritty pumice-coloured substance clinging to the walls of the forlorn buildings they passed.

"Take a lot of elbow grease to get that off," said Dollie.

They arrived at the ancient but well-furbished requisitioned hotel on the outskirts of the town, where they would stay the night.

The transport officer, an RASC captain in shirtsleeves, met them in the foyer. Where itinerant nursing officers were concerned, he was happy to double as the welcoming committee.

"I'll have your kit taken up to your rooms, Sisters, bathrooms are nearby. You'd like some char?"

"Yes, please, sir," they chorused.

The following day, wearing walking-out uniform, they went down to the dining room for breakfast, where June reminded them of an important routine order.

"Mepacrine tabs from now on, girls, daily, even if you go as yellow as Fu Manchu," she said. "This is malaria country. Chargeable offence if you get it."

Nevertheless, the hotel menu lightened their spirits and fully satisfied their appetites.

"Eighth Army's done us proud," said Dollie while they tucked into porridge, bacon and beans, grilled tomatoes and eggs, followed by American flapjacks, maple syrup and real brewed coffee, no doubt also from the Americans. The eggs and tomatoes came from local peasant farmers, who also supplied melons, oranges, peaches and grapes in abundance.

"Haven't tasted oranges for four years," said Colleen, savouring the juicy slices.

Though occupied almost to capacity by male and female officers from all branches of the services, the dining room exuded a relaxed atmosphere. It was spacious, with snowy white cloths spread over the tables and verdant potted palms standing in various niches adding to the pleasing décor. A light breeze stirred the net curtains strung across open windows and triple-bladed ventilation fans fixed to the ceiling rotated soundlessly amid the buzz of conversation.

"Wonder how they got hold of this stuff from the Yanks?" asked Sister Hopgood.

"Paying through the nose most likely, Hoppy," said June. "Or via the black market."

This nefarious commerce was still flourishing, though the Allied occupation had brought some order out of chaos. Although much bomb damage remained, most essential services were functioning and the Herculean efforts of the Allied medical services, aiding hard-pressed local staff, had successfully dealt with the epidemics of typhus and bubonic plague the Allies encountered on entering the city.

"Think you'll keep breakfast down, Coll?" Hoppy asked.

"So far so good," Colleen murmured with a wry smile. "Shall I go sound out the RTO?" she asked, as she folded her napkin, "I've about finished."

"Sure, Coll, go ahead," said June, sipping her coffee.

Captain Fordham, the RASC officer in charge of road transport, was looking harassed. He'd informed them before breakfast that "an unforeseen delay" had arisen with respect to the next stage of their journey.

"The truck that brought you here last night is under the port control, ladies," he'd explained. "Apparently the lorry that was supposed to take you north was one of several that Jerry's blown up lately. His air force still manages to do tip and run raids along the highways from time to time, even as far south as Rome. But don't worry, I'll get you on your way as soon as I can. Come and see me when you've eaten."

Their designated hospital was located near a town above the Liri Valley about fifty miles away, close to a vital road junction. Having earlier received casualties for months on end from the bloody battles of Anzio and Cassino that had raged for the first half of the year, the unit was in the process of transferring to the new battlefront in the hills of Tuscany. For here, in the Etruscan Apennines three hundred miles to the north, the German Army had set up a defensive arc spanning the Italian peninsula, called the Gothic Line.

The enemy would doubtless exact a high price from the advancing Allies in their attempts to breach it.

But part of the hospital was to remain in situ for a few more weeks, caring for long-term patients from the earlier actions. Colleen and her friends would join it as soon as the transport problem was resolved.

She found Fordham at the reception desk. He faced her with a tired smile.

"No luck until tomorrow morning, I'm afraid, Sister," he said wearily. "I've just been on the phone to your unit but unfortunately they can't help either. All their available transport's committed to the moves up north."

Before Colleen could reply, Sister Hopgood sauntered up and audaciously took over the conversation, assuming a most charming look of persuasion. If anyone could get away with such a ploy, slim, vivacious Hoppy could.

"Since we're going to be here another day, sir, any chance we could borrow a jeep and go into town?" she asked. "I can drive and it would be good if we could stock up on – " She paused for effect, "personal items, you know. I'm sure we can find a place to park where it'll be safe."

Fordham pursed his lips, his brow furrowed.

"Hmm," he said finally. "It's not strictly in accord with regulations, but in the circumstances, it's probably the least we can do."

His voice grew more serious.

"Stick to the major roads, Sister, where we've got Redcaps or MPs posted, because the engineers can't guarantee they've lifted all the Jerry booby traps yet and you must get back well before sundown. There's all kinds of riff-raff about after dark. Any problems, just pull into the nearest provost post and ask 'em to contact us, OK?"

"Thank you, sir," said Hoppy sincerely. "It's very much appreciated."

"Fine," he said, adding with a wan smile, "Oh, remember you drive on the right hand side here."

Within half an hour they were on their way, Hoppy relishing the role of driver, looking prim and proper in her walking-out suit with dark khaki jacket, matching skirt, peaked cap, khaki shirt and tie and sturdy but elegant semi-heeled shoes. Her companions were similarly attired; each with two pips up, grey and scarlet lanyards on their right shoulders, brass 'R' badges denoting the QAIMNS Reserve gleaming on their lapels and caps. The day promised to be fine and they were anticipating an enjoyable outing.

"Of all the feminine wiles," said June as she mounted the jeep's passenger step. "You twisted that poor RASC bloke round your little finger. Who taught you to drive, anyway?"

"My brother," said Hoppy. "He was a cabbie before the war; RAF driver now."

Occupying the seat next to Hoppy, June was careful to keep her statuesque form erect and dignified as they motored along the dusty carriageways past deferential military police. Army vehicles to front and rear of them, and from the opposite carriageway, churned up more dust.

The roads were bumpy from the residue of filled-in bomb craters but still lined along some stretches with tram tracks that Hoppy carefully avoided. No public transport was in evidence, however and many buildings lay in ruins along the route.

"Will you let me have a go, Hoppy?" called Colleen, leaning forward. "On the way back."

"Are you licensed to drive, Sister?" June called back over her shoulder.

"Well, no. But I used to ride my dad's motorbike and drive my boyfriend's MG."

"Which one was this?" asked Dollie.

"The Brylcream boy[6]," said Colleen. "When I was a Staffie, the year before I joined up. He taught me how in case he got blotto at any of the do's we went to."

"The one that chucked you for the station WAAF?" June called over her shoulder again.

"That's him, thanks for the reminder," Colleen said in her ear.

Hoppy adroitly changed gears and steered the jeep around a sharp right-angled bend. Another cloud of dust settled over its occupants.

"Did he get sozzled very often, Coll?" she asked, raising her voice.

"Let's just say, he had plenty of booze and I got plenty of practice," Colleen shouted in reply. "So can I drive back?"

"What do you think, June?" said Hoppy.

"Well, OK. So long as neither of you gets blotto."

"Anyone got a clothes brush?" said Dollie loudly, flicking fine floury-like particles off the shoulders of her jacket. "Can you please slow down a bit, Hoppy?"

She and Colleen waved to the MPs who saluted as the jeep drove past.

Occasionally, Hoppy pulled over to ask directions. The provosts, both American and British, obligingly pointed them towards the town centre by stages and about mid-morning, Hoppy parked the jeep outside an American HQ established in an undamaged official building, flying the Stars and Stripes above its ornate entrance. She strode up to the sentry on duty, who briskly stood to attention and brought his rifle up into the position of Present Arms.

"Thank you, soldier," she said warmly. "We've come to do some shopping for essential kit. Could somebody look after our vehicle?"

"Sure thing, Sister," said the sentry enthusiastically. "Take it round the back with our jeeps. The motor pool guys'll keep an eye on it."

He indicated the way. Hoppy thanked him and returned to her friends.

Leaving the jeep with their obliging hosts, the girls shouldered their khaki web bags and ventured into the main shopping precinct. It had escaped most of the bombing and was seething with humanity, both civilians and forces personnel clad in an array of distinct uniforms that contrasted strikingly with the generally drab hues of the citizens' garbs.

"Locals look pretty undernourished, don't they," said June.

She and her friends began window-shopping. Traffic, mostly military, noisily nosed past, supply trucks heading for the docks, troop-laden lorries going in the other direction.

"No shortage of trucks here," Dollie observed. "Can't see why we should be stranded."

"Enjoy it while lasts, Dollie," Colleen advised. "C'mon, gang. We've done enough recceing. Let's try this place."

She indicated an opulent haberdashery and lingerie shop close by. They stepped inside and found the shop's interior to be refreshingly cool.

"You've got an eye for class, Coll," said Hoppy, gazing about her. "Up with Harvey Nick's, this."

"Don't think we should be in here," Dollie said doubtfully. "We still haven't got all the dust off."

A young woman of ample proportions, wearing a full-length black dress, approached them, smiling. She had dark hair and a beautiful olive complexion.

"Buon giorno," she said. *"Inglese infirmiere?*[7]*"*

The woman had recognised the Sisters' lanyards.

"That's a start," Dollie murmured. The four of them returned the lady's smile.

"Er, si," said June hesitantly. *"Parla Inglese?"*

"No, mi dispiace, ma non lo parlo[8]*,"* the lady said self-consciously, shaking her head.

"Oh, hell, what now?" muttered Colleen, though keeping up her smile. The shop lady came to their rescue.

"Ah, ma non si preoccupi[9]," she said and picked up pad and pencils from a nearby counter. *"Imagine di tiraggio, si?[10]"*

"Of course!" exclaimed June. "Draw some pictures and write down our sizes next to them. Come on, girls, let's see how good you are at sketching bras and knickers."

They lady nodded enthusiastically and after examining their pencilled efforts produced large quantities of the most elegant lacy silk under garments the girls had ever seen, along with packets in abundance of the most exquisite sheer silk stockings.

"These are superb," said Hoppy, holding up a matching set. "And she's spot on with the size."

"Talk about value for money, we're quids in," June added. *"Er, quanto costo per favore?[11]"*

"You speak it like a native, June," Hoppy said in admiration.

"Been studying the phrase book, like we were all supposed to, my girl."

Dollie had selected some finely embroidered suspender belts to go with the stockings she'd chosen.

"Eat your heart out, Mr Selfridge," she said.

"Better than anything I've come across in Middlesbrough," remarked Colleen. She doled out a fistful of lire for her manifold purchases.

"Grazie, grazie," the shop lady said joyfully.

"Middlesbrough?" said June. "Where's Middlesbrough? Is it in England?"

"Bog off," Colleen retorted, laughing softly.

Echoing the lady's warm-hearted *"grazies,"* they stepped out into the glare of the thoroughfare.

"Hmm, some people are doing all right," June remarked. "Wonder if she was in with the local *fascisti*? Wouldn't be a problem changing sides, of course. You can bet our brass'll be buying up that gear for their floosies hand over fist."

Some high-ranking American officers had come into the shop to survey the displays, while the Sisters had been completing their purchases.

"Too right," said Dollie. "Even nylons don't compare. Where to, now? Can we get some nosh?"

"Might as well," said June, glancing at her watch. "It's nearly midday."

"Be good to get out of the sun again," said Hoppy.

The noontime heat was intense. They went into a nearby café where they dined on piazza and strong Italian coffee. The establishment was well-patronised and many of the tables were already occupied when the girls entered.

"I'll just try the facilities," said Hoppy after she finished her meal. She got up and went through a side door at the rear of the café. Some considerable time elapsed before she returned.

"They're OK but there's a bit of a queue," she explained.

"Place has got chokka since we came in," said Dollie. "Took quite a while to get seconds on coffee. Normal for this time of day, I expect."

June yawned, placing a hand over her mouth.

"Oh, pardon me," she said. "Be great to have a siesta. How much time 'til we've got to head back?

"Oh, loads more," Hoppy assured her.

"Especially the way you drive," murmured Dollie.

"Well, *you* can thumb a lift then, ducks," said Hoppy, grinning. "Better slip into a pair of those new silks and stick your leg out like Claudette Colbert[12]."

"Let's have a mooch around the old town," suggested June. "Lots of our blokes about, so we should be OK."

They paid their bills, departed the café, and headed in the general direction of the docks.

The back street area they entered was in complete contrast to the town's shopping centre. Here was the real Naples, made worse by uncleared heaps of rubble strewn around bomb-blasted tenements.

Picking their way along a dilapidated sidewalk, the four of them gazed at a labyrinth of twisted streets and alleyways, their nostrils twitching at the stench. Although Royal Engineers and US Army sappers had repaired the sewer mains, it had not been possible to block all of the spillage. Some of it oozed sluggishly in between scattered chunks of masonry strewn over the roads. In addition, uncollected, rotting garbage was piled up in dingy alleys, about which flies buzzed in swarms. High above, row upon row of washing lines were strung between opposing balconies, pegged with all manner of garments, lacing together crowded apartment buildings that had fortuitously escaped the bombing.

"They must sleep six in a bed[13]," said Colleen, looking up at the high-sided blocks. "Especially with so many other places knocked down. Those rooms don't seem any bigger than biscuit boxes."

Here and there, heavy tape with warnings in both English and Italian, prevented access to locations where the presence of unexploded delayed action devices was suspected. Sentries of various nationalities stood guard with rifles and bayonets prominently displayed.

Acutely conscious of the oppressive heat, the Sisters paused for a while in a small plaza, with a stone statue of the Madonna at its centre, chipped and eroded by the scouring of time.

A human tide seethed past them, appearing not to notice their presence. Street urchins chased one another into the alleys, chattering and shrieking in high-pitched tones, most of them semi-naked, half-starved and barefooted. The majority were dark-eyed and olive skinned but a sprinkling of them exhibited fairer colouration with blondish or reddish hair. Yet others displayed the swarthy features of Levantine Arabs. To be Neapolitan was obviously to be cosmopolitan.

The youngest children had no nether garments at all, the insides of their thighs fouled in many cases. Toilet training was clearly a matter of trial and error, especially error. Numerous youngsters rummaged through the garbage, evidently searching for half-eaten fruit, fish ends or cigarette butts.

The nurses' trained eyes immediately discerned the symptoms of rickets, pellagra, scurvy and other maladies.

"Poor little mites, look at that conjunctivitis," said Dollie. "Some of them must be nearly blind."

"With gastro-enteritis, too, I shouldn't wonder," said Hoppy. "And worse."

The particularly emaciated appearances of some of the children, with hacking coughs and distinct lassitude in contrast to their more exuberant fellows, betrayed the effects of tuberculosis.

Several of the youngsters scuttled up to the Sisters, begging with grubby palms extended. The girls couldn't help recoiling from the smell of them.

"Don't give 'em anything," said Colleen. "We'll be inundated. Hang onto your bags, too."

Her companions understood the cruel necessity and desisted, shaking their heads. The urchins quickly lost interest and sped off in loud pursuit of other potential benefactors.

The girls continued on, observing that, as June had surmised, many servicemen besides the sentries were present and definitely not on duty.

"This place is one ginormous brothel," Dollie gasped. "And tavern."

Conspicuous along the byways were the women in skimpy outfits soliciting the servicemen who ambled past, pausing occasionally to negotiate in pidgin Italian before either accompanying the petitioner or lurching on, as they were usually in a semi-drunken stupor, to seek sensual pleasure elsewhere. Colleen and her friends noticed that the deal was often closed with either tins of bully or some other foodstuff, so desperate were the solicitous females for basic necessities[14]. Others obviously craved cigarettes.

The prostitutes were often hardly alluring, resembling half-starved gypsies with lank tresses, gaunt countenances and limbs and hips like scarecrows. Many of them were no more than pubescent girls.

But what particularly shocked the Sisters was that these females were often accompanied by adults of both sexes, who jabbered vehemently at prospective customers, pointing vigorously to the 'ware' on display.

"Mums and dads pimping for their own daughters,[15]" said June.

Not all the servicemen were open to allure. Befuddled by alcohol, some had collapsed amid the rubble, paralytic, several with streaks of vomit spewed from their open mouths, attracting flies in considerable numbers, like the heaps of rotting garbage.

Yet in the midst of the chaos and degradation, street vendors noisily sold fruit and vegetables. Pedlars plied their trade with equal enthusiasm, exhibiting a bewildering array of clothing and trinkets for sale. Shops displaying a multitude of foodstuffs clustered along the kerbsides, competing with the vendors for customers. Haunches of meat, indeed whole carcasses, dangled crawling with flies from awning frames, along with sausages, hams, cheeses and smoked fish, pedestrians brushing by them as they walked past.

"Plenty of scoff about," remarked June. "Suppose you have to be in with the local *Mafioso* to afford much of it, though."

"With a cast iron stomach to ward off the salmonella," Colleen added.

They halted in another plaza. Like the first, it had a Madonna and an arched gateway in its rear wall, leading to a flagstone footpath. Attached to the wall were stone benches. The girls retired to them, taking the weight off their feet.

"This place is a madhouse," said Dollie. "As well as a whorehouse."

"No wonder they had epidemics," Hoppy observed. "Along with the VD. BGHs here had more of those cases than casualties, so I've heard."

"These whores are supposed to be out of bounds," June remarked, with a sigh.

"Tell that to some lad who's just come down from the Apennines with his family jewels still attached," said Colleen. "And hasn't tasted a drop of vino since he can't remember when."

"God help the kids born to them," said Hoppy. She crossed her legs and brushed dust off her skirt. "Congenital blindness from dads who've had a dose and Lord knows what else."

They all knew it was true. Even penicillin couldn't guarantee nil side effects from the scourge. June nodded.

"Brass don't care, of course," she said bitterly. "Apart from the effect on battalion strength."

"Speaking of brass, those drunks won't have any left, when they wake up," Colleen remarked, glancing once again at the soldiers flaked out in the rubble. "Only hope they'll still have their goolies."

"Can see why the army goes in for licensed places," said Hoppy. "Although this lot don't seem to care."

"Too much rigmarole," Dollie remarked. "Boys don't want to be hygienic, they want to get laid."

"Licensed whorehouses," said June, shaking her head. "Where will it end, licensed buggery of minors?"

"What?" exclaimed Dollie, horror-struck, as they all were.

"That's what the Nazis have," June said evenly. "My parents worked in Berlin at the British Embassy for a few years before the balloon went up, and I used to go visit them in the summer. They said Hitler and his crowd were all as queer as coots. It was true. Nazis gaoled a few pansies but only ones that disagreed with Adolph's politics[16]."

"Let's go on for a bit," Hoppy suggested. "These benches are a bit hard."

"OK," said June, getting up. "Mind out you don't get hit by a side of beef. Best to keep in sight of the sentry posts, too."

They didn't venture much further. The streets increasingly turned into precipitous ravines, heading down toward the harbour and congested with military transport going both ways, acrid exhaust fumes adding thickly to the all-pervasive reek of piled garbage, spilt sewage, squalid dwellings and thronging humanity. Debris from the bombing had been bulldozed into nearly continuous ramparts head-high along some verges, to facilitate access for transport to and from the docks.

Amidst the chaos, Colleen repeatedly observed the wayside shrines and statues of saints or the Madonna, like those in the plazas. They seemed to her wholly incongruous in their depressing surroundings.

"I think we've seen enough," muttered June. "I don't fancy having to hike back up these hills in heels."

They retraced their steps to the first plaza, sat down on its benches and waited for Hoppy to remove a stone from her shoe. By now, it was well after two o'clock but the heat was relentless and they took the opportunity discreetly to unbutton their tunics partly and loosen their ties.

"Hullo," said Dollie a short while later. "We've got company. Is it granddad minding the kids?"

A little civilian man of about middle age, wearing labourer's clothes with the sleeves rolled up and a broad-brimmed hat, was strolling towards them, smiling broadly. Two small children, a boy and a girl, accompanied him, each clasping one of his hands. Colleen observed they were rough and calloused, like a workman's. Though his frame was spare, his tanned forearms were noticeably muscular.

"He's a priest," she said. "You can tell from the hat, but as for his other gear, I can't fathom that."

"Kids look well scrubbed," said June approvingly. "Bit of a change."

They adjusted their clothing and rose up as he drew near, smiling their greetings, unsure of what had prompted his approach. To their surprise, he addressed them in perfect English and his comments indicated that, like the shop assistant, he had noticed their lanyards.

"My dear Sisters," he said, releasing one of the children and raising his hat. "Welcome to our city. I am Father Alonzo. I had seen you earlier and I felt I should make myself known to you, to thank you in person for the great help your medical people have given us."

"Thank you, Padre," said June, clearly bemused. "We've only just arrived and thought we'd do a bit of sight-seeing. It is very warm."

She extended her right hand. The priest replaced his hat and shook her hand gently.

"Indeed it is," he said, chuckling. "I wear ordinary clothes for my parish work, as you see, but on days like this, I am never without my good old hat."

"What work do you do, Father?" asked Colleen, intrigued by the priest's incognito garb.

The priest smiled affectionately at her.

"Same as in any parish, Sister. But here it is much easier if I do not look like a priest. I'm also in charge of an orphanage, These – " he nodded to the youngsters by his side, who eyed the Sisters shyly, – "are two of my children. They lost their parents in the bombing and I take them with me, or others who've been through the same experience, else they would hide in the cellars and never come out. Would you like to see the orphanage? It is just through there." He nodded towards the open gateway in the wall at the rear of the plaza. "And I can promise you, it's cooler than in the street," he added invitingly.

June glanced at her companions.

"Let's," said Dollie.

"You probably wonder why I am able to speak your language," the priest said as he conducted them along the path leading from the gateway. "I studied at the English College in Rome and spent some years in an English parish near the Cotswolds. Your country is very beautiful but too damp and foggy for me - though excellent for the complexion."

"You're very kind, Padre," June said demurely.

They followed him and his two charges for about fifty yards until they came to what looked like a run-down chapel building. It had curved oak doors with a large iron ring-shaped handle. Windows on the stone front of the building to either side of the doors were boarded up.

"We were fortunate not to have lost anything but the windows," the priest said.

He twisted the handle to open the doors and led them inside. It was cool, as he had predicted, with a bare stone floor, and spacious, partly because no pews remained. Instead, thin mattresses of straw-filled sacking overlaid with threadbare blankets lined each of the side-walls, about fifty in total. Bright sunlight filtered through the boarded-up window spaces. The air smelt stale, with the distinct odour of urine that Colleen guessed emanated from the mattresses. At the other end of the church stood the altar, a stone bench with two tarnished candlesticks atop it.

"We renew the straw and wash the mattress covers out back, where there is a stand pipe," the priest informed the Sisters. "The children have their duties. They come to learn that this is their home."

He showed them into the kitchen area to the left of the altar space. A blackened range with a large pot on its grating was situated in a grimy hearth, its battered stovepipe reaching up into the rectangular flue. Along the adjacent wall stood a stone sink and work surface. Several large upended crates, some bearing Allied forces markings, served for chairs. Piles of cooking pots, tin utensils and cutlery, scrupulously washed, were stacked on the work surface. A heap of firewood stood beside the stove.

"Please be seated," said the priest.

A little self-consciously, the QAs perched themselves on four of the crates, crossing their legs. In a niche across a narrow passageway from the kitchen, a larger crate stood with its surface covered by sheets of paper. Colleen guessed that many of them were unpaid bills, probably for water, firewood, food, straw and other essentials. Such was the priest's office space.

Seating himself and putting his hat on his knee, Alonzo whispered to the children who scurried out of the building by a rear door. They returned a few minutes later with tins of water that they began pouring into the pot on top of the range.

"We feed them pasta," the priest said. "With macaroni and tomato paste when we can get it. My helpers here will put the ingredients for tonight's meal in to soak. We also get oranges and tomatoes from the markets. You would like some tea? We have what you call the compo variety."

"Thank you, Padre," said June. "That's very kind of you."

His sun-tanned face wrinkled in a smile. The youngsters quickly had a fire going with some kindling wood and the brew was soon ready. The priest poured it into five metal mugs and passed four of them to the Sisters.

Sipping from his mug, he ran gnarled fingers through his sweptback iron-grey hair and gave his visitors a brief description of his mission.

"My aim is to get children off the streets and give them a better start in life. They can stay here until they are sixteen or seventeen, by which time, I hope to have convinced them to seek employment as labourers on farms outside the city, or, with the girls, as maidservants in the big houses of the wealthy families. But," he added with a sigh, "it is one thing to take the children out of the street, quite another to take the street out of the children."

He paused, watching the children breaking open the packets of pasta and tipping the contents into the cauldron.

"How do you get them here, Father?" asked Colleen.

The priest smiled and sighed again.

"I go out and find them, Sister. It is not always easy. Priests are not generally trusted, though most Neapolitans are very religious. But everyone knows me as old Father Alonzo, harmless enough, a bit soft in the head." He tapped his temple with a forefinger. "It helps, that impression. Many of the youngsters confide in me. They are not all orphans in the true sense. Some have left home because of overcrowding, or because one parent is having an affair and there are quarrels, or a girl is being molested by her father or elder brother."

He nodded sadly at the Sisters' shocked stares.

"Yes," he affirmed. "It happens often. Some even bare children by close blood relatives. You have seen the overcrowding. Regrettably, a girl may easily become a prostitute, at a very young age, to help the household income, or a boy take up with a *pederasta*, an older male. Eventually, they decide to shift for themselves. Others, of course, fall into crime, smuggling, pick pocketing, pimping, even for their sisters, or scavenging for food scraps, as you have seen…"

His voice trailed off.

"Who supports you, Padre?" June asked.

Alonzo leant back a little, placed his mug on the work surface and clasped his hands behind his head.

"The local bishop has kindly sanctioned this ministry, Sister. We receive a small stipend from the Church, which allows us to have this building for a token rent only – it is a wreck, of course - and the assistance of a few local patrons. Some nuns assist with the children on a part-time basis, mainly with those who fall ill and many do. We are always on the lookout for medicines."

He placed his hands on the patches that covered the knees of his trousers and his tone brightened.

"In addition, though, the children collect many items that can be sold on, to bring in extra cash," he explained. "Old clothes, scrap metal, sacking such as we have for mattress covers, all sorts of odds and ends, especially from the Allies. You'd be amazed at what your people throw away. It is constructive scavenging. That's what the other children are doing now. They will be back in time for tea, as you say."

"How many orphanages are there here in Naples, like yours, Padre?" asked Hoppy.

"Very few, Sister," the priest said regretfully. "We could establish fifty more and still not have enough."

He leant forward and the tone of his voice took on a fresh intensity. His dark eyes became almost feverish.

"That is really why I approached you, dear ladies, in addition to my gratitude. Please forgive my effrontery but it is folk like yourselves who can really assist our work. I know that you have great responsibilities and little time to yourselves but I would be extremely grateful if you will write to your clergymen, if only one letter to your bishop, urging him to write in turn to the leaders of our Church, even to the Holy Father himself, asking them to help us in our mission, help us get these children out of their corruption and misery, help them get some dignity and live useful lives. If you could approach your own chaplains in the same way, that would be most helpful."

He paused again and spoke softly to the children, who, having completed their task in the kitchen, sped off, out the back of the building.

"They will wash some of the sacking," he said to the Sisters, with a wink. "We have a small laundry space, and also facilities for both boys and girls out back, rudimentary but they serve."

"We would be happy to write, Padre, I'm sure," said June. Her companions nodded in agreement.

"But why doesn't the Church do more for you, Father?" Colleen asked.

"The Church is an organisation, Sister," he said, sighing again. "And it wants to spread its influence. The streets of our city are deemed secure for Mother Church. Even though the people don't trust their priests; they are Catholic from birth to death. Our leaders seek fresh conquests. Besides," he added, with a smile, "we suffer much from what you call red tape. Few bishops are as enlightened as mine, but a word from the outside world may change some minds. We can only hope for the best."

June reached into her shoulder bag.

"I'll like to give you something for the orphanage, Padre," she said firmly. Dollie, Colleen and Hoppy likewise began reaching for their purses. The priest held up his hand.

"No, no, dear ladies, please," he protested. "If you are happy to write, that is more than enough, please, I beg of you."

But June was adamant.

"We'll cover those bills on your desk, Padre," she insisted.

The Father was genuinely moved and deeply grateful as he accepted the proffered lire.

"We're honoured, Padre," said June sincerely. She rose to her feet and discreetly brushed the back of her skirt. "But we really ought to be on our way. Thank you for a most informative time, sir."

"And for the tea," said Dollie, with a smile. She glanced at their empty mugs, now arranged in a row on the stone work surface.

Alonzo accompanied the girls back to the plaza, bade them farewell and returned to his charges.

"He's a sweet chap, isn't he?" said Dollie affectionately. "We write enough to the folks back home, so I'm sure we can pen a few more letters."

"And it might help him," said Hoppy.

They set off back toward the American HQ where they'd parked the jeep.

"No doubt the Yanks'll let us use their facilities," June remarked.

The crowds were thinning but the sun was still harsh and heat radiated steadily of the stark tenement walls. Colleen kept thinking about the kindly clergyman and his ragged orphans, their plight made virtually insurmountable by the overarching indifference of his Church, her Church.

She gazed at the jagged bulk of Vesuvius to the east, still venting smoky haze. It was the first time she'd consciously done so that day and in that moment, the words sounded in her brain, not as an audible voice but nonetheless distinct.

Sister Colleen, your Church has robbed and spoiled this people. You must come out of it.

She stood still, puzzled. She'd never been called Sister Colleen, always Sister McGrath, or simply Sister. It was weird. Hoppy turned around and called to her.

"You OK, Coll?"

"Yeah, just day-dreaming," said Colleen, hastening to catch up. "My turn to drive back," she added.

"After we've powdered our noses," said June. "Definitely not before."

Their American hosts were happy to oblige them in this respect. They then returned to the jeep and Hoppy drove it out of the vehicle park, braked to a halt, slipped the clutch into neutral and handed over to Colleen.

"All yours, Coll," she said cheerfully. Sisters Taylor and Dale exchanged worried glances.

However, despite a slightly jerky start, Colleen smoothly manoeuvred the jeep into the main thoroughfare and blended inconspicuously into the outward-bound traffic, consisting mostly of other jeeps and army lorries.

"Like riding a bicycle," she called to June and Dollie. "You never forget how."

"Just watch the road, dear," June admonished her.

Finding the way back was not difficult, thanks to the military police, who were most helpful when Colleen stopped to ask directions. She was enjoying herself.

"Great gear changes, love," said Hoppy, patting Colleen's shoulder.

Before Colleen could reply, a massive explosion sent a giant mushroom of smoke, dust and debris hurtling skywards. It came from a street on the left, hidden by a cluster of semi-demolished buildings and running parallel to their course. The shock wave searing through the ground made the jeep lurch, though Colleen held firmly to the wheel. The traffic ahead and behind screeched to a halt.

"Delayed action bomb!" shouted June.

Colleen glanced over her shoulder and swiftly backed the jeep up. Looking again to her front, she pressed hard on the accelerator and steered the vehicle down a nearby side street. It would lead them to the scene of the explosion.

"Could be a second one about to go!" June cried.

"Would've gone off by now, surely!" Colleen shouted back.

"We can't help it, anyway, keep going, lass!" June shouted encouragingly.

"Amen to that, June," Dollie said loudly. "You're doing splendidly, Coll."

"Nearly there, Coll!" Hoppy cried out.

Chunks of rubble littered the roadway ahead. Keeping in low gear, Colleen was swerving frantically to avoid both the debris and numerous civilians fleeing the scene, screaming in panic, streaked with blood and grime. The jeep's passengers clung to its sides as it careered forward, other military vehicles following in its wake.

Colleen spun the jeep around a right-angled bend at the end of the side street and drove into the bombsite.

Utter devastation confronted the Sisters.

The device had obviously been well concealed, and extremely powerful. The explosion had collapsed a derelict office block, three storeys high, and catapulted hard-edged stonework in a huge one hundred and eighty degree arc directly at passers-by like a massive shotgun blast. Smoke and dust hung heavily over the terrible scene, filtering out the sunlight. Shocked survivors staggered about babbling incoherently, clothing almost torn off, blood running down their faces or welling from numerous lacerations. Others lay writhing amid the shattered masonry, crying like stricken animals.

Colleen deftly brought the jeep to a halt and the Sisters jumped out, grabbing their bags. Through the haze they saw, to their horror, dismembered torsos, with torn-off limbs and spilt entrails scattered in profusion, one decapitated form still convulsing in its death throes. The sickly smell of blood assailed their nostrils. Dark splashes of it mingled obscenely with the dust of the street.

"We haven't got anything!" exclaimed Dollie.

"Yes, we have," June shouted back. "Put those undies to good use, girls, they'll serve."

Distraught American servicemen were clawing at the jumbled remains of the office block with their bare hands, trying to shout encouragement to those evidently trapped beneath. Piteous cries for assistance arose from every quarter.

The QA Sisters responded as best they could.

Reaching into her shoulder bag, Colleen dropped on her knees beside an Italian man, sitting awkwardly, staring in shock and terror at the fearful rent in his side, from which projected the jagged fragment of masonry brick that had done the damage, blood cascading from all around it. Blood was also coursing from an ugly tear in the man's thigh, from which hung flesh in a lump. His trouser leg was soaked.

"Inglese infirmiere!" said Colleen distinctly, remembering the phrase the shop lady had used. It seemed to calm the man a little.

Next to him a woman, presumably his wife, lay on her side, sobbing, clutching her shoulder, tears guttering through the chalky dust coating her face. One glance at the blood welling from between the lady's fingers told Colleen that the woman's injuries were as life threatening as her husband's and the young QA knew she had to act fast.

The incision in the man's side was his more serious wound and causing him greater distress. Colleen packed a set of underwear around it, fastened with a stocking tied around the victim's waist, relieved that the improvised dressing seemed to be effective. It would only last a few minutes but in that short interval, his life would be saved, because the wail of sirens meant that help was approaching fast.

She took the man's hands in hers, also covered with his blood and clasped them over the wound, pressing firmly.

"Hold, here, yes, *si?*" she urged the man, who seemed to understand.

Colleen quickly bound up the man's thigh, then stepped over his legs to kneel beside his wife.

"OK, OK, *si?*" she whispered and carefully prised the woman's fingers from the wound, smiling to offset the horror she sensed at the sight of the fearful gash, revealing broken bone where nearly a fistful of flesh was gone. Colleen's nimble fingers quickly but gently repeated the process of packing the gouge with nether garments and securing it with a stocking wrapped around the woman's neck and shoulder, stanching the blood loss. She was aware of her three companions carrying out similar ministrations close by, assisted by some of the American soldiers.

The woman herself half-smiled in bewilderment at the 'bandages'.

"OK, *si?*" Colleen said to her. She replaced the woman's hand firmly over the dressing. By now, her own hands were red and sticky to the wrists.

She selected the next casualty, a man sprawled on his back, stammering in panic, blood spreading across his face from a gash on his forehead and with one hand clutching his mangled arm, his lifeblood spilling out in voluminous gouts.

Colleen could see yellowish bone-ends between his fingers. She knelt down again and reached for more silk.

In a short time, Allied medical teams had secured the area. The injured, lying on stretchers under grey blankets, were being loaded into ambulances and the remains of the dead were being placed under canvas on the backs of lorries. Many hands were still helping to shift rubble in search of more buried victims, some miraculously having been pulled out alive, though several corpses were found as well. The sight was still ghastly but the haze was settling and the situation becoming calmer.

"Don't think there's much more we can do," said June. "Our chaps seem to have everything under control."

Jaded and dishevelled, uniforms, faces and hands spattered with blood and grime, they walked slowly back to their jeep, bags looped over their shoulders, bereft of their recent purchases. The sun was low in the western sky. Vesuvius' sinister crater still smoked and plumed to the east.

"We look a sight," said Dollie. "Hope there's enough bath water for us at the hotel."

"And a dry-cleaning service," added Hoppy. She glanced down at her despoiled tunic and skirt. "And some plasters."

Their knees were grazed from kneeling in the gritty dirt beside the casualties.

"Our RASC mate'll have a fit," said Colleen, occupying the driver's seat.

Before they set off, the US Army Medical Officer in overall command of the rescue operation, hailed them.

"You gals did a swell job," he declared as he hurried over to the jeep. "Saved a bunch of lives."

"Glad to help, sir," said June.

"And our WAC ladies're gonna send you gals a heap of new *lingerie*," he added, grinning.

Sister McGrath's prediction proved to be overly pessimistic. Having learnt of the bomb blast, Captain Fordham was full of admiration for the girls and promised that every facility would be provided with respect to baths and dry-cleaning.

He had further encouragement.

"There's an officers' social here tonight, ladies. Swing band, buffet supper, happy hour at the bar. Should be a good do. Starts at nineteen-thirty hours. You're invited, of course."

But even as they expressed their thanks, he relayed some disappointing news.

"Afraid you're transport's going to be delayed until the day after tomorrow," he said apologetically. "I'm really sorry but it's the best I can do."

"In that case, sir, could we please have the jeep again?" asked Hoppy, disregarding her colleagues' sharp intakes of breath. "Might be a good day to go have a look at the volcano."

The officer was taken aback yet responded nobly.

"I don't see why not, Sister," he said. "You'll have to have an armed escort, of course but I'd guess any number of my officers'd be happy to volunteer. I don't suppose Jerry'd bother with any delayed action devices up there. Vesuvius has got plenty of her own."

Four

Capri

Grandma Colleen's personal experiences related in this and other chapters have been reproduced with her prior permission. Grandpa was OK about these disclosures, too. "It was all before we met," he said.

The girls bathed and donned fresh uniforms. Then, as they had promised Father Alonzo, they wrote letters to vicars and priests they were acquainted with in England about the needs of his orphanage, with copies to Father Alonzo's bishop. Dollie included another one to her dad - they had all written to their families the previous day to let them know of their safe arrival,

By the time they had completed this task, the party was well underway. Dulcét strains of Glenn Miller's 'Moonlight Serenade' issued from the hotel's dining area as the girls descended the carpeted staircase from their rooms on the first floor. Exuberant male and female voices intermingled with the clink of glasses.

"Sounds like the world and his wife's cavorting in there," remarked Hoppy, when they deposited their correspondence at Reception.

Entering the dining hall, they saw that the furniture had been neatly arranged around the walls and numerous couples were gliding across the open floor space in time with the music. The band, who occupied a corner of the room diagonally opposite the bar and adjacent to the terrace, consisted of an ENSA troupe, attired in tuxedos.

Above the dancers, the whirring fans circulated fresh air from open windows across which blackout material had been carefully arranged to conceal the light of the candelabras, while allowing in the night breezes. These helped to dispel the accumulation of alcohol and tobacco fumes.

"Good thing it's only one of our do's, place is heaving. Imagine if the Yanks were here too," said Dollie, eyeing the crowd on the dance floor and the press of individuals conversing animatedly at the tables.

"WRNS, QAs, ATS, WAAFs, the works," Colleen observed from the varied hues of khaki, dove-grey, dark and light blue garb of the female personnel. "Servicewomen's jamboree, this."

"And a whole gang of local lassies," added Hoppy.

"Plenty of spare blokes, though," said June approvingly.

And there were, many clustered about the bar or the long tables piled with sumptuous fare; chicken and fish in batter, ham, pork and sliced salami sausage, rissoles, oysters, cheeses, fresh bread rolls and salad vegetables augmented with ripe grapes, together with a varied selection of iced pastries.

The uniforms and voices revealed a panoply of nations; British, Canadians, Australians, South Africans, Czechs, Poles, Free French, Rhodesians, New Zealanders, representing all three services, together with a vast array of regiments and corps. Many of the lads were piling into the buffet as though they'd not eaten for weeks.

"Hope there's some spare grub by the time we get there," said Hoppy, as they edged toward the buffet tables.

"Lads must reckon they'll be back on bully and dog biscuits before long," Colleen remarked. "Can you see where the plates and serviettes are?"

"D'you reckon that stuff's all right," asked Dollie. "And didn't come from the back streets? Last thing we want is an attack of the runs."

"Catering Corps will have their own suppliers, Dollie," June reassured her.

A young New Zealand subaltern with a shock of fair hair falling across his forehead hailed them from the edge of the bar nearest the buffet. He was in shirtsleeves, his jacket draped over one knee and he swayed slightly on the stool he occupied, wine glass held aloft in one hand, lighted cigarette in the other.

"Jeez, you Pommy sheilas are flamin' gorgeous," he exclaimed.

The girls paused and eyed him askance.

"Better put that fag out, soldier," said June imperiously. "You're the one who's liable to go up in flames, with all that Chianti on board."

"Aw, don't be like that, Sis," the soldier drawled, evidently able to recognise their lanyards. "Can I get yez a drink?" he asked generously, swaying in the direction of the Italian bar tender.

"The name is Sister, not Sis," June admonished him. "G and Ts all round, I think?" She glanced at her companions.

"I'll have a shandy, please," said Dollie with a smile.

"Comin' right up, ladies," said the Kiwi lad. He began pounding the mahogany bar top. "C'mon, barman!" he urged. "How about some service? Move along, you jokers," he called to his fellow drinkers. "Make way for these lovely ladies."

The other occupants of the bar obligingly vacated some stools on which the girls elegantly seated themselves, murmuring their "thank you's".

"Are you Australian or New Zealand?" Dollie asked their ebullient benefactor.

"Ar, don't get tangled up with them Aussies, Sister," he warned, placing one hand on the bar top to steady himself. "They're all boozers and womanisers."

"I think that answers your question, Dollie," said June coolly.

Some of their officer hosts had departed for the buffet tables. They returned with platefuls of delicious looking portions that they eagerly proffered to the Sisters. A broad-shouldered captain of Signals, sporting a well-trimmed moustache, served their drinks, having processed the subaltern's order.

"Here you are, Sisters," he said courteously. "You Queen Alexandra ladies are real queens, no mistake."

"Hear, hear!" his companions declared in unison.

The girls smiled appreciatively, feeling a little self-conscious at the abundance of male attention. When they'd finished their meals, their officer companions promptly invited them onto the dance floor, apart from the youngster who'd initiated the hospitality. He was now slumped over the bar top, his cigarette having fallen to the floor. The bar tender collected his empty glass.

As the popular swing music pulsated across the room, Colleen found herself in the arms of the tall Signals officer.

Intriguingly, he looked familiar. She studied his face, noting that he was scanning hers.

"What's your name?" she asked.

"Tony Gatacre," he said. "And yours?"

"Colleen McGrath."

They paused in mid stride.

"I know you!" Colleen exclaimed, putting her hand to her mouth. "We were at school together."

The young officer nodded, smiling.

"Indeed we were," he said heartily. "It *is* a small world."

He gently took her arm when the piece finished and escorted her to the lounge.

Situated next to the dining hall, the lounge area was cool and spacious, furnished with well-padded sofas and easy chairs covered in rich velveteen, arranged around glass-topped coffee tables, overlooked by ornate mirrors and large portraits that hung on the brownish-papered walls. Several couples, enjoying tête-à-têtes, were already ensconced at the smaller tables while groups of male and female officers occupied most of the sofas, drinking, smoking and jovially conversing. Tony ushered Colleen to a vacant table near one of the blacked-out windows.

"Another G and T?" he asked.

"Yes, thanks."

Colleen seated herself in an armchair by the table. Tony came back a few minutes later with the drinks.

"Cheers," he said, as they raised their glasses. "This is amazing."

Colleen nodded. "Must be over ten years; you went to the Brothers' college, I went to the Convent."

"How'd you find it?"

"Absolute hellhole[17], apart from the sports."

"Oh, sorry to bring up unpleasant memories."

"That's OK, it's in the past. How long have you been over here?"

"Best part of a year. Landed at Salerno. When did you arrive?"

"Yesterday."

"Really!" exclaimed Gatacre. "You've had a time of it already, it seems."

"You must have seen the Elastoplasts on my knees."

Colleen rested her glass on a coaster and glanced down. Tony shook his head.

"Before that. My mate Fordham told me," he explained. "I recognised your name and decided I'd keep a look out for you. Glad I did."

Colleen lowered her head slightly and stared at her reflection in the glass top, hoping Gatacre wouldn't see her blush. He placed his glass on the table, took out his cigarettes and offered Colleen one. She declined with thanks. He lit one for himself.

"Where're you bound for?" he asked.

She told him of their intended destination and of their transport problem.

"I know the place," said Tony, exhaling smoke. "Up by the Liri Valley, about thirty miles past Cassino. If Fordy can't sort your transport, I'm sure we can. What've you got planned for tomorrow?"

"Thought we'd take a trip to Vesuvius," Colleen said tentatively.

Gatacre drew on his cigarette.

"It's quite a sight, especially up close, but I've got another idea."

Tony rested his cigarette in an ashtray, leant forward and fixed his gaze on hers. His eyes were deep blue. Colleen thought that with the moustache, he looked like Errol Flynn.

"How about I take you to Capri?" he proposed. "It's a great place. We can catch a boat from Sorrento and we'll easily make Capri by lunchtime if we leave here right after breakfast. Your friends'd be welcome, too. It'd just need a few of my mates to come along, like Fordy said but we can easily take care of that. Have you got anything to swim in?"

"Y-yes. Sounds wonderful."

Colleen felt quite overcome by the proposal.

The lyrics of a familiar ballad, sung by vigorous young voices, issued suddenly from the dining room, interrupting their conversation. The partygoers who'd adjourned to the lounge, took it up, clinking their glasses.

"We are the 'D Day Dodgers[18]*' out in Italy,*

"Always on the vino, always on the spree,

"Eighth Army scroungers and the Yanks,

"We live in Rome and dodge the tanks,

"For we are the 'D Day Dodgers,' out in Italy."

"Our way of giving Nancy Astor two fingers," Gatacre explained. He smiled and stubbed out his cigarette. "We better let your friends know what's happening, and I'll tell Fordy."

Tony stood up and offered Colleen his arm. She eagerly accepted it.

Oh, wow, she thought, I must write and tell Annie[19].

The strains of the ballad greeted them in full force as they re-entered the dining room.

"We landed at Salerno, holiday with pay,

"Jerry brought a band out to cheer us on our way,
"Showed us the sights and gave us tea,
"We all sang songs, the beer was free,
"For we are the 'D Day Dodgers,' out in Italy.

"Naples and Cassino were taken in our stride,
"We didn't go to fight there, just went for a ride,
"Anzio and Sangro were O.K.
"And to us it was just a holiday,
"For we are the 'D Day Dodgers,' out in Italy."

The party broke up around midnight, the revellers dispersed noisily to their billets in varying degrees of sobriety and the hotel staff moved in to clear away the debris.

As they went upstairs to their rooms, Colleen's companions made her a proposition.

"Listen, Coll," said June. "We're not going to be a bunch of gooseberries. You and that Gatacre bloke've really hit it off. He really does look like Errol. You head for Capri and we'll go to Vesuvius as planned."

"But it's all arranged," Colleen protested. "And you can't pass up a trip to Capri, it's the chance of a lifetime. Don't know why we didn't think of it ourselves."

"*You're* the one who's in with a chance, lass," Hoppy insisted as they reached the first floor landing and continued on down the corridor. "And you're not going to miss it."

"Too right you're not," said Dollie firmly. "Don't worry about the arrangements, we can easily sweet-talk the blokes around."

"But you don't know Tony's mates from Adam," Colleen remonstrated. "I don't like to think of you up a mountain with a bunch of strange blokes, even if they are officers and gentlemen, supposedly."

"Don't be silly, Coll," said June, laughing along with the other two. "We're big girls, we can look after ourselves."

"And you can have the rest of our seasick pills," Hoppy added. "Don't want you burking up on the boat to Capri in front of Errol."

A muffled male voice sounded plaintively from the other side of a door next to where they were arguing in the middle of the corridor.

"Can you sheilas pipe down, please? I'm tryin' to get some shut-eye."

"That settles it," whispered June. She gave Colleen the thumbs-up sign, with vehement nods of agreement from Hoppy and Dollie. "'Night all," she added, unlocking the door of her room.

Colleen retired to her room, undressed and climbed thankfully into bed. It had been an exhausting day but here she was with great prospects for the morrow.

It had all happened so quickly. She snuggled between the sheets, too drowsy to reflect that perhaps, it had happened *too* quickly.

Gatacre and three of his fellow officers arrived at the hotel at 0830 hours in two jeeps, having agreed with Fordham about the change of plans. When accosted by Colleen's companions and apprised about the *new* change of plans, the long-suffering RASC officer allowed them the use of *his* jeep as originally intended and Gatacre's brother officers likewise acquiesced to the re-arrangements. Tony voiced no objections.

"You chaps are ever so obliging," said Dollie sweetly.

"What'd we tell you, Coll?" June whispered to her friend moments before the two parties went their separate ways. "Piece of cake. These blokes are putty, you know."

"Best of British, love," Hoppy murmured, with a wink.

"None the worse for wear, Sister?" Gatacre asked cheerfully as he secured Colleen's web bag and steel helmet under the front passenger seat. His belongings were similarly stowed beneath the driver's seat. He wore summer uniform with peaked cap and sleeves rolled up.

"Not at all," said Colleen, smiling.

Instead of her peaked cap, she'd decided to wear her khaki beret, because it was more comfortable. Like Gatacre, she had dispensed with her jacket and wore her shirt-sleeves rolled up.

He courteously extended his hand to help her aboard.

"Thank you, kind sir," she said

Sunlight glinted off the pumice from the volcano still adhering to the hotel's façade and the familiar brown haze from Vesuvius' crater was the only blemish tarnishing an azure sky.

Gatacre climbed into the jeep and started the engine.

"Got your swimmers?" he asked, glancing at Colleen as he drove onto the roadway.

"Sure have. Look."

Colleen hitched up the left side of her skirt momentarily to reveal the lower half of a two-piece cotton bathing suit.

"Take my word for it, the top bit's also in place," she added merrily.

Gatacre was clearly impressed by what he saw.

He manoeuvred the vehicle onto a wide thoroughfare that led around the outskirts of the city and onto the highway that headed southeast to the Sorrentine Peninsula.

Colleen leant back in the seat and loosened her tie. The air rushed past her face now that the vehicle was travelling at speed. It was bracing, and not nearly as dust-laden as it had been the day before, thanks to a brief shower of rain during the night. She removed her beret and carefully inserted it folded into a pocket of her skirt, to allow the breeze to blow through her hair.

Should I have flashed him all that thigh, she wondered. This is supposed to be an outing, not a courting – or is it?

The highway lanced through steep-sided, grey-faceted ravines with green summits displaying rows of orchard trees. Ripening yellow and orange fruits showed distinctly through the surrounding foliage.

"Those are the terraces," Gatacre explained, gesturing with his left hand. "The Ities grow all sorts here; citrus, grapes, olives, melons, peaches. Trouble is, they leave half of it to rot, dig it back into the ground for fertiliser when it drops. Keeps the prices up, they reckon[20]."

"But that doesn't make sense. What about the loss of income?"

Gatacre chuckled and shifted gears to accommodate a long hill.

"Tell that to blokes who've always farmed this way, like trying to argue with a Yorkshireman," he said teasingly.

Colleen laughed.

"Not much debris about," she remarked. "Not like Naples."

They were now driving through more open countryside.

"No real fighting here, Colleen," Gatacre explained. He moved up a gear. "Jerries fell back from Salerno once we'd secured the beachhead, withdrew to the Volturno north of Naples and set up defences ending with the Gustav Line, running through Monte Cassino. That's where it really got stiff."

They were making good progress. Only occasionally did Gatacre have to slow down to steer around a horse or mule-drawn cart plodding sedately along, its driver hunched over the reins. Most of the traffic, virtually all military, was going the other way.

"Coming up from Taranto; or Salerno. It's only about twenty miles further on from where we turn off to Sorrento," said Gatacre as olive drab lorries lumbered past, some of them towing artillery pieces. Many were transporting troops, who waved, cheered and whistled if they happened to catch a glimpse of Gatacre's comely passenger with the knee-length skirt and luxuriant auburn hair. The officer laughed, resting his hands on top of the steering wheel.

"You've boosted more than one squaddie's morale today, Sister," he remarked.

Colleen smiled and glanced over his head to her left, gazing up a long slope, clustered with orchards, toward Vesuvius, whose massive prominence would frown down upon much of their journey.

"Wonder how the others are getting on?" she said.

"Oh, they'll have a great time," Gatacre assured her. "Fantastic sights, solid lava frozen like great black chunks of gun-metal, steam and sulphur spurting up from these huge natural chimneys that go right down to the core. You should have seen it in March, big red flares and great clouds of ash shooting right up into the stratosphere. Noise like all the artillery pieces in the world. Still loads of ash around, as you've seen."

"Sounds quite an adventure."

"Oh, aye. They'll doubtless drop in on Pompeii and Herculaneum, lots to see there, you can understand why the folks back in seventy-nine AD never had a prayer, hit with hot ash and pumice at three times boiling water temperature."

Gatacre took the coast road at the turnoff to the Sorrentine Peninsula. He negotiated a series of hairpin bends around the green wooded tops of grey-white cliff faces that plunged steeply into a cobalt-blue sea, hundreds of feet below. Colleen gazed enthralled.

They passed through several small towns, with square pink and white stucco fronted buildings and trim archways, reflecting the warm sunshine. Evidently, Vesuvius' eruption had not sullied these pleasant environs. Elegant bell towers, constructed on several levels, marked out the churches. All seemed so peaceful.

"Do you know the Sorrento song?" Colleen asked on impulse.

"Sure do!"

Tony broke into a fine tenor refrain.

"Vide 'o mare quant'è bello!

"Spira tantu sentimento.

"Comme tu a chi tiene mente

"Ca scetato 'o fai sunnà."

"Or in English, if you prefer," he said gleefully, grinning at Colleen's wide-eyed expression.

"See the waves of fair Sorrento,

" 'Tis in truth a jewel they cherish;

"Those who've never travelled far 've never

"Seen its like in all the world.

"Yet you say: "Farewell, I'm leaving?"

"You'd desert these loving arms,

"And this very land of beauty,

"Will you nevermore return?"

"That was marvellous!" Colleen exclaimed and gave him a round of applause.

"Pretty rough translation," he rejoined, as he angled the jeep around another bend. "It's the thought that counts, though."

Colleen would have cause bitterly to recall the last stanza before many months had elapsed.

Sorrento nestled at the foot of rugged sea cliffs. It was bustling with shops, hotels and restaurants, clustered about an extensive marina, where numerous yachts rode at anchor as far as the headland, a huge knuckle of dolomite. The Isle of Capri lay beyond it, an hour's journey away by motor launch.

Colleen noticed a large number of Allied officers as Gatacre drove slowly along the seafront, most of whom were accompanied by attractive females, many also in uniform.

Wonder how much those blokes lashed out on silk underwear, she mused.

Gatacre parked the jeep in the rear of a large hotel, amongst other jeeps and some staff cars. He jumped out, collected his kit, then came round to the passenger side and extended his hand to Colleen to help her down.

"Thank you, kind sir," she said again, grasped his hand and gracefully alighted. Donning her beret and refastening her tie, she picked up her web bag with steel helmet attached and looped it over her shoulder.

"It's like our own little Riviera here," said Tony. "We can get a launch at the marina. You'll see the island properly once we get round the headland."

Gatacre paid the fare and they boarded a large cabin cruiser, joining a party of high-spirited RN and WRN officers, all in white summer uniform. Local mariners were doing quite well out of the war, it seemed.

"Reckon we can let this pongo on board," a bearded lieutenant commander called out, with reference to Gatacre. "If he brings his good lady?"

A chorus of voices sounded their approval.

"And he's a good-looking bloke, too," declared one of the WRNs.

Their crossing was smooth, with a mild sea breeze, so Colleen suffered no ill effects. She sat on a padded seat near the stern next to Gatacre, basking in the sunlight that reflected dazzlingly off the gentle swell.

"Maybe you ought to roll your sleeves down, Colleen," he suggested. "The sun here can be pretty fierce on fair skin."

She did so, pleased each time he spoke her name.

On completing the crossing, the cruiser tied up at a marina that resembled the one at Sorrento. A township, also like Sorrento but smaller, was gathered along the far side of the quay. It, too, was thronging with tourists, mostly service personnel. Green fields extended upwards beyond the town to a serrated range of dolomite hills.

"Shall we get lunch?" Gatacre asked as they alighted and ascended a flight of stone steps to the quayside.

"Please, let's," said Colleen. "I'm starved."

They entered one of the cool *trattorias* that fronted onto the quayside, set back beneath a sequence of archways. Service was prompt and they dined with relish on ravioli, lobster salad, fresh fruit salad and cappuccino coffee.

"This place is doing a roaring trade," said Colleen, dabbing the corner of her mouth with her napkin. Allied officers and their escorts occupied most of the tables. Gatacre smiled and sipped his coffee.

"Our little Riviera, Colleen," he said.

After lunch, they decided to take a boat trip round the island.

"They stop off at the Blue Grotto, or *La Grotta Azzurra* as it's known," Gatacre informed her as they strolled along the quay. "When we get back, we can take the funicular over to the Faraglioni Rocks for a swim. We'll see them on the way round."

"Looks like some of our matelots and their lasses've got the same idea."

Colleen observed several of their companions from the crossing stepping into an open boat with an outboard motor and a local pilot at the tiller.

"Come on, sir and Sister! Plenty of room," shouted a voice.

They saw their boisterous lieutenant commander acquaintance, waving them over and patting a vacant space on the planking seat next to him and his buxom WRN companion.

"Be our guests," he said effusively, as they came and sat down. "Righto, pilot!" he shouted to the swarthy fisherman at the tiller. "All aboard, you can cast off now."

Turning to Colleen and Gatacre, he added, "Must keep these Dagos in order," then placed his arm around the WRN officer, who winked at Colleen.

Poker-faced, the pilot complied and then started the outboard motor. With a roar and a cloud of blue smoke, the motorboat set off.

As the craft approached the low, semi-circular entrance to the grotto, it dropped anchor and the passengers transferred gingerly into small skiffs. The local fishermen, who manned them, explained in broken English that the couples needed to lie down in the boats so that the rowers could guide their skiffs through the opening without hindrance.

"Very clean, very clean," they insisted, pointing to the scrubbed canvas mats lining the bottom of the boats.

Ethereal was the only word to describe the interior of the grotto. The water was a transparent, almost celestial blue, shimmering in the sun's rays that filtered through the opening. Several feet above the visitors' heads, the naturally vaulted limestone roof radiated a soft blue sheen that reflected off the visitors' faces. Everyone stared in silent wonderment, the only sounds in the cavern coming from the faint slap of the oars on the surface of the water.

After several minutes, the couples emerged, blinking, into the sunlight to return to the motorboat. Even the lieutenant commander was lost for words.

An hour or so later, cruising at a leisurely speed, they passed the Faraglioni Rocks on the southeastern side of the island, ranked like three rugged sentinels at right angles to the coast.

"See that strip of rock there?" Gatacre said to Colleen. "That's the beach."

A few visitors could be observed splashing about, while others sunbathed on the shore.

When they returned to the marina, most of the naval contingent made a beeline for the nearest bar, the lieutenant commander and his partner in the lead. Gatacre and Colleen boarded the funicular chair lift that conveyed them over the central ridge of the island.

They gazed down at the lush green pasture land, ablaze with multi-hued flora, some of which Colleen thought resembled huge harebells and rich yellow gorse. She breathed in the rich fragrance. On either side of the route, sharp ridges of dolomite thrust upwards into the still cloudless skies. Myriad insects hummed around as the couple alighted on the cliff top above the Faraglionis.

Gatacre and Colleen followed a steep descent of stone steps cut into the cliff face that brought them to the rocky shoreline. Stripping to their bathing suits, they plunged into the limpid blue-green waves that curled along the beach. Gatacre wore a pair of faded, cut-down, cotton khaki shorts.

"Tony, this is wonderful!" Colleen exclaimed when she came up from the cool depths for air, wiping her eyes. "The water's so clear."

Gatacre was backstroking in a leisurely fashion a few yards away. His muscled limbs flashed in the sunlight. Colleen thought he looked like a Greek god.

"Can't beat it," he called. "Do you want to swim out to the rocks?"

"You're on!"

They adopted the crawl position and went gliding swiftly through the sea towards the jutting pinnacles. Colleen remembered that Gatacre had been one of the best swimmers at the junior school and he had clearly lost no condition. She was determined to stay with him and strove to this end with a will.

After nearly forty minutes of strenuous stroking back and forth, Gatacre glanced at his watch, trod water and called to Colleen.

"Sorry to be a nuisance, but we ought to get back to the marina for about eighteen hundred hours, for the motorboat. With a bit of supper in Sorrento, we should make it to your hotel by around twenty-two hundred."

"Fine."

Colleen was floating beside him, lazily kicking her legs and squinting at the sun. "We've got time to sunbath and dry off, though?"

"Sure have. Keep your shirt handy, though. Sunburn's a chargeable offence."

They returned to the rock shelf where they'd left their belongings, dried themselves, then spread their towels out and lay down, the warm sun steadily drawing the moisture out of their thin garments. Feeling drowsy, Colleen positioned herself face-down for a time, with her shirt over her exposed back, cradling her head in her arms.

After a while, Gatacre made a discreet trip behind some dense bushes, Colleen smiled as she positioned her bag for a pillow. Men often had more pressing calls of nature than women.

When Gatacre returned, Colleen was lying on her back, eyes half-closed, reposing full-length, apart from one leg drawn up at an angle. She knew her companion was taking in the alluring sight afforded him of her slender, exquisitely proportioned figure; the taut contours of her upper body, her long, graceful limbs, her hips and thighs that displayed not an ounce of spare flesh, her neat waist where the stomach muscles showed in distinct 'washboard' effect between the component halves of her swimsuit. He slipped down beside her.

"I could stay here forever," she said and placed a forearm across her forehead to shade her eyes.

"Me too," Gatacre said quietly, resting on his side, his well-toned shoulder muscles bunching. "If you were here."

She raised herself on her side and looked into his yearning gaze. Irresistibly, they leant toward each other. Colleen closed her eyes; their lips met and remained pressed together for several seconds.

When they drew apart, Gatacre smiled shyly, glanced down at his wristwatch and murmured, "We should be on our way. I think we're dry enough."

They put their uniforms back on, shouldered their bags and headed for the steep ascent. Gatacre took the lead, stepping easily from one stone stair to the next, Colleen resolved to keep up with him. By the time they reached the top, she was perspiring freely but pleased that her army-issue shoes, the ones with the distinct heels that she'd worn the previous day, had accommodated her feet well.

"Goes to show what you can do if you have to," she said to herself, recalling how she and her companions had desisted from visiting the harbour in Naples, in view of the inevitable climb back up.

Colleen's shirt clung wetly to her skin and the cooling breeze that sighed across the cliff top felt wonderfully refreshing.

When they arrived back in Sorrento, shadows were lengthening across the quayside and the *trattorias* looked idyllic. Gatacre indicated one close by.

"See that little place over there? Serves great omelettes. Do you want to try it?"

"Let's," said Colleen and slipped her arm inside his.

"Everything's so organised here, almost like clockwork," Colleen remarked during the meal.

"Tourist trade's worth a lot of brass, Colleen," said Tony. "Ities can sort themselves if there's dosh to be made. Musso helped, of course." He carved off a thick piece of omelette.

"It amazes me how well-heeled the locals are compared to Naples," Colleen said, slicing through delicately fried layers of egg, ham, mushroom and tomato. "The Allies don't own those boats in the marina and lots of them are really posh."

Gatacre laid down his knife and fork.

"It's only a small percentage; top civil servants – most of 'em former *fascisti* amazing as it sounds, or Mafia, or high-ranking businessmen, the Fiat mob up north for example. But in a country like Italy, with thirty or forty million head of population, that still means tens of thousands of well-heeled toffs."

"It isn't fair."

Colleen told him of the meeting with Father Alonzo.

"Some of those blokes are all right, but they're on a hiding to nothing," said Gatacre.

Colleen's brow furrowed, recalling the letters written the night before but she wasn't about to argue, not wishing to spoil an otherwise perfect day.

"Quite a sight, eh?" Tony remarked as the jeep growled steadily up the winding road from Sorrento in the twilight.

"Certainly is."

Colleen gazed at the deep blue expanse with white edges crinkling along cliff bases far below, an ocean of iridescence in the vast red-orange flare of sunset. As always, Vesuvius, to the north, loomed hugely, its crater still emitting the sinister brown haze from its molten heart.

The return journey took slightly longer than the outward trip but was accomplished smoothly. Gatacre drove through the gathering darkness with dimmed headlights between two lorried convoys.

When he brought the vehicle to a halt outside the hotel, it was only a few minutes after 2200 hours. Colleen stifled a yawn and turned to Gatacre with shining eyes.

"It's been a marvellous day, Tony," she whispered. "Thanks ever so much."

"I'd like to keep in touch," he said, gazing at her intently.

"Of course."

Colleen leant towards him and their lips met again, for a long moment. Then she got out, collected her bag and tin hat and stood waving as he drove off. Joyfully, she turned and walked toward the hotel entrance, humming the tune for 'Sorrento' and nodding to the sentries, who came to attention as she mounted the steps.

The foyer was deserted apart from the uniformed clerk occupying the reception desk, though she could hear sounds of conviviality from the bar and lounge areas.

"Coll!" called a familiar voice. Hoppy was standing in the entrance to the lounge, eagerly beckoning her.

"Must go to the loo," Colleen mouthed back, pointing. Afterwards, she ventured into the lounge.

"Come and sit down," said Hoppy eagerly and patted the vacant place beside her on one of the plush settees arranged around a glass-topped table. June and Dollie were seated opposite and leant forward in anticipation. Like Colleen, they were all in shirtsleeves.

Four cups of hot coffee stood on the table, one with the saucer placed over the cup. June slid the saucer underneath the cup, then pushed both to Colleen.

"Here's your coffee," she said.

"That's great. Thanks, June."

Colleen took a sip of the rich brew.

"And these are for you, too," said Hoppy.

She reached under the table and produced a large shopping bag of goods that she handed to Colleen.

"Oh, the knickers," exclaimed Colleen as she peered at the bag's contents.

"They arrived just as we got back," said June. "Those WACs did a marvellous job. Seems like everything's replaced OK. They don't hang about, our cousins."

"So tell us all about it, Coll," Dollie said excitedly. "How'd you get on with Errol?"

"OK," said Colleen casually. "Looks like we've all caught the sun," she added, glancing at her friends' flushed faces and sensing the warmth of her own in the absence of any cooling breeze. "What was Vesuvius like?"

"Never mind old Smokey," Hoppy retorted. "What was *he* like - Errol, I mean?"

"Yes, come on, Coll," June insisted. "You're not getting away with just 'OK'."

"I didn't lose my virginity," Colleen said coyly, in between more sips.

"Well, neither did we," Dollie said with a grimace. "But that's not the point, how did you get on and are you going to see him again?"

Colleen gave them a resumé of the day's events to which they responded with encouraging "oh's," "ah's" and "hmm's" at appropriate points, especially where Colleen described how "things got a bit romantic at the beach."

"Yes, I am going to see him again, Lord willing," she said finally.

"Well, good for you, girl, he's a first-rate bloke, I reckon," Hoppy concluded with enthusiasm. Colleen settled back against a cushion.

"So how *was* Old Smokey?" she asked.

"Fascinating," said Dollie. "Like the ante-room to hell though, all black chimneys and massive clinker with huge great cracks in it."

"Jets of steam spurting up from below, with that horrible smell of sulphur," June added. "We've left our jackets to air, wore them because it got a bit breezy but that reminds me, our other uniforms are returned, dry cleaned, thanks to Captain Fordham."

"We borrowed a key and put yours in your room," said Dollie.

Colleen expressed her thanks.

"Gatacre's mates – perfect officers and gents, by the way – took us to Pompeii and Herculaneum," Hoppy broke in. "Spooky places, some poor devils are still encased in ash just as it hit them, weird."

"Judging by the artwork on the ruins, they were a pretty debauched lot, and highbrow to boot[21]," said Dollie. She placed her empty coffee cup on its saucer. "The ash was so hot it boiled their brains and blew their skulls apart. So Gatacre's mates reckoned."

Colleen grimaced.

"Anything likely to follow on, with any of those blokes?" she asked.

Her friends looked at each other and shook their heads.

"We got the impression they like to be fancy-free," said Hoppy.

June began to pile up their empty cups and saucers.

"Well, girls, we're up with the lark tomorrow," she said. "Captain Fordy's arranged an early breakfast for us, Colleen, so I think we ought to adjourn for the night."

Back in her room, Colleen decided that she ought to pen a few lines to her friend in Scotland, Nursing Officer Linton, who'd phoned prior to Colleen's departure from Liverpool, to say that she was now officially engaged to Sergeant Bill Harris, of Second Battalion, the Parachute Regiment[22].

Colleen wrote sitting up in bed.

Dear Annie.

Just a quick note to let you know I've arrived and round here it's still covered in grey, like the papers said before we went for interview.

We move up to the hospital tomorrow, patients mostly long-stay from earlier campaigns or otherwise convalescent but we'll be closer to the front soon, I understand.

My other news is I've met this marvellous bloke, Tony, got reacquainted actually. We knew each at junior school and amazingly, he's turned up here. He's Army, looks like Errol Flynn and is a real charmer. Also, he's a great swimmer. Remember how I used to snap at your heels up and down the town pool in our off hours? Well, Tony would give you a run for your money, no risk. Sorry this is brief but I'm knackered and need to get my head down. Love to you and Bill, Colleen.

Sealing the letter in its envelope, she flicked off the bedside light, yawned and stretched out contentedly.

But Dollie's words continued to echo in her mind.

"The hot ash boiled their brains and blew their skulls apart."

And even as she drifted off to sleep, the same Voice that had spoken to her the day before, rebuked her again, so that she slumbered fitfully for the rest of the night.

They were heady, Sister Colleen, high minded, lovers of pleasure more than lovers of God and they reaped what they had sown. Don't you see that you are no different from them?

Five

Base Hospital

At 0800 hours next day, a dun-coloured three-ton lorry drew up outside the hotel. Two ATS drivers descended from the cab, one a comely sergeant with bunched brunette curls, her companion a slightly-built corporal with fair hair and freckled face.

They reported to Captain Fordham, who returned their salutes.

"Sergeant Merryl and Corporal Styles, sir," said the sergeant.

"Thank you, Sergeant, here's your passengers."

Fordham indicated the four QA Sisters clad in khaki drill with sleeves rolled up, gaiters, boots and helmets. They waited beside their kit; bedrolls, web bags and trunks with camp beds strapped to them.

The ATS drivers marched over to Colleen and her companions, who jumped to attention to return the salutes.

"Sorry for the delay, Sisters," Merryl said cheerily. "But we'll get your gear aboard and be on our way."

A soldier leapt from the lorry to assist Fordham's men load the Sisters' trunks and fasten them. He was a Bren gunner, wiry and leathery-faced, his weapon mounted on a frame behind the cab.

"Private Briggs, aircraft sentry," Merryl explained. "Royal Fusilier, Dead-eye Dick with that LMG, too."

The lorry was already stacked with wooden boxes bearing a distinct Red Cross roundel, lashed securely and the Sisters with their kit filled the remaining space, apart from that occupied by Fusilier Briggs. They sat on their cushions, facing each other in pairs.

"Supplies for your hospital," said Corporal Styles with reference to the Red Cross boxes as she fastened the tailboard. "And the one at Avezzano."

"You don't anticipate any air attacks, do you, Corporal?" June asked, glancing up at cloudless skies.

"Don't fret, Sisters, any Jerries come buzzin' about, I'll see 'em off," Fusilier Briggs called out. He patted his LMG.

Styles beamed at him.

"Absolutely nothing to worry about, Sisters," she said, as she returned to the cab.

"Hmm," June murmured. "Not sure I'm convinced."

Their lorry rendezvoused with several others and proceeded along a main highway, unsealed but in good repair.

"REs did a great job here, Sisters," Briggs declared. "Had a lot of shell holes and bomb craters to fill in."

The passengers smiled gratefully as they brushed dust off their clothes. Fastened to its stanchions, the lorry's tarpaulin cover was rolled all the way up at the sides, otherwise the heat inside the tray would have been overpowering but the ventilation space did admit clouds of dust.

Not far beyond Naples, the sluggish brown waters of the Volturno slid beneath the transport as it rumbled across the Bailey bridge that spanned the river.

"Sappers' work again," said Briggs.

Suntanned Pioneer corpsmen, repairing an adjacent pontoon bridge, gave vent to a chorus of wolf whistles before the Sisters' lorry was obscured behind the brush and olive groves growing thickly along the river's northern bank.

"The British soldier's a sharp-eyed chap, ladies," Briggs remarked with a grin.

"So we've noticed," said Dollie, flicking powdery grit off her slacks.

Beyond the Volturno, numerous hulks of battered, burnt-out tanks, artillery pieces and lorries reposed forlornly in ditches by the roadside or lay abandoned in ochre-coloured, churned-up fields.

The girls gazed at them silently, wrinkling their noses at the smell. Here the whole land seemed putrescent.

"Locals crap in the fields," said Briggs.

All around, they could see heaps of dust-laden rubble from semi-demolished buildings, fire-gutted, with charred baulks of timber sticking out. Dislodged iron girders, exposed like the ribs of a butchered carcass, rusted in the sun.

The convoy drove further into the Apennines. Tall trees had once lined this part of the route but most were now fallen, their tangled root systems sticking out above the shell craters half-filled with greasy, fetid seepage.

"We lived in holes like that, when I was with the battalion," Briggs informed his passengers. "Where we could dig in."

A few skeletal trunks remained, their boughs lopped off as if by a giant's axe.

Colleen looked pityingly at the shabbily dressed peasants they drove past, who potted about the ruins of their homes, tending meagre gardens, stoking outdoor fires on which smoking black iron pots were mounted. Ragged garments hung limply from makeshift clotheslines. Scrawny head of livestock chewed at wiry tufts of grass, while a few hens pecked at the dirt.

"What's that over there, Briggsy?" asked June. She pointed to a winding rampart at the base of a bare, saddle-shaped ridge.

"Jerry anti-tank ditch, Sister," said Briggs. "See that excavation next to it and the stumps? Boches cut all the trees down to give a field of fire – stumps become another obstacle. Tanks can't push 'em over, not enough height."

Again and again, they motored past clusters of wooden crosses.

Eventually, another vast, treeless, saddle-shaped peak loomed up. Colleen's keen eyes surveyed its pockmarked slopes, still littered with the debris of battle. The jumble of mauled white stone on the peak's easternmost summit immediately identified it.

"Were you at Cassino, Private Briggs?" asked Dollie. The gaunt Bren gunner nodded, his weather-beaten face grim.

"Cassino," Hoppy murmured, shading her eyes as she looked up at the remnants of the monastery.

Here for the Allies was the gateway to 'the Eternal City.' For so many, it had been the gateway to eternity itself, as the sombre crosses mutely testified.

Colleen leant against one of the lorry's stanchions, blessing her cushion and recalling the last stanza of the ballad sung with such fervour in the hotel.

"If you look around the mountains in the mud and rain,
"You'll find the scattered crosses, some which bear no name,
"Heartbreak and toil and suffering gone,
"The boys beneath them slumber on,
"They're some of the 'D Day Dodgers,' out in Italy."

The words would always haunt her.

A little after midday, they reached their destination, a capacious three-storey building with arched balconies, located on a plateau, amid groves of Cypress pines that gave off a pleasant, resinous smell. On the other side of the road, across a ravine spanned by a viaduct bridge, arose the nearby town, a typical conglomeration of white-walled dwellings, topped by the now familiar fluted red-tiled roofs. A prominent bell tower revealed the site of the local basilica.

"Must've been the noon-time bell we heard on the way up," said Dollie.

Only Merryl's truck halted at the hospital. The remainder of the convoy continued on to the Ordinance depot in the town.

"You go straight in, ladies," Briggs urged, stepping down from his post. "We'll get your trunks sorted."

The four Sisters debussed, taking their bedrolls, cushions and web bags. Several RAMC orderlies led by a stalwart sergeant in Canadian Army uniform came doubling down the front steps to assist with the unloading.

It was then that the girls noticed how happy together Briggs and Styles were, as they helped hoist the trunks off the lorry.

"I thought he fancied Stylesie," June remarked. "How do you suppose he wangled this job?"

The answer to June's question lay in the future. It would be of particular importance for Colleen.

Matron Marian Lovejoy met them in the foyer. She was a diminutive woman in her mid thirties, dressed in the QAs' normal ward uniform of grey cotton frock and white head square. The distinct scarlet cape about her shoulders revealed that she was a Regular. A fringe of brown hair showed on her forehead and her grey-green eyes suggested shrewdness and compassion. She had been with the Eighth Army all the way from Alamein to Cassino, where she'd supervised a CCS.

Boots clicking in unison, the four new arrivals stood to attention and saluted smartly.

The matron drew herself up to attention in response, smiled and urged them to relax.

"Such strapping girls," she said, in a slight West Country accent and continued her introduction.

"We'll show you to your quarters and get you some hot water for a wash – baths are on a strict rota basis, I'm afraid. The engineers have done a wonderful job with the mains but water's still limited, unfortunately."

"We'll change into frocks, Matron?" June suggested.

"Yes, please do," said Marian. "You can have lunch in the Sisters' Mess. It's on the top floor to your left." She inclined her head towards a wide staircase behind her.

The heavy oak door to the foyer swung open to admit the sergeant they'd seen earlier. Towering over Marian, he came briskly to attention and saluted.

"Sisters' gear is stowed, Matron," he said.

Marian drew herself up to her full height again.

"Thank you, Mac," she said.

"This is Sergeant MacHendry," the matron informed the Sisters. "He'll show you to your quarters. I'll see you in the Mess later." They exchanged salutes again and Matron departed.

"This way, ladies," said MacHendry.

He strode to the rear of the foyer and turned left along a corridor that led to a set of double doors. Colleen and her companions followed him, shouldering their kit. To their right, they could look out through open windows across the balcony at the back of the building to wide lawns landscaped with trees and well-tended flowerbeds, where patients in dressing gowns and hospital blues rested on stone benches. Others exercised on crutches, some of whom, Colleen noticed, were amputees. Nursing Sisters and orderlies kept close watch.

"This was originally a hospital?" June asked

Colleen glimpsed QAs attending to patients in a dormitory on their left. She could smell iodoform.

"Pretty much, Sister," the Canadian said over his shoulder. "Sanatorium at one time, so it's fitted out OK, though we're short on accommodation. We're billeted in the town and the nurses are on the top floor, except there are no spare rooms, so your quarters are in the grounds."

"Is that the Burns Unit, Sergeant?" Colleen asked, inclining her head to the ward on their left.

"Sure is," said MacHendry soberly.

"Who looks after the flower beds?" asked Hoppy.

"Ities from the town, Sister. We feed 'em in return. But that reminds me, keep your billet locked when you're not there. I'll give you some keys."

He opened the double doors and led the girls along a concrete path to a squat stone building with several white-painted wooden doors installed in its front wall, adjacent to a rectangular gravel space. Twin wooden shutters, also painted white, were positioned above each door. A gravel driveway led from the rectangular space down the side of the hospital to the vehicle park.

"These stables are very comfortable – and they've been thoroughly disinfected," MacHendry said reassuringly, grinning at their bemused looks. "Your gear's in there and we've set up your camp beds in the loose boxes. Sappers put in facilities out back. After you've washed, use the grey water to fill up the cistern."

He opened a side door and ushered them inside, continuing his commentary.

"We laid tarpaulin on the floor but there are still some bales of straw lying about. Makes the place kinda homely."

The interior of the billet smelt of straw.

"Er, thank you, Sergeant," said June. "You've been most kind."

"Call me Mac, Sister," he said nonchalantly.

"Thanks, Mac, anything else we should know?" Dollie asked.

"Not really," said Mac with a shrug. "But the building's unheated, so I'll get you some extra blankets – it can be cold at night, even in summer. We've got paraffin lamps, so you can find your way back here in the dark. There's also a kitchen niche with a sink and paraffin stoves. Your wash water's heating there."

MacHendry threw open a pair of shutters to let in the light.

"The perimeter is secure after dark?" asked June. She set down her bedroll and other kit in her loose box.

"Patrolled at night, Sister, guard rota's my responsibility," Mac assured her, as he checked the water on the stoves. "Best not to leave food around though. Mice," he added, in answer to their puzzled looks. "Oh, and lizards, these mountains are full of 'em. But don't worry, I've never seen one around here more'n six or eight inches long."

Mac distributed the promised keys and left. The Sisters washed and changed into normal ward uniform.

"If we combined our wash water issue, we'd probably have enough for a couple of baths," Hoppy suggested as they made their way back to the main building. "We could take it in turns to soak."

Their collapsible canvas baths still reposed in their trunks, unused. The nights spent under canvas during training had necessitated only the use of their canvas buckets and washbasins.

Hoppy's idea prompted further speculation.

"While the rest of us pour in the water like Cleopatra's maidens. Worth a go, I suppose."

"I do need to wash my hair. I guess we all do."

"Mine'll need a cut soon. Wonder if there's a salon in town?"

The aroma of vegetable stew wafted down as they ascended the staircase to the top floor.

"Must have their own stove up here," said Hoppy.

On reaching the landing, they heard a male voice, sobbing piteously. Along the corridor to their right, they observed a tall patient in dressing gown being ushered back to his room by one of the Sisters.

"There, there, Major, it's all right," she said soothingly, putting her arm around him. "You mustn't take on so."

The pervasive smell of cooking came from the Sisters' Mess, at the end of the corridor. Entering the room, they encountered two other QAs seated at a long wooden table and sipping compo tea from enamel mugs.

"Hello, you must be the reinforcements," said one amiably, a slender girl with blonde curls and a Scouse accent. "I'm Julie Dalton."

"Helen Goodsall," said the other girl, who sounded Mancunian, also fair-haired, with a carefully aligned parting. "You timed it well. Grub's almost up."

She nodded toward an Aga cooker, set against the wall opposite the entrance, on which a pot of vegetable stew was simmering.

Colleen and her friends introduced themselves.

"I hear you're in the horse box?" remarked Helen.

"Yep, with the lizards," said Dollie.

"First rate concoction there, girls," Hoppy said, admiring the stew.

"We get fresh veg from the town," Julie explained. "Much better for the patients than the usual army stuff. Farms round here weren't blown to kingdom come, fortunately – and they don't use human fertiliser."

"The rest of the gang'll be along in a minute," said Helen.

She arose, went over to the cooker and stirred the contents of the pot with a ladle. Wooden working surfaces stood on each side of the Aga, with a pair of porcelain sinks at one end. Shelves containing piles of enamel plates and mugs were situated on the other side of the room, together with drawers full of cutlery. The Mess windows overlooked the nearby town.

"Sappers installed this Aga," said Julie as she got up to set out plates and utensils. "Wonderful how they got this place functional, water, sewage, electricity, storage heating for the wards, the lot."

"But the power cuts off at twenty-two hundred hours, except for night lights and the cold store," said Helen. "Sappers put that in, too."

"How many places do we need?" asked June. She and her companions moved to assist.

"A dozen should do," said Helen. "We work normal shifts. Julie and I go on after lunch, with the others."

"We're quite self-contained here," Julie added. "Main kitchen only has to cater for the patients - and the lads, of course. I guess Matron'll show you round and get you into the routine."

"Said she'd meet us here," said Hoppy, picking up a handful of knives and forks.

"We've got all sorts," Helen informed them. "Apart from immediate battle casualties. Psychiatric Ward's down the corridor, as you've probably realised."

"Who is the major?" Dollie asked. She stood at the wooden work surface helping Julie to slice tinned spam.

"Major Elkins, Guardsman originally," Julie explained. "Was in the line far too long. His company got overrun at Anzio and only about half a dozen of them came out of it besides himself. Sister Hewitt mainly looks after them. She's marvellous."

"We saw her," said Colleen, who was doling out hard tack biscuits onto a serving plate.

The sound of shoe heels clicking on the wooden floor outside and female voices in conversation alerted them to the arrival of "the rest of the gang." After another round of introductions, Julie and Helen served the portions and Sister Hewitt, who had joined the group, said Grace before they took their places. On the cooker, a kettle of water for their tea bubbled away quietly as she requested the Lord's blessing in the soft Welsh accent that had soothed the distraught Major.

Matron spoke briefly to Colleen and her companions while they were washing the dishes.

"The CO wants me to help him review the stores inventory," she explained. "But Bronwyn can show you around."

"A pleasure, Matron," said Sister Hewitt. "Have a good meeting."

"The CO's a psychiatrist actually," Bronwyn explained as she led the four of them along the corridor. "I work with him a lot."

"What's he like?" Hoppy asked.

"OK," said Sister Hewitt with a tight smile. "Too keen on drug therapy, though, for my liking. That's probably why he's summoned Matron, wants everything accounted for down to the last milligram. And he's a stickler for rules, too, so mind out."

Colleen and Hoppy glanced at each other. The Sister spoke again.

"It's a bit unusual to have a psychiatrist as a CO but the army's very concerned about war neuroses cases. Rightly so, of course."

"Like the chap we saw earlier?" June asked quietly.

The Sister's dimpled features creased into a worried frown.

"Yes, poor Major Elkins," she said with a sigh. "He's still having relapses."

The ward consisted of individual rooms, all of which, to the new Sisters' surprise, were empty. They sniffed at the pervasive smell of tobacco smoke.

"We encourage the patients to get about," Sister Hewitt continued. "I took the major into the grounds after he'd calmed down. We can air the rooms and the bedding, too."

"They chain smoke?" asked June.

Bronwyn nodded.

"Half the night sometimes."

She opened the swing doors leading to the stairwell.

"That's a bit risky, isn't it?" asked Dollie as they descended the stairwell, their heels sounding hollowly on the stone steps.

"We've taken the locks off all the doors," said Bronwyn. "An orderly's always on duty and we keep buckets of sand handy. Oh, we've got SIW patients on that floor, in a separate ward by themselves. There's quite a lot of them."

They came to the second floor landing and another set of swing doors. Sister Hewitt paused to open a wooden box fastened to the wall. She took out five surgical masks.

"You'll have to put these on," she explained. "This is the Infectious Diseases Ward, tuberculosis and diphtheria patients. No typhoid, though, thank God."

They walked slowly past beds occupied by sallow-skinned men, amongst whom moved the Ward Sisters, also masked and gloved, administering medicines or checking their patients' conditions. Colleen heard with disquiet the occasional dry, racking cough.

Passing through two sets of heavy curtain screens, they deposited their masks in a bin marked 'Used' in the intervening space.

"VD," Sister Hewitt mouthed on entering the next ward. "A lot of them, too."

Stifled screams sounded from a space partitioned off by curtains.

"Catheter treatment," said Bronwyn. "We've got some of our long-stay patients beyond here, from Anzio and Cassino. There's an operating theatre and sluice on this floor, too."

They went by several patients in traction, recovering from compound or pelvic fractures. The beds of others were empty.

"Some of these chaps are out in the grounds, then?" said Hoppy.

"Even ones who've been blinded," said Bronwyn, nodding. "Their mates guide them. They go up and down by the rear balcony steps, good exercise for them. You'll have seen the amputees out there. Some of them lost a leg when they stepped on a *Schuh* mine[23], they're terrible things."

"Who's that lad?" Colleen asked quietly. She nodded towards a patient with greyish hair, occupying a niche by himself.

"Private Hinchcliffe," Sister Hewitt whispered. "Sniper got him at Cassino, bullet grazed his spine. It's been slow going but he's reached the stage where someone needs to push him along a bit."

"I'll give it a shot," said Colleen. The others looked at her and Sister Hewitt nodded.

"OK, Sister McGrath," she said approvingly. "You're on."

Bronwyn took them downstairs and through the Burns Ward, where nurses were checking the progress of skin grafts, with patients making prodigious efforts to coax movement back into hands and fingers that resembled lumpy reddish twigs.

Another ward held patients sent down from the units near the fighting.

"It's only a short trip by ambulance from one of the American airfields," Sister Hewitt explained.

She showed them the main operating theatre, X-Ray, Pathology and other essential departments, along with the cold store, kitchen and laundry facilities. Officers' and ORs' messes were also on the ground floor.

"Local women work in the laundry?" June asked as they returned to the foyer.

"They're happy to do it for the extra rations," said Bronwyn. "Also because we're here now," she added soberly. "Hundreds of them, from ten-year-old kids to seventy-year-old grannies, were raped by the Moroccan Goums. Good soldiers but vicious brutes otherwise[24]."

Her listeners were aghast and Sister Hewitt changed the subject.

"In sum, everything's well set up here," she said.

"Thanks to the sappers?" asked Hoppy.

"Yes, indeed," Bronwyn said with emphasis. "Including Lieutenant Andy Somerville and his team. Turn their hands to anything, those lads, even put in some reflective theatre lights for us, made from petrol tins – and got rid of the bugs. Put blowtorches to the metal bed frames. They're up north, now. Andy's a bit too engrossed in his work to notice any of the girls, though, and that's a great pity because he's such a fine boy. Parson's son, you know."

June, Colleen and Hoppy all winked at Sister Dale, who pretended not to notice.

"Well, now," said Sister Hewitt. "I'd better see about your duties."

Colleen was allocated to the Burns Unit with Helen Goodsall and she started on the afternoon shift. Captain Rodwell, the MO responsible for the unit, briefed her. He was a stocky man with receding, gingery hair who dressed untidily but was renowned for his surgical skill.

"You've dealt with burns patients before, Sister, and facial injuries?" he said when she introduced herself in his office.

"Yes, sir," she told him. "At Ormskirk."

"Plenty of work for you here, then, Sister," he assured her.

Colleen's first patient was a trooper who'd been blown out of his tank by a direct hit that had done for his crewmates. Doused in blazing gasoline from the exploding fuel tank, he'd been transformed into a living torch, saved only by some quick-thinking infantrymen nearby who beat out the flames. 'Tommy Cookers' the Germans called the British tanks.

With grotesquely swollen face resembling a scorched potato, the tank-man's countenance was almost that of a ghastly Jack-o-Lantern[25]. His shrivelled eyelids necessitated regular irrigating, his lips were blackened and bulbous, his wrists and hands reduced to the gnarled stalks that Colleen had observed earlier.

Layers of dressing concealed the hideous damage. Colleen's job was to change them. Only now, after weeks, had the man's injuries stabilised sufficiently, in Captain Rodwell's judgement, for grafts to be attempted.

"Tell him that, Sister," the MO had said. "And that I'll see him tomorrow."

"Hello," Colleen said softly to the mummified victim as she halted the dressings trolley next to the bed. "Time to freshen up."

The sound of her voice brought forth a flicker of response from his eyes.

"Captain Rodwell says you'll be ready for grafting soon," she said. Delicately, she squeezed fresh water into his eyes from a small glass dropper.

She carefully removed the cotton mask from his face to expose the used dressing. Soaking it with saline solution via a second dropper, she lifted it from the raw flesh, a strip at a time, with thin forceps held in gloved hands.

Slowly, Colleen cleansed his whole face with saline, soaking away the congealed discharges from the corners of his eyes and his nostrils.

Then she sprinkled sulphonamide powder evenly over the cleansed tissue and covered it with squares of sterilised Vaseline-impregnated net gauze. Carefully sitting the patient up, Colleen overlaid the gauze with a fresh cotton mask, with holes cut for the eyes, mouth and nostrils.

Next, she unfastened the splints that kept his hands extended. On removal of the old dressings, she placed a fresh bowl of warm saline solution on the stand projecting over his bed.

"OK, slide your hands in there," she said gently.

He did so, lowering them until they were submerged above the wrists.

"Move your fingers about, that's fine," she urged. "The captain says he'll take that scar tissue off and straighten the wrists fully for the grafts. He'll tell you all about it tomorrow."

When the patient had withdrawn his hands, she patted them dry, dusted them with sulphonamide powder, wrapped his fingers individually with strips of the Vaseline gauze and re-applied the splints.

The whole ministration took an hour.

"All done," she said.

As she made for the next bed, the bulbous lips parted and a croaky voice sounded.

"Be ye from North Riding, lass?"

"Born and bred," she whispered. "See you later."

The orderlies on shift would irrigate the eyes of this patient and others, at regular intervals, day and night.

But these men had their sight. Colleen's next patient had been blown up by a shell burst, razor-edged shards from the rocky slopes on which it had exploded adding grievously to the blast injuries, an occurrence all too common in the battle for the monastery.

His face was seared like that of the previous patient but his eyes and eyelids were gone, scoured away by the burst, that had also left his hands no more than knobbly stumps[26]. At least he hadn't lost his jaw or nose. That could easily have happened, requiring bone grafts or a flap of flesh transposed from the forehead.

Colleen carried out the same treatment. Another hour elapsed.

"Captain Rodwell says he'll remould your thumbs and forefingers," she murmured as she patted the stumps dry. "He'll explain when he visits tomorrow." She consciously substituted "visits" for "sees".

This patient also spoke to Colleen as she was clearing up.

"You've got a gentle touch, Sister," he said.

She thanked him, feeling her eyes smarting, grateful that she could.

By the time Colleen and Helen had seen to the dressings, their patients were due for their evening meal.

Colleen stood by a man who'd been hit in the face by a heavy calibre bullet. His right eye had been torn out, his right cheekbone and part of the roof of his mouth had all been shot away. He couldn't speak and he was still recovering from the emergency operation that had saved his life.

Moreover, the machine gun burst disfiguring this soldier had caught him in both arms and these lay impotently by his sides, swathed in plaster. Like several other patients, he would undergo a number of operations for compound fractures.

"Supper time," said Colleen invitingly as she eased the meal trolley beside his bed. "If you lean your head on the left side of the pillow – that's it," she advised while helping him sit upright, "we'll get underway."

His meal consisted on chicken vegetable broth, followed by rice pudding fortified with treacle.

"At least you won't get indigestion this way," she remarked.

Colleen carefully delivered the warm broth to the patient's open mouth a teaspoonful at a time. She watched him swallow and gently dabbed the side of his jaw with a towel to clear away any excess that dribbled through the gaping hole in his cheek[27].

"I'll write to your missus, OK?" she suggested, as she spooned in the pudding.

After she'd finished feeding him, she syringed away all trace of food particles from the delicate stitches securing what was left of his palate, collecting the runoff in an enamel basin.

"If they haven't shaved you by this time tomorrow, I'll do it," she said while tidying up. "I can't stand men who don't shave."

The ghost of a smile flickered across the devastated visage.

Sister McGrath's next patient could talk, see and move his limbs. But a blast from a so-called "Bouncing Betty"[28] mine had caused him serious rectal damage, torn out most of his stomach and necessitated a colostomy operation, leaving the characteristic 'appliance' - a rubber bag - attached to his left side immediately below the belt line.

Colleen took his blood pressure, temperature and pulse rate, then checked his appliance for skin irritation at the point of attachment.

"How is it, Sister?" he asked.

"OK," she assured him.

She placed his meal before him, modest portions of scrambled powdered egg and boiled rice with a small dish of tinned peaches.

"Good balance, this," said Colleen. "We'll get some proper eggs tomorrow."

The patient smiled gratefully, dipping a teaspoon into the egg mash. His suffering had aged him prematurely, though his colour was healthy and his eyes were bright.

"MO says I'll be on my way home soon," he remarked, having chewed and swallowed his first mouthful with great deliberation. "Can't wait. Wrote to the missus, 'All things work together for good to them that love God,' she wrote back. We're chapel folk, you see[29]."

"You're lucky to have each other," said Colleen, smiling.

The soldier took another spoonful.

"Known each other since we were kids," he said. "Got married just before I was called up. We'll manage, missus says in her letters. Lord's got plans for us."

Colleen's shift ended soon afterwards. She met up with Hoppy as they'd arranged and, paraffin lamps in hand, they returned to the stables.

"Better do some washing," said Hoppy with a yawn.

Setting aside a portion of their water ration for tea and brushing teeth, they heated the remainder, lathered some soap in an enamel bowl, hand-washed shirts, stockings and underwear, rinsed them out in a second bowl, then hung them on the cord Mac had strung between two posts in the passageway behind the loose boxes. The wet garments would conveniently drip into a drain that ran the length of the passage. Clothing June and Dollie had washed earlier already hung from the cord.

Dollie was asleep nearby, huddled under the extra blankets that Mac had supplied. June was on shift.

"Do some ironing tomorrow," Hoppy said quietly.

They could heat their little flat irons with the paraffin stoves. It made them feel self-sufficient.

On completing their ablutions, they brewed the tea and retired to their loose boxes. Colleen placed the lamp and her mug of tea on the blood box serving as a bedside table, climbed into her camp bed and wrapped the blankets around her.

"Oh, that's good," she said, taking a long draught of tea.

She could feel her eyelids drooping but nevertheless penned a short note to Tony and another one to Sister Linton.

Dear Annie.

Am on Burns Unit, for now. Also have patients in intensive care. One lad said to me, 'All things work together for good to them that love God.'

He must have wonderful faith, because he's had a colostomy...

Tomorrow, she would write to her patients' loved ones.

Dear...

I met your husband/brother/son/fiancé on the ward today. He is doing very well and looking forward to coming home. As you are aware, he has been seriously injured but with your support he can continue to make good progress...

Please do not hesitate to write to me if you wish.

Yours sincerely,

C. McGrath, Nursing Officer, QAIMNS/R.

While she was sealing the letter to Anne, a fragment of Biblical Text came to her.

Dead in trespasses and sins[30]

"God, is that me?" she said out loud, as she extinguished the lamp. "And what am I supposed to do?"

In the morning, Colleen and Hoppy met with June, Sister Hewitt and several of the other girls in the mess. Dollie was on the morning shift. Having a few hours to themselves, Colleen and her friends wore walking-out uniform.

"Eggs over easy?" asked Julie Dalton, looking up from the stove. "Or reconstituted?"

"As we find 'em, thanks, JD," said Hoppy. She seated herself beside Colleen. "How'd you get on, June?"

"Pretty quiet," said June. She put her hand to her mouth as she yawned. "Changing dressings on the amputees and SIWs before settling them down – those holes in their feet'll take weeks to heal. Calming a few who're still having nightmares, then watching the abdominals and chests after that. What about you two?"

"Ready," Julie announced.

"Getting an education from the VD patients," said Sister Hopgood dryly as she queued up. "'We find 'em, feel 'em and in the end forget 'em, with another 'f' in there, Sister,' I was reliably informed. So, you give them a jab of penicillin and help the MO scour off the lesions."

"They don't forget that in a hurry," said Helen, with a wince.

Colleen collected her egg and spam.

"What're we doing today, before we're back on?" she asked.

"Kip," said June.

"Me too," said Helen, who'd worked a double shift.

"It's a nice day, come and kip on the beach," said Bronwyn. "We go whenever we can," she informed Colleen and her companions. "It's only about forty miles away by road. Transport there and back's never any problem."

"Sounds good," murmured June. She glanced at Helen, who agreed.

"I'll do some baking," Sister Dalton proposed. "I saved the fat from all the tinned meat. Handful of crushed-up dog biscuits, couple of tins of peaches and I can turn out a few pies."

"We'll get some extra flour," Hoppy offered. "Coll and I'll go into town – and bring back some more fruit and veg. And eggs, if we can get them."

"That'd be most helpful, Hoppy," said Julie. "OK with you, Coll?"

"So long as we can get our hair done," said Sister McGrath with aplomb, sipping her tea.

"Oh, hark at Lady Muck!" exclaimed Bronwyn with a laugh. "Actually, they've got a pretty good salon and they speak English. Called Enrico's. If you see them first thing, I'm sure they'll fit you in this morning. You'll have to go with Sergeant Mac, though," she insisted. "Or a couple of his merry men."

"Ities've been known to rough up Allied female personnel, even in broad daylight," Helen warned. "And murder our blokes for their boots, after dark[31]."

Returning to the stables, Colleen sat on an upturned blood box in the kitchen annex with her head bent, awaiting the inevitable. The nausea had come upon her suddenly.

"What's wrong, Coll?" Hoppy asked when she came in from making arrangements with Sergeant Mac.

"Wretched mepacrine[32], that, and – well, you know. 'Scuse me."

Colleen hastened to the latrine annex and heaved up her breakfast. When she emerged, Hoppy handed her a mug of water. Colleen rinsed her mouth out and Hoppy gave her a small glass of syrupy medication.

"Thanks," said Colleen in a strained voice.

"Hit me the last night in Naples," her friend said sympathetically.

Having emptied her stomach, Colleen was starting to feel better. She donned her jacket and beret, collected her web bag and went with Hoppy to meet Mac. Several patients waved to them from the hospital balconies.

As they approached the vehicle apron, they saw the sergeant in earnest conversation with Sister Dalton, who was smiling demurely at him.

Sisters Hopgood and McGrath immediately began to speculate.

"Why isn't JD baking pies?"

"Summat else is cooking, I reckon."

MacHendry noticed his two passengers and greeted them with a wave.

"Hi ladies!" he called. "Climb aboard."

He pointed to a jeep nearby.

"I'll see to those extra oxygen bottles for you, Sister," he said to Julie as she discreetly retired to the building.

"Andy Somerville's boys fixed up a couple of iron lungs for the TB patients," MacHendry explained as Colleen and Hoppy clambered into the rear seats. "My buddy Doug Prescott'll be with us in a minute, he's orderly corporal."

Another Canadian, tall, wiry and Nordic like MacHendry, came loping down the steps.

"I got the CO's authorisation, Mac," he declared. "Let's go."

MacHendry started the vehicle and turned left for the viaduct bridge.

"We would've walked for the exercise," said Hoppy, leaning forward. "But Bronwyn said we had to go with you."

Corporal Prescott looked over his shoulder and grinned.

"If you want exercise, wait'll Major Lovejoy corrals you for one of her PT sessions, Sister," he told her.

"How'd you get to join this hospital?" Hoppy asked, as they drove over the bridge.

"We were with First Canadians at Ortuna," Prescott explained. "Then Fifth Canadians relieved us. Figured they'd show us how to win the war[33]. Kraut First Parachutes sobered 'em up, eh, Mac?"

"Amen!" exclaimed MacHendry, nosing the jeep past a couple of mule-drawn carts. "We went back up the line a few days later and ran into the Fifth again. Couldn't decide who was gonna lead the way so First and Fifth Canadians got into a stand-up brawl."

"You shoulda seen it, Sisters!" exclaimed Prescott. "We were down in the valley, with your guys on one hill, Krauts on the other. They must've wondered what was going on."

"You men!" Hoppy chided them. "You're hopeless."

"General Montgomery wasn't best pleased either," MacHendry said. He manoeuvred the jeep along an unsealed street that ran between adjoining tenements with yellowish walls, shuttered windows and arched doorways. Dark-eyed locals gazed at them dully.

"Monty sent First Canadians to the Cassino sector," Mac continued. "That's where we met your outfit. They were down on numbers, so we transferred over on permanent loan."

"Grateful for a quiet spell right now," Prescott added. "We're front line medics mostly."

MacHendry brought the jeep to a halt outside the Ordinance Depot, a multi-storey building with a courtyard where vehicles and stores could be safeguarded. It was located on one side of the town square, opposite the church with its imposing bell tower. Market stalls stood on the cobbled expanse in between and were thronging with shoppers, including a sprinkling of Eighth Army personnel, both men and women.

"I'll tell 'em we've arrived," said Mac. He vaulted out of his seat. "We'll stay with you while you shop and get sorted in the depot when you're in Enrico's. That's his place," he added, pointing to a nearby shop front. "Julie - Sister Dalton - said you're going there first to book in?"

"Sure are," said Hoppy. "Then we'll meet you outside, OK? Sorry it's a bit complicated."

"No problem, ladies," Prescott assured them. "We'll see you in a bit."

The Sisters climbed out and Prescott drove the jeep into the courtyard.

"'Julie,' eh?" Hoppy remarked as Mac headed for the depot's entrance. "What'd I tell you, Coll?"

The four of them returned to the hospital about three hours later, with the passengers cradling boxes of eggs for the patients on their laps and enclosed by splints, crutches and other supplies. MacHendry and Prescott would make another trip for the oxygen bottles. Colleen and Hoppy's web bags were crammed with fresh fruit and vegetables purchased from the market stalls, together with bags of flour.

"We'll sort all the stuff for the patients," MacHendry said to Colleen and Hoppy as he stopped the jeep at the hospital entrance. "You go on up."

"Thanks, Mac," said Hoppy.

"That was a good morning's work," Colleen remarked when they entered the foyer. "And these *coiffures* are OK." She lightly touched her fringe.

"Sisters!" a male voice said curtly.

Instantly, they stood to attention and saluted.

An officer in crisp uniform stepped briskly towards them, a man of medium height with a toothbrush moustache and monocle in his right eye, fastened to a red and black striped cord inserted into the breast pocket of his jacket. His hair showed darkly beneath his peaked cap.

He was Major Ernest Forsythe MC, their CO.

"All purchases of consumables require *my* authorisation," he snapped, ignoring their salutes and fixing his gaze on their bulging web bags.

"Sir?" asked Hoppy, perplexed.

"You are confined to the hospital grounds until further notice."

His voice reminded Colleen of a ban saw in operation.

"We were going to the basilica on Sunday, sir," she said quietly.

Forsythe glared at Colleen, removed his monocle and fiercely twisted the attached cord between his fingers.

"Until then. Dismissed!" he retorted, spun on his heel and strode off to his office.

"Stupid git," muttered Colleen.

"Might have known," said Hoppy with a sigh. "He ticked me off for smiling at VD patients yesterday. Anyway, smart move, mentioning the church. I'm not one of your mob, but I'll tag along."

"Oh, he *didn't*," Julie remonstrated when her friends related the incident.

Owing to other commitments, she'd only started the baking and was most appreciative of what Colleen and Hoppy had brought back.

"It's our fault, really," said Julie, kneading flour into the crushed biscuits. "We ought to have told you when he did his rounds. Mac or Scottie should have, too. I'll have words with those cowboys." She wiped her hands on her apron.

"Don't worry, JD," said Colleen dismissively, seated at the table with Hoppy and sipping tea. "It's only 'til Sunday."

"Coll said she was going to church," Hoppy explained.

"Well, I was thinking about it."

Julie shook her head slowly and reached for the rolling pin.

"I'd like to put *this* round his lug," she declared. "Honestly, if anyone's a nut case around here, *he* is."

Getting on for lunchtime, Colleen was strolling through the grounds, watching the patients exercising on their crutches. One of the attendant Sisters was bringing out the tea trolley.

Colleen noticed Major Elkins sitting by himself on a wooden bench, in the shade of an overhanging Cypress bough, smoking a cigarette.

"Mind if I join you?" she asked. He smiled faintly and motioned to the empty space on the bench beside him. She walked over to him and sat down.

"How long've you been in Italy?" he asked.

"Only a few days, came up from Naples yesterday. What about you?"

He drew on his cigarette.

"A long time, too long, they reckon," he said dolefully.

"You were at Anzio?" she asked gently. He nodded.

"Landed in January, stayed 'til the breakout in May."

He paused. Colleen glanced at him, hoping that her presence would help him unburden. "We need to break that logjam in his head," Sister Hewitt had said.

"Spent weeks in 'The Fortress'[34]," he said, gazing at a set of vapour trails in the sky that indicated a high-flying bomber formation. "Holed-up in ravines, open ground above was just minefields. Trenches full of mud, graves all around, only a bayonet for a marker, stuck in 'em with an identity disc. Had to be careful you didn't unearth any corpses when you extended a trench. Derelict tanks lying about, all sorts of discarded kit – and dead cattle, blown up by the mines. Place stank to high heaven. Most of the action was at night. First the evening stonk – mortars, then the MGs, ours and theirs, echoes off the walls of the ravines sounded like a witches' Sabbath…"

Colleen watched the vapour trails diffusing in the stratosphere.

"Can I get you a cup of tea?" she asked.

"Oh, allow me, Sister, please."

Elkins stubbed out the cigarette and got to his feet.

"Though I'm sure it's only fit for chucking into latrines," he added.

Colleen laughed and thanked him. He strode purposefully toward the trolley, then stopped and glanced over his shoulder.

"You lassies were wonderful, at Anzio," he told her, before walking on.

She leant back against the bench upright and stretched her limbs.

I'm going to be awash, she thought.

But maybe the logjam was breaking.

A while before she went back on duty, Colleen visited Private Hinchcliffe.

He looked up, his deeply lined face creased in puzzlement.

"Hello, Private Hinchcliffe," said Colleen. "I'm Sister McGrath. Sit up for me, please."

Before he could hesitate, she'd removed his blankets and was helping him to perch on the edge of the bed. She passed him his dressing gown and fitted his slippers onto his feet.

"Now then," she continued. "Sister Hewitt says you're from Rochdale?"

"Aye," he said, still bemused.

"Well, in my part of the north, we reckon a Lancashire lad's really a Yorkshireman with his brains kicked out, so it shouldn't hurt you to stand. Here, I'll help."

He grinned hugely and his face lost its vacant look.

She put his left arm over her shoulder and slipped her right arm around his waist.

"Don't do your back in, Sister," he said anxiously. "I'm a pretty big chap."

Hinchcliffe was not heavily built but stood over six feet.

"So you are, Hinch," Colleen assured him. "But we'll manage. Now, ready, stand. Wonderful!"

"What now, Sister?" Hinch asked, pleased with progress.

"We're going to walk around to the other side of the bed. Lean on me if you have to. Let's go."

He shuffled forward. Then he faltered and gasped, but Colleen's firm grip restrained him.

"It's OK," she said soothingly. "You won't fall with me here. Keep going."

Cautiously, they edged forward to the other side of the bed, where both of them sat down.

"Phew!" exclaimed Hinch.

"You're favouring that right leg," Colleen said briskly. "Show me your knee."

Meekly he rolled up his pyjama trouser leg, revealing the telltale scars.

"When did you have your cartilages out?"

"During PTC. Right pain."

"Hmm. Sit on the floor for me, please. And stick your legs out, straight as you can."

Colleen eased him into a sitting position on the floor, felt the space under his right knee, then pushed down on the knee, hard.

"Ow!" protested Hinch.

"Have to be cruel to be kind, soldier. That'll do for now, though, let's get you up."

Colleen got him back to bed, departed for the sluice and returned with a bowl of warm water. She helped him off with his pyjama jacket and began to sponge him. Beads of sweat were coursing down his face from the exertion.

"You've done splendidly, Hinch," she said, dabbing his forehead. "But you didn't get enough physio after the knee ops because you can't fully extend your right leg. How you managed all that time in the infantry, Heaven only knows. You're as tough as teak, lad."

His craggy face widened into a grin again, as she patted the cloth over his chest and shoulders.

"Right," she insisted. "I want you to extend your right leg, every hour on the hour while you're awake, three sets of ten repetitions. Then we'll increase it."

She glanced down at the watch fastened to her blouse.

"I'll come and see you tomorrow," she said. "I'm going on duty now."

"What?" Hinch asked in surprise. "Aren't you already?"

Colleen shook her head.

"This is only a warm-up. I've got lots more lads to sort besides you."

"Pity those poor sods," Hinch muttered.

On the way to their wards, Colleen and Hoppy happened to meet a crestfallen Sergeant Mac.

"I'll make it up to you, I promise," he insisted. "Doug and I'll drive you to church."

"Do you reckon JD used a rolled-up newspaper?" said Hoppy, when they were out of earshot.

"Woof, woof," murmured Colleen.

Matron Lovejoy believed in variety of experience. Not only did she dragoon off-duty Sisters into regular PT sessions on a football pitch that adjourned the hospital grounds, as Corporal Prescott had warned but she changed the Sisters' duties and shifts with calculated frequency.

"You need to be adaptable," she insisted. "At least you won't get bored."

Such was the devotion she inspired that the changes were assimilated with neither complaint nor loss of efficiency.

It was otherwise with Major Forsythe.

Colleen's second *contretemps* occurred not long after she relieved Hoppy on the VD Ward. Like Sister Hopgood, Colleen was observed smiling comfortingly at the patients.

"You're not supposed to smile at us, Sister," one of them said after she'd injected him with the regular dose of penicillin.

"I won't grass if you don't," she whispered.

The CO confronted her on the landing as she was taking the syringes for sterilisation.

"Sister McGrath," he said abruptly. "Nursing officers must not display any amiability towards those patients. They are malingerers. Is that clear?"

"Yes, sir," she said meekly, inwardly resolved to ignore the admonition. But she was vexed nonetheless.

"Sod it," she said to herself when Forsythe had gone. "He knows who I am."

However, her spirits were lifted a few days later when she received a message from Captain Gatacre.

I seem to be touring half the sigs installations in the country, his note said. *But I'll be visiting your patch next week. What about dinner?*

By then, Colleen was due for night duty, overlapping with Dollie on the Infectious Diseases Ward but she'd definitely fit in dinner with Tony.

They met in the foyer at 1900 hours on the day.

"You look gorgeous," said Tony. He gazed at her longingly. Colleen was grateful to the Italian ladies who'd expertly laundered her walking-out uniforms and even painstakingly brushed her headgear.

"C'mon," she said, taking his arm. She noticed a holstered revolver hanging from his belt.

They climbed into his jeep, whereupon she leant over and kissed him affectionately.

"Oh, it's so good to see you," she whispered. "Where're we going for nosh? I'm starved."

"Yeah, I've missed you, too," he said, embracing her. "*Trattoria* in town if that's OK, owned by some bloke named Enrico apparently. I hear it's pretty good."

It was. The food and the wine were excellent and the waiter serenaded them with a violin.

"Your eyes sparkle in the candlelight," Tony remarked during the meal. "And it gives your hair a real sheen."

"Flattery will get you everywhere, sir," Colleen said with a slight toss of her fringe.

But she wasn't prepared for what came after Gatacre had ordered coffee. He held her hand in his and spoke in a voice full of emotion.

"Look, Colleen, I haven't stopped thinking about you since we went to Capri. I reckon the war'll be over by next spring and, well, we're going to keep seeing each other, so, will you marry me, next spring, that is? We'd go straight home, because I'll be due for Blighty then. My priest'll fix it."

Colleen hoped that the hot and cold flushes she was experiencing weren't visible in the candlelight. She swallowed hard before answering.

"I'd like that very much, Tony," she said, feeling quite overwhelmed.

Dollie was open-mouthed when Colleen related events.

"*Marry* him?" she exclaimed. "He *is* smitten, Coll. Guess you are too. Well, Lord bless you both."

Sister Dale would soon discover she was not immune to the love bug herself but first she would be faced with a much deadlier infection.

About 1:00 a.m., Colleen was seated at the ward desk, reviewing the patients' records for the results of X-Rays, blood and sputum tests. She was also composing a letter to the RC Chaplain attached to the hospital, Father St John Montague-Stewart, about Father Alonzo's orphanage and another one to Annie telling her of Tony's proposal.

The patients were mostly slumbering. Occasionally, Colleen heard that characteristic hollow cough and her heart ached. Nevertheless, Sister Dale was on hand keeping watch – and monitoring the ward's remaining diphtheria patient.

Then Dollie tiptoed over to her.

"Coll," she whispered, through her mask. "Could you please see what Hoppy wants? She's waving madly from the stairwell."

Colleen hastened to the sets of double doors and pushed through them to join her friend.

"What's up?" she asked, removing and pocketing her mask.

"Can you help me get Captain Rodwell into bed? He's legless."

"*What?*"

"Drunk as a fiddler's bitch[35]. We can't let the ORs find out. That's why I've come here."

Colleen placed a hand on her forehead and breathed a sigh.

"Where is he?"

"In the CO's car. Scottie too, likewise blotto."

"*Scottie?* How'd he get into an officers' do?"

Colleen was astounded. She'd assumed that another officer would have made up the foursome.

"He's got a BD blouse with pips," said Hoppy sheepishly. "He and Rodwell got tippling with a couple of the Yank flyboys. Helen's gone to fetch Sergeant Mac – he's in charge of the guard tonight, thank God. They'll get Scottie back to his billet, while we sort Rodders."

"God in heaven. Who drove the CO's car back?"

"I did."

Colleen groaned.

"Eyepiece Ernie'll have your guts for garters, Hoppy."

"Another reason for keeping *stum.*"

Colleen quickly apprised Dollie then sped down to the vehicle park with Hoppy. Earlier that evening, Hoppy and Helen had gone with Captain Rodwell to a dance at the nearby American air base. The CO was away. He'd departed that morning with the RC padre to a high-level meeting in Naples in the padre's staff car – a late model Bentley – having expressly forbidden anyone to use *his* vehicle.

The stricture had merely presented a challenge.

MOs' quarters were located on the ground floor and they'd sneak Rodwell in by a side entrance.

"I'll see to the mileage and the petrol. We should get away with it," Mac said when they met by the car.

They did, but rumours circulated and when the CO returned, he looked daggers at the main conspirators, especially Sister Hopgood.

For the present, though, the night had further adventure in store.

Infectious diseases were commonplace in Italy and the RASC driver on Sister Dale's ward was one of several patients admitted in recent weeks suffering from diphtheria. Happily, most had been cured and discharged, thanks to penicillin and anti-toxin serum.

The remaining victim was one of the few individuals who manifested an allergy to the wonder drug and the disease was not yet arrested. Moreover, he had needed a tracheotomy to get sufficient air into his lungs.

Ominously, his increasingly wheezing breaths during the night showed that the device was not functioning properly.

"Get Larry, Coll," Dollie urged.

Colleen dashed downstairs for the second time that shift. Lieutenant Lawrence Jardine was the MO on call.

Colleen opened his door without knocking in accordance with standing orders and said, "Sir, the diphtheria patient…"

Instantly, the Jardine's lanky form leapt out of bed. He donned his slippers, snatched up his dressing gown and charged out the doorway past the startled Sister, whom he'd almost spun like a top, calling over his shoulder, "Close the door, please, Coll."

Immediately Colleen left, the patient's condition rapidly grew worse.

"Father, he's going to choke," Dollie said out loud, aware she couldn't wait for Jardine.

Quickly, she fetched a slim catheter tube and enamel bowl.

Leaning over the patient, she said, "I'm going to shift that blockage."

His breath was issuing in desperate gasps. Dollie placed a restraining hand on his shoulder.

"Hang on," she whispered.

Then she slid the catheter down the tracheotomy tube until she judged it had entered the man's airway.

Dollie placed her mouth over the other end of the catheter tube and cautiously began to draw breath.

Something gave way. Dollie immediately removed her mouth from the catheter, sealed the top with her finger and pulled it clear of the tracheotomy tube.

The man's chest heaved, he uttered a shuddering sigh and his breathing returned to normal. Dollie placed the catheter in the bowl and covered it with a linen cloth. She estimated that the tube would be about half-full of disease-laden mucus.

"Thank you, Father," she said.

At that instant, Lieutenant Jardine came hurrying through the curtained partition, Colleen a few steps behind him. Sister Dale whispered, "Shh," and in low tones described what had transpired. Colleen looked aghast.

"We'd better immunise you, Sister[36]," the MO said gravely.

Providentially, the shadow of death had receded, for now.

Several days later, Sister Dale had another memorable encounter, of a wholly different nature.

Matron had transferred her to the afternoon shift. While on duty, she went to deposit a stack of patient files at the reception desk.

The front door opened and in came a sun-tanned young officer in KDs and beret, wearing the insignia of the Royal Engineers. Startled by his sudden entrance, Dollie dropped several of the files on the floor.

"Oh, I'm sorry, Sister," the officer said. "Allow me."

Nimbly, he gathered up the spilled documents and placed them on the desk. Removing his beret, he smiled and said, "By the way, I'm Andy Somerville."

"Pleased to meet you," said Sister Dale. "Olivia Dale. Most people call me Dollie."

She extended her right hand. He took it gently. She sensed the strength in the lad's fingers and she liked the look of him; above average height, fair-haired, clear-eyed - and sinewy, like many of the sappers were.

"I'm on a routine visit," Andy explained. "We check all our installations first-hand, if we can, periodic maintenance. Also, I'm seeing how much of our Bailey bridge kit down here we can backload for crossings up north."

She nodded, sorting the files into alphabetical order on the counter.

"You installed our billets," she said casually. "The stables."

She smiled at his audible intake of breath.

"Oh," he said. "Hope they're OK."

"Fine. Bit on the chilly side, though, with summer on the wane."

"Hmm, sorry about that," Andy said apologetically. "I'll make it up to you, though. Do you like opera?"

"Opera?"

"Yes. I'm also attending the RE training school at Capua for a course. They have regular performances there, pretty high standard. I'd be happy to escort you."

"Oh, well, fine. I'm on evenings right now but I'll arrange a swap. Will you be around tomorrow?"

"You bet, I'm here for the football match, too."

"Oh, that! One of us is playing, Sister McGrath."

"I know!" Somerville exclaimed, then glanced at his watch. "Sorry, got to dash," he said. "I'm meeting your Sergeant MacHendry to check the boiler and the fridge."

Nevertheless, he accompanied her to the staircase, where they paused.

"Our billets are splendid, really," said Dollie. "You must have worked jolly hard."

The lieutenant smiled, inserting his beret into a trouser pocket.

"Our pleasure, Dollie. Beats what we were doing before, with minefields, opposed river crossings and all that. Chap could come to harm that way. Is it OK if I call you Olivia?"

"Mum and Dad call me Livvie. No reason why you can't, I suppose."

"Thanks – Livvie."

Somerville strode off to find Mac.

"Parson's son, is he?" Dollie murmured. "Hmm…"

The football match was Captain Rodwell's idea and word had spread rapidly, so that participants and spectators came from far and wide. In addition to Lieutenant Somerville, they included Captain Fordham, Dinah Merryl, Mollie Styles and her ever-attentive companion, Fusilier Briggs.

Sister McGrath's intention to take part also caused a stir.

"My dear!" exclaimed Sister Hewitt, when Colleen announced it in the mess one afternoon. "Nursing officers don't play football."

"This one does," said Colleen.

As an only daughter, trying to be the son her father had wanted but never had, Colleen had played football – and rugby, climbed trees, run races and wrestled in the dirt with the sons of ironworkers, navvies, dockers and shipwrights.

At twenty two, she stood tall, long-limbed and lithe, a resolute young woman whom even Queen Boadicea or Queen Alexandra herself would have been proud to call her own.

A game of football with a bunch of army blokes would be a doddle.

Colleen's offer to take part in the game was accepted unanimously by the other players.

To maximise the advantage of speed, she suggested wearing her bathing costume bottoms instead of PT shorts but June was adamant, likewise Matron and Sister Hewitt.

"Absolutely not. Far too skimpy."

Sergeant Mac chivalrously obtained a male jersey for her, less revealing than the normal female PT top. The ground was not slippery so everyone agreed to wear plimsolls for the match.

"It'll be safer," said June. "Especially if anyone kicks your shins."

"Or I kick his," retorted Colleen.

"Even with that jersey, you could wear a bra a size too small," Dollie suggested. "Minimise movement - you know."

On the morning of the match, a Saturday, Mac, Prescott and Briggs scoured the pitch to ensure it was free of stones and strung scrounged camouflage nets for the goalmouths. Rev Allerton, the Anglican padre, would referee. He was in his forties, portly and wore specs but had stamina and was raring to go.

Kick-off was sharp at 1430 hours. Captains Rodwell and Fordham would skipper the opposing sides.

"We'll serve tea and buns at seventeen-hundred hours," Matron promised.

"The Lord's given us a fine day, Matron," Allerton remarked as the teams assembled.

A warm breeze was stirring the Cypress groves, wafting their fragrance across the grounds.

"That's why we asked you to referee, sir," said Andy Somerville, lacing up his shoes. He grinned at Dollie, who tried to hide her blushes.

"Didn't know she was an opera lover, did you?" Colleen whispered to Hoppy and June.

The top balcony of the hospital overlooked the pitch and as many patients as possible were moved there for the event, including Private Hinchcliffe. Those more mobile gathered on the sidelines. Several nearing the end of their convalescence were taking part, including some who'd had an arm amputated but whose lower limbs were sound.

Major Elkins was also playing. He hadn't looked back since his conversation with Colleen and would soon be going home.

Light and fast, Colleen was placed on the wing. She'd change sides with her opposite number at half time.

"Whichever team has you possesses an unfair advantage, Sister," the players insisted.

The game proceeded amid shouts of exultation from the spectators. Colleen succeeded in setting up several goal shots for Jardine, the striker.

At half-time, she ambled over to her colleagues and sank down onto the grass.

"Phew, another forty minutes to go," she remarked.

"You've getting jostled a bit," said June. "But you're playing a blinder."

"Too right," added Hoppy. "Those flashing legs've got the opposition stymied."

"They're going to be black and blue tomorrow," Colleen said with a sigh, glancing down at the grazes on her limbs.

Padre Allerton blew his whistle.

"Go get 'em, Coll," chorused several of the Sisters.

"You're on our side now, Sister," shouted her erstwhile opposition.

The match continued with great exuberance, ending in a draw, amid exclamations of "Well done, Sister," as the players came off the pitch.

After a hot bath that brought ecstatic relief to her battered legs, Colleen changed into ward uniform and tripped up the stairs to the top floor. She'd have tea with the patients there, help get them back into their wards and then resume her shift – after another exercise session with Hinch.

"Think I'll skip church tomorrow," she muttered as she reached the top landing. The decision did not stem merely from anticipated residual fatigue. Her spirit was restive and she was finding the ritual of the mass increasingly hollow.

It's your fault, Annie, she thought, and yours, Dollie.

On the landing, she came face-to-face with the CO. He had viewed the game from the top balcony. She stood to attention and saluted. Forsythe ignored it.

"I do *not* approve of exhibitionism, Sister," he said curtly. "Your conduct is reprehensible and it will be entered on your record."

Whereupon, he disappeared downstairs.

"You sound like a broken one," Colleen hissed when he'd gone.

Hinch was now able to walk several lengths of the balcony.

Colleen accompanied him, helping him build confidence. He leant on her as necessary.

Her nursing colleagues naturally proffered helpful comment.

"He just wants to put his arm around you, Coll."

"You'll have him doing the Lambeth Walk next, Coll."

"No reason you couldn't, Hinch," Colleen suggested encouragingly. "Take the missus dancing, I mean. We'll make sure about the physio back home."

Her tactics varied. Occasionally, she'd provoke him to greater exertion.

"You've seen the Ghurkas holding their own drip bottles when they came down, not taking morphia?"

"At Cassino, oh, aye."

"Well, a Lancashire lad's not going to be beaten by some little brown blokes, is he?"

"I might be maimed and halt, like the Book says," Hinch remarked on one occasion when her alertness had prevented him from losing his balance. "Thank God I'm not blind, though."

Sister McGrath was by nature presumptuous and she was about to incur the consequences – again.

"My mate Annie says I should get a Bible. 'Man shall not live by bread alone, but by every word that proceedeth out of the mouth of God,' she reckons."

Colleen had a good memory for scriptural passages. Her repeated citations to Hinch eventually attracted the attention of her superior.

Several days after the football match, she was summoned to Forsythe's office. Father Montague-Stewart and Padre Allerton were also present.

She stood to attention and saluted.

Seated at his desk, the major glared up at her, twisting his monocle strap as usual.

Montague-Stewart sat to the CO's right, his expression stern. The Father was a thickset man, greyish haired, his eyes cold and penetrating.

Forsythe spoke up.

"It has come to my notice, Sister McGrath, that you have been attempting to minister spiritually to one of the patients, namely Private Hinchcliffe. Is that correct?"

"Yes, sir."

"Then you have exceeded your responsibilities, have you not?"

"Yes, sir."

Montague-Stewart stirred in his chair and held up a paper. Colleen recognised it as the letter she'd sent to him about Father Alonzo.

"You wrote this communication, Sister?" he said severely.

"Yes, sir."

The Father turned to Forsythe. Colleen remained at attention. She could see the town through the window behind Forsythe's desk.

"You have no business meddling in civilian affairs, Sister McGrath," said the CO. "I shall be speaking to your colleagues about this matter as well."

June, Hoppy and Dollie had all written to the Father.

"Have you anything to say for yourself?" the CO asked.

"No, sir."

"Then - dismissed."

Colleen saluted, turned on her heel and marched out of the room.

Rev Allerton later disclosed the rest of the conversation.

"She's trouble, Forsythe," growled Montague-Stewart. "Get rid of her."

"Can you afford to, sir?" Allerton asked.

Forsythe looked from one to the other, scowling.

"Not now, Father," he said to the priest. "Unit's only just up to strength."

Montague-Stewart maintained his cold stare.

"Then we must bide our time." Turning to Allerton, he added, "You appreciate the sensitive nature of this discussion, Reverend?"

"I know my place, Father," the padre said, smiling benignly.

Entering the billet after her shift, Colleen found Dollie seated on a blood box in the kitchen niche.

She'd been crying.

Colleen's companions had all received the Star Chamber treatment during the day, Dollie just before coming off duty.

Colleen pulled up another box and sat beside her, putting an arm around her.

"Thanks, Coll," murmured Dollie. "But it's not the CO and his pals – and Reverend Allerton's OK, no it's - something else."

"Andy?"

"He's fine. We've haven't looked back since the opera."

"He's a good lad."

"Loves the Lord and believes the Book. Can't ask better than that. But while I was up before the CO, I felt - a presence; something – evil, watching…"

"Nasty," murmured Colleen.

Dollie sighed but she seemed to be cheering up.

"Yes, still, it's over now," she said. "Oh, a couple of letters arrived for you. I put them on your bed. One's a note from a patient. I think it's that chap Hinch. He was discharged while you were on shift. Be on his way to Naples now. The other's from Annie."

Colleen thanked her, went and brought back the letters. They often shared their correspondence with each other.

She opened the letter from Anne.

Very happy to hear about you and Tony, she had written. *Our own preparations are mov-*

ing along. Still getting lots of convoys in – often working double shifts – but looking forward to seeing Bill soon.

Have you got yourself a Bible yet, one like mine? Start with the Gospel of John when you do. Proverbs 31 is good advice for wives. I don't know how Solomon managed with a thousand though…

Colleen then opened the note from Hinch. She began reading; then started shedding tears and it was Sister Dale's turn to be the comforter.

"I've got a big mouth, Dollie," Colleen groaned. "See for yourself."

Dear Sister McGrath, the letter read,

Just a short note to say a huge thank-you.

I should explain one thing though. You'll recall I never said owt about my missus. That's because not long after I was wounded I got word she'd left me. As you can imagine, it knocked me for six. Thanks to you, though, I believe that with God's help, I can pick up the pieces – got a letter from my old boss, reckons he's got plenty of work for a chap with my experience of the firm.

Please forgive me for not having said about my ex before now but you and I were having such a great time, I didn't want to spoil it…

"We better get our heads down, Coll," said Dollie gently. "Big day tomorrow."

Colleen nodded, drying her eyes. Dollie was right.

The next day, they would journey north, to join the rest of the unit, near the Gothic Line, where their patients would come straight from the cauldron of battle.

Six

Warriors

Before Grandma's arrival in Italy, events were already shaping the lives of several warriors upon whom her own life would depend. We turn to them now.

North Africa, November 1942.

A sturdy AIF chaplain stood at the sandbagged entrance to the CCS.

Shielding his eyes against the afternoon sun, he gazed at the low ridgeline marking the boundary of Ninth Australian Division's advance against Rommel's Afrika Korps.

The Desert Fox's artillery was cannonading the Australian positions remorselessly. The whole ridgeline was shimmering in the incessant flash and roar of the shell bursts.

"More on their way, Padre," said a tired voice.

The stocky figure of surgeon Captain Fergus Muir emerged from the operating tent in a bloodstained gown. He and Chaplain Beech watched the approaching vehicles.

When they arrived, Beech went to help the orderlies unload. They lined up several dead outside the mortuary.

"Thirty-six," the chaplain murmured. "I buried thirty-six this morning. How many more?"

What of the families receiving the telegram with the words 'killed in action'?

The question dogged him continually.

Seriously wounded were taken to the Resuscitation tent, staffed by an MO and several QA Sisters. The remainder waited under a canvas awning, all but one with dressings wrapped around limbs or shoulders.

They made light of their aching wounds.

"Jeez, mate, look like you had a fight with a threshin' machine and lost."

"Anything to get away from them bagpipes, mate[37]."

When Beech approached the group, they expressed concern for the individual sitting alone, head down, covered in sweat.

"We're all right, Padre," said one heavily-bandaged infantryman. "It's Slim over there we're worried about."

Clad like the rest in khaki shorts, boots and shirt with rolled-up sleeves, the lone soldier was lean, long-limbed and sunburnt, fair-haired and grey-eyed; a typical digger's physique and appearance. He wore sergeant's stripes and looked to be in his early twenties. His knees and forearms were scabbed and his nose had bled under the bombardment but he was otherwise unmarked.

However, the soldier's hands, arms and facial muscles were shaking uncontrollably, the effect of a near miss[38].

He glanced up towards the ridgeline, as Beech came over and crouched beside him.

"My God, Padre," he said. "They're praying up there."

"Can I make you more comfortable, lad?" Beech asked.

The soldier shook his head.

"I'm OK, sir, thanks."

"One of the Sisters will give you a sedative," Beech reassured him.

"Sisters?" the soldier protested. "I can't go in there, Padre, I'm filthy!"

"They won't even notice," said Beech, smiling. "By the way, what's your name, son?"

"Calvert, sir, Matt Calvert."

"I'm ready to go back to battalion, sir," Calvert objected, on hearing Captain Muir's verdict.

After nearly ten days of continuous fighting, the battalion was down to less than company strength. For almost a week, Calvert had led the remnants of his company in desperate assaults on enemy posts, through thunderous barrages, barbed wire, minefields and determined counter-attacks; against the combined fire-power of artillery, machine guns, tanks and mortars; suffering hunger, thirst, exhaustion, mounting casualties, scorching heat by day, bitter cold at night.

A newly promoted sergeant, he'd joined his unit after the action near Tel el Eisa Ridge.

Now another name had eclipsed that engagement.

El Alamein.

Darkness had fallen and in the dimness of the Recuperation Ward, Calvert lay on a camp bed, the shakes having subsided after a shot of morphine and several hours' rest. He reckoned he was OK.

However, the MO was firm.

"You're going down to Alexandria for observation, Sergeant, that's an order."

Calvert sighed and stared up at canvas ceiling as the officer moved off.

He began to doze, despite the monotonous thud of the artillery…

"Tanks! Two waves!"

"Stay in your trenches," yelled Calvert.

The panzers were following up the barrage that had bludgeoned the diggers mercilessly.

High explosive pelted them with a hail of stones and earth, cleaving the air with whirring shrapnel.

Anti-personnel shells burst in hideous black clouds and showers of red-hot splinters. Fire trenches offered little protection against these jagged shards, for anyone unlucky enough to be underneath.

Shock waves forced blood from the men's nostrils, pummelling their eardrums.

Eyes streaming, tormented with thirst, they coughed and gagged beneath dense clouds of dust and smoke.

Calvert blinked away rivulets of sweat to clear his blurred vision, conscious of the heat waves dancing in the glare. Yet he marvelled at the Australian medics, still moving about, rescuing casualties stricken by shellfire.

The barrage was passing over, to isolate the forward troops as the tanks moved in, Rommel's infantry following.

A squealing, sand-coloured armoured monster emerged from the swirling haze, ponderously making straight for Calvert's position.

The earth where the Australians were dug in was like sun-dried clay, yet from between cracked lips, pressing his body to earth, Matt beseeched the God of battles.

"Dear God, don't let the sides collapse."

The metal beast was aiming its track for the trench to crush him like an insect. Face in the dirt under his helmet, Calvert retched at the stink of exhaust fumes.

Crumbly soil cascaded down under the panzer's weight.

Then Calvert felt steel treads pressing like knife-edges against his back. He prayed all the more.

At last, the monster was gone. Those from the next wave passed on either side of his position.

The diggers leapt out of their trenches, clasping rifles and grenades. Several pursued the tanks to lob sticky bombs onto their fuel tanks, transforming them into blazing coffins, except for one that lumbered on, chased for fifty yards by big Hughie Donovan, who hurled three bombs in succession at his quarry, with shouts of exasperation.

"Blow up, you dingo[39], blow up!"

It did. The A/T gunners, together with the doughty Rhodesian battery, would cripple the rest.

The remainder of Calvert's men tackled the German infantry, tossing grenades, then charging down on their foes through the smoke of the detonations with bayonets fixed. Even when reinforced by the bombers returning from pursuing the tanks, the Ninth Division men were grossly outnumbered.

They didn't care.

Shouts arose.

"On, Australians! C'mon, Australians!"

Rifle shot, bayonet thrust, rifle butts against skulls and jawbones, blood splashes on faces and tunics, screams of shock and pain, the whipped and demoralised enemy fell back, leaving their dead, dragging their wounded.

But the barrage descended anew, sending up geysers of dirt and debris. Hauling wounded comrades with them, the Australians scrambled to their trenches.

Except Calvert.

A near miss knocked him flat. Dazed, he stood up. Though miraculously unhurt by the zinging shrapnel, he couldn't stop shaking. Disorientated, he staggered toward the German lines, his rifle slipping from his grasp.

"Jesus, Matt!"

Hughie Donovan's bulky figure slammed sideways into Calvert, hurling him prone, then tugging him back up the slope, through clumps of stunted scrub. Calvert felt them scratch his limbs. Despite the shells crashing around, Lance Corporal Ken Lassiter crawled over to help.

Crouching low, stumbling over sun-bleached rock, metal splinters whizzing close, they got to a fire trench and tumbled in.

"Hang on, Matt," gasped Hughie. "We'll get you out, mate."

"Please, God, make 'em drop wide," Lassiter was praying.

"Medic!" Hughie was shouting.

Eventually, they got Calvert down into an ambulance. He was still shaking.

Calvert sat bolt upright, sweat coursing down his brow. Only then did he realise his mind had been reliving the previous day's events.

"You all right, mate?" said the man in the next bed.

"Yeah."

Calvert observed that the other man's whole face and upper body were glistening with perspiration.

"Hey, Barney, you're sweatin' buckets, mate," he said.

"It's nothing."

"I'm getting Sister."

Sergeant Barney French had been operated on for shrapnel wounds to shoulder and chest. With the anaesthetic having worn off, they were giving him hell.

"No need, Matt," French protested through gritted teeth. "She'll be round soon."

But Calvert had already disappeared through the tent flap.

Casualties from the Ninth Australian were being cared for by British medical units because their own had returned home as part of the build-up against the Japanese.

Amongst the RAMC personnel with this responsibility were Sister Jane Griffith[40], QAIMNS/R and her MO, Captain Muir. Hitherto, Sister Griffith had nursed men of all the other nationalities in the Eighth Army, and Greek and Yugoslav partisans. Muir was confident she could cope with all comers.

The diggers nearly proved him wrong.

Already swathed with dressings, now sweat-soaked, Barney got a dressing down from Sister Jane.

"Silly man, why didn't you call me or an orderly?"

"I'm from Balmain, Sister. Balmain boys don't cry[41]."

"Stuff and nonsense! You Australians, you're the giddy limit[42]. Well, you're getting a short of morphine, Sergeant French, whether you want it or not."

"Thank you, Sister," he said.

She injected French and by the light of a hurricane lamp, gently sponged him down, towelled him dry and replaced his dressings. She also gave Calvert a sponge bath and got them each a cup of compo tea.

Having settled them down, she went to double-check for other Colonial Spartans holding back their agony through clenched teeth in the darkened wards.

His discomfort blunted by the morphia, French quietly continued talking with Calvert. They were from different companies, so did not know each other well.

"Berrima," whispered Calvert, in answer to Barney's question about his hometown. "Eighty miles south of Sydney."

"Southern Highlands, eh? Great place."

"It's home."

"Yeah."

"Padre said you were a theolog."

"Lay preacher, property developer by trade. What about you?"

"Sydney University, studying classics. Joined the AIF from SUR when I'd finished. Reckoned I ought to see it through, for Mum and Dad."

"Yeah, sure. Why didn't you go for officer training – Duntroon, even?"

Calvert hesitated.

"Girlfriend gave me the elbow," he said finally. "For some RAAF bloke at Richmond."

"Permanent home posting, eh?"

"Well, you know the air force."

"Muscovy ducks, heh."

"Yeah, only one in every thousand flies. I wanted to get away."

"Don't reckon you'd have stayed out of it, Matt, once you'd graduated. As for the other, God's got somebody else, mate."

They had already spoken of their respective conversions, in which their families had been instrumental.

"What if I'm killed first?" Calvert asked, sitting up in bed again.

"Then 'For me to live is Christ, and to die is gain,'" said French.

The following day, the casualties' transport assembled outside the Recuperation tent, its engines noise almost drowning out the battle.

Inside the tent, another battle was brewing.

Long-suffering Captain Muir was being harangued over Sergeant Calvert.

Breakfasted and fully clothed, dressings changed, their few belongings gathered about them, the evacuees were refusing to budge.

"Sergeant Calvert must go to a neurological ward," the dour Scot insisted.

"We're stickin' together, Doc," said a defiant voice, the statement prefixed by an oath.

"Steady on, mate," French interposed quickly. "Sister's here."

"Yeah, well, sorry, Sister, but we're still stickin' together."

"We're all from the same mob, Doc," said another voice.

Jane Griffith tactfully broke the *impasse*.

"Sergeant Calvert is stable, sir," she said to Muir. "And being more mobile, he could assist the others. I'm sure the neurologist wouldn't mind just seeing him occasionally."

The mood changed instantly on Muir's acquiescence.

"Yer a bobby-dazzler, Doc, you too, Sister."

"I am most grateful to you, Jane," Muir said with considerable relief.

"Hey, boys, give us a cheer!"

The crowd clustered around the pier where the troopship would berth, overjoyed at the sight of the returning veterans, yet puzzled by their silence.

Leaning on the ship's railing, flanked by his comrades, Calvert had gazed unbelieving at the sights of Sydney Harbour. He looked up at the huge arch of the world-renowned bridge.

Only big Hughie could find his voice.

"It's like a dream, Matt..."[43]

"This is a flamin' nightmare."

"Pipe down, Hughie," said Platoon Sergeant French. "And watch out for those yellow men."

Second Lieutenant Matt Calvert's platoon was trekking through dense rain forest up steep-sided slopes of the Atherton Plateau, north Queensland. In the sultry climate, loaded with weapons, ammunition and kit, the men were lathered in sweat.

Sounds of slithering in the brush as their boot-falls alerted the reptiles didn't help matters. Neither did the insects.

The rain forests, with their lush drooping fronds and abundant waterfalls had looked picturesque when Ninth Division first saw them on arrival at their new training ground.

Toiling through the gloomy undergrowth up and down slippery slopes, laden with gear, carrying out fire and movement exercises, had dispelled the illusion.

Calvert tried to keep things in perspective.

"You'll look back on this place with fond memories," he warned his command.

The New Guinea campaign was about to enter its next phase, the conquest of the Huon Peninsula, its ports and airfields. Ninth Division, with its sister formation, the veteran Seventh, would effect that conquest.

And the time of departure was drawing near.

"I don't like your attitude, Mr Calvert."

Matt couldn't have cared less.

"I don't think we appreciated that of your men, sir," he said to the American Army colonel.

Calvert's CO cleared his throat.

"Gentlemen, I think a letter of apology from me is the best solution. We must keep it quiet at all costs."

It was a humid day and the atmosphere around the table in the Nissen hut housing the enquiry was as close as it was tense. Calvert could feel the wetness beneath the armpits of his shirt.

"OK, Colonel, you win," the American drawled. "Let's get on with the war."

The incident precipitating the enquiry had occurred the previous day, during embarkation for amphibious landings at Lae, the jumping-off place for the Huon invasion.

Calvert had been at the bottom of the gangplank, checking off names as the men boarded, with full kit and loaded weapons.

Without warning, a truckload of American GIs careered to a halt some distance from the Australians. Waving whisky bottles, the Yanks had started taunting the diggers.

"So long, Aussies, we'll look after ya gals for ya!"

The Ninth Division men raised rifles and promptly opened fire.

Brandishing his revolver and shouting, "Cease fire!" Calvert succeeded in restoring order – not without risk to himself, so at the subsequent enquiry, he'd been plain-spoken. The Yanks had asked for it. Their brashness had also marred the excellent rapport between Ninth Division and the American Amphibious Engineers, forged by dint of hard training in preparation for Lae.

Providentially, neither side suffered casualties. All was successfully hushed up and embarkation delayed by only twenty-four hours. Nevertheless, Calvert's company commander delivered a fitting admonition to his men.

"You'll get plenty of shootin' up north – and Tojo won't drive up in a truck."

Mrs Irene Calvert picked up a tea towel and looked out the kitchen window at the eucalypt gums. Their characteristic resinous smell wafted in on the evening breeze. The setting sun was bathing the valley beyond in a mellow golden-green light and she could hear the murmur of rustling leaves.

Fewer dishes needed drying now.

Daughter Becky lived on her husband's dairy farm, where she and her CWA pals also did the shearing, now that her husband and most of the men had joined up. She also managed the local riding academy and had turned it into a most profitable venture, helping Tom to become an automotive engineer and Matt to attend university.

"'But my God shall supply all your need, according to His riches in glory by Christ Jesus,' Mum," her daughter would say.

Irene had needed those scriptures, when her husband, Tom senior, had died a few months back, finally succumbing to wounds received in 1918.

Irene's elder son, Tom junior, was with RAEME workshops in Port Moresby. She glanced at his photo on the shelf next to the cooker. At least he was safe.

Not so her younger son, Matt.

He was now in the battle for the Huon Peninsula.

She'd been overjoyed to greet him at the little station under the towering pines when he'd come home on leave in February, bronzed and fit, with his kitbag slung over his shoulder. His leave had passed quickly but at least he'd been able to see his dad for one last time.

The Calverts, like all their friends and neighbours, were of conservative Protestant stock, who loved the old country and fought to resist her manifold foes, both for her sake and that of their own land.

Irene well remembered how William Morris 'Billy' Hughes, Australia's far-sighted prime minister during the last war, had warned of the traitor Mannix, RC Archbishop of Melbourne[44]:

"He has only one objective...the destruction of the Empire."

Billy Hughes had warned further, *"The British Empire now surrounded by ene-mies...Bolshevism, Sinn Feinism, Germanism...was a League of Nations, bound together by the ties of blood and race, and if they broke Great Britain, they broke Australia."*

Mannix and his acolytes loathed these ties of blood and race but twice in a lifetime, the young men had defended them with honour – and with their own blood, for in 1914, the then Australian PM declared:

"If England goes to her Armageddon, Australia will go with her."[45]

Irene finished the drying and hung up the towel, reflecting on the high price of loyalty. In addition to her recent bereavement, she had lost a brother and a cousin in the Great War.

And her son was in the firing line again.

She put the kettle on and smiled at the cackling of the kookaburras in the eucalypts. Jack, as the canny bird was known, kept the long grass about the homestead free of snakes, so that Irene's youngsters and their friends had been able to run around barefoot in complete safety during the warm summer days.

"Snakes in the grass," she murmured, in reference to Mannix and the Axis. Irene did not differentiate between them.

She stacked the dried crockery on a shelf in the cupboard by the sink. Her eye took in the poem on a sheet of paper pinned there.

It was a dedication to the native New Guineans, whose close-set locks earned them the nickname of 'Fuzzy Wuzzy Angels' and who had served as stretcher-bearers ever since the Kokoda Trail, the battle that stemmed the Japanese advance across the rugged Owen-Stanley ranges in New Guinea the previous year.

Mrs Calvert knew the words by heart.

Many a mother in Australia, when the busy day is done,
Sends a prayer to the Almighty, for the keeping of her son,
Asking that an angel guide him, and bring him safely back,
Now we see those prayers are answered, on the Owen Stanley track.

For they haven't any halos, only holes slashed in their ears,
And their faces worked with tattoos, and scratch pins in their hair,
Bringing back the badly wounded, just as steady as a hearse,
Using leaves to keep the rain off, and as gentle as a nurse…

"Matt," she said softly, gazing at his photo on the shelf next to Tom's. A lump constricted her throat.

The kettle was whistling. She placed her well-worn bible on the kitchen table and took the kettle off the stove. Irene usually had devotions about now. With a cup of tea, it was a winning combination.

The landing craft eased into the beach and its ramp dropped with a splashing thud[46].

"Follow me!" Calvert commanded the heavily laden infantrymen at his back, clad in jungle green.

Anticipating Jap gunfire any second, he sprinted through the shallows, sub-machine carbine poised at his side and made swiftly for the jungle fringe.

To right and left, other LCPs were disgorging the rest of the assault wave. Smoke from the naval bombardment overhung the shoreline, through which the remnants of palm trees were visible, shattered by shell explosions.

"Two section up, Ken," Calvert muttered to Corporal Lassiter as they regrouped amongst a profusion of splintered trunks and fallen fronds.

Lassiter nodded. Stealthily, he assumed the point position.

With hand signals, Calvert aligned the rest of the platoon to follow, his HQ forming up behind Lassiter's section.

They edged forward, boots squelching in mud.

A spasm of thunder sounded and before long it was teeming. Platoon Sergeant French grinned at his officer. Water cascaded off the broad brims of their slouch hats.

"Doesn't look like a sun shower, mate," said French.

The advance toward Lae took several nerve-racking days of sweeping the brooding wilderness for enemy positions. None were found in strength, though solitary machine gunners and lone snipers, sometimes camouflaged in trees, persistently harried the Australians, before concerted retaliatory fire took them out. Two of Calvert's men suffered gunshot wounds and were evacuated, white-faced, with blood-caked dressings.

At night, the men bivvied down in total darkness, wet through, rain crackling off the jungle growth that closed in all around.

By day, Allied fighter-bombers pounded Lae relentlessly and smoke from the devastation rose sluggishly into overcast skies.

"Be nothin' but matchwood by the time we get there," grunted Hughie.

In the meantime, Seventh Division AIF advanced from the Ramu and Markham valleys further west. Like Ninth Division, they encountered mainly delaying actions.

In mid-September, Seventh and Ninth Australian joined hands.

"What took you so long?" soldiers of the Seventh wanted to know.

Typical.

Nevertheless, together they raised the Union Jack with the Southern Cross over the captured town.

What was left of it.

"You were pretty right, mate," French remarked to Hughie as the platoon trudged along the sodden main street strewn with scattered timbers, gutted houses on either side. "Matchwood."

Several days later, the LCPs grounded again, at a place called Scarlet Beach. Again, Lieutenant Calvert led his platoon up the muddy foreshore.

The invaders' objective; the port of Finschhafen, with its airstrip, on the tip of the Huon Peninsula, sixty miles east of Lae, six miles south of Scarlet Beach.

This time, the landings were effected before dawn, advantageous because the darkness was alive with flashing Jap tracer.

But the barges landed in the wrong sector. With splintering crashes, the plywood craft slammed against submerged reefs and the impact threw their occupants into a heap.

"Come on!" urged Calvert. He leapt over the shattered bows, dashed across the rocks and onto the beach, his men at his back.

Fortunately the firing was wild and Calvert's men formed up amongst the close-set palms and fetid undergrowth, ready to deploy.

They had spotted a key Jap position.

"Woodpecker," muttered French. "See the flashes from the embrasure?"

Barricaded with logs, the heavy machine gun thundered its savage bursts, the brilliant tracer arcing way out to sea. The post, about sixty yards to the Australians' front, was protected by light machine guns spitting like fiery serpents, and would have infantry in support.

"Keep the Brens on 'em, Barney," Calvert ordered. "I'll take a couple of sections round to the flank."

The tactics were fraught with risk but clatter of small arms and crack of grenade explosions elsewhere indicated that resistance was stiffening. The battalion had to do its best to break it, as soon as light allowed.

Calvert pushed warily through matted vines and overhanging, broad-leaved foliage. You had to be careful. Some of the plants were natural irritants that could raise blisters on the skin. All the more important, therefore, to roll sleeves down after dark, in addition to ensuring protection against the malarial mosquito. As they'd experienced during the advance to Lae, leeches would also attack the men's bodies. When eventually dislodged with lighted cigarettes, their anticoagulant saliva would delay the congealing process, spreading dark patches of blood through the victim's clothing.

For now, the Jap obstruction had to be dislodged.

Barney's Brens were sending splinters flying from the log fortifications, drawing the defenders' fire. Calvert earnestly hoped that ammunition parties following the platoon would keep French's LMGs well supplied.

The sections edged to within grenade throwing range of the post. Lance Corporal Mick Bolster led his Bren team to the cut-off position.

Forehead clammy with sweat, Calvert nodded to Corporals Vince Naylor and Ted Rice, on either side of him. First light was approaching.

Calvert gave the signal.

Together, they pitched flares at the flank of the enemy position. The instant these ignited, Calvert's assault team hurled grenades and charged the moment these burst, OMCs firing on automatic, riflemen with bayonets fixed.

Hopefully, the grenade bursts would also detonate any booby traps. And hopefully, the action elsewhere would distract Jap mortar men from bombing their own position once it was attacked – a callous tactic, but effective.

It was a lot to hope for.

The Japanese position consisted of a bunkered system with interconnecting trenches. This much had been visible in the light of the flares. Reaching the sandbagged parapet, Calvert glimpsed a Jap LMG crew, dead beside their weapon.

"Grenade!" he yelled and hurled a 36M into the nearest traverse. Rice simultaneously lobbed one into the second traverse.

The attackers ducked down as the devices exploded with terrible booms. Calvert and Rice leapt through reeking smoke into the pit of the trench, firing their OMCs, the others following. Calvert felt his boots thudding onto a Japanese corpse.

"Sayonara, Tojo!" snarled an Australian voice.

"Bomb out the saps!" shouted Calvert. "Don't shoot each other!"

That was a potential hazard in the half-light of the gloomy dawn.

Shadowy forms lunged at each other, Japs charging from concealed positions. Muzzle flashes, bayonet thrusts, automatic bursts, shrieks of pain, blood blotches on faces and chests, the assault team stumbling forward over dead and dying. Rice fell, pole axed by a Jap bullet. Lance Corporal Des Havelock took his place.

Calvert and he riddled the Jap who'd shot Rice. They ducked back to avoid an enemy grenade, then tossed two more 36Ms into the next traverse. Deafening bangs and shrill screams followed. Calvert swiftly changed magazines.

Vince and the boys were tossing grenades down the side trenches, routing out the surviving enemy, regardless of whether or not any Jap put his hands up – he might be concealing a live grenade. A few of the foe escaped to be cut down by Bolster's group and French's, at close quarters.

Calvert's ears were ringing, his eyes watering. Bunkered enemy defences were to be expected in New Guinea but the connecting trenches had made the action seem like the First War – and as horrendous. Though the Japs had clearly foreseen the landing site, this position had fortunately not been completed. It was not entirely roofed over or fully strengthened and thus more open to attack. Otherwise, it would probably have been a job for the fighter-bombers, consequent delays in the advance notwithstanding.

Matt's diggers cleared the bunker system from end to end. The scene was a charnel house, the air thick with the stench of blood and cordite.

However, retaliatory mortar bombs had not descended. Calvert realised they'd got away with it – though not without cost.

"We lost Ted Rice and Pete Brady, sir, Mick Bolster, Johnny Atwood, Ross Owens and Curly Warren wounded," Calvert reported to his OC. "Got twenty-seven in all."

They were crouching beneath a coconut palm. Rain pattered down. Private Owens, a wiry lad of about nineteen, sat sipping tea from an enamel mug, flecks of blood on his face, a thick band of dressing around his head.

The OC nodded.

"Well done, Matt. Mr Bowery's platoon will move through yours."

Calvert observed the dark-skinned, barefoot men in shorts, gently hoisting the stretchers carrying his wounded comrades. The fuzzies were on the job again.

Sattelberg Road, mid-October, 1943.

Inexorably, Ninth Division had pressed towards Finschhafen, enfilading the Japanese opposition at the Bumi River, investing the town itself a few days later, supported by artillery and Allied fighter-bombers, which had the additional task of beating off remaining enemy aircraft.

By then, Calvert's men were verging on exhaustion but their training and resolve were paying dividends.

Patrols through rain-forested half-light transformed enemy ambushers into the ambushed; sudden, brutal bursts of fire slaughtering them in the process.

Hordes of brown-clad foes that came screaming through coconut groves in suicidal Banzai charges were cut down in swathes by concerted MG, rifle and mortar fire from expertly sited weapons pits.

And Jap infiltrators never got back.

In earlier campaigns, these had overwhelmed individual sentries and shoved meat skewers through their ears. Such tactics against Ninth Division earned any intruder a bayonet through the throat.

"No Geishas where you're goin', Tojo," was his epitaph.

By sheer determination, the men withstood fatigue, exacerbated though it was by carrying wounded down slippery, treacherous tracks – for the native bearers were too few for the task – returning burdened with ammunition and rations, in alternate soaking rain and stifling heat, when the sun broke through sullen cloud, bringing the voracious insects.

Good equipment and organisation also offset the difficulties. The men's brass-studded boots sustained a steady grip on the slushy ground, their calf-high gaiters helped keep their feet dry and relatively free of leeches, double doses of atebrin kept malaria at bay, company cooks produced marvellous hot meals from a limited menu of bully beef, biscuits, dehydrated fruit and vegetables[47].

Hygiene was strict, from the siting of latrine pits to washing, shaving and brushing of teeth - whenever conditions allowed.

And the diggers never lost their sense of humour.

"No water to be drunk unless passed by the RMO," French warned with a perfectly straight face.

"Tastes that crook it must be OK," remarked Hughie, after dissolving up the required chlorine tablets.

Best of all, from Calvert's perspective, Padre Beech was always up at the front, his calm demeanour a morale booster to all ranks.

"We are about God's business, boys," he would say.

More of that business was about to be transacted.

Australian Intelligence had discovered that the Japanese were preparing a major counter attack, to cut the Sattelberg road, west of Finschhafen, its initial objective the town of Jivenaneng, a collection of bamboo-poled and grass-thatched huts.

And here, Calvert's battalion was concentrating.

Encumbered by weapons and ammunition, web straps cutting into their shoulders, Calvert's men crept laboriously uphill through bamboo, jungle scrub and six-foot-high kunai grass, boots digging into the root-veined soil. Clinging morning mist shrouded the hostile slope, where Japanese assault troops had been sighted assembling to the Australians' direct front.

The battalion had pushed out strong fighting patrols before first light to counter enemy flanking parties. These would intercept any attempts to reinforce the Japanese centre when it was itself attacked, by two Australian companies.

The company containing Calvert's platoon would engage the western half. With its other companies poised to repel additional attacks, the battalion was now fully stretched.

Aggression would count for everything.

Matt's men reached the designated area where the vegetation was thinner, then deployed, crouching in the dew-soaked grass, fingers poised on triggers.

Movement.

Shadowy, pot-helmeted forms were approaching, slipping through the dank undergrowth. These were the skirmishers.

The Australians let them pass.

The main group followed, bayoneted rifles at low port, the nearest only yards from Calvert.

He fired a burst from his OMC, the pre-arranged signal to start the battle. Pandemonium erupted. A crescendo of rifle, Bren and SMG fire shredded the advancing foes, stricken further by rifle grenades fired into their midst.

Shrieking in shock and terror, the assault group fell apart.

Slapping on a fresh magazine, Calvert led his men forward, the other platoons on either flank, Company HQ in the centre. With bullet and bayonet, they weighed into the survivors, trampling the blood-splashed, corpse-strewn kunai.

More gunfire sounded as the fighting patrols tore up the flanking parties and battle was joined to the east.

"First wave's coming back!" shouted French.

The skirmishers were climbing frantically up to reinforce their comrades.

They ran into a flurry of bursting 36Ms.

"Put that in your saki, Tojo!" shouted a voice.

"Matt!"

Calvert turned abruptly to see Barney collapsed in a welter of blood, an onrushing Jap intent on delivering a bayonet *coup de grace*, determined to avenge the humiliating rout.

The burst from Calvert's OMC nearly tore the attacker in half. Frantically, Matt dragged the sergeant behind a huge kunai tussock where the medics could see to him. Barney's agony from the rough handling showed in his face.

"Barney, I'm sorry," Matt exclaimed.

"Don't be, mate," French gasped. "Not when people are tryin' to kill you[48]."

Attacks continued until early November, when the battalion was relieved. It held firm throughout, according to its motto, *What We Have, We Hold*[49].

The reserve brigade subsequently captured the key feature of Sattelberg Ridge. With its fall, Huon, and indeed New Guinea, would soon be secure.

"You still whingin' about goin' home, mate?" asked Hughie.

"Don't want the Yanks runnin' the show, Hughie," Calvert said with a grin.

Donovan drew on his cigarette and shrugged.

"Can't get their hands on our sheilas, mate, not if they're out there."

"Gotta get your priorities right, Matt," Ken Lassiter affirmed.

It was Christmas Day, 1943.

Calvert's battalion had come back from reserve to join in the pursuit of the beaten enemy. Pushing northwards, they'd encountered mainly Japanese dead, corpses rotting in the hundreds.

Matt, Ken and Hughie were standing on a promontory of the peninsula's north coast, gazing at the huge American armada bound for the invasion of New Britain, a step closer to Japan. Around them, many others from Ninth Division were taking in the sight, conscious of how their efforts had made it possible.

They shared the victory with their sister division, the Seventh, the Allied air forces and the Militia battalions. Though disdained as "Chokkos" by the all-volunteer AIF, the conscripts had fought well.

Calvert and his comrades were also conscious of the cost. Sixty of their battalion mates had died since the first landing in September. Hundreds were wounded, or evacuated sick, despite all precautions.

Among the dead was kindly Padre Beech, not from enemy action but scrub typhus, despite the expert nursing he'd received at the Australian General Hospital established in Lae. The disease claimed fewer victims than malaria but killed up to one in ten of them and unlike malaria could not be countered by suppressants.

All ranks had been saddened by Beech's death, but with French repatriated, Calvert had lost his closest companions.

The padre had been an unfailing support, ministering to the wounded, guiding Salvation Army canteens as close to the forward positions as possible, challenging men with the Gospel in his courteous fashion.

"Christ died for our sins, soldier, shed His blood for them on the cross, everyone's."

"Even the Japs, padre?"

"Even the Japs."

"After what they did in Singapore and Hong Kong?"

Reports of enemy atrocities against British and Australian nurses and their patients had made the diggers' blood boil[50]. The oriental foes were regarded as *brute beasts, made to be taken and destroyed*[51].

St Peter's words applied to all men in rebellion against God but the Australians reckoned the Japs to be in a class by themselves.

"I'll never get that feeling out of them," Beech confided to Calvert and French. "But it's wrong, even so."

"They know, Padre," French had said quietly "We all do. 'The true Light lighteth every man that cometh into the world[52].' Doesn't mean we'll admit it."

Watching the invasion fleet, Calvert wished he had some light for the future. Seventh and Ninth Divisions were to return to the Atherton Plateau, while, in Matt's opinion, the war passed them by.

He didn't know what to do. The problem would vex him for months.

Kachin Hills, Burma, summer 1944.

"Red Two to Red Leader, baling out, Glaz."

Flying Officer Jonathan Gray, Hurri-bomber pilot, heard the response of his flight commander, Flight Lieutenant Gordon 'Glasgow' McKenna, in his earphones.

"OK, Jonny, we've got your position, Godspeed, lad."

With controls sluggish, oil pressure dropping, brown smoke whipping back from the engine cowling, Gray knew he could not keep the Hurricane airborne much longer. He unbuckled his seat harness, pulled down his goggles and slid back the canopy.

Choking smoke hit him in the face. Pushing hard on the control column, he tipped the aircraft over and fell into space.

Cool air rushed past him.

He pulled the ripcord handle. The unfurling parachute slowed his descent.

His doomed Hurricane exploded against a green hillside. Forlornly, Gray watched the rest of his flight become dots in the distance.

"It's Thee and me, Father," he whispered.

Dense foliage came rushing up. Gray bunched himself tightly, pressing his head into his chest, eyes shut, covering his face with both hands.

Then he was crashing through a tunnel of splintering, snapping branches slapping his face and snatching at his clothes, his boots scraping off the heavier boughs. Several of them thumped him like quarterstaffs.

Involuntarily, he screamed at the sickening sensation of what seemed like a red-hot sword blade slashing through his trouser leg and up the outside of his left thigh. He felt warm blood welling and fainted.

The 'chute snagged and Gray came to, hanging by his harness several feet from the ground, dripping blood from his injured thigh.

In dismay, he smelt ether and realised that the branches whipping his body had broken the phial stashed in the first-aid kit attached to the front of his web belt.

"Get down," he muttered. Ripping off his goggles and helmet, he stuffed them in a pocket of his undamaged trouser leg. He pulled his Ghurka knife from its scabbard and sawed through the rigging lines, gritting his teeth at the unrelenting throb in his thigh.

He collapsed onto damp leaf-mould, crying out at the pain that stabbed him on impact.

Gray detached the parachute harness, took the container of sulphonamide powder from his first-aid kit and poured the antibiotic into the bloodied slash. Everything in the kit smelt of ether but it had largely evaporated.

He extracted a needle and threaded it with surgical twine.

Using his left hand, Gray pressed the sides of the incision together and thrust the needle into his flesh with his right.

Teeth clenched, streaming tears, he made stitch after stitch.

"Don't stop, don't stop," he sobbed, until he had closed the inches-long gash[53].

At last, he tied off the twine and severed it with a small pair of scissors. Smearing on gentian violet jelly, he dressed the wound, then wiped his face on his sleeve. He threw away the broken bits of the ether phial. The blood on his hands was drying. He would find a stream to wash it off.

"Did the nails hurt like that, Lord?" Gray whispered, looking upwards.

Above him, somewhere, was the presumably shorn-off, sharp-edged branch with his name on it.

Shafts of sunlight filtered through the trees. Gray rolled up the sleeves of his bush jacket, only now conscious of the heat.

Gingerly he stood up, encouraged that he could place weight on his left leg. Grasping nearby saplings, he took some hesitant steps. His injured leg ached but did not buckle.

Gray rested on a moss-covered log and spread out his linen survival map to assess of his situation.

Apart from his leg and, no doubt, a few bruises from being pummelled by the boughs, he was unhurt. He had emergency rations for forty-eight hours, a medical kit – already put to good use – chlorine tablets for water, map and compass, a knife and his service revolver, with spare rounds. He'd been immunised against various ailments, including malaria and tetanus.

He had cigarettes, a lighter and wax matches for burning leeches off – ordinary match heads turned to mush in the damp.

And he had his Bible, in a waterproof container, tucked into a pocket of his bush jacket.

Against that, he was in the midst of mountainous jungle, challenging terrain even without a leg injury.

His base at Imphal lay one hundred miles to the west, on the other side of the Chindwin River and unaccounted numbers of Japanese retreating from Imphal were between him and Fourteenth Army.

Moreover, soon it must rain, for the monsoon season was not over. However, Glaz and the boys at base would have already contacted the bush telegraph and Kachin Rangers might find him.

Gray stood up, looking towards the summit of the hillside where he'd landed. It lay in his direction of travel.

He cut off some lengths of parachute cord and consulted his compass. Taking up a fallen bough that would support the weight of his wiry frame, he stepped cautiously forward, grimacing at the fiery pain in his thigh.

"Could use an umbrella," he muttered, as the first drops began to fall.

Gray crouched motionless, gripping his revolver. He was being watched.

For two days, he'd trekked through mountain and scrub, enduring steaming heat, drenching rain, tenacious insects and gruelling slopes; burning off leeches, vigilant for cobras, scorpions and nests of red ants, battling increasing fatigue. Night had brought little rest. He'd spent them propped against hilltop trees, listening to jungle sounds and waiting for dawn. He was hollow-eyed, footsore and stubbly-chinned, his uniform begrimed and sweat-stained.

But his wound was definitely healing and he had no shortage of water. And he'd not encountered any Japs – it was a big jungle. By counting paces, tying a knot in a length of parachute cord after every thousand, he reckoned that, allowing for detours forced on him by terrain and injury, he had progressed about fifteen miles due west.

That was the problem. Still eighty-five to go.

Then he'd felt eyes upon him.

Some fronds moved, not with the wind. Gray swallowed. Any second now…

A brown-skinned little man stepped from concealment. He wore a cloth cap, khaki shirt and baggy trousers, with a machete and bandolier of ammunition slung across his chest. He carried an American M1 carbine.

Gray sighed with relief and got to his feet, replacing the revolver in its holster. The little man beckoned into the brush and a tall, bearded occidental appeared, similarly armed and dressed but shod with canvas boots.

"Frank Mildenhall," he said in a Mid-Western drawl. "Colonel, American-Kachin Rangers and OSS."

"Jon Gray, Flying Officer, RAF," said the airman thickly. "I'm very glad to meet you, sir."

They shook hands.

"We'd better get you back to camp, Jon," said the American. "Let our MO see that leg. Guess you've not eaten much lately?"

"No sir, not much," said Gray, striving to maintain the stiff upper lip.

The MO was a beautiful young Kachin lady, with rich, shoulder-length, black hair and clothed in a red and gold *longyi*.

"I'm Dorothy, in English," she said.

Gray lay on a bed of bamboo interlaced with matting, while Dorothy carefully inspected his injuries, confirming that his bruises were minor and complimenting him on his stitching.

"You did a good job, Jon. I'll put some more gentian on and change the dressing. We've got plenty of medicines now, thanks to Colonel Mildenhall."

She fetched a bowl of warm water containing disinfectant and began to sponge the incision gently.

"You're probably wondering why I'm the MO?"

"Yes – if that's not being discourteous."

Dorothy gently patted the wound dry with a towel.

"Not at all. My husband is the local chief," she explained. "We were both at Cambridge a few years before the war. We met through the Evangelical Union."

Gray nodded. That explained the absence from the village of Japanese heads stuck on poles as trophies. The hill tribes had some rough customs.

"I was at Cambridge," he said. "Tripos in maths, along with rugger, swimming, athletics and the university air squadron. That last one took over."

The doctor laughed, her slim fingers skilfully wrapping the new dressing.

"The Lord's plan and purpose, Mr Gray. I'll bring you some wash water and you can change into some of the colonel's clothes. Then I think you'll be ready to eat."

Gray was conducted to the colonel's premises where a feast of roast pig, fresh fruit and vegetables was set out, augmented by American C rations. Jon could smell coffee brewing. The American greeted him, indicating a wicker chair.

"Hi, Jonny. Come and sit down."

Gray did so.

The Kachin chief, wearing fatigues, was also present, with a British major, tall and dark-haired, loose-limbed and immaculately uniformed. They sat with Mildenhall around the bamboo table on which the meal was spread.

"My name is Nigel in English," the Kachin explained, shaking Gray's hand.

"Delighted to meet you, Gray. I'm Peter Waverly, SOE," the major said. "We'll get you out by L-Five as soon as we can."

Gray recognised the name.

"Are you Lord Waverly, sir?" he asked.

"My father's the earl but, yes, I'm the heir apparent."

"I remember your name from the Oxford eights, sir and the first fifteen."

"You guys can reminisce over lunch," Mildenhall said good-humouredly. "Time's a wasting."

Nigel gave thanks and they fell to.

"So what happened, Jonny?" the American asked.

""We were beating up a Jap logistic unit on the other side of these hills, sir. It was guarded by some light AA – well guarded, too well, for my liking."

The weather closed in after Gray's rescue, delaying the arrival of the L-5.

"I know you guys fly in conditions like this, Jonny, so do ours," Mildenhall explained, as they stood on the veranda of his hut, watching the lightning flash. "But we want you to get back OK."

By the time the L-5 arrived, Dorothy had removed the stitches from Gray's leg and he was walking almost normally.

Mildenhall accompanied him to the aircraft as it taxied to a halt.

"Thanks again, sir," said Gray. "Give my regards to the major."

"Sure will, buddy," said the colonel. He shook Gray's hand. "God speed."

In the meantime, Waverly's Kachin patrol had penetrated to the Chindwin River, where they crossed by makeshift raft under cover of darkness.

On the other bank, they found vast numbers of putrefying Japanese bodies, the vanquished of Imphal. Waverly's patrol members had to tie handkerchiefs soaked in mosquito repellent around their faces to count the corpses without vomiting.

Waverly was glad of his task, despite the revulsion. It stopped him thinking about Collette. But inevitably his mind would return to that last mission.

They waited to drop, Ed Russell, OSS, Marçel Surcouf and Peter Waverly, both SOE. Their task: assist the Maquis of this part of rural southwest France to hinder German reinforcements moving north.

They had not worked together before but were veterans and could do the job well. It was a vital one. The cross-Channel invasion had started.

They sat on the edge of the dark hole in the Halifax's fuselage, flexing their shoulders against the straps of parachute and kit. Waverly could just make out his companions' features in the dim greenish light.

The engine note changed, the pilot was lining up.

"Blue bloods first, Pete," said Russell above the noise of engines and vibrating airframe, a grin creasing his high cheek-boned face.

Waverly forced a smile as the green light came on.

The dispatcher shouted "Go!"

Waverly exited into the warm summer night.

His parachute blossomed open and he noted the distinct 'T' on the ground, from torch-light, denoting the DZ. After the others had dropped, the Halifax made another run, to release the containers carrying arms and ammunition.

They were off to a good start.

A few hours earlier, Madeleine Veron had listened intently to the message from Base in England, confirming that the drop was on.

She acknowledged receipt, closed the set down and hid it in its niche.

Dressed in black fatigues and gym boots, she slung her Sten gun over her shoulder, slipped four extra magazines into the pouch fixed to her belt next to the sheath that held her fighting knife and climbed down from the attic.

She crept out of the cottage and set off along the forest trail behind it to alert her colleagues.

She had also donned a black balaclava as an extra precaution. The Gestapo had shot her predecessor, a female Marquisard, when they'd intercepted a supply drop in April.

Madeleine suspected an infiltrator and therefore accompanied the Marquisards only after dark, masked and speaking as little as possible. Apart from her radio network, all trusted local folk and Alain, grey-haired Great War veteran and local Marquis leader, they knew her only as "Collette."

She jogged along at a pace that would cover the half-mile distance to the RV in about three minutes.

Madeleine's papers indicated she was from Lille and her explanation for moving south was to care for an aging aunt, with whom she shared the cottage, located on the outskirts of rustic village.

'Aunt' Renée was a fearless patriot with a mane of white hair and piercing gaze. Even the local *Gauleiter* held her in awe. However, her arthritis was getting worse and Madeleine had been so kind.

Olivier had nothing on Madeleine's 'aunt.'

No-one had any suspicions. Madeleine wanted to keep it that way, because Madeleine Veron wasn't her real name, she was from Lewes not Lille – her mother was French - and she was SOE; a trained radio operator, medic, saboteur, martial arts and small arms expert, fluent in French and German.

A lot to assimilate for the twenty-four year-old lass, who had studied to be a veterinary.

Part of the team's responsibility was to train Maquis recruits in guerrilla warfare but first they had some pre-arranged demolition to carry out, with an elite group.

"Breakfast by sunup, *mes amis*," Alain promised, as they trekked for miles along the forest trails, perspiring under the weight of weapons, ammunition and explosives.

Collette went with them. Waverly observed that she moved as lithely as the men, though carrying the same load.

The target was an iron bridge that spanned a deep gorge.

Alain's party halted on a bluff overlooking it. They crouched, concealed beneath the trees.

"Two sentries this end," Collette said quietly.

Waverly could make out the dim helmeted figures, one on each side of the bridge abutment with the approach road. They appeared to be armed with automatic firing assault rifles.

"Should only be two more at the other end, according to our scouts," Alain said to Waverly under his breath. "This area's been pacified. *Les Boches* are not expecting trouble and reinforcements are only a few minutes away by road."

The Resistance in the vicinity had been scattered or executed in a recent enemy coup, all its arms, explosives and ammunition seized.

"That's why we had such a long jaunt, *ma cher*," Collette whispered to Waverly. Her lips curved sensuously. Peter reckoned she must look lovely under the balaclava.

Waverly smiled in return and the trio turned their gaze to the twin arches, visible in the moonlight, set in the steep-sided slopes. The heavy-duty timbered roadway, eighty yards in length, formed a tangent with the arches at their centres and rested on vertical stanchions bolted into the long, bow shapes.

They would attach a hundred and fifty pounds of plastic explosive on timer detonators to each end of the bridge. Its destruction would delay by several days an elite SS panzer battle-group now concentrating in the next valley.

"Jacques, Reynaud, OP," Alain whispered, pointing to a looming crag on the far side of the gorge. 'Jacques' was Marçel's alias. Russell and Waverly were 'Justin' and 'Guillaume' respectively. The watchers departed. Reynaud, the tough ex-Legionnaire, carried a Bren gun, Marçel extra Bren magazines and his Sten.

"Far side, Collette," said Alain in French. "With Guillaume, Joffroi and Michel. Fifty minutes. We signal each other from under the bridge, OK?"

Collette nodded. Her group began the descent upstream of the bridge, where thick brush gave good cover. Waverly noted how she and the others negotiated the rough slope like chamois goats.

The water at the bottom was icy. Waverly felt it lapping his calves.

They began the steep ascent.

"Alain's turn next time," Collette whispered in French when they'd gained the ridge. Wearing Denison smock and battledress, Waverly was bathed in perspiration.

"Must be hellishly hot, that headgear," he remarked to Collette.

"We'll make it hotter for Les Boches," said Joffroi, an ex Alpine Chasseur.

"*Très bientôt*[54]," murmured Collette.

She led them over the brow of the ravine, where they sighted the other two sentries, positioned like their comrades on either side of the junction where the bridge met the road.

The four concealed the explosives in scrub and crept via dead ground to the base of the nearer arch. Joffroi and Michel climbed over the cross-supports to the other side. They would attack on a pre-arranged signal. Waverly felt his mouth drying.

Alain glanced at his watch. He nodded to his group of four. Like Collette's, they deposited their explosives, then filed silently under cover of gorse bushes to the massive concreted buttress of an arch, where two of them clambered through to the arch opposite.

Alain glimpsed the pinpoints of light. He answered with his pocket torch.

The pairs dashed uphill for their quarry. Halfway up, Russell slipped and fell with a gasp, slithering backwards.

"*Wer ist dort?*[55]" said a voice. "*Hände hoch!*[56]"

The sentry fired the instant Alain flung himself flat, wincing as he landed in gorse. The automatic reports rocketed along the ravine.

As the second sentry rushed to assist his colleague, Alain's companions felled both guards with dagger thrusts from behind. They then helped Alain to his feet.

"Where's the Yank?" asked one.

"Fifteen minutes," Alain urged. "The charges, *vite!*"

"Damn," muttered Russell, limping up the slope. "My ankle's twisted."

"Can you get to the RV?" Alain asked anxiously.

"Sure, good luck."

Painfully, Russell hobbled off.

Strangely, the American's injury disappeared the moment he got to the forest trail…

The watchers in the OP shook hands when they heard the shots.

"*Pour la France, mon brave.*"

"*Pour la France, mon brave, allons*[57]."

In the present eventuality, they were to resist the SS riposte, for as long as possible.

Marçel and Reynaud made their way downhill, placed Gammon bombs in the road and assumed their firing positions.

Collette leapt like a cat up to the roadway on receipt of the response from Joffroi's tiny torch, Waverly at her heels.

She seized the sentry around his nose and mouth, plunged her knife into his right kidney, forced him back on the blade, then pulled it out and deftly slit the man's throat.

Joffroi executed the other sentry likewise. Waverly smelt the blood. It was everywhere.

Then they heard the shots.

"*Mon Dieu!*" cried Collette.

"Fifteen minutes," said Waverly.

It took three for Collette, Waverly and Michel to retrieve the explosives, transport them to the arches and climb to the end pair of stanchions. Chasseur Joffroi stood watching a cutting on the approach road, Gammon grenade poised.

Collette's demolition team lashed the charges by their long web straps, set the detonators and hastened back onto the slope.

They had four minutes left. All hell was loose on the roadway.

Marçel and Reynaud's Gammon bombs destroyed the first SS vehicle and blocked the road.

With deadly automatic fire, Reynaud and Marçel took out thirty of the foe before enfilade fire killed them both.

Unblocking the road took time, though.

Joffroi hurled the Gammon when he saw lights emerging from the cutting.

The bomb burst set the vehicle aflame. A second collided with it.

Joffroi tossed a white phosphorous grenade to encourage the blaze and calmly picked off survivors with his Sten, until he fell from a Schmeisser burst.

Collette and the others dashed onto the bridge, bullets cracking around them, splintering planking and ricocheting off the iron guardrails.

More SS vehicles arrived to shove the burning wreckage from the cutting, clearing the road but making their infantry better targets in the firelight for Alain's Brens, manned by the remaining two Maquisards in his group.

Red tracer snarling from their expertly sited weapons was scything down the foes.

Firing Sten bursts into their attackers, the three saboteurs fell back across the bridge. Collette hurled a smoke grenade to cover them.

Them Michel was hit.

"Ma fois!" he cried and collapsed, clutching his thigh.

Waverly hoisted him with a fireman's carry.

"I'll hold them," said Collette.

"Two minutes, Collette," Waverly gasped as he lurched forward.

She laughed.

"If Alain's charges don't go up first, *ma cher!"* she called over her shoulder.

"Guillaume!"

Waverly saw Alain beckoning.

He stumbled on with his burden amid the crescendo of gunfire, until he got to the other side. Alain took Michel and Waverly turned about, Sten at the ready.

He saw Collette, standing in the middle of the bridge. She had placed a Gammon bomb on the road beside her.

A half-track came nosing through the smoke, grenadiers to each side, tracers flashing from its machine gun as the gunner tried to silence Alain's Brens. Collette opened fire with her Sten.

The vehicle's machine gunner toppled into the cab, the grenadiers fell back, the vehicle faltered.

Collette tossed her Gammon bomb at the half-track and turned to run. The bomb burst under the grill, engulfing the bonnet in a sheet of flame.

"Collette!" shouted Waverly.

She came sprinting towards him like a gazelle. The SS did not shoot at her. They were fleeing in the opposite direction.

Waverly and Collette dropped into a ditch. He put his arm around her. They covered their ears. The charges exploded.

With a horrendous shriek of tearing metal, the twin arches collapsed, crashing down in a gargantuan roar. Choking smoke and dust filled the narrow valley.

An elite SS panzer group would be late for the battle of Normandy.

"We must get you both out," Alain insisted. "I have radioed for a Lysander. It will be here tonight."

Waverly frowned. They were conferring in a derelict farm building, where Alain's wife had brought breakfast by bicycle; bread, cheese, boiled eggs and fresh milk.

"Les Boches are beside themselves," she told them. "They hardly noticed me."

"The Gestapo have the bodies of our friends," Alain went on. "They will make thorough checks. We must disperse, standard procedure."

Waverly nodded. Seated on a mass of straw, he nevertheless felt wretched about it but Alain reassured him.

"Last night was a major success, Guillaume. We fight another day, eh?"

"We killed a lot of Jerries, though, Alain."

The veteran *poilu* nodded gravely.

A back-up party from Madeleine's radio network stretchered the casualties in stages via back routes on foot and by horse and cart to the cottage, Madeleine anxiously monitoring Michel's wound. It exhibited ugly entrance and exit holes but no bones were broken and no artery severed so she was able to stop the bleeding, much to the young man's relief.

Madeleine and her aunt turned the study into an infirmary and while Renée kept watch, her niece continued to administer first aid.

She cleaned Michel's wound, changed his dressing and gave him a shot of morphine.

"We'll get you away after dark, Michel," she whispered.

"*Merci*, Collette," he said drowsily and drifted off to sleep.

Madeleine smiled at Russell, also recumbent in the study, then went and changed into skirt and blouse, concealing her bloodstained garments.

"We're quite a way from the bridge," she explained to Russell when she came back. "We should be able to get you out OK."

The rangy American was reclining on a mattress.

"Good cover here," he said.

Collette checked Michel as she spoke. He was stable.

"I send messages on my vet rounds. Clients shift the radio around for me. Makes it hard to get an RDF fix."

Russell nodded.

"Smart move. By the way, you look much better without the mask. And in proper clothes. Madeleine's a nice name, too."

Madeleine blushed, running her fingers through her dark tresses and adjusting the sleeves of her blouse. Lightly, she felt Russell's ankle, noting the curious absence of swelling or bruising.

"I'll fetch some ice," she said and got to her feet. "As the local vet, I've got a cold store."

When Madeleine returned, the study windows were open and American appeared to have gone. But she smelt chloroform.

Puzzled, Madeleine stepped inside the room and went first to the windows. Suddenly, she was tightly grasped from behind and a cloth smothered her face. The chloroform, from her own medical kit, overwhelmed her[58]. Crushed ice scattered on the carpet.

Russell acted quickly.

He throttled Michel.

Before Renée even sensed his approach, the garrotte was around her throat.

Russell was pleased that the cottage had a telephone.

"The local vet is well equipped," he remarked.

Russell picked up the receiver and dialled.

"Albrecht," he said, when a voice answered. "Von Hollstein here…[59]"

At the conclusion of his call, Russell glimpsed Madeleine stirring. He reached for the chloroform.

A dash of cold water hit Madeleine in the face and abruptly she awoke, shocked to discover that she was tied to a chair in Renée's parlour.

She could hear screams and commotion from outside in the village. God, they're rounding everyone up, thought Madeleine, in dismay.

Then she raised her head and stared horror-struck at the sight in front of her.

'Justin' was leaning against her aunt's dining table, in SS uniform. Beside him stood a sour-faced civilian, who was placing an empty bucket on the floor.

Gestapo, Madeleine realised, almost sick with fear. The *Gauleiter* would not intervene; even if he'd wanted to.

"Now, you will answer our questions," Sour-face demanded.

Madeleine tried to sound defiant though she knew it was futile.

"Go to hell."

The resounding slap left the side of her face stinging. Dazed, she heard Justin speaking – without an American accent.

"Steady on, Albrecht. We must be considerate to Mademoiselle, especially since I've bumped off her aunt and her comrade-in-arms."

"*Meurtrier!*[60]" Madeleine snarled. She strained at the cords holding her, tears springing to her eyes.

"Calm down, Mademoiselle," said Russell. "We're all expendable in war. And there's no point in being defiant," he added for Albrecht's benefit. "We can loosen your tongue if we have to."

"W-who are you?" Madeleine stammered. Terrified, she knew Von Hollstein's threat was real.

"Count Franz Von Hollstein, Mademoiselle," Russell informed her. He got off the table and clicked his heels. "Herr Albrecht is my associate. I played the double agent game for years in the States. It's paid dividends."

That explained everything, Madeleine realised, with palpitating heart; the screw-up at the bridge, her predecessor's murder, the uncanny success of the pacification and earlier missions compromised, with Maquisards publicly bayoneted as a warning, their eyes and tongues gouged out[61]. According to Alain, Justin had made previous sorties to the area. Even though he would not have known the precise location of a mission, for security reasons, he would still have been able to warn Albrecht to be on the alert at a particular date and time, using a clandestine radio in England.

Probably one like mine, Madeleine reckoned. Oh, God.

And only Alain's adroit preparations had thus avoided total disaster at the bridge. When his ankle ruse misfired, Von Hollstein would have had no option but to see the mission through, in order to locate the Resistance nerve centre - Renée's cottage. That was doubtless his objective, even at the cost of the bridge. And he'd achieved it.

The count spoke again, his voice sinister.

"I lost my sister, on assignment in England[62], and England will pay, Mademoiselle."

Cruelly, his gaze bored into her. Madeleine trembled at the iciness of those piercing blue eyes. Then she noticed that the noise outside had died down. That meant the hapless villagers were corralled somewhere, condemned to their fate. The efficient Nazis would have accomplished the task in less time than it would take to conduct a normal school assembly.

Someone knocked at the front door.

"Come in," said Von Hollstein.

An SS lieutenant entered and saluted smartly.

"Orders from Berlin, sir," he explained. "Reassignment, effect immediate. Your transport's waiting. And for you as well, sir," he said to Albrecht, who grunted in response.

"Very well, Lieutenant," Von Hollstein said decisively. "Take her to the church, with the rest," he ordered, nodding toward his captive. "We can dispense with the interrogation, Herr Albrecht, evidently now the bigger game's afoot."

The count's Gestapo crony smiled wickedly.

Madeleine was aghast. She had guessed what was coming.

"That's – inhuman," she gasped.

Von Hollstein leant close to her, his voice a serpent's hiss.

"Your allies turn our cities into crematoriums with their air force. Don't lecture me about humanity, Mademoiselle."

Madeleine spat in his face.

Von Hollstein's fist slammed against her jaw and she blacked out. The force of the blow sent the chair toppling backwards.

"Cut her loose," Von Hollstein said to the lieutenant. "Dump her in the crematorium."

Madeleine slowly came to. She tasted blood in her mouth. Lying on her side, wreathed in choking smoke and feeling searing heat, she heard shrieks and crackling flame.

The thought flashed through her disoriented brain.

God, I'm in hell!

A terrifying crash sounded, followed by more and the shrieks rose to hysteria.

Vicious automatic firing broke out. Madeleine pressed her body down. Lethal missiles cracked past. Red-hot cinders scorched her.

A falling object hit something soft and liquid spurted into her face. She vomited, spitting blood.

Gripped with terror, she saw that in this hell, the fiends used German weapons and wore German uniforms. She glimpsed them at apertures through the smoke and flame.

And, like her, the damned bled.

And they had the appearance of women, children and babies.

In horror, Madelaine saw stick grenades pitched in amongst living, screaming forms. Again, she pressed herself to the floor, covering her ears as the hideous blasts sprayed out bloodied flesh.

More objects plummeted down, smashing living forms beneath. Madeleine cried out as her thigh and hip received hammer blows. Reaching down, she felt more blood.

"God, I've been shot!" she croaked.

Under cover of smoke, she crawled on her stomach towards a sidewall; desperately praying the fiends would not pick her off. She got to it and lay huddled on the tiled floor, broken glass all around. Her jaw hurt, her face was swollen, her aching thigh was dripping blood. She was soaked in perspiration from the scorching heat of the flames.

Above her, light from a window space showed through the murk.

"Get the blokes, now," shouted a guttural voice.

The fiends spoke German. Madeleine remembered Von Hollstein's order.

They had started the fire with phosphorus and smoke grenades. Madeleine now realised that from the stench of the fumes. And they had probably taped incendiary to the wooden furnishings. That would explain the intensity of the blaze and why the weakened rafters were breaking away so quickly. Slabs of roofing and stonework fell with them.

"Please, God, help," Madeleine whispered.

She clutched a stone carving, dragged herself to her feet and reached for the windowsill.

Somehow, she heaved herself through the window space, disdaining glass edges that scoured her legs. Falling awkwardly, she crawled into long grass behind ancient tombstones, where she passed out again, the roar of the inferno and screams of the damned still ringing in her ears, and the clatter of weapons used by the fiends.[63]

"Madeleine, Madeleine."

The voice was Alain's. Madeleine felt water moistening her lips.

She awoke – and saw she was in bed in Alain's cottage, with him and his wife at her side.

"Alain!" she gasped. Madeleine seized his sleeve and sat bolt upright. "We've got to get away. Oh, God, I ache!"

"Madeleine, I know, everything," Alain said softly, helping her lie down again. "We went back after the SS left. Found you and a few of the men. You were shot twice but we've treated the wounds and you'll be OK."

"We put you back to sleep for that," said Alain's wife. "Chloroform."

With a tender smile, she handed Madeleine a cup of coffee.

"Thank you, Madame," said Madeleine. "Everything's a blank, after I got out of the church."

"We will leave soon," Alain promised. "And get you to England when you are well."

"Guillaume!" Madeleine exclaimed.

"Gone," said Alain. "Lysander. Couldn't wait for Justin. We thought at first he'd been captured."

"I will kill that son of a bitch with my bare hands," Madeleine vowed.

Waverly was reassigned to the Far East. Russell's infiltration had compromised him for Europe.

Madeleine recovered and returned to her parent unit in WAAF Intelligence, where, in addition to her assigned duties, she undertook to trace Guillaume. Her initial efforts were thwarted because, officially, SOE was divulging nothing about agents still active.

But Madelaine was determined to find him.

And Von Hollstein.

Franz would be rediscovered ...   *who was among the thousands of*
Allied troops to b   *rquis and others who had gone*
b   *y now.*

...er Lieutenant Stephen Graham ...moved along the pitching deck inspecting ...ull AVREs, Armoured Vehicles Royal Engineers.

Keep 'em secure."

...ighed forty tons.

...s squadron was part of the unique Seventy-Ninth Armoured Division, known as ..s Funnies," after their ingenious commander[64]. It had a vital task, to breach Hitler's ...antic Wall, using its specialised armour; amphibious Sherman 'Duplex Drive' or DD tanks, with all-round canvas screens and propellers, enabling them to 'swim' from the landing craft as infantry support, Sherman 'crab' tanks with chain 'flails' for destroying mines, armoured bulldozers, 'crocodile' flame-throwing tanks, and AVREs, Churchill tanks modified to carry a multiplicity of assault equipment; SBGs for crossing thirty-foot gaps, road-laying mesh, canvas or paling 'carpet,' paling bundles called 'fascines' for filling A/T ditches and 'petards,' mortars firing forty-pound 'dustbin' charges with a range of ninety yards, to shatter concrete.

Graham's half-troop of three petard Churchills would be in the first wave.

Sea-spray lashed his youthful face. His lean, well-muscled frame shivered beneath battle-dress and camouflage smock. A northern lad of twenty-five, tough as the Sheffield steel of his hometown, he was nevertheless finding the cross-Channel voyage uncomfortable.

"Still OK this side, sir!" shouted Sergeant Tyrell, his second-in-command, a stalwart ex-furnace mechanic from Rotherham. Most of the squadron were from the steel towns of the Rother and the Don, or the mining villages of West Riding, Notts county and Derbyshire.

"Let's get back inside!" Graham shouted above the howl of the wind.

The dim passageways stank of diesel fumes, blocked latrines and vomit. Having been confined aboard for nearly forty-eight hours in the tossing waters of the assembly anchorage before their LCT got underway into a considerable swell, many of the men had been sick.

Graham was due to attend an O Group convened by his friend and troop leader, Captain Don Winstanley, but dropped in on his crews first.

"At-ten-tion!" barked Corporal Hazeldene as Graham and Tyrell approached the nest of hammocks where the half-troop resided.

Sixteen pairs of boots crashed on the steel floor. Hazeldene, a stocky youth from Doncaster in his early twenties with short fair hair, brought his hand up sharply to his khaki beret in salute.

"Stand easy," Graham said quietly, returning the salute. "We disembark in ninety minutes, everyone raring to go?"

"Yes, sir, I think we've thrown up all we can," said Hazeldene, to growls of wry amusement.

"Get something to eat if you can keep it down," Graham urged. He observed that the lads were all washed, shaved and wearing fresh clothes, as ordered.

"Try to, sir. Best we'll get for a while."

After months of standard army rations, the sappers had been delighted to savour RN cooking, until seasickness set in. Sod's law, they reckoned.

"Nothing from Sally?" said Graham. The question provoked ironic laughter.

"Not 'til zero seven forty-five, sir," Corporal Crittenden interjected. "We'll miss it, unfortunately."

Crittenden, ex-electrician from Selby and ace scrounger, had tuned into Radio Paris the previous day with his AVRE's wireless, filling the well deck with the syrupy tones of Axis Sally, enemy propagandist broadcaster with Hollywood accent known as "the Berlin Bitch."

She'd made an unexpected announcement.

"You Limey boys of Seventy-Ninth Armoured can sew your bullhorns[65] back on, we've got your number."

Someone had made an obscene proposal.

"Better not, mate," Crittenden had advised. "We don't want any more like her."

Normandy, June 6th, 1944, H Hour.

The invasion fleet stood to off the misty shoreline, smoke from the bombardment spreading over the beaches. Naval escorts' guns banged away at Nazi shore batteries and Allied fighter-bombers with their D-Day stripes streaked in to strafe the enemy positions.

Growl of engines, roar of gunfire, shriek and boom of shells, clamour of ships' claxons and loud hailers created an amphitheatre of noise never to be repeated along this sleepy stretch of coastline.

Earphones over his beret, standing on his pedestal behind petard operator Sapper Ferrarby and beside his wireless operator/co-ax Besa gunner, Sapper Shoreland, hunched over the AVRE set, Graham tried to moisten dry lips, his head and shoulders projecting above the vehicle commander's open hatch. Enemy shells were exploding near the vessel, spouting water, sending waves of concussion slamming against the hull. Elsewhere, the German guns had scored direct hits.

A battered LCT drifted into Graham's line of vision to port, on fire and billowing smoke. Survivors were launching life rafts. Steve bit his lip, feeling the heat of the inferno against his face. The vessel was carrying flail tanks and an armoured bulldozer, intended for supporting his half troop in securing their objective. It meant an added burden for the remaining vehicles.

Abaft of Graham's LCT, a barge-like rocket ship was firing salvo after salvo, a series of multiple flashes and whooshing roars.

Graham's landing craft stopped with a shudder. Its ramp thudded down. Ratings released the chains. They fell with a grinding clash and the sailors quickly rewound them around their capstans, dodging between the six behemoths with their engines already idling.

Steve spotted the church spire through his binoculars, projecting above the mist. Their main landmark, it stood directly beyond where half of Winstanley's One Troop would help breach the coast road retaining wall that sloped up several feet above the dunes. Winstanley's tasks were to cover the Churchills laying fascines for gapping the concrete-lined anti-tank ditch gouged through the dunes and any AVREs surmounting the wall with SBGs, then reinforce the attack against the fortified houses on the landward side of the coast road.

The objective for Graham's three AVREs lay to the left, a sturdy ramped beach exit of concreted stone, cutting through the wall and extending beyond the dunes. Steve knew from studying aerial photographs that the slipway was guarded by gun emplacements on each side and would be surrounded by mines. Though beyond the anti-tank ditch, the ramp was choked with massive angle iron entanglements along the entire length of its high-sided slip road through the wall.

And these looked firmly fixed in place.

Steve saw obstacles in the water; tall wooden poles, topped by Teller anti-tank mines, beyond them clusters of projecting angle iron, known as 'hedgehogs,' doubtless booby-trapped. Landing at low water, the AVREs were to dislodge them.

Crabs from adjacent LCTs would move through the gaps thus created to flail the mine-fields. They then had to provide long-range gun support until the DDs could be landed 'dry' because the seas were still too choppy for them to swim in.

The forward half of One Troop, Amazon, Arrowhead, Alligator, surged down the ramp, with Amazon, Winstanley's Churchill, in the lead.

The trio of AVREs detonated the Tellers with bursts from their Besa machine guns and drove down the poles. They blasted the hedgehogs to twisted fragments with petards explod-ing in massive *"crumps"* and brilliant flame.

As the treads of the first three Churchills thrust clear from the seawater, Winstanley's drivers detonated the Cordtex explosive taped beneath the waterproofing fabric around the turret ring, mortar and Besa mountings. Huge bangs ripped away the yards of heavy, imper-meable cloth.

"Drivers advance!" Graham called into his mike.

Lance-Corporal Talbot let in the clutch and with a mechanical roar, the Churchill lum-bered forward, Tyrell's and Crittenden's following.

AVREs Armadillo, Arquebus and Adamant were on their way. It was 0730 hours[66].

Everything depended on the first wave making rapid progress, not only to prevent succes-sive waves from piling up but also because the rising tide would conceal remaining beach obstacles.

Winstanley's voice crackled in Graham's earphones over the B set for communications within the troop.

"Able One to Delta One. Going for the anti-tank ditch, Steve. Over."

"Understood, Able One. Godspeed, Don. Out," said Graham into his mike.

"Follow crabs to the beach exit," he instructed Talbot.

Crabs were now churning through the gaps Winstanley's AVREs had created, flailing the sand. Graham's Churchills splashed through the shallows after the reserve crab troop making for the concrete ramp.

"Stand by to jettison waterproofing!" Talbot called through the intercom. He slammed shut the driver's rectangular porthole with its armoured glass visor and Graham ducked his head beneath his hatch. Talbot activated the Cordtex switch. More strips of fabric were sent flying, to loud accompaniment.

Lumbering down the ramps of adjacent LCTs, fascine and SBG carrying AVREs from the rest of the squadron ranged themselves to span the anti-tank ditch and the retaining wall. Others would transport bulky bundles of steel mesh carpet to cover stretches of treacherous blue clay. Yet more petard Churchills joined Winstanley to bombard the defences. More crab tanks followed.

Machine gun bullets and mortar bursts tore up the sand. Graham closed the hatch and re-sorted to his periscope.

Flashes of gunfire were visible from concrete pillboxes near the wall, amid the grass-entwined dunes and from the heavily fortified houses further back. With each flash came the hiss of death-dealing missile.

The specialised armour took the positions on.

Winstanley's petard trio and Major Blackstone's Zero[67] Troop savaged the enemy gun emplacements, blasting huge holes in house wall and concrete shield, aided in their task by the disposition of many German eighty-eight mm and one hundred and fifty-five mm batteries, sited to enfilade the beach at high tide and therefore unable to counter the petard fire from nearer the water's edge. Even many Spandaus, protected by concrete, had only limited traverse[68].

One by one the enemy batteries were silenced but not before some of them registered.

With a massive bang, one shell exploded against the flail roller of a crab, tearing it askew and immobilising the tank. Another blew a tread off one of Three Troop's Churchills. Pieces thumped into the sand forty yards from the AVRE as surviving crewmen scrambled out, the able-bodied helping the injured. Then it exploded. Another mighty bang and a second AVRE suddenly stopped dead, in a welter of smoky flame.

"Sergeant Ingles and Corporal Stringfield, sir," said Ferrarby, aghast, staring through the turret aperture. "God help 'em!"

Regimental medics appeared on the scene, having landed from a support vessel and began tending the casualties. Unwounded crewmen, armed with pistols or Stens, bravely continued their advance, in the lee of the intact vehicles.

Graham felt a surge of anguish for the men who had not escaped.

"One fifty-five!" exclaimed Talbot, in reference to the German gun. Crabs to the right of Armadillo were pouring round after round of seventy-five mm shells at its position.

The three crabs on Graham's left edged doggedly for the concrete ramp, smoke, mud and sand flung upwards from their beating chains.

"Flails approaching exit!" Graham called over the intercom.

But the enemy one fifty-five managed to impede progress once more, before it was knocked out.

A sudden *"whoosh"* followed by a deafening bang caught the crab nearest Graham's Churchill. Smoke belched from its turret.

Talbot swung the tiller bar to pass the stricken Sherman on the lee side. Two crew members, begrimed and bleeding, were helping a third out of a hatch, his legs pulpy strips of blackened and red-raw flesh mixed with splintered bone. A medic rushed to his aid in a crouching run.

Graham swallowed, sickened and fearful.

"Get Crab Able Three!" he called over the intercom to Shoreland.

"Over to you, sir!" Shoreland called back a few seconds later. He had homed in on the frequency almost immediately. Steve switched to the A set.

"AVRE[69] Delta One to Crab Able Three," he said. "Ready to engage exit, Chris. Over."

"Roger, Delta One, all yours, Steve. Out."

Graham switched to the intercom.

"Embrasure eighty yards direct front, fire!" he ordered Sapper Ferrarby.

The mortar discharged with a metallic crash. Acrid fumes from its propellant charge mingled with the stink of sweat and petrol fumes.

The bomb exploded on the pillbox to the right of the exit. Concrete shards flew like confetti.

Sapper Illingworth, Armadillo's co-driver/gunner, seated on Talbot's left, reached out of a hatch below the stubby barrel and broke it open like a shotgun. Hazeldene, Armadillo's explosives NCO, hefted another round to him. Illingworth rammed the charge into the barrel and slammed it shut.

Graham's three Churchills devastated the pillbox with petards and its neighbour on the other side of the ramp. Covered by the AVREs, Cavendish's two crabs flailed both sides, then joined in the fire support, their seventy-fives and machine guns barking and spitting at the wire-entangled enemy positions.

Armadillo hurled more dustbins at the exit. Angle iron shot skywards.

Infantry assault craft were arriving. Heavily laden squaddies were wading through waist-high water.

Mortar bursts and staccato snarls intensified. Spandau rounds caromed off the Churchills' hulls, magnified like terrible drumfire for those inside, lethal for foot soldier flesh targets. Graham switched to the B set again, praying that Tyrell and Crittenden would be listening in, according to procedure except when they had to use their intercoms.

"Echo One, engage anti-personnel fire to right, Fox One, follow me!" he shouted into his mike, relieved to hear the prompt acknowledgement, "Roger, leader, wilco," from Arquebus and Adamant in turn.

"Engage strong points beyond pillbox left of exit!" Graham ordered Ferrarby and Adamant. Leaving Arquebus to assist Winstanley's trio, Armadillo and Adamant trundled after the crabs, now both on the far side of the ramp.

More petards burst forth from the two AVREs, shattering more concrete emplacements. Together with the crabs, Shoreland, manning the turret co-axial, flayed the enemy Spandau and mortar posts. Illingworth joined in with the hull Besa, in between reloading the petard mortar. Crittenden's gunners did likewise.

AVREs from Zero Troop and the rest of One Troop swept the enemy blockhouses, MGs, and mortars to the right of the exit with petards and Besas. Fascine carriers from Two and Thee Troops in turn dropped their chespale bundles into the A/T ditch and a large shell crater in the dunes. They traversed right to make way for vehicles following. The first, an SBG-carrying Churchill, crossed the ditch, slammed its bridge against the retaining wall and mounted the steel ramp, like crusaders on a scaling ladder storming castle battlements. Two more Churchills surged over the ditch and filled-in crater up onto the wall where the dunes rose higher. The armoured trio crashed four feet to the esplanade below and petarded the enemy in the fortified houses opposite, the lead tank driving down a house shell still standing. Several other AVREs, the fascine layers among them after loosing their bundle cradle mountings, ploughed across shattered German gun positions in the higher dunes and through smashed sections of the wall to widen them for vehicle lanes, extended in one place by another Churchill that used its SBG to span a wide culvert. Crabs went ahead, flailing more mines. Aggressive infantrymen

110

scrambling over the beach and into the dunes mopped up enemy survivors there. Several fortified houses were ablaze and choking smoke rolled along the esplanade.

The AVRE crews toiled incessantly, loading, firing, reloading, drivers striving to maintain their headings amid the chaos.

Even though Armadillo's ventilator fans were working at full capacity, choking cordite smoke and reeking gun oil vapour stung the crew's throats and nostrils. Their eyes streamed tears. The staccato Besa reports beat mercilessly at their eardrums, adding to the discomfort of the engine noise. Graham drew back from the rubber-padded eyepiece of his periscope to wipe his eyelids. The sleeve of his smock was soaked. Spent cartridges and belt links clattered in hundreds onto the AVRE's floor.

An armoured bulldozer was emerging from an LCT, backup like Cavendish's crabs for the machines lost in the sunken craft. The dozer had to shift residual debris on the ramp without hindrance.

Armadillo and Adamant ground across the shingle past the ramp.

"Delta One, halt! Fox One, halt!" Graham ordered. The Churchills lurched to a stop, still engaging their targets.

"Ronny, with me!" the lieutenant shouted to Corporal Hazeldene.

Steve unfastened Churchill's left-hand side door and leapt through the aperture. Ferrarby and Hazeldene handed him two twenty-six pound General Wade explosive charges, one after the other. Ronny then jumped out himself, to receive two more from Ferrarby, assisted by Talbot, while Shoreland and Illingworth kept up a steady rate of Besa fire. Adamant and Cavendish's crabs likewise continued raking the dunes left of the ramp.

Graham and Hazeldene scrambled onto the slipway, wedged the charges in amongst the remaining iron thicket as far as they could, primed them, jumped down to the left of the ramp and flung themselves earthwards, covering their ears.

With stultifying blasts, the charges detonated. Pieces of angle iron flew overhead in all directions. Some plummeted into the sand several yards from where Steve and Ronny sheltered by the ramp, in shallow craters gouged by the flail-exploded mines.

The dozer surged up and pushed the dismembered metal clear with a grinding shove.

As Graham and Hazeldene made for Armadillo, infantry were plodding through the shallows and panting up the beach. Cavendish's crabs and Graham's AVREs maintained covering fire.

Suddenly a scream arose like the frenzied braying of panic-stricken mules.

"Moaner!" yelled Hazeldene. He and Graham fell flat again.

The six bombs burst with horrific violence a split second later. An avalanche of sand showered down. Something soggy bounced off Graham's back, like a football.

It was half a human head.

"Jesus," muttered Hazeldene. "Sorry, sir."

"OK, Ron," gasped Graham, after he'd thrown up.

Infantry survivors were scrabbling for cover, some with blood streaming from shrapnel lacerations, one with half an arm nearly severed, the side of his face torn open, blood spreading in the sand.

The armour didn't have an immediate answer for this menace but the air force did.

Two RAF Typhoons promptly silenced the killer mules. The fighter-bombers flashed overhead, each with its four twenty-mm cannon ablaze.

Again, the medics were quickly on the scene. An RAMC orderly knelt tending the casualty with facial injuries and mangled arm, another a soldier with his thigh slashed open, exposing the pulsating femoral artery. The medic jabbed him with morphine and began suturing the injury with safety pins.

Brens, Lee-Enfields and Stens were thumping and crackling as the rest of the infantry joined battle in the dunes, supported by the armour. Graham heard the cracks of bursting 36Ms and then it was over. Steve saw enemy in field-grey with their hands up.

Graham's half-troop came rumbling up the slipway in the wake of the dozer, the vital exit now secure. Steve and Hazeldene rejoined Armadillo at the top, where the lieutenant contacted Major Blackstone via Armadillo's A set, as Cavendish's crabs reversed and clanked onto the ramp. Unlike the vulnerable infantry, they and the Churchills had emerged unscathed from the mortar salvo. Though susceptible to enemy heavy guns, their metal hides were too tough for the 'moaner.'

"Well done, Mr Graham," his OC radioed back. "We're through the wall and on the esplanade. Join us there. Out."

"Dad would be pleased with us," Steve said to himself as Armadillo swung onto the coast road.

Fred Graham had served with the fledgling tank corps in WW1.

By 0830 hours, D-Day, 1944, his son's squadron had broken the Atlantic Wall.

Margaret Graham pegged out the last of the washing and glanced toward the fells overlooking their cottage on the outskirts of Sheffield, the hills where their two lads had trained year in year out until they were as hardy as mountain goats.

She and Fred had suffered agony when Neil, their younger son and RAF Pathfinder navigator, had been reported missing after the Nuremberg[70] raid in March but last week they'd wept with joy on learning from the Red Cross that he was a POW in Germany and uninjured.

Now they faced fresh anxieties.

She went back into the house, switched on the radio, and in an attitude of heartfelt prayer, held her breath at the broadcast.

"D-Day has come. Early this morning the Allies began the assault on the northwestern face of Hitler's European fortress… Under the command of General Eisenhower, Allied naval forces supported by strong air forces, began landing Allied armies this morning on the northern coast of France."

At the rush of tears, Margaret reached for her handkerchief, then for her Bible. She knelt by the sofa.

Having followed the experiences of those upon whom Grandma would later be so dependent, we return to her service in Italy.

Seven

The Gothic Line

Up in the snow on Cisa Pass...we were British proud to be British
- Roy Farran, Adventures on Special Service

"On the road again, girls," said June as clad once more in KDs, boots and helmets, she and her companions climbed aboard Dinah Merryl's lorry, their trunks, camp beds, bedrolls and web bags stowed on the tray.

"Dinah and Mollie must specialise in QA transport," remarked Colleen, clambering after June, followed by Hoppy. They were pleased to see their ATS friends again and Captain Fordham, who was in charge of the convoy, having been reassigned north.

Settling onto her cushion, Sister Dale voiced one reservation. "Just hope Briggsy still doesn't get any targets."

The tough fusilier was accompanying them for a second time and winked at his passengers as he hoisted himself up.

Sister Hewitt and Helen Goodsall would be travelling with them. Almost everyone else had already gone north, as part of a staged handover with the new unit. Colleen and her friends were among the last to leave.

"You'll soon wish you were back here," the incomers warned.

Their departing colleagues were inclined to agree. About an hour's drive up the unsealed highway through the inevitable clouds of dust, they came upon a scene of devastation.

"Jerries called this the Caesar Line," said Briggs, glancing down from his station. "Yanks had a hard time here, in the breakout from Anzio."

The sights reminded Colleen of Cassino's ruins. Former buildings were battered heaps of bomb-blasted stonework and masonry, with their skeletal timbers starkly exposed. Open ground on either side of the road was a lunar-like landscape of shell holes and savagely torn-up earth. Amid rusting hulks of burnt-out tanks and vehicles, the bleaching bones of hapless cattle slaughtered during the fighting gave the area the appearance of an abandoned abattoir. Repeatedly, the trucks were forced to nose carefully past piles of rubble spilling onto the roadway.

"Jerries could've mined 'em," Briggs explained in his off-handed way.

Wooden crosses marked the graves of GIs killed here.

And the sickly-sweet smell of death lingered, a ghastly, invisible shroud.

Grimacing, Colleen glanced up into a brilliant sky, acutely conscious of the sun's heat on her back and shoulders. Her helmet pressed into her forehead, from which she was repeatedly mopping perspiration. Patches of sweat under her armpits and between her shoulder blades were forming a consistency of starch with the powdery grit settling on her clothes. With sleeves rolled up, her arms looked like she'd been milling flour.

"Hope we can get a wash," Hoppy said to her. "Our hair'll be like wire after today."

Briggs uncorked his water bottle and passed it around.

"You're a gallant gentleman, sir," said Sister Hewitt. She took a draught and daintily wiped her mouth.

Eventually, the convoy descended onto flatlands with occasional copses of trees. They were approaching Rome.

"Looks like the Vale of York," said Colleen.

"Jerries pulled back from here," said Briggs. "That's why there's no signs of fighting. We got to Rome just before D Day, Normandy, that is."

The transport halted for a brew and necessary break where two copses grew conveniently close by on either side of the road. The passengers nimbly alighted.

"Lovely spot, this," June remarked. "Hear those birds?"

"And the insects humming in the grass," said Helen. "Pity we can't set up camp."

"That's ours," Sister Hewitt informed them, pointing to one of the clumps of trees after she'd conferred with Fordham. "Take a spade with you."

Briggs grinned at them as he and Mollie tended the spirit burner for their tea.

"He's nearly domesticated," she said proudly.

Soon after the journey resumed, the dirt road gave way to a paved stretch and honey-coloured tenements came into view. The vehicles cruised along a stone bridge across the mud-coloured expanse of the River Tiber. It smelt foul. Glancing over the side of the tray, Colleen was shocked to see the bloated carcass of a mule in mid-stream and even more horrified when she glimpsed a human corpse floating face down close to it[71].

"Muleteers just chuck 'em in if they peg out," Briggs called nonchalantly above the noise of the traffic. "Locals get rid of anything dead that way, except cats and dogs. Ities eat 'em."

"What about the dead man?" Dollie asked, still aghast. Briggs shrugged and leant on the butt of his LMG.

"Probably a Fascist. Wops are mostly on *our* side now that Musso's got the push," he said sardonically. "Like to show they're doin' their bit."

A multi-storeyed circular ruin with Romanesque arches set in its lower three tiers arose before them. The lorries followed the road around to the right. Helmet tilted back, Colleen leant her weight on one arm and stared up at the ancient limestone façade.

"Well, we can say we've seen the Colosseum," said Helen. Her blue eyes twinkled with satisfaction.

Their transport threaded its way northwards through the city's venerable byways. Unlike Naples, Rome was almost undamaged and most civilians appeared well-to-do.

"Folk seem to be doing OK here," June remarked.

"Only the townies, Sister," said Briggs. "There's thousands living in shanties on the outskirts, or in caves even[72]. Sight to behold, eh, Sister?" He glanced at Bronwyn, who spoke out fervently.

"It's terrible. Most of them have got pellagra and malaria, permanently. Typhoid hits them summer and winter[73]. Hardly any can read or write."

From time to time, the Sisters waved courteously in response to the customary wolf whistles their appearance elicited from passing servicemen, both lorried and on foot.

Hoppy nudged her friend.

"There's St Peters, Coll," she said. "We ought to drop in on the Pope if we can[74]."

Colleen nodded slowly, arching her back against the tray's wooden railings as she gazed at the distinct dome shape in the distance.

Together with Hoppy, she would visit the Vatican a few months later and, in doing so, change the course of her life.

The ugly spectacle of war was manifest again once they left the capital. Many villages and towns north of Rome had either been destroyed by Allied bombing or demolished by the retreating enemy. The jumbles of wreckage sprawled in obscene contrast to the picturesque, undulating green countryside round about.

Where dwellings were intact, Italian families gathered in the doorways of sandstone-hued houses, their dark eyes watching the lorries trundle past within a few feet of them.

"Bet they've got a lot of homeless neighbours bunking in," Dollie remarked, as she lifted her helmet to run fingers through her blonde locks. Colleen felt sorry for her. Dollie's normally immaculate hair was a mess. Like mine, she thought.

The route occasionally took them across rivers where the sappers had replaced blown bridges with Baileys, like the one over the Volturno. Italian women at the waters' edge carried on with their washing without looking up but their children paused from play to wave and shout at the passing Allies.

The girls smiled and waved back.

"Look healthier than the mites in Naples," Hoppy remarked.

"Northern Italy's different from the south, Sister," Briggs called down. "Locals look more like Swiss, or Austrian. They're still as poor as church mice[75], though they've got a bit more to eat, except for the war."

"Then it's boiled grass for some," said Bronwyn.

"We were lucky where we were," Helen added. "At the base hospital."

Briggs nodded.

"Italy's like that, good and bad side by side," he told them. "You've got a few that are permanently stinking rich of course, like the Fiat gang and His Holiness. Vatican museum'd knock your eyes out."

Colleen was silent, thinking over the similar conversation she'd had with Tony at Sorrento and their efforts to assist Father Alonzo. Italy, showpiece of her religion, displayed the contrast between rich and poor far more sharply than at home. She felt ashamed.

Late in the afternoon, the trucks halted outside an abandoned villa. Its roof was gone but, according to Captain Fordham, it was habitable. They would leaguer here for the night.

"About eighty miles to go," said Briggs, debussing and taking his Bren with him. "Be in Tuscany well before noon tomorrow. We best put all your gear inside, ladies," he advised. "Easier to guard."

While Captain Fordham liased with the local holding unit, Briggs and the orderlies lit paraffin stoves and heated dixie pots of water filled from Jerry cans, for cooking, and washing utensils.

"Dinner on the grounds, folks. Ladies first," Briggs announced when the *alfresco* supper was ready. It consisted of spam, meat and veg stew and treacle pudding heated in their tins, hard tack biscuits and, naturally, compo tea.

"Can we have some water for rinsing out socks and – er – smalls, please, love?" Mollie asked Briggs with a winsome smile as she dunked her dixie tins and KFS preparatory to collecting the meal.

"And a dollop or two for our hair?" added Hoppy, likewise smiling like the Cheshire Cat.

Of course they could.

"I like wall-to-wall stars," said June. She gazed up from her bedroll through the jagged hole where the ceiling of an upstairs bedroom had been.

Their quarters reeked of the mosquito repellent applied to faces and hands, because they had decided not to string their nets for the one-night stay. However, various washed garments hung from improvised clothes lines, including their shirts. Everything, even their woollen socks, would dry quickly in the warm summer air.

Before they could attend to these necessities and that of washing themselves, the bedroom had needed sweeping and emptying of damaged furniture, the pieces of which went to augment the fires.

But now, supper over, they were comfortably settled, with the men located on the ground floor or on sentry. The orderlies had also dug a latrine in the grounds so that the ladies could use the inside facilities. These were functioning, thanks to the holding unit's efforts.

Captain Fordham and Briggs had kindly collected some straw from the out buildings and placed it in sacking for the girls to put under their bedrolls.

"You lads are so chivalrous," Sister Hewitt had said.

The eight of them conversed informally, disparity in rank put aside, apart from deference due Bronwyn as their superior.

"Been in the Med for nearly two years but I can never get over how bright they are," Dinah murmured drowsily, taking up June's comment.

"Compared to Bermondsey, anyway," said Mollie. "Especially after the Blitz[76]."

"Bermondsey?" exclaimed Hoppy. "I'm from Wandsworth. I trained at Guy's."

"My gran was a tea lady there. That's how she met Granddad. He was a delivery driver. Runs in the family," Mollie said with a laugh.

"Bit before your time, Hoppy," Helen interposed, joining in the laughter.

"Shh," said Sister Hewitt. She put a finger to her lips. "You don't want to wake the boys, now."

"This lamp won't keep anyone awake, will it?" asked Dollie. She was writing to Andy by the light of a hurricane lamp. Seated beside her, Colleen was sharing it to write to Tony.

"Not me," Helen reassured her. "Give Andy our love," she whispered seductively. The last word came over as "loov," in rich Mancunian.

"I will *not*," said Dollie, stifling a giggle.

Sister Hewitt looked up at the stars and recited a verse from the Psalms.

"'He telleth the number of the stars; he calleth them all by their names.'"

And He's calling me, Colleen reflected, also glancing upward. By name.

The next day, after breakfast, they went back upstairs to pack away their dried washing and apply some lipstick. Men patients always appreciated femininity. Gentle shafts of sunlight through the roof cavity and knocked-out window spaces reflected off minute dust particles spiralling in the still air.

"Can I have your attention, girls?" Sister Hewitt asked.

The others turned to her from folding away their clothes.

"We're going into an operational area," she continued, hands clasped behind her back. "We should all kneel down and make our peace with God and His Son, or make sure everything's right between us and Him – out loud. I'm not asking you to be goody two-shoes. Not with the monkeys in this group. No, this is an honourable and womanly thing to do, especially if you're in uniform. And our men folk will be much better for it in the long run."

Obediently, they slipped to their knees. Colleen felt embarrassed at first but when her turn came, she managed to pray "Dear God, keep us in Your love and mercy, for all our sakes and for those we love and care for, Amen. And Lord save me," she added under her breath.

Her sincerity surprised her.

So did the warmth of assurance that her personal prayer was answered.

"If you'd like to talk about this, you know you can speak to Marian or me at any time," Sister Hewitt said after they stood up.

"Do you suppose she meant us, when she said monkeys?" Hoppy asked as she came down the stairs with Colleen and Helen, all of them carrying their bags and bedrolls.

"Well, who else, Hoppy?" said Helen with a mischievous grin.

The impromptu prayer meeting would have repercussions, monkeys notwithstanding.

From the rolling hills of Tuscany's farmlands, the convoy turned east into the northern Apennines, where the road snaked around one hairpin bend after another in its steep ascent.

Clouds of choking dust once again enveloped the passengers as Corporal Styles skilfully manoeuvred their lorry along the twisting mountain track in the wake of Fordham's vehicle, scarcely visible through the billowing haze. Occasionally, she and the other drivers had to stop, reverse and drive forward by stages to get round the sharpest curves.

Colleen and her companions tied handkerchiefs around their faces to filter the dust and exhaust fumes.

"So much for femininity," June called out wryly.

"We look like a gang of bank robbers," said Bronwyn.

Yet the scenery was awe-inspiring. On the one hand, the girls had to crane their necks to see the summits of the almost sheer mountain sides that rose beyond the road, terraced with jutting rock, laced with coarse, tangled shrubbery. On the other, they could gaze at vast green slopes that chasmed away to fertile river valleys far below, veined by glinting watercourses.

"This isn't too bad," said Briggs, raising his voice above the grinding of gears. "Roads turn to mud in the autumn rains." He didn't seem bothered by the dust.

"How do they keep them open?" shouted Dollie through her handkerchief.

"Sappers chuck on road base, Sister," Briggs called back. "Gets washed away in the mountain floods so they have to keep at it. They also bulldoze the snow off in winter, or we all pitch in to shovel it by hand. Keeps you warm for a bit. Mr Somerville digs it out with the best of 'em."

His knowing wink provoked refreshing laughter.

They emerged onto a wide, grassy saddle that displayed the scars of recent fighting, for the Allied offensive to break the Gothic Line had already begun. As usual, all buildings had either been dynamited by the enemy or destroyed in the Allied bombardment that had also uprooted extensive belts of German barbed wire. Nevertheless, the Wehrmacht had fought back stubbornly. Three wooden crosses stood poignantly beside a disabled Sherman tank as one of many reminders. Again, Colleen sensed the smell of death. As the lorry drove past stunted fir trees, she glimpsed dug-in German tank turrets, now abandoned, tree stumps to their immediate front indicating clearance for fields of fire.

"Smiling Albert's[77] idea," Briggs informed them. "Jerries put 'em here because they're short on fuel. Armour makes 'em harder to knock out than normal gun positions."

The lorry bumped over an uneven stretch of road. Colleen and the others held onto their tin hats.

"Anti-tank ditch," said Briggs. He leant against the back of the cabin. "Sappers've filled it in. Camouflaged originally. That's why there's no spoil. A lot of mine clearance hereabouts, in front of the buildings." He nodded to either side of the road. "You can see where the ground's been dug up. Hope there's none left for any kids around here to set off. Happens occasionally."

Colleen noticed that for all his dourness, Briggs did not mention Andy in this context. He had no doubt guessed what Dollie was thinking.

As Mollie steered around a corner, the Sisters were startled to see a sinister-looking gun barrel poking at them from a huge hole in the wall of a wrecked two-storey dwelling. It was still attached to the parent tank that displayed a black cross on the turret.

"Jerry Mark Four," Briggs explained. "Backed in for cover."

A little further on, the lorries edged past a column of British infantry in khaki, with weapons slung over their shoulders, plodding along the road in two files, a Sherman tank between them, moving at a walking pace. Grimy and gaunt, these squaddies were apparently too parched to whistle at the Sisters as they passed but wearily raised their heads with affectionate smiles and were generously rewarded in kind. The dust having subsided, Colleen and the others had removed their handkerchiefs.

"Lincolns or KOYLIs[78], I reckon," said Briggs. "Comin' up from reserve."

"Reserve!" exclaimed Colleen. "They look dead beat."

Briggs grinned at her. "They've only got a few miles to go, Sister," he said. "No use hurryin' to a battle, not here. It ain't Waterloo."

He inclined his head to the forbidding ranges that rose up beyond the broad saddle they were traversing.

Colleen and the others cocked their ears. The truck's engine was quieter now that Mollie was motoring along a level stretch in high gear and the Sisters could distinctly hear the rumble like thunder, though no storm clouds were visible.

"Ours and theirs," Briggs informed them, pushing back his helmet. "Sounds like Jerry's still got plenty of eighty-eights."

Beyond another cluster of firs, dark brown tents with distinctive Red Cross roundels emerged, set in rows amid stones and gorse, backing onto the next escarpment.

"Here we are, girls," Sister Hewitt announced. "Hello, what's got into Scottie?"

Corporal Prescott came dashing up as the lorries wheeled into the hospital's vehicle park.

"Sister Hewitt!" he shouted. "CO wants you. Battle-fatigue cases. His HQ's right there."

Scottie pointed to one of the smaller tents. Briggs quickly unlashed the Sister's gear, then he and the others passed the items to a couple of orderlies who had debussed from Fordham's lorry. He was already making for the tent to report to Major Forsythe.

"Rest of you can stay put," Prescott continued. "CO wants you to help out at the ASC. You can give me a lift."

He jumped onto the cab's running board beside Dinah, exchanging grins with her and Briggs. Colleen thought the corporal looked extremely jaded.

Bronwyn stood waving for a few moments as the others drove off, likewise waving.

"Goodbye, my boon companions," she called. "I'll see you soon."

Mollie drove across a shallow stream spanned by a Bailey bridge. She sped through a narrow gorge, with the sound of artillery growing louder. Two sharp roars followed by sudden explosions on each of the ridgelines sent earth and stones tumbling down onto the road behind the lorry.

"Probably safest to lie down, ladies," Briggs advised.

"Why are they shooting at us?" cried Dollie.

"We're coming to a Forming Up Place, Sister," Prescott called out. "Besides the casualty clearing stations, there's dumps, stores, vehicles, guns, HQs and company bivouacs hereabouts."

"Jerry's ranging on them, not us," Briggs added. "But they'll be tucked away in gorges like this where he can do the least harm and we're too far back for his mortars."

They smiled reassuringly at the girls as the shelling continued.

With thumping heart, Colleen joined the others on the floor of the tray. Consciously, she tensed her insides and returned her companions' sickly grins.

"Hope I don't wet myself," she said.

The lorry emerged the gorge and Mollie swung left down a banked track to brake on the vehicle apron in front of the ASC.

"Just yourselves, Sisters," Prescott urged, as he jumped down. "Head for the marquee straight in front."

"We'll stash your gear," Briggs called, detaching his Bren. "Keep in single file."

He tossed the bedrolls and bags to Prescott, Dinah and Mollie, then began untying the Sisters' trunks, to which their beds were attached.

The ASC was a smaller version of the main hospital, with several tented wards, quarters and facilities. These were situated in a scrubby, high-walled re-entrant as protection against shellfire, as Briggs had said. Outside the wards, portable generators for lighting and cold store hummed steadily. Kettles for sterilisation were continuously on the boil, while incinerators smoked and burned.

Some distance from the tents, enlisted men with shovels were working on a burial area.

"Hope that's only for arms and legs," said Helen, vaulting over the side of the tray. "But I don't guess it will be." She too had been at Cassino.

Following Helen, Colleen and the others sprinted for the nearest ward, tin hats held securely on their heads by tightened chinstraps. Shells were bursting in gouts of flame near the bank top to their right, filling the air with hissing fragments and sending showers of earth down on them during the thirty-yard dash. From olive-drab, Red-Crossed ambulances, parked on the stony vehicle apron, orderlies were carrying men on stretchers under grey blankets to the same ward.

Colleen realised she would be tending them almost immediately.

But she nearly screamed at the sight that confronted her upon coming through the tent flap[79].

Everywhere she looked, distraught men lay on stretchers or camp beds, gasping, groaning, sobbing, covered in blood-soaked dressings that the duty staff were in the process of changing, after administering plasma, whole blood, morphine, anti-tetanus serum and penicillin[80].

Blood-clotted gauze came away to reveal lacerated limbs, stumps or ugly holes in chests, abdomens or buttocks.

"Could put a fist in some of those wounds," said June, aghast.

Colleen's heart went to her mouth at the sight of burns and facial injuries such as she had treated down south but in the raw here. Even gunshot and shell-fragment casualties would likely need treatment for burns, from the scorching effect of the missiles that had felled them.

The suffering victims came from many nations and regiments; Sikhs, Ghurkas, Poles, British, Canadians, New Zealanders, South Africans, with even some Wehrmacht wounded amongst them. In horror, Colleen recalled the night of the party in Naples. Were any of the boisterous young men in that multi-national gathering now here?

God, she thought, Tony. Are you OK?

The ward stank of blood, sweat, bodily discharge and suppurating flesh, intermingled with disinfectant. Colleen noted that, despite the warmth of the day, casualties were kept wrapped in blankets as part of treatment against shock and hot tea was given to those able to drink.

"You can scrub up here, Sisters," said familiar voice. They turned to see Sergeant MacHendry indicating bowls of hot water on a trestle table, heated by paraffin stoves. "We've got some head cloths for you," he added as they doffed their helmets.

Colleen thought he looked dead on his feet and remembered that Prescott and he had been helping to stretcher wounded down from the barren, seven-thousand-foot peaks of the battle line, for days on end, from outposts where even jeeps couldn't go. Army mules were the only alternative transport, carrying casualties seated in panniers slung across their backs. The enduring animals also assisted the carrying parties, transporting additional ammunition and supplies.

And they brought back the dead, slumped in the pannier saddles.

MacHendry went outside, to help unload the newly arrived casualties.

"Wonderful, you've almost doubled our nursing complement. Is Sister Taylor here?" said another voice.

June introduced herself to a tall MO, capped and gowned, who stepped out from one of the surgical annexes that had been operating round the clock.

"I'm Mike Halliard," he said in a tired but friendly voice. "You've been assigned to me so Matron can get back to Resus. We're a bit swamped today."

In a second annex, Lieutenant Jardine laboured over the operating table, assisted by an Ulster QA named Karen Treloar. In a niche to her right, Colleen saw Julie Dalton with Captain Rodwell preparing another patient. Orderlies hastened past carrying a variety of loads; begrimed, bloodied clothing and discarded bandages for incineration, dressing packs, bedclothes, blankets, splints, trays of used instruments for cleaning and sterilisation, or trays covered with linen cloths containing fresh instruments.

"This way, Sisters," an orderly said to Helen, Dollie and Hoppy, when they'd completed their preparations. They followed him to assist with the most recent casualties.

"Colleen, over here," said another voice that she recognised. It was Matron Lovejoy, in boots, khaki and headscarf. Opposite Rodwell and Julie, she was kneeling by a waxen-faced soldier with a huge swathe of dressing around his middle. Quickly, Colleen went to help her set up the drip bottles. These were hung from loops of cord in the ceiling of the tent, or fastened to metal stands.

"Usual," said Marian. "One of saline, one of plasma." Colleen knelt down and inserted the cannula for the twin bottles into the man's pallid arm. She removed the tube of the near-empty bottle containing whole blood that the RAP medics had used for an emergency transfusion, taping over the hole left by the detached cannula. The medics were well trained, Colleen noted. It wasn't always easy to find a suitable vein in the limb of casualty in shock whose body was involuntarily directing blood to the vital organs but the RAP lads had kept this soldier alive. Colleen and her colleagues would do their utmost to ensure that he stayed alive.

With an orderly's help, Marian and she then lifted the old dressing that was dripping blood on the tarpaulin floor. The exposed wound went clean through the man's body, shattering one side of his lower rib cage. Colleen bit her lip momentarily but then turned her gaze to smile at the anguished young face before her.

"I'm giving you morphine," she whispered, swabbing the lad's arm, then inserting the syringe. Marian Lovejoy nodded and they renewed the man's dressing.

Colleen had almost forgotten about the shelling but she looked up at the sound of an explosion that was closer than the others, cringing at the tearings in the marquee wall that appeared as if by magic, aware that Marian and she were instinctively leaning across their patient.

Startled by a terrible cry of pain, Colleen glanced over her shoulder, horrified to see Julie collapsed on the floor of the theatre annex, struck by shrapnel.

"Bring her here."

Matron Lovejoy's calm, clear voice galvanised two orderlies into action. It also seemed to settle everyone else, patients and staff alike. Work had to go on.

"Sister!" said Rodwell. He beckoned Colleen.

"You go," said Marian quietly, as the two orderlies deposited the pain-wracked, white-faced Julie on a stretcher beside her.

Colleen got up and stepped over the stretcher. Rodwell's orderly, Lance Corporal Burrows, quickly tied Colleen's gown while she donned surgical gloves, cap and mask. As she did so, she noticed the ashen look on Sergeant MacHendry's face when he came back into the tent, holding one end of another stretcher.

The patient lay on one of the two trestle operating tables in the annex. He was breathing through an oxygen mask. Colleen leant to check his respiratory rate and saw out of the corner of her eye that she was standing into a patch of Julie's blood.

"Abdominal, Coll," Rodwell said as he cleaned away strips of damaged flesh. "Usual eight-inch incision."

She handed him the instruments. Burrows monitored the patient's heart rate, breathing, and IV drip.

"Now for the intestines," Rodwell muttered, after cutting open the cavity. Colleen helped him clamp off flaps of incised flesh and blood vessels. She passed him the probe. Sometimes even a small hole concealed fearful internal injuries and the original wound was not small. Fifty percent survival rate for abdominals was considered normal.

Rodwell probed for bullets, shell fragments and shards of stone - as at Cassino, these too were adding significantly to the toll of mutilations.

"Have to cut off some of the bowel," Rodwell said through his mask.

Colleen nodded, again handing him the necessary devices. She remembered the soldier with the colostomy at the hospital down south. When he'd finished probing, Rodwell sewed shut the holes made by the slivers he had removed. Several minute metal pieces, close to the surface, he extracted with a magnet, minimising damage to tissue.

"Stitch up the incision, Sister, while we get the next chap ready," Rodwell told her. He nodded towards a casualty with an open chest wound placed on the other trestle table. Hideous sucking sounds were audible.

"Leave a loop of bowel for temporary venting, as usual," Rodwell continued. "I think this chap will mend OK, thank God. Sulfa powder and standard Vaseline gauze dressing, finally, of course and penicillin." He sounded relieved but desperately tired.

The whole procedure had taken over an hour, while the guns thundered on, uncomfortably close, but Colleen lost track of time. When the abdominal was carried out to Post-Op, she turned to assist with the chest casualty.

After him, they performed an amputation, right leg below the knee, where the limb was necrotic, stinking and grey with gangrene. Colleen arranged the drip Pentothal for the patient's anaesthetic.

"This'll put you under," she said, encouraged when the man's taut countenance relaxed in response to her voice and the smile in her eyes.

She fastened the tourniquet and Rodwell meticulously cut the flap. Colleen tied off the blood vessels. She watched the MO saw through the yellow bone laid bare and drop the severed limb in a bucket, boot still attached. Handing Rodwell the needle and sutures, she helped him close the flap.

Burrows took away the bucket.

Rodwell examined the semi-comatose individual who followed the amputee. The left side of the man's head and neck were almost pulpy with bloodied flesh. His left arm was crushed, blood-sodden and limp as a rag, his left eye horribly blackened and torn up by shrapnel, the right also blood-black.

"Left eye's a write-off," said the surgeon. "I think I can save the right and his arm, though he'll have limited use. Eardrum's burst, permanent damage there. A shot of anaesthetic, Sister, adjust his drips and we'll start on the eye."

When that operation was finished, orderlies stretchered in the next patient, heavily drugged. A shell burst had shattered his hip, carrying away his leg, part of his buttock and a portion of his colon[81].

"He's going to need a hip amputation, Coll, it's like a jigsaw," said Rodwell when Colleen removed the sticky, sodden gauze covering the hideous cavity. "And he'll have to stay on heroin for Post-Op. Morphine won't do."

The soldier was semi-delirious until Sister Hopgood injected him with morphine.

She and Corporal Prescott then arranged his IV fluid drips and Hoppy administered a penicillin shot.

"OK, Doug," she said. "Let's get this dressing."

With Prescott supporting the casualty, she prised off the sodden layers, piling them in a bucket for disposal. The machine-gun burst had left fearful entry and exit wounds. In the midst of the perforated and still bleeding midriff before her, Hoppy could see splintered rib ends protruding. Using instruments to ensure her hands did not touch the casualty's flesh, she carefully packed the holes with sulfa powder and fresh gauze, then gently wrapped on a new dressing.

"We'll have to keep an eye on him, Doug," she said. "Be a while before he's stable enough for theatre."

"Sure thing, Sister," the tall Canadian said, smiling.

"Call me Hoppy," she whispered and moved to the next stretcher.

"WP," she said, noting the wet dressings. "We'll double check for any that's left, mate," she told the casualty. "Pick it out and put a cellophane bag around that arm, with soda bicarb and sulphate solution. That'll ease the pain – and stop you glowing in the dark. MO'll stop by later."

Despite his distress, the casualty a smile while Hoppy injected him with morphine, then penicillin.

"Another penicillin jab in three hours," she said to the lad, as she noted the time. "One of the Sisters'll be around, OK?" He nodded again, looking calmer.

They used *Tulle Gras* dressings or saline-filled bags to encase the burnt limbs of other men, some of whom had been in tank conflagrations, or scorched by liquid fire spewing from German flame-throwers that sometimes fused flesh and bone together into a grotesque, amorphous mess. Glucose and saline drips augmented the treatment, to counter fluid loss. Even where victims incurred fifty percent burns, diligent nursing often brought them through to recovery, despite their desperate injuries and terrible pain.

Again, like Cassino, the terrain of the Gothic Line meant that the ASC would receive many head and facial injuries. Hoppy ministered to one soldier brought in straight from the battle because the RAP was full. His jaw had suffered multiple fractures. A thick wad of dressing, wet with blood, covered the lower half of his face and he had been kept upright, first in a mule pannier, then on a stretcher in the ASC, in order not to choke. His breathing issued forth as bubbling wheezes.

Hoppy carefully unwound the soiled dressing, disposed of it and encouraged the soldier to open his swollen mouth a little wider. He did so, gingerly. She helped him lean forward to drain a mixture of blood and saliva.

"I'll get any loose bits out," Hoppy said softly. "Then give you a drink."

Using forceps, she delicately removed fragments of broken teeth and deposited them in a bowl.

Then she held the patient so that he could take some careful sips of water. The young woman's arms and her voice helped reassure him.

"MO'll stabilise your jaw. And we'll get you down to a Max-Factor unit."

Hoppy gently taped a new dressing over the wound.

Like their colleagues elsewhere on the Resus ward, she and Prescott tackled many different tasks; setting up blood transfusions, applying splints for cruelly fractured limbs, cutting away boots with heavy scissors so fractured feet could be set, arranging tractions for men with splinted limbs on which casts would be placed, helping convalescing men out of their blood-stained and soiled clothing into fresh pyjamas, a manoeuvre requiring considerable skill owing to the patients' manifold injuries.

"We're well equipped, Doug," said Hoppy, when they paused for a tea break several hours later.

"We've had too much practice, Hoppy," Prescott said with a grim smile.

As part of their duties, Helen and Dollie had continued the penicillin round. Each patient received an intramuscular injection every three hours, in the buttocks, thigh or directly into knee or shoulder wounds.

"We'll mix it with some local anaesthetic[82]," said Helen as they prepared the syringes. "They won't complain so much."

Passage of the thick yellow fluid into muscle tissue was nevertheless still uncomfortable and some recipients were apprehensive.

"Come on, you're a big lad," Dollie would chide them. "Not scared of a little needle, are you?"

"Only if it's goin' in me bum, Sister," retorted one Cockney infantryman.

"Wait'll we do you on nights," said Helen. "It's known as the wake-up call."

Then they were confronted with two emergencies, almost simultaneously.

A casualty was rushed in spurting blood from a sudden haemorrhage. Prescott and Hoppy came to assist them. The patient consumed several bottles of whole blood before the crisis was averted. An orderly cleaned up the floor.

In the midst of these events, Jardine called "Gas!" Alerted by the smell, Dollie injected the patient with penicillin straightaway, while Karen administered six thousand units of anti-gas serum.

Jardine had admitted a casualty directly from ambulance to surgery and called out the instant he had removed the dressing. The stench like a sewer, and the telltale bubbly tissue in the ugly black mouth of a gash that stretched from armpit to elbow, signified gas gangrene. Thanks to the antidotes, the patient and his arm could be saved but he would have to be isolated, the annex scrubbed and disinfected, everything in it re-sterilised.

Jardine and his team moved to a spare niche. Their next patient was Julie Dalton.

"She's going to lose her appendix," Jardine said, on inspection.

"So long as we don't lose *her*, Larry," Sister Treloar rejoined.

"Pelvis definitely fractured, Sister," said Mike Halliard.

June guessed that from the mixture of blood and urine soaked into the trousers she had cut away. The bullet had torn through the patient's hip and come out through his opposite thigh, leaving a hole almost the size of a teacup.

Halliard was inspecting the bullet track with a pencil torch.

"Nicked the bladder but missed the urethra, thank God," he told June. "A lot of bone splinters, though. I'll have to open it some more."

She handed him the thin knife he needed and long forceps. After Halliard removed the fragments, they cleansed the wound and affixed the drainage tube.

"Sulfa and penicillin, Sister, as normal," Mike said finally.

Facial casualties, such as the one Hoppy and Prescott had tended, were also admitted. Rodwell and Jardine also received a share.

"I can carry out a tracheotomy and wire this fellow's jaw to get him back to main[83]," Halliard said of one such patient. "Also immobilise the cheekbone, what's left of it. He'll need bone grafts. Max-Factor people at base will see to them. Have to take out his front teeth, though, so we can spoon-feed him."

June handed Halliard the wire and extraction pliers.

"Right eye, cornea damage," he said on inspecting another patient.

Mike pointed the pencil beam at an eyeball that looked like a globule of blood set in a thick ring of mucus. He continued his diagnosis.

"Several bits of metal have gone through, now sitting in the gel. I can get them out with the magnet but he's got some retinal damage. Need to get him to the specialist unit at main for some spot welding as we call it, to prevent detachment. He'll probably have fifty percent vision in this eye. Like looking at a mirror with the silver flaking off."

June gently dabbed away the mucus and Halliard applied the magnet.

She delicately shaved the next patient's head.

"Severe scalp laceration and depressed cranial fracture," Halliard muttered. "I'll have to drill to relieve pressure on the brain and deal with any haemorrhaging."

June supplied the requisite instruments in succession. Mike released the trapped fluid. It squirted out with a slight hissing sound.

"Sulfa-impregnated dressing and plaster of Paris seal, June," said Halliard when he'd finished.

She carefully applied both in turn. Private Elsdon, Halliard's orderly, had prepared the porridge-like mixture.

"He'll be comatose for days," Halliard concluded. "Nasal drip for glucose feeding and regular sponging until his brain starts regulating his temperature again."

"Going to be hard getting them down to the base hospital, Mike," she said, remembering the trip up.

"There's a better road, June," Mike told her. "Not so steep. Drivers'll be able to use that for the most critical cases fairly soon, I hope."

"Jerry's got it under observation, Sister," Elsdon explained. "That's why you had to come up that bleedin' goat track."

June smiled. Elsdon and his fellow orderlies were a jaunty lot and supremely competent, thick as thieves with their two Canadian counterparts. She and her friends could surely thank Providence for this posting.

But Elsdon had disturbing news about one particular patient.

"We've got a UXP, sir," he told them and held up a chest X-Ray photograph. "Radiographer thinks it's a twenty millimetre. They've left him outside for now."

Halliard glanced at June.

"Marked 'Caution,' I suppose," he said. "Well, we'd better bring him in, hadn't we?[84]"

"Sister!"

Hoppy hastened over to where Prescott was kneeling beside the abdominal case they'd treated earlier.

"Oh, God," she groaned. "Tie his hands, Doug."

The staff had tried to watch him but with responsibility for so many, gaps of a few minutes had occurred where the patient had remained unobserved.

During one of those gaps, having relapsed into delirium, he'd pulled his dressings loose. Heaps of sticky red gauze lay on the floor.

Prescott fastened the soldier's hands to the stretcher handles while Hoppy applied fresh dressing.

"'She hath done what she could,'" Hoppy murmured. "Dollie and her Bible readings, and Bronwyn's" she said in response to Prescott's quizzical expression. "Getting to us all."

"I'm down to the heart," said Halliard.

June handed him the retracting clamps to secure the opening. She could clearly see the palpitating cardiac wall.

"It's right by the heart membrane," Mike continued. "See the bulge?"

June nodded and swallowed hard. She felt frightened.

"Better mop all our fevered brows, Sister," said Mike, grinning behind his mask.

June did so and handed him the fine silver probe with which he dissected the tissue, a stroke at a time, until he exposed the sinister black bullet shape.

Pulling it out between thumb and forefinger, Mike gave the shell to Private Elsdon, who would arrange for its disposal.

They ate brief meals outside the annex and exchanged their soiled theatre clothing for fresh garments when they returned.

"We can take it in turns to get some more compo cubes for the tea," said Halliard, glancing at the bubbling urn. "Feel free to make any necessary detour."

"Thanks, Mike," said June.

Elsdon had mentioned the location of the hessian-walled enclosure, thoughtfully roofed over.

It was late afternoon the following day before the ASC staff could rest.

Halliard, in overall command, sent the original duty staff to their quarters, including MacHendry and Prescott.

"We'll relieve you this evening, ladies," Mike said to June and her companions before he and Rodwell departed. "You've all done splendidly and I'm happy to report that Sister Dalton is stable."

"Thank you, sir," said Helen said. They were greatly relieved about Julie.

Karen remained to assist Jardine with the remaining operations.

When they were complete and Larry had turned in, Karen and Colleen stood sipping compo tea at the entrance to the ward. Hoppy had said she'd "join them in a bit."

It was night and the first shift had returned so that June, Helen and Dollie had gone to the Sisters' Mess before retiring. Though some of the patients groaned and muttered incoherently in drug-induced sleep, the ward was comparatively calm.

The artillery was still firing intermittently and small arms could be heard crackling up in the mountains but the enemy pieces that had menaced the ASC earlier seemed to have shut down.

"We're well set up here," said Colleen. Karen nodded, taking another sip of tea.

"Better than before," she said. "We were amputating in holes for while, in front of Cassino and living in them. Never forget the looks on those poor boys' faces. Guess the others told you?"

Colleen nodded. "How's Barry?" she asked.

Flight Lieutenant Barry Congreve, RAF, was Karen's fiancé.

"OK. You know he was flying ground-attack Tiffies in Normandy? Well, he's chasing buzz bombs these days, in one of the new Tempests. So I'm still wearing out my knees praying. Have you heard from Tony lately?"

"Write as often as we can."

"Mike was right. You folks did well."

Colleen topped up Karen's tea and hers.

"I nearly screamed my head off when I came in."

Karen smiled sympathetically.

"Perfectly normal. But not everyone can adjust. One of the girls got sent home pregnant a few months back."

"One way to get chucked out of nursing and the army double quick,[85]" said Colleen, holding the hot mug with both hands. "Why didn't she speak to Matron or Bronwyn if she couldn't cope?"

Colleen felt little sympathy, even if the girl had entered into the affair in genuine need of solace. Many QAs had sweethearts amongst serving men but personal integrity was a matter of honour. Any deviation brought both the Corps and indeed the entire profession into disrepute[86].

Karen sipped her tea.

"Too embarrassed, I think."

"Who fathered the little bastard?"

"A senior officer. He got sent home too. That's how we ended up with Eyepiece Ernie for a CO, in the reshuffle. But changing the subject, where's Hoppy got to?"

Colleen glanced around. Sister Hopgood was nowhere in sight.

"She'd have come and told us if she was going straight to the mess," Colleen remarked, puzzled.

"We better go find her. She shouldn't be on her own."

Karen and Colleen were drawn toward the sound of crying. They found Hoppy seated on one of the empty blood boxes outside the ward, her head in her hands.

She looked up at their approach. The tears streaming down her face glistened in the dark.

Her friends pulled up another pair of boxes and sat beside her. Karen put an arm around Hoppy's shoulders and they waited for her to speak.

"Y-you know the lad who pulled his dressing out?" she said after a while, in between sobs.

"You had to tie his hands," Colleen said gently. Hoppy nodded and wiped her eyes.

"I came back to see him and he'd died," she told them. "I meant to check him sooner but we had so many to see to…"

Given the welter of serious injuries the centre had coped with, the dead were mercifully few but a tragedy like this was a terrible blow.

"You did all you could, love," said Karen.

Colleen lightly touched her friend's arm.

"C'mon, Hoppy," she whispered. "While there's still some spam left in the mess – or whatever else's come to light from those compo boxes."

"Trust you to be thinking of your stomach, McGrath," Hoppy said, smiling through tears.

Together they got up and strolled toward the mess tent.

Going through the tent flap, the trio immediately sprang to attention.

"Er, at ease, ladies," said the high-ranking visitor. It was the corps commander. His response notwithstanding, he appeared most ill at ease. Major Forsythe, standing beside him, looked mortified.

Seated at the trestle table, June, Dollie and Helen stared open-mouthed, their spam and veg forgotten.

Their supremo had come from Corps HQ to visit the unit and to express his concern over Nursing Officer Dalton but he hadn't reckoned on Matron Lovejoy's reaction.

Colleen, Hoppy and Karen had arrived just in time for it.

Marian's eyes were blazing. She held an ugly metal fragment up to the commander's face - he stood more than a foot taller than she – and addressed him in no uncertain terms.

"This is the piece that hit my girl, General. Thank God we didn't get any more casualties but it could happen again at any time. If you want your men cared for as they should be, General, then you'd better give us some extra protection."

"I'll get the sappers to work immediately, Matron," the commander promised.

Too right he will, Colleen reckoned.

Snarling tracer flashed back and forth across the ravine. Opposing mortars coughed harshly in repeated crumps. Livid flashes and bellowing bursts rent the night air, echoing and re-echoing from the chasm walls.

With its steep sides, the ravine was a serious obstacle even in summer.

Autumn rains transformed it into a raging torrent.

"Dozer up, Sergeant Gilfillan!" Lieutenant Andy Somerville shouted above the noise.

He stood in the centre of the Bailey's first planked section, beckoning. Smoke jetted from the dozer's exhaust, the growl of its engine intensified and Gilfillan nudged the boxed metal platform with its five-foot-high load of stringers forward. It grated on its rollers.

When the rear end of the load was level with the edge of the Bailey section, Gilfillan gave Somerville the thumbs-up signal, halted the dozer and backed it away.

Attached to the bridge's second section was a third, partially complete and joined by transoms. This section thrust out cantilever fashion over the void. If the whole span was pushed a little further, a fourth section with a launching nose for the far side would close the remaining gap. Armour could then follow up the infantry assault in progress, via rough mountain defiles that were nevertheless wide enough for tanks. Somerville's sappers had already reconnoitred them in the shadow of late afternoon, ensuring they were free of mines.

Much depended on heavy sustained fire keeping the foe occupied. Thus far, the plan was working.

A team of ORs hastened to help Andy unload and secure the stringers between the transoms of the cantilevered section.

The enlisted men pulled the platform back and loaded it with steel planking that Gilfillan dozered onto the bridge. Reversing the vehicle, he climbed down and joined the remainder of the sixty-man platoon, positioned on either side of the two completed Bailey sections. Andy and his team quickly laid down the planking on the third section. Then the ORs lined up with their sapper colleagues while Andy stood in the centre of the span, facing the gap.

"Heave away, lads!" Somerville shouted. He waved his arms forward.

Immediately, his sappers began straining every sinew to shove the construction along its rollers.

The duelling machine guns and mortars hammered each other unceasingly, joined by the roar of shell bursts from Allied mountain howitzers that lit up in spasms the towering crags on either side of the gorge.

Showers of earth and stones cascaded into the ravine.

"Hope the gunners don't drop any short, sir," said Gilfillan as he and Somerville conferred to bring forward the next load of stringers. "Don't want the Boche to see us in the flash."

Somerville nodded.

"Like you, Sergeant Gilfillan, I'm a modest chap. Hate being the centre of attention," he said.

But the location had been chosen because the crags helped conceal the operation and the sappers completed the bridge by midnight. Tanks, SP guns and towed artillery promptly began crossing to reinforce the hard-pressed infantry, who had earlier gone over under cover of darkness and Allied gunfire.

Somerville's platoon was preparing to move up in support when a jeep halted outside his tented HQ. Its driver, Sergeant MacHendry, went inside, stood to attention, saluted and handed Somerville a written communiqué bearing the corps commander's signature.

"From the highest level, sir," Mac said.

"Marian Lovejoy?" said Andy, scanning the document.

They exchanged grins.

"We'll build up the bank with sandbags, Matron," said Somerville. "Try and get as much done before the morning stonk. We can work by the light of your incinerators."

Matron and he stood on the vehicle park outside the operating tent. The CO and his august visitor had departed.

"Thank you ever so much, Andy," said Marian. "It's been a bit of a shooting gallery here this past week, though the other day it was much worse."

"Ranging," said Andy, nodding. "They won't be looking for you, though. Bigger fish for them to fry hereabouts. We should push 'em back soon but the bags'll stop any shrapnel. How's Julie? Mac seemed to be taking it pretty well."

"She's doing fine. I know they appreciate you praying for her. But I better let you get on. We'll keep you fed and watered, of course."

"Thank you, Matron," said Andy. He touched his helmet. "Sergeant Gilfillan!"

"And I'll make sure you get a few minutes with Sister Dale," said Marian in parting.

The pioneers had filled in the craters from the earlier bombardments but the sappers had plenty of spoil for filling the bags. They had built a barrier eight feet high at the outer wall and several feet thick by the time the shelling started again, so were able to work on, sheltered by the bags already in position.

Numerous splinters tore into outer wall during the day but none damaged the hospital. Under the blazing sun, stripped to the waist, Somerville, Gilfillan and the rest toiled away, sweat dripping from lithe bodies and sinewy arms.

"Magic, thanks, mate," said Gilfillan when orderlies brought out tea. He ran fingers through his sun-bleached hair. "Reckon we'll be done by dark, sir," he said to Andy "Pioneers can throw up some spoil to protect the outer wall."

Somerville nodded. That was his estimate. Sean Gilfillan and he had soldiered together since North Africa and thought very much alike.

Towards sundown, they rigged up some perforated canvas buckets for showers, under which they each stood for a minute, in KD trousers and boots. It was still so hot, they rapidly air-dried.

"Matron's marvellous," Sean remarked, with respect to the shower water that had come from the hospital's precious store. The various units used huge amounts each day and every drop had to be tankered up, though pipeline construction was underway - courtesy of the Royal Engineers.

About the time Somerville and his men were showering, June, Helen and Colleen hitched a ride back in an ambulance to visit Julie Dalton. They would also monitor the patients the vehicle was carrying. It had been another harrowing day in the ASC but they were coping.

Sister Hewitt greeted them outside the huge convalescent ward. Bronwyn would go back with them to relieve Marion Lovejoy as Senior ASC Nursing Officer.

"Julie's in here," said Bronwyn, taking them to a partitioned section by the admissions desk. "She'll be ever so pleased to see you."

She was. Colleen noted how the colour came to Julie's pale cheeks immediately they went in. They each kissed her on the forehead, pulled up blood boxes and sat around her bed, anxious to express their professional opinions.

"C'mon, JD, let's see Larry's needlework."

"Ghoulish lot," said Julie, grimacing as she pulled up her pyjama top. Her friends voiced approval.

"Send that pattern to *Good Housekeeping*, JD."

"Be on all next year's embroidery."

"Ow, don't make me laugh," Julie wailed.

"Reminds me of the first appendectomy old Bridger let me sew up at the General. 'Ever thought of moonlighting as a sail maker's apprentice, Staff?' he said."

"That one's got whiskers on it, Coll."

"Ow, ow," said Julie.

The partition screen moved and they looked up as Sergeant MacHendry entered, smiling self-consciously. Julie blushed.

"We shouldn't keep you too long, JD," Helen murmured. She and her two companions bade their friends goodbye and discreetly retired.

Well after dark, when Colleen and the others had returned, Sister Dale ventured inside the mess tent where, between shifts, several of her friends were finishing supper.

"Could you all stay here for a bit, please?" she asked. "I'd like to have a few minutes with Andy. Our sleeping quarters are the only private place, really. Matron says it's OK."

When the rest of his platoon had departed, Andy remained to supervise the pioneers. Mac would take him back to his command after he had seen Dollie.

June looked at her watch.

"Five, and counting, Sister Dale," she said sternly. Dollie hastened away. "Love to be a fly on the wall," she heard someone say.

She met Andy outside the tent she shared with her companions, pulled him inside, wrapped her arms about him, kissed him fiercely, then wept on his neck. He held her close.

"Oh, Andy, I've been so worried," she sobbed, dismayed at how fatigued he looked.

"It's OK, Livvie," he whispered and stroked her hair. She felt comforted by his voice and reassuring embrace. "Listen, I want to ask you something. We better sit down."

They sat on her bed. Looking her in the eye, his hands in hers, Andy came straight to the point.

"We haven't known each other long but I think we know our own hearts. Will you marry me, Livvie?"

"Yes, Andy, I will," she whispered. Their lips met again, for a long moment. Flushing hot and cold, Dollie didn't know what to say next, except "Would you like some tea, Andy?" She indicated the small paraffin stove mounted on an empty blood box.

"Yes, thanks, very much," he said eagerly.

"I'd better go get some water and cubes," said Dollie, getting up. "Be back in a tick."

June and the others generously gave her an extension of time. They were surprised when she came back almost immediately, looking flustered.

"It's Andy," she gasped. "He's asleep."

"What? Where?"

"On my bed. I can't wake him."

Astonished laughter.

"Sister Dale! Well, I never!"

"What are we going to do?" Dollie asked plaintively.

"Get Mac," said Karen. The sergeant had also returned from the visit to Julie.

Duly summoned, Mac led a chortling entourage to the sleeping quarters.

"You don't *all* have to come," Dollie protested.

"Wouldn't miss this for the world, love," said Helen.

They trooped inside the tent and saw Lieutenant Somerville seated, with his head slumped to his chest.

"At-ten-tion!" barked MacHendry, startling everyone.

"Peel me off the ceiling," Hoppy muttered.

The effect on Somerville was electric. In an instant, he was standing ramrod straight, returning MacHendry's salute.

"Your transport's ready, sir," said MacHendry.

"Very good, Sergeant," Andy said crisply. Turning to Dollie, he kissed her on the cheek, murmured, "Bye, love, another time for tea, eh?" and departed with Mac.

All eyes turned to Sister Dale.

"Andy asked me to marry him," she explained. "And I said yes."

Andy Somerville and Olivia Dale married the following spring. Over sixty years on, they are still a devoted couple. For the time being however, a particular crisis was imminent.

Rain.

Early in September, the deluge started. Heralded by forked lightning and growling peels of thunder that burst like an avalanche through the mountain passes, autumn storms unleashed water in sheets. The dust-laden roads of summer became tracks of glutinous mud. Dry streambeds were suddenly rushing with turgid, foaming runoff, often breaking their banks to undermine the Baileys that spanned them and wash away road surfaces.

When not supporting the forward troops by clearing mines, blowing away barbed wire and bridging tank-trap canals, the long-suffering sappers were on gruelling road and bridge maintenance, extricating bogged vehicles and repairing Bailey sections, even with timbers scavenged from deserted houses, still under the menacing gaze of enemy gunners, who consistently sent down harassing fire.

At times, the counter-barrages seemed like one continuous cacophony, continuously throwing up mud and earth. Only when the German artillery spread its arc of fire could the sappers resume their tasks.

"These things are sent to try us, Sergeant Gilfillan," Andy Somerville remarked.

"And they do, sir," said Sean.

They were sheltering beside an ancient aqueduct that provided some cover from the shells but none from the rain.

The wreck of an ark bridging tank lay skewed and smoking from a direct hit in the middle of a four-foot-deep watercourse barring a brigade advance. Its detached ramps were wholly submerged. To front and rear, water was lapping the chassis of the arks still in position.

"Fascine in the gap, Sergeant," Somerville ordered. "Then we'll have to top up with sandbags and rubble."

"Plenty of that about, sir," said Gilfillan. Somerville's men were already collecting it, with the help of the ark crews.

The sergeant beckoned forward an AVRE cradling the eight-foot-diameter, twelve-foot wide bundle of interconnected palings forming the artificial roadway. Under its commander's direction as he clung precariously to the top of the bundle, the AVRE slithered ponderously on the slippery road base the sappers had laid to the bank, drove into the river along the ramps of the first ark, dropped its load into position and gingerly reversed, guided by Gilfillan and its commander. Shells burst on the far side of the aqueduct but did not hinder the operation.

Somerville's wireless operator appeared at the entrance of the Platoon HQ dugout, with an urgent message.

"It's the brigadier, sir," he said. "Wants to know how long this job's going to take."

Somerville trudged back through the mud to his HQ, acutely conscious that neither he nor his men could look forward to rest or food for some considerable time.

"Yes, Corporal Ashbourne," said the lieutenant. "I'm sure he does."

Drainage ditches prevented the wards from being flooded but the vehicle parks became quagmires. Ambulances sunk in grey-brown, viscid mud almost to the axles. Mountain trails were impassable for jeeps. Chronically over-worked stretcher-bearers and the mules now brought back all the casualties, soaked and shivering in their filthy battledress, suffering as much from exposure as wounds, for the infantry had little protection against the elements.

Like Somerville at the front, Colleen and her friends trudged through mire that was often calf-deep to go on duty either in the ASC or the main hospital according to the rota, now wearing BDs, leather jerkin, Macintoshes, balaclavas and mittens to keep out the cold and the wet.

All rubbish had to be buried in deep pits. The rain decisively put the incinerators out of action.

But the tales of horror from the battlefront continued.

During one shift in the ASC, Colleen leant close to an infantryman lying on his stomach, to catch his voice above the drumming of the rain on the roof of the tent. She had injected him with penicillin and was cleaning the multiple, purplish-red gashes in his back oozing quantities of pus. In places, razor-edged fragments had stripped his flesh down to the rib cage and she could see pink lung tissue pulsating beneath the bone.

"'Twas all shell craters and smashed houses, Sister," he said hoarsely. "Jerries'd hide from the barrage behind the reverse slope, then come back and hammer us when it lifted. Broke their line in the end, Canadians, Ghurkas and ourselves - Canucks went as far as Rimini on the coast but our tanks got held up by a river in flood. When some of 'em tried another route, Jerry eighty-eights on high ground blew 'em to bits."

Colleen knew about the havoc wreaked on the tank crews, having ministered that day to many of the burnt and mutilated survivors. For her, this was more significant than the salient fact that the Gothic Line had actually been breached.

September blended into October and the rainstorms into snow, hail and freezing sleet. The mud turned to chocolate slush, then treacherous ice and even fast-flowing mountain streams, brown with erosion, eventually froze over.

Paraffin stoves were kept burning as long as possible each day to heat the wards. Fuel was like gold dust.

For Colleen and her friends, life was mainly a constant round of duty punctuated by brief intervals for eating sleeping, ablutions – such as standing shivering in a canvas basin of tepid water to sponge themselves down – and particular necessities like airing their clothes to prevent mildew.

"Must make sure we still look feminine," said June.

The snow falls intensified and the girls trudged through calf-deep whiteness to and from the wards.

"Keeps the boots clean, anyway," said Karen, from between numbed lips, her hands under her armpits. "We won't have to scrub the mud off."

As the year waned, more and more trench foot and frostbite cases were brought in, men with feet blackened and hideously swollen, often necessitating immediate amputation, after the nurses had first sliced off their boots. So numerous were the victims that the bearers carried many on their backs individually, rather than by stretcher.

No-one was surprised when the number of SIWs multiplied, men not only shooting themselves in the hand or foot but also inflicting cigarette burns on their private parts to simulate syphilis.

Court-martial and disgrace was the inevitable outcome but as one soldier said ruefully to Colleen, "Sister, it's better than a packet of shrapnel up the arse."

Other men simply went AWOL. Gangs of Allied deserters were still rumoured to be terrorising the Adriatic coast near Barletta. On top of the battle casualties, it added up to a serious manpower shortage, particularly in the infantry, where rifle companies were often only at half-strength. The Allied armies who'd attacked in August would lose over thirty thousand men by Christmas, about evenly divided between the Americans and the British.

On the credit side, everyone was delighted when Julie Dalton returned to duty but the occasion was sobered for Colleen by a letter from Annie.

Dear Colleen, it read. *You will know of the big operation over here. Bill is missing. Please pray for us. My unit has now moved up the line. Thinking of you and Tony. Love, Annie.*

Colleen replied immediately, trying to comfort her friend, urging her to keep hoping[87]. She and her friends still wrote to patients' families and of course to their own loved ones at home. Naturally, their mums and dads would worry, especially those like Colleen's with only children but the girls themselves didn't.

"Too busy, too knackered, or too much of both," said June succinctly.

Oddly enough, Colleen had been less pre-occupied with Tony than she'd expected, though they faithfully exchanged letters. His unit was somewhere on the Adriatic coast. Had she accepted his proposal too quickly, she wondered?

She would have to give the question some thought.

In the meantime, the life and work of the unit went on, with various highs and lows.

Such had been the welter of suffering and the scarcity of anything but the most basic rations that the forthcoming festive season was destined to pass without great celebration, though when the time came, the girls improvised makeshift decorations to brighten up the wards.

"You'll put the mistletoe above my bed, won't you, Sister?" they were asked more than once, not only by patients.

A couple of soldiers needed no mistletoe. One was Andy Somerville, who still managed to make the occasional visit to Dollie during the autumn campaign.

"You'll need chaperoning, Sister Dale," the others would say, yet the vibrancy of the couple's faith and the warmth of their love managed to reach out and embrace everyone.

It seemed that, in the midst of the heartache and suffering, a beneficent influence was at work.

One night, before going off duty, Karen was sipping tea with June by the entrance of the ASC, as she had done with Colleen weeks earlier. Though many patients were muttering and groaning in their sleep, once again the ward was relatively peaceful.

Bronwyn Hewitt joined them.

"Thanks again, girls," she whispered. "By the way, June, I think you're quite a comfort to Captain Halliard. He lost his wife in the Blitz, you see. They had trained together. He was in North Africa when it happened. Devastating blow but he's got such a strong faith, it's carried him through. Nevertheless, it's so good you're here."

June bit her lip, astounded at the frankness of Bronwyn's disclosure and determined to avoid Karen's whimsical gaze. But something had occurred to her.

"His wife. Would that have been Ruth Halliard?" she asked. "She was a lovely lady and a wonderful doctor. I met her when she visited Bart's and I heard that she was killed. I'm so sorry."

Bronwyn and Karen both nodded.

"That's her," said Bronwyn, touching June's arm. "A wonderful lady. She shared Mike's faith, of course. That's why it's so good you're here. 'Night, girls."

"Have some more tea, June," said Karen mildly when Sister Hewitt had gone. "You look like you need it."

"I-I don't know what to say," said June, flabbergasted.

Karen topped up June's mug.

"She seems to spot prospective couples," said the Ulster girl. "Pulls strings to get them together. Heaven knows how. She helped Mac and Julie take the first steps, and Jardine and Helen – they've kept it very quiet, for Mac and Julie's sake, but you've probably sensed something?"

June nodded as she sipped her tea. Karen continued with the disclosures.

"Not to mention Briggs and Stylsie. Probably had a word in Dollie's ear, too. Leaves a trail of torn-up regulations in her wake but she reckons you ought not to worry about them or the war, just keep praying and let the Lord look after you. Of course, you shouldn't feel you're under any pressure, June."

June gasped with mirth.

"Is Marian in cahoots with her?"

"Up to her neck. We call them 'Two M, Two B,' Marian and Bronwyn, the Marriage Bureau."

For Corporal Prescott too, mistletoe was irrelevant, as Colleen discovered, one evening in November.

If anyone in the unit could find a social event in the sombre surroundings and the means to attend, Prescott and Hoppy could.

The adjacent American Fifth Army held many dances behind the lines, often in marquees with makeshift wooden platforms for dance floors. Prescott no longer bothered with his officer's jacket. Their American cousins seemed to ignore disparities in rank totally now and took no notice when a Canadian corporal showed up with an English nursing officer on his arm. They had become very close, without any encouragement from Sister Hewitt to "take the first steps."

Their friends considerately paid no attention to the blossoming romance and the couple were wisely discreet, for a time, but Colleen was astounded at what happened when Prescott dropped Hoppy off in the vehicle park of the main hospital where she and Colleen were doing a spell of duty.

Returning from a late night trip to the facilities, Colleen saw the jeep drive up. Though the night air was freezing, the weather was calm and the road to the Yank base negotiable, with care, so the pair had contrived to attend the latest function. Moreover, Scottie was an expert driver but Colleen was nevertheless glad that her friends had arrived back safely.

However, she was shocked by the lingering kiss they shared and intercepted Hoppy on the path to their quarters - strewn with gravel to prevent anyone slipping on the ice.

"Hoppy, what d'you think you're doing?" Colleen whispered vehemently.

"That's my business, Coll," Hoppy snapped, her eyes flashing.

Colleen desperately tried to make her see sense.

"Look, Hoppy, it's OK about the dances – Yanks don't give a tinker's cuss about rank. But snogging an enlisted man in the hospital lines. That's insane! What if Eyepiece Ernie finds out?"

They stared at each other for several seconds, speechless. Then Hoppy lowered her gaze.

"I'm sorry, Coll," she muttered. "You're right. But you know how it is with Doug and me." She raised her eyes. "Guess we have been pushing the boat out a bit far, though."

Colleen put an arm around her friend's shoulders.

"C'mon, Hoppy," she said. "Let's get the tea on."

Many of the hospital staff were experiencing their second winter in Italy and the rigour of the past few months was threatening morale.

Marian Lovejoy therefore made a declaration one evening in the mess while a gale buffeted the tent walls and the girls had gathered around paraffin stoves to warm their hands before taking their places.

"We'll have a snowball fight on New Year's Eve, weather permitting, since Christmas was such a damp squib. Boys versus girls, tea and buns afterwards, like the football match, while the patients have their meal. Bronwyn and I'll organise that with the NAAFI in Florence – and get some goodies for the patients too."

"We meant to last year," said Sister Hewitt. "But we never managed it. And I think the weather'll be on our side, Marian."

So was the absence of the CO, at another high-level conference with Montague-Stewart, this time in Pisa. Some ungracious souls had asked, "Could Andy and his boys make the tower fall over and land in the right place?"

Halliard, Rodwell, Jardine and the rest of the lads eagerly took up the snowball challenge. "We'll smother 'em," they reckoned.

But they had forgotten how fit and agile their QA companions were, originally recruited for their stamina and predisposition to sports, many having excelled in ball games at school. They could throw snowballs straight and hard – and, as it turned out, exploit natural advantages afforded by the day.

December 31st dawned grey and still, with a heavy mountain mist rolling down the slopes by the main hospital. A vacant expanse beside the vehicle park, under eighteen inches of snow, was the venue for the contest. Visibility was less than twenty yards.

The girls' team smiled with satisfaction.

"Perfect," said Karen.

Marian blew a whistle and the combatants starting pelting each other. Whichever side kept their formation under the hail of snow would be the winner and receive extra NAAFI goods.

"Pound 'em, lads!" shouted Rodwell exuberantly. "We've got 'em on the run!"

The girls had indeed fallen back, though keeping up rapid and accurate volleys. It was all part of the plan. The boys had also forgotten the battle of Hastings.

They remembered too late – when showered with snow from behind, handfuls of it being stuffed down their backs.

"We're outflanked!" shouted a male voice.

Colleen, Hoppy, Helen and a few others had slipped through the mist to attack from the rear while the lads were intent on the advance. Several boisterous wrestling matches ensued that prompted Matron wisely to step in and declare the girls the winners.

"Fix!" gasped Halliard, brushing off snow while extricating himself from beneath June and Karen, who'd both piled into him.

By this time, contestants and onlookers alike, including well-rugged patients who could venture outside, were helpless with laughter.

"Get inside now before you catch your death," Sister Hewitt urged breathlessly as tears of merriment ran down her face. "And get some hot tea and nosh inside you."

"Any time you want a roll in the snow, girls, just ask," cried Jardine. "We planned it all along, eh, boys?"

"Bollocks!" shouted a chorus of female voices.

However, Colleen's hospital was eventually facing a dilemma that eclipsed both personal entanglements and recreational distractions.

It arose from the Allies' failure to reach their ultimate objective of the Po Valley by the end of autumn, despite having broken the Gothic Line and captured the strategically important towns of Rimini and Ravenna. It meant they would be stuck in the mountains until next spring, still facing formidable enemy defences.

So, the opposing armies settled down in the snow-covered wastes on either bank of the

River Senio, with deep drifts blocking the mountain passes near its source and, as Briggs had predicted, continuously occupying the sappers and pressed volunteers who toiled night and day to keep the roads open, assailed by stinging blizzards that resumed in the new year and howled through the bleak ravines that honeycombed the river line, blasting the road gangs with thick flurries of powdery ice.

As January wore on, the temperature continued dropping and the RAMC staff knew they would have to take decisive action. Numbers of fresh battle casualties had declined but Colleen's hospital moved by stages during the fighting to keep up with the front-line units and was therefore still choked with convalescents. All hospital units in the mountains were in a similar predicament.

Mike Halliard summed up the position.

"We can't keep the wards warm enough now, or our own billets. We're going to have to find a town, or freeze to death.

Eight

Friends from Afar

Grandma's service on the Gothic Line would come to an abrupt end early in 1945 but in the aftermath, she would find new friends. We consider them now.

Calcutta, September 1944.

It had been a wonderful wedding.

Together with the other well-wishers, Nursing Officers Robyn Fairlea and Trish Calder bade farewell to their friend, Nursing Officer Gwen Lewis and her husband, Dai, a spruce young subaltern of the Royal Welch Fusiliers, veteran of Arakan and Kohima.

"My name's Dafydd," he'd explained to Trish and Robyn, when Gwen introduced him at the officers' club in Calcutta (actually the attached single-storey building on the lawn where officers could entertain their wives, fiancées or girlfriends – and hold wedding receptions). "But you'll never pronounce it right, so you'd better call me Dai."

With the main Imphal-Kohima battles having been won, many personnel were being sent via C-47 to Calcutta by rota for rest, including those of the RAMC. They'd needed it. At times, the casualties, brought in by jeep, ambulance or mules, had been an endless stream, often arriving in heavy rain, to be resuscitated and operated on wherever space could be found in the crudely thatched, earthenware-floored bamboo huts known as *bashas* that housed the wards.

His battalion now in reserve after weeks at the sharp end, Dai had been granted special leave. Gwen had lived through an agony of dread.

On alighting from their C-47 at Dum Dum airport, she had flagged down the first available jeep to take the girls to their billets at the university.

"You can manage with everything, can't you, Sergeant?" she'd said sweetly to the RASC driver as the girls boarded the jeep with their holdalls and web bags. "I'm getting married tomorrow, you see."

He managed.

Dai's padre conducted the ceremony in the imposing, high-ceilinged St John's Church. A senior official of the Indian Civil Service and long-standing friend of the padre's, Lieutenant Colonel Charles Dalrymple, Royal Artillery, retired, had kindly given the bride away.

Now the couple were on their way to Kalimpong, in the shadow of the Himalayas, for a short honeymoon.

"Camellia trees in full bloom all around the hotel, they reckon. We'll bring you a post-card of Kanchenjunga," Gwen called to her friends from the departing jeep, driven by Dai's best man and brother officer, who would take them to the train station.

"I've heard it's higher than Snowdon," said Dai. "We'll have to see for ourselves."

Trish and Robyn returned soon afterwards to their hall of residence, catching a taxi with a voluble local driver who honked the horn furiously to get through the thronging streets. On arrival and after freshening up, they took tea in the cool of the courtyard garden, relaxing in shirtsleeves, surrounded by fragrant ferns and deep-hued orchids.

"What it is just to sit here and do nothing," Trish murmured. She crossed her legs, leant back in her chair and closed her eyes.

"Amen," said Robyn drowsily, doing likewise.

The multi-purpose lawn annex to the officers' club also catered for non-conformist Sunday services. Flying Officer Gray arrived by taxi during the first hymn. He selected a spare hymnal, removed his cap and discretely joined the back row. Jon was halfway through his survivor's leave and had been taking long walks through the botanical and zoological gardens to exercise his leg.

He reckoned he'd try the university's running track near his billet on the morrow.

The congregation was mostly made up of European middle-aged civilians, the women gently waving fans, although some service personnel were present, representing all the forces and all ranks, both male and female.

Gray noticed that the auditorium's windows had been opened for maximum ventilation, yielding an added bonus in that the service would have the widest possible circulation too.

Today's speaker was a sparely built man in a safari suit, with aquiline features, commanding blue eyes and carefully combed white hair. An elder from the regular attendees introduced him as Reverend Henry Simpson, long-term missionary on the border with Nepal.

Gray reckoned that Simpson looked the part. His physique was that of a man used to long treks on mountain trails and his face was permanently tanned but as he spoke, the regal, hawk-like features easily softened into an affectionate smile, traits no doubt essential for any man ministering to Ghurkas.

His message was about God's guidance for staying on the right path, according to the promise of Isaiah.

"'And thine ears shall hear a word behind thee, saying, This is the way, walk ye in it, when ye turn to the right hand, and when ye turn to the left.'

"My wife and I have proved this Text many times," Simpson assured his congregation. "So can you."

Recalling his trek through the Kachin Hills, Gray was inclined to agree.

Most of the worshippers lingered after the service, with several besieging the Simpsons. Gray was standing absently to one side when a heavyset man in a white tropical suit ambled over and introduced himself.

"Haven't seen you before, young man, but very pleased you could attend. Charles Dalrymple, Lieutenant Colonel, ex Royal Artillery. ICS these days."

"Jonathan Gray, sir. Very glad to meet you."

They shook hands.

"Delighted to meet you, Jonathan," said Dalrymple. "Would you like to join us for lunch, if you don't mind a trip out of town?"

"That's very kind of you, sir. Thank you very much."

As an officer and gentleman, Gray could hardly do otherwise, especially when "us" included two stunning blondes in QA uniform, who joined them in company with Mrs Dalrymple, a grey-haired, matronly lady radiating calm dignity and poise.

"Good crowd today," said Dalrymple. "William Carey[88] had a lot of influence here, of course. Some of us Baptists have carried on."

The blondes introduced themselves as Robyn and Trish, presenting Gray with a serious dilemma, namely whether or not he could be partial to either of them and if so, which one.

He needed the wisdom of Solomon. Providentially, One wiser than Solomon was at hand.

"Twenty-eight Bentley, sir?" Gray asked as the group took their seats in Dalrymple's vehicle, the ladies in the back, Jonathan sandwiched in the front between the colonel and his Indian driver.

"Indeed yes, wonderful tourer," said Dalrymple. "All right there, girls?" he called over his shoulder, adding, "Away you go then, Dhanesh," to his driver upon receiving confirmation from the others that all was well.

From the city's environs, the journey took them across dun-coloured flatlands with scattered clumps of thicket and occasional trees, past clusters of huts constructed of hardened mud bricks, roofed with layers of saplings and grouped near primitive village wells. Children and livestock scattered noisily at the vehicle's approach. Though the day was humid, the movement of the vehicle helped to dispel the odours of both town and country.

"Roads are pretty damp at the moment," Dalrymple remarked. "Just enough rain here to settle the dust for a while."

They negotiated a couple of sluggish brown streams at intervals, by means of ancient punts operated with rope and pulleys harnessed to bullocks. These crossings added about half an hour to the journey.

"Have to get you back before sunset," Dalrymple informed his guests. "Punt drivers knock off then. Be capital if you could stay over but we've got a bunch of high-level visitors descending on us. Semi-official business, you know."

"Mostly Charles's old pals from the regiment," Edith Dalrymple interposed. "He's going up country with them for some game shooting."

Dalrymple winked at Gray.

"Missus always puts me right," he said.

The Bentley drew up in front of a two-storied bungalow with thatched roof and spacious upstairs verandah. Rows of low, green shrubs spaced at regular intervals grew in front of the house at right angles to its whitewashed façade. A wisp of smoke curled up from the back of the house, where Gray guessed that the kitchen was situated[89].

Dalrymple gestured at the shrubs.

"Grow tea here ourselves," he said. "Nothing like our plantation up north but we get a fair crop."

"I'll see to the kitchen, dear," said Edith. "You can show our friends where to wash."

The colonel conducted Gray and the girls around the side of the house to some outhouses, each partitioned into bathroom and WC of pan-style design. Tin basins of steaming water, heated by the servants on fuel stoves, stood on benches in the bathroom annexes with fresh towels beside them.

"I'll go organise drinks," said Dalrymple. "Come up to the verandah when you're ready." He indicated the outdoor staircase up the side of house.

Gray glanced at the flight of steps. That would be useful exercise for his leg too.

A little later, the four of them were seated comfortably on cane chairs, sipping homemade lemonade. Edith came up the stairs and sat with them.

"All's well in the kitchen, so I thought I'd join you," she said.

"Bet you've not seen an oven like ours," interjected Charles. "Four-foot high brick wall with holes in for the air. Get a wood fire going in the bottom, cook everything above that, in pots and pans on grids. Smoke goes straight up into a suspended hood and out the flue. Marvellous invention. You must see it before you go."

"It's like a big barbecue, really," Edith explained. "But Charles is very proud of it because he set it all up. It's his new baby, now that ours have all flown the nest. He'd cook on it himself except it would give the servants a fit. We all have our places, you see, even us."

Charles nodded with a wistful sigh and Edith replenished the drinks from a pitcher on the table.

Nearby, a small boy kept a loosely woven grass mat soaked with water. The breeze blowing through it produced a pleasant cooling effect, with the smell of mown hay. Green gecko lizards scuttled up and the down the verandah posts and along the railings.

"Splendid little chaps," said Dalrymple. "Keep the insects down. So, what has the air force got you doing, Jonathan?" he asked, turning to Gray.

"Hurricanes, sir," said Gray. "Close support. We don't mix it with the Jap fighters unless we have to, rely on Spitfires for top cover. Our fighter blokes reckon that us Hurri-bomber lads get giddy if we fly above tree-top height."

Gray was delighted by the obliging female laughter.

"How long have you been out here, Jon?" Edith asked.

"Since last November, ma'am. We were down in Arakan earlier this year and then moved to Assam."

"Hmm, and before that?" asked Dalrymple.

"Tank busting with the Desert Air Force, sir. Then Sicily and Salerno, close support again."

"Splendid," said Charles approvingly. "I believe our Beaufighters have been pretty successful out here, too?" he asked, leaning forward with evident keenness.

"Very much so, sir. I've trained on them. They're brutes to fly with those big engines but they've got a long range and big bomb load. Got a very quiet approach, too. Japs call 'em 'The Whispering Death.'"

"We see quite a bit of your chaps, of course," said the older man. He set his glass down on a straw place mat. "And the army IOs, as do the Simpsons, because we know Assam so well. Still got a market garden there along with the plantation, and a duck farm. Army's keen to build those up. They'll help supplement the troops' diet, especially the native chaps. Don't want another shindig like the mutiny. My granddad was in the thick of it, you know."

Gray noticed Mrs Dalrymple wink at Trish and Robyn, a gesture that plainly said, "He's getting into his stride now. One of you had better head him off."

Robyn got in first.

"How do you manage all that up country, Charles?" she asked, crossing her legs and placing her cap on her knee. Gray reckoned that Robyn had gorgeous legs, as did Trish but his brow furrowed at the mention of the colonel's Christian name. He would never have dared use it himself. Robyn and Trish had a natural advantage, of course.

"Estates manager. Solid chap, salt of the earth, ex gunner like me," their host explained. "Known each other since Gallipoli. We met Bill Slim[90] there, as it happens, although he was with a battalion and we were in divisional artillery – "

The gong sounded for the meal, interrupting the soliloquy. They set aside their glasses for the servants to collect when they went down to the dining room.

"Perhaps you'd be so kind as to escort my dear wife to the table, Jonathan," Dalrymple proposed as he got to his feet. "While I accompany these charming young ladies? Well, they'll *all* charming young ladies, but you know what I mean."

They took their places in a large, well-ventilated room with two window spaces, around an oval table covered with a white embroidered cloth. The servant boy resumed his task of soaking a grass mat hung from an adjacent doorway. Fragrant moist air wafted around the diners.

Dalrymple sat at the head of the table, with Trish and Robyn to either side of him, then Mrs Dalrymple and Gray. A nice arrangement, the young airman decided. He observed that the utensils and napkins were set out with military precision and hoped that he would remember enough RAF etiquette from formal mess nights to get by.

The Indian servants distributed the first course, steaming bowls of vegetable soup with a distinct savoury aroma. "Grow these veg locally," Dalrymple said. He and his four companions bowed their heads while the colonel said grace, simply but sincerely. Wholesome food could not be taken for granted in India.

A scuffling sound made them look up. Pointed indentations in the ceiling cloth sped diagonally across it.

"Tally the Mongoose," said Dalrymple, unfolding his napkin. "Lives up in the rafters a lot of the time. She's pretty good at catching snakes. We made sure there weren't any in your bathrooms, by the way. They've been known to crawl up via the drainpipes – that's why we have wire covers over 'em."

Successive servings of fish and chicken followed, then the main course, roast antelope with vegetables in season, followed by a light milk pudding with fresh pineapple.

After the meal, they adjourned to the verandah for coffee. Another boy servant took over the job of soaking the grass mat.

"So, tell us more about your trek through the Kachin Hills, Jon," said Dalrymple.

They had broached the subject during lunch and the others were keen to elicit more details. It had transpired that Gray's Kachin succourers were part of what Dalrymple called "the gang." "Marvellous you met up with Nigel and Dorothy. Real answer to prayer, eh?" he had said, adding an apposite citation from Job:

"'But He knoweth the way that I take: when He hath tried me, I shall come forth as gold.'"

Gray related the events as objectively as possible, heartened by the murmurs of sympathy from the ladies, especially when he mentioned having to sew up his leg.

"Splendid testimony, Jonathan," Dalrymple said warmly when Gray concluded his narrative. The colonel turned to the girls.

"I know you've told Edith all about yourselves," he said. "But I'm still none the wiser. However, let me guess. You're from Norfolk, young lady, like the RAF gentleman next to you[91]," he said to Robyn.

"Charles has a keen ear for accents," said Edith. "Picked Jonathan's right away."

Gray smiled courteously. He guessed Robyn came from his home county but Dalrymple's perceptiveness was remarkable.

"Got used to them in the regiment," Dalrymple explained. "My lads came from all over the place. So, am I right, Miss Fairlea?"

"Yes," said Robyn, laughing. "My mum and dad own a farm on the way to Thetford."

Robyn spoke briefly about her training, enlistment and service with Gwen and Trish during the Imphal battles. Dalrymple nodded with satisfaction and fastened his gaze on Trish.

"I'd put *you* nearer Oxford, my girl," he said. "But I'd wager you're no stranger to India, from what you've said already."

Gray still couldn't decide which of the young ladies to be partial to, though data was accumulating. Over lunch it had emerged that the girls were about a year or so younger than him, which was nice and he was pleasantly surprised when Robyn hadn't mentioned any deep involvements.

He listened intently to Trish's response.

"I'm from Banbury originally," she said, smiling. "But we lived in India from when I was three until I was nearly ten. My dad was a missionary. He had a station near Ranchi but we went home when my mum fell ill. The fever affected my dad, too but he never said anything. Ellie and I were spared, thank God. She was about two years old, then."

"Your sister would be going on fifteen?" Dalrymple asked.

Trish nodded.

"Bit of a handful for Dad," she said.

"I think all you girls are at that age. Ours were," said Charles facetiously. "They're in the forces, now, like you splendid folks. How are your parents these days?"

"I'm afraid Mum died the year I started training," Trish explained. "Dad's still unwell but he still doesn't let on. The work continued, though. A curate took it over, chap named Evan Dane, one of my dad's former students. When the war started, he went home and joined the navy. He's an RN Chaplain now. Lovely man, about twelve years older than me but – we get on very well."

Gray continued to pay close attention.

"Lucky fellow," said Dalrymple.

"Charles," said his wife with a look of embarrassment.

Trish smiled graciously.

"We've had – an understanding, for a few years," she said.

Gray's mind was made up, for now, anyway.

"Nice lad, very athletic – and handsome," said Trish after she and Robyn had parted from Gray at the university. He was staying in a different hall but they had agreed to meet for supper.

Wrapped in towelled dressing gowns, the two girls were waiting in Robyn's room, while their baths were being run. Robyn was seated cross-legged on the bed, writing to her parents, Trish reclining in a chair by the open window – barred to exclude thieves.

"Must be tough as old boots, sewing up his leg like he did," said Robyn, wincing.

"Amazing he only lives down the road from you, back home."

"I could tell that as soon as he opened his mouth."

"Certainly took a shine to you."

"Only after you explained about Evan. Poor lad, strung him along a treat, didn't we?"

"Thanks to dear old Charles. Could hardly get a word in edgeways until he started quizzing us."

"He *is* a dear, isn't he, and Edith? Wish we could have stayed. Would love to make friends with Tally the mongoose. She sounds like Miss Tiggywinkle, only bigger."

"They can be very affectionate. We used to have one at Ranchi. But speaking of friends, are we going to take up Charles' suggestion and tour the Sunderbans with our gallant F/O Gray?"

A discrete knock on the door and the servant's muffled voice told them that the baths were ready. Robyn put aside the letter, swung her legs over the edge of the bed and slid her feet into her slippers.

"I'm game if you are," she said.

"So what *do* you think of our Jonny?" Trish asked, standing up and stretching.

"Well, let's see what happens in tiger country," said Robyn with a shy smile.

Gray and the girls arranged for their passages the following day through some of Dalrymple's contacts, after which they took a sightseeing tour of the city, partly on foot, partly by tonga, partly by motorised taxi.

"Haven't seen much apart from the zoo and the gardens," Gray remarked.

"Might as well while we're here," said Trish. "But keep your sidearm handy, please, Jonathan."

Gray wore a Webley revolver in a webbing holster attached to his belt, as a precaution.

The contrasts they encountered were astounding, from the dignified government buildings and imposing Victoria Memorial, set in its spacious lawns and resembling St Paul's, to the teeming masses of beggars amid the squalor and vermin of the city's vast railway platforms and along the sidewalks of Chowringee Road, the conurbation's main artery. Here, in yet more bizarre contrast, the American forces had installed a vehicle repair track[92].

Elsewhere, mothers in bare feet helped dig out stinking open drains, while their children scuttled in the dirt and male supervisors stood watching, hands in pockets.

But the most memorable sights were the ghats, Calcutta's open-air crematoriums numbering at least half a dozen, some situated on the banks of the Hooghly River, a tributary of the Ganges that flowed through the city. With family members watching, corpses were incinerated every few minutes atop stone cairns so that the funeral pyres blazed non-stop, day and night. Corpses about to be cremated lay beneath sheets of rusted corrugated iron. The stench given off in the humid heat was overpowering.

"Good thing we're not stopping," Trish murmured as their taxi chugged past in a cloud of dust. "Be very hard to get that smell out of your clothes."

"I've only seen them from a distance until now," said Gray. "Think this is as close I want to get."

"Don't fancy having to ward off those urchins, either," said Robyn, with distaste. "Make it seem like some sort of exhibition."

They watched grimy youngsters with human skulls and oddments of bone looped about their necks or waists, gesticulating to curious US servicemen, offering to show them where to take photographs, for a small fee.

"Says something about a nation, the way it treats its dead," said Gray soberly. "Spiritually, I mean."

"Plenty there to pick up from where Carey left off," Trish added, sighing.

"Welcome aboard, ladies and gentlemen, sahibs and memsahibs. I am Purser Chaudhary at your service. I promise to do my utmost to make your voyage with us a most pleasant and interesting one."

The effusive Indian gentleman greeted his passengers with a broad smile as they stepped off the gangplank onto the deck of the coastal steamer that would be home to them for the next three days. Gray immediately took in the gleaming brass, freshly dried white paint, scrubbed decking, polished railings and complete absence of rust.

"Could stand C-in-C SEAC's inspection, this, or even your matron's, I reckon," he said to Trish and Robyn.

Jon set their web bags on the deck and slipped his off his shoulder.

"Thank you, my man," said Trish.

"Ditto, kind sir," echoed Robyn.

Gray touched his cap. The girls had seen him exercising on the university's oval, so when he had offered to carry their bags, they'd cheerfully let him.

Purser Chaudhary rubbed his hands and went on with his welcome. In spotless white suit and turban, scarlet cravat and expertly polished Black and Whites, he looked as spick and span as his ship.

"I'll show you your cabins and the rest rooms," he said obligingly. "Then please come to the stateroom for drinks. It's just through there to your left. We set sail in an hour."

His passengers voiced their thanks. Thirteen in all, they were mainly senior officers or civil servants and their memsahibs, who gazed benevolently at the three youngest members of the party.

They had accomplished the first stage of the Sunderbans' journey by train, a thirty-mile trip across grey-clay flatlands to a tiny river port named Fort Canning. From there, the steamer would negotiate the narrow channel into the Bay of Bengal.

For now, after the closeness of the railway carriages, in spite of the early morning start, drinks in the stateroom were well received.

"Trust an air force chap to fetch up with *two* QA lovelies," said a beefy colonel with white handlebar moustache. He'd paused on his way to the bar to ogle Trish and Robyn. "Couldn't possibly spare one to cheer up a couple of old sweats, could you, young fellow?"

He glanced at his cronies, who were sitting at a table sipping sherry and smoking cheroots. They had clearly egged him on.

Gray smiled thinly. He leant back against the polished mahogany panelling of the booth where he and the girls were seated.

"They're actually my sisters, sir," he said casually. "Father was most insistent I accompany them. I answer to him if anything untoward happens."

With a confused grunt, the interloper ambled off.

"Thanks, Jonathan," said Trish. She raised her glass and placed her hand on Gray's arm. "I think you've saved us some trouble."

"Amen, Jonny," said Robyn, touching his other arm.

The colonel's lady was in earnest conversation with Purser Chaudhary about cabin amenities during the incident and did not observe anything.

Gray and his two companions leant on the steamer's railing and watched the flaring orange-red sunset over the vastness of the bay.

As Kipling's poem[93] implied, they had even seen some flying fish.

To the north, the dark streak on the horizon indicated the shoreline of the Sunderbans, where they would make landfall the next day to begin the tour proper, extending as far as the main estuary of the Ganges, about two hundred miles to the east.

The ship's captain wisely remained close enough to the coast to run for port if a squall blew up but far enough offshore for his passengers to enjoy the comfort of sea breezes as they slept - and sleep came easily after they had sampled the vessel's excellent cuisine.

Purser Chaudhary was a man of his word.

The steamer dropped anchor about a quarter of a mile from a fringe of evergreen mangrove forests and the visitors transferred to a motor launch. As it nosed in towards a small jetty of palm and bamboo poles adroitly lashed together, it passed several fishermen's skiffs, gliding silently by like floating black scimitars.

"The fishermen have to keep an eye out," said the Indian guide who accompanied the launch. Also named Chaudhary, he was a cousin of the purser. "The tigers may swim out this far to attack them. Many are man-eaters because humans are such easy prey."

On shore, they followed a trail fenced in by high bamboo poles each several inches thick to a well-concealed viewing site, roofed over with palm branches. The fence notwithstanding, a couple of Indian police, armed with Lee-Enfields, accompanied the tourists. They were older men, in their fifties. Gray reasoned that their younger companions were most likely in the forces.

"We must be patient," the guide explained in a low voice. "But we should see something."

Gray gazed at the dense green mantle surrounding them, conscious of the heat and the ceaseless singing of insects. Red-blue kingfishers darted low across the waters gradually creeping up the tidal mudflats bordering the mangroves.

"Some of the islands float when the tide comes in, though not this one," the guide assured them.

Small, grey, newt-shaped creatures with bug-eyes crawled out of mud burrows to climb the stilted mangrove roots on flipper-like fins.

"Mudskipper fish," said the guide.

A majestic bird of prey swooped silently across their line of vision, drawing astonished gasps from the onlookers.

"White-bellied sea eagle," the guide explained.

"Shil[94]," said Robyn.

"He's a kite," said Gray.

"Don't spoil it," Trish protested, digging Jon in the ribs. "We're romanticising."

At successive hides, the visitors' patience was rewarded by the sight of spotted deer, wild boar and a huge python that slipped into the murky watercourse with scarcely a ripple.

"Kaa[94]," said Robyn, as the giant reptile slid beneath the surface.

"He's a rock python," whispered Gray.

"Jonathan," said Trish menacingly.

"Kaa *can* go in the water, if he wants to," Robyn added with spirit.

The trek around the forest took most of the morning and was tiring in the oppressive heat, despite lengthy rests. At noon, Chaudhary took his party to a small, chalet-type building, constructed of bamboo with woven matting on the floors and walls. The chalet overlooked one of the native villages situated in a forest clearing, where smoke arose from several wood fires.

The visitors were served drinks and a light lunch.

"Rest rooms are adjoining," the guide said helpfully. Gray discovered that they were similar to those at the Dalrymple's and well-maintained.

"After lunch, we will go by motorboat for the rest of the tour," the guide announced while they ate. "It is the best way to see the forests."

"Good show," grunted the colonel who had spoken to Gray the previous evening. He was enjoying a whisky.

"Be quiet, Benji," his wife admonished him, tapping him on the wrist. "The man's not finished yet." Gray winked at his companions. With their memsahibs present in addition to Gray, the senior officers' behaviour towards Trish and Robyn was impeccable, though the older men were feeling uncomfortable with the heat.

"It is possible we may see a Royal Bengal tiger," the guide continued. "Of one thing you can be sure, as they say in these parts, 'The tiger is always watching you.'"

Trish raised her eyebrows, as she delicately dabbed her mouth with a snowy white napkin.

"Shere Khan[94]," she said. "And don't you say a word, Jonathan."

The Indian pilot navigated the launch slowly through a multiplicity of water byways, where the tourists glimpsed more wildlife, including Ganges crocodiles that slithered splashing into the streams at the boat's approach – no python-like subtlety with them.

At various locations, parties of woodcutters and honey-collectors could be seen picking their way through the gloomy undergrowth, most of the men wearing thin boards on their backs or heads, displaying paintings of grotesque masks.

"The tiger always attacks from behind," said the guide. "These masks are supposed to frighten him off."

"Do they?" Gray asked. The guide shrugged.

"It is better not put to the test, Gray Sahib," he said gravely.

"He's like the devil," Robyn said with a shudder. "Looking for someone to devour."

The tiger – undisputed king of the Sunderbans, mostly unseen but always watching. Robyn's analogy was a good one.

During the still heat of late afternoon, the pilot began to steer back towards the jetty. They had to return well before sunset, not only for safety's sake but also to avoid the mosquitoes that were most active then.

As the boat rounded a spit of land, Gray began to tense. Many operational sorties had imbued in him an acute sensitivity to potential danger.

"'The tiger is watching,' Chaudhary Sahib," he said quietly, indicating with his arm the mangrove fringe at the tip of the land spit.

"Ah!" exclaimed the guide.

A collective intake of breath sounded from the tourists. From less than twenty yards distance, they could see the massively shouldered beast, with its rippling, black-striped orange flanks, tufted black-edged ears, protruding white whiskers and glaring yellowish-green eyes. It was beautifully camouflaged in the jungle shadows.

Baring its terrible fangs with a blood-chilling hiss, the tiger padded softly away into the mangroves, a living embodiment of immense, silent power, flicking its thick, j-shaped tail in a gesture of contempt before blending invisibly into its surroundings.

"'Tiger, tiger, burning bright, in the forests of the night, What immortal hand or eye, Could frame thy fearful symmetry?'" whispered Trish in awe. Both she and Robyn had each taken hold of one of Gray's arms.

The young airman would soon discover that even more sinister creatures were watching them, beings that did not feature on any tour.

A refreshing rain swept across the bay that night but its waters remained calm. Early the next day, the steamer entered the broad, shimmering brown mouth of the Ganges, passing between large islands of more mud and mangroves. Another bright but sultry day promised.

Greyish-brown torpedo shapes with bulbous heads and elongated snouts like proboscises repeatedly broke the surface of the water and plunged back into the depths, displaying pink underbellies.

"*Susu*, fresh water river dolphins," Purser Chaudhary said to his visitors watching from the railings. "They are blind and swim by feel of the riverbed with one flipper."

"Blind and grubbing in the dirt," said Gray to Trish and Robyn. "Remind you of anyone?"

The steamer eased further upstream, past docking facilities where modern merchantmen were moored alongside much older vessels with canvas furled. Two square-rigged river packet boats laden with jute headed downstream, brownish sails taut and full with a following wind. Dockworkers were packing fawn-coloured bales of raw jute into the hold of another boat tied up at a small wharf behind which stood the mill and its adjoining village of typical native *bashas*. Nearby sprawled an extensive bazaar, replete with brightly hued stalls, clamouring voices and typical smells.

"No-one packs jute like my countrymen," Purser Chaudhary proclaimed with a paternal smile.

It was easy to see what he meant. A line of dockers had formed a bridge of bales along the length of the hold. In time to a low chant, they were rhythmically jumping up and down on the bales, forcing them simultaneously deeper into the hold.

"You wouldn't get a cigarette paper between those bales when they're finished," exclaimed Colonel Benji, puffing on his cheroot. He and his smoker cronies were leaning on the railings downwind of the other tourists, at the insistence of their wives.

"And those mills are all owned by whisky-swilling Scotsmen, drinking themselves into an early grave," Mrs Benji said loudly with disapproval. She was small, plump, forthright and never seen in the open without her bright green parasol.

"You girls ought to get one each," she'd said to Trish and Robyn. "With the work you do, you can't help getting suntanned but it's no good in the long run for a couple of English roses like you. Sun here'll turn your skin into parchment. And the sooner you can stop taking those pills the better. They make you look jaundiced. Same goes for you, young man," she added for Gray's benefit.

"And here's me thinking mepacrine yellow was all the rage in the West End," Robyn whispered to Trish afterwards.

"Ladies and gentlemen, we will dock at the wharf here," the purser announced. "You can visit the bazaar for a couple of hours and then we will take the elephant ride out into the country. Quite a lot of interest to see there and we will be back to the ship for lunch. I suggest make yourselves comfortable now."

"Or it's a convenient bush when you get off the elephant and watch out for red ants," Gray warned the girls, who scowled at him.

The stalls offered a seemingly limitless array of fabrics, pottery and weavings together with metal, ivory, linen and leather goods, all of which one was supposed to bargain for in the traditional fashion.

Trish was good at haggling, so that she and Robyn obtained some beautifully hand-woven scarves and blouses at knockdown prices.

"I used to go to the local markets with Mum and Dad," she explained.

Out of respect for Mrs Benji's genuine concern, they also bought a couple of parasols.

"We'll hold them over you during the ride, Jon," said Robyn. "I don't think a chap in RAF khaki should be seen twirling one of these."

The girls also obtained items of high-quality lingerie and even pairs of nylons, no doubt originally acquired from the Americans.

"Whatever you're thinking, Jonathan," Robyn said stiffly as she hid the garments in her web bag away from Gray's admiring gaze, "it's unbecoming for an officer and a gentleman."

"Yes, milady," he muttered.

"Let's get measured for some high heels, Robbie," Trish suggested when they came to a cobbler's stall. "They can make them up in a couple of hours and we can collect them on the way back."

"Excellent idea," said Gray.

Robyn winked at Trish.

Gray especially enjoyed the elephant ride. They sat comfortably on the leather carriage strapped to the animal's back, with a boy seated behind it waving a large fan to keep the flies off. The beast lumbered along a dirt track, squelchy from recent rains, at a surprisingly good pace, meekly obedient to the terse commands of the *mahout* astride its massive neck. Gray was developing a distinct affection for the patient creature.

"He's doing OK, is Jumbo," said Gray. "And these parasols of yours make me feel like one of the Raj, with a couple of mem servants."

"Don't push it, Jonathan," Trish admonished him. "Or we'll make you change places with Mrs Benji."

"And his name's Haithi[94], not Jumbo," Robyn insisted. She reached over the side of the carriage to pat the tough hide beneath its gold and scarlet saddlecloth.

The surrounding countryside consisted of green flatlands blending into acres of rice-paddies in the direction of the Ganges. Low hills arose in the direction of travel, covered with numerous palm trees and thicket of darker green.

"Comilla's over that way," said Trish. She pointed towards the hills.

"We were at the hospital there when we first arrived," Robyn explained to Jonathan.

As they went on, the travellers sighted the various species of deer that abounded in the area. These invariably leapt for the hillside scrub at sight of the elephant train.

"Aren't they lovely!" exclaimed Robyn.

"Bet Shere Khan'd like to sink his teeth into their haunches," Gray said teasingly.

"I'll hit you with this, Jonathan," warned Trish, eyeing her parasol.

The track meandered toward a wooded slope, where a crumbling stone building abutted its base, carved stone *chinthes* adorning each side of the flight of steps to its entrance. Instantly, Gray had a feeling of unease.

The elephants halted and knelt down for their passengers to alight.

"This is one the most ancient temples dedicated to Kali," Chaudhary explained. "We have permission to enter and explore. I am sure you will find it fascinating."

"We'll wait outside," Gray said quietly but firmly. Trish and Robyn nodded and drew up beside him, folding their parasols.

The rest of the party looked at them quizzically but before anyone could reply, a tremendous shrieking burst out from the canopy of trees that cast their shadow over the brooding structure. The tourists were pelted with a hail of bark and twigs. Gray glimpsed spindly brown forms leaping through the branches[95]. The stone *chinthes* suddenly seemed *alive* and it was as if a silent scream surged out of the temple entrance, rolling up against the visitors like an invisible wave of sheer malevolence[96]. To the rear, the *mahouts* and their boys had their hands full to prevent the elephants from stampeding.

"I must apologise, ladies and gentlemen," said Chaudhary breathlessly when the party had withdrawn a safe distance down the trail and the handlers had pacified their mounts. "Sometimes, the monkeys get agitated when visitors arrive. I think it best if we take a detour that will nevertheless provide some more interesting scenery."

"So long as it doesn't throw anything," said Mrs Benji. She and a couple of the other ladies had looked quite flushed, prompting Trish and Robyn unobtrusively to distribute some mild sedative tablets.

"My dad said that missionaries always avoided temple areas, in case they got attacked by monkeys or whatever else was about," said Trish when they'd resumed their seats atop the elephant.

"Devil's domains?" asked Robyn. Trish nodded.

Gray desisted from making any jokes about the *Bandar-Log*[94].

The ship replenished essential supplies from a government terminal and headed down-river about mid afternoon with the ebbing tide.

Daylight was fading by the time the steamer emerged from the estuary and manifold jungle sounds emanated from the forests and swamps around the mouth of the river, easily drowning out the throb of the ship's engines.

Gray's abiding memory was that of high-pitched shrieks, coughing grunts and shrill screeches issuing across a limpid watery expanse from black jungle fringes silhouetted in stark relief against a blazing orange sunset.

At the time, he wished he could have put his arm around Robyn, who was standing beside him at the rail with Trish but decided that would have to wait.

"Either of you feel like a turn around the deck?" said Gray, rising to his feet. They had been relaxing in the stateroom after supper, with the comfortable surroundings to themselves, their older companions having already retired following a long and unexpectedly exciting day.

"Think I'll have a wash and turn in," said Robyn, with a yawn.

Trish agreed. "You've started me off, now, Robbie," she said, yawning herself.

"Good night and sleep well, then, ladies," said Gray as he adjusted his cap. "Your shoes really are superb, by the way."

"You said that," Trish responded haughtily, angling her left foot up and down. The elegant high heels of burnished leather were of excellent fitting and quality, though costing only a few rupees. They were totally impractical for QAs and completely non regulation wear but none of the passengers minded when Trish and Robyn had worn them, together with nylons, at supper, not even the memsahibs.

"Well, why shouldn't you lasses be allowed a bit of glamour?" Mrs Benji had declared in her inimitable style. "Don't you think so, Benji?"

Colonel Benji had thought so all along.

The girls bade Gray goodnight and he stepped out onto the deck.

Jon headed for the stern, then paused when he heard Chaudhary's voice, sounding agitated. The purser was clearly in conversation with someone else but Gray couldn't hear the other individual. Cautiously, he continued on until he came to the shadow of an aft companionway. From its concealment, he could plainly see the pair of speakers in the pale gleam of a nearly full moon, standing abaft of the quarterdeck.

Gray had to clench his teeth to avoid gasping in horror.

Confronting Chaudhary was a creature that, although a biped, was unlike any being the airman had ever seen.

It stood over seven feet tall and had a black, glistening hide with an extended dorsal fin down its back. The creature's head seemed to be part fish, part reptile[97] and its arms were as long as a gorilla's, ending in broad, webbed hands with curved talons.

But what struck Gray particularly were its eyes.

They blazed like red-hot coals.

After a couple more minutes of apparent dialogue, the creature sounded a guttural hiss and abruptly heaved itself over the side, hitting the water with a distinct splash. Gray observed wide, flipper-like feet as it disappeared. He heard the purser heave a mighty sigh.

"Chaudhary," he said and stepped from concealment. The other man turned toward him abruptly.

"You saw?" the purser asked hoarsely. Gray nodded.

"Come on," he said. "You need a drink."

They returned to the stateroom, now deserted, where Gray fixed Chaudhary a double brandy. He drank in sips with shaking hands.

"What on earth was that?" Gray asked. He was seated opposite the Indian and trying not to sound frightened himself.

"You must understand, my friend," said Chaudhary earnestly, his voice shaking like his hands. "Kali is no figment of the imagination[98]. She has servants everywhere and we all live in fear of her. Something has alarmed her master. You call him," Chaudhary lowered his voice, "the Devil and Satan. He has commanded her to find out more. That is why," the Indian paused, shuddering, "her servant spoke to me just now."

"What is this - alarm? Was it this afternoon?"

Chaudhary shook his head.

"No, though that alerted Kali, too. That is why her – servant – was asking about – *you* and the young ladies. But her master is alarmed about something else, something that you and your friends are – or will be – part of, because of your beliefs."

Gray was finding the explanation hard to comprehend but he was anxious for Trish and Robyn.

"What did this – thing – ask about us?" he said, swallowing hard.

"If you were the Enemy's Watchmen[99]. I said you were among his Enemy's followers but that I knew no more. Eventually I persuaded him and as you saw, he left."

"Will he come back?"

"Not on this voyage. What is more, I believe you and the ladies are protected, for now. Kali's master does not have permission to harm you, not directly."

Gray nodded. He sensed that otherwise neither he nor the girls would still be breathing.

"How did it get aboard, that thing?" he asked.

Chaudhary drained his glass and set it down. He continued to speak in a strained whisper.

"It was here all along, Gray Sahib. Rest assured, no-one will report the missing crew member. He has from Kali this terrible power to – change[100]. It will eventually kill him because your Master's power is far greater than Kali's but in my country, she is like the tiger in the mangroves, always watching."

Gray still felt bewildered but of one thing he was sure. He looked Chaudhary in the eye and spoke firmly.

"You need to make peace with my Lord and Saviour, Chaudhary Sahib. Your own life could be in danger."

Gray's dire warning tragically proved to be true. Purser Chaudhary mysteriously disappeared during a later voyage, though not before he had left written testimony that he lodged with the Dalrymples, affirming his newfound faith.

His bold stance resulted in martyrdom.

In the wider context, Gray could not then know about the impromptu prayer meeting that Sister Hewitt had convened in Italy or its reverberations beyond the material realm.

Or how, like Purser Chaudhary, some of its participants would seal their own testimonies in death.

Dai and Gwen arrived back from honeymoon the day after Gray, Robyn and Trish returned from the Sunderbans.

They met up with the newlyweds at the Grand Hotel, where the couple would stay overnight, convening by the poolside for pre-lunch drinks.

All five were due to fly back to their units the following day.

In the meantime, the girls were gleeful at being together again and Trish and Robyn were agog over the pictures of Kanchenjunga. Prompted by the muggy atmosphere, they decided to go for a swim before lunch.

"Water's supposed to be chlorinated but use your earplugs just in case," Gwen advised.

The Grand had largely been converted into an officers' transit camp but Dai and Gwen's room was in the more secluded married quarters part that retained its pre-war elegance and amenities, including the pool.

Seated opposite Dai at a poolside table, Gray watched the lithe female forms gracefully gliding back and forth through the water.

"Like guardian angels you chaps were," Dai said appreciatively, with reference to the recent campaign. "Came in so low over those bunkers, it's a wonder you didn't have a Nip or two hanging onto your tails when you landed."

Gray glanced at him and grinned. Dai was easy to talk to – when he took time to draw breath.

"Hard to winkle 'em out," said the airman reflectively. "Only the five hundred-pounders or the rockets could crack open their best dugouts. Had to get down low to be on target – and do our best to miss you lads."

"We very much appreciated that bit."

A servant brought the drinks. Dai called to the girls and they nimbly climbed out of the pool to go and get changed.

"We'll only be a couple of minutes," said Gwen, picking up her towel and gown. "Mind you behave yourselves."

"You can count on me, dear," Dai retorted. "I'm a respectable married man now. Not sure about this fellow, though."

He winked at Gray, who was gazing at Robyn and reckoning that, like her companions, she carried not an ounce of spare flesh.

"Can't take your eyes off her, eh, boyo?" said Dai with a chuckle when the girls were out of earshot.

"No."

"Then marry her, mate, before some other bloke does. You Englishmen, you're so reserved you wouldn't even lead in silent prayer. I've been married nearly a week now and I'd recommend it to anyone."

"I should pray about it first," said Gray mildly. He fingered the condensation on the side of his glass.

"Oh, by all means, boyo. Gwen and me, we've known each other since we were sprogs, back in Llangollen. You can't rush into these things, you know."

While they were having drinks, Gray related the bizarre events of the previous evening. Dai shook his head slowly.

"I know it sounds daft," he said. "But could it have been a frogman[101], with a red light on his chest, so a boat could pick him up in the dark and you saw it reflecting off his goggles? We've got them and I've no doubt the Japs have."

"Could he have been standing on something, so he just looked tall?" Gwen asked.

"Frogmen don't dive overboard head first from a ship's upper deck, Dai," Gray said quietly. "What's more, he went like a kangaroo. And it was only the bare planking around him."

"And it doesn't explain Chaudhary's story," said Robyn uneasily.

"Well, if you say you saw something, Jonno, then as far as we're concerned, you saw it," Dai affirmed. He glanced at the girls, who murmured their assent. "Lord knows what it means but we better watch and pray, eh?"

The summons for lunch brought the discussion to a close and the group's impending business on the morrow ensured that the subject was not raised again.

But it would resurface, nevertheless.

Jon, Robyn and Trish spent the rest of the day with Dai and Gwen, taking leave of them after supper at the Grand.

"Think I'll go straight up," said Trish considerately when the taxi dropped them off at the entrance to the hall. "Still haven't finished that letter to Dad. See you tomorrow, Jon." She gave Gray a fierce hug and hastened into the foyer.

"Do you want to walk for a bit?" Gray said to Robyn.

"Fine," she said softly.

Gray thought she looked lovely in the moonlight. They strolled along the flagstone path leading from the halls' courtyard to a small fountain, where they paused. The water jets were making a bubbling sound and the night air seemed cooler.

Gray gently clasped Robyn's hand.

"Robyn, could I please – kiss you?" he asked, trembling.

"Yes, Jon, of course," she whispered.

Folding his arms around her, he drew her close, sensing the litheness of her slender frame, his lips feeling the warmth of hers.

Afterwards, they walked slowly back to the hall, Gray with his arm around Robyn's shoulders.

"I'll be praying for you night and day now, Jonny," she said with emotion. "You've made me go all schoolgirly."

Such were the local logistics that Dai, Gray and the three girls would fly back to Assam on three different aircraft. Gwen, Robyn and Trish were the first to leave and bade tearful farewells to their menfolk at Dum Dum Airport, in the early morning, during a downpour.

The girls piled into a jeep with its hood fastened to take them across the airfield to their waiting C-47. They wore jungle greens, trench macs, bush hats, boots and short puttees.

Helping the crew shove their kit through the doorway, they climbed aboard and sat on their holdalls, wedging themselves in between boxes of supplies lashed to the ribs of the airframe. Built for cargo rather than troop transport, this particular aircraft was not equipped with seats, unlike the one on which they'd flown earlier.

The crew chief, a warrant officer, handed the girls some piles of old newspapers.

"Just in case, ladies," he said apologetically. "Probably get some turbulence on the way up."

"But we had quite a smooth flight on the way down," said Gwen.

The airman shrugged. "Luck of the draw for this time of year, Sister," he responded casually and made off towards the flight deck.

Shuddering in sympathy with the vibrating fuselage, the girls clung to the ribbed supports as the C-47 gathered speed down the runway, occasionally veering from side to side. Rain splashed against the windows.

Trish glanced at her companions, aware they were praying as hard as she was that their aircraft would safely get airborne, reckoning that Dai and Jon would be doing likewise.

Together the Sisters heaved a mighty sigh when the transport rose into the sky.

But as the C-47 flew through the storm, it hit turbulence as the crew chief had predicted, plunging and dipping like a bucking bronco through a succession of air pockets.

In turn, the girls were violently airsick and the newspapers were fully utilised[102]. The smell of vomit persisted for some time.

"At least the boys weren't here to see this," croaked Gwen as she wiped her mouth. "Thank Heaven for small mercies."

Gradually, the air became colder and the girls dug into their holdalls for their bush jackets, donned them and then, wrapped in their macs, tried to doze for the rest of the journey, once the buffeting from the air pockets had subsided.

The crew chief took pity on his charges and gave them a blanket each. He then produced mugs of well-sugared black coffee from a thermos that the girls gratefully received and cautiously sipped.

A few hours later, the C-47 dipped towards an ochre-coloured expanse surrounded by jungle-covered hills. The girls folded and packed away their macs.

They were about to rejoin their unit on the plain of Imphal, scene of the great battles from which they had tended so many cruelly injured victims.

It was time to pray for a safe landing.

Shakily, the girls descended the small ladder from the aircraft, when the crew chief opened the door. He handed them their holdalls and they stood on the edge of the runway, blinking in the dazzling sunshine, immediately conscious of the oppressive heat.

Trish noticed that the strip was constructed of sheets of interconnected PSP, the all-purpose artificial surface. All around, she could see blasted, burnt-out remains, not only of vehicles but also, to her horror, several aircraft, reduced to fire-ravaged heaps of twisted metal.

"Let us know when you're travelling again, ladies," the crew chief called cheerfully.

Trish and the others smiled hesitantly but expressed their thanks for his concern during the flight.

"Phew, too hot for these," said Gwen, stashing her bush jacket in the web bag slung over her shoulder. Her companions followed suit and they rolled up their sleeves.

"Over here, ladies," called a male voice.

"Oh, there's Sergeant Nicholson," said Robyn. "Hello, Sergeant Nick!" she called back. They waved to the familiar figure standing beside a one and a half-ton truck and hastened to get aboard.

Nicholson conveyed them along a rutted track to their unit, where they were surprised to see stores and equipment hurriedly being loaded onto vehicles.

On reporting to the CO's tent, they discovered why, though their major's austere face creased into a welcoming smile.

"Congratulations, Sister Lewis," he said to Gwen and got up from behind the table serving as his desk to shake hands with her.

"Just as well you all got back when you did," he continued. "We're moving down the Tiddim road with one of the MFTUs, following the advance. The town's about a hundred and forty miles away through the Chin Hills, across the Manipur River. We'll set up shop as close to the front as we can. Lance-Corporal Wood's[103] your driver."

Trish glanced at her watch. It was 1000 hours. They were in for a long day.

The Tiddim Road.

The CCS convoy ploughed through viscid mud as the track thrust deeper into the hills.

Alternatively assailed by sudden rainsqualls and searing heat, Trish and her friends sat grasping the sides of Wood's canvas-topped jeep as it bounced over water-filled potholes. Stashed around them were their holdalls and web bags with the rest of their gear stowed aboard lorries. The jeep was cramped because the girls had not had time to transfer the kit from their holdalls into their trunks and then flatpack the canvas containers in the trunks as well, according to the usual procedure for a field move.

"Used to get the odd Jap shell from time to time," said Wood in between a couple of bounces. "But they've been pushed back out of range now."

Trish felt hot, damp, thirsty, jaded and in need of a loo and a wash but those would have to wait. She glanced at her arms, spotted with mud thrown up from the tyres and smeared, like her face, with oily, pungent-smelling insect repellent. It was effective but materially increased one's discomfort.

"Not much coming the other way," said Gwen. "Would have thought we'd have seen ambulances because we were still getting patients, right up until when we went on leave."

"They'll go up the Kabaw Valley, Sister," Wood explained. "About twenty miles east on the other side of the hills. More malaria there but the road's a lot better."

At 1300 hours, the unit stopped for lunch, consisting of spam, biscuits and chlorinated water that at least assuaged the thirst. It was also refreshingly cool, being carried in *chagals* affixed to the jeep's grill. The edibles weren't particularly palatable but, for Trish and her friends, they filled the void left by the airsickness.

The engineers had widened the road at this location and dug latrines, screening them with hessian. Female and male personnel used them in turn.

"Embus!" the CO shouted at about 1320 hours and the convoy drove on.

Numbered wooden posts marked the miles, the occasional one with a grinning Jap skull nailed to it. These were easily identifiable by their noticeably large eye sockets. Small white crosses along the way showed the graves of Fourteenth Army dead.

"Seventy-five, ladies," Woods exclaimed, with reference to the latest milepost. "We're in Burma now. Another five miles to camp - easily make it before sunset."

"Sooner the better, Woody," said Gwen, seated beside him. Even an expert driver like Wood could not prevent the vehicle from slewing sideways through the muck now and then during successive ascents, descents and sharp, near one-eighty degree bends.

Trish gazed to her left. From the edge of the road, a few feet away, the hillside fell steeply to a stream at the bottom of a ravine. She observed several rusting and burnt-out vehicles that had probably been torched after sliding over the edge and proving impossible to retrieve.

"I wouldn't look down, Sister," Wood called cheerily over the growl of the jeep's engine, glancing at Trish via the rear vision mirror. "Or up, either, come to think of it."

They rounded an interior bend to be confronted by an almost sheer wall of soggy earth, covered with hundreds of square feet of tarpaulin sheets that the REs had fastened as securely as possible to prevent subsidence.

Though successfully negotiating this part of the route, Geordie Wood bogged the jeep a little further on. It had already happened earlier – and to most of the other vehicles. Stalled lorries had needed a tow.

"Time to get out and push again, ladies," he announced. "Canna block the traffic."

Trish and the others stepped into ankle-deep mud and leant with all their strength against the rear of the vehicle. Taking stodgy paces forward, they listened with amusement to Wood's exclamations of encouragement as he pushed from the side of the vehicle, with one hand on the steering wheel.

"Nearly there, lassies!" he exclaimed. "Champion, man, all aboard now."

Cheers and whistles arose from troops round about. Stumbling through the patch where the jeep had foundered, Trish felt slimy water rising above her calves.

"Mind how you go, Sister," several male voices called.

Perspiration trickled down Trish's face and welled under her arms. She glanced at Robyn's mud-spattered countenance. They couldn't help grinning at each other.

"Bet Haithi wouldn't have got bogged," said Robyn.

Their camp was at the bottom of a slope where the gradient allowed for a slip road to be constructed, spreading out into a roughly circular vehicle park, hardened by a considerable amount of road base.

Here the gorge became more of a shallow valley but the stream still churned noisily through it, replenished by repeated spasms of monsoon rain, carrying with it copious amounts of assorted flotsam, including tree trunks, empty tins, broken boxes and, occasionally, animal carcasses. The air was dank with the threat of more rain during the night.

In the fading light of day, the girls noticed the battered bones of a decaying elephant skeleton on the far bank as they climbed out of the jeep with their kit. They grimaced at the stench of unburied corpses issuing from the same direction.

"Japs over there were probably caught by an air strike," said Wood.

The distinct figure of Major Trenholme, their CO, came striding through the gloom, puffing his pipe.

"So he can't smell the dead Japs," whispered Robyn. The three girls sniggered.

"Ah, we're all here, now," said Trenholme. "Well done, Corporal Wood. We've cleared a space in the back of a couple of the lorries for you to kip, ladies. They're just over there and Vera's broken out some rations - cold I'm afraid, but you'll have enough water for a brew and a bit of a wash. And those are your facilities."

He indicated a familiar type of hessian enclosure, dimly visible beyond the lorries.

"ORs' quarters are on the other side of the park, Corporal," he said to Wood. "Sergeant Nicholson's got everything organised. We leave at zero nine hundred tomorrow."

"How long to go, sir?" asked Wood.

"About three days, Corporal," said Trenholme, stoking his pipe. "Can't get into Tiddim[104] itself yet so we'll fetch up just short. Only about another sixty miles or so but the going's a bit tougher from here on and we've got to cross the Manipur. That reminds me, drivers' O Group at nineteen hundred hours, so I'll see you there, Woody."

"Get a good rest afterwards, Woody," said Gwen when the CO had gone. "We're relying on you."

"Soon as my head hits the pillow, Sister," their driver said firmly. "Or whatever I'm usin' for one."

Vera Jeffries, the senior Sister, was a sturdy and thoroughly practical woman. She and the other Sisters had made ready the rations and compo brew.

"You can change into dry clothes in the truck there," said Sister Jeffries. "Your bedrolls are under the mosquito netting and your trunks for sorting your holdalls."

Vera and the others had also set out canvas basins of water to wash and rinse out clothes that were then hung on cords stretched between the trucks. Socks and smalls would dry out inside the backs of the lorries.

Most of all, the other girls were eager to hear about Gwen's wedding. Being at opposite ends of the convoy, the two groups had not been able to meet up for any length of time until now.

The unexpected acquaintance with F/O Gray fuelled the conversation further and they talked on until Major Trenholme came over and told them to get to bed.

But before retiring, they read some scriptures by pinpoint torchlight and prayed for their loved ones and the men to whom they would be ministering.

Trish felt keenly for her closest companions. It would be some time before the unit received any post, probably by airdrop as they had during the Imphal battles, longer again before Dai and Jonny received replies.

"I can't wait to see what Jonny writes to her," she said to Gwen out of Robyn's hearing.

"And what she writes back," said her friend eagerly.

In the morning, the girls tumbled bleary-eyed from the backs of their lorries to retrieve the shirts and trousers they'd hung out. Though these were wet from rain during the night, the Sisters dressed in them again, packing away their dry clothes. A few minutes of vigorous movement warmed the wet garments and the humid heat of the new day would gradually dry them, apart from sweat. Their macs and the jeep's cover would keep off most of the rain.

After a breakfast that was similar to last night's supper, Trish sprinkled powder on a small brush, cleaned her teeth scrupulously, rinsed her mouth out, spat back into her mug, emptied the contents into a small slops pit and rinsed out the container.

She then completed her dental ablutions with a wooden toothpick, combed her hair and applied a small amount of face cream, scent and lipstick before slapping insect repellent on her face and arms.

"That's the bit that spoils everything," said Robyn, who was going through the same ritual along with the other girls. "Makes you smell like a factory."

With the vehicles refuelled and the lorries used for sleeping quarters repacked with their loads, mostly tents and wooden furnishings, the convoy set off at 0900 hours.

At the Manipur River, one hundred and twenty-six miles south of Imphal, the sappers had constructed a raft ferry, floating on steel pontoons and attached by wire ropes to a heavy moveable block fixed to a three-inch steel cable stretched from bank to bank.

Trenholme's convoy queued for a couple of hours in broiling heat and annoying insects, for the rain had subsided temporarily. The girls then sat motionlessly as their vehicle was hauled across the one hundred and ten-yard width of swirling brown water by means of another cable attached to the block. The raft was also carrying a lorry and another jeep, plus their passengers.

"Canny contraption, this, Sisters," said Wood as they reached midstream. "Like some of the block and tackle kit we had in the pits. They lost a couple of the sapper lads 'cause of the current when they were stringin' the cable but at the end o' the day, lads did a canny job, like."

With moisture in her eyes for once not from sweat or rain, Trish prayed silently.

Lord, help us to do a canny job, amen.

After they left the Manipur, the weather deteriorated. Rain spattered on the jeep's windshields, to be swished away by the whirring wipers. Mist enveloped the crests of the ridges above the road and rolled clammily across the line of slow-moving vehicles.

Huge tarpaulin sheets, like they had seen on the first day, had been staked into the slopes to try and prevent mudslides. The traffic wound carefully past gangs of sappers and pioneers still shovelling away the remnants of earlier slippages, in order to restore the full road width.

Again, they drove past rusted, abandoned vehicles, including Jap tanks and the crumbling skeletons of mules and men. Trish hoped that the human remains were those of the enemy. They still came upon small white crosses, the price of the battles to secure the roadway. She felt sorry for the columns of infantry they passed from time to time, slogging through mud up to the ankles in full marching order.

"Feel like I'm sitting in a sauna," Robyn remarked to Trish, who was dabbing perspiration from her eyes with a square of towelling.

"Like driving through boiling fudge," Gwen said to Corporal Wood. The road seemed to have that consistency over this stretch.

"Aye, well. They call it the 'Chocolate Staircase,'[105] Sister," their driver explained. "Champion drive, this, man. Gans up three thousand feet in seven miles, thirty-eight hairpin bends and an average gradient of one in twelve."

The girls only had to get out and push on average once per mile.

"Never mind, girls," said Gwen on about the fifth occasion. "We've still got plenty of Sunlight soap."

The going was easier beyond the Chocolate Stairway. The road still rose, fell and twisted sharply between frowning, jungle-choked ridges ascending two and three thousand feet but the surface was firmer.

They had to overnight by the road on the third day but arrived reasonably refreshed at their destination well before noon on the morrow.

It was located at milepost one hundred and forty-four, close enough to hear the muffled clubbing and boom of battle as the forward troops invested Tiddim itself. The campsite was in a patch of cleared jungle at the bottom of a widened slip road similar to that where they had stopped at the end of the first day. A shallow stream, about twenty yards wide, bubbled noisily over a stony bed at the other side of the clearing and beyond it arose forested slopes, each in turn rising higher than the one before it until the summits disappeared into pinkish-golden mist. Bright sunlight bathed the camp area and a delicate rainbow could be discerned in the direction of Tiddim. Faint birdcalls issued from across the stream.

The advance party had already set up the tents and ambulances would soon be arriving from the regimental aid posts.

"Thank you, Woody," said Gwen as they climbed out onto the hardened vehicle stand. Her companions added their heartfelt agreement.

"Anytime, ladies," the corporal said jovially, slinging a haversack over his shoulders. "I reckon that'll be yours," he added and pointed to the hessian screen to the right of the vehicle park. "And those'll be your quarters, where Sister Jeffries is." He indicated the dark shape of a nearby tent, from which Vera had emerged and waved. "For now," he said philosophically. "I better gan and report to sarge."

Before he could depart, Major Trenholme summoned them to his HQ tent.

"Good to see you again," their CO said. "Please sit down."

He gestured to some foldable wooden and canvas chairs around his table.

When Wood and the girls were seated, Trenholme picked up a pointer and turned to the large-scale map mounted behind the table on an A-frame.

"We've had an urgent call from a battalion commander on top of this trig point here." He tapped the location on the map. "He's got a number of scrub typhus cases that can't be moved yet and he's asked if we can send some nurses up. It's about a four-hour journey and the chap assures me the nearest Japs are holed up in bunkers on the other side of the crest. I should ask for volunteers but I've already got the other girls getting ready for a batch of wounded on their way now. Will you go, soon as you can?"

"Of course, sir," said Gwen quietly. Trish and Robyn each nodded.

"We'll organise a mule train and you'll lead the party, Corporal Wood?"

"Aye, sir, glad to."

The CO looked visibly relieved.

"Right, I'll go over the details of the route with you," he said. "And I'll have us radio the battalion you'll be there around seventeen hundred hours. That'll give you time for something to eat before you push off as well as get your kit together. As you know, we've lost dozens of chaps from scrub typhus recently and the situation up there seems pretty desperate."

Trish, Robyn and Gwen waited by the stream while Wood and two other orderlies helped the mule handlers finish loading the beasts. They sat on their bedrolls that they'd wrapped in gas capes and buckled to the base of their large packs. Perched along the edge of the wet, grassy bank, they absently dug their boot heels into the sandy soil sloping down to the water. On the other side of the stream, the russet coloured blossoms of several flame trees stood out against the varied greens of the jungle foliage.

"I'd love to have one of those in the garden back home," said Gwen, poking a stick into the sand. "But it wouldn't be warm enough in Llangollen."

The ambulance convoy had still not arrived so Vera and a couple of the other girls came over to see their friends on their way.

"My dears," said Sister Jeffries, "you're packing more than the mules."

"All the essentials, Vera," Trish explained. "You know, cosmetics and everything. Must look feminine."

Among the girls' loads were containers of surgical alcohol that they would use to sponge the typhus patients down in an effort to regulate their temperatures. They were also taking with them copious amounts of quinine for IV drips and other medicines. These drugs could not prevent the onset of the disease but seemed to alleviate its effects, provided the patient could ingest regular meals. For that reason, much of the total load consisted of extra rations, to be replenished daily by mule train.

"Once we start getting some air drops, you should get better food," Vera said hopefully. Their designated drop zone was a couple of miles back towards the Manipur.

Robyn tossed a pebble into the stream. She looked up and smiled from beneath the brim of her bush hat.

"Until then, I've got my favourite cook book, *Fifty-Seven Ways to Fry Spam*," she said.

In sum, the girls would be carrying their own body weight, with large pack, haversack, gas cape, bedroll, full *chagal* and, though it contravened the Geneva Convention, a Sten gun and four full magazines each. Bitter experience had taught the medical services in Fourteenth Army that the Japanese had nothing but contempt for non-combatants, whether male or female, something the framers of the Convention had not contemplated. The girls had been taught how to fire the weapons and only on the wards were firearms strictly prohibited[106].

They had also packed lipstick and other cosmetics, including lotions to suppress prickly heat, because they would definitely try to look feminine.

"At least it isn't raining," said Robyn. She glanced up at clear skies.

"Yet," murmured Gwen.

"Here comes Woody," said Trish. "See you when we see you, I guess," she said to Vera and the others.

The trio got to their feet, donned their packs and slung their weapons.

"God speed," said Sister Jeffries as the groups embraced. "You'll be in our prayers – and we won't forget to air your things for you."

We will follow up these events shortly – and the correspondence between F/O Gray and Nursing Officer Fairlea. But now, we must turn again to those young men who would support Grandma Colleen in days to come.

Nine

Longsuffering

Normandy, June, 1944.

L ieutenant Graham was seated at a foldaway table beneath the canvas awning attached to Armadillo's turret and spread out with tent poles.

He stared down at the sheet of paper in front of him.

Dear Mrs Tyrell, it read.

Apart from the date, that was all he had so far. Bearing the same date, another piece of paper lay on the table. It was a message from the hospital, sent by dispatch rider.

Sergeant J.M. Tyrell died of his injuries at 1630 hours today, it read, citing Tyrell's army number.

With the message came the sergeant's red identity disk, for divisional records. The green one would be buried with him.

Graham glanced over to the lads sitting under the awning rigged up to Adamant, or on the ground beside it. They were smoking cigarettes, sipping compo tea and not saying much[107]. Two members of Arquebus's crew were with them. Two others were in hospital and the remaining two, including Tyrell, would soldier no more.

The padre's visit had been beneficial. A jovial, rotund little man who wore specs and possessed shrewd insight into human nature, he'd also landed in the first wave on June 6th, with the medics. Graham liked him. Reverend "Tubby" Potter and he were very much alike on biblical matters.

"It's the balm of Gilead your lads need now, Steve," the chaplain had said, on meeting Graham at the gap in the hedge forming the entrance to the troop's leaguer. One Troop's Churchills were parked in a field of hitherto waist-high corn, now largely macerated by the tanks' treads.

Tubby had buoyed the men up a little. They trusted him, knowing he was always close at hand during any action.

More action was pending on the morrow and a new Arquebus would be brought up from divisional reserve, though it wasn't certain when reinforcements would arrive.

"I think Bill Crittenden should take over as Arquebus commander, sir and become my second-in-command," Graham had recommended to Major Blackstone at the debriefing.

"He's earned his third stripe. I'd like to put Ronny Hazeldene in charge of Adamant and make Illingworth up to lance-jack as explosives NCO in Armadillo."

Winstanley, also present, voiced his approval and that was sufficient for the major.

Everything would be sorted but for now, the lads needed to recuperate, on their own patch of ground, surrounded by typical Normandy *bocage*, the hedgerows that were both a protective barrier and a major impediment to the Allied advance – and often the bane of AVREs.

Graham leant back in his chair, looked up and sighed. The very success of the specialised armour during the landing had repeatedly prompted frantic calls for "funnies here, funnies there!" from the hard-pressed infantry advancing inland through meadows and orchards that the enemy had ranged to the last inch with Spandaus and mortars, including the dreaded moaners.

Loyally, the AVREs had responded and accounted for many enemy strong points but suffered considerably in doing so, from long-range A/T weapons concealed in the *bocage* that should first have been destroyed by artillery or RAF Typhoons in support.

Winstanley lost Alligator that way, on D plus 3, though the crew had baled out and One Troop was restored to full to strength with a replacement Churchill. Until today, it had been notably fortunate to incur no further losses but the enemy was "writing off" Allied armour at a frightening rate. Graham and his companions time and again witnessed disabled Churchills and Shermans being carted back for salvage or lying abandoned and burnt out in the fields.

A harsh *"crack"*, a ringing *"clang"* and whirling bits of jagged metal amid a blossom of blue and orange flame would spell the end of another Allied victim, picked off from a mile away by eighty-eight mm dual-purpose flak guns, or hull-down German tanks, sometimes the mighty Tigers, also armed with the lethal eighty-eight mm, more often the Panthers, carrying the smaller, seventy-seven mm gun, though the difference was academic for a Churchill.

The divisional commander had therefore stepped in and appointed senior officers to oversee all requests for AVREs.

Unfortunately, even their expertise could not entirely counter the unexpected, as Graham's crews had discovered earlier that day.

Steve got to his feet, placed his beret on his head, picked up his enamel mug and strolled over to Adamant. He was reassured by the crews' welcoming looks. Crittenden gestured to the spirit burners on the Churchill's track, where the tea was brewing in a couple of large dixies.

"Fresh lot, sir," he said.

"Thanks, Bill," said Graham. He filled his mug with the concoction and glanced at the young faces before him.

Like Graham, his sappers wore denim trousers and KD shirts with sleeves rolled up, though some were stripped to their string vests. Recently they'd experienced a brief, blustery interval with accompanying storms in the Channel that had greatly disrupted ship to shore transport and severely damaged the artificial harbours but made little impression inland. High summer in Normandy had therefore largely meant baking sunshine and bursting new growth – *bocage* and woodland blind with heavy foliage, where wild beasts lurked unseen until it was often too late.

It also meant that if the severely wounded fell out of sight into the long grass of the orchards, they could die before help came. The medics were having a desperate time. So were the Graves Registration units. Corpses putrefied rapidly in the summer heat and buzzing hordes of bluebottles were ever present, attracted manifold by the hideously bloated and stinking carcasses of slain cattle. When these ruptured, frequently through the agency of a bullet, the resultant stench from the gases released was nauseating in the extreme.

At first, the lads were distressed by the slaughter of the helpless beasts; often driven stampeding mad by the battle tumult before expiring – unless directly blown to bits through being too close to strafing runs by RAF Typhoons, the dreaded "Iron Tommy" as the Germans called them.

Now the sappers simply regarded the animal massacres as part of the general unpleasantness.

Taking casual sips, Graham squatted down and apprised his command of the reorganisation.

"You might as well break out the rations now," he said afterwards. "Rest of the troop is."

Graham inclined his head towards the other AVREs leaguered in the field. This area had good cover but the troop had to be alert for possible air raids and had dug slit trenches for this purpose. Providentially, the fighter-bomber "cab rank" was in the air throughout the hours of daylight and an anti-aircraft battery maintained station in a field nearby - though its zeal in challenging any overhead droning after dark with loud *"booms"* and angry flashes drew protests from neighbours, especially those subjected to falling shrapnel.

For this reason, One Troop often slept in the Churchills. Lithe men of pre-war experience working in the confined spaces of pit galleries in addition to their wartime service with the armour, they adapted easily to their makeshift "dormitories".

Crittenden nodded at his officer's suggestion.

"Will do, sir," he said. "We'll give you a shout when it's ready."

Hazeldene and a few others got up to light more spirit burners and access the boxes of compo rations. These had replaced the twenty-four-hour individual packs they'd been issued with for the landing and the lads preferred them, though the MO had expressed doubts about the long-term nutritional sufficiency of the compo supplies.

"Any chap who's pale and feverish and says he's got the runs, send him straight to me," the doc had said at an officers' briefing. "Like as not it's compo sickness[108]."

It was but one more potential nuisance for the ordinary soldier.

Thus far however, the squadron had not lost anyone through this malady and the men appreciated the modest variety of the composite rations. Besides the usual bully beef or spam, compo tea cubes and packets of hardtack, the tins yielded Irish stew, beef sausages, steak and veg, treacle pudding and other delights.

"Anyone for tinned pineapple?" Graham overheard Hazeldene ask, as he trudged back to Armadillo, still sipping his tea.

"Just make sure you read the label this time, Ronny," growled a voice. "Don't want carrots in vinegar again."

Graham smiled. They were getting back to normal, though God knew, their loss was small compared to that of the infantry battalions and gun tank regiments, with no letup in sight.

But when your mate is dismembered in an instant beside you, or almost incinerated, you don't recover in five minutes.

Graham was still stunned himself.

Seated again at his desk, the lieutenant tried to reflect on the day's action, in the hope it would help him compose something suitable for Tyrell's widow, a twenty-year-old bride of less than five months.

Steve closed his eyes and sought to reconstruct in his mind the terrible sequence of events, beginning with the stupendous bombardment of the morning...

The barrage had been bludgeoning away since breakfast; twenty-five pounders roaring from adjacent fields, huge blurred bullet-shapes thundering overhead, some from battleships in the Channel in addition to Second Army's guns. Fighter-bombers skimmed the treetops to batter the enemy defences with rocket, bomb and cannon fire.

Though obscured by hedge and woodland from One Troop, who stood by their vehicles awaiting the summons to go up in support of the attack, the target was nevertheless distinctly marked by what a British Second Army poet/correspondent had termed *the evil smoke shouting in the air*[109].

Eventually, the guns subsided and a strange silence descended until Sapper Shoreland stuck his head out of Armadillo's turret. The half-troops' wireless operators waited by their sets for incoming orders.

"It's the OC, sir," Shoreland called to Graham, who nimbly climbed up to the turret and slipped his earphones on, immediately conscious of the familiar hum indicating the set was netted in.

"Major Kinross from the Lowland Brigade, Steve," said Winstanley. "Got two companies of Jocks held up near the village's outer defence ring. Doesn't want to risk more artillery or even the Tiffies. His lads are too close to the Boche, he says. So it's crocodiles or us and we're available."

Winstanley stated the grid reference, near the bombardment's main target, a notorious fortified hamlet blocking Second Army's intended encirclement of Caen, its prime objective.

"Wilco, Don," said Graham. "On our way, out."

It was his turn, Winstanley's half-troop having carried out a similar task the day before, including using their dustbins to blast huge holes in the *bocage* for the passage of gun tanks.

Graham alerted the rest of his half-troop, who by dint of physique and repeated practice swiftly assumed their cramped positions. The three AVRE engines roared into life and the vehicles rumbled out of the gap in the hedge onto the road in single file, Armadillo leading. Graham stood on his commander's pedestal, leaning out of the turret hatch.

The Churchills chugged noisily past groups of infantrymen bivouacked in a field with a devastated cottage at its roadside border, the vehicles' sharp-edged treads scooping up white dust in billows. Despite the filters on the AVREs' air intakes, the annoying particles easily made ingress, coating everything and everyone.

"Aw, sod off!" shouted a dozen helmeted, brown-clad figures. Several lifted two fingers, others pointed indignantly to a roughly painted sign displaying an unequivocal message:

DUST MEANS DEATH! WE WANT TO LIVE HERE!

The possibility of a well-aimed enemy response to a dust cloud had diminished the AVREs' earlier popularity with the foot soldiers.

Traversing ground fought over was a depressing business. First came the smell, thick and loathsome, of rotting animal carcasses mixed with the lingering tang of HE, then the sight of formerly rich farmland, pitted with shell and bomb craters, its trees splintered, hedges torn up, long-cherished barns and houses blown apart. Constructed of white Normandy stone, many were now roofless, tumbledown, blackened and forlorn.

Inevitably, you saw the charred vehicle remnants; lorries, armoured cars and tanks that were mostly, in a sustained blow to morale, British. Many of the tanks remained gutted in the ravaged fields, mute witnesses to yet another thwarted Allied advance. Steve recoiled from the bitter-tasting smoke drifting into his face from still-smouldering abandoned transport.

Buried Allied dead lay beneath wooden crosses rough-hewn from boards of ammunition boxes or rifles shoved part-way into the chalky soil, with the dead men's helmets looped over the butts. To each grave marker was affixed a note of the deceased's details, written in indelible pencil.

A number of immobile forms awaiting burial were ranked along the roadside, under grey blankets, boots and gaiters protruding stiffly.

Then Graham noticed several grotesquely swollen Wehrmacht corpses scattered by the verges. These did not enjoy the same priority as friendly dead.

For one thing, they would have to be checked for booby traps, before, probably, being deposited in a mass grave.

"Our lads at work, sir," said Talbot over the intercom.

Graham glanced at the plots of ground taped off by sappers from the field companies, with painted signs displaying the warning VERGES UNCLEARED. REs on foot were continuously sweeping suspect ground with their metal detectors, digging gingerly by hand to determine if the detection device had located a mine or merely one of the myriad metal shards that peppered the terrain. Usually, the object was inert but each find had to be treated as "live" until proven otherwise. Even something apparently mundane, like a nail, could conceal an explosive destroyer of life and limb. A fortunate victim of an A/P mine might lose a foot to the blast, if less fortunate, both legs, or his stomach and possibly his life as well. Any man who set off an A/T mine lost all of these.

So the sappers' work was vital.

"What would they do without us, eh, Corporal?" Graham said, to murmurs of "Hear, hear," from the rest of the crew.

"This road has been swept for Tellers, sir?" asked Hazeldene.

"As of yesterday, Corporal," said Graham, trying to sound confident. A Teller mine explosion could easily tear off a track.

It was another worry they had to live with. Graham glanced down at the others, their faces impassive, displaying an unnatural hue from the red glow of the wireless indicator light and the white turret illumination light, needed inside the vehicle even in daytime.

Each man was an island of apprehension.

Climbing into his tip-up seat, Graham checked his map and resumed searching with his binoculars, staring *into* the hedgerows, scanning any adjacent copses or deceptively innocent-looking building debris. The nearest enemy were supposed to be the panzer grenadiers pinning down Kinross's companies but given the Boches' talent for infiltration, who knew for certain?

The Churchills growled steadily forward, bumping over filled-in holes gouged out originally by shell bursts, surrounded by unnervingly white dust, their commanders scanning constantly, in perpetual fear of the distant eighty-eight's terrifying, supersonic *"crack"* or the flash and *"whoosh"* closer to hand of the *panzerfaust*, the one-shot enemy infantry anti-tank weapon in the form of a finned, HE rocket head, attached to half a wooden broom handle, for flight stability.

The wobbling demon could fly a hundred yards. On impacting a Churchill at the correct angle, it instantly drilled a pencil-sized hole in the armour and unleashed a witch's cauldron of molten metal. The Germans also possessed a bazooka-style weapon that was reloadable and did the same job from a greater range. Compared to the eighty-eight mm A/T shell, whose tungsten-carbide armour-piercing round could ricochet repeatedly around the inside of a tank before its energy was expended, one couldn't say which was worse.

That the Allies had similar devices was cold comfort on viewing the results of enemy A/T work. It was best not to view them all.

Even when one passed a given point unmolested, safety could not be guaranteed. All vehicle crews understood the danger:

"They'll let you go on for a bit, then hit you up the backside."

Recognising the risk to "Tail-end Charlie," troop and half-troop leaders rotated their vehicles accordingly. Today it was Crittenden's worry.

The pall of brownish-grey smoke coming into view told Graham the AVREs were nearing their destination.

"Get the Jocks' OC, Tom," he muttered.

Shoreland nodded and gave a thumbs-up sign when he'd made contact via the A set.

"AVRE Delta One to Greyfriars," Graham said into the mike. "ETA in five minutes."

"Roger, Delta One, over and out," said a quiet Scots voice.

Graham zipped up and buttoned his camouflaged smock over his string vest, then buckled on his Webley revolver. By feel, he adjusted his beret, not wishing to appear scruffy before

Major Kinross. Wouldn't do for the squadron image at all. He was glad they'd all been able to wash and shave that morning – and even wash their clothes yesterday, a satisfying task requiring a deceptively small amount of the strong Sunlight soap. Unlike the infantry, the assault engineer squadrons could obtain plentiful supplies of water from their well-organised logistics tail.

Steve halted the Churchills in file behind Kinross's armoured scout car, on the edge of a laneway littered with fallen foliage. A broad field to the left enclosed part of the battalion assembly area, where numerous casualties had congregated in a tented RAP. The area was partly obscured by drifting battle-smoke, acrid with the smell of cordite and HE.

Away to the right, beyond the veil of smoke, issued the rattle of automatic fire, both British and German, and the *"whoomp"* of opposing mortars.

Taking his Sten gun and binoculars, Graham jumped down from Armadillo and jogged to the three officers leaning on the rear of the car, examining their maps.

One of them drew himself up and shook Graham's hand. He was tall, raw-boned, with steely gaze, weathered features and dark hair showing grey at the temples beneath his steel helmet.

"Steve Graham, sir," said the lieutenant.

"Pleased to meet you, Steve," the major said. "Ian Kinross."

Kinross introduced his fellow officers, both subalterns and added, "Stalemate at the moment. Hopefully you and your lads can break the deadlock. Come on, Steve, I'll show you the form."

Kinross picked up a Sten from the back of the car and beckoned Graham to follow him along the lane into the haze.

They passed a T-intersection down which Graham glimpsed a line of ambulances, then came upon about a score of infantry, begrimed and nervous-looking, crouching in the brush on either side of the lane.

"My reserve," muttered Kinross as he took up position beneath a spreading broad-leafed bush a few yards beyond the infantrymen. "I'll send them up with your lads. We'll also put down smoke to the right with our mortars to screen you some more from any interference over that way. Save you the trouble." He gestured into the field opposite, to where the distant exchange of fire was taking place.

"Thank you, sir," said Graham. His crews would have their hands full without handling the Churchills' two-inch smoke mortars as well.

Steve ducked under the bush and raised his binoculars to examine the cornfield adjacent that under its dirty grey-brown pall resembled acres of moonscape more than mother earth.

"Ian's the name, lad," said the major with a wry grin. Pointing to the upward sloping field he went on. "You can see my companies. A couple of spits would bring them into the Hun positions on the skyline there, too close for artillery or even our mortars but I don't want to pull the lads back because one more bound brings us to the village. The right-hand battalion cleared this lane up to where it intersects one that goes behind the Boche position. That'll be your approach road. There's a field on the other side of it, sloping down, so the far bank will help conceal you from it. Anyway, we'll drop smoke there, too."

Through his enhanced vision Graham could see khaki forms crouching in craters at the top end of the field before him, angling their weapons toward the enemy. A few lay further back, corpses waiting collection, frozen in contorted attitudes of sudden death.

Graham scrutinized the line of heavy growth, twisted saplings and thick blossom that denoted the German position. He discerned sinister-looking Spandau barrels.

"They let us get close," the major said grimly, still peering through his binoculars. "The barrage didn't touch them, though it made quite a mess of the field. They're very well dug in and camouflaged – roofed-over bunkers, for sure. We lost a third of the assault force."

"Likely they'll enfilade if you send your reserve onto the lane unaccompanied," said Steve.

"My reasoning, too," said Kinross. He glanced away from his binoculars at Steve. "They'll no doubt have all-round flexibility. That's why I hope you'll blast your way through."

"We'll try. My map shows the top lane coming to a crossroads."

"That's right," the Scot affirmed. "Continues on as a rough track. The through road dips down over dead ground, mostly wooded. From there, as you'll have seen from the map, you're almost into the village."

"When we're done, we'll form up past the crossroads and wait for your companies," said Steve. "Hopefully, we can forestall any counterattacks and your lads can move up before the Boche mortars interfere."

Kinross nodded.

"My companies will hit them with everything as you go in, Steve," he said, lowering his binoculars. "Especially the first corner where you turn – don't want any intrepid Hun dropping a grenade on you. The sides of the lane are sheer just there, according to the right-hand battalion. And it's not mined. We heard Jerry vehicles using it during stand-to. This lane's been swept too, by the way."

"That's reassuring," Graham said, also lowering his binoculars. "We'll get a few mortars into that corner as we go up."

"Aye, should be possible. The hedge growth's lower on this side near the T. We'll also spray the trees along the lane for snipers, so keep your heads down."

They withdrew back the way they had come, past the Jocks in reserve.

"We'll see some fireworks noo," Graham heard one mutter.

"Drivers advance!"

The half-troop lurched ahead at Graham's command and clattered up the lane at their top speed of thirteen miles per hour. The reserve Jocks followed on the run. Kinross's companies were whiplashing the enemy strip of hedge with Bren and rifle fire while brown smoke from his mortars was sealing off the battle area with an opaque L-shaped cloud that spread across the AVREs' line of advance.

The three commanders stood partway out of their hatches for best observation but were careful to heed Kinross's warning, Steve having relayed it to the others.

"Mortar, oblique left, fifty yards!" Graham yelled to Ferrarby as the corner of the field became visible beyond the adjacent hedge growth. The turret motor whirred as Ferraby adjusted the angle. Steve ducked below the hatch opening. Then, with crashing report, the dustbin hurtled from the stubby barrel to burst with devastating roar and smoky plume of debris on its target. One followed from Arquebus, another from Adamant. Automatic fire from Kinross's companies tore into the position.

Armadillo's petard barrel clanged shut, Illingworth having replenished the round.

At the corner, Talbot swung Armadillo sharp left into the top lane, through billowing smoke. As Kinross had said, the banks were sheer for about thirty yards before settling into scrub-covered mounds. The left mound, about five feet high, housed the enemy position.

Graham drew his Webley and settled it in his left hand.

A fallen tree lay in their path, felled by their own petards. Armadillo's forty-ton bulk crunched it to matchwood.

"Mortar, oblique left, fifty yards, sustained fire!" Graham shouted as Armadillo cleared the shattered tree. "Co-ax and hull, oblique left, sustained fire!"

Armadillo thundered along the lane, mercilessly petarding and machine-gunning the enemy. Arquebus and Adamant closed up on the leading Churchill. Their Besas flayed both banks of the lane.

Armadillo's dustbins plummeted into the German line and smashed it to smoking, churned-up earth. The weapon noise inside the AVRE was tremendous, with the banging of the mortar and the bark of the Besas emptying belts of 7.92 mm rounds into the tortured strip of exploding soil. The Bren rounds snapping overhead ceased as Kinross's LMG teams concentrated on the bank. No tree-bound sniper could have lived through the petarding.

In between ducking down as successive dustbins burst, Graham stared in horror at the body parts flung up with the smoke, dust and hedge growth debris from the petard barrage. Sobbing screams issuing from within that cauldron of death turned his stomach. His eyes and those of his crew were streaming from the propellant and cordite smoke. He earnestly hoped the assault would eliminate any *panzerfaust* operators.

As arranged, the Jocks in reserve deployed onto the right bank, Bren gunners up front, in support of the Besa barrage, firing bursts along its length to take out any concealed *panzerfaust* assailant or sniper.

"Not in the road!"

Illingworth's frantic shout was intended for the panzer grenadiers stumbling across the lane in an effort to escape.

But it was futile.

Easy targets, cut down by Brens and Besas, they fell beneath the AVRE's treads.

Graham cringed at the sight of the ghastly, sticky red mess staining Armadillo's tracks.

Part way out of his hatch, Steve turned sharply in response to a half-perceived movement.

He came face-to-face with a jack-booted German youth in coal-scuttle helmet and camouflage SS smock, white-faced with fury, brandishing a Luger pistol, two potato-masher grenades thrust through his belt. Somehow having avoided the maelstrom of blast and metal deluging the German position, he had clambered onto Armadillo's hull with astounding agility, too quickly for Tyrell's Besa gunners to pick him off.

Graham swung his left hand out in a vicious backhander, catching the grenadier smack in the mouth with the Webley chamber. The youth fell backwards, the revolver banged and jolted as Graham pumped two .45 calibre rounds into the SS boy's chest.

"Get off my tank!" snarled the lieutenant. The corpse thudded to the roadside.

Armadillo emerged from the lane and roared over the crossroads.

"Driver, traverse right!" Graham ordered Talbot, who swung the heavy vehicle through ninety degrees to face into the wooded patch by the downhill through road. Arquebus chugged out from the tunnel of smoke filling the laneway, with Adamant visible behind. The Jocks were cheering and swarming over the erstwhile strongpoint, joining hands with their comrades who'd followed the Churchills.

"Deploy left, past the tanks!" Kinross was shouting. Graham could see him at the corner of the enemy position, directing his men along the cart track. They obeyed promptly, hustling along some incredibly fortunate Germans who'd survived. An enemy mortar salvo could be expected anytime.

But the initial riposte was even more terrifying.

In shock, Graham saw the armoured monster lurch up from concealment in scrubby dead ground ahead, fifty yards away.

It was a Tiger tank.

And it had taken them by surprise, the general din of battle masking the sound of its approach.

The monster's massive gun bellowed in smoke and yellow flame.

Aghast, Graham saw the split-second flash terminate in a direct hit on Arquebus, setting the Churchill ablaze.

Five figures tumbled into the roadway, out of the hatches and side doors, three of them alight, rolling to smother the flames. In desperate haste, dragging a couple of the injured, the survivors made for the ditch on the far side of the lane, doubtless fearful of an imminent stonk.

Horrified and enraged, Graham saw the five go sprawling. Simultaneously, he heard the stutter of the Tiger's hull machine gun and saw the spitting flashes, even while shouting orders to his crew.

"Driver, advance, mortar, direct front, open fire, Besas, open fire!"

With the engine roaring at full power, Talbot charged Armadillo straight for the enemy behemoth, whose turret was swivelling menacingly to meet them. Graham was aware of Kinross shouting "PIATs up!" and Bren and Besa bullets bouncing off the foe's seven-inches-thick armour. At the same time, he saw Adamant bashing across the narrow ditch and through the underbrush bordering the adjacent field, charging the Tiger's left flank. Crittenden's driver had swerved instantly to avoid Arquebus's crew.

Armadillo's petard burst with a terrific *"bang"* and gout of flame against the enemy tank's turret ring. As Illingworth rapidly reloaded, Adamant also lobbed a petard that struck home.

At up to ninety yards' range, the forty-pound, two hundred and ninety-mm dustbins were effective even against a Tiger – and the enemy tank had ventured inside that distance.

The twin blasts wrenched monster's turret askew at an angle.

"Cease fire!" Graham shouted over the intercom, then via the B set to Adamant. Kinross was bawling the same order to his infantry.

Three survivors hoisted themselves out of the yawning aperture beneath the Tiger's dislocated turret, flames licking around them.

Arquebus blew up with a gigantic roar and sheet of flame. Jagged bits of flaming metal flew in a 360-degree arc. Graham felt the searing heat of the blast rush against his face as he ducked into the turret.

As if in sympathy, the wrecked Tiger vomited a vertical column of flame accompanied by a gargantuan bellow as its fuel and ammunition exploded. More fiery metal fragments spewed out over the landscape. Graham and everyone else ducked again.

When the debris had settled, Steve saw several grim-faced Jocks line up the surviving Tiger crewmen and begin marching them at gunpoint down the through road to the Scotsmen's original start line. They would be put with the other prisoners, mostly wounded, who had miraculously lived through the petarding, though several, Graham discovered subsequently, were unhinged by the experience.

"They're only kids," said Shoreland, astounded at the evident youth of the Tiger captives, who looked to be no more than seventeen or eighteen.

"Hitler *Jugend*[110]," muttered Graham. "Keep your eyes peeled for the rest of their troop," he ordered his crews but thankfully, no more enemy juggernauts appeared.

Several ambulances had moved onto the through road and then reversed direction, to get the casualties away with minimum delay.

Graham climbed out of the turret, leapt to the ground and sprinted over to where eight brawny Jocks had placed the most seriously wounded member of Arquebus's crew onto a stretcher made up of four rifles.

A medic was holding a blood bottle aloft, its stem inserted into one of the casualty's arms. Blackened bones and sinews were showing through the charred flesh of his other forearm, above which a blood-stained tourniquet was secured and an already reddened dressing was covering the bullet holes in his side where the Tiger's machine gunner had caught him.

"Steady now," the RAMC man muttered to the bearers. "But quick as you can."

In anguish, Graham saw that the wounded man was Jack Tyrell, though scarcely recognisable, his face scorched and swollen.

"I've filled 'im with morphine, sir," the corpsman panted to Graham as he hurried past. "But that arm's a write-off, I'm sorry to say."

Eight more Jocks were transporting Sapper Irvine, Tyrell's co-driver, on another improvised stretcher, his lower left leg heavily bandaged. He too was burnt but from swollen lips grinned up at the lieutenant as he was carried past.

Bringing up the rear were two more infantrymen, helping Lance Corporal Lennox, Tyrell's driver, whose right arm hung limply, courtesy of the Tiger hull gunner, and heavily wrapped with dressing. His eyes were bandaged and what could be seen of his face was streaked with blood and smoke-grime.

"Aye, lad. Your officer's here," said one of the Jocks. "On your right."

"Thanks, mate," said Lennox. Turning his head, he said to Graham, "We did OK, didn't we, sir?"

"We sure did, John," said Graham. Steve felt his throat constricting.

He then hastened back up the road to Kinross's new HQ. The infantry were entrenching themselves in the woods, several chains' lengths from the crossroads where the armoured remains were still on fire. Graham saw through the smoky haze covering the battle area that the sun was almost overhead and his watch confirmed that it was nearly noon. A mere twenty minutes had elapsed since his order to advance.

Armadillo and Adamant had also pulled back along the rutted cart track, the two remaining sappers from Arquebus clinging to Armadillo's turret.

"Splendid work, Steve," said Ian when Graham joined him. The major looked up from inspecting the ravine in front of his position through his binoculars. It was overgrown with thicket.

"I'm sorry about your lads," he added quietly.

Graham thanked him. "We'll get back to leaguer, now, Ian but call us when you need us," he said.

"Right enough, Steve. I'd anticipate we'll be investing the village tomorrow - "

He was interrupted by the heart-stopping *"whee, eee!"* of the killer mules. The moaners crashed violently around the former German defence line.

Hastily excusing himself, Graham sprinted to Armadillo, sprang onto the turret, seized his mike and ordered both AVREs back to leaguer.

"Take the shortcut!" he shouted to each driver in turn. "Hang on, boys!" he yelled to the unhurt members of Arquebus's crew.

The two Churchills crashed through a barbed wire fence into the field beside the rutted lane. Cornstalks flew from their tracks where they ploughed through patches of ripening crops undamaged by the morning's artillery barrage.

Looking back, Graham saw what a superb target his vehicles would have presented for *panzerfausts* from the position they had just petarded. Kinross had done them a favour in choosing the approach road ahead of time.

The return journey scoured most of the mess from the tracks. The crews sloshed water over them anyway, when they returned to their leaguer.

In the aftermath of any sortie, manifold chores awaited them; engine and transmission maintenance, track, wireless, mortar and Besa maintenance, clearing the thousands of expended cartridge cases from the vehicles, replenishing petrol and ammunition.

The sappers always reckoned that it was like "knocking off work to shovel coal."

While the maintenance was underway, Steve donned his shirt to report to Winstanley and Blackstone for the debriefing. He had to look regimental. String vest and smock wouldn't do.

On his return to the leaguer, Graham discovered that scrounger Crittenden, who had quickly absorbed a good portion of Norman French, had managed to trade some compo chocolate at a nearby farm that was still functioning for enough eggs to fry up a fourteen-man omelette for a late lunch. The farmer's wife highly prized the specially enriched confection that didn't melt even in the heat of the Normandy summer.

Despite the chaos inflicted by the invasion, sturdy Madame de Richelet welcomed *"Les bon soldats Anglais"* and cursed vehemently in colourful *patois* whenever she mentioned *"Les Boches, cochons."*

When Crittenden broke the news of Sergeant Tyrell and his crew, she wept copiously, crying, *"Ah, ces pauvres garcons."* Drying her eyes on her apron, she then gathered up another batch of eggs, marched over to the leaguer with Crittenden and cooked omelettes for the whole troop.

She also instructed her husband to brew the coffee and bring it over on a handcart in an insulated container.

"I don't think it's a breach of security, Don," Graham said to Winstanley.

With their mess tins full of home-cooked omelette and Madame distributing home-brewed coffee, neither officer thought so.

Crittenden's summons to supper interrupted Steve's reflections. They normally ate at this time, if circumstances allowed, but Steve reckoned that this meal, like Madame's ministrations and Tubby's visit, would also help the lads recuperate. It was essential that they did. "We have to get on," Steve told himself.

He got to his feet and strolled over to join the group beside Adamant.

A little before sunset, Crittenden and Illingworth fetched the replacement Churchill from divisional reserve, having cadged a lift to the beachhead after the evening meal.

"She's all gunned and primed, sir," said Crittenden with a grin, patting the flank of the new Arquebus. "Thanks for busting me up a stripe, by the way."

Illingworth emerged from the side door.

"Goes for me too, sir," he added.

"You've earned it," said Graham sincerely. "And welcome to the gang, lads."

Steve here addressed the two replacement crewmen who came up with Crittenden and Illingworth; sandy-haired, slightly-built Sapper MacGee, from Belfast and long-limbed Sapper Tomlinson, from Preston, dark-haired, taller than MacGee.

"It's an honour, sir," said MacGee in his Ulster brogue. Tomlinson nodded.

"Aye, sooner here than a Bevin boy[111], sir" the lanky Lancastrian declared, grinning.

They would be making up Crittenden's crew, with Sappers Kendle and Young, the two survivors from Tyrell's original team.

"Sorry you'll be a bit shorthanded, Bill," said Graham as Crittenden climbed down from the Churchill. "As we will be, Tapper," he added to Illingworth, whose nickname derived from his foundryman's background.

"Not a problem, sir," Crittenden assured his superior. "Give us a bit more elbow room."

"Chance for me to show my breadth of talent, sir," said Illingworth, fastening the Churchill's side door.

The four enlisted men went for a brew. Graham climbed inside Armadillo to complete the letter to Lorraine Tyrell, using the turret illumination light, with the hatches closed.

Dear Mrs Tyrell, he wrote.

You will by now have been officially informed of your tragic loss. I am writing on behalf of all the lads to express our deepest sympathy and to assure you of how much you are in our thoughts. For reasons of security, I cannot reveal to you the precise circumstances of Jack's death but I can vouch for the fact that, as always, he fought bravely and well. As my second-in-command, he enabled us to maintain the highest standards of discipline and professionalism. We shall all miss him greatly, both as a staunch comrade-in-arms and a close friend. We earnestly hope that you have those near you for support at this distressing time but if you feel that we could be of further encouragement, please do not hesitate to write to me.
Yours sincerely,
S.J. Graham, Lieutenant, Royal Engineers

He then wrote three more letters, to the families of Lance Corporal Lennox, Sapper Irvine and Sapper Knowles, the other fatal casualty from Arquebus.

With yet more action pending, he turned in without writing to his parents. They'd received a letter from Neil the day before the War Office telegram had arrived. Trust my stupid brother, Steve again reflected wryly. He'd wept openly on learning that his gangly sibling and lifelong best mate was safe but he didn't want that situation to arise again.

The next day, the weather broke and Graham's squadron lumbered through drenching rain along byways quickly dissolving into mud to the start line, where it would support the Lowland Brigade.

"The final bound, Steve," said Kinross over the wireless.

Alongside flame-throwing crocodile Churchills, the petard AVREs charged across more mangled cornfields and rampaged like steel Visigoths through the rubble-strewn ruins of the village and its shell-torn environs, pulverising the enemy trench and bunker systems to churned-up detritus and obliterating the occupants, who nevertheless fought savagely to the last with Spandaus, bazookas and *panzerfausts*.

They wrote off a couple of crocodiles and an AVRE from Three Troop but in cold military parlance, "the bale-out factor was high."

Throughout the attack, the roaring gouts of red-centred black smoke from the petard bursts joined in horrendous harmony with the slapping hiss of red-tongued infernos slipping like fiery serpents around enemy trench traverses and licking fiercely through pill-box embrasures.

Shrapnel-pocked, skeletal walls left over from the opening barrage crashed down in billows of masonry dust. Stone fragments and glass shards from shattered windows were ground in the rain to gritty paste beneath the Churchills' squealing treads. Their crews suffered repeated drenching from rain pulled in by the same air intakes that had earlier showered them with dust.

"Can't win either way," the boys reckoned.

Likewise soaked through, the Jocks battled stubbornly forward from one broken-down building shell to the next, winkling out enemy remnants with gunshot and grenade burst.

Green and red flares shot up into the streaming downpour, arching above the smoke of battle.

They signified trouble. Urgent wireless messages intensified over the A sets – with unexpected consequences.

Graham heard Blackstone's voice.

"Gamekeeper here. Enemy armoured column advancing down eastern approach road. Squadron regroup!"

"Homebrew and Woodpecker, prepare to resist counterattack!"

Steve recognised the voice of "Scoutmaster," the officer coordinating the petard/crocodile thrust in this sector. The same voice appeared to speak again.

"No counterattack. Squadron stand down and withdraw!"

"What?" exclaimed Graham, perplexed.

"Wilco, Scoutmaster, withdrawing as ordered," said another voice, followed by an expostulation from the real Scoutmaster.

"That's a Jerry, you great steaming clot! You're broadcasting on an open frequency. Counterattack still on, prepare to resist!"

The identical voice came back on the air, chilling Graham's blood.

"We're onto you, AVRE Delta One. We'll roast you to cinders next time."

"Not if I see you first, Boche!" the lieutenant snarled into his mike.

Blackstone's voice cut in.

"Calm down, Steve. Gamekeeper here. All troops listen in. Our own batteries'll see off the Boche. Stand by."

"Affirmative, Gamekeeper. Twenty-five pounders engaging. Homebrew and Woodpecker, stand by," said Scoutmaster in a mollified tone.

The counterattack was blunted and the Churchills withdrew as darkness wetly closed in, leaving the infantry sheltering under gas capes in slimy, hastily dug weapons pits to contend with snipers and infiltrators.

Despite the armoured help, they had sustained significant losses. Kinross was now the only officer in his battalion from its original cadre.

One Troop's sole casualty was Lieutenant Graham, who burnt his wrist on a hot exhaust pipe when helping with vehicle maintenance after the troop had leaguered for the night in another wasted cornfield.

"You ought to leave these jobs to us grease monkeys, sir," said Sergeant Crittenden as he wrapped a dressing around Graham's wrist.

After maintenance was completed, Graham hitched a ride to Squadron HQ, where he spent a few minutes with Tubby Potter. The enormity of so many souls, both friend and foe, thrust into eternity so quickly had suddenly pressed in grievously on the young lieutenant.

"Drop in on our lads, if you can find them," Winstanley called to Graham as the HQ jeep drove off. Steve was going to the divisional dump, where he would organise the delivery not only of ammunition and rations but also of spares, including tracks, for the AVREs were in dire need of new parts, having been hammered hard day in day out since the landing.

The battle rumbled and flickered to the east but the jeep splashed away in the opposite direction through laneways that were now ribbons of grey-black mud streaked with yellow.

"Wish you could keep on 'til Yorkshire," Graham said to the driver, Sapper Birkett. The day was cold, drizzly and overcast. Both men wore BDs and leather jerkins over their smocks.

"Drop me at Worksop, sir and you can have the jeep all to yourself," came the cheery reply.

When the logistics liaison was completed, they drove to the hospital complex near the Bayeux-Caen road, known as "Harley Street."

After making initial enquiries, Graham directed Birkett to park opposite a long, grey-brown marquee with Red Cross roundels painted on its canvas roof and an identification sign at its entrance.

"Not sure how long I'll be," Steve said as he climbed out.

"Take your time, sir," Birkett said casually, reaching for his newspaper and cigarettes. He then switched on the jeep's radio and tuned it to some dance music.

WIPE YOUR FEET! The sign said.

Graham obediently rubbed the soles of his hobnailed boots on the coarse matting placed before one of the hessian-covered, duck-boarded paths linking the hospital tents.

He made his way to a particular tent and on mounting the threshold, wiped his boots again. As he entered, he noted the warmth inside and the comforting atmosphere, the smell of iodoform notwithstanding. The tarpaulin-laid floor had been raised on wooden pallets to keep it dry.

Two lines of camp beds stretched as far as he could see, occupied by bandaged men in hospital blues, many with limbs splinted or in traction, some without a limb. MOs and orderlies moved amongst them – and nurses. Graham's heart leapt.

"Can I help you?" said a quiet feminine voice.

The speaker arose from a desk set back on Steve's left. She wore white head square, grey frock and cardigan. She was dark-haired, blue-eyed, Geordie and gorgeous.

Graham introduced himself.

"I've come to see two of my lads, if they're still here," he explained.

"Val Norwood," said the QA. She smiled and proffered her hand. Graham shook it gently, sensing the young woman's delicate skin. "Take a seat, Steve and I'll check," she added, indicating a camp chair by the desk.

Graham occupied the seat, whereupon he noticed a framed photograph standing on a blood box behind Sister Norwood. It displayed a uniformed officer with the distinctive hackle of the Royal Northumberland Fusiliers affixed to his beret.

To my darling Valerie, all my love, your Jamie, XXX, its inscription read.

Mentally crossing his name off the list of Sister Norwood's potential suitors, Graham gave her the details of his wounded comrades.

Val consulted the documents in front of her and confirmed the two were still on the ward.

"We've treated them for burns and Corporal Lennox will have the sight of one eye," she said gently. "The surgeon saved his arm but it will be partly paralysed, I'm afraid. We had to amputate Sapper Irvine's leg but he'll have a knee. I'll take you to them now."

Graham was almost tongue-tied when he stood by his crewmen's beds but the two sappers were nevertheless cheerful and most appreciative of the chocolate Steve brought them, though partaking of the cigarettes would have to wait.

"I'll save the fags for you," Sister Norwood promised. She helpfully did most of the talking.

"You shouldn't have to manage without us, sir," said Lennox. "Between us, we could make up one crew member, right, Reg?"

"Too right, Johnno," mumbled Irvine, his lips still swollen. "It's the experience that counts, sir."

Graham smiled and nodded, still finding speech difficult.

When the visit was over, he followed Sister Norwood back to her desk, trying not to glance at other patients who were heavily sedated and in a particularly bad way.

Steve was about to depart but the Sister restrained him.

"Hang on, Steve," she said. "I'll take a look at your wrist."

"It's nothing, Val."

"I knew you'd say that but I can change the dressing while you have a cup of tea."

She indicated a spirit burner with a compo brew on the go.

"An offer I can't refuse, Sister," said Graham, seating himself again.

Sister Norwood was unwrapping Steve's dressing when a slender, auburn-haired QA with her grey and scarlet cape over her shoulders swept past.

"See you in a bit, Val. They need some help in Resus," said the redhead, obviously a southerner. "You're in excellent hands, Lieutenant," she added with a wink as she departed. Graham thought that, like Val, the redhead was gorgeous.

"OK, Pippa," rejoined Sister Norwood. She applied some anti-burn cream to Graham's injury while he sipped his tea. "Philippa Conniston-Price," Val explained. "She'll be one of our equestrians at the next Olympics after the war, I reckon. Her fiancé's in the Royal Marines."

She expertly applied the new dressing and Graham deleted his name from another imaginary list of suitors.

"Your lads'll be going home in a few days," said Val, wiping some streaks of surplus cream off her fingers. "I'll write to their families as soon as I can. Your wrist'll be right in no time."

When he'd taken leave of Sister Norwood, Graham stood reflectively outside the tent for a short while.

He shrank from the prospect of suffering like the men on the ward.

But if that was what it cost to prevent Axis foes and their sadistic cronies; the Muslim Waffen SS[112], the Japs and their Jiff hangers-on, the Grand Mufti's Arab saboteurs[113], the mass rapist Goums in Italy[114] and the Soviets, Allies both but only by default, from getting their hands on girls like Val or Pippa, then so be it.

After securing the village, the Lowland Brigade and its sister Highland Brigades carried their attack to the next fortified town in their drive to the Odon River west of Caen, where leapfrogging assault forces captured the main bridge intact.

In the follow-up, Shermans were supposed to consolidate the bridgehead extending a couple miles beyond the crossing, around two key prominences each a few hundred feet high called Hills 112 and 113.

From there, it was another three miles to the River Orne. Once the Allies crossed it, British and Canadian forces east and west of Caen would converge on their opponents like two halves of a giant pincer and chase them down the Caen-Falaise road. There, fleeing towards the Seine, the foes would become easy prey for the fighter-bombers.

That was the plan.

In practice, the Scots' advance over three miles of scarred earth to the Odon and their efforts to punch the two-mile deep salient further into enemy territory, were so costly that the fighting became known as the battle of the Scottish Corridor. The name stuck, even after the Wessex and Welsh Divisions came in to relieve the Jocks.

Moreover, massive traffic jams prevented the AVREs from supporting the infantry attacks and when the Shermans did cross the Odon, the eighty-eight mm nemeses of the battlefield, invisible in the woods and orchards, hammered the leading tanks into scrap iron. A flight of Messerschmitts machine-gunned the surviving armour falling back across the Odon and shot up their thin-skinned logistic tail, adding substantially to the clusters of burnt-out tanks and lorries around the river.

The derelict Shermans became lairs for enemy snipers and a seventeen-pounder A/T gun had to be hauled up to eliminate them.

The advance to the Orne then metamorphosised into desperate battles of infantry and artillery attrition for Hills 112 and 113, augmented by rocket-firing Typhoons and rivalling in their intensity the Pyrrhic struggles for *Le Morte Homme*[115] at Verdun in 1916.

When troops of gun Churchills charged up Hill 113 to support the Lowland Brigade, eighty-eights hidden in fields of flax on the crest promptly reduced them to blazing hulks and the attrition went on.

From the end of June throughout most of July, convoys of ambulances ran the gauntlet of enemy guns and mortars across the Odon valley. Seeing them go past One Troop's leaguer, Graham reckoned that glam girls Val and Pippa would have their hands full.

Though the Allied persistence at least yielded the city of Caen, captured on July 9th.

However, Blackstone's squadron was often inactive during this period, apart from carrying out various bridging and gapping jobs, regular maintenance and essential repairs like replacing worn gun barrels and damaged engine or track parts. For the rest of the time, in the major's words:

"We sit here on our backsides and do sod all."

To make matters worse, one of the few forays undertaken at this time in anger led to the unfortunate loss of an AVRE to the enemy. The crew gallantly disabled a Panther tank with a petard while supporting an attack on a village but when they reversed to escape counter-attacking panzer grenadiers, the Churchill mounted a heap of rubble and overturned into an adjacent sunken lane. Though dazed and shaken, the crew managed to leg it but the Germans captured the AVRE.

Blackstone paraded the whole squadron and delivered a scathing harangue.

"The blasted Boche will know all about our kit now!" he declared fiercely[116].

Thankfully, the foe appeared to make no use of any information they had gleaned though as Winstanley said, "I think we all feel suitably chastened."

The squadron crossed the Odon in July, only to leaguer again behind a wrecked village, amongst piles of debris, because minefields ahead had not been cleared. For several days, the sappers were confined to the AVREs, in stifling heat, harried by mortars and occasionally snipers. Though these could not physically harm the buttoned-up crews, the continuous *"crash, crash"* of falling bombs and *"ping"* of bullets frayed their nerves.

Yet they coped as best they could.

Unable to establish the usual hessian-enclosed latrine pits, they used spent shell casings they'd scrounged and emptied them out the side door.

For the other, it was a case of "Got your spade? Right, out you go!" and a dash behind the nearest heap of rubble, trusting in the Churchills' bulk as protection against snipers.

Water was strictly rationed and in the heat they drank most of what they had, so while that stricture applied, the crews could neither shave nor wash, though Ferrarby produced a pair of scissors and gave everyone a respectable back and sides, including himself.

Sleeping, despite the heat, was less awkward than it might have been, because AVRE seats were padded, unlike those in other tanks that weren't called "bum-numbers" for nothing, with reference to feeling, not numeracy.

And with the aid of a pencil torch, Graham could at least continue his Bible reading, while the others were slumbering. He thought of Val and Pippa occasionally, to shut out his surroundings, including the lowbrow conversation of four fed-up blokes, although they all spent considerable time writing letters.

Then in early August, orders came to move. The mines had been cleared and the enemy forced back.

"We're heading for the Orne," Blackstone informed his command.

The members of One Troop shook off their lethargy and Graham packed away his Bible.

But the *bocage* slowed them down again and the AVREs crept along tight little lanes constricted on each side by the thickest hedges the sappers had seen in Normandy. No breeze stirred the thickets and the heat was oppressive.

In gathering darkness the squadron came to the battle line, a crescent of fire on the crest of rising ground, farmsteads, woodland and haystacks burning fiercely in the aftermath of the initial clashes. Graham and the others had heard the bickering of small arms from a mile back.

Blackstone convened his O Group by shaded hurricane lamp in the lee of Hannibal, his Churchill, wedged on the verge beside a farm gate.

Graham was delighted to see Kinross present, as liaison officer. They exchanged grins of recognition.

With a sharpened pencil point, Blackstone showed the way on the map.

"We go in at first light," he said.

Unfortunately, in the clinging mist of dawn, the leading AVREs got bogged in marshy ground. The Churchills following extricated them with tow hawsers but the element of surprise had gone and SS grenadiers, resisting viciously with hull-down tanks, Spandaus, moaning Minnies, bazookas and *panzerfausts*, cut up the attackers with gusto.

"Able Zero mined!"

Heart in mouth, Graham heard the shout over the A set, while waiting in reserve behind a bend in the approach road screening the action. The location made for gnawing anxiety punctuated by sudden calamities, many details of which only became known later.

An undetected Teller mine had blown a track off Hannibal, Blackstone's Churchill, effectively blocking the renewed advance.

Covering fire from the infantry and Horatio, the second HQ Churchill, enabled Hannibal's crew to evacuate, although Blackstone's driver and co-driver suffered compound fractures from the mine blast.

Another frantic voice surged through Graham's earphones, jangling his nerves afresh.

"Baker Zero gunned! Four bale outs!"

A seventy-seven-mm round from a hull-down Panther had brewed Horatio.

Then Graham heard Blackstone's voice, charged with frustration that he wholly shared.

"Squadron fall back under cover of smoke. Regroup at start line!"

Blackstone was using the A set from Hercules, his third HQ Churchill.

"Complete and utter balls-up," was the crews' consensus as they complied with the order.

Nevertheless, wild-eyed, stubbly-chinned, sweat-streaked Jocks clung tenaciously to half the collapsed brick and timber wasteland, so at least something had been gained, though their equally stubborn teenage opponents held fiercely to the other half.

Kinross, who'd survived again, tried to sound consolatory at the debriefing.

"As the bard said, lads, 'The best laid schemes o' mice an' men gang aft a-gley'[117]."

He then went to oversee his Jocks and didn't eat or sleep for the next thirty-six hours. Graham's squadron was at least able to spruce up and wash clothes.

For several days another stalemate ensued but other units captured an undamaged bridge across the Orne. Despite heavy German counterattacks that brewed up many Allied tanks, the bridgehead held.

Then came the final strokes.

One night, seemingly endless formations of four-engined Lancasters dropped thousands of tons of bombs on the approaches to Falaise, where the enemy was concentrating after falling back from Caen.

"Neil would like to have been up there," Graham remarked to Winstanley.

"He's done his share, Steve," said Don.

Together with their crews, they were watching the sky to the east shimmering in the glare of bomb burst and shell explosion from the artillery barrage augmenting the air raid.

The Germans held Falaise for a fortnight, under incessant bombardment. Then they began withdrawing eastwards, pounded relentlessly by the fighter-bombers until roads, lanes and fields were choked with smoking, shattered remains of vehicles, animals and men.

The enemy opposing Graham's squadron and the Jocks disappeared in the general retreat.

"They waded the Orne in the dark," Kinross reported.

The battle of Normandy was over.

No-one was more relieved than the local civilians, salvaging what they could from the wreckage of their homes, the citizens of Caen burying their dead in thousands. Remembering Madame de Richelet, Graham reflected that *"Les soldats Anglais"* were not perceived here as quite so *"bon"*.

In the meantime, Seventy-Ninth Armoured rendezvoused beyond the Orne.

"We're going to practice rafting and bridging, lads," Blackstone informed his command. All the AVRE squadrons were concentrating in a particular area east of the Orne for this purpose.

Unfortunately, they about to suffer again from the truth of "the best laid schemes."

Low-lying, rank with putrefying animal remains and a haven for flies, wasps and mosquitoes, the concentration area very soon afflicted the men worse than the Germans had. An epidemic of "Normandy Tummy," so-called, compounded by bouts of forewarned compo sickness, broke out and virtually everyone came down with stomach cramps and recurring diarrhoea.

"Troops at Agincourt had the runs," Winstanley gasped to Graham on one occasion when they emerged white-faced from the latrine. "Things aren't all that different."

"Dastardly Frog plot that the Boche borrowed," muttered Steve, glad for once that Val and Pippa were not present, however effective their ministrations might have been.

Several days of unremitting, heavy rain exacerbated the general discomfort but after hygiene units disinfected the area and regimental field kitchens were able to send up vacuum-packed, hot cooked meals more often, the ailments subsided.

When their training was complete, the AVRE squadrons swept in a triumphant procession northeast, along roads restored by Second Army sappers, through battered heaps of towns and villages, roaring past their bemused inhabitants, into virgin territory towards Rouen. Blackstone's squadron eventually concentrated in the spacious grounds of an undamaged chateau.

"We are about to astound the world with our unique talents once again, gentlemen," the major said at an O Group convened in the chateau's elaborate dining room. "Our job is to capture the Channel ports, starting with Le Havre."

After the O Group, Graham collected the letters for One Troop from the orderly room on the ground floor of the chateau. He noticed one addressed to himself, in unfamiliar handwriting.

It was from Lorraine Tyrell.

Dear Lieutenant Graham, it read.

I am writing to thank you very much for your most kind letter and to assure you that you and your men are always in my prayers. As you can imagine, I nearly screamed my head off when I got the telegram and I am still trying to come to terms with the fact that my husband is gone. I am staying with my mum at present. She has been such a wonderful support and since I'm working from dawn to dusk, just about, that has helped too.

We can only hope and pray that this terrible business will soon be over so our men can come back to the safety of home and loved ones.

Once again, thank you for your kind thoughts and prayers.

Yours sincerely,

Lorraine Tyrell

"Ask Bill Crittenden if he'd like to write to her," said Tubby Potter when Graham showed him the letter. "I know he's got a soft spot for her and so he won't put himself forward, of course. Just an idea."

Graham folded away the letter and went to look for his second-in-command.

Owing to the complexity of the Normandy operation, this section has occupied considerable space but events that would prove equally important for Grandma Colleen were taking place at almost the same time, far away in Burma.

Kachin Hills, autumn 1944.

Frank Mildenhall drew his pipe stem from his mouth. He turned from watching the hill men collecting the containers from an air drop and spoke to Waverly.

"Figure you should have your own column now, Pete," he said casually. "Detachment G, or DG they call themselves. They're operating under a local leader at present but with you, we can bring them under command and re-supply 'em regularly."

Waverly nodded. In the warmth of the afternoon sun, he gazed at the little men scurrying in among the spread out parachutes. His period of induction to the Kachins had ended with his successful mission to assess the strength and condition of the Japanese forces falling back from the Chindwin.

"Where are they, Frank?" he asked, removing his bush hat briefly to wipe his brow. The American withdrew a map from a case hooked to his belt. He took a bamboo sliver fastened to the map's edge by a small dog clip and pointed to a location where the contour lines were compressed close together.

"Here," he said. "It's a coupla days hike. Take Okey and Wes with you and two of the mules. Hector – that's the local leader – and his boys'll appreciate some extra ammo and medical supplies. Rough outfit but they gotta a good record against the Japs. I'll radio 'em to expect you."

Okey and Wes, to use their Anglicised names, were seasoned Kachin scouts and experienced mule handlers. Waverly was satisfied with the choice.

They trekked through the gloom of jungle and teak forest for two days. The monsoon rains made the ground slushy underfoot, hindering both men and mules, bringing out the insects and leeches in large numbers. Both animals and men suffered.

Nevertheless, urged on by Okey and Wes, the laden beasts waded obediently across slippery streambeds with the water swirling to their girths and plugged steadily up and down the intervening slopes. They made only the occasional snort. Mule Detachment veterinarians had severed their vocal cords to prevent braying that might have alerted the Japanese.

Sweltering in the heat, enclosed by the all-pervasive noise from jungle birds and tree creatures, Waverly felt his pack straps cutting, his binoculars banging his chest and his boots sinking in mire, perspiration streaming down his face and body. The grenades on his belt jarred against his elbows, his revolver holster, Ghurka *kukri* scabbard and other belt equipment rubbed against his hips and thighs. Determinedly, he put one foot forward and then the next, his eyes constantly following the movement of his carbine, up, down, right, left, searching the gloomy thicket for a possible ambush or sniper niche.

He was also on the lookout for lurking leopard or tiger.

"Advantages are all with them, Father," he murmured, too weary to be startled by the greenish snakes that slid away at his approach.

On the third day, the rain ceased but a cotton wool-like mist descended. Waverly's party advanced warily onto a ridge corresponding to DG's map reference and was challenged by two Kachin sentries. Known as Jesse and Moe, they eagerly exchanged greetings with Waverly's mule handlers.

"Ready for our next mission, sir," Moe said heartily to the major.

"Splendid," said Waverly, wishing he could lie down and sleep.

Jesse guided the newcomers into the encampment, the usual rows of thatched bamboo *bashas* set beneath overhanging trees, raised a few feet off the ground by means of teak posts, with platforms in front.

All at once, Waverly heard the sound of raised voices.

"What's all the row?" he asked.

"Two prisoners, sir," said Jesse. "Undergoing interrogation."

Thanks to missionary efforts, these Kachins spoke good English, though not all had embraced Christianity, as was apparent from the sight that greeted the major through the thinning veil of mist.

Waverly was appalled. He knew that Gestapo or Kempi Tai[118] interrogations could mean bamboo slivers under the finger or toenails. The Kachins had easier access to the devices and inserted them in a different place.

However, an overtly bloodier outcome seemed imminent in this "interrogation."

On the grass apron in front of one of the huts, several scouts were haranguing a terrified Japanese in mustard-coloured jungle fatigues and puttees, kneeling, with blood coursing from his nose and mouth. Another Kachin, his supple frame stripped to the waist, held aloft a bloody *dah*, with it having obviously sword-whipped the prisoner.

Now he intended it for a different purpose, one that was also obvious because a second Jap lay on the ground, face down, except that he was decapitated, a huge splash of blood staining the grass in front of the severed trunk. One of the Kachins, a youth, danced around, squealing with delight. He held high the gory head by its short-cropped hair.

Waverly sprinted to the scene. When the captors looked up at his approach, the major saw that the would-be double executioner possessed eye teeth filed to needle-like points, so that he resembled a swarthy, diminutive vampire.

"Hector, stop!" shouted the major peremptorily – for he reasoned the vampire must be his second-in-command.

Waverly aimed his carbine at the Kachin's chest.

"If you harm the prisoner any further, I will shoot you," Waverly said firmly.

The Englishman understood the brutality. Japs had invaded Kachin villages during the Allied retreat from Burma in 1942. With few weapons to protect themselves against overwhelming numbers armed with machine guns and supported by light tanks, the hill men had been massacred. The invaders raped any girls and women left alive, then hacked the genitals off the men and boys who hadn't escaped, leaving them to bleed to death. Some they skinned alive. Other survivors were herded into *bashas* that the Japanese then soaked in gasoline and torched[119]. Kachin loyalty to the Allies could still provoke similarly bestial reprisals.

Nevertheless, Waverly would not allow his command to degenerate into bandits and terrorists. Slicing the ears off Japs KIA as trophies and setting their heads on poles as symbols of victory were, in Waverly's view, practices sufficiently abhorrent. He wasn't about to condone worse. Murder had been done, but it would go no further.

The major didn't take his eyes off the little man with the razor-edged *dah*, poised over the cowering captive. Waverly would not back down, though he knew that the men of the village were in sufficient numbers to hack both him and the petrified Jap to mincemeat in minutes if they so chose.

They chose not to.

"This meat's exceptionally good," said Waverly. "What is it?"

They were seated on the matting-covered floor of Hector's *basha*. The womenfolk had prepared the midday meal for the scouts, who were using the village as their current base of operations. Most of the young men among the villagers served with DG.

With the meat came boiled rice and bamboo shoots. After weeks of American K rations, the meal was for Waverly a pleasant change.

"Python," said Hector succinctly. He grinned, flashing his vampire teeth as Waverly swallowed hard, nodded and forced a smile.

"Excellent," he said with a discreet cough and received another vampire grin.

After the initial *contretemps*, all had been smoothed over and the surviving Jap was on his way back to Mildenhall's encampment under close guard. Waverly had no doubts that the prisoner would arrive safely. Hector and he now understood each other.

DG was, above all, keen to augment its "good record against the Japs."

The Railroad Corridor, Mytkyina-Indaw, autumn, 1944.

During the spring and summer, men of many Allied nations had fought to seize the air-strip and railhead at Mytkyina, then force the Japanese back southward in order to capture the Mandalay-Mytkyina Railway, for a subsequent advance into the Irrawaddy Valley in support of Fourteenth Army.

The battle to secure the eighty-mile stretch of terrain from Pinbaw to Indaw, enclosing the rest of the "Railroad Corridor," was still in progress.

Throughout the months of the monsoon, Chinese artillerymen, British infantry of the Thirty-Sixth Division, British, Ghurka and West-African long range penetration Chindit brigades and the American 5307th Brigade, known as "Merrill's Marauders[120]," pushed doggedly forward, re-supplied by air drop. From hilltop fortress and thickly forested river line, their enemies resisted with characteristic fanaticism, retaliating with concentrated artillery and mortar fire, followed by savage banzai charges whenever the Allies tried to consolidate their gains.

Mauled repeatedly in such attacks, the Chindits and Marauders were withdrawn towards the end of summer. Hundreds of them were dead or wounded but thousands more had succumbed to malaria, dysentery, typhus and a plethora of other diseases. Less than half would ever be fit for active service again.

Kachin Rangers had been fully engaged throughout this period, scouting, patrolling, raiding and setting up ambushes, protecting the flanks of the larger forces, frequently in hand-to-hand encounters with the Japanese. Both they and their OSS supervisors[121] had suffered losses.

That was how Waverly, though still SOE, came to be under command of Oklahoman Colonel Frank Mildenhall.

After his initiation to jungle warfare at the training centre in wild, scrubby country around Deogarh in India, Waverly was flown by C-47 to the American's base in the Kachin Hills, where he parachuted in at the head of a supply drop, carried out during a break in the weather.

Landing with a thump in grassy earth, he quickly removed his harness and glanced round at the jungle fringe, inserting a full magazine into his carbine and briskly folding his canopy while keeping an eye out for descending containers, especially any that might have "candled"[122].

Waverly observed the rangy American in bedraggled fatigues striding towards him. Mildenhall was also grasping an M1 carbine.

"Not only manna from heaven, but today a British major," he said, a grin creasing his craggy features. "I'm Frank Mildenhall. Glad to meet ya, Pete."

The two shook hands warmly.

"Ready to go over the form, Frank," said Waverly as he gathered up his weapon and pack.

"All in good time, buddy. Let's have some coffee first."

Waverly mused on these things while he lay concealed in elephant grass, index finger against the trigger guard of his M1, alert for the first sign of movement down the trail. Beads of perspiration trickled down his forehead and dripped onto the stock of his weapon. The mist had lifted but not the heat. Weak sunlight filtered through the thick tree crowns above.

Insects buzzed close and ants crawled on him but the major stayed motionless, fearful of the slightest movement that would betray his presence.

Hector, Okey, Wes and the rest of the patrol were also hidden in the undergrowth, deployed for best fields of fire. Jesse and Moe each manned an LMG to enfilade the trail.

This intended ambush was one of many the Kachins were conducting. Their aim was to harass the enemy patrols protecting the railway. Here it cut through a gully the nearer crest of which ran about fifty yards to the right of Waverly's position.

Waverly held his breath. He could see the lead scout, stepping warily along the track, brown face visible beneath his pot helmet camouflaged with foliage, rifle and bayonet poised.

The major waited until the lead scout was only yards away, his sharp oriental visage clearly discernible.

Waverly fired twice. The carbine's reports sounded obscenely loud in the heavy, still air.

The bullets struck the Japanese in the chest. He lurched backwards and a crescendo of gunfire broke out from the rangers' concealed positions, scything down many of the patrol members, who collapsed shocked and screaming. Others flung themselves into the brush on either side of the trail, some shrieking as they fell impaled on the *pungyi* sticks, planted invisibly in the jungle growth. These two-foot long bamboo stakes were fire polished to the hardness of steel and as sharp as a Kachin *dah*.

"DG withdraw!" shouted Waverly above the din.

He leapt to his feet to count the rangers as they dashed past to regroup on a wooded knoll about a quarter of a mile to the southwest. They had inflicted enough damage. Waverly estimated that twenty Japanese lay dead or dying.

He intended to reconnoitre further into what was still enemy territory, coordinating his probings with those of Mildenhall's and other Kachin columns. That was another reason to vacate the scene of action promptly.

But they were too late.

"Banzai! Banzai!"

A second Japanese patrol was bearing down on Waverly's men from his left flank. Inwardly he cursed. His flanking scouts must have been overwhelmed before they could raise the alarm. He could see the pot-helmeted figures charging between the trees, shouting in frenzy, brandishing rifles and bayonets, officers and NCOs with Samurai swords or SMGs they fired from the hip. Bullets cracked and zipped past him. One or two scouts tumbled over, crying in pain.

"Grenade!"

Even as he shouted the warning, Waverly had torn the pin from a 36M and hurled the device thirty yards at the nearest Japanese, the striker lever flipping away with its characteristic "ping." On either side of him, the Kachins were doing likewise. More shouts of "Grenade!" filled the air, more striker levers pinged away and a score of knurled objects thudded onto the forest floor in the path of the enemy.

A line of smoky brown, yellow-flamed explosions with their defiant *"bangs"* momentarily obscured the attackers.

Some fell, crying in anguish but the survivors came on until bayonet and Samurai sword clashed chillingly with *dah* blade and carbine stock. Horror-struck, Waverly saw a Jap cut Okey down at point-blank range with a sub-machine gun. Moe's LMG thundered and Okey's assailant died. In the same instant, Waverly warded off a bayonet thrust and shot his frenzied attacker in the midriff. Hector slashed at a Samurai-wielding Jap officer, who sprawled to earth thrashing in death throes, blood and brain oozing from where Hector's *dah* had split his head like a melon.

"Rearguard, to me!" shouted Waverly.

Hector, Moe and Wes rallied about their officer to hold off the rest of the Japanese and enable their comrades to escape. Led by Jesse, the able-bodied rangers half dragged, half carried the casualties, who strove to stifle their groans of anguish.

Three of the wounded, including Okey, lay where they had fallen, too seriously injured to be moved, their blood spreading onto the ground.

For several minutes, Waverly's rearguard blazed away at the foes, who, seeing the slaughter inflicted on the initial wave, had taken cover. Hector, braving the enemies' sniper fire, elbowed to the seriously wounded and pressed a plug of concentrated opium paste into each man's mouth. It was stronger than morphine and highly addictive, though that wouldn't matter.

"Disengage on my signal!" Waverly called to the others.

They had to be quick, before enemy reinforcements came up. Their fusillade of counter fire had kept the Japs' heads down but ammunition was getting low.

From behind the tree stump where he'd taken cover, Hector turned to the major, his brown, battle-begrimed face streaked with tears.

"I will see to our friends, sir," he said.

"No, Hector," said Waverly. "I will do it."

It was imperative that the Japanese did not find any of the wounded alive.

The Kachins poured another huge volley of semi and fully automatic fire at the Japs from their M1s and Moe's LMG. Forcing down his anguish, Waverly crawled rapidly to each of the badly wounded rangers and dispatched them in turn with a single shot to the head from his Webley revolver.

Then, alternatively firing and moving in pairs, the rearguard made its getaway. Waverly was distressed they had to leave their dead.

"Good work, Pete," Mildenhall's voice came crackling through the earphones in response to Waverly's report of the ambush. "Yeah, sorry about the boys. We'll send some mules for the others, then meet up as planned for the next drop. So long, buddy."

Waverly took off the earphones and gave them back to Wes, who packed away the set. Durable, reliable and even with its batteries a light load, the radio was Wes's pride and joy.

Dug in among the boulders and tangled tree roots that interlaced their pre-determined hill-top position, the rangers stripped, cleaned and reassembled their weapons. The casualties' wounds had been dressed and they were being kept quiet with small amounts of the opium paste that Hector had administered earlier. Tomorrow, as soon as the mules arrived, they would all vacate the knoll.

As was customary, the men assisted each other to remove leeches from their limbs, bodies and the backs of their necks.

"We'll use salt, sir," Hector said, flashing his eye teeth. "No cigarette lights."

The rangers then partook of their K rations, so Waverly returned to his fire trench to break open one of his own packs. He would have appreciated a wash and a shave but neither was feasible

He hoped to get some new footwear from the drop. His boots were wearing out and one's feet were perpetually damp in the current climate, bringing problems of fungal infection in addition to everything else and requiring the application of copious amounts of anti-fungal powder. "Too bad you can't run around barefoot like us, sir," Hector had remarked in his toothy way. Kachin feet had soles like rhinoceros hide.

"Get your head down for a couple of hours, Wes," Waverly said to his wireless operator. "Then we'll go refill the *chagals*."

A stream meandered past the base of the knoll.

"Kraits and cobras be thirsty by then, sir," the little man warned, grinning crookedly.

"As long as they don't crawl into the *chagals*, Wes," Waverly said with a tired smile. But they would have to be careful, nevertheless. Anti-venine was scarce and a bite from either reptile brought death in twenty minutes.

In the meantime, Waverly planned to get a couple of hours' sleep himself. He placed his carbine between his knees and leaning back against the dirt wall of the pit, reflected on the day's events before nodding off.

Five dead, including the two flanking scouts. Another six wounded, though they should recover if the mules could transport them along the twisting jungle trails and across the *chaungs* still swollen by the monsoon rains to the nearest RAP.

And if they didn't see any Japanese – for the campaign was often a desperate game of hide-and-seek in the all-encompassing wilderness.

But the rangers had written off a platoon of the enemy. They'd not had time to check the dead but that was a fair estimate. And Waverly could make good his losses from his reserves.

Yet he had much to ponder, in preparation for the next sortie.

Should he have used more men? Should he have positioned more flanking scouts? What was the likelihood of more enemy patrols on parallel axes?

Much depended on training and they would need time to train the replacements, most of whom would be virtually adolescent boys. How much time could they afford?

As usual, his thoughts eventually converged on a name.

"Collette," he whispered. The gentle sound seemed to palliate the day's ghastly experiences.

But she was a shade, like the numberless jungle shadows around him. His faith notwithstanding – for it was constant – he had never felt so alone.

Many miles to the south another operation was taking place that also needed a trained contingent.

Ten

To the Chindwin

Chin Hills, Burma, autumn, 1944.

Following Lance Corporal Wood, Trish, Gwen and Robyn waded across the slow-flowing stream, the mule handlers and their beasts bringing up the rear.

"Nice and cool," remarked Gwen.

"No crocodiles," muttered Trish.

They reached the other side without mishap but Robyn accidentally disturbed a nest of black scorpions when she nudged a piece of driftwood partly sunk into the grey-brown sand sloping up from the water's edge. The scaly, shiny arachnids scuttled to the shelf of grassy earth overhanging the bank.

"Ugh," said Gwen. "Glad we don't have them in Llangollen."

"From now on, check your boots every time you put them back on, not just in the mornings," Robyn advised, as they strolled over to where Wood was hacking at some bamboo trunks with his machete. The trunks were up to six inches across.

"Widen the trail out for the mules," the corporal grunted in between slashes at the stubborn green stalks. His face was already glistening.

"We'll help," said Trish. She stripped off her pack and pulled her machete out of the scabbard attached to it. Her companions did likewise, although, like the corporal, they kept their Stens slung across their shoulders.

"Aye," said Wood, hardly pausing between strokes. "Hit the trunk at right angles, in the shaft, Sister, not that knuckle-type joint, else blade'll glance off, see? That's it, you're deein' canny, Sister," he said when Trish took a firm but cautious strike at the stalks on the other side of the trail. "Mind out for kraits[123], like. They get in the bamboo. And watch when you cut that young stuff. Splits with a razor's edge, it does."

The mule handlers, some of Wood's fellow orderlies, were impressed at the sight.

"You're doin' a grand job, Sisters. You too, Corporal."

"You'll have a track like the Great North Road in no time, ladies."

"Can we have a smoke, Woody?"

"Why-aye, Donny, man! We've not halted, like," exclaimed Wood. He aimed another expert blow at the springy growth while wiping his forehead. "Temporary obstruction, this. Oh,

197

you'll have to hack it top and bottom, Sisters," he added. "It's too tangled at the top to fall over if you only cut it at the base, like."

After forty-five minutes of bamboo bashing, at which all took turns after the mules were tethered, Trish felt her head swimming. She was soaked in perspiration that evaporated unnaturally slowly, owing to the rank humidity of the still air and the oily film of insect repellent on her face, neck and forearms. Her arm muscles ached and the palms of her hands were stinging from broken blisters raised by the chopping.

Wood extracted a block of whetstone from his pack.

"Give us your blades, ladies and we'll re-sharpen 'em," he said "You might as well have a smoke, lads," he told the other orderlies, who were also reaching for their sharpening stones.

Wood and his mates sat on their bedrolls by the side of the trail re-honing the machetes, conversing casually with lit cigarettes dangling from their lips. The girls seated themselves on a fallen log and swallowed a few mouthfuls of chlorine-tasting water from their bottles. Robyn, the farmer's daughter, voiced her admiration for the men's technique.

"Spit 'n stone," she remarked. "Like my dad uses. Now, where's that gentian, so these blisters don't get pus?" She twisted around to sift through the contents of her pack.

"Use mine," said Trish. She handed a phial to Robyn, who applied some of the violet liquid and passed the bottle to Gwen. On receiving it back, Trish then dabbed the medication onto her own raw skin.

"Good for the prickly heat, too," Robyn murmured. "We'll have patches of it under the armpits."

"We'll look like Boadicea's warriors," said Gwen with a laugh. "Covered in woad."

"Time to go, ladies," Wood announced, returning their machetes. He and his mates didn't need any gentian. They seemed to have palms like leather.

They took up their packs and plodded along behind Wood through a tunnel of green. Shrill bird and insect noises enveloped them. Mottled sunlight streamed through the breaks in the tree canopies.

"We've hardly started and I'm worn out," gasped Gwen. She flexed her shoulders against the weight of her pack. "I'll burst if I get any hotter."

"Probably best to down sleeves," Robyn suggested. "Stop some of the cuts." Thorns and prickles from overhanging bushes were tearing at their arms.

The trail was considerably overgrown. Each member of the party kept a safe distance from the person in front, in order not to get slapped in the face by branches springing back. Using their hands to assist with climbing by clinging onto the saplings by the track, they pushed through twisted vine curtains that hung like matted ropes, each strand as thick as a finger, and clambered over twisted, mossy tree roots strewn in the way like natural hoops. Repeatedly they had to detach themselves from "wait-awhile" creepers that dug barbed tufts into their packs or shoulders. Insects buzzed about them incessantly.

"They seem to like this repellent," Trish said to Gwen and Robyn.

And despite the protection of their bush hats, the girls felt leeches dropping onto the napes of their necks, apparently from every nook and cranny in the dank undergrowth, and wriggling down inside their shirts. Trish knew the little fiends were probably also feasting on her feet, having elongated themselves to squirm through her boot eyelets. You couldn't feel them feeding, because they anaesthetised the incisions.

"Half a dozen on you I can see," Gwen told Robyn. "They're definitely down your back. There's a patch of blood under your pack."

"Little perishers," said Robyn. "I hope they all get mepacrine sickness[124]."

Occasionally they got on the girls' faces. You had to be quick to dislodge them because any bite left a little scar that persisted for months.

Trish bit savagely onto one intruder that landed on her cheek and tried to crawl into her mouth.

"Pests," she muttered and spat out the loathsome remnants that resembled bits of slimy black rubber.

They trekked on up the gloomy slope, past thickets of lantana, teak, bamboo, elephant grass and other types of growth that the girls couldn't name but thought of only as a living prison with the smell of compost. They slipped and staggered as their boots sank into leafy mould and viscid mud. Muttered comment issued from behind as the mule handlers encouraged their laden beasts forward. Most of it was sanitised, out of respect for the Sisters.

"Like Christian's burden, this," panted Robyn in reference to her pack. "Something's digging into my ribs."

"Let's hope we get to the wicket gate, soon," said Trish, breathing heavily.

She looked up sharply at the sudden hiss. Through a film of sweat, she saw the descending sweep of Wood's machete take the hooded head clean off a risen cobra. The corporal flicked the body to one side and wiped the blade on some grass.

"Nivver mind, ladies," he called over his shoulder. "It's only an ordinary one. No more than eight or nine feet long. The kings're twice as big. Most of 'em slip off when they hear us coming. Not often they stand their ground, like."

"So much for Nag[125]," muttered Robyn as they circumvented the writhing remains.

"Watch out for Nageena[125]," whispered Trish.

Wood called a halt a little later, when they came to a rocky clearing. He and Donny soon had a spirit burner going for a brew of compo tea.

"About another hour to the top, ladies," the corporal said. "We're through the worst of the scrub by the looks."

The orderlies started getting the leeches off the mules. Their fetlocks were glistening where the bloodsuckers had attached themselves. The handlers dislodged them by rubbing in tobacco.

In addition to removing their packs, shirts and boots, the girls stripped off their string vests and went after their unwelcome guests with lighted cigarette ends, assisting each other. Wood and the other males chivalrously looked the other way – while similarly ridding themselves of the vermin after having seen to the mules.

"I like jabbing 'em in the behind with a glowing end," said Trish maliciously.

"Well, there's the vicar's daughter for you," Gwen remarked to Robyn as she pulled off a sock blotched with blood from leech bites. "Repressed pyromaniac."

"Ow, my aching back," said Robyn with a grimace, sitting bolt upright on her rock. "We'll need to do some washing. Our shirts look like we've been wrestling with Count Dracula." She looked distastefully at the red patches in the material.

"The little beggars inject you with an anti-coagulant," Gwen remarked. "I'll get out the alum."

Driblets of blood were running down their bodies and intermingling with the perspiration. Gwen retrieved a bottle of crystalline substance from her pack. They helped each other apply it after they'd got the leeches off.

"We might have them where we can't get at them now," said Trish when they had dressed again. "Though I can't see any blood there."

"That reminds me. We should take it in turns behind a bush," murmured Gwen. "Serves those little blighters right if they get drowned in the process."

"Forceps work OK, or even bamboo slivers. On blokes, too," said Robyn with a grin. Trish grimaced.

"They can sort themselves out," she said, standing up. "Mind if I go first?"

"Be our guest but watch you don't get bitten by red ants or anything," Robyn warned. "Don't forget your Sten."

"Brew's up, ladies," said the lance corporal, who courteously refrained from looking over his shoulder.

"Let's have a look at that, Donny," said Trish when they all gathered around for tea. Though blister proof, the orderlies' hands had suffered abrasions from the mules jerking their heads and pulling roughly on the halters to chew on bamboo leaves. Trish and her companions cleaned and dressed the injuries.

"Champion, Sister, thanks," said each of the men in response.

Rain began to fall when they set off again, the drops pattering on countless leaves.

"It'll help wash the blood off," said Gwen stoically.

Through streaming rain and clammy mist, Trish saw two figures approaching as Wood's party neared the reverse side of the crest. The forest still pressed in on them but she could discern the dim outline of the ridge summit.

She paused to lean against a nearby teak trunk and breathed deeply. They'd been taught to walk up and down hills carrying loads by taking the weight on their thighs but her legs were wobbly nevertheless and she still felt trapped in an open-air greenhouse with the humidity turned full on. Perspiration continued trickling down her face and chest.

Robyn glanced at her watch, exhaling in gasps.

"Four and a half hours, allowing for the bamboo bashing," she said. "The CO was about right."

The two figures spoke briefly to Wood, then came over to Trish and her companions. They wore tattered, sweat-stained JGs and broad-brimmed bush hats. Their boots and puttees were mud-caked, scored and scuffed. Each man was heavily moustached and carried a Sten gun. One was of medium build with gingery hair, the other broad-shouldered and brown-haired. Their epaulettes bore no insignia of rank and Trish immediately noticed how under-nourished they were.

"I'm Colonel Keith Bedser, Sisters, battalion CO. Very glad you're here," said Ginger. His voice sounded tired. "This is Major Trevor Hudson, battalion medical officer," he added, nodding to his companion.

"Ladies," said Hudson and respectfully tapped the brim of his hat.

"We've concentrated the typhus cases in some dugouts just up the slope there," Bedser explained after introductions had been completed. "Took a risk, bringing 'em from all parts of the crest – it runs north-south and goes for quite a way – but it'll make your job easier."

"Thank you, sir. Can we see them now?" Gwen asked, flexing her shoulders against her pack again. The CO nodded.

"Trev'll show you the form, Sisters," he said. "I'm off to visit our positions. Again, very glad you're here."

Touching the brim of his hat, he moved away through the trees to where he was joined by two other Sten-toting troops who materialised out of the mist and rain.

"This way, folks," said Hudson. He gestured up the slope and the party followed him across a carpet of fallen leaves to what looked like a bus shelter cut into the ridge, using stout teak poles for vertical supports. A bank of rocky earth was piled up along its length about waist high and two sheets of tarpaulin screened the interior. The dugout nestled beneath an extended bluff topped by trees and bamboo thicket.

Hudson pulled one of the tarpaulins aside.

"Corporal Proctor," he said.

A muscular man in shirtsleeves, about five and a half feet in height, with shaven head, emerged.

"Show Corporal Wood where they can unload and tether the mules," the MO ordered. "And where they can set up their tent under the bluff."

"Yes, sir," said Proctor. "Over here, lads."

Trish thought she detected a Brummie accent. Hudson's orderly helped Wood and the others to guide the mules to some makeshift stables, also partially cut into the slope, with natural protection afforded by large boulders.

To Trish, the area appeared to have been hacked fairly recently out of virgin jungle. The rain was easing and some distance away, through the gathering dusk and curtain of drizzle, she discerned several crosses, constructed of bamboo. She silently prayed, Father, may we not lose any more.

"Drop your packs inside here for now, Sisters," said Hudson. He leant his Sten against one of the teak supports, held aside the tarpaulin again and conducted the girls inside the shelter.

"We've brought medicines, Trev," said Trish. "Extra rations as well."

The MO beamed.

"Marvellous," he said. "We've got another dugout for a field kitchen. Sappers blasted it out with explosives, you see, like the ward here. Up 'til now, we've only been able to give scratch meals to the lads."

The shelter was sturdily raftered with thick bamboo stems pinioned by pairs of teak trunks set at right angles to them, slotted and fastened into teak supports sunk into the ground. The walls were braced with more bamboo poles and backed with corrugated iron sheets. Additional sheets served as a ceiling. A couple of flickering hurricane lamps, affixed to the rafters in gaps between the corrugated iron, revealed a line of patients lying on stretchers the ends of which were balanced on forked teak sticks sunk into the earth. Mosquito nets, slung from the rafters, were draped over the convalescents and their boots were placed under their beds, together with a haversack containing personal possessions. They were unshaven and hollow-eyed, with sunken cheeks, naked apart from under shorts. Even through the nets, Trish could easily make out the reddish-brown rash characteristic of the men's affliction. Several moaned in delirium, turning restlessly on their beds. All were doubtless running high temperatures.

"We burnt their clothes to get rid of the bugs," Hudson explained. "Then did a whip-around for extra under shorts. The CO's ordered replacement clothing. Should arrive any day by air drop."

The air smelt of paraffin, sweat and bodily secretions. Tarpaulins and hessian covered the floor, except where the bed supports were inserted. A variety of containers stood in several empty medicine boxes arranged as shelves. Among the containers were the men's mess tins, their KFSs in a heap beside them. Other empty crates were close by, to serve as table and chairs.

"What's that?" Robyn asked. She pointed to a pile of objects in a corner at the rear of the dugout, covered by a frayed piece of crumpled canvas.

"More empty tins, Sister, for patients' personal needs," said the MO. "Some of them have got a touch of dysentery. We disinfected the tins with carbolic and brought 'em in out of the rain to keep down the rust. Men's latrine is on the edge of the perimeter past the stables. You'll find yours on the opposite side, by the way."

"Thanks, Trev," said Gwen. "We brought plenty of carbolic with us - and quinine."

"And chloride of lime," Robyn added, wrinkling her nose.

"Great," said Trev appreciatively. "We've only had mepacrine tabs up 'til now and as you can see, all of 'em have got sores – ulcers almost down to the bone in some cases."

Muffled explosions and the unmistakable popping of small arms sounded from above.

"Evening stonk," said the MO, grinning as the Sisters looked up. "We dug the ward in to avoid mortar bombs and set up the bank outside to help stop splinters – CO wanted proper shelters and the lads worked like Trojans. We got the corrugated iron from a deserted village up top. Your quarters're dug in the same way – except for the latrine. We've got another couple of wards like this, a bit further around the ridge, so I guess you'll take one each."

"You have this one, Gwen," Robyn suggested.

"OK by me," said Trish.

Gwen smiled her thanks and her friends helped her transfer several medicine bottles from her pack to the boxed shelves.

"How far away are the Japs, Trev?" asked Gwen. She extracted IV drip components from her haversack and placed them on a spare box.

"Beyond our lads, Sister," Hudson said reassuringly. "The crest is fairly spread out. Tojo's on the other side, holed up in bunkers. Probably need some Hurris to shift 'em."

Trish and Gwen glanced at Robyn, who raised her eyebrows.

"What about battle casualties, Trev?" Robyn asked.

"I've got a separate RAP now," Hudson explained. "As soon as we can, we send them back by mule to the CCSs. I'm more concerned about these chaps here for now, though. It'll be touch and go with some of them but as soon as we see the Japs off, we can get these lads back by a jeep track on the far side of the ridge, when they can be moved. Ah, here's your orderly. I'll get back to the RAP."

As he left, Hudson held back the tarpaulin to admit Corporal Wood, who was carrying one of the primus stoves brought via the mules, together with a can of paraffin.

"Have it going in no time, Sisters," he said cheerfully. "I'll set up a couple in your kitchen after this. Lads're putting them in the other wards."

"Better dab these blisters with gentian again when we can," said Robyn. "And cover 'em with Elastoplasts. I'm glad Trev didn't put us on a charge for SIWs."

She and Trish started collecting the tins in the corner, using the canvas cover as a sack.

"These go outside," said Trish between gritted teeth. "Rust or no rust."

Wood got the burners alight and left to install the stoves in the field kitchen. Gwen poured water from her *chagal* into two enamelled bowls she selected from the shelves and placed them on the stove.

"Glad we brought loads of loo paper," said Robyn when they returned from depositing the tins. "Can't waste time collecting grass."

Gwen dissolved flakes of Sunlight soap in one of the bowls for washing her hands and let the other come to the boil to sterilise the syringes for the IV drips.

"We should boil up all the dixies and KFSs too," she remarked.

"And break out the carbolic for those *other* containers," Robyn added.

The three of them briefly reviewed their plan of campaign as Gwen scrubbed her finger-nails and dried her hands on a square of towelling.

"So, it's temperature, pulse and respiration rate and quinine drips with an alcohol bath," she said in sum.

"And note it all down," Trish added.

"OK, we'll get along then," said Robyn.

They departed and Gwen went over to the nearest patient. She lifted the net and he stared at her in amazement.

"Nurses?" the man gasped, almost inaudibly. Even those lying closest to the entrance were too debilitated to notice the girls as they came in.

"Yes, mate," Gwen whispered. "Nurses, and we're going to get you better."

The expression on the sick man's face told all.

'Sister's here. We'll be all right, now.'

Trish and Robyn cleared the lavatory containers from the other wards and turned to their individual responsibilities.

Trish deposited her pack, bedroll, haversack and weapon at one end of her ward, made preparation as Gwen had done and began the treatment, sponging the men with alcohol to help stabilise their temperatures.

She noted again how weakened they looked and she was particularly anxious about the shallow breathing of some. However, these patients too were delighted by the arrival of real nursing Sisters.

Wood came in with a can of paraffin to replenish the stove. Donny and the others were helping Gwen and Robyn.

"Whenever you're ready for the drips or whatever, Sister," he said. "Proctor'll be here in a bit to help."

"Thanks, Woody. I decided to do the baths first," said Trish. "Then we'll follow up with TPRs and drips." She applied her sponge to a patient's chest and he smiled crookedly. "We'll get you well, mate," she said encouragingly, eliciting another smile.

"We'll start preparing some broths for them as soon as we can," Trish said to her orderlies when the initial tasks were completed. "Use nasal drips if we have to. We have to keep up their fluid intake – even if it's only with compo tea."

The occasional muffled explosions from the crest suddenly intensified into a continuous chain and the thuds reverberated through the earth. Clods of earth spilled down from between the iron sheets. Some of the patients became agitated so Trish and the others went to calm them.

"Our lads and the Nips chuck grenades at each other after dark," Proctor informed Trish. "Hundreds of 'em."

"Sounds like they're really getting stuck in," said Trish, trying not to sound anxious.

"Aye, same as at Kohima," Wood added nonchalantly. "Could gan on all night."

The girls decided on a watch system of three-hourly shifts during the night and at any time, two of them would be resting in their dugout. Colonel Bedser was adamant in this respect.

"Any of the lads would volunteer to keep you company," he said when he visited them again after inspecting the battalion positions. "But that's not quite the form."

With the orderlies' help, Trish gave the patients each a dose of sulphonamide as a precaution against dysentery and applied gentian and sulfa powder to their sores, many of which were suppurating and, as Hudson had said, penetrating to the bone.

She then inspected the field kitchen dugout, adjacent to the wards.

It was rudimentary, consisting of metal ammunition boxes for the spirit burners and for use as working surfaces or seats. The orderlies had stacked the compo ration boxes close by and, for safety, stored the kerosene cans outside. Wood had assembled two stoves and they were ready for firing. The dugout would double as a laundry. A couple of paraffin lamps were available for lighting by night.

Robyn came in, carrying a couple of caterers' dixies in which to do the cooking and a *chagal* of water. Gwen was overseeing all three wards, with the help of orderlies.

"Right, let's get on," said Trish. She carefully ignited the stoves. "Slice everything as small as we can for making gruel – I've marked those boxes for working surfaces. Only wish we had something better than compo rations."

"I asked Trev about that," Robyn said as she began opening one of the compo boxes. "He's arranging to get extras from the locals."

"That's good," said Trish. She peeled open a tin of bully by means of its metal key. "And we'll use some of the clean containers for giving the lads a proper wash tomorrow."

"They smell like they could use it," said Robyn.

Several hours later, they had cooked the patients' meals, fed them, sedated them so they wouldn't dislodge the IV drips by tossing in their sleep, washed up and organised all the utensils, washed themselves and their clothes using their canvas buckets and changed into spare garments that had stayed relatively dry, wrapped in gas capes in their packs. They tipped the used washing water into the scrub and piled up the cooking waste for incineration.

"Burn it whenever you like, ladies," Hudson had said. "Japs won't see the fire at night from their positions – crest is too high. Any tins you don't want to save, too. The lads'll bash and bury 'em."

"Use these for sleeping in," said Gwen about the dry clothes, as the Sisters prepared their own meal. "We'll probably be wet most of the day while the monsoon's on."

"If we hang the others up in the sleeping dugout, they'll be damp-dry by morning," Robyn suggested, pouring compo tea into three mugs. "It's still pretty warm."

"Has anyone used our loo, yet?" asked Gwen. She was stirring a large dixieful of beef and veg compo stew. Her washed socks were tied around the metal handle as insulation, for lifting the container off the blue paraffin flame when the stew was ready.

"Bamboo arrangement over a hole," Trish informed her. "Quite functional. Lads put tarpaulin around it and they've set up a string connecting it with our quarters, so you won't have to use your torch until you're inside. There's an ammo box with chloride of lime in it, too, courtesy of the MO. Take your own loo paper."

She began breaking out hard-tack biscuits.

"And your Sten," said Robyn brightly, placing a tin of treacle pudding in a simmering bowl of water. "Mind out for snakes, although they'll probably scarper when they hear you coming. At least we won't get rained on for a bit. It seems to have stopped."

Trish rinsed their utensils in scalding water.

"Just as well," she said. "The loo hasn't got a roof, so wear your mac."

"Keep that rinse water for washing up afterwards," Robyn suggested.

"I hope I can mostly go late at night. More privacy, you know," said Gwen, as she doled out the stew.

"Thanks, Gwen," said Trish and dipped her spoon in the concoction. "Less likely to get stonked, as well. But we better go in pairs after dark."

The others agreed.

"It would be safer," Gwen acknowledged.

"We'll just have to synchronise ourselves," said Robyn.

They had finished giving thanks when a voice sounded from outside.

"Sisters, Corporal Wood here. I'll sort your Stens for you. Have 'em back in a jiffy. Everything's quiet on the ward. Proctor's there."

"Here they are, Woody," said Robyn. She handed him the weapons through the tarpaulin. He would strip, clean and reassemble them, then transfer the rounds into fresh magazines to prevent the springs from weakening.

"Nasty little contraptions," said Gwen with distaste. "My Dai says if they jam and that bolt thing comes forward while you're trying to clear it, it can take the tops of your fingers off."

Robyn dipped a biscuit in her stew and eyed her other hand, fingers splayed.

"Wouldn't do your nails any good, that," she remarked.

After supper, they burnt the waste among rocks behind the kitchen.

"Not too much," Robyn advised when Trish tipped on some paraffin before starting the fire. "Don't want third degree burns."

"Hot bunking," said Robyn, on inspection of the interior of their sleeping dugout. "I'll see you around zero three hundred, Trish – or sooner, if there's a crisis. Proctor'll fetch you." It was nearly midnight.

Two stretchers, arranged like those of the patients', stood side-by-side on canvas mats. The orderlies had transferred the Sisters' gear into their quarters and unfurled their bedrolls. Bedser's men had laid rock fragments beneath the tarpaulin to help keep the floor dry.

"They've done a marvellous job all round," Trish remarked. "For medical wards, I think we're better kitted out than we would be at Imphal."

This was paradoxically true. Medical units close to the front were often well equipped compared to those further back that were becoming backwaters as the fighting progressed.

Gwen and Trish looped parachute cord over the bamboo rafters, hung out the washing, arranged their bedrolls on the stretchers and strung mosquito nets.

Before turning in, they brushed their teeth, combed their hair, spread lotion over their blisters and applied face cream.

"I'll leave the cream out for you, Robbie," said Gwen.

"Thanks, Taff," said Robyn as she departed for her shift, with the usual refrain:

"Mind you keep those Stens handy."

Wood had serviced and returned the weapons.

"I'd rather have Dai," Gwen murmured wistfully.

"I'm glad you haven't," retorted Trish, stretching herself on top of her bedroll and yawning. "I'd have to sleep in the kitchen with all the pots and pans."

For the next couple of days, their routine was undisturbed but on the third, having been relieved by Gwen and returning to bed, Trish awoke at six o'clock to the crash of mortar bursts. The shock waves caused the tarpaulin screen in front of their quarters to billow like a sail until its bottom pegs tore loose and it flapped freely.

"Let's get to the wards!" Trish exclaimed. She threw aside the netting and reached for her boots. "Gwen'll have her hands full."

"Morning stonk, how inconsiderate!" Robyn cried, doing likewise. "Watch out for iggie wiggies and creepie crawlies."

They shook their boots vigorously and banged them against the walls but nothing emerged.

"They've mildewed again," Robyn observed. "Grown whiskers like Father Christmas." This happened frequently in the damp climate.

In a couple of minutes, they had donned their boots, fastened their puttees, buckled on their haversacks containing their medical kits, grabbed their hats and weapons and were crouching behind the bund in front of their quarters. Looking up, they saw the next salvo of bombs descending and waited for them to impact.

A string of yellow flashes accompanied by gouts of brown smoke and harsh bangs mingled obscenely with the dissipating morning mist. The girls observed Wood, Proctor and a couple of others going helter-skelter for the stables, to prevent the panic-stricken mules from pulling their halters loose.

"Lads're taking a risk," exclaimed Robyn. "Mules'll trample 'em, surely."

The bombs had detonated in jungle beyond the perimeter but shrapnel and debris whizzed unnervingly close.

They had a few seconds before more rounds descended.

"Go!" said Trish.

They sprinted across the slanting, uneven ground to Trish's ward and ducked behind the earthen bund.

Robyn tensed for the dash to her ward after the next salvo had exploded. Amazingly, Wood and the others seemed to have got the animals under control.

"Look!" shouted Robyn, pointing upwards. They'd both seen the unmistakable silhouettes and heard the powerful hum of the Merlin engines. A flight of RAF Hurri-bombers was descending like avenging Valkyries to maul the enemy positions with cannon and rocket fire. Through the thinning mist, the girls could discern the sinister, black, pencil-like shapes slung on rails beneath the wings.

"Get stuck in, Jonny!" Robyn shouted. She waved exultantly to the Hurri flight.

This time, the mortar bombs landed further up the slope. Shorn-off saplings tumbled down. Robyn was off like a deer.

Then all was drowned out by the staccato cough of the Hurris' cannons and the *"whoosh"* of the rocket salvoes.

Trish watched anxiously until her friend had reached the bund in front of her ward. It was disconcerting that the plunging fire had bracketed the position but they could only trust in the protection of the shelters and the efficiency of the airmen.

Trish pulled aside the tarpaulin screen, placed her Sten against the wall and doffed her hat and haversack. Several of the men were distinctly alarmed. In their panic, they had pulled away from the IV syringes and their arms were dripping blood on the floor. One of Hudson's orderlies, a small-sized man named Saville, was trying to reassure them and restore the drips.

Clods of earth lay scattered about, loosened from the roof by the detonations.

"Calm down, lads," Trish called out. "It'll be finished soon. Just lie still while Sav and I fix your drips. Then we'll sweep up the mess."

Her words had the desired effect. Sister was here. Everything would be all right.

Though Sister was desperately hoping the men wouldn't hear her heart pounding like a drum - and not from her recent athletic effort.

"The CO whistled up this air strike peremptorily," Hudson explained to Trish when he dropped in for a visit. "With the mist clearing on top, we reckoned the Nips were going to attack in force and try and overwhelm us – that's what the mortars were for, cut off any rein-forcements. Sorry for the inconvenience. Our chaps got off pretty lightly, thanks to the RAF, one reason I'm swanning around here and not at my RAP."

"We were OK, thanks, Trev," said Trish. She looked up from the box she was using as a table to compile the patients' documentation.

Desultory sniper fire could be heard from the crest but the mortaring had stopped. The mist was gone and the day seemed to be brightening, consistent with the forecast end of the monsoon.

"Hopefully it won't happen again," said the tall MO. "Hurri boys caught the blighters forming up and blew 'em to hell. They're lying about like cordwood. Place'll stink to high heaven in a day or so, I'm afraid. No way we can bury 'em now but the Hurris also took out some of their bunkers – devilish hard to find – so there's a chance Tojo might pull back sooner than we expected. How long do you think it'll be before these lads can be moved?"

"Several more days, I think," said Trish. "Though they're responding to treatment pretty well, as you can see from the records here." She displayed a summary of the patients' condi-tions. "The main thing is to keep their strength up, with all the food and fluid we can get into them."

"Ah!" exclaimed Hudson. "Could I ask you to step outside briefly, Sister and I'll intro-duce you to our visitor."

Emerging from the ward, Trish was momentarily taken aback at the sight of a stocky, browned-skinned, bare-footed man wearing a sari-like garment that ended at his knees, revealing muscular calves. His hair was shoulder-length and it shone glossy black in the sun. With powerful arms, he held a plaited wicker basket on his head and welcomed the Sister with a wide grin that revealed prominent teeth stained with betel juice.

"One of our Chin friends," Hudson explained. He nodded to the villager who placed the basket on the ground. Trish stared with delight at its contents. These consisted of eggs, sweet potatoes and fresh fruits, including bananas, limes, mangos and papayas.

"Should help the chaps' diet," said Hudson with approval as Trish knelt down to examine the foodstuffs more closely. "Plenty more where that came from. Locals're quite happy to trade for our compo rations and American fags. We should get a few cartons with the next airdrop. Oh, by the way, the whites of those eggs look a bit funny when cooked, green actually and the yolks turn a funny yellow, too, not what you or I are used to. But they're OK."

"I'm sure we'll manage, Trev," said Trish, looking up, her face radiant. "Thank you and tell him, 'thank you, thank you very much'."

Manage they did. And the patients' health improved. As their fevers broke, they gained in strength to the stage where, donning their boots and with assistance, they could walk to the men's latrine. Gradually, the convalescents were able to get into a morning routine of washing and shaving – and even buffed their boots.

"Must look our best for you, Sister," they would say. "Do yours if you like."

They also received fresh clothes that came up via the mules from the airdrops. The girls undertook to mark the men's clothing with indelible pen for the purpose of washing, so that their patients always had some clean items to change into. It was easy to string clotheslines inside the shelters with parachute cord, or between trees on the slope above when the weather was fine.

The mule convoys had continued regularly since the arrival of Wood's party, bringing medicines and rations from the CCS. Colonel Bedser generously supplied mule handlers from his battalion in order to enable the medical orderlies to remain at their primary duties.

Bedser had no shortage of volunteers for the supply trains, and not simply because it was a change from daily confrontation with the Japs.

"Lads won't miss an opportunity to chat up you lasses," the CO explained.

Trish and her companions sought, therefore, whenever they could, to make sure at least one of them was around to be chatted up when the infantrymen came down to lead off the mules and when they came back.

"Another chance to put on some lipstick," remarked Trish. They invariably smeared a little on when they went on the wards and applied some scent, if time and opportunity allowed.

It helped offset the grim surroundings and the stench of corpses from the fighter-bomber strike. As Hudson had predicted, even the rear echelon area stank but, as Gwen said, "We'll just have to put up with it, like my Dai says."

With the ending of the monsoon season, brief periods of sunbathing were feasible for the patients, in order to help dry out the prickly heat and their jungle sores. The unremitting heat, of course, exacerbated their need for fluids, a problem compounded by the diminishing rainfall that necessitated more quantities of the precious liquid occupying the mules' loads and battalion water parties having to forage further afield.

"At least it's up to us when we want to get ourselves wet now," Robyn said philosophically. "Or our clothes. Blisters've dried up, too."

The girls also snatched a few opportunities for sunbathing, outside their sleeping quarters, discreetly, of course.

"Those airdrop chappies are marvellous, you know," said Gwen one morning, when they were preparing the patients' breakfasts on the tenth day after their arrival. It consisted largely of eggs and fruits regularly supplied by the Chins.

Trish and Robyn exchanged winks. 'My Dai says,' Robyn mouthed.

"My Dai says the crews have a terrible time, sometimes, finding the DZ – drop zone, that is – especially at night or in bad weather," Gwen went on, stirring the green and yellow scrambled concoction. "Sometimes the storms are so severe, they'll damage an aircraft quite badly, or even force it down, as if it wasn't hard enough navigating through all these hills. Then they might have to make several run-ins to be sure they're on target and that's dangerous in those narrow valleys with all those updrafts and downdrafts and what have you. Yet, the Daks never failed them, Dai says."

Although for Gwen and Trish, one airdropped item that arrived by mule the following day was cause for disquiet.

It consisted of a crate of several live chickens.

The handlers deposited it outside the field kitchen when the girls were clearing up after the patients' breakfast. Farmer's daughter Robyn immediately pulled back the wood-framed wire door, reached in to grasp one of the squawking birds firmly with both hands and deftly wrung its neck.

"Come on," she said to her companions. "Don't be squeamish. We'll make the lads some chicken broth for supper."

A little hesitantly, Trish and Gwen followed suit, wincing as the neck bones cracked beneath their grip.

"We could do this bit first," said Robyn as she sliced the head of her victim with a fighting knife. "But it's messy. If we rig up a clothesline and hang them by the feet, the blood'll drain easily enough. Maybe use some mozzie netting to keep the flies off."

Trish and Gwen each made a face.

"Just as well our patients are all BORs," Gwen remarked while they plucked the birds preparatory to gutting and cleaning them. "My Dai says that IORs wouldn't eat chickens killed the way we did it. They slit the poor birds' throats and let them run around bleeding to death. Horrible business."

"When's your Dai going to write his memoirs, Taff?" Robyn asked. She pulled out several body feathers from a chicken and winked at Trish again.

"Do you think he should?" asked Gwen as she wiped her hands on her trousers to remove some feather down. "I suppose I could mention it. He does seem to know an awful lot."

That evening was the last they spent in the area. The following day, Bedser's patrols confirmed that the Japs had quitted their portion of the hill and the battalion could continue its advance – to the next enemy-fortified position.

In the meantime, the scrub typhus patients had recovered sufficiently to be evacuated via the vehicle track hitherto under enemy surveillance. Bedser's redoubtable infantry, together with a field company of sappers, set about making it passable for ambulances as well as jeeps.

Thanks to expert nursing, improved diet and round-the-clock monitoring, all the patients would be making the journey.

During that last afternoon, while the broth for supper was warming, Major Hudson came to express his gratitude. Trish thought that Trev wasn't looking quite so gaunt as when she'd first met him. The Sisters' intervention had clearly been a load off his mind.

"Keith'll be up to see you later," he told them.

The CO duly arrived and conveyed his thanks.

It was the first of two visits he paid to the field kitchen that evening.

The second took place several hours later when Trish was brewing tea for the patients before settling them. Whichever Sister was on duty carried out this task because she took responsibility for adding the measured amount of sedative to help the men sleep, still not easy in the heat and with skin infections that were slow to heal.

She would distribute the tea with the help of the orderlies.

"High point of the day, Sister, being tucked in by you," the patients often said, adding in reference to the orderlies, "Wouldn't be the same with just you ugly blighters."

She could rejoice at what their ribaldry signified, compared to their general condition two weeks before. It was worth the feeling of alarm the girls experienced as and when a snake slid away from the path of their feet during journeys to and from the wards at night.

Bedser's voice roused Trish from her musings.

"May I come in, please, Sister?" he said.

His plaintive tone put Trish on her guard but she acceded to his request and smiled congenially as he pushed past the tarpaulin.

"Nice to see you, Keith. Have a seat," she said casually and gestured to one of the empty ammunition boxes. Gratefully, Bedser sat down, took off his hat and placed his Sten on the floor. Trish noted that a bloodied bandage was wrapped around his upper arm, where the sleeve of his bush shirt had been cut away.

She placed a mug of compo tea before him and said quietly, "I'll have look at that for you."

He thanked her for the tea but declined her offer.

"Nothing to worry about, Sister. A memento from this evening's set to. My batman fixed me up."

Gently, she persisted, reassured that he harboured no ulterior motive. Otherwise he wouldn't have kept calling her "Sister."

"Medicine kit's in my haversack," she said. "Be useful to get some practice. Haven't dressed any battle injuries for a while."

"OK, Sister," the CO said with a chuckle. "Go ahead."

Trish pulled up an ammunition box to sit next to him and carefully unwrapped the old dressing, depositing it in a kitchen waste receptacle tin. She cleaned the laceration with alcohol, warning Bedser with a smile that "It'll sting a bit," then applied gentian and sulfa powder and wrapped on a new dressing.

"I'll give you a shot of anti-tetanus," she said. "Just a pin prick."

She filled a syringe, swabbed a patch on his arm with alcohol and inserted the needle, easing the plunger forward.

"Thank you, Sister," the CO mumbled, his voice breaking.

Unlike the MO, Bedser appeared to be as jaded as ever, in the glow of the paraffin lamps. And his moustache was unkempt, most unusual for a senior officer, regardless of the circumstances.

Trish wasn't surprised when Keith started to weep. She laid aside the empty syringe, put her arms around him and he sobbed on her shoulder like a distraught child.

Please, Father, she prayed. Don't let Woody or Brummie call me just yet.

When Bedser had composed himself, Trish sat back and he began to unburden to her.

"I came out with the retreat in forty-two. We were fighting the Japs all the way. Had to leave any seriously wounded that couldn't walk, put a bullet through 'em because of the Japs. Lots of civilians in the retreat too, women and kids. Tens of thousands of 'em died. Everything got 'em; snakes, tigers, Japs, disease, drowning, starvation, exhaustion, you name it. I've been at the sharp end ever since, one way and another. I was the last of the old gang, apart from Hudson, so they made me CO."

He paused and put his head in his hands.

"I haven't seen my wife and kids for five years. They're back in Blighty," he said, with renewed sobs. "Wife was going to come out after she'd had Keith junior but the war stuffed that up. Don't even know if I've still got a wife. I know the post's slow but she hasn't been answering my letters. I've never seen my son. Don't suppose he or my daughter would even know me now."

"*I'll* write to her, Keith," said Trish firmly. "I'll tell her about the work we've been doing here and how much you're looking forward to seeing her and the children again. I can easily explain we got talking while you were my patient." She glanced pointedly at his wound.

"Would you do that?" he asked, his eyes brightening. "That'd be wonderful. Have you got a pen? I'll give you our address."

He did so, finished his tea and bade her goodnight, departing in apparently a much better frame of mind.

Wood and Proctor arrived straight afterwards.

"Was that our CO, Sister?" the Brummie asked.

"Yes," said Trish evenly. She gave them each a large dixieful of steaming liquid from the paraffin stoves. "Came to have his dressing changed. Reckons us nurses have got a special touch. You've set out the mugs then, all spick and span?"

Later, she overheard part of a conversation between her two helpers.

"Sister Calder? Haddaway, man!" Wood was expostulating. "Ne funny business with her, like. Straight as a die she is, man."

Trish smiled inwardly. Before the night was over, she would have written the promised letter. If Mrs Bedser then put two-and-two together and got five, that was her lookout.

Perhaps it would encourage her to be a better helpmeet in future.

Major Trenholme sent a three-ton lorry to rendezvous with his personnel, who came down in jeeps piled with their gear.

Before tidying up the scene of their endeavours – a task that included spading their latrine full of earth, the girls supervised the carriage by stretcher of their former patients over the hilltop to the waiting vehicles. Most were still too weak to walk the distance.

Trish and the others did walk it, however. It was their first sight of the position and not one they relished. The area was scarred with holes and ditches, littered with discarded weapons, barbed wire and abandoned kit, strewn with putrefying enemy remains grotesquely swollen in the tropical sun, some of them partly submerged in putrid green water half filling the craters torn out by the Hurri bombardment. Flies droned in swarms.

"Best soak a handkerchief in mozzie repellent, Sisters and tie it round your face, like this," Corporal Wood advised the girls. "Keep out some of the smell."

They were not slow to follow his example.

A clear line of sight existed between the opposing British and Japanese positions. Intervening trees were but stumps, the fallen trunks scattered around at all angles.

"We lost about the equivalent of a company," Hudson told the Sisters as he trudged along beside them. "Including quite a few to malaria, though not enough to get the CO sacked[126]. You didn't see them because they went straight to the MFTUs. Thanks to the Japs, I've got about a dozen lads buried near my RAP site."

"And we pick up where all this has left off," murmured Gwen, glancing at a knocked-out battalion mortar position.

The transport took them to a new site beyond Tiddim, because the fighting was progressing towards the Chindwin and medical units were leapfrogging each other to keep up with the forward troops.

Trish and her friends jumped off the truck when it pulled up in late afternoon among a collection of tents and *bashas*, acquired from the Chins, marking where the CCS had ensconced itself atop a ridge.

The three of them joyfully embraced Vera and the other off-duty Sister, Sarah Monaghan, a dark-haired Irish girl.

"The prodigals return!" exclaimed Sister Jeffries. "Your *basha's* over there. Stash your gear, then come along to the mess for tea. It's this tent here. We're expecting another convoy before sundown but the post's caught up with us."

"We aired everything for you," said Sister Monaghan. "It's all packed safely in your trunks. They're in your *basha*."

"Oh, thanks, Paddy," said Gwen, still with an arm around her friend. "It's ever so good to see you both."

They read their post in the mess while sipping tea and exchanging voluble accounts of how they'd fared since parting by the stream.

Gwen was relieved to discover that, as one of the most experienced officers, Dai had been promoted to captain and was now in a Brigade HQ job.

"'It's all to do with Intelligence, so I don't know why they picked me,'" she read out, laughing. "'Still, I suppose it'll please you, dear.'"

"You certainly look pleased, Gwennie," said Sister Jeffries.

Trish received several letters from her father and sensed that he still wasn't well but Ellie seemed to be settled into the school year so that was a relief. Evan's letters seemed more distant in tone. That puzzled but didn't distress her - something she found odd in itself.

They were all keen to learn what Gray had written to Robyn and clustered round her in anticipation as she unfolded his letter.

"Give me room to breathe," Robyn protested. "If you *must* know, this is what he says."

"'Dear Robyn'," she read out, "'I know that communications from your neck of the woods are a bit sporadic right now and I can understand any delay in reply.

"'However, you are continually in my thoughts and it's with this in mind that I am writing to ask a very serious question.

"'Will you marry me?

"'I wrote separately to the Dalrymples, to ask their advice. Turns out, it's very simple: Do God and Robyn each say, 'yes'?

"'I realise this may come as a surprise but I genuinely felt I had to ask you.

"'Yours sincerely,

"'Jonny.'"

Patients and other staff were startled by the spontaneous exclamations of delight from the Sisters' Mess.

"Well, what are you going to say?" asked Vera eagerly.

"The right thing, I hope," said Robyn, as she refolded the letter and inserted it into a shirt pocket.

"You weren't all that surprised, were you?" asked Sarah, placing her partially drained mug on the trestle table.

"I suppose not but I better think about it," murmured Robyn.

Vera topped up the mugs.

"The smile on your face is giving you away, Robbie," she said. "However, I'm sure another cup of tea will help make up your mind."

Robyn wrote to Gray, thanking him for his proposal but stating that she wished to seek some guidance herself from the Dalrymples. He replied saying that she should take as long as she wanted to decide.

Now that the post was functioning regularly, Gray received Robyn's reply about two weeks later.

Before evening mess, he sat on an upturned crate in his tent and opened the letter, his hands clammy, his heart beating wildly. Glaz McKenna sat opposite, watching, drawing on his cigarette. With his mate there, Gray felt reassured.

Dear Jonny, the letter read. *Charles and Edith have given us their blessing. Gwen and Trish have too, so it's fine with me.*

We only have to decide when, where and how. Not easy, given our mutual circumstances but I believe that With God all things are possible.

All my love,

Robyn.

P.S. Gwen and Trish had quite a lot to say but I'm sure you'll see the funny side of it.

P.P.S. Were you anywhere near a hilltop on the following dates...?

Gray heaved a mighty sigh and passed the letter to his friend. Glaz read it, stubbed out his cigarette and shook Gray's hand.

"Calls for a celebration, Jonno, though as usual I don't suppose you'll imbibe anything stronger than lemon and lime. Deplorable state of affairs. I wonder why she's asking about hilltops. Must have seen some Hurri strikes."

Gray's brow furrowed.

"Hope she keeps her distance," he said.

Trenholme's CCS and its sister units were continuing to follow the advance. Their convoys plugged up serrated ridges of dense tropical forest and descended into the intervening gorges slashed with rushing rivers that the transport crossed by the pontoon Baileys the sappers had established.

"They won't get washed away for a few months, at least, ladies," Wood remarked cheerfully to his three passengers as he steered the jeep across the first Bailey they encountered. "Not with the monsoon finished."

"You going to be a rally driver after the war, Woody?" Robyn called from the back. Judging by the way he took the hairpin bends, the lance corporal seemed to look on each leg of the journey as a fresh challenge to his driving skills.

"Divvent think so, Sister," he said over his shoulder. "Missus'd reckon it was too risky."

In the battles for the desperately fought-over crests, the assaulting troops had been forced to ascend eight thousand feet or more through stifling heat and sudden cloudbursts. Time and again, the girls witnessed expanses of shattered trees, devastated jungle and torn-up earth.

Occasionally, they happened to glimpse the devastation in progress, as formations of RAF Hurri-bombers roared overhead to blast Japanese strongpoints on the next enemy-held peak, transforming the disputed height into an exploding horizon of smoke and flame. Such sights had prompted Robyn's PPS to Gray.

"That's my boy, Jonny!" she would shout from the jeep, clutching Trish's arm with glee until Sister Calder protested, "Robbie, you're giving me pins and needles, again!"

And if Wood ventured to join in with, "Champion, man!", Sister Fairlea's two companions would be impelled to cry, "Don't encourage her!"

In relays with their sister units, they tended the brutally torn-up victims of the actions, because air power notwithstanding, the final victories were down to the men on their feet wielding rifle, machine gun, grenade and bayonet; British squaddies, Chin guerrillas, Ghurkas, sepoys and askaris from the East African Division continuing their advance from the pestilential Kabaw Valley further north.

Bonds of suffering blurred the racial distinctions.

This was the real significance of the names on the map that had been unknown pre-war and would soon return to oblivion; Kennedy Peak, Fort White, Vital Corner, Kalemyo, and Kalewa, almost on the banks of the Chindwin.

Except in the minds of those who'd either fought there or striven to save life and limb afterwards.

All their lives they would remember the cost of the Burma victory.

Yet, in a strange way, that cost served to reinforce the Sisters' faith. When a Hindu died, the man's comrades incinerated the body as though on a ghat, to the grisly accompaniment of raucous chanting. For a final, macabre touch, the charred remains were then gathered up and flung into the nearest stream.

"They hope what's left'll eventually flow into the Ganges," Trenholme explained. "Geography's a bit off."

By contrast, the Christian burial service for a British soldier succumbing to wounds was always dignified, simple and moving. The dead man would be gently consigned to earth usually within sound of murmuring stream and melodious birdcalls from the jungle-green backdrop, beneath brilliantly blue skies, now that the weather was usually fine – hot during the day, cold at night. When not on nights, the girls slept fully clothed and woke to a layer of frost around the campsites.

Trish and her friends always tried to attend the Christian ceremonies if they were off duty. The words of scripture intoned by the padre invariably brought comfort, especially for whichever Sister would be writing to the soldier's family.

"'I am the resurrection and the life: he that believeth in me, though he were dead, yet shall he live.'"

For other casualties, their lot was steadily being improved by the establishment of air-strips as the Allied formations moved beyond Kalemyo into the dry belt of Burma during November.

"Goodbye jungle," said Gwen as the jeep motored along. "Hello dust."

The wheels of the vehicles were throwing it up in billows as the convoy drove through open countryside past banana groves and scrubby copses. The Sisters kept brushing it off their clothes.

"There's a stretch of *bithess* up ahead, Sisters," Wood remarked. "That'll keep the dust down a bit."

"What are those mounds, Woody?" asked Robyn. She pointed to some heaps of red earth that dotted the route on either side.

"Termite hills, Sisters," said the corporal. "Don't ever disturb 'em."

For the first time, they sighted the distinctive, tapered spiral shapes of Burmese pagodas, sun-bleached white with an occasionally gilded appearance.

"Monuments to heathenism," said Robyn.

Trish nodded. She felt the same aversion for the structures as she had for Kali's temple near the Ganges.

A name has been changed in the part of the narrative that follows, for reasons that will become apparent.

The sun was low in the west when they reached their destination, an undulating patch of scrubland on the edge of paddy fields, to the rear of Kalewa, where battles were in progress for the vital bridgehead to the Chindwin. An advance party had already set up most of the CCS's tented facilities.

A surprise awaited them when Trish and her friends alighted from the jeep, carrying their web bags and bedrolls.

Vera Jeffries greeted them accompanied by a young nursing Sister who had arrived that day by L-5 from a base hospital in India. The advancing Fourteenth Army had captured a nearby airstrip, strengthening the supply chain and enabling more patients to avoid the arduous overland journey back to Imphal through the Kabaw Valley.

"This is Gracie Quentin, our welcome reinforcement," said Vera. "I think she should work with you so we'll have two lots of four."

Sister Quentin nodded nervously. "Happy to," she murmured, tucking up some ash blonde locks that had strayed beneath the brim of her beret.

Trish saw at a glance that the girl could hardly have been more than a few weeks out of England. She looked so delicate and her JGs were spanking new.

"We're expecting a convoy of patients first thing tomorrow," Vera told them. "I suggest get some nosh and turn in. It'll be a long day."

"Well, how about you team up with me, Gracie?" Trish suggested to the newcomer as the four of them trudged through red dust to their tent. "Gwen and Robbie are partners in crime from way back."

"Fine," said Gracie. "Can I wash?"

"We'll sort something out," Robyn reassured her, holding open the tent flap. "Get you a bush hat, too, like ours. Save that nice complexion of yours."

"And don't believe a word Sister Calder says about Robbie and me," added Gwen cheerfully.

Gracie smiled self-consciously and said nothing. Trish was already having misgivings. She sensed that the base hospital CO had sent out his most junior neophyte in order not to break up an established staff cadre. It was grossly unfair.

Sister Calder's misgivings would be fully justified on the morrow.

The ambulances came early because the battle had been flaring and thudding throughout the night. Quickly consuming compo tea, biscuits and spam, Trish and Gracie hastened through the half-light to one of the Resus tents as the first casualties were being unloaded, wiry, dark-skinned men from the East African Brigade.

Some were able to go straight to theatre where Robyn and Gwen had been allocated to assist Major Trenholme and his second-in-command, laconic New Zealander, Captain 'Kiwi' Mostyn.

Others groaned and grunted with laboured breathing as ambulance men and orderlies placed the stretchers in two rows along the tarpaulin floor beneath the flickering orange glare of the paraffin lamps.

The two Sisters briskly scrubbed up and knelt beside an askari whose forehead was swathed in thick dressing. He was convulsed and making a succession of guttural noises.

"Shouldn't we have an MO?" Sister Quentin asked nervously.

"Usually," muttered Trish. "But they're busy in theatre, or with Vera's lot. Must've been one hell of a battle. Never mind, we'll manage. Help me hold his arm down and I'll sedate him. Stop him thrashing about."

Hands trembling, the other girl obeyed and Trish injected the African with a syringeful of morphine.

"Now for his dressing," said Trish. "Keep his head still."

When she unwrapped the bloodstained gauze, Trish saw that part of the man's forehead had been shot away, exposing his brain.

"We'll clean the wound and fill it with sulfa powder," Trish advised. "Then he'll need a new dressing, saline and plasma IVs. Note him down as first priority for theatre as soon as he's stable. We'll keep monitoring him for secondary shock."

Gracie seemed numb. Trish did most of the work herself.

The next askari they saw to was drowsy but conscious. He looked up with touchingly trustful brown eyes that blinked at seeping tears. His breathing was a succession of rasping, rattling noises and beads of sweat coursed down his face and chest. A huge swathe of dressing was fastened to his side, beneath a bush shirt that clung about his torso, secured by safety pins, the fabric stained deep red. Trish didn't need to look at the card looped around the African's neck to see they had doped him to the eyeballs at the RAP – though she knew the morphine would soon be wearing off.

The pain was ready to claw him like a savage beast, as the analgesic lost its hold.

"My charm's in there, lady," the askari said hoarsely to Trish. He pointed to a waist pocket. "Could you please get it for me?"

Trish carefully inserted her hand into the pocket.

And immediately withdrew it, thankful the askari seemed not to notice.

Saturated with blood and sweat, the dressing had partly collapsed. Trish's fingers had gone straight into the man's stomach cavity[127], ruptured by shrapnel.

"In a bit," Trish said firmly and tried to smile. "We ought to change your dressing and sort your drips first. I'll give you morphine, too."

Or heroin, she thought, with disquiet. Keeping the pain at bay without overdosing the casualty would be a fine balance.

His trusting eyes showed assent. Again, Trish carried out most of the ministration, while her companion stared uncomprehendingly.

"Why don't you go and sit by the desk?" Trish suggested as she fastened the new dressing. "We'll need to document everything."

Marionette-like, Gracie obeyed. Trish caught Woody's eye.

"Get her out of here," she said between gritted teeth when he could join her. "Don't let anyone see you if you can help it. I'll square it with Trenholme."

"Will do, Sister," Wood reassured her. "Back in two ticks."

"Sister!" called Donny from the other end of the ward.

Trish hastened over to help with a patient whose face was as pale as an askari's could get. A shell fragment had torn off a chunk of his thigh and buttock. With the sudden rupture of an artery, the blood was spurting onto the tent floor almost as fast as Trish and Donny could replace it with plasma.

"Another priority for theatre, Donny," said Trish, feeling for a pulse when they had stanched the wound, eyes on her watch. "Soon as he's up to it. I better start on the penicillin round."

"Aye, Sister," rejoined the stocky Westmorlander. "I've noted him – and we've set out the solutions."

Early in the afternoon, Trish and Gwen were able to take a brief break in order to farewell Sister Quentin. She would travel in an ambulance with several patients to be flown out by C-47.

"Take care, love," said Trish. "We'll send the rest of your kit on. Don't worry."

"Thank you, Sister," Gracie mumbled.

Gwen and Trish hugged her and she climbed aboard the transport, her face still tear-stained with bemusement.

"It's best," said Gwen as they waved to the departing vehicle. "So dreadfully unfair, sending someone new like her."

The CO had insisted on Sister Quentin's immediate return to her unit, though he'd tactfully let Trish and Gwen deal with her.

"But I'll play war with 'em in my next report," he promised darkly.

Perspiring in the heat of another cloudless day, the two Sisters trudged back to their duties.

"Be a nice Christmas present," said Trish. "Getting up to strength with a lass who can cope."

Christmas Day, 1944, was only three weeks away.

"Amen," said Gwen. "Pray for one, eh?"

Though not in time for Christmas, she would soon be on her way.

Kalewa fell a few days later and by the middle of December, Trenholme's CCS was crossing the broad stretch of the Chindwin by means of the longest Bailey bridge in the world, with a span of nearly twelve-hundred feet.

"Sappers've done a canny job again, eh, Woody?" said Robyn from the back of the jeep.

"Why-aye, Sister!" came the jaunty response. "You'll be an honorary Geordie, yet, man!"

But all were preoccupied with the prospect of Sister Fairlea soon becoming Sister Mrs Gray. Circumstances had combined to make this union a distinct possibility.

Advancing further into Burma's dry belt, Fourteenth Army was concentrating amongst the rolling scrubland of the Shwebo Plain, its eyes set on the great eastward bend of the Irrawaddy River and the objective on the far shore – the city of Mandalay.

In this open country, the army commander intended to exploit to the full his overwhelming superiority in armour and air power.

Undoubtedly, Trenholme's CCS and similar units would have much work to do with the Irrawaddy crossing.

But for now, all was in preparation and a comparative lull prevailed.

During which time a letter of great import arrived from Jon Gray:

Dear Robyn

You'll be interested to know I've been pushed up the ladder to Flight Lieutenant. Some of the lads, including Glaz and myself, are converting to new aircraft when we finish our current tour - any day now. We're going back to India for the course but I'll be exempt parts of it because I've already trained on similar aircraft.

The base is near a hill station in sight of the Himalayas – beautiful place. See the PO Box details below. I should be able to wangle a fair amount of free time.

Any chance you could get a few days off and fly up so we can tie the knot? Daks go pretty regularly between there and Dum Dum.

All my love,

Jonny.

P.S. I know we're presenting folks back home with a fait accompli but Mum and Dad'll be over the moon when they meet you.

"Will you come with me, Trish?" Robyn asked when she shared the letter with her companion in their tent after they came off duty – for several patients with minor afflictions had arrived as soon as the unit had occupied its new site. "I know it sounds selfish."

"Nonsense!" exclaimed Trish. "I'd love to. All we have to do is sort out Trenholme. I'm sure we can both be back before the balloon goes up again in earnest. I only wish you and Jonny could have more time together."

"So do I," said her friend wistfully. "But, thanks, hugely. And I promise, I'll dance at *your* wedding, or something."

Robyn and Trish successfully appealed to their CO's romantic nature.

"Didn't know he had one," said Sister Jeffries in the mess the following day. "Wonders'll never cease."

"Don't be like that, Vera!" protested a chorus of female voices.

Ironically, Gray's squadron was at the time located not many miles from Robyn's CCS. The Hurris had transferred to a fighter strip in the dry belt only hours after advancing Allied infantry supported by tanks drove the Japanese out.

Soon afterwards, McKenna's flight filed into the briefing tent to receive their orders for what would be Glaz's and Gray's last sortie in Hurri-bombers. The following day, they would depart for India.

In a vest pocket of his bush jacket, Gray was cherishing the letter from Robyn stating that she could join him for the wedding as planned, with Trish as her bridesmaid.

Great! he'd written back. *Glaz'll be my best man, DV. Charles has said he can be there to give you away and guess who'll conduct the service? Our friend Rev Simpson. Wonderful how Father has taken care of us. And we'll be there over Christmas.*

Gray was therefore in an unusually light-hearted mood prior to a sortie.

But not for long.

"Sorry, lads," said the CO brusquely. "Your turn, I'm afraid."

He then gave them the details, using a slim pointer to pick out the route and the target on the large-scale situation map behind him. They also viewed aerial photographs. Gray felt sick.

Afterwards, they dispersed to their aircraft, saying nothing.

The mission was simple enough. Fly deep into enemy territory, with Spitfires for top cover, and shoot up enemy transport – like the Hurris had often done with Jap lorries and locomotives.

Except that this time, the transport consisted of elephants, requisitioned by the Japs from their Burmese allies[128]. The CO had recently led Blue Flight in a similar sortie and could sympathise with McKenna's lads.

Blue Flight was still coming to terms with the experience.

"We'd thought one bash at this might have put the Japs off," the CO said. "But evidently not. Tojo's desperate to consolidate his defences east of the Irrawaddy."

Operational flights in Burma had exposed Gray to monsoon weather that tore the fabric from the Hurricane's fuselage, intense anti-aircraft fire that had once deposited him in the Kachin Hills and targets buried deep in jungle ravines where smoke and haze from the Hurris' attacks made avoidance of the surrounding ridges the most hazardous part of the mission.

Going through the familiar cockpit drill, Gray would rather have faced any of those hazards than do the present business.

But do it they must.

In brilliant sunshine, the aircraft streaked over the silver loop of the Irrawaddy and continued on a bearing south-east, past Mandalay, in the direction of the Shan Hills, across wide open country sun-baked yellow-brown in hue, interspersed with native villages, half-filled *chaungs* twisting through the earth like tiny veins, barren rocky outcrops and scattered patches of greenish jungle scrub.

Gray heard Glaz's voice in his earphones.

"Red Leader to Red Flight, target sighted. Assume attack formation."

Gray's stomach tightened. The intelligence was spot on. Their objective lay in plain view.

A line of ponderous grey beasts with handlers atop them, heavily laden and plodding along a bush track that cut through acres of what looked like wild tea trees.

Gray shifted his gun-button to the Fire position, easing the control column gently forward.

The flight zoomed down in a shallow dive until their prop wash was furrowing the tea tree foliage, the Hurris making a staggered approach to dispatch the target in a single pass, if possible.

With long-accustomed precision, Gray lined up through his gun sight. Perspiration trickled from beneath his flying helmet. His thumb was poised over the gun button.

"Open fire!"

Glaz's order burst into his earphones at the precise second when Gray would have pushed the button himself.

He obeyed, gritting his teeth. A broadside of twenty-mm shells lanced from the Hurris' wings. Gray's aircraft shuddered with the coughing reports, the smell of cordite filling the cockpit.

The effects were immediate and horrific.

Gray was fighting to keep formation as he pulled back the control column, dry retching at the same time. So was everyone else, it seemed.

Glaz's voice issued stridently over the W/T.

"Sort yourselves out! We'll have some collisions in a second!"

They reformed for a second pass but nothing was left except meat for the vultures – already butchered. A few unhurt animals were stampeding through the tea trees, having thrown off their handlers. A couple of others were dragging themselves pathetically along by their forelegs, with hindquarters shattered and slopping blood.

The rest were carcasses.

Tearful and furious, Gray imagined he could hear the trumpeting shrieks of anguish from the doomed beasts.

The flight rendezvoused with the Spitfires and set course for home.

"Jesus," said a voice over the W/T. It sounded like a prayer.

Haithi – God, what'll I tell Robyn, cried Gray inwardly.

"It's beautiful," said Robyn in awe, shading her eyes as she gazed over pine-covered slopes towards the majestic white peaks beyond, beneath an azure sky. "Like we're in the Alps with all these chalets, except it's even better. Incredible."

"We came here on holidays a few times," said Trish. "You'll have lots to do, even pony trekking and there's a lake to swim in."

"Oh, Trish," said her friend impulsively. "You'll have to come back with Evan."

They were standing at the little railway siding where Gray had promised to meet them. Amazingly, all their connections had gone like clockwork, beginning with the flight accompanying patients from the strip near their CCS and in the warmth of the late afternoon amid rustic, fragrant surroundings, they were looking forward to a joyous reunion with Jonathan.

Gray arrived by taxi. He wore a fresh uniform and was looking fit and tanned.

Robyn hugged and kissed him eagerly.

"Oh, Jonny!" she exclaimed. "So wonderful to see you. You can give Trish a hug, too."

He did but perfunctorily. Clearly, all was not well.

The airman seemed about to attend a wake the next day, instead of his own wedding.

He helped the driver stash the girls' holdalls in the boot of the taxi and held the rear door open for them to climb in.

"Let's get to the hotel," he muttered, trying to smile.

The three of them were seated around a table in the hotel restaurant, an ornate room with its own bar, well patronised at that time of the evening.

"This looks scrumptious," said Robyn when the waiter brought the food. "Shall we say our own grace?"

Trish spread her serviette.

"Please do," she urged. "I'm ravenous."

After giving thanks, they both started tucking in but Gray hardly touched his meal, instead maintaining a moody silence.

After a few minutes, Robyn laid down her knife and fork.

"OK, sweetheart, what's wrong?" she asked. "This is no way to start a marriage."

Trish made as if to depart.

"Perhaps I'd better go and speak to Charles about the arrangements and your mate Glaz?" she suggested.

Many service personnel on leave were residing at the hotel where Trish and Robyn would overnight. A smaller establishment nearby catered for the overflow, including Glaz and Gray, who had journeyed up that day from their base on the plains some miles distant. Colonel Dalrymple was also staying there.

"No, please," Gray rejoined hastily. "I think – you should both know."

Haltingly, he told them about his last sortie.

When Gray had finished his account, Robyn rested her hand on his.

"I love you, Jonny," she said gently. "And I'm looking forward to writing my name as Robyn Gray. Now, eat up, there's a good chap. Do as Nurse says."

"I've had an elegant sufficiency so I'll go find the others," said Trish, getting up. "Bye for now, Jonny. We should all pray that you can put it behind you and think about tomorrow."

"Amen," said Robyn.

Trish placed a sisterly hand on Gray's shoulder as she departed.

Jon glanced after her gratefully. He then resumed his meal, only to have Robyn interrupt him.

"Jonny," she said anxiously. "Did you see that chap who's just left?"

One of the bar patrons, a rough-looking individual in a dishevelled uniform, had lurched up off his stool as Trish went out.

"Hefty bloke, looked like an orang-a-tang?"

"Yes. I think he's gone after Trish."

"Has he now? I'd better head him off, then."

Gray got to his feet, donned his cap and strode out of the restaurant.

"Jonny - " called Robyn, hastening after him. Though alarmed for Trish, she was nevertheless reassured to see the Hurri pilot definitely back in control.

Trish walked briskly through the warm dusk along the hotel driveway arched by overhanging trees. The insect noise around her sounded like all the cicadas in the world.

Then she realised she was being followed. Glancing over her shoulder, she recognised the shambling shape of the oaf from the bar. She had noticed him staring at her as she'd left the restaurant but had reckoned him too drunk to stand, let alone walk.

Clearly, she'd been wrong.

"Please, Father, encompass me now," she prayed out loud.

She reached into her handbag and drew out a vial of dark brown powder that she poured into the palm of her right hand.

Her stalker sidled up to her from the left and put his right arm around her shoulders, as she'd expected. Most individuals were right handed and she'd observed him holding a drinking glass in his right hand.

The stink of alcohol nauseated her. A voice spoke in a thick, slurred, Scots accent.

"Weel ye no take a walk wi' me, lassie?"

Fighting panic and revulsion, Trish turned her head in a deceptive smile. It put the accosting Scot of his guard.

She flicked the handful of pepper straight into his eyes, then pulled away.

Her assailant staggered backwards roaring in rage and pain.

She heard hurrying footsteps.

"Trish!" called a voice.

"Jonny, Robyn! Oh, thank God!"

"Look after Trish, Robyn," said Gray. "I'll see to his nibs. Half the garrison will be here in a minute."

The miscreant had staggered back up the drive, pawing his eyes and screaming "Water, water!"

Gray caught up with him and guided him into the waiting arms of a couple of MPs.

"Bet you've not begged for water in a long time, Jock," said Gray grimly. "On its own."

The wedding and the reception that followed went off splendidly, unmarred by the incident of the previous evening. A local jeweller managed to supply the rings on the morning of the ceremony.

"We're quite used to doing things at a moment's notice," he assured the purchasers.

McKenna had even arranged to have an RAF photographer present. The bride and groom both wore crisply laundered uniforms – courtesy of the hotels where they were staying – and Gray noticed to his satisfaction that Robyn was wearing the high heels purchased during the Ganges trip and scrupulously well maintained.

The wedding couple and their bridesmaid enjoyed a time of renewed fellowship with Charles Dalrymple and the Simpsons.

And in Trish's case, it would be happily prolonged.

"*I'll* be your escort all the way back to Dum Dum, young lady," Colonel Charles insisted. "And Mrs Dalrymple says you're to stay with us for a day or two. Don't worry. Our bush telegraph goes all the way up to Uncle Bill[129]. Rest assured your CCS can do without you for a bit longer."

Trish hugged Robyn and Jon fiercely before they boarded the *tonga* that would transport the newlyweds to the chalet by the lake where they would honeymoon.

"Your turn next, Trish," whispered Robyn, amid happy tears. "It won't be long, I know."

And it wouldn't be, though not in the manner Sister Calder anticipated.
In what follows, some personal details have been interpolated, with kind permission.

Jon and Robyn arrived at the chalet a little after dark and were conducted by the porter to their upstairs suite. A magnificent view of the Himalayas dominated the window space.

The porter placed the couple's holdalls inside the room and bade them good evening.

"Thank you, sahib," he said as he departed, on receipt of the tip from Gray.

They'd had supper at a café near the depot where the *tonga* driver halted to change horses but the porter assured them they would be able to get snacks until midnight from the chalet cafeteria.

"At last," said Robyn with a sigh. She closed the door behind them, removed and hung up her cap, jacket and tie, then partly undid her blouse. "Could you please pour us a drink, Jonny?"

She nodded toward the tumblers and pitcher on the cane table by the windowsill.

Dutifully, Jon obliged. When he turned around holding the filled glasses, he nearly dropped them.

The sight took his breath away.

Robyn's blouse and skirt were lying on the back of a chair. She was wearing the fine *lingerie* purchased at the bazaar during the Sunderbans trip. It complemented the nylons and high heels perfectly.

His earlier assessment had been correct. She wasn't carrying an ounce of spare flesh and what she did have was perfectly arranged, right down to the ridged muscle tone of her midriff.

Nonchalantly she squirted on some more perfume and placed the bottle back in her purse.

"The drinks can wait," she said, smiling. Jon put aside the glasses and Robyn stepped into his arms. Running a finger lightly down the nape of his neck, she pressed her lips to his.

"You can think what you like, now, Jonny," she murmured. Robyn rested her head on Jon's shoulder and flexed one knee to rub against his trouser leg.

"And put it into practice?" Jon asked fondly, bathing in the fragrance of her perfume.

"Amen," she whispered. "But I suppose you better draw the curtains first."

Gray awoke a few hours later, roused from slumber by the all-too-familiar awareness of danger.

Yet the room was quiet, the wide-bladed fan turning almost soundlessly above the bed. Robyn was still asleep, her breath falling lightly on his cheek.

Gray looked towards the drawn curtains. Carefully, he arose, put on his dressing gown and crept to the window. He decided against unpacking his revolver. With Robyn there, the last thing he wanted was flying bullets.

Standing to one side of the window, he pulled the curtain back a fraction and looked out.

The slope beside the chalet lay in pale moonlight, its flowerbeds and pine groves peaceful and deserted.

Except for the balls of light.

They floated shimmering, ghostlike across the moonlit landscape.

Gray caught his breath.

"What is it, Jonny?"

He turned to see Robyn sitting up in bed.

"Come and see," he said quietly and opened the curtains a few inches.

She climbed out of bed, slipped on her robe and came and stood by him at the window. He put his arm around her.

"What are they?" she whispered.

The lights glided eerily toward the roadway that ran past the chalet.

"I guess back home we'd call them corpse candles," said Gray. "Though I didn't think they existed. I wonder if they were up here - and how long they were hanging about before I woke up."

The lights were slipping through the trees on the far side of the road. They dipped towards the stream that fed the lake and were lost from view.

"Kali?" said Robyn, apprehensively. Her husband nodded.

"Sending another recce, maybe," he said. "Like the fish man I saw. Must think we're more than twice as dangerous, married."

"Married and dangerous," said his wife. "I like that. Let's get back to bed."

Kali was indeed active that night. One of her agents helped Sister Calder's would-be molester escape custody.

Eventually to join the dark forces gathering around Grandma Colleen.

Eleven

Dangers, Toils and Snares

Valley of the Senio, January 1945.

The town stood on one of the foothills overlooking the river. To the east, a vast plain extended to the Adriatic, great stretches waterlogged where the Germans had demolished irrigation canal banks to impede the Allied advance.

West of the foothills, brooding limestone peaks, veined and capped with snow, thrust massively upwards. The temperature still hovered around freezing.

With other units occupying all available coastal sites, Colleen's hospital, moving in stages, took over the town's jumble of red-tiled, whitewashed buildings, including a deserted convent - for most local inhabitants had fled the area.

The fighting had bypassed the town so it was largely undamaged but many troops had been quartered there, with the inevitable consequences.

"Place is a tip, Coll," Hoppy remarked while they were scraping and sweeping up frozen mud and assorted rubbish from the rooms on the convent's top floor in preparation for receiving the remaining patients. Huddled under blankets and supplied with hot water bottles and thermos flasks of tea laced with rum, these waited in the ambulances parked outside.

"At least the windows have still got their shutters," said Colleen.

Though wearing BDs, they still felt chilly despite the activity but Lance Corporal Burrows was preparing a brew in the upstairs scullery halfway along the corridor. Julie and Helen were clearing out the rooms beyond while Karen, Dollie, Dinah and Mollie worked on the ground floor.

The move was almost complete but over several raw, sleeting days, lorries, ambulances and jeeps had ploughed noisily up and down the gritted access road to relocate the hospital. Halliard and his fellow MOs organised theatres and other departments while MacHendry, Prescott, Briggs and several orderlies sorted the vehicle park, stores and maintenance areas. With June's assistance, Bronwyn Hewitt supervised the setting up of kitchen, washing and ablutions facilities and the layout of the wards.

Today, they were seeing to the Sisters' quarters.

Bronwyn was now Matron, Marian Lovejoy having returned to England after five years' service overseas. With the departure of several other long-serving QAs, June had been promoted to Senior Sister, an appointment that pleased everyone, even though she had been with the unit less than twelve months. All the remaining girls, including Dinah and Mollie, looked upon June as an elder sister – and speculation was mounting that she would eventually become Mrs Halliard.

By nightfall, installation of beds, stoves, instruments, operating tables, storage heaters and other equipment and furnishings was complete and all patients were accommodated in the new wards. The ubiquitous paraffin stoves would heat them until generators were available and the REs had laid the cables for the heaters.

"Do that in a day, Matron," Andy had promised Bronwyn. They would, in between helping with road clearance and bridge maintenance. "Sewage seems OK, thank the Lord, but we'll still have to tanker up water. Wells here won't be sufficient," he'd advised.

"Dollie says Andy and the lads'll have the heaters going by the end of the week," said Hoppy. She dragged the waste bin across to where they had piled up the trash.

"She reckons he can walk on water, ever since he bought her that rock," rejoined Colleen, wielding brush and shovel against the pile. Using an RE shovel, Hoppy dropped a load of empty ration cans in the bin.

"Hark at you!" she exclaimed. "First clear day we get after New Year and you're off to Florence in Captain Tony's jeep making a beeline for the jeweller's with the Somervilles-to-be canoodling in the back"

Colleen smiled. It had been a wonderful break from the usual austerity. They'd purchased the engagement rings from the town's most reputable jeweller, toured several of the famous sights and had a delightful supper in the Regency-Firenze[130].

"You should talk!" retorted Colleen. She emptied the last of the trash into the bin.

"Doug and I are behaving ourselves," Hoppy assured her as they headed for the next room, dragging the bin. "At least when Eyepiece Ernie's around, or his mate Montague."

This wasn't often. Together with Montague-Stewart, Forsythe seemed to be semi-permanently on assignment in Florence so that Halliard was effectively the unit's CO, something that suited everyone, especially Sister Hopgood and recently promoted Lance Sergeant Prescott.

Not that they had much time for socialising. Prescott and MacHendry were often away with the fighting units holding the line of the Senio.

Orderly Burrows' cheerful summons for tea issued along the corridor as Colleen and Hoppy were brushing cobwebs off the ceiling of the room they'd entered.

Once evidently a supervisor's quarters, it was adjacent to the centre stairwell, with scullery and storage annex beyond.

A modest little niche, but one Colleen was destined never to forget.

"Come on, Coll. We'll go see the Pope."

Hoppy made the suggestion while they were sipping tea in the novices' dining room that was their mess during a break. Outside, the skies had cleared and sunshine beamed in through small square windows, brightening the bare whitewashed walls and austere furnishings. Colleen and Hoppy huddled around the paraffin stove on which they'd made tea.

"Yeah," said Colleen, both hands clasping her mug. "We could manage it on a forty-eight."

Since the new year, Halliard had been arranging brief spells of leave for his staff because, despite the number of convalescent patients, the workload was now fairly routine. Colleen had used part of hers with the day trip to Florence but she had enough left for a couple of nights in Rome.

"Briggsy'll take us to the strip at Ravenna," Hoppy said eagerly. "We can hitch a flight on a Dak with the Nightingales – they won't mind some extra help –and Briggsy'll pick us up when we get back."

The RAF was still shuttling casualties back to base hospitals in the care of RAF nurses during the journey. They were known as 'Flying Nightingales'[131] and were quite happy to accept in-flight assistance from QA colleagues seeking transportation.

"Blizzards have blown themselves out for a bit," Colleen remarked with a yawn. "Let's give it a go."

On the morning of the trip, Hoppy offered to assist Briggs change the jeep's spark plugs.

Provided the CO was absent, for he disapproved of such activity, Hoppy frequently helped with vehicle maintenance when off duty, having a natural mechanical curiosity.

And the lads never objected.

Grasping a spanner, Hoppy leant over a fender watching Briggs delve into the engine bay. A powerful lamp hung from the bonnet catch, connected to a generator humming away at the back of the requisitioned shed that served as the workshop.

Out of the corner of her eye, she noticed Prescott approaching but didn't let on.

He slid his arms around Hoppy's slim waist and kissed her ear lobe.

"Not while I'm holding a spanner, you idiot," she admonished him. "I really ought to fend you off with it. We're not supposed to mess about on the premises, remember."

"Guess not," said the Canadian apologetically. He backed off and touched his beret. "Hi there, Briggsy."

"Wotcher, Doug," said the lean fusilier, who glanced up from unclipping the distributor cap. "Do you want me to go for a quick cuppa?"

"No, no," Scottie insisted. "In fact, you can be one of the first to know."

"Know what?" Hoppy asked.

"I'd like you to come back to the Rockies with me after war, Marjie," Prescott said earnestly. "Reverend Allerton can marry us when this is over. Mac and Julie'll be our neighbours. What do you say?"

He always called her Marjie now, instead of Hoppy.

"I'd say it sounds wonderful, Doug," she murmured, straightening up, her eyes shining.

"Congratulations, mate," said Briggs. "I'd shake hands but they're all mucky. Stand you a drink later."

"Thanks, Brian," said the sergeant. "Look forward to it."

Hoppy glanced past Prescott to check that they were otherwise unobserved, then kissed him warmly, her eyes still aglow.

"Naw, gawn, hop it," she whispered, in her best Cockney. "Can't you see we're busy?"

Colleen knew she faced a crisis.

It had been looming ever since her prayer for salvation on the way to the Gothic Line. Despite Bronwyn's invitation, Colleen had kept her decision to herself, apprehensive about the implications of disclosure.

But like a new-born child clamouring for sustenance, Colleen's new life was desirous of *the sincere milk of the word*[132], in spite of herself.

A few days before the Rome trip, unable to resist the inner promptings any longer, she'd gone to the arched alcove in the convent that Rev Allerton used as an office and asked him for a Bible.

"Like the one you use, Padre," she'd said.

"You'll find it a great assurance, Colleen," he told her, on handing her a copy.

It had been, in all she had read so far.

He that heareth my word, and believeth on him that sent me, hath everlasting life[133].

I give unto them eternal life and they shall never perish, neither shall any man pluck them out of my hand[134].

As she helped monitor the patients lying on their tiered stretchers during the flight to Rome, Colleen realised the journey would be decisive. Because she knew she was at a crossroads about the Church and already sensed which way she would go.

"Bet you'll be pleased, Annie," she said quietly, while carrying mugs of coffee to the pilot's cabin.

Events unfolded uncannily.

They started with the billet, a five-star hotel, like the one in Florence.

They continued with the guided tour around the Vatican Museum. Colleen and Hoppy gazed awestruck at the priceless paintings, sculptures and artefacts that adorned the vast galleries.

"This is but a fraction of our collection," their dapper Italian guide assured them.

"How much is it worth?" Hoppy asked.

The guide shrugged. "God only knows, *Inglese* Sister," he said with a toothy smile.

And while we revel in all this, a few miles away, the faithful are eating boiled grass, Colleen reflected indignantly. The knowledge distressed her now even more than her experiences in Naples.

Then came the sight of His Holiness himself, waving from his balcony at the huge throng below.

"He's just a little old gagee in a white cloak and a funny hat," said Colleen, shocked at her own irreverence. "Why's everyone so gobsmacked?"

Hoppy looked at her quizzically.

But Providence had saved the worst for last.

They returned to Saint Peter's Square in the late afternoon, having arranged to meet there with the transport to their hotel.

Colleen noticed the shadow of the obelisk lengthening as the sun declined and approaching the open entrance to the Basilica.

The realisation sickened her.

Sun worship.

Here it was, masquerading as the true church, yet performing this obscene rite of Baal worship[135], *daily*.

Once again, the Voice came to her, this time in ultimatum.

Sister Colleen, this is wickedness. You must come out of it.

She would.

On the morning of their flight back to Ravenna, they had an hour or so to wait in the Quonset departure hut by the airstrip. The building's wooden walls offered little resistance to the brittle cold of dawn and most of the passengers in transit had drawn their chairs up around the pot-bellied stove at one end of the hut, where they sipped hot black coffee dispensed with doughnuts by chatty American Red Cross girls.

Colleen used the time to write to Tony.

Dear Tony, I have decided that I must leave our religion, she wrote. *I believe from the scriptures and from what I have seen here God is prompting me this way.*

She tried to elaborate, contrasting the opulence of the church with the destitution of most ordinary people – including Father Alonzo's orphans.

It's hard for me to say this, she concluded. *But I hope and pray you will understand and agree with what I've written.*

Otherwise, I regret I will have to end our engagement.

She also penned a note of explanation to her parents.

Over to Thee, Father, she thought as she walked to the red box by the door and dropped the letters in. Posted from here, Tony's letter would be delivered very quickly.

"All right, love?" Hoppy asked when Colleen resumed her seat.

"I had to do it, Hoppy," she said, swallowing hard.

Hoppy patted her shoulder, having listened intently to Colleen's explanation for her decision on the drive from Saint Peter's square.

"Bronwyn's got to us all, Coll, along with Dollie and Andy," she'd said simply. "Even Doug and me. 'Whither shall I flee from thy presence,' Reverend George said when I went to see him. There's nowhere, is there?"

Briggs was waiting with the jeep when the girls alighted from the C-47.

"Weather's holding up," he remarked, as he helped them stash their holdalls and web bags. The sky was bright.

"Can, I drive, Briggsy?" Hoppy asked with an ingratiating smile.

"OK, Sister," said the fusilier cheerily. "So long as we swap over in sight of camp."

Colleen settled herself on a rear seat next to Briggs' Bren, wedged by its butt beneath the front passenger's seat.

They followed the highway to where Hoppy turned off onto a minor road that led into the mountains. It ran along a rocky embankment that merged with gorse-like bushes at its base.

Shivering in her BDs and leather jerkin, Colleen heard the drone of an aircraft and observed a single-engined fighter swooping low over the foothills.

"That one of ours, Briggsy?" she asked.

Before he could reply, the machine looped around and came whizzing toward them like a huge wasp.

"Stop, Sister!" Briggs shouted. "Take cover down the bank!"

Hoppy jammed on the brakes. Colleen and Hoppy grabbed their kit, Briggs his Bren. The three of them scrambled out of the jeep and down the embankment. The Sisters lay flat in the marshy scrub at the bottom, while Briggs was prone behind some rocks.

The fighter came hurtling in. Colleen glimpsed flashes from its cowling and wings. Dirt and gravel spurted up from the road and with a massive explosion that sent heat waves searing over the escapees, the jeep disappeared in a red-orange mushroom of flame.

As the fighter flashed past, Fusilier Briggs, in a kneeling position, brought his LMG up, the stock pressed firmly against his right side. The weapon sounded its staccato beat and the aircraft was suddenly trailing a ribbon of brown smoke, its engine whining as the pilot fought to gain height. It arced high above them and a white canopy blossomed. The doomed fighter then turned over and spiralled into a hillside with a gout of fire and smoke[136].

"Bullseye, Briggsy!" shouted Hoppy.

"I'll bag that Jerry!" he shouted back.

Briggs went loping across the plain.

"Sapper's have cleared this area, thank God," remarked Hoppy, as they stood up and brushed gritty soil off their trousers.

They saw the parachute settle and the enemy flier getting to his feet with his hands up after divesting himself of the 'chute.

A grim-faced Fusilier Briggs marched the prisoner back at gunpoint.

The pilot's right sleeve hung in strips and blood was dripping off his forearm. His face, too, was cut and bleeding.

"Sit down, *ja*?" said Hoppy, motioning the prisoner to sit on the embankment. He meekly obeyed. Colleen and Hoppy pulled dressings and tubes of Gentian Violet gel from their web bags to tend the airman's injuries.

"Briggsy, the weapon," Colleen said with a smile.

"OK, Sister," he said obligingly and pointed the Bren to one side, though never taking his eyes off the German.

"Either of you want his Luger for a souvenir?" Briggs asked.

He had frisked the prisoner and held up the pistol by its barrel.

They declined the offer, with thanks. Briggs stuffed the German's weapon in his web belt.

"Our blokes're on their way," he remarked.

A column of vehicles was approaching from the main highway.

"You're in luck, Fritz," he added, eyeing the injured pilot coldly. "These ladies outrank me."

On arrival back at the hospital, they encountered Major Forsythe, who was paying one of his brief visits.

He appeared very chagrined at the loss of the jeep.

When Colleen and Hoppy related the events to Corporal Burrows while they were priming the stoves for the patients' evening meal, he told a bizarre tale.

"Oh, he's Bullseye Briggs, all right," said the shrewd little NCO as he tipped compo stew into a container. "*And* Bogeyman Briggs, too. He was a gamekeeper, see? Best scout in the Eighth Army, they reckon, better even than the Goums and the Ghurkas. Does these one-man night-time recces right up to German HQs and brings back all sorts of gen – knows their lingo, he does. His CO gives him time off, in between, unless there's a strafe on and he stays with the lads, like when you arrived in the mountains. That's why he disappeared straight after."

Burrows lowered his voice and his listeners leant closer.

"They reckon Jerries've put a price on his head," he continued. "If he finds two Jerries asleep in a foxhole, he'll slit the throat of one of 'em with his kooker and leave the other one to find out when he wakes up[137]. Cuts off an ear, for proof. Don't tell Mollie. She'll have kittens."

"We won't," Hoppy whispered. Her hand shook as she stirred the compo tea.

A few months later, some startling information would emerge from one of the fusilier's night-time forays, with peace-time repercussions.

Tony's reply arrived a couple of days later. Colleen was disappointed that all he wanted was for them to see the priest.

She then received a letter from the priest and read it by hurricane lamp after coming off duty, nestling fully clothed beneath two blankets on the wire-framed bunk in her unheated novice's cell. The winter wind howled outside and matched her mood.

Tony had obviously shown the priest her letter and that incensed her. Wasn't he man enough to consult her first?

But the vitriol that poured from the pen of the august cleric astounded her.

Though her fingers were numb from cold, she wrote a curt reply.

Dear Father,

I always believed that freedom of worship is one of the reasons we are fighting this war. It is most disappointing to see you taking the enemy's side in this respect.

As for your remarks about my professional and personal integrity, I have no doubt that they are legally actionable. For now, I choose to treat them with the contempt they deserve.
 Yours sincerely
 C. McGrath, Nursing Officer, QAIMNS/R

Before extinguishing the lamp, Colleen addressed an envelope to Tony, put in the engagement ring and sealed it.

Recriminations were swift. The CO summoned her before the week was out.

Major Forsythe occupied the superior's office. It was luxuriously carpeted, with heavy drapes about the windows, plush mahogany furniture and a roaring fire in the hearth – even though firewood was at a premium.

Montague-Stewart sat malevolently at a corner of the CO's desk. Colleen stood smartly to attention and saluted.

The firelight reflected in the CO's monocle but his voice was icy.

Her letter to Tony's priest lay in front of him.

"Your conduct towards a senior member of the Chaplaincy has been intolerable," he said. "Have you anything to say for yourself?"

"No, sir."

"In that case," Forsythe continued haughtily, "you are to be transferred from this unit as soon as formalities are complete. I understand that your special circumstances no longer apply and you should therefore arrange for an issue of tropical kit. Be thankful you are not facing a court-martial."

Oh, hell, thought Colleen. Fourteenth Army. End of the earth. How do you do it, McGrath?

"Yes, sir," she said aloud. "If I'm to get my arse kicked, then so be it."

"Dismissed," Forsythe snapped.

Colleen saluted, about faced and strode out of the office.

Her friends were distraught but as Mike Halliard said ruefully, "Ernie's quite within his rights. SEAC's more stretched for nurses than we are. They're combing the woods for them, as is Lady Edwina[138]."

They tried to commiserate with her about Tony.

"Mr Right's out there, Coll," said Hoppy as they mounted the stairs to the first-floor ward for a spell of night duty.

"Busier than usual tonight," she remarked, changing the subject while they were scrubbing up. "Bunch of shrapnel cases to keep tabs on."

"Sounds like it's on again," said Colleen. She reached for a towel. The thudding of opposing guns could be heard, growing louder.

Artillery of both sides had been ranging recently, from the mountains down to the plain, friend and foe probing each other's positions. The hospitals had begun to receive the inevitable victims.

It would indeed be a busy night, and a tragic one.

The guns were thundering on, shaking the convent's walls and breaking off bits of plaster. Colleen and Hoppy were continually on the move, pacifying the patients and brushing debris off their beds.

As a precaution, they extinguished and removed all the paraffin lamps, hanging up hand torches in their place to give at least some light.

"Captain Halliard says to get as many of the patients under their beds as possible, Sister. Doug and I'll help."

Colleen looked around at the sound of MacHendry's voice. The sergeant stood in the doorway to the room in which she was overseeing several of the shrapnel casualties.

"Thanks, Mac," she said. "We can start here. I guess Doug'll be helping Hoppy."

He nodded, grinning. They began lifting the first patient.

The hospital staff would be doing the same on all the wards, under Halliard's supervision, Forsythe having decamped again, this time to Rome.

Some patients, such as those in traction, would not be moved. Likewise, a casualty with a head injury whom they'd placed in the supervisor's room.

"I'll stay with him, Coll," said Hoppy when Doug and she had relocated all the patients they could. "Can you get some extra pillows and whatnot?"

"Sure," said Colleen and headed for the storage annex. They'd arranged spare bedding around the immobile patients, for maximum protection.

Colleen was sorting the items when the bombs hit.

Though Luftwaffe activity was now rare, the enemy still made occasional fighter sweeps, as Colleen and her friends had experienced[139].

And the odd tip and run raid.

Tonight, one aircraft achieved complete surprise amid the darkness and noise of the guns.

The raider released two bombs. One smashed into the first floor ward end-on. Miraculously, it failed to explode but the impact choked the end staircase with fallen debris. The missile stuck fast in the rubble, fins protuding diagonally.

The other bomb ploughed through the convent's roof and exploded in the centre stairwell. It collapsed with a roar. Clouds of billowing dust and pungent HE smoke filled the floors. A huge hole rent the shattered ceiling and the roof fell apart. Tiles and rafters crashed down, shutters were blown out, partitioning walls caved in.

Screaming patients were struck with falling wreckage. Half the upper ward was devastated.

Colleen was flung against a wall and blacked out.

When she regained consciousness, she felt something smothering her. It was a mattress. Pushing it off, she discovered blood was trickling down the side of her head and reached up. Her fingertips came away glistening wet from a cut above her temple. Her eyes were streaming. The air was thick with dust and acrid with HE fumes.

Dazed, Colleen struggled to her feet, relieved that she was unhurt, apart from the abrasion above her temple and a dull ache in her left hip from where she'd cannoned into the wall.

"Sister! Sister!"

The cries penetrated the ringing in her ears. Male voices were shouting – meaning some patients were alive. She was dimly aware of more voices from outside above the growl of engines as rescuers converged on the scene.

As the dust settled, she began to see better, her vision aided by torchlight still diffusing from somewhere.

She could smell chemicals. The medicine chest had fallen sideways and burst open, spilling its contents. Colleen gathered up as many intact ampoules of morphine and dressing wads as she could locate in the semi-darkness and stuffed them into a medical satchel she found, along with cords for tying on splints – she'd come back for those later. She slung the satchel by its strap over her shoulder.

Colleen groped her way forward, past the wreck of the scullery, and realised it was raining, drops splashing off dislodged timbers around her. They hissed and steamed and she thanked God the rain had doused any fires, as well as helping settle the dust.

The floor sagged beneath her feet and she paused. Its beam supports ruptured, the jagged cement apron was all that remained of the landing.

"God, don't let it fall through," she prayed.

Then Colleen saw in horror that the ceiling of the room where the head patient lay had caved in.

"Hoppy! Hoppy!" she cried, scrambling over splintered timbers, her fear of the weakened flooring temporarily forgotten.

She was able to pull some beams aside enough to see amid the rubble that Sister Hopgood was collapsed across the patient, having shielded him with her body.

"Sister," said a voice behind her. More light shone around.

It was Mac, with his torch. He'd come from the undamaged end of the ward, also having safely negotiated the rickety floor.

"Mac, thank God," said Colleen. "We've got to get through to Hoppy."

"OK," he said, coughing in the dust haze. "But careful we don't bring any more junk down."

They gingerly wormed forward and the torchlight revealed that Hoppy's head and shoulders were covered in blood and dust. A bloodstained hole gaped in her back.

Colleen knew her friend was beyond hope but she felt Hoppy's throat, nevertheless. Her skin was fearfully cold to the touch.

"Mac, I can't find a pulse," Colleen sobbed, in a desperate effort to stave off the awful truth.

"If *you* can't find it, Sister, it isn't there."

Move the body, Colleen told herself, fighting down her emotions. Get to the patient.

Together they shifted Hoppy to one side and discovered that the patient, though unconscious, was stable and had not suffered any further injury, thanks to Sister Hopgood.

Colleen re-adjusted the bedding around him.

"Let's check the rest, Mac," she said. "Some of them must have a chance if they're yelling their heads off."

Cries of distress were still coming from the adjacent rooms. Colleen tried to sound calm as she shouted back, encouraged that the ringing in her ears was subsiding.

"Right, lads, we're coming for you. Sister McGrath and Sergeant MacHendry."

In response, the cries grew more coherent.

"Please hurry, Sister," said an anguished voice. "I think my leg's off."

"I should take a look at that gash first," MacHendry said to Colleen.

"No time," she said firmly. "Blood's clotted, anyway."

"Anyone hear me!"

Halliard's voice came from the ground floor. The rescuers would be evacuating patients downstairs. Dollie and June were down there. God, were they OK, Colleen wondered anxiously.

"Sister McGrath, Sergeant MacHendry," she called back. "At least one fatal staff casualty, Sister Hopgood."

Colleen's voice choked on the words but they had to know.

"Main staircase is gone but the stairwell took a lot of the blast," Halliard informed her. "We'll get you out, Coll but we'll have to clear the staircase at the end of the building. It's full of rubble. We got shook up down here, knocked off our feet but we're OK."

A couple of sturdily built anterooms separated the ground floor wards from the main stairwell. Though now wrecked, they, too, had absorbed a lot of the concussion. Moreover, the ward immediately below the bombed wing was unoccupied, having been cleared for possible incoming patients. Again, Colleen thanked God.

"Thanks Mike, we're going for the patients," she called down.

"Take care!" he shouted back. "And hang on."

Boots crunching on plaster and masonry fragments, almost unaware of the still falling rain, Mac and Colleen eased underneath fallen timbers into the room next to the supervisor's quarters.

"Over here, Sister!" voices were urging.

Mac's torch beam fell on the nearest patient, a shrapnel casualty grunting and in shock with a fresh wound, from which his intestines were pushing out like bloodied ropes. Colleen carefully scooped them back into the stomach cavity with both hands.

"Get a dressing on him when I move my hands, Mac," she said. "That's it, perfect timing."

MacHendry secured the dressing and Colleen injected the casualty with morphine. She sensed movement and glimpsed some of the patients who'd miraculously escaped further injury trying to stand.

"We'll help, Sister," said one.

"Thanks, lads," said Colleen. "Help Mac with those beams."

They discovered two patients who had suffered fatal head injuries and then the man who'd feared his leg was severed. Colleen was able to reassure him.

"OK, mate, traction's away west but your leg's still on. I'll give you a jab."

The end of a ladder grated against the room's ravaged windowsill and another familiar voice sounded. Through the gloom, Andy Somerville and Colleen recognised each other.

"Dollie's OK, they all are, Mike says," she blurted out. God, he must have been worried on the way in, she thought.

"I know, Coll, thank God it wasn't a blockbuster," he said calmly. "Any that we can take down via the ladders? We can use fireman's carry as necessary."

"Any takers, lads?" she said to the patients. A couple of them shuffled to the window space. In the meantime, other REs got in through windows by standing on truck cabs, where their mates hoisted them up to help shift debris, even while the fire escape stairs were being cleared – where a sinister discovery was made.

"UXB, sir!" called a voice from below. It was Sergeant Gilfillan.

"On my way, Sergeant!" Someville called back. "'Scuse me, Coll."

He rapidly descended the ladder and headed for the end staircase.

Andy and Sergeant Gilfillan supervised securing the projectile. It was the safest strategy in the circumstances.

Gilfillan then organised placement of joists on the ground floor to brace the ceiling. On the top floor, Somerville oversaw the stabilisation of the caved-in roof, while several of his sappers conveyed the less seriously injured down ladders.

Orderlies followed the sappers, to assist Colleen and MacHendry. By the light of torches, they bound dripping wounds, injected morphine, splinted fractures and transferred the more severely wounded to stretchers. They discovered another fatal victim of crush injuries but the remaining patients had survived, though many needed more surgery. Teams of orderlies and sappers removed the patients from the entire upstairs ward. Where necessary, they strapped them onto their camp beds or stretchers and hoisted them out windows – all panes were shattered, even in the undamaged wing - down ladders fixed at low angles in the trays of lorries parked close to the walls.

Andy crouched beside Colleen.

"We'll get everyone out through the window spaces, Coll," he said. "Can't risk the end stairs. I've told Mike. We'll detonate the bomb with a controlled explosion when everyone's clear."

"And pray it doesn't go off in the meantime," said Colleen shakily. She was kneeling by a semi-conscious patient covered with a blanket and still in shock, binding his broken arm.

"Amen," said Andy.

Then the muted glow divulged one more casualty. He lay comatose beneath several broken timbers. Blood from a chest wound had soaked his battledress.

"God, it's Scottie!" exclaimed Colleen, reproaching herself that she'd forgotten about him.

As soon as possible, willing hands carefully stretchered Prescott out a window into the back of a lorry, along with other serious casualties.

Providentially, nearby farm buildings included a combination barn and stables that had earlier been converted into an overflow ward. The wounded were conveyed there. When the bombed ward was emptied, Colleen and MacHendry made their way across the intervening field to the stables, gas capes about their shoulders. Their boots squelched in soggy ground patched with snow partially thawed.

It was still raining but the artillery had subsided. Colleen noticed that the ache in her hip was nearly gone. Her hearing had almost returned to normal.

Then she heard the sound of more aircraft engines and looked up, startled.

"They'll be our night fighters," Mac explained as he ushered her into the barn. "Pity they weren't here earlier."

Inside, the REs had rigged up emergency lighting and already theatre staff were operating, Dollie, Helen and Karen among them. Directed by Halliard and Matron Hewitt, Sisters and orderlies tended the men on stretchers or those sitting on bales of straw with arms slung or heads bandaged. Colleen glimpsed June and Julie helping with the emergency Resus. For now, it was all hands to the pumps.

"You wait right here, Sister," said Mac. "I'm gonna clean up that injury."

He made her sit down on the edge of a set of straw bales and went to scrounge a basin of hot water. Colleen settled herself, thankful that her surroundings were warm and dry.

"Sister," said a voice huskily. It came from a form lying on a stretcher close by, in semi-shadow.

Colleen recognised Prescott. His face was like chalk. Her heart sank at the sight. She knew his wound was mortal.

Colleen knelt beside Doug and clasped his hand.

"Thanks, Sister," he said weakly. "You should have that cut sorted."

"Mac's looking after me," she said, smiling. "Can I make you more comfortable, Doug?" She realised he was heavily drugged.

"No, I've not long. I asked to be put aside. Will you pray with me, please?"

She did so.

"Marjie didn't make it, did she?" he asked hoarsely.

Sadly, Colleen shook her head.

A shadow fell across them.

"He is my communicant, Sister McGrath," it said. "I will see to him now."

The figure held aloft a metal crucifix. It resembled a devil's trident in the half light.

Colleen looked up, brushing stray hairs from her forehead with her free hand. She felt like a tigress, protecting her young.

"You go to hell," she said thickly. "Take that demon magnet with you."

Abashed, Montague-Stewart moved away.

"Fixed him, eh?" said Prescott. His eyes gleamed in his waxen face. "I love you, Sister…"

He stiffened, then relaxed. His hand in hers went limp. He was gone. Gently, she closed his eyes and folded his arms across his chest, hot tears spilling down her face. She wiped them away and sat back on the bale.

MacHendry returned with dressings and a bowl of hot water. Halliard was with him.

"Doug's died," Colleen whispered. Her friends nodded soberly.

"I'll make arrangements," said Mac. Halliard thanked him and the sergeant departed.

"Right, let's have a look, Colleen," Mike said and took out his pencil torch.

"I'm sure it's nothing, Mike."

"I'll be the judge of that," said Halliard. He shone the torch in her right pupil. "And when we're finished with you, you're going to rest. That's an order. By the way," he added, "Jim Rodwell says the bloke Hoppy shielded will pull through, also the lad whose guts you retrieved. Well done."

Colleen's wound required only an outsize strip of plaster after it had been cleaned up. Halliard gave her an anti-tetanus jab, nevertheless. Accompanied by Lance Corporal Burrows, Mac returned with a blanket and towel over his shoulder and another bowl of water for Colleen to wash her hands, for they were still smeared with blood and dust from the rescue operation.

Mac placed the blanket and towel beside Colleen, then he and Burrows took hold of each end of Prescott's stretcher.

"We'll take Doug away now, sir," MacHendry said to Halliard, who nodded gravely.

"I'll see you later, Coll," he promised, before returning to his rounds.

"You take care, Sister," the lance corporal said kindly.

Colleen smiled and thanked them. When she'd washed and dried her hands, she wrapped herself in the blanket and lay down on the straw bales.

She fell asleep in an instant and didn't even stir when the REs' controlled explosion dealt with the UXB.

Colleen awoke a couple of hours later, to find that things had settled down considerably, though the theatre lights were still on, where Rodwell and Jardine were operating. Others of her colleagues quietly monitored slumbering patients by torchlight or hurricane lamp. She could hear a generator hum above the pattering of rain.

"Feeling better?" someone said. Colleen looked up to see Halliard coming over to her. She nodded.

"My head's clear."

"Good. Could do with your help, Coll. Some more casualties are on their way from tonight's shindig."

"Be with you in a tick," she said, standing up. "I'll just go to the bathroom."

The latrines were located in an outhouse near the bombed building.

"Fine. Oh, by the way, there's a bloke to see you. He's been waiting in his jeep for an hour or so. Seems a bit agitated."

"Captain Gatacre?"

Halliard nodded.

He handed her a garment. It was her waxed leather raincoat. They'd all recently been issued with them.

"We carted everything over from the Sisters' wing when Andy's boys secured it. Best see your visitor when you've been."

"Thanks, Mike." Colleen put on her mac. "I won't be long."

Immediately he sighted Colleen, Tony hastened to meet her. They stood facing each other, Colleen with the mac's hood over her head, her arms clasped about her, Gatacre spreading his hands in an imploring gesture.

The conversation was brief.

"Colleen, you can't mean it."

"I meant every word. And you had no business betraying my confidence. That's why you got the ring back."

"Colleen, surely…"

"*No*, Tony. It's *over*."

She turned on her heel and trudged away through the storm without a backward glance.

Halfway to the stables, the floodgates burst.

"Oh, God, I can't take it," she sobbed, her boots half submerged in a patch of slush. "We've lost Hoppy, we've lost Scottie. I've dumped Tony and I'm being posted to God-knows-where in Burma, and all in the pissing rain."

Ironically, she recalled the last stanza of Sorrento, from all those months ago.

"Yet you say: "Farewell, I'm leaving?"

"You'd desert these loving arms,

"And this very land of beauty,

"Will you nevermore return?"

"No, I won't" she said through gritted teeth.

But ten years later she did, in the company of her husband and their two children, one of whom was destined to become my mother. During the visit, Colleen would meet an old friend, with some important information for her. For now, we must continue with Sister McGrath's then current dilemmas.

The dead were buried with full military honours and a special service was held for Nursing Officer Hopgood and Sergeant Prescott.

Despite the tragedy, Forsythe, who had returned, was adamant that Sister McGrath's posting would proceed but he granted an extension for her to attend the funerals.

Naturally, her outburst at Montague-Stewart hadn't helped her case.

When the rain eventually stopped, the temperature dropped again and snow squalls beset the town. The staff set about breaking up the ice on the paths and spreading gravel.

In the brittle air of early morning, the Apennine wind whipped ice crystals into the faces of the ranks marching to the hillside cemetery.

A platoon from Mac and Scottie's old regiment led the way, followed by Andy Somerville's Royal Engineers, then the Royal Army Medical Corps contingent, crisply turned out in battledress, leather jerkins and peaked caps or berets.

Dinah and Mollie marched with the QAs, Fusilier Briggs with Andy Somerville's platoon.

"Parade, halt! Right - turn! Right – dress! Eyes – front!"

The shouts of the parade commander, a Canadian warrant officer, resounded across the bleak landscape.

His charges drilled with precision.

They formed a hollow square around the open gravesites containing their fallen comrades wrapped in canvas shrouds.

The parade stood at attention, bareheaded, as Reverend Allerton intoned his funeral oration during which he quoted from the First Letter of Saint John.

"'This is the victory that overcometh the world, even our faith.'"

The reverend placed a handful of snowy earth on each of the shrouded figures. He resumed the position of attention, repositioned his cap and brought his hand up in salute. The rest of the parade followed suit.

The WO then summoned the firing party. At his command, the weapons fired as one. Their reports rocketed across windswept ridges.

Then a lone Canadian piper sounded The Flowers of the Forest, while the parade maintained the salute.

Blinking away tears, frozen snowflakes stinging her face, Colleen listened to the solemn notes of the lament drifting up the valley of the Senio.

She thought on the words.

I've seen the morning,
With gold hills adorning,
And loud tempests storming,
Before parting day.
I've seen Tweed's silver streams,
Glittering in the sunny beams,
Grow drumlie[140] *and dark,*
As they rolled on their way

But Hoppy and Doug would see the morning, of that Colleen was sure.

Thus did the young men and women of Britain and the Empire bid farewell to fallen comrades.

An abundance of letters would go to the families of those killed.

Captain Halliard sighed heavily and looked up from the report form on his makeshift desk in the groom's annex of the stable.

"Three patients, Sister Hopgood, Sergeant Prescott," he said moodily to June, who was standing beside him. "Twenty others needing surgery. And as if the butcher's bill wasn't enough, we're still going to lose Sister McGrath."

Irritably, he flung his pen down on the report, rose to his feet and stared at the wall.

June lightly touched his sleeve.

"Mike," she said softly. "We have to get on."

"I'll see you on the ward in a bit, June," he said, nodding.

She was about to depart when he spoke again.

"I've got to attend one of these regular conferences with some RAMC brass in a few days' time. They're held jointly with the Yanks, so it means a trip to Florence. Matron usually accompanies me to give the nursing perspective." He paused, with a shy smile.

"However, Bronwyn insisted that Sister Taylor went this time," he continued.

"Just say when, Mike," she said warmly, her deep blue eyes sparkling.

Irresistibly, they drew together, Halliard's arms enfolding June's trim waist, their eyes closing, their lips meeting and sealing.

They were glad that the groom's quarters were reasonably private.

The weather had grounded all flights, so Sergeant MacHendry drove Colleen fifty miles to the recently restored railhead at Rimini, little more than a bare platform in the war-ravaged town. It was January 31st, raw and misty.

Colleen and Mac stowed her trunk, camp bed and bedroll aboard the goods van, crated and clearly stencilled for onward transfer to the transport she'd join at Naples.

"So long, Mac," she said, her voice breaking as she hugged him. "Look after Julie."

"I will," he promised. "Come see us after the war. We'll tour the Rockies."

"You bet," she said, then boarded the train and located her compartment. She would be sharing it with some WRN officers, pleased to be leaving their bleak Adriatic station.

"Sunny Italy," remarked one. "You could have fooled me, ducks."

"Hullo there!" said another to Colleen as she entered. "Shove up, you lot, make way for the Queen Alexandra's."

Colleen thanked them, stashed her holdall and web bag on the luggage rack above her seat, smoothed her skirt and settled down to what promised to be a convivial journey.

At the same time, a nondescript individual in civilian clothes had also entrained. He was not so kindly disposed to Sister McGrath. Moreover, he served the same master whose acolytes had already taken note of Sister McGrath's friends-to-be in the Far East.

And he was charged with a deadly assignment.

The journey lasted twelve hours. On the way to Naples, the train clattered past coastal towns shattered by battle and then through mountains witness to so much blood.

But for Colleen, the trip was pleasant enough. Her WRN companions were chatty and sociable and she was glad of their company.

"We're off to Trincomalee," explained the one who'd welcomed Colleen. "Suits me. My bod's out there on HMS *Wyvern*."

A tall, fair, athletic girl named Sue Lentaigne, she was serving with the Queen Alexandra's Royal Naval Nursing Service.

Eventually, the train jolted to a halt at the terminus by the Naples docks.

"End of the line, girls," said Sue. She got up to don her mac and reach for her baggage.

The others followed suit. Colleen had been reading her Bible by the brownish glow of the compartment light and she placed the Book in a top pocket of her mac.

When they emerged from the station, Sue managed to hail a covered one-and-a-half ton lorry nosing through the rainy gloom with dimmed headlights. The bereted driver leant out of the cab.

"Can we be of service, ladies?" he asked.

"Can you please give us a lift to our billet?" said Sue with an engaging smile.

Their billet was a pre-war hostel for young *fascisti* that the American Red Cross now ran as a rest and transit centre, complete with dorms, dining and catering facilities. It was up the road from the station.

"Sure thing, ma'am," said the driver. He and his mate climbed out to assist their passengers into the back, a slightly awkward operation because the girls were all wearing skirts though Colleen reckoned the RASC boys wouldn't mind the unavoidable displays of leg.

"Be a bit of squeeze with all our gear but that'll keep us warm," Sue remarked when they were all aboard.

None of them noticed the battered taxi-cab that followed unobtrusively, with its shabbily dressed civilian passenger.

Colleen checked into the centre and then headed for the dining room, intent on a quick supper and early night. Sue and the others had gone to a local *trattoria*.

The dining tables seemed to be fully occupied but as Colleen stood with a laden tray and tried to locate a spare seat, she heard a voice to her left.

"Hey, over here, honey!"

Colleen turned to see an American Nurse Corps Lieutenant, seated at a nearby table with an empty place, beckoning her. She noticed that the American girl was the same slim build as herself, with similarly coloured hair, cut short like hers.

"Thanks," said Colleen gratefully. Setting down her tray opposite the American, she eased into the seat. "Must be about the only spare space."

"Yep, chow-time sure is popular – and the ham and eggs are great. By the way, I'm Naomi Sullivan, from Amarillo. That's in the Lone-Star state of Texas."

They shook hands.

"Colleen McGrath. I'm from Yorkshire."

"In England, right?"

"Sort of. Like Texas and the US, I guess."

Naomi laughed.

"I get the picture, hon."

Colleen placed her serviette on her lap, mentally said Grace and started tucking in. Naomi was right. The food was marvellous.

"Where're you off to, Naomi?" Colleen asked.

The Texan had finished her meal and was sipping coffee. She responded enthusiastically to Colleen's question.

"Stateside, yippee! I've been in the Med since Kasserine[141], so it's rotation time for me. What about you, Coll?"

"CBI. Burma probably."

"Well, God speed – hey, is that the time?"

Colleen glanced at her wristwatch and then at the American's.

"Checks with mine." she said.

"You'll have to excuse me, Coll," said Naomi, getting up in haste. "I gotta catch the PX. It closes in a few minutes. Anything I can get you?"

"Oh, thanks, Naomi. Soap, toothpaste, lipstick, please – nylons if they've got any. I'll pay you."

"Forget it, my treat. I guess you'll take the same size as me. Oh, wait a second, is it still pouring cats and dogs out there?"

"Was when I came in."

Naomi grimaced.

"Left my mac in my room, by the time I go fetch it, the place'll be shut."

"Take mine. I left it at Reception," said Colleen. She reached into a breast pocket. "Here's the chit."

"Thanks a million, Coll. I'll be back in a jiffy."

The Texan girl hurried to the foyer.

The quarry was there! Lurking in an alleyway, Colleen's pursuer saw the girl in the PX, just across from the centre, the hood of her British Army raincoat folded back to reveal that unmistakable red hair.

He had been considering his next move when fate had presented him with this opportunity, one he would not pass up.

Naomi did her shopping, stuffed it into the pockets of the mac, then re-crossed the street to the centre. The rain beat down relentlessly and she pulled the mac about her.

As she neared the steps, a figure wearing a balaclava dashed out of the darkness. She saw the danger too late.

The knife-blade's razor edge slashed the victim's outer garment, the needle-like point aimed at the American girl's heart.

But it hit an obstruction that deflected it from the intended vital spot

The blade pierced Naomi's abdomen nevertheless and she cried out in pain and fear, her knees buckling.

Torchlight glared in her face, as the hood of her mac fell back.

Her attacker cursed, seized her handbag and fled. Naomi lurched to the balustrade, pressing her hand to the wound, blood streaming from between her fingers.

She dragged herself up the steps, forced her way through the doors and collapsed on the floor.

"Naomi," Colleen whispered as she entered the cubicle.

The other girl looked toward her and smiled, her nose twitching with the oxygen tube inserted therein. Following an emergency operation and transfusion at a nearby American hospital, her condition was thankfully now stable. A guard of white-helmeted MPs had driven Colleen to the hospital.

Provost officers had already seen Naomi but she had been able to tell them little.

"Hi, Coll," she said weakly. "I'm usually the one looking down."

Colleen sat by the bed and grasped Naomi's hand.

"Oh, Naomi," she said, tears in her eyes. "I should have gone with you."

"You weren't to know, hon. My fault, leaving things to the last minute. Disorganised, like my mom says."

"I got some things from the hospital kiosk while I was waiting to see you," said Colleen, reaching down. "Here, I'll put them in your locker."

"You shouldn't have, but, hey, thanks. And your share of the shopping's in there, too - ."

Naomi coughed. A spasm of pain rippled across her face. She held a towel to her mouth and spat blood into it.

"I'll get the MO," Colleen said anxiously. Naomi shook her head.

"No, I'm just clearin' my throat. Take more than a Dago footpad to finish this Panhandle gal. Good thing you'd left your Bible in the pocket, though."

"Praise the Lord for that."

"Amen. Sorry about your mac, and your Bible's got a rip in it."

"Don't worry. Just get better."

Naomi smiled and nodded. Then her voice grew grave.

"Listen, Coll," she said earnestly. "In spite of what I said just now, I don't think it was just a bag snatch, even if the provost guys do."

"What do you mean, Naomi?"

The American girl spoke in a fearful whisper.

"When that guy stabbed me, he shined a torch in my face and got a closer look at me. He cursed in some foreign lingo and made off. Might have lifted my bag just to make it look like a robbery. If that's true, then somebody's got your number, honey. We're about the same height and in a British raincoat with the hood down, I look like you, especially from the back. He could have caught sight of me in the PX and mistook me for you. I hate to worry you, Coll, but it sure seems that way to me."

The duty nurse discreetly approached.

"Your transport's here, Sister," she tactfully informed Colleen.

Colleen collected her share of the shopping, leant over and kissed Naomi gently on the forehead.

"Bye for now, love," she murmured. "Safe journey home."

"Come visit after the war, Coll," Naomi urged. "Amarillo, the Sullivan spread, I'll send you our box number. Definitely my treat but 'til then take care, OK?"

Colleen was driven back to the centre with an armed escort.

Naomi's warning reverberated in her brain. Was it a random attack – or not? Twice recently, her life had been in danger but those incidents were accidents of war – or were they?

The events were in fact harbingers of terrors to come.

Colleen and Sue stood leaning on the AMC's top deck railing, watching Naples' bomb-scarred docks recede into grey morning mist as their ship cruised past the protruding masts of bombed vessels still resting on the bottom.

"A lot's happened since I last saw those," said Colleen. The two of them had quickly become friends, not only by virtue of their shared calling but also because the other girl came from Bridlington.

Sue drew on her cigarette and exhaled smoke.

"You've been pushed from pillar to post, Coll," she said sympathetically. "Any more repercussions from last night?"

"Provosts still think it was robbery," said Colleen, shaking her head. "Can't blame them. It's happened before, even in broad daylight."

Sue nodded reflectively and voiced their shared hopes.

"Well, here's to a relaxing sea voyage, anyway."

At first, their hopes seemed to have been fulfilled. The sea stayed calm and Colleen was able to enjoy the fine repasts from the galley without upset.

"Merchant Navy's done us proud," Sue remarked at the first meal to murmurs of agreement.

After a night passage through Suez, Colleen and her companions came on deck to gaze at the glittering expanse of the Red Sea, after which the days slipped by in leisurely fashion. The girls basked in warm sunshine, played deck games – when they'd recovered from the various inoculations they had to receive from the ship's MO – and socialised. The other passengers were male and female officers from all the services so an almost holiday atmosphere prevailed, enlivened by an ENSA troupe that provided nightly shows in the ship's ballroom and orchestral backing for dances.

Though Colleen preferred to volunteer for duty in the sick bay when these were staged. She realised now how Dollie must have felt ill at ease on these occasions, until Andy had claimed her, in his kindly and manly way.

"I don't feel right about dancing any more," Colleen explained to Sue, who usually kept her company. "Ever since Matron staged a prayer meeting on the way up to the line. Our Lord got a hold of me and He hasn't let go."

Colleen never forgot Sue's response.

"I think He's under your skin, too, Coll."

One evening, as the ship entered the Gulf of Aden, the troupe staged a number where everyone could join in the chorus.

"On the road to Mandalay,

"Where the flyin' fishes play,

"An' the dawn comes up like thunder outer China 'crost the Bay!"

"Had to come, didn't it," said Sue during the applause, when she and Colleen went for a round of drinks at the bar.

But after they'd retired for the night, something happened that no one expected.

Colleen woke to a violent lurch that nearly pitched her out of bed.

"I think we've hit something," said Sue. She swung her legs over the edge of her bunk. "Better get dressed."

"Ship's stopped," said one of the other two WRNs who shared the cabin.

"No power," said the other, flicking the light switch. The cabin remained in darkness.

They quickly donned their JGs, plimsolls, life jackets and steel helmets. These were all placed ready to hand in the event of an emergency.

A loud knock on the door and a steward's urgent voice confirmed that such had arisen.

"Make for your lifeboat station, ladies. Ship's hit a mine."

They heard him hurrying off to alert others.

Slinging their survival bags over their shoulders, they made for the companionway dimly visible at the end of the corridor, gripping handrails for balance because the vessel was wallowing to and fro.

Along with her Bible, torch, First Aid kit, stationery, cosmetics, manicure set and other personal items, Colleen's bag contained the lingerie acquired in Naples and the nylons Naomi had bought her. She wasn't about to lose that gear.

"We're going uphill," she remarked.

"Ship's settling by the stern," said Sue. "That's usually where a mine hits. Must've been a drifter."

"I'm glad we didn't go straight down," Colleen said nervously.

"They'll close watertight doors," Sue told her. "That'll help keep us afloat. Just hope no-one's trapped."

They met the other WRNs in the passage and merged with a stream of passengers who filed quietly up the companionway onto the boat deck. Everyone knew the drill. Colleen noticed Verey light distress flares arcing above them in the warm tropical night.

"No fire by the looks," said one of the WRNs. "That's a blessing."

The ship's davits had been swung out and lifeboats were already descending, each with a couple of ratings aboard as crew.

"Saves time to get them launched first," Sue said to Colleen. "See they've unrolled the nets for us."

"This way, ladies," a petty officer called, confirming Sue's remark. "You can go down the scramble nets. Lads'll catch you at the bottom."

"Bet they will," Colleen said as she and the others hoisted themselves over the side and grasped the thick rope strands.

"Chance of a lifetime," said Sue.

As each boat filled up, crew and passengers rowed it away from the sinking vessel. The WRNs in Colleen's boat handled the oars like veterans. She observed that the ship's stern was almost awash. They had taken to the lifeboats with minimal time to spare.

"There's someone in the water!" shouted a voice. Colleen saw a splashing figure.

Several pairs of hands heaved the castaway into the boat. He was one of the ship's boys.

"I'll see to him," said Colleen and put her arms around the shivering lad. All at once, he vomited bile and seawater over her slacks.

"That's it, mate," Colleen whispered. "Get it out of your system."

She called for some drinking water from the boat's provisions and helped the boy take a few sips. "Gently does it," she said.

A huge shape loomed out of the darkness and a searchlight swept across the watery scene. One of the escorting destroyers had drawn alongside to pick them up. Colleen observed more scramble nets unravelling and navy crewmen lining the deck. One of the ratings in Colleen's boat called to them.

"We've got a castaway."

A bosun's chair was lowered for the boy, after which Colleen and the others ascended the nets into willing hands that assisted them inboard.

"Quite an adventure," remarked Sue, as they were conducted below decks to be fortified with cocoa.

"Anyone got a comb?" asked another WRN. "Remember, we're not supposed to look like survivors[142]."

It turned out that everyone had survived, a small counter balance to the hecatomb of lives lost at sea in the last five years, including dozens of QAs in transit.

Wearing navy fatigues while her slacks were being laundered, Colleen was shown into the destroyer's cramped sickbay to meet Boy Nesbitt.

He lay under a blanket on a bunk fixed to a white-painted bulkhead. Despite his pallor, he smiled broadly when Colleen entered and eagerly grasped her extended hand.

"I was right aft when the mine hit and fell down a companionway," he explained in a voice scarcely broken. "Sea flooded in and washed me out when the ship heeled over. Seems the mine wrecked the screws, so that was good but I kept getting doused in the swell. Thanks for looking after me, Sister."

"My pleasure, Nezzie," said Colleen, smiling.

What's a kid like him doing in this mess, she wondered.

Several hours later, the destroyer dropped anchor in the port of Aden where the AMC's crew and passengers were dispersed to various billets. RN transport conveyed Colleen and her WRN companions to tented accommodation next to an RAF base.

"We better insist they do something with us quick sharp," Sue advised when they detrucked amid swirls of sand kicked up by a desert wind like the blast of an oven. "So we're not stuck here."

Unimpressed by the arid surroundings, the flat-roofed, sun-bleached dwellings of the town and the bare hills beyond, her colleagues were in full agreement.

Ascertaining its location from their driver, they trooped to the station commander's tent. Sue put her head through the tent flap.

"May we come in, sir?" she asked.

"Of course, ma'am," said the moustached squadron leader in khaki shirt, shorts, long socks and polished boots. He sat behind a trestle table with paper work spread over it. "How can I help?" he asked when they assembled inside, five WRNs and a QAIMNS/R.

"Thank you for accommodating us, sir," said Sue tactfully. "But we need to continue on to our postings as soon as possible; Trincomalee - and Calcutta," she added, glancing at Colleen. "No doubt those will be the best places to get rekitted."

"I've actually been working on your problem, ladies," the squadron leader said, rising to his feet – and the occasion. "But for now, would you like to take a shower and then have a drink in the mess? I'll show you the way."

The showers were perforated canvas buckets mounted in an ablutions tent above duckboards placed over cement soakaway drains. The girls stood under them fully clothed, the refreshingly cool water helping to wash the sweat out of their garments. They stood about in the sun afterwards and quickly dried off.

"Here's the plan," said their benefactor when they convened in the tented officers' mess and were sipping ice-cold shandies. "One of our Liberators is due here at zero seven hundred hours tomorrow. She'll be ready for take-off by zero nine hundred hours and go via Karachi, Dum Dum and Trincomalee. You should all be where you need to be in a day or so[143]."

"We're very grateful, sir," Colleen said sincerely. Sue and the others echoed her thanks.

"Our pleasure, ladies," said the airman. "Until tomorrow, I trust you will continue to enjoy our hospitality. Evening mess is at eighteen hundred hours and you are all cordially invited."

Colleen was to remember the flight mainly as endless skies, clear blue and fleecy white by day, diamond-pointed velvet black by night. The RAF crew went out of their way to ensure the girls' journey was as comfortable as possible.

The Liberator landed on Dum Dum's concrete apron about midday local time, approximately twenty-four hours after leaving Aden.

Colleen's first stop after the WC was the transit hut. Her initial posting was a base hospital at Comilla, two hundred miles east. From there, she was determined to wangle a transfer to a CCS in Burma itself.

"When can you get me to Comilla?" she asked the RAF flight coordinator, a pudgy warrant officer with thinning hair. "I'll be taking all my kit, though I need to get reissued first. Our ship was mined."

"Daks go pretty regularly, Sister," he said, eying her up appreciatively. "I'll get you on the zero nine hundred flight tomorrow."

"Thank you, Sergeant-Major. You're most kind."

"Lecherous old coot," she muttered under her breath on her way out. "Still, it's to my advantage."

The Liberator wasn't flying out until the evening so the WRNs insisted on accompanying Colleen to the huge SEAC depot where she drew her kit issue and then to the Grand Hotel – stopover point for innumerable servicemen and women.

As in Naples, they commandeered another one-and-a-half ton truck for transport.

"Safety in numbers, Coll," Sue advised. "We'll just hover in the background but as senior service, we're bound to impress the army QMs. It'll help get you a room at the Grand, too."

It did, on both counts.

Following a poignant farewell in the hotel foyer, Colleen went up to her room and lay down on the bed. She soon fell asleep beneath the gently whirring fan.

When Colleen awoke, she summoned a maidservant to run a bath. About an hour later, feeling much refreshed and wearing her newly issued walking-out uniform – minus the jacket because it was too warm – she went down to the restaurant for an English meal.

She took a spare seat on the restaurant balcony among some obliging ATS officers and ate her meal while gazing at the ornate, old world surroundings. They seemed so anachronistic.

When she'd finished supper, she decided to turn in. Her nap notwithstanding, Colleen was finding the climate quite enervating.

"Knocks you for six, at first," said one of the ATS girls sympathetically.

But first, Colleen visited Reception to ensure a taxi to the airport would arrive for her at zero seven hundred hours sharp.

"Or there'll be hell to pay," she warned the Indian clerk.

Her prediction proved true but not as she expected.

Heading for the staircase, heels clicking on the tiled floor, she passed in full view of some rowdy Special Forces officers at the bar, all in JGs. They were recently returned from Burma and tippling as if anticipating no tomorrow.

A deluge of wolf whistles followed her.

"Hey, sweetie, come an' have a drink," several slurred voices called.

She continued up to the first floor landing.

Heavy footsteps came pounding after her.

"C'mon, sugar, join the party," urged a gruff voice with beery breath.

"Sod off," said Colleen irritably.

She heard a mischievous chortle and felt a hand slide onto her hip.

Forbidden territory.

On one side of the landing, conveniently within Colleen's reach, an exquisite vase, over a foot high, reposed on a wooden stand.

Colleen grasped its curved brim, whirled about and smashed the vase across the interloper's head. A long-limbed individual with fairish hair and beard, he tumbled back down the stairs

But a crony had followed him, an Oriental whom Colleen took to be a Nisei[144].

Muscular, agile and enraged by his colleague's humiliation, he confronted Colleen on the landing.

She was holding the rim of the shattered vase, a collar of jagged porcelain teeth.

With a snarl, the Oriental tried to kick it out of her hand but Colleen was too quick for him. He howled in pain as she gouged his shin with razor sharp ceramic.

"That's one for our girls in Hong Kong," she snapped and hurled the bloodied shard at him as he, too, lost his balance. The rebuke was grossly unfair but Colleen wasn't disposed to be fair at that moment.

She dashed to her room, hastened inside, locked the door, shoved the heavy teak dresser against it and leant back on the dresser, exhaling heavily.

"God, what next?" she cried.

That question was easily answered. The Provost Marshall placed her in protective custody and she was deposited on the C-47 next morning by two hulking red caps, who grinned hugely as they helped stow her kit.

"Cracking job, Sister," said one of them.

"Don't tell anyone we said so, though," his mate added. "We're not supposed to have a sense of humour."

Seemingly endless rows of hospital tents and *bashas* stretched across the flat, muggy environs of Comilla.

After she'd sorted Colleen's accommodation, the senior Sister put her on night duty with a ward full of Sikhs, brought from Arakan with hideous jungle sores. Her tasks included supervising local VADs in cleaning the infections, changing dressings and forestalling some distasteful patients' proclivities.

"Watch 'em like a hawk, Sister," Colleen's superior warned her. "I don't want them buggering each other[145]."

They seemed too emaciated for that. God, what must it be like in Burma, Colleen wondered, to do this to grown men? She reckoned Comilla unpleasant enough, with its climate like a sauna, the huge beetles that flew into your hurricane lamp during tours of the wards, the frogs and reptiles that hopped and slithered across the pathways in the dark.

"Always check your boots before putting them on," the senior advised.

Colleen was returning to her quarters about midnight some days after her arrival when an orderly intercepted her.

"Post's caught up with you, Sister," he said, handing her a bundle of letters. "Sorry I took a while to find you."

She thanked him and hastened to her tent.

Most were from the girls in Italy. June's revealed that Major Forsythe had been transferred to Eighth Army HQ and that Halliard was now officially the CO. *Mike and I are engaged* she'd added.

Reading in bed by torchlight beneath her mosquito net, Colleen whooped for joy, startling the other off-duty QAs in the tent.

"Sounds like you've won the pools, McGrath," said a tired voice. "You better pipe down if you want to live to enjoy it."

A letter from her parents quietened her. Like Tony, they were hurt by her decision. However, she knew of one person who would both understand and rejoice.

With the torch in her lap, she began writing to Annie, first apologising for the delay[146]. She had to write to everyone again because all the letters penned aboard ship had gone down with the purser's safe.

After breakfast, Colleen put in a request for transfer to a CCS and received an early morning summons from Matron two days later.

Matron was a buxom woman with rich, dark hair. She habitually wore a white starched cotton uniform, though everyone else was in JGs. She sat to attention behind her trestle table desk when Colleen came in and saluted.

"Seems like trouble's your middle name, McGrath," she said abruptly. "I've been reading your record." She glanced at the file on the table. "But you're also a top notch nurse, so I'm approving your transfer as requested. They certainly need people of your calibre. Here are your orders."

She handed Colleen a slim brown envelope.

"Thank you, Matron."

"Your transport takes off at zero nine hundred hours. Dismissed."

Colleen saluted and went out.

The crinkled green of the Chin Hills faded into the vast dun-coloured dry belt of central Burma. With the V-shaped confluence of the Chindwin and Irrawaddy Rivers reflecting muddy brown in the afternoon glare off the C-47's port wing, Colleen gazed at the array of paddy fields, scrub patches, rocky hillocks and scattered villages that slid beneath the aircraft as it began its descent.

She glanced at her watch, the greenish painted strap reminding her that everything needed green camouflage here. Touchdown was not far off.

The transport was ferrying supplies and equipment to the CCSs in support of Fourth Corps.

Beginning about the third week of February, the Corps had been engaged under cover of darkness in crossing the Irrawaddy, shifting troops, vehicles, ammunition and supplies across the vast watercourse, over a thousand yards wide in places, to join battle on the eastern shore.

Fourth Corps' prime objective was the railhead town of Meiktila, seventy miles south of Mandalay, the old capital and another Fourteenth Army objective.

Resistance would be bitter, the fighting bloody. The C-47's other passengers, men en route to their units, sat subdued, like Colleen wedged in between the panniers and crates of supplies secured by straps.

Not even the presence of their glamorous QA fellow traveller could allay their apprehension.

The aircraft's array of in-flight stretchers were folded up and fastened against the fuselage to admit the supplies. They would carry their own precious cargo on the return flight.

When she climbed down the C-47's steel ladder onto the PSP strip, web bag and bedroll over her shoulders, Colleen adjusted her bush hat to shade her eyes from the glare.

The heat hit her like the breath of a furnace.

Almost immediately, she noticed lines of jeeps and ambulances, with the all too familiar sight of injured men on stretchers, limbs and bodies displaying the bloodied yellow of dressing swathes.

Several C-47s would fly out today.

Other vehicles waited to convey cargo and men to their destinations.

A wiry little man behind the wheel of a waiting jeep hailed Colleen.

"Over here, Sister," he called with a welcoming grin and an unmistakable accent. "Geordie Wood's the name. I'm your driver."

"Pleased to meet you, Corporal," said Colleen, smiling. The vicissitudes of her Odyssey notwithstanding, her connections from Comilla had, amazingly, proceeded satisfactorily.

Following after Colleen were a couple of ORs. They were helpfully carrying her trunk to which her folded camp bed was attached by straps.

"Pleasure's all mine, Sister," said Wood warmly, as he assisted Colleen to stash her gear. "Thanks, lads," he said to the ORs, who deposited Colleen's trunk and bed in the jeep. "I'll look after Sister McGrath from here."

And indeed he would, to the war's end.

They drove in convoy with a couple of lorries through a tunnel of red-brown dust, flanked by cactus clumps and stubby trees with leaves stained like rust.

Colleen observed decayed corpses of animals and men – invariably Japs to judge by the tattered footwear and clothing remnants – sprawled amongst rocks and sandy ditches of the fields on either side of the road.

As the convoy skirted villages, the region's many reddish-white pagodas could be seen. Colleen now understood they had the same significance as the Masonic obelisk in Saint Peter's Square. She felt revolted.

"We've had quite a time of it this last week," Wood remarked, steering around an abandoned ox cart. "Came more than a hundred miles down from the Shwebo Plain. Had to cross the Chindwin by barge, made us all pretty tense, not your average beck, like."

Colleen nodded and tied a handkerchief around her nose and mouth. She could feel the perspiration under her arms and knew she'd have to apply calamine after every wash. And foot powder. And that loathsome insect repellant.

"Aye, good idea, that, Sister!" Wood exclaimed. "Fourteenth Army's makin' crossings along a hundred mile stetch of the Irrawaddy," he continued. "It'll keep Tojo on the hop, Uncle Bill says. Kept us on the hop, too. Oh, we're nearly there."

Wood pointed through the dust haze to a collection of *bashas* and tents.

Colleen noticed that vehicles were dispersed, under tree canopies or camouflaged tarpaulin. Her ears caught the sound of gunfire.

"Aye," said Wood. "Bridgehead battle's full on."

They both looked up at the high-pitched growl of approaching engines. Aghast, Colleen glimpsed angry red roundels on silver wings and glistening green fuselages.

"Jump off here, Sister!" yelled Wood. "I'll see to your gear. Head for that tent. That's Sister Calder."

Engines racing, the trucks sped beneath trees.

Colleen ripped off her handkerchief, leapt onto the sandy earth and sprinted toward the willowy blonde girl waving to her. She could hear the heart-stopping racket of strafing and bombing runs, the pounding of light anti-aircraft weapons and the whine of superchargers as Spitfires on station screamed in to intercept the Zeros.

"You must be Colleen," cried the blonde, grasping Colleen's hand. "Trish Calder. Sorry about this, they're after the forward dumps, not us. SEAC reckons Jap air activity is not significant but Tojo up there doesn't know that."

A fleeing Zero howled past, almost overhead, chased by a Spitfire with Browning machine guns chattering. Spent cartridge cases spattered down.

"Don't worry, it's happened to me before," said Colleen.

She took off her hat and followed Trish into the tent where two lines of patients lay apprehensively on stretchers, recently arrived Colleen judged, by their haggard appearance and blood-wet dressings.

Some were crying out in fear, orderlies trying to placate them.

"What's happening, Sister?" one casualty shouted at Trish.

"You're safe here," Trish rejoined calmly, I think, she mouthed to Colleen. Pointing to a canvas basin half full of soapy water, she added, "Scrub up here, Coll. Oh, loo's that way. Hessian box out there."

She indicated the ward entrance.

"Thanks, Trish," Colleen said and made a hasty exit.

By the time she returned, Corporal Wood had reappeared after safely parking the jeep.

"Your gear's in Sister Calder's tent, Sister," he said to Colleen. "I'll break out some more ampoules," he added, turning to Trish.

"Thanks, Woody," said Trish as she gathered up dressing packs. "You'll be bunking with me, Coll. Robbie and Gwen are in theatre. You'll meet them in a bit and Vera and the other girls later on. Fighting's so spread out we've split into two groups."

Colleen scrubbed up and joined Trish in preparing the casualties for theatre.

They knelt by an Indian OR in severe shock from his stomach wound – an injury sustained with alarming frequency in the close-quarter fighting the infantry had to endure. He made piteous groaning noises.

Together they began resuscitation. But while Colleen was arranging the man's drips, she was startled when Trish unpacked the dripping gauze to see three bloated leeches in the sepoy's gut.

"These pests are more of a problem during the monsoon but this chap must've have been lying in the marsh by the sand banks before they found him," Trish explained.

They detached the parasites with alcohol and applied a suppressant to stop the bleeding.

Trish took a ball of what seemed like gum from a small tin and pressed it into the sepoy's mouth. It smelt of alcohol.

"Concentrated opium paste," she said. "We give it now to anyone in really severe pain. It's stronger than morphine. Against regulations but the CO doesn't fuss, though we have to be careful patients don't get addicted."

Colleen grimaced.

"We used heroin, sometimes. In Italy."

"Same effect. We use that, too."

They set about cleaning the wound, preparatory to renewing the dressing.

After him, they tended a sepoy whose lower left leg was a dark grey gangrenous mess of crushed bone and festering tissue. He would need amputation.

The next casualty was a Ghurka, trembling, sweating and lying on his front, his lower back and buttocks covered in dressing.

Colleen eyes almost smarted from the smell when the layers of blood and pus-clotted material were removed. The stinking red-black cavity was crawling with maggots.

"Pity we have to kill them," she said, reaching for an alcohol swab. "Doing a good job on the infected bits."

Other casualties arrived with blood dripping onto the sandy floor from saturated dressings. They promptly needed massive amounts of intravenous fluid – and penicillin injections.

One such victim was a tousle-haired Scots Carabineer tank commander. As she lifted the reddened gauze about his face and upper body, Colleen saw the Jock had been slashed diagonally from jawbone to hip as if by a giant butcher's knife.

"Nip with a Samurai, Sister," he explained. "Jumped onto the turret out of a tree. My Number Two's turret MG gunner's a canny shot, or I'd not be here."

Trish injected him with morphine and they arranged his drips.

Colleen realised the Jap aircraft had gone. But they'd left their mark. Though unable to locate the ammunition stocks, they'd scored hits on vehicles, stores, guns and men – who would soon be arriving at the CCS.

The four of them sat on blood boxes beneath the canvas roof of the Sisters' Mess. The next lot of wounded was not expected until after dark so the girls were enjoying a late afternoon meal of compo tea, hardtack, bully and veg. The sides of the tent had been rolled up for ventilation and they sat inside as a precaution against the kites.

"They can swoop down and steal your grub right off your plate," Trish warned Colleen. "Keep an eye out for the spiders, too."

They were ugly, hairy creatures, some with the leg span of a dinner plate.

Wood had bashed a couple into caramel-like pulp with a spade while heating the Sisters' meals.

"Aye, check your boots first thing, Sister," he told Colleen. "We get the odd krait, like, and scorpions. Cobras, too, biters *and* spitters but divvent worry, I'll sort 'em for you."

He was now heating more water, for washing their utensils, themselves and their clothes. After supper, Colleen would unpack her canvas basin.

"Change from Spam," she remarked, dipping a spoon into the bully-hardtack concoction.

"Smoked salmon on the next airdrop, Coll," said Robyn, tongue-in-cheek. "My Jonny'll fix it."

"Thought he was flying Mosquitoes," said Gwen. She flicked away an inquisitive wasp.

"He is but I reckon he'll pull strings for us."

"Wish I could tug a few for a posting to Corps HQ. My Dai's there now. He doesn't know whether to be flattered or annoyed, he says."

"What and leave all our exotic surroundings?" said Trish, winking at Colleen.

Trish was overjoyed with Colleen. She was superb. Throughout their gruelling stint in Resus, replete with emergency cases, she'd done everything right, a real veteran.

"Enough of this frivolity," said Robyn with aplomb. "We're neglecting our new arrival. Tell us more, Coll. Where were you before dear old salubrious Comilla?"

"Gothic Line, since last summer."

"D Day Dodger, eh?"

"That's it. Sodding Nancy Astor."

Trish took a sip of tea.

"Well," she said, "you'll find it cold here at night, strange to say but at least you won't get snowed in."

It was dark when Trish and Colleen trudged back to the wards, wearing their bush jackets over their shirts because, as Trish predicted, it was getting cooler. Dew covered the vehicles' windshields. Croaking lizards scuttled up trees at the sound of the girls' bootfalls.

Robbie and Gwen would relieve their friends at midnight.

"Can't wait," Colleen had said, yawning. "I'm knackered."

Her companions sympathised.

"You've come a long way in short time, lass," Gwen had remarked.

The bridgehead battle still flashed and boomed.

"Next lot'll be coming across in the barges now, Coll," Trish murmured.

Pausing outside the Resus tent, they looked again at the flickering sky.

Neither of them could know that among the Fourteenth Army soldiers poised for the maelstrom of battle across the river was a young Australian from southern New South Wales.

Or that before the year was out, Trish would marry him.

Twelve

Meiktila and Beyond

Burma, March 1945, Meiktila Railhead[147].

Despite the layers of blanket and bush jacket over his shirt and string vest, Private Leigh Grafton shivered. After blazing hot days, nights in the Dry Belt could be bitter.

He looked beyond the barbed wire to the expanse of rock-strewn soil and stunted cactus. Weird shapes cast grotesque shadows in the moonlight but they didn't move. His rifle resting on the gas cape spread in front of the fire trench, Grafton listened intently for the slightest rattle from the empty tins fastened to wire strands stretched across likely enemy approaches.

He heard nothing, except repeated croaks of "Tuck-too! Tuck-too!" that drew muttered ribald responses from occupants of the perimeter pits.

A figure was approaching, traversing the reverse slope of the embankment where the pits were dug, one hand gripping a carbine.

Grafton and his mate, Private 'Stony' Rockford, recognised the rangy outline of their platoon commander, doing his rounds.

"All quiet out there?" the officer asked, in his distinctly Antipodean tone.

"Like a morgue, sir, apart from that blasted lizard," Stony whispered, in reference to the reptile making the noise, erroneously called the "Tuck-too bird."

"Yeah, pity the Japs don't eat 'em, eh?" said the subaltern. He edged away to continue his inspection of the perimeter.

"'E's a right one[148], is our Mr Calvert," muttered Stony.

Grafton nodded, smiling as he thought back over the platoon's introduction to its new subaltern, voluntarily seconded from the famous Australian Ninth Division.

The shock of recent events had receded a little and Grafton was able to start taking stock.

The battalion was in reserve, camped across typically sunbaked, hillocky plain when Mr Calvert arrived on a late afternoon C-47 flight.

Grafton had met him with a company jeep by the PSP strip and was immediately impressed by the tall Australian's easy-going manner, firm handshake and shrewd but benevolent gaze.

"Private Grafton, sir, usually known 'Gruffie,'" Grafton explained. "Welcome to the West Yorks and the Black Cats[149]. I'm your driver-batman."

"Thanks, Private Grafton," said his officer congenially. "I'm much obliged."

Wearing JGs, boots, puttees, bush hat and web gear, carrying a Lee-Enfield carbine and kit bag, the suntanned Calvert seemed already acclimatised, unmindful of the heat.

"A lot of dead Japs hereabouts," the Australian remarked. He nodded to some uneven earth as he placed his gear in the back of the jeep.

"Yes, sir," said his driver in surprise. "Not obvious, though, not now."

"Cactus on those heaps is new, Gruffie," said Calvert, climbing into the front passenger seat. "What you'd expect from filled-in mass graves."

Grafton had driven the subaltern to Battalion HQ, where he was feted in the tented officers' mess.

"But 'e never touched a drop, apart from lemon an' lime," said an incredulous Private 'Badger' Benfield, swarthy ex-sand blaster and mate of Grafton's from Shipley. He'd been barman for the evening. "Never thought I'd run across an Aussie that didn't drink. Never saw 'im take a fag either. But I reckon 'e's on the ball."

Calvert was, as Benfield in particular would find out.

Grafton continued gazing to his front, wryly reflecting on Mr Calvert's second full day of command. He'd been largely absent on the first. After a meticulous inspection of weapons, kit and feet – "Get some foot powder from the MO," he'd said to Grafton and several others - Calvert had departed to make preparations. "That you'll soon find out about," he'd explained cryptically, adding, "I don't want anybody smoking in fire trenches. I've noticed a few cigarette burns on palms[150]."

Some platoon members gasped. Platoon Sergeant Warwick told them to shut up.

"Platoon, battle order with chagal, riflemen one hundred rounds ball ammunition, Bren gunners and number twos, six mags a piece, fall in!"

Warwick's shout of command when they'd cleared up after breakfast brought the sections hastening to form three ranks.

Rifle slung over his shoulder and wearing an extra bandolier of ammunition, Calvert addressed them succinctly.

"A lot of what we do today will be old stuff. But I want us to find out what we can expect from each other. Sergeant Warwick!"

The sun was not yet shedding its full heat, so on Calvert's summons, Warwick shouted, "Platoon, to the range, double!"

Their boots kicked up a trail of red-brown dust as the men jogged to the improvised rifle range a mile or so distant, laid out over some cleared flatland, elsewhere riven by thicketed ravines.

Mouthing curses, his charges observed how effortlessly Calvert loped along beside them.

"Aussie kangaroo," somebody muttered.

"Sections form up behind the butts!" ordered Warwick when they arrived, panting and sweating. "First firing party fall in, numbering targets from the right, prone position, move! Rest of you, stationary double-time."

The first section scrambled to the sand-bagged stop butts. Rhythmic thumps sounded as with muted groans, their mates continued jogging on the spot.

Targets improvised from ammunition boxes stood upright two hundred yards away, with replacement targets stacked nearby.

"I want to see how we shoot after exertion," Calvert called out, taking up a flank position. Perspiring faces glared from beside rifle stocks pressed to shoulders.

"Firing party, at the targets, five rounds rapid, fire!" Warwick commanded from the rear.

In the course of half a day, enlivened by nearly continuous small arms racket, the platoon discovered that Mr Calvert was a match for any of them, on all weapons. Company transport brought up extra LMGs, SMGs, carbines and spare ammunition for the range practice.

"He's a bushranger, Gruffie," Benfield concluded.

"And thorough," remarked Grafton.

After the exertion shoot, Calvert had ensured that all rifle sights were correctly aligned, or zeroed. He inspected everyone's five-shot groupings and Sergeant Warwick made adjustments to the sights as necessary.

They cleaned weapons at midday, tipping boiling water through the barrels to facilitate removal of carbon deposits. Afterwards, they congregated in sections around campfires kindled by bits of bullet-shredded target boxes and broke out rations from their small packs, boiling up the tins of compo stew in which they would mix hard tack oatcake biscuits, brewing tea with chlorinated water cloudy with silt in the seven-pound jam tin each section carried. A mosquito net bag contained the pungent-smelling tea leaves, replenished after every couple of brews. The men saved the compo cubes for occasions when the real thing wasn't available.

Flavoured by sugar and condensed milk, either beverage, known as "char" or "chae," was "an acquired taste," the lads reckoned.

It was the same with the food.

Grafton glanced at the expectant faces of his comrades, their gaze focused on the steaming dixies. The alfresco setting eminently suited them, the marked contrast of the harsh surroundings with West Yorkshire notwithstanding.

Grimy, sun-browned, tough as gristle, the men were at one with their adopted environment.

It was a long way from where he'd worked in his dad's booksellers in cool and leafy Harrogate, Private Grafton often reflected.

"By 'ell, that's good," remarked Benfield, alternately spooning up mouthfuls of steaming 'conner' and sipping mud-brown brew from his enamel mug. He was sitting against a dead tree stump, his sturdy legs stretched out in front of him.

"Thee looks too comfortable, Badge," said Stony Rockford, similarly reclining. "Sarn't Warwick'll have thee on stag."

The lads kept an eye out for food-pilfering kites but the shooting had temporarily scared them off.

Calvert visited each section in turn and made sure all his men were fed and watered before he himself ate anything.

"Volunteered for selection, passed the tests and I'm here[151]," he explained to the groups. "Better than kicking my heels training in North Queensland."

"We'd give it a shot, sir," remarked Private Moorcroft as he drew on his clay pipe. "What with all those Aussie sheilas."

"Have to see off them Yanks first," Benfield remonstrated. "Not to mention the Aussie blokes, eh, sir?" He flung away the dregs of his tea and reached for his cigarettes.

"I'm sure you'd find everyone hospitable, Badge," said Calvert tactfully and moved off towards Corporal Fell's section. Fell was a stringy lad from Keighley with an infectious grin and clearly keen to impress his new superior.

But others were suspicious.

"What's 'e got planned for this afternoon?" growled Rusty Weatherlake, another of Grafton's mates.

The plans began with a series of simulated platoon attacks, with grenades and live firing, supported by two-inch mortars, putting down both smoke and AP. A team from Support Company brought the mortars up by jeep and trailer while the platoon was finishing lunch. They also brought extra grenades.

The angular figure of leathery-faced, bushy-browed Company Sergeant Major Petrie, from Huddersfield, debouched from the jeep with the team.

"Reckoned I'd see what you lot are up to," he explained dourly.

As the men stumbled cursing and sweating up and down rocky defiles, Grafton noted how Calvert kept pace with the toughest of them, wiry, rugged veterans like Petrie, Warwick, Weatherlake, Benfield and Corporals Fell and 'Brickie' Dymock, lads who'd trekked all the way down the Tiddim Road and across the Chindwin from the Imphal boxes. Keeping up with his officer was for Leigh an arduous business.

The lieutenant also practised the sections extensively in movements via hand signals, both for stealth and sheer necessity – the din of gunfire and explosions could drown out voice commands in action.

"Lance corporals take over section command, section leaders become riflemen!" Calvert shouted at one point during the exercises. "Private Grafton, take over Corporal Barraclough's section."

Like Grafton, Greg Barraclough, a slightly built ex-bank clerk, was new to the platoon and younger than most of its members. Greg was a lance corporal who'd earned his stripe as a clerk at Battalion HQ and had been given command of a section to help bring the rifle formations up to establishment for junior NCOs.

His section contained some old sweats, namely Benfield, Moorcroft and Weatherlake.

"They're always waiting for my next cock-up, so they can put me to rights," Barraclough confided to Grafton.

"Oh, well, my turn now, Greg," said Grafton sympathetically.

During the afternoon, Calvert led the platoon to a low, scrub-covered hillside into which Jap bunkers had been dug, their frontal openings visible amid heaps of rubble and collapsed timbers.

The lieutenant produced from his pack several cylindrical devices with cup shapes at one end. He placed them on a ground sheet with a box of blank cartridges. Sergeant Warwick did the same.

"We're going to hit those bunkers with rifle grenades. That's why our Support Company colleagues brought along the extras," Calvert explained. "I want every man to get a grenade through one of those openings at fifty yards."

The cylinders fitted over rifle barrels and clipped onto the stock. The cup held a 36M grenade with an attachment for yanking out the pin when the blank cartridge was fired. The system could be very effective, at up to seventy yards range but nobody liked it.

"*I* want a good, deep funk hole if there's a misfire," grunted Weatherlake.

Such a mishap could drop the primed grenade almost in front of the firer, with potentially fatal results.

Calvert divided the platoon into firing parties of four and lined them up in turn behind some piles of protective rocks, while the rest of the platoon retreated down a nearby gully.

Calvert and Warwick stood with each party as it discharged the weapons.

"Good work," said the Australian when the firing was complete.

In his turn with the rifle grenades, Calvert once again demonstrated superior marksmanship.

But the *piece-de-resistance* emerged during the final exercise.

In a dry streambed littered with rusted derelict kit and weapons lying among bleaching bones bearing shreds of Jap uniforms, Private Rockford, acting as a forward scout, discovered another bunker, ostensibly empty. Like the hillside bunkers, it had been excavated from the earthen bank, then reinforced and skilfully camouflaged. A manhole-sized aperture showed through a tangle of wizened branches.

Stony summoned his superiors.

"It's not been cleared, sir," muttered Warwick suspiciously, levelling his rifle at the opening.

"Get everyone back behind cover, Sergeant," Calvert said firmly.

"Yessir," said Warwick.

With the platoon safely dispersed, Calvert crept forward to the bunker, carbine at the ready. Grafton saw him pause a few feet from it, extract a 36M grenade from his belt, pull out the pin, toss the grenade through the entrance, retreat hastily and duck behind a crevice in the bank.

The resulting roar and shower of debris far in excess of an anticipated Mills Bomb explosion startled everyone.

"Suicide Jap with a bomb!" exclaimed Corporal Fell at the sight of blackened, bloodied human remains plopping down with the rest of the detritus. "Must've been watchin' us the whole time."

Such enemy ploys were common[152].

"Used to do that on the Huon, just to make sure," Grafton heard Calvert say to Petrie and Warwick. "Fall the men in, Sergeant. Transport's on its way."

Grafton followed Calvert's gaze to the approaching cloud of dust.

"Eh, Gruffie," drawled Benfield as they formed up to embus. "If in doubt, blow 'em to bits. And we don't even have to walk home. I'm startin' to like our Mr Calvert."

Major Renshaw, their gimlet-eyed company commander with distinctive black moustache, arrived by jeep to confer with Calvert about the day's training. Renshaw was over six feet tall but Calvert could look him directly in the eye.

"You got a Jap into the bargain?" remarked the OC, raising his eyebrows. "Well done, Digger."

"He's a right one, is our Mr Calvert," said Petrie.

Crouching in the fire trench, Grafton felt a nudge in his ribs.

"Just makin' sure you're awake, Gruffie," muttered Stony.

"Thanks, mate. My turn next time," Grafton rejoined and pulled his blanket closer around him.

"And up you, too," grated Rockford, with reference to the vociferous lizard.

Grafton glanced at his watch. Their stint was due to end in fifteen minutes. Resting his elbows on the parapet, Leigh recalled the air drop, when Calvert and he accompanied the collection party, consisting of Greg Barraclough's section.

"For the experience," Calvert had said.

Benfield, Moorcroft and Weatherlake seemed none too pleased. It would soon be apparent why.

Grafton parked the three-tonner in the rows of lorries lined up beside a vast bone-dry paddy field marked out in zones for the various formations, British, Indian and Ghurka, waiting to be re-supplied[153].

"It's your party, Corporal Barraclough," said Calvert when they debussed. "I'm just one of the hangers-on, for now."

Calvert had divested himself of badges of rank.

Barraclough reported to the RASC warrant officer coordinating the drop and received their allotted area.

The engine noise heralded the approach of the C-47s, silhouetted in the brilliant sky as they unleashed containers from an altitude of two hundred feet.

"Free drop," remarked Moorcroft. "Bales'll bounce like tennis balls, so keep your eyes open."

Parachutes were reserved for fragile items, like bottled medicines, so boxes of ammunition, food, weapons or clothing were pushed out in padded canvas bundles. They impacted the ground with a thunderous *"whump!"* and rebounded, as Moorcroft had predicted, like huge tennis balls.

The drop teams pursued the bundles across the plain, sliced the fastening cords with *kukri* or *dah* and carried the contents back to their respective lorries – where the WO and his surly assistants ensured that nobody was collecting more than their specified portion. The surplus would go into the RASC depot.

In the searing heat, the work was exhausting. Sweat streamed from the men's bodies and though hardened by his months in the infantry, Grafton found his limbs aching with the exertion, his heart and lungs heaving.

But again, Calvert impressed one and all.

"Right Trojan he is," said Weatherlake, watching the Australian jog smoothly to the lorry with a box of ball ammunition held on each lean shoulder.

When the collection was complete, the section washed themselves down with the remaining water from the *chagals* they had brought – having drunk the rest – donned fresh shirts and, along with the other drop parties, formed up beside their truck while the WO's assistants made one last check of the lorry loads.

When they gave the OK, he dismissed the formations.

"Form the men up again, Corporal," Calvert said quietly. "Behind the truck. And hand me that *chagal*, Gruffie, it's one we've drunk from."

To Grafton's surprise, the container felt heavy.

Calvert removed the stopper and tipped some white crystals into his palm.

"Sugar," said Calvert, sampling a few grains. "I've heard of water into wine but this is also miraculous."

When the section formed up, Private Moorcroft was first in line. Calvert paused in front of him.

"Would you please remove your hat, Private Moorcroft?" he asked casually.

"My hat, sir?"

"Yes, Private Moorcroft, your hat."

Moorcroft obeyed, with a look of resignation. Several packets of cigarettes and tubes of condensed milk cascaded off his sandy coloured hair.

"Hmm," said Calvert, smiling. "So long as it all gets distributed to the platoon, I don't suppose there'll be any recriminations."

Barraclough looked mortified. It was soon evident that the wide boys in his section had purloined a huge amount of ration extras, secreting them inside shirts, trousers and under hats. Several of the *chagals* contained loose sugar or tea.

"You can embus the men now, Corporal," said Calvert, heading for the cab.

"Might've known," muttered a lugubrious voice. "Australians. Could steal the shine off your buttons, those blokes."

"I'll drive if you like, Gruffie," Matt suggested.

"How *did* you know, sir?" asked a still bewildered Grafton, as he occupied the passenger's seat. Even during the clean-up, the lads had contrived to keep everything hidden.

Calvert started the engine and steered the lorry past the WO and his acolytes who were piling the canvas covers into their one and a half-tonner.

"Like Moorcroft said, Gruffie, you keep your eyes open," the Australian answered laconically.

The incident soon receded. The next day, with the bridgehead secure, the battalion crossed the Irrawaddy to take the battle to its next decisive stage.

The advance to Meiktila.

Moorcroft and Corporal Howard, the new section commander, relieved Grafton and Rockford, who then trudged back to the bivouac area.

They passed Calvert huddled asleep in the narrow pit that consisted of Platoon HQ, his carbine between his knees.

Grafton recalled the morning of the Irrawaddy crossing – and the approach to Meiktila.

Battling the current, DUKWs and barges churned across the fast-flowing river, transporting men and vehicles. When the barges ground into the shore, the lorries disembarked onto sandy gravel, collected their passengers and drove through steep-sided gullies that bisected the hundred-feet high bluffs lining the bank.

Not far away, hundreds of pagodas, red-white or gleaming gold, poked through the morning mist, adorning ancient temples half-hidden by swathes of green foliage.

Temple bells could faintly be heard tinkling in a light breeze.

"City's called Pagan, sir," remarked Corporal Dymock, a long-limbed ex bricklayer from Dewsbury – thus known as 'Brickie'. Though aloof from the other subalterns in the company, Lieutenants Abercrombie and Lorrimer, lads not much over twenty like Barraclough and Grafton, Dymock had formed an immediate respect for Calvert.

"Was the old capital of Burma before Mandalay," Brickie added.

"It's well named, Corporal," said Calvert, glancing at the pyramidal spires.

Calvert's Christian convictions were by now well-known. He had even taken a Sunday service for non-conformists, stressing the simple Text, *Man shall not live by bread alone, but by every word that proceedeth out of the mouth of God*[154].

"The Lord said that in a desert place surrounded by the enemy," Calvert had explained. "He knew what it would be like for you and you can trust Him with your life."

Grafton, from a chapel background, attended out of a sense of duty but was pleased he'd done so.

"What about the Japs, sir?" he'd asked Calvert after the service. "Does the same apply to them?"

"Yes," said the Australian firmly. "Not easy to believe that, I know."

Especially when from the back of the lorry, you glimpsed the wooden crosses signifying the Allied cost of the bridgehead battle.

The dust and glare intensified. Bare metal was soon scorching to the touch. The vehicles lurched and bumped over the uneven track, jolting their passengers. Some men tied handkerchiefs around their mouths and noses, others donned full face masks that made them look like Dick Turpin in JGs.

All were wearing tin helmets instead of the usual bush hat, an unpopular stipulation but the CO was insistent.

"The Japs're bound to see us first," he had warned.

The convoy would stop briefly by small clumps of palms, threadbare oases in the surrounding desert, to allow the men to wash off the dirt with water from their *chagals*, gulp down assiduous quantities of the precious fluid, relieve themselves and rest in the meagre shade by the trucks.

Only the villages broke the monotony of the landscape, with their white-plastered brick buildings, wooden huts, artificial pond surrounded by tamarind trees and the inevitable pagodas, like man-made stalagmites.

In the course of a few days, the battalion advanced ninety miles, sleeping by the roadside at night, with double sentry posts, for with the enemy concentrating around their vital supply depots at Meiktila, desperate rearguards sought repeatedly to delay the Allied advance.

One group attacked Renshaw's company with machine gun and rifle fire as the column drove across a dry *chaung* bed west of a town called Taungtha, near commanding heights about halfway along the Fourth Corps' dog-leg route to Meiktila.

The *chaung* was unusually wide and the slow-moving vehicles presented a good target for the enemy concealed in bunkers dug into the banks.

However, Shermans from the accompanying tank brigade opened fire with their seventy-five mm guns and blasted the opposition to oblivion.

A Ghurka battalion winkled more snipers out of the town, following up the Shermans that shot and smashed their way through the abandoned houses.

"Won't be as straightforward at Meiktila, will it, sir?" Grafton asked as battalion transport rumbled past smoking devastation and Jap corpses already fly-blown.

The Australian gravely shook his head.

Approaching Meiktila, another Ghurka formation captured a dusty set of dwellings named Thabuktong – and its airstrip.

Renshaw's company leaguered for the night near the strip while sappers worked away with their bulldozers, repairing shell damage to the runway and laying down PSP.

Everyone was apprehensive.

The West Yorks were scheduled to attack Meiktila the next day.

The battalion debussed astride the Thabuktong road, in front of the northern outskirts of Meiktila. One of the town's two broad lakes lay to the right, blue and glimmering in the sun's pitiless glare.

The road cut through a low earthen bund and Renshaw's company formed up in extended lines to the right of the thoroughfare.

"Would've been part of the old city walls, that," remarked Sergeant Warwick, eying the extended mound.

The men wore full battle order, with extra grenades and ammunition. Japanese seventy-five mm artillery was ranging as the West Yorks waited to advance, mouths dry and hearts pumping. Dirty brown mushrooms shot up in roaring flame from Jap shells exploding near the bund.

Tracks clanking, Sherman tanks growled forward and bellowed retaliatory fire from their turret guns. Close support Hurricanes, P-47 Thunderbolts and twin-engined Mosquitoes whizzed overhead to flail the Jap defences with rockets, bombs, cannon and machine gun fire.

Divisional artillery boomed from the rear, the shriek of their shells adding to the tumult. Foul-smelling HE smoke half hid the town and its environs.

The gargantuan noise made Grafton want to curl up like a hedgehog. His throat was parched but he couldn't touch his bottle yet.

But the thought of the water bottle hanging from his web belt nevertheless brought a grin to Grafton's cracked lips as he recollected what had happened that morning, shortly before they'd embussed.

Warwick had assembled the platoon for Calvert to inspect each man's weapons, ammunition and kit.

Pausing in front of Benfield, he had said, "Show me your water bottle, Badge."

"My water bottle, sir?"

"Yes, Badge, your water bottle."

Reluctantly, Benfield had handed it to the lieutenant, who removed the cork and sniffed the contents.

"Get over to the water truck, Private Benfield and get yourself a full *chagal*," Calvert ordered. "Be back here in two minutes."

"Ready to embus, Mr Calvert?" CSM Petrie had called from the front of the vehicle column, moments after Benfield returned on the run, perspiring and panting, with the extra container affixed to his belt.

"Ready, Sergeant-Major!" Calvert called and handed Benfield back his bottle. "Embus!"

"He was collecting whisky behind the bar the night of my welcome," Calvert explained to Grafton when they'd boarded their lorry. "He didn't line up at the water truck with the rest of you, so I reckoned he must have kept it until now."

Calvert's voice, issuing from a few yards away, abruptly brought Grafton back from his reverie.

"Big show, this Gruffie!"

The Australian was grinning. His teeth showed whitely in a face streaked with sweat and topped by a steel helmet enclosed in camouflage netting.

Major Renshaw fired a coloured Verey rocket.

Grafton swallowed hard.

"Come on, mate," he heard his officer say.

The lines of jungle-green advanced toward the bund, bayonets fixed.

Rockford joined his section mates in the second line of pits. Occupying a trench next to the signallers' lean-to adjacent to Platoon HQ, Grafton settled himself in his blanket, his rifle close by. He yawned and downed a few mouthfuls of water from his bottle.

The lizards seemed to have wandered off. Grafton could hear only the faint hum of the wireless set. Signaller Mick O'Hare was on watch, sitting with his back to Grafton. A gas cape concealed the soft green glow of the set's dials. His mate, Signaller Terry Hogarth, lay sleeping opposite Grafton.

A silent scene, in contrast to the pandemonium of a few days ago...

Battalion mortars were putting down thick red smoke to obscure the lines of advancing infantry.

Grafton found himself scrambling over loose earth, his heart pounding, aware of forms to either side of him.

As the mortar smoke diffused, he glimpsed before him a panorama about two hundred yards square, of smoking, burning chaos. Trim stone houses had crumbled beneath the bombardment into piles of fragments. Bamboo and thatch dwellings were blazing bonfires, lapping the troops' faces with their heat. In between the wreckage of the houses, clumps of shrubbery, water channel cuts, mounds of earth, stood in the way of the advance.

"Keep moving!" Calvert ordered. "Sections in extended line!"

He gesticulated to Fell's, and Barraclough's men. Warwick relayed the order to Dymock's section. The jungle-green lines plodded on, up to a swathe of thickets and ditches.

"Ground's not dug over," Calvert observed, ducking beneath some low branches. "No minefields. They've not had time, here, thank God."

Elsewhere the Japs had, as the company discovered later and the advance slowed while divisional sappers lifted the lethal devices.

"Booby traps, sir?" Grafton asked anxiously. He could feel sharp prickles scraping his clothes.

"The Japs themselves, Gruffie," said his officer grimly. Matt continued to wave the sections forward.

Battalion mortars were switching to HE. The bombs burst some chains' length in front of the platoon and threw up more debris.

On the right of the platoon, two Shermans had rumbled over the bund. Their seventy-five mm guns belched smoke and flame.

Then the defenders retaliated.

Grafton saw Calvert fling himself to earth almost as the Japanese machine guns opened fire and likewise dived flat, worming frantically into the dust, petrified by the spiteful snapping above his head, clipping off bits of cactus and thorny scrub.

"Bunker, eighty yards, eleven o'clock!" yelled Calvert. "Bren gunners engage!"

He was firing repeatedly at a grassy mound, pausing momentarily to shout his orders.

Grafton pressed his rifle to his cheek and began loosing off rounds at the mound, bracing himself to absorb the jolting recoil.

The machine gun fire intensified.

Japanese seventy-five mm shells shrieked in from somewhere. They were known as "whizz-bangs," with good reason. Rubble and dirt flew in all directions from the explosions. The enemy appeared not to have mortars in this sector but the whizz-bang field pieces were trouble enough. Fighter-bombers from the 'cab rank' roared down to assail them.

"Corporal Fell, bunker thirty yards left of first!" shouted Calvert. "Concentrated fire."

Fell's section, on the extreme left, poured fire into the left hand bunker.

"Bunker thirty yards right of first, sir!" Warwick called from Dymock's flank. "Interlocking fields of fire!"

"Signaller, relay enemy position!" Calvert ordered.

Close by, Mick O'Hare bellowed into his set. The Sherman guns thundered. Seventy-five mm rounds of solid shot slammed into the bunkers. Earth and debris spurted up. The enemy automatic fire faltered.

White billows of covering smoke mixed with red were suddenly obscuring the mounds.

Calvert's voice rang out.

"Come on!"

Led by their officer, the Yorkshiremen charged across the broken ground before them at a crouching run. Smoke bombs launched from both the mortars and the tanks were screening the attackers, who rushed to within thirty yards of the bunkers. Their loopholes and embrasures were clearly discernible, spitting bullets anew as the smoke cleared, answered with an avalanche of small arms fire from the platoon and more solid shot from the tanks.

The shot silenced the right hand bunker, creating a patch of dead ground relative to the centre position. Corporal Fell's section had the left hand bunker fully occupied.

Calvert's voice sounded again.

"Sergeant Warwick!"

The lieutenant dashed towards a tangle of scrub in the dead ground, Grafton at his heels. Barraclough's and Dymock's sections followed up, pouring fire into the centre bunker as they assumed position.

In a lather of sweat, panting with fear and exertion, Grafton noticed that Weatherlake was missing.

"Rusty's missing, sir," he gasped.

"Didn't make the last rush," said Matt anxiously. "But we've got to get on."

Warwick dropped down beside the Australian, who had crawled almost to within line of sight of the bunker's nearest embrasure.

"Reckon you could get a rifle grenade through there, Sergeant?" asked Calvert.

Warwick nodded – and calmly did the business. Grafton shuddered at the sounds of screaming above the cracking of exploding ammunition that followed the grenade burst. Gouts of smoke-veined flame leapt from the embrasures.

Fell's lads swarmed forward and cut down a handful of survivors exiting the left hand bunker. The platoon pressed on between heaps of wreckage and shattered houses.

"Watch out for snipers and MGs!" Calvert warned stridently. He fired on one knee at a smouldering bamboo frame about ten yards distant.

A pot-helmeted figure collapsed sideways through the frame. In among the crackling heat, sinister shrubs and lethal rubble heaps, Calvert's sections were closing with individual enemy positions, supporting each other with fire and movement, subduing the defenders with Mills Bomb, bayonet, rifle shot and automatic burst.

The sudden sound of heavy staccato beating indicated that Vickers gunners from the MMG Platoon were adding their considerable firepower to that of the mortars in hammering the foe.

Who nevertheless hit back.

A sudden bang culminated in a roaring flash.

One of the Shermans lurched drunkenly to a fiery halt. Its surviving crew members scrambled from the hatchways, clothes and hair alight. Grafton glimpsed Corporal 'Stitch' Kelsey and his RAMC mates beating out the flames.

The tank's killer was one of the notorious Jap seventy-five mms.

"A/T gun, stone house, one hundred yards, one o'clock!" Calvert called to O'Hare, who got busy on the wireless again.

The other tank edged forward, engine muttering, its Indian crew seeking to bring their gun to bear on the A/T menace.

"Keep moving, keep moving!" urged Calvert.

He waved his sections on again. Desperately frightened, temples pounding, his throat almost aflame with thirst, Grafton knew this was the wisest course of action, keeping the foe off balance.

He cringed at the constant crack and whine of bullets and strove to utilise all cover he could find, levelling his rifle and squeezing off rounds at whatever targets were spotted – frequently by Calvert and Warwick.

Perspiration dripped continuously from Grafton's face and arms, coursing down the rifle stock as he reloaded, a wary eye on his diminishing stock of ammunition. The carrying parties from the company in reserve would have to find them soon.

In response to O'Hare's message, mortar bombs were crashing down about the A/T post and the remaining tank joined in, its turret gun banging away steadily.

The multiple explosions threw up a wall of debris that engulfed the position. The A/T gun was no more.

"Cease fire!" O'Hare yelled into his set. The mortar rounds stopped.

But the last one fell short and burst with deafening violence near Barraclough's section.

Too near.

"My eyes!" screamed Greg.

He was thrown backwards, writhing in shock and agony. Grafton saw with horror that his friend's face and chest were splashed with blood and rushed to aid him.

But Calvert got to Barraclough first, yelling for the section to keep moving and for Stitch Kelsey.

"Hold his arms," Calvert gasped to Grafton, who desperately tried to prevent Greg from pawing at his blood-splashed eye sockets.

Calvert tipped half his bottle of water onto Barraclough's face and wrapped a field dressing around Greg's eyes. He then inserted a couple of morphine tablets into the corporal's open mouth. These were easier to administer than a syringe.

Kelsey dashed up with his team.

"We'll see to him, sir," he cried.

"Come on, Gruffie," Calvert ordered. Weapons raised, they hastened through streams of smoke to catch up with the platoon.

Tenacious enemy snipers, machine gunners and artillerymen continued to fight back from culvert, foxhole, spinney, tumbled-down building and rubble-choked thoroughfare. Shouts of "Corporal Kelsey!" sounded again and again.

But the carrying parties had come up and replenished with ammunition from them, the platoon doggedly returned fire from their own places of concealment, fending off mad rushes of shrieking foemen.

In open-mouthed admiration, Grafton saw Calvert trip up a samurai-wielding assailant, bashing away the blade with his carbine stock and then finish his attacker with a quick bayonet thrust.

The battle raged on. Flames and smoke from the burning wooden buildings obscured both friend and foe. Grafton wiped away sweat and tears provoked by the stinking fumes of battle.

"Seventy-five mm, cactus clump, thirty yards direct front!" cried Calvert, bringing his carbine to bear. Bren and rifle fire carved the clump to bits and felled the gunners. With cracking burst, a rifle grenade disabled the enemy gun.

"MG post, water cut - " Warwick shouted but the vicious *"knock-knock-knock"* of the weapon drowned his words – and claimed a victim.

Benfield collapsed, crying in anguish, his right leg twisted and blood-drenched from thigh to ankle.

Calvert and Grafton dragged the white-faced Badge into a ditch and wrapped dressings around the worst of the perforations. They were quickly reddened.

While Grafton shouted for Kelsey, Calvert placed morphine tablets into Benfield's mouth, then unfastened the wounded man's bottle, pulled out the cork and pressed the neck to Badge's lips.

"Here, mate," urged the Australian.

"Thank you, sir," croaked Badge. He took several swallows.

Stitch Kelsey arrived with orderlies and a stretcher to evacuate the casualty.

A boom and flash from the lone Sherman's turret gun put paid to the Jap MG and its crew.

It was keeping with the platoon, thanks to Dymock's men who were acting as flank guards. They had dispatched several Japs concealed in trenches, grasping aerial bombs between their knees, ready to detonate them when any tank drove over the position.

"Needed to be quick on the trigger," Private Hogarth later told Grafton. Warwick had sent Terry to reinforce Dymock's depleted riflemen.

"Let's get on, Gruffie," Calvert muttered.

In short dashes and using all available cover, they rejoined the platoon. With the tank in support firing from the lee of a collapsed house, the sections were blazing away at the window spaces set in massive stone walls. Bullets spat back from ornately carved alcoves.

"Town monastery, sir!" O'Hare called, crouched over his set. "Full of Japs. Whole battalion advance is stalled."

"Can you raise battalion mortars?" Calvert asked.

Grafton saw that the men were digging in amongst piles of debris from the wrecked houses. He seized his entrenching tool and chopped away at the water cut into which he and his officer had leapt, where O'Hare was ensconced.

"Supporting left-hand company, sir," Mick reported. "Getting low on bombs. They'll give us a team when the carrying parties come up again."

"Let me know, Mick," said Calvert. Grafton thought that his officer looked tense.

A tall figure approached them, holding binoculars. It was Major Renshaw, JGs stained with sweat, helmet tipped back over his head. Company HQ had kept with the assault force all day.

"You've done very well, Matt," said Renshaw. "But looks like we'll be stuck here until the fighter-bombers come back tomorrow."

The major glanced toward the declining sun.

"We'll be ready for counter attacks, sir," Calvert reassured him, inserting a fresh magazine into his carbine. "You should get down – "

The sniper's shot interrupted him.

It came, not from the monastery strong point as Calvert had feared but from an innocent-looking mound in a cactus patch twenty yards to the right of the water cut.

Renshaw toppled back. Blood spurted from his chest. Grafton frantically dragged the OC into the ditch, scrabbling for a dressing.

He saw Calvert dash obliquely to the mound from cover to cover while the platoon poured fire at the strong point to distract its defenders. The Australian kicked open the camouflaged trap-door, fired twice into the foxhole beneath and sprinted back to the water cut.

The sniper's bullet had left ugly entrance and exit wounds. Grafton and Calvert desperately tried to stanch the blood. Renshaw's breathing was issuing in agonised gasps.

Dodging behind wreckage and scrub clumps for cover, Kelsey and his orderlies got the major away on a stretcher. Another RAMC man held up a plasma bottle with cannula inserted into Renshaw's arm.

"What d'you reckon, sir?" asked Grafton anxiously as he mopped the major's blood from his hands with a soiled rag.

"I wouldn't lay odds, Gruffie," the Australian said through gritted teeth.

The carrying parties returned with extra grenades. They were needed. With night would come the Jap reprisals.

Grafton stared enviously at the slumbering Hogarth. For some reason, he couldn't sleep, bone weary though he was. He watched his breath condensing in the chill air and glanced up at the stars. They were brighter than he could ever recollect at home and seemed close enough to touch.

Leigh was still coming to terms with the savage dislocation of the company's familiar fabric.

Despite the devoted efforts of the medical staff, Major Renshaw had died in the CCS.

Rusty Weatherlake had been killed, along with CSM Petrie. The company sustained several fatal casualties that day, with nearly two score wounded.

But outwardly, it was business as usual.

Corporal 'Shemp'[155] Howard, tough, experienced, quietly spoken, was seconded from the reserve company to take over Barraclough's section. Robust Captain 'Granny' Stobart, Renshaw's second-in-command, took his place as OC. Granny was so named because the lads reckoned his pedantic instructions drew forth the proverbial granny-suck-eggs comparison. But he knew his job.

Warwick became Company Sergeant Major. "I'll still be keeping a close eye on you lot," he'd warned Calvert's men. They believed him.

A few men, including Rockford, sustained slight injuries during the grenade duel that eventuated on the first night of the battle, as Calvert had predicted. The foes made short, desperate rushes, terminating in bombs thrown at random and a helter-skelter retreat to the monastery.

These forays were called "jitter parties."

"They scared the hell out of me right enough," Rockford had said. He was listed as "Wounded – at duty."

Many 'jitterers' paid in full for their bravado when flares caught them and they fell poleaxed by retaliatory grenade bursts or Brens firing on fixed lines.

Nevertheless, hundreds of explosions had jarred the men's nerves and senses all night long. At dawn, fighter-bombers, aided by battalion mortars and Shermans firing solid shot pulverised the monastery walls and the advance resumed. Stobart's company now acted as ammunition carriers for the reserve company who had taken over the attack.

They also acted as spare stretcher-bearers. Kelsey and his lads were flayed out.

And as gravediggers.

The dead had to be buried quickly before becoming black and bloated in the unremitting sun.

After the burials, the dead men's kit was laid out for the survivors to exchange any items as they saw fit. Grafton selected Weatherlake's haversack. It was in better repair than his own.

Fourteenth Army fatalities received a brief burial service. Japanese corpses, where they could be collected, were flung into mass graves.

Meiktila fell after four days of fighting. The West Yorks carried on past the town's towering principal pagoda to the railway line, where Calvert's platoon blew several Jap snipers out of goods wagons with rifle grenades.

"Well worth it, the range practice, sir," remarked Fell to Calvert when the company bivouacked for the night in the midst of shell-battered rolling stock and marshalling yards. "Reckon we'll make thee honorary Yorkshireman after this."

Watching a meteor flash across the night sky, Grafton smiled at the recollection of Stony's *résumé* after the push to the railway line.

"Japs make moles look like camels when it comes to diggin' in."

The battalion proceeded northeast from the marshalling yards, bypassed the formations investing the town's airfield and established its own strongpoint along the earthen bund, where Calvert seconded his batman to help man the trenches held by Howard's section. They strung wire along the length of the forward slope, dug and fortied weapons pits in the bund's broad and scrubby crest, with HQ and reserve trenches in the rear – and established latrine pits further away.

Hacking holes in the hard-packed earth was arduous in the extreme but everyone went at it with assiduity because even with the town secure, the fighting wasn't done.

The enemy cut the Meiktila-Thabuktong road, regained the Taungtha heights and remained in strength within a two-mile radius of the town.

Somehow, the Japs then summoned up fresh forces and tried to recapture the town's airstrip – with tanks.

"That's the worst of Johnny Jap, never knows when he's beat," Moorcroft observed.

Thankfully, the enemy were thrown back, even while Allied reinforcements from the 'Ball of Fire' Division[156] were being flown in under fire. Without the strip, more airdrops would have been necessary, precarious in the circumstances.

In the ensuing days, the beleaguered battalions had sent out raiding parties to penetrate the fortified villages and copses around Meiktila, punching great gaps in the enemy encirclement, though at a price.

During a sweep of some wooded ravines northwest of the airfield, Grafton saw Kelsey take Lieutenant Abercrombie back, blood dripping from an arm and soaking his shirt, one of several sniper victims.

Lieutenant Symonds transferred from Support Company's mortar platoon to replace Abercrombie. It was 'KO' Symonds, taciturn, stocky, about Calvert's age, who with the help of aerial photographs, had liased so effectively with the assault companies during the seizure of Meiktila. His mortars repeatedly knocked out stubborn enemy positions.

The small number of friendly casualties the mortars caused was reckoned "acceptable" – except by those who'd suffered in the process, like Greg Barraclough.

Nevertheless, coordinated Allied firepower continued to pile up Japanese corpses in windrows.

Providing more meat for the vultures.

This macabre memory stayed with Grafton.

It eclipsed the recollections of bone-shaking rides on the scorching metal backs of the Shermans and the frenzy of ensuing fire-fights.

It blotted out the ordeal of clearing a line of brick and bamboo dwellings that had gone on for hours, though the village street was less than a quarter of a mile in length.

And the manifold discomforts of heat, thirst, exhaustion and battlefield din.

Because in honour of the Rising Sun, the Emperor's bravest warriors had become mere carrion prey.

Yawning, as at last he slipped into sleep, Private Grafton felt disquiet when he thought on an old Text.

I will give thee to the ravenous birds of every sort, and to the beasts of the field to be devoured[157].

The Text referred to something future. Japanese dead in Burma were but an overture.

Trenholme's CCS crossed the Irrawaddy in the wake of the Black Cat Division.

With a new driver.

"I can drive a jeep, sir," Colleen told the CO. "That'll free up Corporal Wood and take some of the strain off Kitty and Rach. They reckon I'm OK."

Along with Paddy Monaghan, Kitty Earnshaw and Rachel Greenock made up Vera Jeffries' foursome. Owing to the shortage of QAs, the pair had come to the unit from the FANY. Although only about nineteen or twenty, they could shoulder many of the nursing responsibilities and were trained ambulance drivers.

Colleen had persuaded them to let her drive on several occasions when they'd gone by jeep to collect stores from the nearby base depot.

Trenholme was seated at the trestle table in his HQ tent, conferring with Captain Mostyn.

He looked doubtful. "What d'you reckon, Kiwi?" he asked.

The gangly New Zealander shrugged and spun his bush hat on a forefinger. "Makes sense to me, sir," he drawled.

"Oh, go on, sir," Colleen urged. "I'd love to be able to tell my grandkids I drove a jeep in Burma during the big war."

Mostyn guffawed and Trenholme capitulated.

Sister McGrath fell in with her two FANY friends who'd been waiting outside Trenholme's tent.

"All done and dusted, Coll?" Kitty asked eagerly, her freckled face animated.

"Yep, let's go have a cuppa," said Colleen. She placed a hand on each of her friends' shoulders and they strolled off to the Sisters' Mess.

"Good work, Coll," said Rachel, patting Colleen on the back. "We knew you could twist him round your little finger."

Thabuktong contained some intact *bashas* that could be used as theatres and Post-Op wards. Tents again would have to suffice for the remaining facilities, including Sisters' quarters.

"We'll need a bath," exclaimed Colleen.

She and her friends alighted from the jeep, untied the handkerchiefs around their mouths and brushed the dust from their clothes. "Patients'll think we've been dug up with the pharaohs."

"All this place needs is a few pyramids instead of pagodas and you wouldn't know the difference, apart from the cactus," Gwen remarked.

It had been a long, exhausting drive in the searing heat and all commended Colleen's stirling effort. Their CCS had leap-frogged other units receiving casualties from the fighting between the bridgehead and Meiktila but the battle for the railhead would start the next day and Trenholme's staff braced themselves for a night of preparation.

Sweltering in theatre clothing, Trish was in an operating *basha* with Mostyn and Wood. Robbie and Gwen were in Resus, Colleen was assisting Trenholme in a second *basha* operating theatre.

Vera and Kitty were in Post-Op. The Sisters would work staggered shifts, so Trenholme had sent Rach and Paddy to get some sleep.

The first patient carried into Mostyn's theatre was a corporal from the West Yorks, in great distress, thick dressing covering his face.

"My eyes," he kept repeating, in between sobs.

The orderlies placed him on the table and departed. While Wood and Mostyn gently restrained the patient, Trish carefully removed the wad of gauze, biting her lip at the sight of the blood-black lacerations beneath.

She grasped the corporal's hand and leant close to him.

"What's your Christian name, mate?" she whispered. He seemed no more than a boy. Trish fought to keep her voice steady. She'd had this kind of experience all too often.

"Greg," the lad sobbed.

"Listen, Greg," said Trish earnestly. "We're going to put you under and Captain Mostyn will examine your eyes. When we've finished here, we'll transfer you to the specialists at Comilla. The airstrip's just next door, so you'll be on your way very soon."

"Thanks, Sister," he murmured. His sobs subsided a little.

Wood handed Trish the syringe containing the anaesthetic and Mostyn stood poised with pencil torch and fine forceps. Trish rewashed her hands after carrying out the injection.

"Be touch and go," the surgeon said when they'd finished. "So, who's next?"

The stifling little cavern of bamboo and thatch became a prison. Trish felt the perspiration sliding down her arms as she handed Mostyn the instruments and sutures. Many a towel got soaked through with sweat from mopping their faces.

The line of patients seemed endless – Gloucesters, Ghurkas, East Yorks, West Yorks and numerous others.

Trish lifted a sticky red mass of dressing from the badly shot-up leg of one, Private Benfield.

"What do they call you, mate?" she asked, smiling behind her mask and taking his hand.

"Badge," said the patient hoarsely. His dry lips hardly moved.

"OK, Badge," she said. "Captain Mostyn's going to tidy up that leg and then we'll get you back to Comilla."

He looked reassured as Trish injected the anaesthetic.

"Leg's going to be a mass of blood and pus for God knows how long," Kiwi muttered when the orderlies carried Benfield to Post-Op. "They'll have to watch him like a hawk for gangrene but he might keep his leg."

Trish hoped so. They'd done some amputations that day.

Private Weatherlake was another leg casualty, brought in comatose with a fearful rent in the back of his thigh, where shrapnel from a seventy-five mm shell had slashed the flesh down to the bone.

He'd been blown into a ditch obscured by scrub and lain unconscious a long time before the medics found him.

Too long.

The loss of blood, combined with shock, proved too much even for Mostyn's skill. Weatherlake died on the operating table.

A similar death that day caused particular anguish for the surgeon.

"God, it's my mate, Ricky Renshaw!" Kiwi exclaimed when the major was brought in.

The damage wrought by the sniper's bullet was mortal.

"We're losing him!" said Mostyn anxiously when the major's heart rate inexorably slowed despite the team's efforts to stanch blood loss and restore it via saline and plasma.

Mostyn cut open Renshaw's chest cavity and Trish massaged the faltering heart with her bare hands.

To no avail.

Mostyn mouthed a curse and Trish stared blankly at the wall when the orderlies took the major away.

Trish realised it was night and that they had been operating by the hurricane lamps that Wood had installed.

The battle boomed until the end of the shift.

One of the patients admitted to Resus was an airman.

"Hit by ground fire and had to bale out. He's pretty badly burned," Sergeant Nicholson explained to Robyn.

The man's visage was predictably swollen and blackened, with flesh hanging in strips. His clothes had caught alight and in places on his arms, skin and fabric were fused into a charred mess, down to the bone.

"OK, Nick, we'll cut the clothes off him first," said Robyn, kneeling beside the semi-conscious flier. "Then the usual. Penicllin in the thigh, plasma, saline and *Tulle Gras*. We'll dust him with sulphonamide when we put the plaster on. Trenholme can decide what else needs doing."

With these ministrations, the airman's condition gradually stabilised. Stoically, he bore the agony that savaged him despite pain killers – the anguish caused by burns cut through the strongest of them.

"We'll hang on to him for a bit," said the CO when he'd seen the patient. "I reckon he'll pull through but we'll have to put him by himself in a day or so."

"When the plaster's crawling with maggots and stinks to high heaven," said Robyn, forcing a smile.

After Paddy and Rachel relieved them, Gwen and Robyn trudged to the Sisters' Mess, where Robyn burst into tears.

"Oh, Jonny!" she exclaimed, her fists clenched. "When will you come off ops?"

Gwen put an arm around her.

"Pull yourself together, Robbie," she said quietly. "Just like you made me do when I was all upset about Dai at Kohima."

Robyn wasn't the only one in distress that night.

When Colleen entered their tent, she found Trish seated on her camp bed, sobbing. Virtually in tears herself after the exhausting stint in theatre, Colleen sat beside her friend and put an arm around her shoulders.

"I'm sorry, Coll," moaned Trish, her head bowed. "Today's been so awful."

"C'mon, lass," Colleen murmured, giving Trish a hug. "Let's get to the mess before Vera and the rest scoff all the conner."

They joined the others in the mess, where their Senior Sister spoke comfortingly to them.

"I've been in this war since Norway[158] and you are the best people I've served with."

Vera took her Bible out of a pocket of her bush jacket and read from the letter of James.

"'Confess your faults one to another, and pray for one another, that ye may be healed. The effectual fervent prayer of a righteous man availeth much.' Or woman," she said, smiling. "And I think the stew's just about done," she added, with a nod towards the paraffin stoves. "Smells like it, eh?"

Cheeks stained with sweat and tears creased in grins. Vera's gang was getting back to normal.

"If the Japs try to rape you, Sister, just pull the pin," the youth gasped. "You won't feel a thing."

Colleen had sat him up on the operating table to remove the swathe of dressing that covered one shoulder and half the lad's chest.

He had promptly pulled his trouser leg out from beneath the puttee with his good hand, extracted a grenade he'd concealed there and proffered it to Colleen.

"How did you get in here with *that*?" she exclaimed. "Never mind. Thanks for your concern but I'll have to give it to the orderly. Better not let the MO see it."

Colleen slipped the bomb into the map pocket of her JG trousers. Beneath her gown, it was almost invisible.

"Better give it to Woody when I can," she said to herself as she washed her hands again.

Trenholme was temporarily absent, helping Wood bring over some oxygen bottles. Some patients with chest wounds, like the lad Colleen was seeing to, would need assistance with breathing.

The Japanese had cut the road to Meiktila and from Taungtha, so that Thabuktong was isolated, though its airstrip still functioned. Fourth Corps was striving to re-open the roads and the casualties were coming in from both directions.

Some, like Colleen's patient, were extremely apprehensive about the nurses falling into Japanese hands and Trenholme, mindful of the danger, had ordered them to be armed at all times, except on the wards.

He asked Geordie Wood to help them practise with their Stens while they were off duty.

"You just have to fire 'em, ladies," the corporal declared. "Divvent worry if you don't hit anything."

He gestured to the line of improvised targets. They'd set them up in a derelict back yard.

"We'll show him," muttered Robyn, taking aim.

By the time the crisis was past, Colleen and her friends had become quite accomplished markswomen with the SMGs. Wood was suitably impressed – also with Colleen's grenade present that she bestowed on him.

Calvert's platoon stood revelling in the cool of the canvas container showers rigged above their heads, enabling them to enjoy at least a token wash simultaneously of bodies and clothes steeped in grime and sweat.

Stobart's company was enjoying a brief rest period by the shore of the northern lake, where in the words of the company commander, "You can all spruce up."

They always spared enough water from the copious quantities they drank for shaving and brushing teeth but Granny Stobart was here in his element.

"Wonder he doesn't issue us all with dolly pegs," muttered Howard, watching the water cascade through his clothing.

They could have used the cords of rope each man carried as clotheslines but so quickly did everyone dry out in the heat, it wasn't necessary.

After days of subsisting on individual forty-eight ration packs, they were also pleased to have local fruit and vegetables. The fresh food was obtained by barter from townspeople living near the lake whose particular community had escaped the ravages of the battle.

However, the troops' beaming, brown-skinned benefactors inevitably incurred some Yorkshire scepticism from Grafton's hard-bitten cronies.

"Bet they'd be just as friendly with Jap," grunted Moorcroft.

That the locals would probably have had no choice made no odds.

Tiger patrol[159].

Hatless, shod in Plimsolls, the four-man formation proceeded stealthily beyond the wire, past the platoon OP manned by two of Dymock's lads and crept in diamond formation through the scrub towards the nearest village. Calvert was leader. Grafton, Hogarth and Rockford, with the Bren, were the others.

They kept in shadows, using the pale moonlight to guide their way but avoiding its direct illumination.

The eerie silence unnerved Grafton. Even the tuck-too lizard seemed to have taken the night off.

Navigating by compass bearings, Calvert found the village they were meant to reconnoitre easily enough. It stood like a ghost town in the whitish glow of the moon, *bashas* and houses abandoned and forlorn, charred debris everywhere.

An earlier patrol, on a different mission, had reported movement there, prompting a terse reaction from Stobart.

"Check it out, Matt."

The patrol edged along each side of the main thoroughfare in turn. At times, Calvert halted them, evidently sensing something ahead. When nothing definite could be discerned, they crept on. Once or twice, Grafton thought he saw – something. The hairs rose on the nape of his neck and his heart beat wildly. His throat drained of saliva.

But whatever it was had vanished.

Calvert abruptly signalled another halt and pointed. Half-hidden by the shadow of a collapsed *basha*, a Japanese corpse lay spread-eagled in the sandy soil. He was newly dead. Matt ensured that the body wasn't booby trapped and retrieved the soldier's identification disk. The Australian seemed puzzled.

"What is it, sir?" asked Hogarth in a whisper.

"Look at his face," Calvert muttered.

It was a death-mask of frozen horror. Grafton broke into a cold sweat at the sight.

Then Calvert angled his carbine at a house across the street. The others quickly adopted firing positions. A minute elapsed. Nothing happened. Calvert glanced at his watch.

"Time to go home," he said. His voice sounded scared as well as tired.

"What was it?" Stony asked tremulously when they regained the concealment of the scrub beyond the village.

Grafton shook his head. "Only saw a shadow," he muttered. "But it did move."

Back in the ruined village, hate-filled eyes from another realm glared at the retreating patrol, whose members it had not been allowed to molest – unlike the unlucky enemy straggler.

But the shadow would assume substance on a different and totally unexpected battleground, one where Matt Calvert, among other friends of Grandma Colleen's, would be very much at the sharp end.

Towards the end of March, the battle of Meiktila ended and Mandalay, eighty miles to the north, fell to Thirty-third Corps, Fourth Corps' sister formation.

The Ball of Fire Division had also swept the Taungtha heights clear of the enemy.

Yet one particular event marred the success for the Black Cats, experienced though they were in the loss of those close to them.

The son of the Divisional Commander had been killed in the fight for Mandalay, while serving with the 'Golden Dagger' Division[160]. Brigade and battalion commanders sent messages of sympathy to their CO[161].

For Stobart's company, it compounded the sense of loss evoked by Major Renshaw's death.

In the meantime, the enemy was falling back southwards, in the general direction of the Pegu Yomas, a hilly spine of trackless jungle, with crests about a thousand feet in height, stretching almost two hundred miles towards Rangoon.

Opinions in Calvert's platoon varied about the likely strength of the remaining opposition.

"Jap's marchin' on his chinstrap[162]," declared Rockford one day at a section brew. "Must be, after Mandalay *and* this shindig here. Reckon he'll pack it in any day now."

"Will he hell," grunted Moorcroft, drawing on his cigarette. "Johnny Jap'll fight for every yard between here and Rangoon."

"Aye, best is yet to be, boys," added Howard lugubriously. "Mr Calvert says he's dug in around Pyawbwe now, waitin' for us to come up."

"Where?" asked Rockford, with furrowed brow.

"Pyawbwe, another railway station" said Grafton. "OC mentioned it at his O Group this morning, so Mr Calvert says."

"Ah, well," said Rockford resignedly as they helped themselves to char. "Then charge your magazines, boys. Why change the habits of a lifetime, eh?"

Nevertheless, with Meiktila's airstrip secure, regular fly-ins did much to raise morale. Along with various luxuries and an abundance of post, the men received a necessary issue of fresh clothing and footwear – and on the next day, a visit from the Army Commander[163].

He addressed them informally in the lee of the bund where Stobart's company had dug its weapons pits.

Though dressed almost identically to his men, their Field Marshall was instantly recognisable, by his sturdy features and Ghurka hat with puggaree and the brim turned up on the left side. His very presence commanded immediate respect. When he spoke, it was with overwhelming reassurance that the enemy would soon be defeated and sincere appreciation for all that the battalion had achieved.

"You only have to keep the pressure on," he told them simply.

The CO then introduced the Field Marshall to the battalion's officers.

"This is our Australian, sir," said the colonel when he came to Calvert. "Lieutenant Matt Calvert, from Ninth Division, AIF."

"Pleased to meet you, Mr Calvert," said the Army Commander, shaking Calvert's hand. "What battalion?"

"Second Seventeenth, sir."

"Ah, Jivenaneng[164]."

"Yes, sir," said Calvert, clearly taken aback.

"I like to keep up with what our Allies have been doing. Glad you're here, Mr Calvert."

"Thank you, sir."

It was one of two occasions when Grafton saw his officer pleasantly surprised.

The other came about a few months later, via a letter from a certain Nursing Officer Calder.

But much would happen before then.

Starting the following day, when the battalion embussed for Pyawbwe.

After Meiktila and its environs were secure, Colleen and her friends asked Trenholme if they could go there by jeep to purchase fresh food.

"Be good for the patients, sir," Trish advised.

As usual, they managed to persuade him but he insisted they take their Stens, with spare magazines in their web bags.

"I feel like the Wicked Lady[165] with all this weaponry," said Robyn as she climbed into the vehicle. "Film'll be out soon, according to *SEAC*."

"Calm down, Robbie," Trish admonished from the back. "You're a respectable married woman, now."

"Jonny *did* call me that once, on our honeymoon."

"Wicked lady or respectable married woman?" Colleen asked, starting the engine.

"None of your business," said Robyn merrily.

"Now you've *got* to tell us!" her three companions chorused.

"Find a Ghurka *naik*," Robyn suggested when Colleen parked the jeep by the northern lake, within walking distance of a village that seemed relatively untouched by the fighting. "Our lads'd be fine but for Sister Memsahib, Johnny Ghurk'll guard our jeep like it was the coronation coach."

They found a smiling Nepalese NCO, eager to oblige, who volunteered the help of his half-section. With their brims of their bush hats turned up smartly on the left side and wearing fresh uniforms, the Ghurkas looked as if they had recently come off parade, instead of having endured a month's fighting.

The girls were able to buy and barter for fresh eggs, vegetables and fruit, including sweet potatoes, mangoes, limes, strawberries and plump red bananas. Their Burmese vendors were very grateful for the medicines the Sisters gave them in return.

"Don't suppose Trenholme will mind when he sees the loot," said Gwen. Stens over their shoulders, they made their way back to the lakeside with web bags bulging, followed by a barrage of wolf whistles from the British ORs who caught sight of them.

The girls responded with customary smiles and waves and Trish was moved to quote Kipling.

"'The wind is in the palm trees and the pagoda bells, they say,

"'Come ye back you British soldier, come ye back to Mandalay.' It's a Burmese girl who says that in the poem, so I suppose I can."

"And Mandalay's only just up the road," said Gwen.

"Plenty of tinkling pagoda bells about, too," remarked Robyn, glancing around.

Unfortunately, the OC of the Ghurka Company, a major, was not at all pleased when he caught sight of the girls.

Tall, moustached and immaculately uniformed, with aquiline features like the Duke of Wellington, he strode forth angrily as the Sisters neared the jeep. Colleen noticed that his left hand and forearm were wound in grimy strips of bandage, in contrast to his spotless attire.

The Ghurkas discreetly withdrew – after Robyn rewarded them with several tubes of condensed milk, highly prized by the Nepalese.

Their officer gave vent to his ire in a voice that could probably have been heard on the far side of the lake.

"What the hell do you mean by parking your jeep in my company lines? We've only just cleared this area of Japs. Last thing I want swanning around here is a gaggle of nurses!"

Colleen was incensed. Rank or no rank, she was about to give the major an earful when Gwen interposed with soothing Welsh charm.

"I think you should have that dressing changed, sir," she cooed. "Why don't you sit here in the jeep and we'll look after you?"

The mood immediately relaxed and they fussed about the officer like four doting aunts.

"Sorry for blowing my top," he said meekly. "Arm was giving me hell. Perhaps you'd like a drink - and a chance to meet my officers?"

It was an invitation they couldn't refuse.

"Just in time, Gwennie," murmured Robyn as the major was summoning his subordinates. "I saw those green eyes flash, Coll."

"Yes," said Trish. "Nearly copped a load of Teesside Billingsgate, didn't he?"

"Sure did," said Colleen, with a self-conscious smile.

She saw the Ghurkas grinning hugely. They had witnessed the whole scene.

Drinks were served in the officers' mess and a most convivial atmosphere prevailed. When the time came for the girls to depart, their hosts volunteered an additional courtesy.

"You'll let us escort you back, ladies?" the OC asked.

They returned to the CCS in convoy with their officer escorts and a platoon of Ghurka riflemen.

Trenholme's astonishment gave way to deep appreciation with the gift of several bottles of whisky from the Ghurka OC. The MO decided against asking any awkward questions.

"Well, praise the Lord for feminine wiles," said Robyn when the four of them retired giggling to their quarters.

"And all those boys," she added softly.

Pyawbwe, April 1945.

Stobart's company was in reserve but the lads climbed to the summit of a rocky bluff where they could view the assault.

A few hundred yards away, the Border Regiment[166] attacked up a long bare slope through bursting white shrapnel clouds and a shimmering heat haze to capture the railway station located on the crest.

Watching the jungle-green lines advance unwavering, the Yorkshiremen were like a football crowd as they urged on their comrades-in-arms of the Western Marches.

"Gan on, marras! Git stuck in!"

"Show 'em your cap badge, Border![167]"

They broke into a raucous rendition of the Border's famous Regimental March.

"D'ye ken John Peel, with his coat of gray?

"D'ye ken John Peel at the break of day?

"D'ye ken John Peel when he's far far away,

"With the fox and the hounds in the morning?"

"I think we've seen history in the making today, Gruffie," Calvert remarked. "You don't often get the chance."

After Pyawbwe fell, Fourth Corps continued its southward advance down the Rangoon Road, through country that was refreshingly verdant compared to the Dry Belt, bordered on the east by the Sittang River and on the west by the Pegu Yomas.

The Japanese were not yet defeated but many of their formations had lost cohesion. Large numbers of the enemy were trying to escape across the Sittang or trekking through the Yomas wilderness, in retreat from Thirty-Third Corps' thrust west of the range.

Driving and marching down parallel axes of the Rangoon Road and the accompanying railway, a few hundred yards apart, Fourth Corps was carving out the deepest, narrowest offensive salient in history. Ball of Fire Division led the way, but the Black Cat's men established strong defensive positions at every overnight stop, with extensive fire trenches. Each vehicle received a night-long double guard.

"Mustn't get jumped by Jap in the dark," Stobart stipulated.

And they weren't.

Until they reached the crossroads, north of Pegu, fifty miles up the road from Rangoon, where the Black Cats passed through the Ball of Fire Division.

The battalion arrived during the afternoon, in the rain – because the pre-monsoon showers had begun and for the past few days, the men had been wet through and needed all their skill to light fires for brew-ups.

During intervening dry spells, the countryside steamed in the humidity, adding to the men's discomfort.

But at Pegu, those inconveniences were the least of their worries.

The Japanese 'jitter party' stormed forward from the cover of ditches and scrub in long swaying, screaming ranks to the insane blare of bugles as Stobart's company debussed.

"Platoons deploy in extended line!" shouted Warwick, firing off a flare.

Grafton remembered subsequent events as a few frantic minutes of stunning grenade blasts, flashing tracer, ear-pounding gunfire and vicious cut and thrust of close-quarter fighting in the pelting, flare-lit rain.

A horde of howling dervishes died but the company, despite its prompt reaction to the danger, suffered a dozen casualties, including Signaller O'Hare.

"Good thing they missed the radio set, Mick," Grafton muttered as he buckled it on and secured his pack beneath it.

"You'll mean it before the night's out, Gruffie," O'Hare gasped, bloodied gauze covering his chest where a Jap bayonet had struck.

And according to Sod's Law, Stobart, Symonds and Lorrimer were among the wounded. Abercrombie had returned from hospital but he was acting adjutant for the battalion.

That left Lieutenant Calvert as the one remaining company officer.

He went to confer with Stobart while Warwick directed Dymock's, Fell's and Howard's sections to their start lines, preparatory to the advance on the town.

In the soaking rain, Grafton, who accompanied Warwick, glanced apprehensively at the brooding houses ahead.

"Be a night to remember, this, Gruffie," said Rockford shakily, as he trudged past his mate en route to the start line.

Grafton nodded, conscious that Stony's prediction, like O'Hare's, was bound to prove true.

Trenholme's CCS moved to the outskirts of Pyawbwe while the fighting was in progress and soon afterwards joined the general advance south, always in company with a screen of protective infantry, who leaguered around the unit at night.

Although after weeks in the Dry Belt, the girls preferred their greener surroundings, with the impressive sight of the Yomas chain to the west, the new environment soon manifested problems of its own.

Colleen likened the pre-monsoon showers to the autumn rains of Italy.

"I haven't seen anything like this since the Gothic Line," she affirmed.

Drainage ditches dug around the tents were soon overflowing with liquid red mud.

"You've got a treat coming, Coll," her friends warned.

And the chill nights of the Dry Belt were now replaced by the cold of the rains, when everyone shivered at night, only to be discomforted after sunrise by stultifying humid heat when the storms let up temporarily.

During which intervals, clouds of annoying insects emerged - necessitating recourse to the loathsome repellent - together with an army of leeches.

And even less welcome local inhabitants.

Colleen was hurrying to fetch some more plasma from the CCS store when she saw the sinuous grey-brown shape in the grass, not ten feet away.

Usually, they slithered off.

This one didn't.

It reared up, fanning its hood.

Colleen froze.

"Cover your eyes, Sister," said quiet voice. "It's a spitter."

Instantly, she did so. Geordie Wood had observed her predicament. He circled around the reptile and took its head off with a swipe of his machete.

"Thanks, Woody," said Colleen, trembling with relief.

Wood wiped the blade on the grass.

"Aye, Sister," he said. "I'll get rid of it but keep an eye out for its mate, like."

Then problems arose over patient care. Supply lines were now severely stretched and to speed up the advance, everyone was on half rations, so that more and more wounded were admitted with signs of malnutrition.

"At least we can fly them out from Toungoo," Trenholme remarked stoically as several underfed Post-Op patients were loaded onto ambulances. "Be hard for them going back by road."

Toungoo lay halfway between Meiktila and Rangoon. Fourth Corps secured the town in the latter part of April, together with its vital airfields and Trenholme's CCS encamped nearby.

But owing to the continuing proximity of the enemy, the Sisters still could not risk leaving the CCS perimeter and the problem of patient diet persisted until the protective squaddies were able to bring in quantities of eggs, fruit and vegetables from surrounding villages.

The scarlet-skinned jungle bananas proved a great favourite.

"Three times as big as any I've seen on my dad's barrow," Kitty said admiringly. Her family operated a market stall in Stratford-Upon-Avon, so the other girls often called her Puck, though not when any males were around.

And eventually, the post arrived, with some wonderful news for Colleen, from Anne.

Dear Colleen, Bill is SAFE! He's a POW in Austria[168]. *I can't thank God enough. We'll be getting married in the summer, DV.*

Everyone shared in Colleen's joy.

"We suffer and rejoice together,[169]" said Trish.

Gwen and Robyn received reassuring letters from their husbands.

I'm in Corps HQ now, Dai wrote. *Going so high on this Intelligence ladder, I'm getting dizzy.*

Mostly doing aerial photography these days, wrote Jon. *See you in Rangoon, love.*

But before Rangoon, there would be Pegu – and the monsoon.

"Now you know what 'a multitude of waters in the heavens[170]' is like, Coll!" Trish yelled above the roar of the deluge when they were dashing to Resus the afternoon the monsoon broke – two weeks early.

"Like a million fire hoses!" shouted Colleen.

The monsoon capes with which they'd been issued helped to keep out some of the drenching.

Though they would soon be caught up with circumstances in their own way as tumultuous as the storm itself.

This chapter has skipped over Grandma's Colleen's short absence from the CCS during April 1945, when she was flown by air ambulance to help tend wounded Karen levies in the hills east of Toungoo. The experience proved to be most poignant for her and she didn't re-late the details to her friends for several weeks. This is why the description of that episode has been deferred to Chapter 14. For the present, we must return to other theatres of operations.

First, it is time to 'fast forward' a few months and reveal the true identity of a young lady encountered earlier in this narrative – now beset with divided emotions after an unexpected success.

Spring, 1945, Occupied Germany.

WAAF Officer Kate Bramble scrutinised her reflection in the mirror, brushed some min-iscule strands of lint from her jacket and adjusted her cap.

She wanted to look her best for Steve, the note on her dresser notwithstanding.

They'd met as a result of his report that had constituted a breakthrough.

Their friendship had progressed from there, in turn helping Kate come to terms with the apparent failure of another line of enquiry.

But after months of frustration, some vital information concerning that inquiry had ar-rived by DR the previous day – with an uncanny link to their current investigation into the Von Hollstein case.

Major, The Lord Peter Waverly, DSO, MC. Domicile, Waverly Manor, Derbyshire, the note read. *SOE, Alias Guillaume.*

Kate's heart had almost stopped when she observed the location. It matched what they knew about Von Hollstein's apparent destination. It couldn't be coincidence

Satisfied at last with the angle of her cap, she gazed through the window at the pink blos-soms on the trees in the manor grounds and thought on the additional implications of the missive on her dresser.

Suppose Waverly *was* Guillaume – her Guillaume? How would that affect things with Steve?

A jeep was entering the manor grounds. It halted in the vehicle park and a young officer in peaked cap and crisp BDs climbed out.

"Well, forget it for now," Kate said to herself.

She took up her shoulder bag and hurried downstairs.

Thirteen

Liberators

The friendship between Steve Graham and Kate Bramble developed through a series of events spread over several months. We trace them now.

Boulogne, September 17th, 1944.

Lieutenant Graham stood with Captain Winstanley beside Armadillo. They were surveying the low, grassy hills a mile distant.

"The outer ring," said Don. "Concrete pillboxes dug in. Mines in front."

"Be tougher than Le Havre," Steve said.

Le Havre had fallen the previous week. Thousands of tons of HE had savaged the defenders, from the RAF, RN battleships and corps artillery, after which two infantry divisions forced the garrison's surrender. Dazed civilians groped through the ruins as army engineers and naval logistics personnel strove to get the port back into working order.

Now Boulogne was about to suffer the same fate.

Plumes of smoke arose from the rocket salvoes unleashed by RAF Typhoons, roaring down in steep dives, pulling out at perilously low altitudes.

Both officers glanced up into fair summer skies at the intensifying engine noise.

"Heavies are on their way," said Winstanley.

The vast formations filled the western sky and soon the officers could discern sinister black bomb sticks falling earthwards, their bursts smothering the hilltop positions in a stygian artificial fog bank, spouting red tongues of flame. Steve felt the ground shuddering beneath his feet. The noise was immense, augmented by the massive barrage from Third Canadian Division's artillery, whose shells shrieked low above the sappers' heads.

"Too low," the lads reckoned.

Third Canadian's infantry would assault the town.

Once they broke through the chain of hills.

"Flails are coming back," said Graham.

The crab Shermans were reversing across the field on the other side of the road along which One Troop was deployed. The field, not the road, was the line of advance. Undulating and partly screened by copses of trees, it gave better concealment than the road.

"Crews, mount!" Winstanley shouted. He sprinted to Amazon. Steve leapt onto Armadillo's turret.

"Hang on, sir!" Shoreland called out as he handed Graham his headset and mike with connecting leads. Steve grimaced, donning the earphones over his beret.

Graham shoved his right boot between two adjacent horizontal stakes. He reached up to grasp another of the wooden palings comprising the eight-foot diameter chespale fascine. With a core of rigid hollow tubes for drainage and secured by wire ropes, its four-ton, twelve-foot wide bulk lay crossways over the forepart of Armadillo's hull.

Steve climbed to the top of the bundle, clinging on like a spider, his boots wedged into the bundle for stability.

"Driver advance! Oblique left!" he said into his mike.

Armadillo chugged across the metalled road and ploughed into the field. Freshly pitted earth showed where the crabs had carved paths through the mines.

The AVREs' destination was a stream running at right angles to the line of advance. Armadillo and Amazon would drop their fascines in parallel to enable the remaining vehicles to cross.

Steve felt himself swaying with Armadillo's movement. The palings beneath him pressed creaking into his thighs.

"Left, left!" he yelled in his mike to Talbot. "OK, straighten up!"

Graham was thankful for the smoke obscuring the enemy positions. Otherwise, as on D-Day, fascine-carrying AVRE crews had to rely on quick glances out the side doors to aid direction, because the bundle's cradle mountings partly obscured frontal vision.

"Stop!" Graham ordered. Armadillo lurched to a halt on broken turf lining the bank of the stream. Amazon stopped some distance to the right. The lieutenant scrambled back via his hatch to the commander's seat.

"Stand by to drop fascine," he said over the intercom.

The wire ropes holding the bundle merged in a Y-junction with the main cable affixed to the AVRE. Several pounds of guncotton were wrapped around the junction and could be detonated via a trigger mechanism inside the turret.

Graham ducked his head below the hatch opening and pressed the trigger. The guncotton exploded with a sharp bang, severing the ropes. The bundle tumbled neatly into the watercourse.

Everyone cheered. If the release mechanism malfunctioned, it meant an awkward job to detach the fascine manually.

All the crew except Driver Talbot then exited through the side doors. Unfastening the cumbersome angle-iron cradle and the main cable, they hauled them to one side and hurried back inside Armadillo. Recovery units would collect the discarded items.

"Swinging turret to main axis," said Graham through the intercom.

The turret revolution gear whirred, bringing the housing to face dead ahead. An AVRE had to turn the petard mortar through ninety degrees, in order to accommodate a fascine.

"Driver, reverse," Graham ordered.

With Amazon's fascine also in place, the AVREs pulled back to enable the crabs to cross first and continue flailing. One Troop was to follow in support of the infantry.

"Let's hope the Boches are still blind with smoke, Steve," said Major Blackstone over the wireless when Graham reported the successful crossing of his half troop.

Blackstone's HQ Troop was pushing towards the northern outskirts of the town, his remaining two troops in reserve.

Though they would not be starved for action.

One Troop's Churchills charged in parallel columns through the billows of smoke and dust, the drivers weaving skilfully between yawning bomb craters that littered the rising ground beyond the stream. They re-crossed the approach road in the process as it curved between the hills.

A crab lay on its side where the road verge had caved in. The Sherman's flails hung impotently.

But the crew had taken some two-score Germans prisoner. Steve recognised his friend Lieutenant Cavendish, brandishing a Sten. Cavendish's crabs had flailed the beach exit at Normandy.

"Well done, Chris!" Graham called.

"Keep on, Steve!" Cavendish shouted, his youthful face manifesting a plucky grin.

The AVREs roared on towards the hill fortifications, accompanied by a troop of flame-throwing Churchill crocodiles, with armoured personnel carriers right behind.

To Graham, staring from his hatchway through goggles, it seemed that the air inside and out of Armadillo was all choking grit. He cringed at the combined clamour of engine, air intake fans, clattering tracks and slamming gear changes as Talbot sent the forty-ton vehicle surging fiercely up the slope like a rally bike. Armadillo's intrepid driver was known as 'Crash' Talbot.

Steve glimpsed a squat concrete shape through the drifting smoke.

"Pill box, eleven o'clock, fifty yards! Mortar, open fire!" he yelled into his mike.

Ferrarby brought the turret to bear and discharged the weapon. Illingworth reloaded and Ferrarby fired again.

The dustbins blew great chunks out of the pillbox's front.

Deeply dug in, protected on top by many feet of earth, the hill forts had suffered little from the bombardment. Spectacular though it was, the rain of bombs and shells had materially done little more in this sector than blast away topsoil.

But though physically safe, the defenders were still stunned by the shock of the explosions. They had insufficient time to bring their A/T guns to bear before petards smashed great holes in the blockhouse walls into which the crocodiles poured liquid flame. The enemy could not withstand this dual assault.

"Cease fire!" Graham ordered but the gunners had already seen the cheering Canadian infantry swarm out of the carriers to surround the bunkers and collect survivors. Dozens of gleeful, sturdy young faces grinned up at their armoured protectors from beneath scrim net camouflaged steel helmets.

"You guys are gold!" called an enthusiastic subaltern, his Sten levelled at a group of sullen-faced POWs.

"Glad to join the party, mate!" Graham called back.

As neighbouring pillboxes were subdued, the assaulting flails, crocodiles and AVREs churned down the reverse slope into the town's cobbled lanes, past battered shells of trim façaded houses, flames licking at their timbered frames. The RAF heavies had departed but the howl of high-powered engines, shriek of shells and flashing booms revealed where artillery and fighter-bombers were still ravaging German fortifications in the dock area.

"Heading for the river, Don, over," Graham informed Winstanley.

The River Liane cut through the town. The bridges spanning it led to the docks.

"OK, Steve," Don radioed back. "Travelling on parallel course. Will inform OC. Out."

Treads scraping harshly on cobbles and shattered stone, Armadillo, Arquebus and Adamant edged cautiously along a twisting thoroughfare, engines muttering. Alert-eyed drivers peered through visors as they nudged the AVREs around gaping pits left by bomb and shell blast. Canadian infantry crept along in the rear of the Churchills.

Heart-stopping bangs and cracks sounded to left and right, where other vehicles in the column were encountering resistance. Thick puffs of smoke drifted skywards.

Graham brushed brick dust away from his goggles and stared intently into the ruins ahead for likely enemy positions. He heard Blackstone's voice in his earphones.

"Engaging Citadel with petards."

The Citadel fortress was the lynchpin of the enemy defence.

A few minutes later, Graham heard an agitated voice.

"Gamekeeper wounded, lead troop pinned down. Two Troop moving up. Retriever assuming command."

Steve swallowed hard. The speaker was Blackstone's wireless operator. The right-hand column had struck trouble and the major was a casualty. Captain Julian Yeardley, squadron second-in-command and Two Troop commander, was now in charge, bringing his AVREs up from reserve to reinforce HQ Troop.

Then the enemy to Graham's front reacted.

Steve heard the 'whoomping' of the mortars, saw the ugly projectiles arcing upwards and glimpsed the spurt of bluish smoke from a camouflaged gun pit together with the instant flash. He heard the supersonic whip crack combined with the crashing roar of collapsed masonry as the A/T shell smashed through a skeletal tenement building.

Steve ducked into the turret, slamming the hatch shut. He pulled his goggles down around his neck and thrust his face to the eyepiece of his periscope, frantically relaying his orders.

"A/T one hundred yards, two o'clock! Pak Forty-three[171]. Co-axs engage. Drivers, stay out of his line of fire!"

His voice was drowned in the banging of the mortar explosions and Shoreland's burst from the turret Besa. The AVREs would have to reduce the distance to the German gun if they were to use their petards.

More whip cracks followed. To right and left, Graham spotted additional telltale puffs and the stabbing flashes. So had Crittenden and Hazeldene.

None of Graham's AVREs were hit but he saw a Sherman crab slew to a stop from a direct hit and a sheet of flame burst from a crocodile's trailer, engulfing the tank. Survivors scrambled out to join infantrymen sheltering amid rubble heaps and bomb craters.

"Fox One engage target left," Graham ordered. "Watch for *panzerfausts*!"

Retaliatory bangs sounded from the turret guns of adjacent tanks. Adamant chugged down a side street between several smashed houses to get into position.

Then came the terrible flaring hiss.

"Pak Forty-three flamed," Graham informed his half troop.

And Adamant got close enough to attack a second A/T position.

"Petard away, sir!" Hazeldene reported over the wireless. "Bang on!"

Armadillo was within range of another A/T position.

"Target ninety yards. Present heading, mortar, fire!" Graham called to Ferrarby. The round flew between a pair of gouged out walls, blew away a sandbagged redoubt and upended the gun. Crouching infantrymen dashed forward to occupy the position.

Screening themselves via heaps of debris, the armoured vehicles pushed on, gunning, petarding, flaming the stubborn opposition. Although the collapsed buildings at times hindered the Allied tanks, they obstructed enemy fields of fire so that the terrible eighty-eights, nemeses of Normandy, could not be used to full advantage. Armour and infantry acting in concert dealt decisively with enemy mortarmen, *panzerfaust* operators, machine gunners and more A/T emplacements.

But one menace remained.

Though several feet deep and at times half a road width across, the craters left by the Allied bombardment often proved difficult to spot in the congested streets, especially with dusk falling. Several vehicles thus came to grief, including Armadillo.

As Talbot swerved to avoid a pile of stonework, Graham felt the Churchill suddenly lurch at an angle and stop dead.

"Sorry, sir," Talbot said plaintively over the intercom, amid the chaos of cursing bodies pitching sideways. Graham had instinctively clung to the turret hatch handle to steady himself.

"Sod's law, Corporal," said Steve. "Everybody out. Echo One, get ready to tow," he radioed Crittenden. "And any blighter who thinks it's a joke will be court-martialled tomorrow."

"Wilco, sir," said Crittenden, audibly gasping with mirth.

As he scrambled out the turret hatch, Graham observed that Armadillo was perched half in, half out of a bomb crater, nose down, with a gap of four or five feet beneath the sunken tread.

"A considerable list to starboard, sir," Talbot said ruefully, on climbing out a side door.

Shoreland leapt down from Armadillo's turret.

"OC'll mark your card for this, Crash," he remarked with a malicious grin. Ferrarby and Illingworth were unfastening the towing hawser from the Churchill's hull.

"Start piling rubble under that tread," ordered Graham. "You might be able to drive her out, Crash," he said to his driver. "With the tow."

The thoroughfare was too narrow for Arquebus to get past so Crittenden detoured around a couple of side streets to position his AVRE for the tow. Fortunately, the area had been subdued although gunfire continued from about a block ahead and the dismounted sappers kept their Stens handy. Quickly they slipped the hawser's hooks through each of the AVRE's towing rings.

Sergeant Crittenden ordered his driver, Sapper Kendle, to let Arquebus take up the slack.

"OK!" he called when the hawser was taut. He and his lads then piled into the road to help Armadillo's crew collect chunks of fallen masonry.

"We've got company, sir," said MacGee. A line of civilians was hurrying towards them, mostly middle-aged men and women but including a couple of teenage girls.

"Where did they come from?" asked Ferrarby, slinging an armful of half bricks into the void beneath Armadillo's tread. "Thought most of the locals would've hightailed it by now."

"Church crypt most likely," said Crittenden, as he and his wireless operator, Sapper Young, pushed a slab of stone into the crater. "There's a chapel back there, what's left of it."

"Nous aiderons, oui?[172]" asked the leading Frenchman when the group arrived.

"Yes, please do," said Graham. He indicated to the new arrivals they should pass pieces of rubble to his men who were chocking the tread.

The French understood immediately and the two girls smiled at the lithe young lieutenant.

"They don't seem too bothered we've knocked their town to bits," Crittenden observed. The citizens' stoicism in the circumstances was indeed admirable.

Their combined efforts soon bolstered the tread. Talbot climbed in and started the Churchill's engine. Kendle edged Arquebus forward. With a grinding of metal on stone, Armadillo regained the roadway, then closed up on Arquebus, to slacken the cable.

A cheer went up and Talbot's face, visible through the driver's aperture, looked mightily relieved. Ferrarby and Illingworth quickly detached and stowed the hawser.

"Crews mount!" Graham ordered. The sappers sprinted to their AVREs. *"Merci beaucoup,"* Steve said to the French.

One of the girls, a supple, olive-skinned brunette, impulsively threw her arms around Graham's neck and pulled him close.

"Je m'appelle Monique, je t'aime, soldat Anglais[173]," she said softly.

The lieutenant was slightly bemused but his men weren't.

"Go on, sir," they called. "Don't be shy, give her a kiss!"

Graham did so – and greatly appreciated the tender warmth of the girl's lips against his.

The resulting cheer far surpassed the earlier one.

It was well after dark when Graham's two vehicles rendezvoused with Adamant, parked in the cobbled courtyard of what was left of a school.

To ensure that Armadillo and Arquebus did not blunder into any more craters, Graham had gone ahead on foot to guide them through the rubble-littered streets. The grey-haired Frenchman from the rescue party voluntarily accompanied him.

"La, la," he would whisper, pointing out various detours.

Graham was extremely grateful for the help. The route to the river had been planned with the help of the local FFI[174], one of whose personnel was accompanying Blackstone's column but darkness and the destruction would have greatly slowed progress for Steve's AVREs without the guide.

Foul-smelling smoke haze hung about the area, glowing red in areas where timber frames were still slight. It seriously restricted vision.

Shoreland in the meantime established radio contact with Hazeldene, who confirmed that the town was clear of enemy up to the river and Steve was glad to see the gleaming strip of the Liane come into view across a heavily rutted and unsealed esplanade.

Before the lieutenant had time to thank their guide properly, the Frenchman said, *"Bon, Anglais,"* to Graham, shook his hand and disappeared into the night.

Armadillo and Arquebus had emerged onto the esplanade only a short distance from their objective, a stonework bridge – now blown. But it served as a landmark for Graham and Hazeldene to reunite the half troop via directions passed over the wireless.

Nearing the courtyard, Graham heard French Canadian voices raised in drunken hilarity and glimpsed shadowy forms lurching about a street corner diagonally opposite.

"What's all that, Ronny?" he radioed Hazeldene.

"Bunch of Chauds[175], sir," the corporal responded. "They found some cellars full of cognac and they're pissed rotten."

Hazeldene and his crew had carried out essential maintenance on Adamant. They were now brewing tea and heating tins of compo rations on primus stoves set up in the ruins of the school but concealed by the remains of adjoining walls.

Graham's other two crews would set about the same tasks in turn. Hazeldene came up and reported to him.

"There's a big hole in the floor of the school there, sir," he said. "We've dragged some beams across. It'll do for a latrine."

"OC's on the line, sir," said Shoreland.

"Thanks, lads," said Graham.

He replaced his earphones, apprehensive at the sound of Yeardley's clipped tones. What had happened to Major Blackstone?

"Major's been evacuated, Steve," Julian told him. "He should pull through. I'll give you the details when I arrive."

Because Graham was with the centre column, Yeardley decided to use the courtyard for the O Group. He and Winstanley would converge on it from opposite directions, using the blown bridge for a marker.

Graham hoped the Frenchman had made it back to his friends OK.

Alan J. O'Reilly

All along the riverfront, troops were consolidating their positions for the night. Lorries brought up ammunition and food, having gingerly threaded their way through the devastated streets by means of dimmed headlights.

One Troop gratefully replenished its stock of petards.

The troop officers convened inside Battleaxe, Yeardley's Churchill, while Julian's crew joined Hazeldene and the others for a brew.

Julian informed Don and Steve of Blackstone's fate as he spread out a map of the sector.

"He got out to reconnoitre a better field of fire to knock down the Citadel gates. Jerry shell blew down a wall and the major was hit by falling debris. He also took shrapnel in the chest."

"You got in, though?" Winstanley asked. Yeardley nodded.

"After Zero Troop petarded the gates off, the Jerries ran up a white flag. The FFI bloke[176] with the troop took the Canadians in by a secret entrance. Seeing they were surrounded, the Boches called it quits. We bagged nearly three hundred of 'em."

Yeardley described various positions on the map in the dock area west of the river, indicating them with a pencil point, his aristocratic features taut in the turret's illumination light. He outlined the plan of action for the morrow.

"Infantry'll go over at first light. Crabs and crocs will shoot 'em across[177]."

"River is a bit wide for petards," said Graham.

His scalp felt prickly beneath his beret and he was sweating underneath his BDs and smock. He wished he could have had a bath but a quick wash and shave after stand-to in the morning would be all they could manage. The mobile shower unit was miles in the rear and the troop would have no opportunity to dig bathing holes and line them with groundsheets, like they'd occasionally done in Normandy.

"FFI's shown us where the main German positions are in the docks – also which villages they've fortified along the coast up towards Calais," Julian went on. "We'll be going for them as soon as we're finished here. Three Troop's already on their way from reserve."

"When can we expect the arks, Julian?" asked Winstanley.

"Day after tomorrow. They're coming up from Le Havre."

"Brew's up, sirs," whispered a voice. Sergeant Crittenden and Sapper Tomlinson proffered three steaming mugs of tea through a side door to the officers, who received them with thanks.

"Any word about a Class Forty[178]?" Graham asked.

"Maybe end of the week," said Yeardley. "It's priority but the lads are at full stretch even now."

Steve nodded. He knew that the field companies would be toiling round the clock, dozering away rubble, getting power lines and water mains back on stream and repairing the sewers.

"What if they gave us the kit? We could put up the Class Forty ourselves," Winstanley suggested.

296

"Don't think we'll have time, Don," said Yeardley, with a regretful shake of his head. "By the way, Steve, your lads are to be commended for the brew but they must've needed bolt cutters to stop it pouring."

"Corporal Hazeldene, Julian," Graham explained. "Noted for his generosity with compo cubes."

"And the cognac dollops, too," Don remarked and tilted his mug in appreciation.

Yeardley put his mug to one side and stretched his long-limbed frame – a difficult manoeuvre in the confines of an AVRE.

"Well, we might have something to drink to by the end of the week," he said, taking up his mug again. "First Allied Airborne Army's invaded Holland today. War could be over very soon."

It wasn't, although two of the troopers taking part in the airborne invasion were destined to become Steve Graham's life-long friends. They were Sergeants Jim Grant and Bill Harris, of the First and Second Battalions, the Parachute Regiment, respectively[179].

Lieutenant Graham's half troop watched the Canadian infantry pile into the phalanx of terrapin amphibians, DUKWs and motorised rafts by the water's edge.

A continuous *"crash-crash"* was sounding up and down the riverfront, from the seventy-five mm turret guns of the supporting tanks. HE smoke tasted bitter in the damp morning air and swirled across the water. No counter fire came back.

"Those Chaud boys must be sufferin' from all this noise, Ronny, with their hangovers," Sapper MacGee remarked to Hazeldene from the shelter of Adamant's hull while Graham was inspecting the vehicles. Among the embarking assault troops were the French Canadian revellers of the night before.

The corporal shrugged, pleased with having convinced his officer that all externally stowed kit was securely in place.

"So long as there's a fight going, mate, they won't give a tinker's cuss," he said.

The day after the infantry crossing, the turretless ark Churchills with their twelve-foot ramps affixed front and rear arrived on the esplanade. They plunged in succession into the river to create an artificial causeway that quickly enabled the armoured columns to cross over.

At first, the enemy in the dock area resisted stubbornly but lacking heavy weapons, they were forced to surrender within two days, resulting in hundreds more prisoners.

And a couple of surprises for Lieutenant Graham.

They emerged from the remains of a warehouse in company with a Lieutenant Ben Hedges, the young Canadian subaltern of the North Shore Regiment, who'd hailed Graham during the hilltop battle.

"Say, Steve," he called. "Over here."

Summoning Crittenden, Graham climbed down from Armadillo and went to meet the two strangers who were dressed like French civilians but carried Stens.

One was fair-haired and rangy, slightly taller than Graham, the other shorter and squatly built, having darker hair and a pugnacious expression.

"Major Pitcairn, SOE," said the tall one. He shook hands with Steve. "This is Sergeant Stroud," he added, nodding to his companion. "We were landed here to link up with the Resistance but had to take shelter when the stuff started flying. Any chance you could get us to your Divisional HQ?" he asked.

"I'll write you a pass for my squadron commander, sir. His HQ's that way," Graham answered, pointing.

"Thank you, Lieutenant," said Pitcairn.

"Boys have got a brew going, sir," Crittenden informed the major. He indicated where the half troop was setting up their primus stoves. "You'd be welcome to a cuppa before you go."

"Thanks very much, Sergeant," said Pitcairn. "But we'd best be on our way."

He folded the pass into a jacket pocket. Then he and his stolid companion hurried off along the dockside towards Yeardley's leaguer.

Graham, Crittenden and Hedges exchanged puzzled looks.

"We found 'em hidin' behind some packing cases," said Ben. "Kinda pacifist for your SOE."

"Very much so, Hedge," said Graham.

"I reckon even the SOE would stop for tea, sir," Crittenden ventured.

"And the FFI's all over the place," Graham added. "So how come they couldn't make contact?"

Hedges shouldered his Sten.

"Well, at least your report'll be on file, Steve, if anyone wants to check," he drawled. "You guys don't mind if I take you up on the cuppa?"

Graham learned later that Pitcairn and Stroud obtained a further pass from Yeardley, were conveyed back across the river and disappeared into the town. Steve filed his report and soon forgot the incident, because more urgent tasks were in the offing.

Including the capture of Calais.

"We're giving you blokes a wide berth."

Winstanley and Graham waved at the speaker, a Lieutenant 'Shep' Tyson, as he led his troop of crocodile Churchills past Winstanley's AVRES. Tyson's nickname derived from his dad's occupation, a sheep farmer in the Yorkshire dales.

Towing trailers loaded with four hundred gallons of flame fuel, the crocs were reckoned as the most hazardous vehicles in Seventy-Ninth's menagerie but today, Amazon, Armadillo and Arquebus were also towing trailers, filled with an even more dangerous fluid.

Nitro-glycerine. Each trailer carried a ton of it.

The explosive would be used to breach the minefields encircling Calais. The armoured column containing One Troop would break in from the west, while a second column attacked from the south.

Following the customary RAF raid, the all-too-familiar cloud of HE haze shrouded the town that nestled below a distant rise.

Now it was the AVREs' turn, with the new weapon, known as the 'conger'.

Winstanley gave Graham the thumbs-up sign and ordered his driver to take Amazon into the grassy meadow adjacent to the road. It formed a shallow basin between a nearby headland and the far slope above the town.

Graham watched from the verge, a sharp drizzle spitting in his face. Dull cloud and a biting Channel breeze had replaced the fair skies of the Boulogne attack.

Amazon halted on the edge of the mine belt. Sapper foot patrols had mapped its location during the night. They'd had to prod gingerly with bayonets for anti-personnel *Schuh* mines and non-metallic devices that didn't respond to the detectors and feel for trip wires with long twigs.

Nasty things, the A/P mines. Some could take a foot off, or half the lower leg, or both legs. Others jumped up several feet when detonated and sprayed out ball bearings. They were laid as a screen, in case anyone came looking for the A/T mines.

Graham observed Don and his explosives NCO, Corporal Jevons, unhook the tracked carrier containing the conger device.

Amazon came rumbling back to the rest of the troop.

Jevons primed the rocket launcher. With a sharp bang and blue puff of smoke, it discharged a three-inch-diameter fire hose. Two hundred yards long, the hose looped over the meadow and flopped onto the ground.

After carrying out the statutory checks with Winstanley, the corporal then rejoined the troop.

Graham watched Winstanley reach down to open the discharge valve and start the pump.

The idea was for the pump to fill the hose with the explosive liquid, after which it would automatically stop. The pump operator would then retreat to the safe area, trailing the wire for the detonation device. The resulting explosion was intended to clear a path through the minefield at a single blow.

Only it didn't always work out in practice.

Graham saw the flash and threw himself flat. So did everyone else outside the vehicles.

A terrible yellow-black mushroom of flame shot forth, followed by a gargantuan roar and a huge shower of earth.

Shock waves and a rush of heat beat against the horrified onlookers.

"Oh, my God, Don," wept Graham, ears ringing, his face pressed to earth.

Smoke hung heavy over the scene as Graham leapt up to Armadillo's turret. White-faced, Shoreland handed Steve his headset.

"Crab leader, sir," he said stiffly.

Chris Cavendish's voice spoke in Graham's earphones.

"I'll take my troop forward, Steve."

"Thanks, Chris but we'll do the job with the other congers."

"They might all blow, man."

Cavendish sounded distraught.

"Then you can use the flails, mate. Out."

Graham ordered, "Driver, advance," and Talbot nosed Armadillo cautiously across the heavy turf to the edge of the mines and halted. It was imperative to avoid jarring the explosive.

Graham and Illingworth unhooked the trailer and Talbot drove off.

Steve almost retched from the stench of cordite. Where Amazon's trailer had stood was a crater in which a man could easily have hidden.

Illingworth activated the rocket launcher. It successfully unfurled the hose.

"I'll do the rest, sir," he offered.

"Push off, Tapper," said Graham, with a sickly grin. Illingworth obeyed.

Graham then started the pump, his heart pounding, his hands clammy. He heard the motor whirr and watched the hose bulging. After a short interval that seemed to Graham like hours, it tripped out.

The conger was successfully deployed.

Steve returned to the safe area and detonated the device.

A rippling roar sent waves of soil flying, right and left, accompanied by multiple secondary blasts.

A full vehicle lane width was clear, as far as the foot of the slope above the town. By inspection through his binoculars, Graham reckoned the conger had spanned the mine belt.

"Brilliant job, sir," said Jevons warmly. The nuggety NCO shook his officer's hand as Steve walked past Amazon.

"Thanks, Jev," muttered Graham, his voice constricted by having to clench his teeth in order to stop them chattering. Everyone else was cheering.

Sitting atop Arquebus, Crittenden had ordered his AVRE forward, towing the last conger. The advance ideally needed two lane widths.

"I'll take it, Bill," Graham called but Crittenden shook his head.

"My job, sir," he said firmly.

It would not have been proper to insist, so Graham returned to the protection of Armadillo's hull, where he slipped to his knees, acutely conscious that Crittenden and Lorraine Tyrell were now in regular correspondence.

The sergeant successfully cleared a second lane, prompting more rousing cheers. Packed with Canadian infantry, the troop carriers surged toward the distant crest, with the flails and crocodiles in support. One Troop's sacrificial effort had gained valuable time.

Graham climbed into Armadillo's turret to contact Yeardley, coordinating the squadron's efforts in another sector.

"Cleared two lanes with congers, Julian," Steve reported. "One Troop commander killed by premature conger explosion. No other Troop casualties."

"OK, Steve," came the calm reply. "Return to reserve as planned. Out."

"Wilco, Julian, out," said Graham.

He switched to Armadillo's intercom.

"Driver, return to leaguer," he ordered, then relayed the instruction to Arquebus and Arrowhead, commanded by Sergeant Kinnear, Winstanley's senior NCO.

And now his.

"Four years ago, Steve, I stood on those cliffs," said Tubby Potter.

Hands thrust into the pockets of his greatcoat and with a pair of earmuffs projecting from beneath his peaked cap, the chaplain was standing with Graham on the headland adjoining the meadow where Don had died.

They were gazing across the Channel at the White Cliffs of Dover.

The skies had cleared and the headland's grassy sward shimmered green in bright sunshine that bathed the deep melting blue of the narrow sea. A stiff breeze was whipping up the white caps.

"Good to be looking the other way," said Graham, hands clasped behind his back.

Steve wore only his camouflage smock with his BDs and beret but the brisk October wind didn't bother him. He remembered from D-Day how much colder it could be down in the swell.

"Folk over there'll be getting their first decent night's sleep since nineteen-forty," Tubby said.

His prompt visit to the troop after Winstanley's death had heartened the men. Morale was boosted further by the news that the specialised armour and their Canadian allies had captured the great Channel batteries of Cape Gris Nez and Sangatte, whose sixteen-inch guns had long menaced the Kentish towns.

Still in reserve, One Troop did not participate in the guns' capture but it assisted with the assembly of a Class Forty Bailey bridge near the seafront of Calais, to gain access to the town across ground the Germans had flooded.

Calais fell soon afterwards.

Tubby withdrew a gloved hand and pointed to several small warships in line astern, carving through the choppy seas on a southwest heading.

"Minesweepers from the Dover Patrol," he said. "They'll be clearing the fairways[180] into Boulogne."

"I've written to Barbara," said Graham quietly.

Winstanley had been a pre-war regular, married for five years, with two children.

"So have I," Potter murmured.

So would Blackstone, Yeardley and the CO. Officially confirmed as One Troop's commander, Graham couldn't help wondering when his own number would be up, though he took comfort from Tubby's exhortation from the Psalmist.

"'My times are in thy hand,' Steve. And it was a soldier who said it."

During October, the squadron moved into Holland, first destination Eindhoven, at the end of a one-hundred-and-sixty-mile drive spread over several days and conducted through repeated rainstorms.

With the enemy having been pushed back beyond Eindhoven, the AVRE crews motoring along interminably straight roads flanked on either side by endlessly flat landscape, suffered mainly from the weather - and tiredness, thanks to the demands of vehicle maintenance at the end of each day.

"Not like Buxton, Steve," said the lanky youth standing next to Graham during a midday halt.

The speaker shook his shoulders and droplets cascaded from his gas cape. His fresh-complexioned, freckly face was spotted with rain. The showers came sweeping in over the bleak expanse before them, where only the odd line of poplars and occasional cluster of farm buildings broke the monotony of the view.

Lieutenant Mark Napper, straight from officer training, had been given command of Winstanley's half troop, under the paternal guidance of veteran Sergeant Kinnear.

"We'll soon bring him round to our way of thinking, sir," the doughty NCO assured his troop commander.

Napper was twenty years of age. He came from Buxton, in the Derbyshire Peaks, so Steve could sympathise.

"Brew's up, sirs," said Hazeldene cheerily. He handed each officer a steaming enamel mug.

"Thanks, Ronny," said Napper. "I hear your brew's renowned throughout the regiment."

"Chock full of goodness, sir," Hazeldene assured him. "Another fifteen minutes for lunch, sir," the corporal said to Graham.

The Churchills were parked along the grassy verge of a lay-by, one designated free from mines. The lads had rigged tarpaulins on the hulls in the lee of the rain and were crouched beneath them, cooking the midday meal on spirit burners.

Graham sipped his tea, noticing immediately Hazeldene had been generous with dollops of fortifying rum. As usual, the tea almost had the consistency of syrup but Graham relished the feeling of warmth it imparted, all the way down.

"Is B Echelon still sending up the revitalised stuff, Ronny?" the lieutenant asked.

"Fresh meat and veg, too, sir," Hazeldene affirmed. "Someone's looking after us."

"Reverend Potter's influence on high," said Steve, winking at Napper. "And that of the divisional commander."

So many men had suffered from dietary deficiencies in Normandy that the army had sought assiduously to improve the quality of the compo rations.

And Seventy Ninth Armoured's senior officers made sure the forward units did not suffer from 'selective' pickings – an old supply chain trick.

Advancing into Holland, the specialised armour spread out in a wide arc, from Bergen-op-Zoom, roughly halfway between Antwerp and Rotterdam, then forty miles east to Venraij, on the west bank of the Maas, then approximately thirty miles south-southwest towards Bourg-Leopold, in Belgium.

Much of this salient had to be wrested violently from the enemy, at substantial cost in men and material.

One of the most vital tasks after the fall of the Channel ports was the clearing of the Scheldt Estuary and the subjugation of the island of Walcheren, to enable the Allies to use the port of Antwerp. An assault regiment of Royal Engineers was instrumental in the success of the operation but not the one containing Yeardley's squadron.

When it reached Eindhoven, that particular formation was diverted to a relatively unspoiled strip of country northwest of the town. Farms and villages in this area were as picturesque as they had been pre-war. Even the windmills were undamaged. As natural havens for enemy snipers and artillery spotters, these had mostly been flattened in areas blighted by the fighting.

And the local citizens were overjoyed to billet the incomers.

Yeardley ordered his men to clean up and buff their boots before descending upon their hosts. They also changed into fresh uniforms and underclothing, sent courtesy of B Echelon, along with consignments of fresh socks.

Graham borrowed Shoreland's steel mirror and scrupulously ran a comb through his shock of light brown hair. Napper did the same with his own reddish thatch.

"Mind you boys set a proper example," Yeardley admonished his two subalterns as they climbed into Hazeldene's jeep, en route for their billet.

Mark and Steve were quartered with the Vanderveers, who lived above the drycleaner's shop that Mama and Papa ran as a family business, with the help of their two daughters, Katrijn and Marijke. Slender, blue-eyed blondes, they were aged eighteen and sixteen respectively. The guests found that the family could all converse well in English, provided one didn't speak too quickly.

"We'll be very happy to do your laundry, boys" said Mama, when she showed the officers to their room. It was on the third storey of the building and heavy oaken rafters sloped down to a few feet above the window. Thickly carpeted, the room contained two beds, a dressing table mounted with a mirror and a spacious built-in wardrobe. It had an adjoining bathroom and loo.

"Give you a good discount, ja?" Papa said jovially as he deposited fresh towels on the beds, fetched at Mama's request.

Mr Vanderveer was a portly man in shirtsleeves, wearing matching grey-flannel trousers and waistcoat. He had a trim moustache, beard and grey-white hair.

Mama, fair, slim and bright-eyed, like her daughters, wouldn't hear of it.

"Papa, we would be scandalised!" she protested as she bulked up the pillows on each bed. "You give your laundry to me, boys. We will clean and press everything."

"Mama has spoken, boys," said Mr Vanderveer meekly.

"Now, Papa," Mrs Vanderveer continued. "You start running the bath. Our guests will be tired after their journey."

"Do you want to flip a coin, Mark, for who goes first?" Steve asked. Napper shook his head.

"Seniors first, Steve," he said. "That's what they taught me at Sandhurst."

"Yes," said Graham. "I remember something about that."

Before they retired, Steve and Mark joined the family for tea in the parlour.

The room reminded Graham of something out of Hans Christian Andersen, with its spotless furnishings, exquisitely carved woodwork and lounge suit "that could have graced Buck Palace," Steve said to Napper afterwards.

The tea was comparatively weak for the officers' palates but after the Hazeldene brew, that wasn't surprising.

Mama plied her guests with delicious homemade iced cakes, while Papa smoked his clay pipe with its long, curved stem and the two daughters sat with their mother on the sofa.

Graham sensed that Katrijn and Mark had taken an instant liking to each other and hoped it wouldn't give rise to complications.

"Some of the local boys were lost in nineteen-forty, of course," Mama explained, pouring the tea. "But many others escaped to England and either joined your air force or the Princess Irene Brigade[181]."

Napper carefully grasped the willow-pattern cup and saucer Mama offered him.

"Did any of them join the Resistance?" he asked.

"Quite a few, ja," interjected Papa. He removed the pipe stem from his mouth to sip his tea. "The ones left are either with the Irenes or acting as guides for other units – a lot of them up near Njmegen."

"It is terrible there and over the Rijn, in Arnhem," said Marijke vehemently. "They are having to eat tulip bulbs![182]"

"We can't be sure, Marijke," said Katrijn.

"I bet it's true," Marijke insisted.

Katrijn acquiesced in response to her sister's vehemence and smiled warmly at Napper, who courteously reciprocated.

"I fear it may be so," said Mama with a sigh. "The Germans kept back food here, from the shops," she explained to the subalterns. "We got by thanks to local farmers and Papa's kitchen garden."

The failure of Market Garden had been a great disappointment, made worse by the knowledge that the enemy were bound to take reprisals.

Mama passed around the plate of cakes again. "But your air force has been marvellous," she said. "They have dropped hundreds of food parcels in occupied areas. We got some here last winter."

"A big help to us at the time," said Katrijn, smiling at Napper again.

"My brother flew on some of those missions[183]," Steve remarked. "He's an RAF navigator, although he's POW now. Shot down over Nuremberg."

"Then we will pray for your brother every day, Lieutenant Graham," said Papa firmly. He leant forward and knocked his pipe out into the scuttle by the fire. The chimes of the hall clock sounded the hour, reminding Steve of the one at home.

Papa spoke again.

"It is time for bed for you youngsters. Mama and I will clear up."

So ended the most enjoyable evening Steve could remember for a long time.

Though billeted in private homes, the squadron members continued to mess in their individual troops. The army worked diligently with local authorities to restore civilian infrastructure in the areas of Holland now liberated but insisted it be kept separate from that of the military.

Nevertheless, Mrs Vanderveer always gave Steve and Mark morning coffee before the transport arrived to take them to Squadron HQ. The other ladies of the village did likewise with their guests.

"We should give them some compo boxes," Mark suggested as they waited outside the house for Hazeldene after their first night with the family. Frost sparkled on the cobbles.

"Against regulations and we don't want to offend Mama," said Steve. His breath condensed as he spoke. "Maybe when we go," he added on reflection.

The officers usually returned well after dark, dog-tired, for the day was spent in intensive training and preparations for the next operation, aimed at bridging the River Maas. And, as always, vehicle maintenance took hours.

But Mama ensured that plenty of hot water was ready for baths – and returned their crisply clean clothing from the previous day for them to change into.

Afterwards, the officers invariably met with the family for tea.

It was the high point of the day. Sometimes, they studied the scriptures together, for the Vanderveers were strong Mennonites.

"Reckon Tubby organised this billet, Steve?" Napper asked when they'd retired one evening. Like Graham, Mark came from an independent Baptist background.

"I reckon," said Steve, yawning. The growing closeness between his second-in-command and Katrijn still worried him and he was considering broaching the subject with Mark.

But a development in Graham's own circumstances would soon render this impossible.

Army policy notwithstanding, Mrs Vanderveer and her companion housewives wrote to Regimental HQ and insisted that they be permitted to provide Sunday lunch and high tea for any of the soldiers billeted with them who wished to attend church.

In the face of such a determined onslaught, the CO relented.

Major Blackstone, who had resumed command of his squadron after recovering from his wounds, relayed the decision.

"The colonel feels a bit put upon," Blackstone said.

Another pressure, less welcome, issued from Divisional HQ, who directed that AVRE squadrons be reduced from four troops to three, to help even out losses in men and vehicles and to provide experienced personnel for divisional workshops and training wings.

Blackstone's Three Troop fell victim to the reorganisation but out of it, One Troop's crews were brought up to strength. Armadillo acquired a new explosives NCO in the robust form of Lance Corporal Stoker, called 'Drac' by one and all[184]. Stoker, like Graham, came from near Sheffield and was a long-term crony of Armadillo's wireless operator, Sapper Shoreland.

"Try gettin' the BBC World Service, Boff," said Drac over the intercom, during a lull in a squadron exercise the day after he joined One Troop. "They play swing classics about this time." 'Boff' or 'Boffin' Shoreland was so-called by dint of his interest in all things electronic.

"Shut up, Drac," Graham interjected. "It'll be me swinging from the nearest windmill if we get a message from Squadron halfway through Moonlight Serenade."

When Napper and Graham accompanied the Vanderveers to church on the officers' first free Sunday, Steve was pleasantly surprised to see Tubby Potter occupying the pulpit as guest preacher.

His Text, from First Peter, was shrewdly chosen to encapsulate the Gospel.

"'For Christ also hath once suffered for sins, the just for the unjust, that he might bring us to God, being put to death in the flesh, but quickened by the Spirit.'"

He spoke slowly, for the benefit of the locals in a congregation that included numerous Allied service personnel. The readings and hymns were conducted alternately in Dutch and English. Graham kept quiet during the singing, so he could listen to Mama and the girls, whose voices were beautiful.

After the service, Marijke introduced Graham to a young man in grey suit and blue cap, tall and thin, who eyed Graham warily.

"Uncle Steve, this is Jan Brinker. We were in the same class at school and Jan's family are the local timber merchants. Jan, I would like you to meet my Uncle Steve."

Steve reckoned that, as troop barber, Ferrarby could have done a useful job on Jan's thick brown locks but he appreciated the firmness of the youth's grip when they shook hands and the way that Brinker looked him straight in the eye.

"I am very pleased to meet you, sir," the lad said courteously. "Thank you for liberating our country."

Steve was tempted to say, "I won't liberate anything else," but desisted.

Lunch at the Vanderveers was sumptuous.

"The butcher had got in some geese from one of the farms," Mama explained.

The after-lunch walk in the countryside proved to be quite entertaining. The ladies changed from their church attire into brightly patterned cardigans, woollen skirts and calf-high leather boots.

"Sorry to disappoint you," said Katrijn to the guests. "But we don't wear clogs anymore."

A chilly autumn wind buffeted the walkers as they ambled along the gravely path beside what seemed to Steve like a limitless canal. With Mark and Katrijn stepping out in front, Steve and Marijke in the middle and Mama and Papa sedately bringing up the rear, the party strolled for a couple of miles past farm fields replete with livestock, sturdy barns, heavily gated canal locks, wooded thickets and imposing windmills, their huge timbered arms turning ponderously in the breeze.

Marijke demurely clasped Steve's arm. She was a mine of local information.

"Hardly a place hereabouts we haven't been pirates, red Indians or crusaders storming a castle when we were youngsters," she said, her blue eyes twinkling. "Jan and I always seemed to be in opposing gangs. I don't suppose he really believed you are my uncle but you *could be*, sort of, as a fellow believer," she added with a mischievous laugh.

"I'm surprised your sister didn't already have a special admirer," said Steve. He noted that Katrijn had taken Mark's arm.

"She did," Marijke told him. "He was with the Resistance. His group raided a Luftwaffe airfield but it went badly wrong. Heiko and most of the group were shot by the Germans. Only Jan and a couple of others got back."

Graham bit his lip, wishing he hadn't raised the subject.

Especially since Mark probably stood as much chance of being shot by the Germans as Heiko had.

Eindhoven afforded a host of amenities. The cinema and ENSA shows were the most popular.

One afternoon, Steve and Mark borrowed Hazeldene's jeep and took the sisters to see *Gone With The Wind*. Katrijn cried through much of it while Mark held her hand.

"My sister gets so emotional," Marijke whispered to Steve. "It's just a film."

Outdoor recreation was also well patronised.

Despite the increasingly bitter weather, the citizenry turned out in great numbers to watch the football matches organised between the soldiery and local teams – for B Echelon's kit issues included everyone's sporting gear.

Katrijn and Marijke faithfully supplied thermos bottles of hot coffee after each match, tactfully sharing them equitably between their officer guests and Jan and his friends.

The Dutch were also keen to follow the Rugby tournament staged between the different units in the area (with improvised goal posts).

As inside centre, Steve was entirely satisfied with his own performance but waxed enthusiastic about Napper's on the left wing, although the sisters were nonplussed by his terminology.

"A blinder? But it must be against the rules to interfere with somebody's vision?"

Needless to say, the players returned their togs to B Echelon for laundering.

"We can't inflict those on Mama," Steve said to Mark.

After several weeks around Eindhoven, the squadron moved due east towards the Maas, its objective, the fortified town of Blerick on the west bank, opposite Venlo.

"Hard saying goodbye," said Napper, when Hazeldene drove up to fetch them on a raw November morning. Mama and the girls had been in tears – in contrast to the night before, when Steve and Mark slipped some compo boxes to the sisters, who giggled at the officers' embarrassment.

"Don't worry," said Katrijn. "We'll talk Mama round."

"She'll be very grateful, really," Marijke added.

All along the route to Blerick lay burnt-down buildings and burnt-out tanks, guns poking impotently at odd angles, at times with two or three rough-hewn wooden crosses sunk into the soil beside them. Discarded weapons and kit, British and German, littered the verges.

Friendly armour, often vulnerable on the dyked roads, had mostly been written off by enemy tanks or SP Guns. Occasionally, a twisted hulk of one of these could be seen hull down in a copse of trees or amid the incinerated remains of a haystack, where the fighter-bombers or Allied armour and flame throwers had sussed the attacker's hiding place.

Rain fell during most of the drive and as always, the Churchills' air intakes sucked in showers of droplets so that the crews were cold and wet the whole time.

The sappers found what shelter they could in smoke-blackened buildings by the wayside, first double-checking that the area was clear of mines, then lighting small fires in an effort to dispel some of the chill that penetrated to the bone. RE field companies had cordoned off many abandoned dwellings with white tape and the sinister warning sign, DANGER – BOOBY TRAPS.

Similar signs marked out the round, cake-tin shaped Teller anti-tank mines unearthed and lying by the roadside, awaiting disposal.

"It's dismal, Steve," said Napper, watching the squalls advance across acres of flatland before a driving wind. They were sheltering beneath the eaves of a farm's out building, where the troop was leaguering for the night. As usual, the lads had already got the brew going.

Steve knew how Napper felt. The little crosses by the knocked-out armour had deeply distressed the lad.

"Face of war, Mark," he said. "And the Normandy smell."

As in Normandy, numerous animal carcasses rotted in the fields, butchered by the fighting. Many of their erstwhile owners had found refuge in Eindhoven and a destitute farming family now resided with the Vanderveers.

The troop bedded down on stone floors in damp clothes, grateful for the self-warming cans of Heinz soup[185], manufactured by ICI, that augmented the compo rations, saved on primus fuel and definitely raised morale.

"Must be a healthy life we lead, lads," said Crittenden. "No-one's caught a cold in the entire squadron, so I hear."

But then came the mud, as they approached the river flats, like a vast expanse of black porridge. Movement off road was impossible and all thoroughfares to the Maas became choked with queues of vehicles, disappearing into the mist.

Blerick stood on firmer ground but it promised to be a tough objective. The enemy had thickly sown its environs with mines, both anti-tank and anti-personnel, then ringed the town with slit trenches and a cavernous anti-tank ditch topped by barbed wire. The slim-façaded, white-fronted buildings facing the Allied advance were filled with snipers, machine gunners and *panzerfaust* operators. Across the Maas, enemy guns were deployed around Venlo.

Blackstone summoned his officers to the briefing, inside his spacious command vehicle. It was warm, dry and fitted with a well-fired urn by means of which Blackstone's orderly dispensed mugs of piping hot char.

"The weather is too unsettled for air strikes," said Blackstone. "But we'll have enough artillery support to keep the Boches heads down in Venlo. Our guns'll put down smoke, too."

He tapped the large-scale map fastened to the wall behind him with a pointer.

It displayed the intended battlefield.

"Crab flails will beat paths through the mines," he continued. Steve noted that they included Cavendish's troop.

"Conger has been withdrawn from service," Blackstone added succinctly.

"None too soon," said Yeardley to Graham amid the general outburst of relief.

An accident in another squadron, in which no less than three tons of nitro-glycerine had exploded during an unloading operation, had killed over thirty men and injured more than a hundred. Eleven AVREs had been destroyed.

"The A/T ditch is too wide for fascines, so we'll use SBGs – the wire won't be a problem," said Blackstone. "But we'll drop fascines into the trench system. Fix any Boches underneath at the same time."

Several liaison officers from other units attended, one of whom was Ian Kinross, now brigade major. The Lowland Brigade, following the AVREs, would assault the town in their Kangaroo tracked armoured personnel carriers, with petard Churchills and flame tanks, including Shep Tyson's troop, in support.

Graham introduced Napper to Kinross after the briefing. The Scot had some sage advice for the youngster.

"Keep with your troop commander, Mark. Best chance of staying alive, barring accidents of war, of course."

Graham smiled modestly but declined to comment. Such accidents were alarmingly unpredictable.

The attack on Blerick began in cold, driving rain on December 3rd, 1944, at 0745 hours.

Allied artillery bludgeoned the enemy positions. Graham watched the barrage from his commander's hatch and reflected sadly on the destruction being wrought on yet another fine old town.

The leading troop of flails growled forward, mud dripping from their treads.

Shoreland had tuned Armadillo's radio to the flail troops' frequency, where he intercepted a frantic message.

"Troop bogged one hundred yards forward of start line! Send in reserve troop and recovery vehicles."

Graham tensed, fearing disaster. He watched Cavendish's Shermans lumbering into the smoke left by the barrage, praying they would find solid earth – and obliterate the mines.

Some time later, amid the roar of opposing guns and the hammering of the Spandaus, Steve was relieved to hear Chris's voice sounding triumphantly in his head set.

"Three lanes clear to A/T ditch. Ready to support AVREs. Please acknowledge, over."

"AVRE Delta One to Crab Able Three. Wilco, Chris, over and out," Steve called into his mike. He switched to the intercom, then the troop frequency.

"Drivers, advance!" he ordered.

Armadillo's engine roared. A thirty-foot span of box-girdered bridge fastened to the front of its hull, the Churchill plunged ahead like a huge metal giraffe, the rest of the troop following. Black sludge squelched from the treads.

The attack went superbly. Enemy counter fire showered the advancing armour with avalanches of mud but inflicted little damage. While the flails pounded the German defences with their turret guns, Graham's troop spanned the obstacles even as other AVREs from Blackstone's squadron helped recover the bogged Shermans.

Kangaroos came churning up, laden with Jock infantry, who quickly secured the town. Accurate, sustained support fire overwhelmed both *panzerfaust* operators and enemy machine gunners.

So decisive was the action that Graham heard Kinross make a remarkable announcement over the A set.

"Greyfriars to Crocodile Baker Three. Flame won't be needed, boys."

"Thanks, Greyfriars, don't mind sitting this one out," Graham heard Tyson reply.

Blackstone was eminently satisfied. "A good party" he called it. Blerick's citizens came rushing ecstatically out of doorways and cellars to greet their liberators.

Steve, too, was pleased because Napper had shown great skill and steadiness throughout the action and Graham asked his OC to let Mark spend Christmas with the Vanderveers.

"The amount of post he gets from the daughter is amazing, sir," Corporal Jevons confided to Graham. "I hope we can see him through."

Steve was delighted when Blackstone acceded to the request – as indeed was Napper. It had worked out because the squadron commander would be sending batches of his men on leave via a rota system during the Christmas-New Year period, with offensive operations winding down in the sector, owing to the weather.

It steadily deteriorated as December advanced, with sleet and snow supplanting the rain, prompting Regiment to order that the AVREs be whitewashed for winter camouflage. Like ghostly mammoths, Blackstone's AVREs crawled sluggishly nose to tail along ice–encrusted highways some fifty miles northwest of Blerick, to heath and woodland in sight of the slim church spire of Tilburg, past the abandoned German defence line of the Wilhelmina Canal. Vast amounts of derelict equipment littered the empty trench system, where silent eighty-eights poked their long barrels towards the former British line of advance, breech mechanisms sabotaged by their own crews.

"How's your Gothic, Boff?" Graham asked Shoreland.

Heads out of Armadillo's turret hatches, Steve and his wireless operator were gazing at the lettering of the enemy's broken-down road signs.

"About as good as my Dutch, sir," said Shoreland.

"We can't billet in the town," Blackstone explained at the first officers' briefing, held on the stone-floored kitchen of a farm vacated during the battle for Tilburg. "Too full of troops as is and the folk from these farms, who probably won't be back before spring. But we should be OK. Woods'll provide plenty of firewood."

Once again, the squadron adapted deserted farmhouses, stables, barns and outbuildings for winter accommodation, the sappers' personal comfort considerably enhanced by the heavy winter coveralls called 'zoot suits' that B Echelon had helpfully issued.

Not long after the squadron had settled into its new surroundings, Graham received an official letter.

It was to affect the rest of his life.

> *Dear Lieutenant Graham,* the letter read. *I am authorised to arrange with your commanding officer for you to attend a conference with me and my assistant, Section Officer Bramble, at RAF Intelligence HQ in Eindhoven. The matter concerns your situation report of September 20th last.*
>
> *Could you please acknowledge receipt of this letter by W/T communication with our signals unit? We will send a driver to collect you at 1000 hours the following day.*
>
> *Yours sincerely,*
> *Victoria Leonard, Squadron Officer.*

Graham reported immediately to the farm kitchen where Blackstone had established his HQ.

The major was seated at the heavy oak kitchen table. His dark brows became progressively more elevated as he read the letter.

"This Vicky Leonard[186] has got quite a reputation," he said. "Her job is to trace our missing special agents. She makes regular requests for items of information, which is why your report must have eventually landed on her desk."

"I don't think I can tell them much beyond what's in it, sir," Steve said uncertainly.

The major shrugged his broad shoulders.

"Make the most of it, lad," he said with a chuckle. "They're bound to put you up in the best hotel and there's a lot worse ways of spending the festive season than with a couple of comely WAAFs – as I'm sure they'll be. Spare a thought for the rest of us, though, won't you, stuck here with our frozen feet and subsisting mainly on compo rations again."

Blackstone's predictions proved to be correct.

RAF Eindhoven had taken over a five-storey hotel near the town centre. The light blue ensign with its Union Jack and RAF roundel mounted on a slanting wooden pole graced the hotel's arched stone entrance.

The two WAAF officers met Graham in the high-ceilinged foyer. Both were tall and slim, their blue uniforms expertly tailored and complemented perfectly with grey silk stockings and black semi-heels. Squadron Officer Leonard looked almost regal, with magnificently styled chestnut hair, high forehead and commanding gaze.

But it was the section officer who captivated Graham. Her dark hair was neatly waved, her eyes, beneath elegantly pencilled brows, almost violet, unsettling in their intensity. Her lips, exquisitely curved, were set in a finely formed oval face of flawless complexion and displayed beautiful white teeth when she smiled. Steve reckoned the girl's supple figure seemed made for conquering the fells back home.

She'd conquered him, at any rate.

"Vicky Leonard," said the regal one, who extended her right hand and smiled warmly. "This is Kate Bramble," she added, indicating her companion. "We're delighted to make your acquaintance, Steve. But your hand's like ice. You must have had a terrible drive."

"Snow squalls all the way," said Steve, conscious now of the melting flakes dripping off his beret, leather jerkin and kit bag. The RAF jeep driver sent to fetch him had managed the fifteen-mile journey in under an hour despite atrocious conditions.

"An orderly'll show you to your quarters, Steve," said Vicky obligingly. "And we'll see you in the officers' mess when you've had a chance to freshen up."

Steve could hardly wait. Section Officer Bramble wasn't wearing an engagement ring. That was a start.

Graham's room was furnished with delicately fashioned woodwork like the Vanderveer's parlour. The pinewood bed had a firm, deep mattress and was made up with crisply laundered sheets and thick woollen blankets.

The adjoining bathroom glistened in white marble, with gleaming gold coloured fittings. Graham noticed the abundance of soap and bath salts provided.

"Just leave your laundry in one of the linen bags, sir," the RAF orderly advised. "The hotel staff will have it sorted by tomorrow evening and they'll do your boots too."

Graham felt overwhelmed. He thanked the orderly and set about running the bath.

Wearing his spare BDs and second pair of boots, Steve rejoined his hosts at the appointed time, in the spacious dining room, to discover that the hotel's cuisine was excellent. The trio sat on carved mahogany chairs around a table spread with snow-white cloth, set with napkins of a similar material. The cutlery consisted of the finest silverware and the meal was on a par with Sunday lunch at the Vanderveers.

"Everything's gradually getting back to normal, with Antwerp and the other ports functioning," Vicky explained, over bowls of thick vegetable soup.

After the meal, they retired to Vicky and Kate's office for coffee. A large room, it had been used by the hotel's accounts staff, who'd transferred to the lounge. The office contained two desks, two telephones, filing cabinets and a glassed-in bookcase, almost filled with alphabetically labelled case files.

The three of them occupied an L-shaped divan settee arranged around a low, glass-topped table. Vicky placed a slim manila folder on the table beside the coffee things and poured out three cupfuls from a silver pot.

"We'd like to discuss your report in more detail, Steve," she said. "Then tomorrow, I'll visit Lieutenant Hedges and Kate can have a word with your Captain Yeardley, since he was the last known person to see these alleged SOE chaps."

Graham nodded.

"First, we'd like you to describe them," said Kate.

She got up and fetched a sketchpad, pencils and an eraser from her desk.

Graham loved watching her move. And listening to her voice. She was quietly spoken, with a cultured Home Counties accent.

"What's all this about?" he asked.

"As you know, Steve, our job is to investigate what happened to our missing agents," Vicky explained. "But we're also on the look out for Nazis trying to infiltrate our side."

Graham sipped his coffee. He understood.

"Alias Pitcairn and Stroud, for example," he said.

"Yes," said Vicky. "The Fuhrer regards Himmler as 'the new Loyola[187].' The true Sons of Loyola are the core of the SS and their aims are unchanged, even though we're bound to win the war. We have to resist."

Kate rested the sketchpad on her knee.

"My mother is French, Steve," she said. "Her family were Huguenots. She can tell you all about the dragonnades. These days it's called Blitzkrieg. If that fails, infiltration and deception have always been the alternative, usually effective."

"And even the precursor," Vicky added with a sigh. "We know it as appeasement[188]."

An hour or so later, the sketches were complete.

"You're a dab hand at artistry, Kate," said Graham in admiration.

"Part of my training when I was in SOE but I've always painted for a hobby," she explained.

"What do you think, Kate?" asked Vicky.

"That's them," said Kate firmly. "Von Hollstein and Albrecht. They match my other ones, don't you think?"

She produced two more sketches from Vicky's folder. They were almost identical to the new ones.

"I did them while I was in hospital," said Kate. "But I'll get the photographic unit to make copies of the ones we've done, Steve. They'll be more up to date."

"Hopefully, Hedges and Yeardley will confirm them," Vicky remarked. "Then we'll see what we can piece together. You've been a tremendous help, Steve."

"Thank you, Vicky," said Steve. "But how did you get to be in hospital, Kate, if that's not classified?"

Vicky and Kate smiled at Graham's bewilderment.

"It isn't," said Kate and recounted the experience of her last SOE operation.

When she'd finished, Graham felt more apprehensive than he had even on the verge of D-Day.

"It's another war, Steve," said Vicky soberly. "And the other side will make a pact with the Devil to win it."

Her words were literally true.

Vicky arranged for a jeep to be put at Steve and Kate's disposal. This was unorthodox but Squadron Officer Leonard cut through red tape with alacrity.

Graham didn't wonder that she had a reputation.

The following day was clear. Sappers had bulldozed the road clear and carpeted the surface with a heavy layer of grit, so Graham almost halved the journey time of the pervious day.

"Half the troop's on forty-eight hours' leave but the others'll be very glad to meet you," he said, glancing at Kate, who occupied the jeep's front passenger seat. She wore RAF BDs, boots, gaiters, peaked cap and leather jerkin, in accord with Graham's advice – "You better be ready for anything."

"I'm looking forward to it," said Kate eagerly, her exhaled breath visible when she spoke. "I'd especially like to speak to your Sergeant Crittenden."

"He'll no doubt be happy to oblige," said Steve. Crittenden was fortunately still available, because Napper and his crews were the ones on leave.

"Didn't expect you back quite so soon, Steve," said Blackstone when Graham and Kate reported to the farmhouse. "But I'm delighted to meet you, Miss Bramble. We've an exercise planned for today. Perhaps you'd like to watch?"

"Could I possibly have a go with a Besa, sir?" Kate asked. "I trained on them in SOE."

The major had arranged for his remaining crews to carry out live firing exercises, over some of the open heath and Two Troop was already on its way. Kate would be able to confer with Yeardley afterwards.

Blackstone glanced at Graham.

"What do you think, Steve?" he asked.

"I'm game, sir, if Kate is," said Graham.

That settled the matter. Graham's crews were overjoyed.

"You'll let Kate ride with us some of the time, won't you, sir?" Crittenden and Hazeldene each petitioned him.

She proved a dead shot with the MG. Ferrarby, with Graham's permission, let her fire the petard mortar.

"Yes, I trained with mortars in SOE," she said over the intercom when the lads applauded the results.

Kate revelled in the exercise, oblivious to the fumes and stink of petrol, sweat, gun oil and cordite. One Troop accomplished its tasks without a hitch.

On the way back to the leaguer in Armadillo, Kate asked if she could take the controls.

"I've driven tracked vehicles before," she explained. "In SOE."

"Give her a go, sir," the rest of the crew chimed in, Driver Talbot foremost.

Kate changed places with him and adjusted her goggles. She grasped the gear levers and adroitly steered the AVRE back to base, unmindful of the plastering of slush and sticky dark earth that she and everyone else received from the suction of the Churchill's air intakes.

"Keep the goggles as a souvenir, Kate," Talbot urged when Kate brought Armadillo to a halt on the vehicle park. "You can have my job any day."

Kate bade them thanks and hurried off to see Captain Yeardley, clutching a brief case containing copies of her sketches.

"Julian confirmed the likenesses," Kate told Graham breathlessly when she came hastening back from Two Troop's HQ. "And he's given us some more to go on with. I'd like a word with Bill when you've done with maintenance. Anything I can do to help?"

"You trained for that in SOE, I suppose?" said Graham casually.

"Why, yes," rejoined Kate. "How did you know?"

After they completed vehicle maintenance, One Troop convened for a brew in the barn they were using as their billet. The lads had a further request for their commander.

"Can Kate come back tomorrow, sir?" Crittenden asked. "We've got quite a spread lined up."

"And you won't know this place, sir," added Hazeldene, gesturing at the austere surroundings.

Graham remembered it was Christmas Eve.

"I'd love to," said Kate enthusiastically. "Don't worry, Steve. I'll sort it with Vicky."

"I think it's unanimous, Kate," said Steve, to rousing applause. "We'd better be getting back, though, or Vicky'll think you've been kidnapped."

"Kate Bramble, you mucky pup!" Vicky exclaimed when she met the couple in the hotel's foyer. "What *have* you been doing?"

"Having a *whale* of a time," said Kate joyfully. "And I've got some more useful gen."

"Well," said Vicky, with an indulgent smile. "You can tell me about it over supper, *after* you've had a bath *and* a change of clothes – you too, Lieutenant Graham."

On Christmas morning, the three of them attended the church where Graham and Napper had gone with the Vanderveers on their first Sunday.

The service was packed. The Dutch were experiencing their first unoccupied Christmas for four years.

Tubby Potter was preaching again. His Text was from Luke 2:10:

"'For unto you is born this day in the city of David a Saviour, which is Christ the Lord.'"

As Graham anticipated, Tubby challenged the congregation head on.

"Is He *your* Lord, dear friends, is He *your* Saviour?"

"He is now," Steve heard Kate murmur. She had told him about asking the Lord to save her, following her escape from the church.

Tubby smiled benevolently as he shook hands with them at the door after the service. His kindly face displayed a definite "I'll speak to you about her later, Steve," expression.

The Vanderveers, along with Napper, exuberantly greeted the couple.

"You don't look lonely any more, Steve," said Napper.

"Jan looks so relieved, don't you think, Uncle Steve?" said Marijke. She gave Graham and Kate a hug in turn.

"I'll explain later, Kate," Steve said.

"So much in common, we're both Katherine!" exclaimed Katrijn, when she too hugged Kate.

"I haven't got a sister named Mary, though," said Kate, looking a bit overwhelmed.

"Would you like one, for Christmas?" Katrijn asked eagerly.

"You must visit us on Boxing Day, if you can," said Mama.

Papa winked at Steve and puffed on his pipe.

Graham parked the jeep as near to the barn as possible, so Kate wouldn't have to walk in slush up to her ankles.

However, Steve's half troop had with typical forethought spread brick and stone fragments in front of the entrance.

"Sapper touch again, Steve," Kate remarked, as she alighted from the vehicle.

Steve held the door open for Kate and she went inside.

"Something smells good," she said, taking off her overcoat and cap. Graham carefully placed them on his foldaway table set up by the door as Troop HQ. He marvelled at the transformation of the old barn's interior.

A delicious aroma of roasting meat permeated their surroundings.

The whole place had been thoroughly swept and tarpaulins placed on the floor. Long strips of coloured paper hung from rafters and adorned the walls. Wooden slabs mounted on ammunition boxes fixed end-on were arranged in the central area for the dining table and it was spread with blankets. For seating, rows of wooden benches and bales of straw were placed along its edges. Mess tins and sets of KFSs were neatly laid out and the lads had even scrounged some candles from somewhere. Hurricane lamps provided additional illumination.

And it was warm.

"They've got an oven behind there," said Graham in amazement. He pointed to a loose box in a corner of the barn, from where the aroma was emanating.

316

A flue fashioned from interlocking seventy five-mm shell containers projected through a wall of the box. It bent at ninety degrees via a makeshift elbow and then, tied to one of the barn's vertical beam supports, poked out of the roof. The metallic segments radiated a considerable amount of heat, augmented by flaring paraffin stoves on which food tins placed in dixies of water were heating.

"Who's doing the cooking, Ronny?" Steve asked when Hazeldene came to greet them.

"MacGee and Tomlinson, sir," said Hazeldene. "Eager to volunteer."

"Guest of honour, ma'am," he said to Kate and indicated a place at the head of the table. "Next to our illustrious troop commander. Make yourself comfortable and we'll bring it to you."

He poured a quantity of mulled wine into two enamel mugs.

"Eindhoven NAAFI," said Graham, when they raised the containers. "Cheers."

"Cheers," said Kate happily, crossing her legs. To save time, she'd decided not to change after church.

"I think I'll manage in a skirt," she'd said.

Graham was glad. So was everyone else.

The main feast consisted of two large roast geese and a roast pig.

"Managed to barter some coffee and chocolate for these, sir," said Crittenden. With his usual acumen, Bill had located some farms not far distant still functioning, bypassed by the battle.

"What did you do for the stove?" Kate asked as Crittenden passed them the compo vegetables.

"Lashed it up with rubble, ammo boxes and various odds and ends," the sergeant explained. "Tipped on some petrol to set the wood going – was a bit smoky at first but it's OK now. We've rustled up treacle duff for afters – it's on those heaters. Plenty of condensed milk to go with it. No end to our talents, really."

"Hear, hear!" chorused the rest of the assemblage, clinking their mugs.

"At least they haven't incinerated themselves," Graham said to Kate.

Hazeldene rose to his feet.

"Here's to our distinguished visitor," he declared.

Another round of strident "Hear, hears!" followed, with more clinking of enamel and a sincere "Thank you, One Troop," from Kate.

Graham couldn't help wondering how many of them would see next Christmas.

That evening, Steve accompanied Kate to an ENSA pantomime in Eindhoven. When they walked back to the hotel afterwards, she slipped his arm through his.

It was another clear night with abundant stars overhead and their footsteps scraped noisily on the gritted pavement.

They paused in a secluded spot beneath some willows. Steve put his arms around Kate and she easily yielded to him.

"It's been wonderful, Steve," she whispered.

"You can say that again," he said earnestly.

The heartfelt kiss they shared precluded any further discussion.

Kate lay staring up at the ceiling for some time after she'd gone to bed. She was falling for Steve. She knew it.

But Kate couldn't help herself. She'd been unable to trace Guillaume. Surely Steve was her reality.

Or was he?

Fourteen

Enemies at Bay

Karen Hills, Burma, April 1945.

A snorting grunt broke forth, amid a desperate scrabbling of hooves.
The terrified beast pitched over the edge of the trail and tumbled down the slope, a macabre tangle of jerking head, twisting body and thrashing legs, leaving a broad mud slick in its wake. Still burdened with its load and smashing through clumps of scrub, it eventually plummeted thirty feet into the swirling *chaung* at the bottom of the gorge, to be instantly swept away, still frantically kicking impotent hooves.

"Follow me, Sergeant," said Waverly between gritted teeth.

Clinging to tree roots protruding from the sheer slope on the other side of the track, Waverly plunged back down through the sticky morass past the leading members of his patrol to where the nearest mule handlers, young Karens, were struggling to restrain their charges, panicked by the accident that had befallen the animal in between them.

Waverly's wireless operator, brawny Ulsterman Sergeant 'Thompy' Devlin, followed at his officer's behest, splodging through calf-deep slush.

Together they helped the handlers calm the animals. The Karen whose mule had fallen to its death stood covered in muck, tears on his muddied brown face mingling with the rain that cascaded off the jungle growth.

"You're all right, Leo, that's the main thing," Waverly reassured the diminutive youth, patting his bare shoulder. "Join the front of the patrol."

He indicated the line of stocky little men in shorts and bush hats carrying carbines and Stens who crouched alertly further up the trail.

Sniffling, the Karen nodded and splashed off towards them.

"Slipped the halter just in time, or he'd have gone too," said Devlin.

As it fell, the doomed mule had dragged Leo to the ground but he had quickly released the bridle attachment.

"We'll leaguer on top," said Waverly. He pointed to the densely thicketed crown of the ridge that they could dimly see through mist and rain. The major glanced at his watch, pulled a compass looped round his neck with parachute cord from beneath his sodden bush jacket and checked the bearing.

"We're still on schedule, Sergeant," he said.

Waverly's tour of duty with the Kachin Rangers had ended in December and he had returned to SOE's HQ in Ceylon for a rest and a spell of training duties.

His next assignment materialised soon after the fall of Meiktila.

With Fourteenth Army advancing down the Rangoon Road, the army commander had sent signals by wireless and native courier for the tribes in the Karen Hills east of the Sittang River to rise against the Japanese.

The network of contacts was born of SOE sacrificial efforts[189] earlier in the war. Now it enabled arms and ammunition to be dropped, followed by seventy SOE personnel who would lead the Karens' operations.

Waverly and Devlin were two of them.

The irregulars' prime task was to delay Japanese columns falling back towards the crossing place opposite Toungoo. Fourth Corps was pressing hard to seize the town, before Japanese formations retreating from Meiktila through the Pegu Yomas could concentrate there with their comrades heading for the east bank.

If the two arms of the Japanese withdrawal joined hands, the combined force might hamper the Allied advance indefinitely.

But the enemy were experiencing serious delays themselves, thanks to Karen intervention in the form of roadblocks, ambushes and demolitions.

During night forays, the stealthy hill men even succeeded in cutting hobbles that secured elephants used by the Japanese for transport. They then stampeded the beasts into the jungle with bursts of automatic fire.

"Save the air force from havin' to massacre the poor critters," Devlin remarked.

Although SOE personnel coordinated many air strikes themselves – renewing for Waverly an old acquaintance when he had radioed a reconnaissance mosquito seeking to pinpoint one of numerous enemy depots dispersed in dense undergrowth.

"Peter!" exclaimed the pilot. "Good to hear from you."

"Jon!" said the major exuberantly. "Likewise, old chap."

Pleasantries were kept to a minimum. Waverly directed Gray's photographic runs to capture the depot's entire perimeter. The fighter-bomber's precision equipment enabled Gray to carry out his task before Japanese ground fire could range on him.

The next step was foreordained.

"Better retire to a safe distance, Peter," said Gray as he departed. "This place is going to get very hot, very soon."

A stupendous rain of bombs and rockets had devastated the depot well before sunset.

Air and ground teams would doggedly seek out more caches but Waverly's Karens were now embarked on a different mission of destruction, that of a bridge spanning a tributary of the Sittang.

The task inevitably reminded Peter of a similar escapade. He strove to suppress the thought.

After a brief rest on the heights overlooking the river, the column accomplished the descent thankfully without mishap. The rain gradually eased and Waverly's team made good progress through the scrub to the bridge's approach road, despite insects and leeches that assailed both men and mules.

On arrival, Waverly, Devlin and the two senior Karens, known as Amos and Luke, unloaded the consignment of plastic explosive. The handlers then led the animals back into the jungle and tethered them.

The major ventured cautiously up the stony causeway onto the bridge. Planters had built it pre-war and it was mounted on sturdy piles to convey mechanised transport.

Waverly beckoned the others to follow and crept along the bridge to the set of piles closest to the far bank. Swinging himself over the timbered railing, he braced his boots against the stout teak and bamboo support frame, then unslung the charges fastened across his back. His long arms and nimble fingers quickly had them lashed in place with manila cord. Devlin carried out the same procedure for the opposite pile. Amos and Luke did likewise for a set of supports near the other bank.

Dark water swirled beneath. The current was strong and the depth at least a fathom.

"Sheer vandalism," Waverly said under his breath. Deftly he set the detonators.

"I'm done here, sir," whispered Devlin.

They climbed back onto the span's logged roadway and rejoined the two Karens, who came clambering up over the railing.

"All set, sir," Amos said quietly, with a toothy grin.

Waverly nodded. They linked up the detonator wires and retreated into the jungle. Waverly carefully paid out the detonator wire until he and Devlin rejoined the main group. He shivered. The prevailing sensation in the environment was one of rank humidity but he had been feeling alternatively hot and cold since noon and feared the condition was worsening.

"You OK, sir?" asked Devlin. He was crouched beside his officer as Waverly positioned the plunger device on the ground.

"A bit off colour, that's all."

"Aye," rejoined the Ulsterman. "I've got some spare mepacrine tabs in the medicine kit. Charge yourself up with 'em."

"Thanks, Thompy," said Waverly. "In the meantime, we better charge up this bridge."

He pressed the plunger. The resulting thunderclap panicked the mules and they tried to bolt but the tethers held firm.

Waverley and Devlin stealthily went forward to check the damage and through the lingering veil of HE smoke saw to their satisfaction that the span had vanished and the piles were shattered.

"Bet the Nips have got a sinking feeling about that bang, sir," said the laconic Ulsterman.

Waverly's column had earlier established the location of the Japanese force bound for the bridge. They would now be about an hour's march away and definitely have heard the explosion. The enemy column would be forced to divert.

"A timely delay, Sergeant," Waverly said grimly. "We'll meet them at first light."

The track dipped into a gully where the river gradually spread out, grew shallower and slowed its pace. A narrow band of cotton wool-like mist hovering above the watercourse thinned rapidly as the sun ascended.

Figures began to emerge from beneath the teak trees on the far side of the gully. Many were ragged and barefoot, grasping bamboo canes for support but pressing doggedly on, their objective the junction of the track with the east-west Mawchi-Toungoo Road.

To Waverly, lying hidden in a dew-soaked clump of elephant grass and staring through binoculars, they looked like scarecrows.

"Starving, poor beggars," he said.

The leading members of the column advanced down the bank, waded across the *chaung* and began climbing the other side.

A long Bren burst from within the forest two hundred yards to their front sent them scurrying back into the shelter of the gully. The rest of the column scuttled after them.

Negotiating fallen trees and mounds of earth where the banks had partly caved in, the Japanese column entered the widest part of the stream.

Waverly nodded to Amos. The Karen pressed the trigger of his carbine.

None of the column escaped the storm of bullets that whiplashed it from end to end.

Waverly splashed into the river to count the corpses. He noted forty-one in all.

Amos and Luke joined him in the centre of the killing space. The water was crimson.

"Usual verification, sir?" Luke asked, reaching for his *dah*.

"Yes," said Waverly. He kept his carbine trained on the nearest bodies as a precaution. "Double-check they're all from the same side of the head."

He would send a couple of his patrol members back over the hills to the clandestines' HQ, with a uniform set of Japanese ears to verify the kills. Many of the opposite numbers would doubtless replenish individual Karen collections. As with the Kachins, sterling missionary endeavours pre-war had Christianised many of the hill communities but the grisly habit of souveniring enemy body parts as trophies was nevertheless ingrained – until the stench of the severed organs necessitated disposal.

The tendency had been exacerbated by Japanese atrocities in recent years, every bit as savage as that inflicted on the Kachins and augmented by the age-old animosity of the native Burmans, who actively assisted the invaders in persecuting the hill men.

Devlin and his Bren gunners rejoined Waverly and the rest of the patrol.

"Good work, Sergeant," said the major.

"We continue on to the road, sir?" the Irishman asked.

The major removed his bush hat and wiped his brow. His temples were pounding and he felt exhausted, alternatively clammy and sweltering. Aided by the extra mepacrine dosage, his body was fighting the fever but the effort was taking a huge toll. It didn't help being on half-rations. He earnestly hoped Devlin wouldn't succumb and envied the Karens who seemed to possess a natural immunity.

He nodded in response to Thompy's question.

"Column of route, Sergeant. We want to be in position by nightfall."

Despite the effectiveness of the Allied delaying tactics, sizeable parties of Japanese were breaking through to the vital road link and pushing west to the Sittang, Their determination elicited admiration from their opponents.

"Japs are doin' their country proud, sir," said Devlin succinctly as Waverly's patrol deployed among the teak scrub bordering the highway.

In intermittently searing heat and pelting rain, the next few days bore witness to a series of running battles as the Japanese tried again and again to batter their way to the crossing place, charging the very muzzles of their antagonists' weapons, to be dispatched with edged steel.

In these hand-to-hand encounters, the irregulars inevitably sustained casualties and Waverly's patrols suffered several seriously wounded. The tough little men could endure transport by mule and stretcher to the nearest village and the Karens possessed remarkable medical skills but Force HQ wanted the utmost professional care for their doughty warriors.

"Give HQ the map reference and the state of the casualties, Sergeant," Waverly told Devlin as they prepared to evacuate a batch of wounded. "Request a surgical team to be flown in by air ambulance as soon as the weather allows. Tell them the strip will take an L-Five."

He gazed at the bloodstained bandages and the strained faces of his injured men, one of whom was Leo. Waverly tried to smile at them. The inside of his head felt like a hammer pounding an anvil. He was standing upright almost by sheer will power alone.

"We can but try," he murmured, in the knowledge that HQ would be relaying numerous requests like his.

Clear skies throbbed to the sound of Spitfires' Merlin engines. One flight was already in the air, a second taxiing down one of the PSP runways laid out across the airfield's hardened brown apron.

At one end of a shorter stretch of PSP, away from the main flight paths, several figures toiled to transfer operating kit and medical supplies from a jeep's trailer to the cabin of the waiting L-5. It was one of several that would undertake mercy flights that day, escorted by Spitfires.

When all the gear was loaded, Geordie Wood stepped back toward the jeep to salute Captain Mostyn and Sister McGrath.

"I should be goin' with you, sir," said the corporal, as Kiwi and Colleen returned the salute.

"Sorry, Geordie. No room," Mostyn said apologetically. "And someone's got to drive Paddy back."

Mostyn gave Sarah Monaghan a quick hug before climbing aboard. The brash New Zealander and the quiet Irish girl had grown very close over the past few months.

"Wedding bells in Rangoon, you bet," Vera Jeffries had predicted.

"Look after my man for me, Coll," Paddy urged as she hugged Colleen.

"Don't worry, Paddy," said Colleen. "And don't forget, our relationship is strictly personal." She winked at Corporal Wood.

"Glad to hear it," rejoined Paddy, raising her voice above the noise of the L-5's engine. "What, say that again!" she shouted as her friend, grinning cheekily, hoisted herself into the cabin beside Mostyn.

The aircraft came to rest on the patch of white gravel in the midst of a hilltop clearing and the passengers immediately deplaned. Colleen was startled at the sight of several olive-skinned figures, who materialised from the surrounding bush and jogged towards them. They wore khaki shorts and seemed armed to the teeth – teeth that showed white in their Oriental faces via gleeful grins.

Many of them seemed to be mere boys and Colleen realised they were - Karen boy soldiers, as tough as Ghurkas and she felt greatly relieved at the sight of the distinguished-looking officer who followed them. Colleen noted he was clean-shaven and wore freshly washed JGs. He had also buffed his boots and his bush hat looked new.

Lee-Enfield Carbine slung over his shoulder, the officer walked with the limber grace of a professional athlete and stood over six feet tall, with a gangly physique, like Mostyn's.

Indeed, the two knew each other and shook hands heartily.

"Very glad to see you, Kiwi," said the newcomer in a resonant, cultured voice. "I'll have the boys unload everything, so your pilot can get on."

The American airman was due at another jungle strip to pick up a couple of stretcher cases.

"We'll do all we can, Peter," Mostyn promised. "First, let me introduce my colleague, Nursing Officer McGrath. Colleen, meet Major Peter Waverly, SOE."

"Pleased to meet you, sir," murmured Colleen. The major shook her extended hand and she noted the strength of his sinewy grip.

"Peter, please," he said earnestly.

Colleen observed that Waverly's eyes were deep blue and they were gazing intensely into hers. Bit of a toff, she thought, but he must be OK.

A strange expression had passed over his face at the mention of her name and that made her curious. She also realised that despite his efforts to keep up appearances, Major Waverly was a sick man, gaunt and feverish.

Mostyn looked on benevolently, though keeping an eye on the unloading operation. It was proceeding smoothly. The Karens knew they were handling the means by which their comrades' lives would be saved and they did so with care.

"This way," said the major. He indicated a trail as several of his men helped the pilot to turn the L-5 around for take-off. "You can see the village from here," he added, as his visitors fell in beside him. "We're well protected with standing patrols and we're chasing the Japs off to the south. My sergeant's in charge of a column doing that right now. We hope it'll stay fine enough for a couple of days, so you can fly anyone out – including yourselves."

The trail, also of crushed gravel, took them between thatched bamboo houses with plaited walls, raised a few feet off the ground on stilts with small platforms in front, serving as porches.

Dressed in brightly coloured *lungyis*, dark-eyed women with jet-black hair emerged from several of the houses with their children to watch the group, staring at the tall newcomers. Colleen felt embarrassed.

"Where are the patients?" Mostyn asked.

"There," said Waverly and pointed to a long hut at the end of the left row of houses. "It's the village church. We've partitioned off the pulpit end for your operations."

He conducted Mostyn and Colleen inside. The weather was warm but the interior of the building was well ventilated. Wounded Karens lay on improvised bamboo litters arranged in rows along the plaited mat floor. They looked up at the party's approach. Waverly said something in their language and they all smiled, despite the greyness of their faces that told Colleen the extent of their suffering, to which the heavy swathes of dressing also testified.

"Let's know how you want things set up, Kiwi," said Waverly. "The boys'll get to it right away."

Mostyn nodded.

"Thanks, Peter," he said. "While you do that, Coll and I'll examine them and get them ready for theatre. We'll need to wash up, of course and sterilise syringes and instruments."

"The women have already got water on the boil in their houses," Waverly explained. "There are some good nurses amongst them. Have to be."

After examining the patients, Mostyn arranged them in order of priority. He and Colleen set up saline and blood plasma drips, changed the casualties' dressings and administered antibiotics, with the help of some of the Karen women, including the head man's wife, a doll-like beauty named Natalie.

"The serum is thick like honey," Colleen said to her on demonstrating how to inject a casualty with penicillin. "Once you've inserted the syringe, keep a steady pressure on the plunger and don't take any notice if he says it hurts, even though it does. We'll give them another lot in three or four hours."

The little woman smiled. "I understand," she said quietly. Her English was hesitant but precise.

Each candidate for theatre was placed on a bamboo table with a woven grass covering that one of Natalie's companions replaced after each operation.

These went on until well after dark, when flaring paraffin lamps provided general illumination, while Mostyn scrutinised injuries and peered at bloodied flesh by torchlight, Colleen watching and passing him the instruments.

Kiwi updated his diagnoses as they dealt with each individual.

"Depressed skull fracture – rifle butt, probably," he said, bending over one patient. "I can relieve the pressure but we should get him flown out as soon as we can."

"Grenade fragment lodged next to the windpipe. Just missed the jugular."

The patient's breathing was a series of rattling gasps.

"Look like this fellow's been on the wrong end of a samurai."

The man in question was Leo. He received fourteen stitches in the scalp.

"Bullet's broken the clavicle and gone down into the lung. Missed the spine and the kidney on the way out, thank God but we'll have to open up the bullet track, Coll."

"I can save the arm but he'll have a scar from the elbow to the shoulder, half an inch deep."

"Depressed cheekbone. Another rifle butt I reckon, but I can incise and reposition."

"We'll have to reset the tibia. Then I'll sew up the gash and we'll splint the leg."

After the operation, the patient's limb was attached to a crude but effective traction device. They dealt with a number of fractures this way.

At regular intervals, Natalie held the torch while Colleen checked and noted the patient's condition, temperature, pulse, respiration and blood pressure.

"Several of these chaps will need to be flown out," Mostyn remarked when he and Colleen were re-scrubbing their hands. "They're stout fellows, though."

The stoicism of the little men was astounding.

"Save that for my friends," Leo said to Colleen when she came to inject him with anaesthetic.

"OK," said Kiwi. "We won't argue the toss. Keep your head still."

The lad did and bore his ordeal with fortitude.

The surgeon and his helpers were exhausted after their efforts and stumbled thankfully out the back of the building into the cool night air – for it had grown stuffy in the operations area with the lamps and the precaution of covering the windows with mats for a blackout.

"You get some kip, Coll," Kiwi advised. "I'll do the post-op first and wake you in about four hours, unless there's an emergency."

"Fine," said Colleen, yawning.

"Come with me, Colleen," said Natalie. "Everything's made up."

Natalie and her husband Damian had provided both beds and facilities for the visitors in their house.

"God has been so good in sending you. It is the least we can do," she added.

Late the following day, Waverly dropped in to visit the convalescents. The weather was still holding up so the man with the depressed skull fracture and the Karen shot through the lung, together with two of the more severe fracture cases, had been taken to the CCS by L-5s.

The remainder of the patients were in good heart and pleased to see their officer. Waverly knelt by the litters and spoke with each man individually.

When he'd finished, Colleen intercepted him before he left.

"You better drink this, Peter," she urged and poured out a medicine glass of dark, thick liquid that she handed to him. "Before you keel over."

"Don't you need to take my temperature or something?" he asked.

She placed a hand on his forehead. "No," she said firmly. "Now, do as you're told."

Meekly he took the potion and swallowed it in one gulp.

"It tastes foul," he spluttered, his face contorting.

"Cure you or kill you," said Colleen nonchalantly. "Extra dosage of quinine all sorts. Have a chaser."

She poured him a mug of water from her bottle and handed it to him with two tablets.

"What are they?" Waverly asked.

"Sulphonamide. For any dysentery. I'll give you some more later. Now, get all that down."

He did so.

"You should get some sleep," she said.

He shook his head.

"Going on patrol," he explained.

"Oh," said Colleen. "Well, I hope that hefty sergeant of yours is there to carry you back, because I'm not doing it."

Waverly thanked Colleen for her ministrations and departed, grimacing.

The convalescing Karens watched the proceedings with great glee.

That night, Colleen sat on one of the benches removed from the church to admit the litters. It had been left in front of the building and she leant her back against the bamboo frame. Her Sten gun lay within easy reach, just in case.

Mostyn had conducted his round of examinations and retired to complete his reports.

"I always hate this bit," he said to Colleen. "But I'll kip when I've finished and relieve you as planned."

All was up to date with the patients, including drips, fresh dressings and penicillin jabs. They'd been fed, watered and made comfortable and were now resting in the tender care of Natalie and a couple of the other women, who'd also cooked a meal for the visitors.

Colleen was taking the opportunity to sit outside in the fresh air. It was warm and moist. Gecko-type lizards scampered across the gravel path by the building, giving her a start but Damian had assured her that no snakes were about.

"All the buildings have gravel stands," he'd told her. "And we keep the grass down. The lizards are too fast and there's no other prey so they stay away."

Listening to the animal and insect sounds of the jungle, Colleen stared up enthralled into an indigo sky, iridescent with full moon and countless stars, a breathtaking sight.

"Mind if I join you?" said a quiet voice.

Colleen glanced sharply to her right, one hand immediately gripping her Sten. She exhaled audibly at the sight of the angular figure by the corner of the church.

"Holy Mother, you nearly scared the life out of me!" she exclaimed. "But please do."

She moved her weapon so Waverly could sit down.

"Aggressive kit for a QA," Peter remarked. He leant his carbine against the end of the bench.

"CO insists we carry them everywhere outside the CCS perimeter. How're you feeling?"

"Much better, thanks. I took your advice. Got my head down this afternoon. Pleased that I woke up."

Colleen laughed softly.

"So am I. It was a bit of a gamble."

"*Now* you tell me," said Waverly, in mock indignation. "Thanks for everything, though."

"Glad to help,"

Colleen gazed into the sky again.

"It's beautiful here," she said.

"You should fly out tomorrow if you can," said Peter. He placed his hat on his knee and took a deep breath. "Monsoon'll be early this year[190]. You can tell from the air."

Colleen asked about something that had puzzled her.

"Why aren't there any old people here? Damian seems so young to be the head man."

"This is a new village. Japs burnt the other one. Took the elders hostage and their wives. Lined them up, made them kneel down and then cut their heads off. However, the young folk escaped, thank God."

Colleen sat silently for a while, appalled. Then turning her gaze toward Peter, she posed another, more personal question.

"Why did my Christian name affect you?"

The major smiled.

"You're as observant as you are curious, Sister. I once knew someone named Collette. She's dead."

Colleen thought it wise to change the subject.

"What'll you do, when all this is over?"

"Manage the family estate back in Derbyshire – and take care of any foreign office jobs that come my way."

"Cloak and dagger?"

"Pen and paper, more likely."

"Mrs Waverly'll be relieved, then."

"There isn't one, not even senior. My mother died not long after I was born."

"Oh, I'm sorry."

"Thank you. A governess brought me up, the redoubtable Miss Heythorpe. Dad still depends on her as a kind of family retainer."

Colleen placed her hat on the bench and ran her fingers through her hair. She'd wash all over when she went to her quarters. Glancing at the watch fastened to a top pocket of her shirt, she saw she still had an hour to go before Mostyn relieved her.

"No brothers or sisters?" she asked.

"No."

"Nor have I. That's something in common."

"Parents still living?"

"Yes."

"Anyone else?" Waverly asked. "Special, I mean."

"I was engaged for a while last year. It fell through."

"Sorry to hear that."

"Bet you're not."

Colleen glanced mischievously at Waverly, smiling at his embarrassment.

"Ignore my wicked sense of humour. How'd you get to be here?"

"By stages," said Waverly. He sounded relieved. "Was in the tank corps in the Western Desert until Alamein. Then joined SOE. Served with the Jeds[191] in France until I got seconded to OSS and the Kachins last summer. Came back to SOE in December."

Colleen's curiosity got the better of her.

"That where you met Collette, in France?"

"Yes. She was with the Resistance. SS captured her. They killed her."

"Oh, Peter," said Colleen tenderly, realising that the loss still bore heavily on this brave and honourable man. She placed a comforting hand on his arm.

He took it gently, thanked her and digressed.

"So how did you get to these exotic climes?"

Colleen told him. The account elicited a further question.

"What will you do, after the war?"

"Finish my term as a QA. I've still got about half of it to go."

Peter's voice took on a new intensity.

"Would you like to do it in England? There's a military hospital near our home, for psychiatric cases. I'm sure I could pull a few strings if you don't mind working in a looney bin."

"I'll think about it," said Colleen casually. He was still holding her hand and she was happy for him to do so.

She watched a meteor flash across the sky. With her free hand she extracted a small cylinder from her top pocket, eased the top off into her lap with thumb and forefinger, then gently applied some lipstick. Repositioning the cap, she dropped the container back into her pocket and pressed her lips together for a few moments.

Waverly edged closer to her.

"Sorry all else I've got on is Chanel Sweat Number Five," Colleen whispered.

"OK with me," said Peter.

He put his arm around her shoulders and she inclined her head to his.

The kiss brought comfort to them both.

"Better see what they're up to in there," Colleen said when their lips parted. She glanced toward the church entrance.

"Yes, I'd best be getting on my way," said Waverly. He stood up, replaced his hat and picked up his carbine. "You'll think about what I said?"

"Of course. 'Night Peter."

She rose to her feet and lightly kissed him again. He bade her good night and soundlessly departed. Colleen put on her hat, collected the Sten and deposited it inside the church entrance. From within, the figures of the Karen women were visible in the lamplight, moving between the patients, some of whom were groaning and muttering in their sleep.

Colleen set about preparing sedatives for them. Though still tingling with excitement over her unexpected close encounter with Peter, she couldn't help wondering about Collette. What was the full truth?

Events half a world away were even then framing the answer to that question.

Northern Italy, April 1945.

The final offensive was underway, to prevent the retreating German Army from reaching the *Alpenfestung* via the Brenner Pass, where Nazism could regenerate itself in the mountain fastnesses of Austria, the Fuhrer's personal fortress.

One million men under arms stood ready to do his bidding.

Their forward troops had breached many of the high banks along irrigation channels feeding the cultivated plain north of the Senio and flooded much of the low-lying countryside.

And from behind fortified river lines, laced with deep minefields and interlocking gun positions deeply dug in, they battled resolutely to resist the two-pronged Allied advance, the Americans attacking west of Bologna and the Eighth Army striking for the narrow stretch of navigable flatland west of Lake Comacchio, called the Argenta Gap.

Argenta suffered days and nights of relentless Allied bombing and artillery. Soon after mid April, it fell to the British Fifth Corps, following a series of brilliantly coordinated attacks by all arms.

Recently arrived crab flail tanks cleared minefields to enable assault forces to get up to the edge of the river lines. By firing directly *through* nearside flood banks, seventeen-pounder A/T guns blasted out German positions on the far bank previously marked by patrols.

Under heavy mortar and artillery support, aided by cab ranks of fighter-bombers, infantrymen quickly got across in storm boats and assault rafts to seize the opposite banks.

Often simultaneously and likewise braving enemy gunners who hit back viciously despite the preponderance of opposing fire, Allied sappers forced ark and Bailey crossings over the watercourses.

Andy Somerville lost several men in the process.

"Too many rivers, Sergeant," he said bitterly to Sean Gilfillan on seeing two of his most experienced NCOs stretchered away.

But their efforts enabled the tanks to get over and assist the infantry to secure Argenta, doggedly battling the enemy from house to house in the devastated streets.

Among the assaulting troops was Fusilier Brian Briggs, back with his battalion, "for the last big strafe," he said.

"Jerry's still tryin' to invent somethin' to kill 'im," said his mates, though not to Mollie.

At the time, Corporal Styles and Sergeant Merryl were moving up from Ravenna with a supply column.

The convoy negotiated the congestion in what was left of Argenta, crossed the flood plain via a causeway and entered undulating wooded country beyond, following Fifth Corps as it pursued the enemy to the valley of the River Po.

"This is more like it," said Dinah.

"Let's hope it stays fine," said Mollie.

Of all the obstacles the Allies had faced, the weather wasn't one of them. It had been warm and sunny throughout the battle, the road surfaces were good and the line of vehicles was cruising along at a steady twenty-five miles an hour, passing many stationary enemy vehicles en route, bereft of petrol and abandoned.

"Amen," said Dinah. She steered the lorry around a slight bend, maintaining the regulation distance with respect to the vehicle in front.

At that moment, the driver's windshield shattered.

Dinah's head and shoulders jerked against the back of the cab. Blood spurted from the hole in her chest and spread through her battledress.

"Dinah!" cried Mollie.

She grabbed the wheel and steered the lorry to the nearside ditch, instinctively crouching down in the seat. Dinah's body slumped on top of her and Mollie retched as she tasted Dinah's blood trickling down her face and into her mouth.

Two more rounds punctured the driver's door and punched holes in the seat back above Mollie's head.

The truck lurched into soft soil where it stalled. Mollie couldn't reach the ignition so she pushed open her door and stumbled onto the earth, dragging Dinah's body with her.

Shocked and sickened even as she reached for her sidearm, Mollie lay quivering in the crumbly soil of the ditch, next to the body of her friend.

An armoured car came charging up from the rear of the column, overtaking the trucks that had pulled up behind the stalled lorry and halting beside it. The car's machine gun lashed the woods from where the shots had issued.

The trucks to the front also stopped and their crews piled out into the ditches on both sides of the road, weapons ready.

Several RASC lads from the vehicles behind came running up, armed with Stens.

"You OK, Mollie?" one of them asked anxiously. His mates covered Dinah with a groundsheet. The bullet had struck her in the heart.

Mollie had taken cover by the nearside front wheel of the lorry, grasping her Webley revolver.

"Yes," she gasped, in tears.

The officer in command of the armoured car joined them, his face sombre.

"You go sit in the car, Mollie," he said. "We'll sort things here. Fetch a tow rope from the lads up front," he ordered the RASC man beside Mollie.

"Yes, sir," he said and immediately set off along the ditch. The car's machine gun was still firing intermittent bursts.

Mollie wiped her eyes with her sleeve. She stood up, holstered the Webley and went to fasten the goggles around her neck across her eyes.

"Thank you, sir," she said as calmly as she could, though she was still shaking. "But I need to get back on the road."

The car's machine gun stopped firing and debussed troops were scouring the woods.

"No," said the officer firmly. He took Mollie by the arm. "That sniper only shot at Dinah and you. God knows why but I'm not taking any chances. You ride with us for the rest of the way."

It was a wise precaution.

The assassin had escaped through the trees even as the car made its approach.

"Got one, at least," he said with satisfaction.

Thanks to good intelligence and powerful Zeiss binoculars, his efforts had not been marred by mistaken identity, as in Naples.

Inconspicuous in partisan dress, he merged with the groups now harassing their former allies and several days later met his liaison officer in a white stucco church building in Bologna.

The officer wore priestly garb and thanks to his fluency in several languages, was taking confession. The assassin entered the communicant cubicle in his turn.

"I got one," he said through the wire grill. "The sergeant, Merryl. But they reacted fast. I had to get away."

"No matter," said the priest. "You did well. The money will be in your account by this evening."

"If only you'd let me take a *panzerfaust* – "

"Patience, my friend. Remember, above all, not too much zeal. We'll get the rest in due course. Let them agonise. As it happens, another has been accounted for."

"Another?"

"Yes. Seemingly natural but I know our Master's work."

He related the details of the tragedy.

"So what now?" the other man asked.

"We need you in England, because the war is ending quicker than we'd hoped," said his confessor. "I will arrange a job for you."

"Whereabouts?"

"In the north midlands. Out of the way but not too far from our operations."

A few minutes later, communicant and confessor went their separate ways.

The priest doffed his clerical attire and left the building in full uniform.

He strode briskly along a dusty thoroughfare through throngs of civilians and service personnel to the Allied HQ. Armed sentries stood to attention as he entered.

The priest gave a number to the female signals telephonist at the switchboard.

"I'll take the call in my office," he said.

Seated at his desk, he picked up the phone.

"You're through, sir," said the telephonist.

The officer spoke into the mouthpiece.

"Forsythe? Montague-Stewart. Our man is on his way."

When he'd finished the conversation, Montague-Stewart leant back in his chair, lit a cigarette and gazed out the window into the sunshine.

It was all going according to plan.

"Indeed, above all, not too much zeal," he said quietly, exhaling smoke.

Before the April offensive opened, Captain Halliard's MGH moved down from the mountains to a town south of Argenta, where it joined other RAMC units, as close to the fighting as patient safety allowed.

Wards and theatres were set up in a town hall, an extensive building with two floors that fortuitously sustained only minimal damage during the preliminary bombardment.

Soon it was teeming with casualties. Stretchers covered both floors, laid in rows with their groaning occupants connected to life-preserving drips and swathed in blood-sodden gauze.

The noise of artillery pounding, bombs bursting and fighter-bombers roaring in for low-level attacks virtually drowned out patients' cries and almost forced staff to shout to each other as they made their way between stretchers.

"Another lot of packs, Dollie!" Julie Dalton called. "Sulfa sachets and compression splints."

"We can start on the penicillin when we've finished this row," Dollie told her as they renewed dressings and dumped the old ones into waste buckets. "Karen's got the solution made up."

"OK," said Julie. "We'll manage but I wish Coll was here."

"And Mac," said Dollie, smiling at a lad with a fearful laceration exposing his rib cage.

Julie heaved a heartfelt sigh.

MacHendry, the tower of strength, was no longer with the hospital, having been recalled to his unit when the Canadian Corps in Italy had transferred to northwest Europe.

Julie and he wrote to each other regularly but no-one would have time for letters today.

"Soon have you in theatre, mate," Julie told the casualty, whose face showed a typical chalk-like pallor. He smiled at the Sister's reassuring voice.

"Hope so," said Julie to Dollie when they'd moved on. Rodwell, Jardine and other surgeons were operating non-stop in converted ante-rooms.

So great was the congestion that the girls had to crawl on their hands and knees between the rows of stretchers. Their hands were reddened time and again from changing dressings, necessitating Elsdon the orderly to keep up a steady supply of bowls of hot water and disinfectant for washing. Seeing to the patients' personal needs was an added and unending burden for the staff.

All the while, they sweltered in their battledress.

The near-incessant explosions brought down showers of dust and plaster flakes. Dollie carefully brushed the debris from the blanket covering a pallid youth whose sweat-streaked face was twisted in terror.

"Can't have the MO seeing you like that," she said, leaning over him. The sound of her voice seemed to calm him. He was on her list for morphine. "This'll make you feel a bit easier," she added as she injected him.

She and Elsdon followed Julie to the next patient.

"As busy as it's ever been, Sister," said the orderly. "Even compared to Cassino."

Dollie nodded – and tried not think about Andy.

In the formal mayoral residence, Bronwyn and June were caring for a particular set of casualties requiring isolation. Their stretchers covered the parlour floor and filled the hallway.

The overpowering stench and the festering tissue that showed bubbly black when the dressings came off immediately identified the malady.

Gas gangrene.

"Must be because of the marshes they're fighting in," remarked Bronwyn when she and June set about preparing penicillin and anti-gas serum. "Some of them are going to lose a limb, poor lads."

Halliard was operating in what had been the mayor's office, assisted by Helen Goodsall and Orderly Corporal Burrows. June knew how desperately tired Mike was but also that the suffering men were in the best possible hands.

Tragically, the marshes claimed one more victim even as the Argenta Gap was secured.

The swampy areas not only exacerbated the gangrenous infestation but also bred the malarial mosquito. Thankfully, victims at the hospital recovered with large doses of quinine – all but one.

Bronwyn had volunteered to complete the latest patient reports in the lull after the fighting. She and June shared an upstairs study for the purpose.

"Are you sure, Bronwyn?" asked June as they ascended the stairs. "You don't look well. Why don't I give you a check-up?"

"I'm fine, June," said her friend. "You get the brew on."

When June returned with the tea, she found the matron slumped on the desk, almost comatose.

"Mike!" she called.

Halliard came running. They placed Bronwyn on a stretcher in the office and set up an IV quinine drip.

June loosened Bronwyn's clothing and began sponging her with alcohol. The matron was sweating profusely and shivering uncontrollably.

"I think it's MT[192], Mike," June said anxiously.

Halliard was monitoring Bronwyn's temperature and heart rate. "Keep at it, June," he urged. "We've got to cool her down."

But despite their efforts, Bronwyn died, two hours after June had found her. Feeling shocked and helpless, the couple remained kneeling beside their dead friend.

"Why, Mike, why?" June asked, turning a tear-stained face to him.

Mike placed a hand on her shoulder.

"I don't know," he said quietly. "It doesn't make sense. There'll have to be an autopsy. I'll make the arrangements," he added.

June dried her eyes and covered the matron with a blanket.

The autopsy confirmed cerebral malaria, of a particularly virulent strain.

"Unusual for these parts," the pathologist said to Mike and June.

Unusual indeed.

Bronwyn's untimely death stunned everyone and the news of Sergeant Merryl's assassination bore heavily on emotions already raw with grief.

Mollie's escape brought comfort to the mourners but no-one believed that the twin tragedies were accidents of war, though there seemed no alternative to accepting them as such.

However, one man was resolved on a day of reckoning.

Fusilier Brian Briggs. His determination would inspire others.

When his battalion closed up on the Po, it went into in reserve and Briggs acquired the job of company dispatch rider. He managed to visit Mollie, now with ATS HQ quartered in a villa as spacious as the one they had stayed in during the drive to the Gothic Line but intact and almost on the shores of Lake Comacchio.

They walked for a short time in the grounds. The solitude enabled Mollie to unburden. She clasped Briggs's hand.

"Oh, Brian," she sobbed. "Hoppy, Bronwyn, Dinah. What's happening? It *can't* be coincidence."

They were standing on a grassy terrace, from which the shimmering surface of the lake could be seen through some trees. The lean fusilier gazed at the line of vehicles drawn up on the approach to the villa, his weathered face expressionless. He spoke quietly, earnestly.

"I've been talking to the partisans, love," he said. "Not much happens they don't know about. They've given me a couple of leads and a description. Very interesting."

Mollie glanced at him. Brian squeezed her hand and spoke again, cryptically but reassuringly.

"All in good time, sweetheart. Once we're over the Po, it'll be hell for leather for Austria or Venice, but first chance we get after we're married, we'll take a quick trip to Bologna."

In the meantime, the crossing of the Po was underway, with the Corps sappers fully involved.

River Po, April 1945, a cloudless morning.

"So much for aerial photography," said Lieutenant Somerville.

He and Gilfillan stared at the stationary vessel. Her crew were trying ineffectually to pole her off the submerged obstruction.

"River's like soup, sir," the sergeant said despondently. "All that silt."

Somerville's platoon had painstakingly put together and launched a Class Forty[193] assault raft, with its outboard motor attached. The components of a second raft, awaiting assemblage, reposed on their heavy duty wheeled trailer, parked some distance back from the bank, in the cover of a grove of trees.

The rafts would ferry a troop of Churchill tanks across the six hundred-foot stretch of water to help support the infantry who had already crossed by means of storm boats under cover of darkness.

Having blown a hole in the near flood bank, the sappers bulldozed a shallow earthen causeway to the water's edge that they then laid with logs, for stability. An AVRE had carefully backed the trailer into the water, where the raft's pontoons, each weighing a couple of tons, were floated off to enable Somerville and his men to finish the raft's construction, working in water up to their waists.

On completion of this task, the raft's crew had manoeuvred their unwieldy craft parallel with the shore and swung out its ramped Bailey section to take the bulldozer aboard, so it could build another causeway on the far bank, after it, too, was gapped by explosive.

With its load secure, the raft's engine growled and the crew turned it to head for the opposite shore.

It had made good progress for twenty yards and then stopped.

"We're aground, sir," called the NCO in charge of the crew. The raft had struck a mud bank, invisible beneath the turgid waters.

"Try the poles," called Somerville.

"Not budging, sir," said the NCO after a few minutes of unsuccessful exertion.

"OK, Sergeant," Somerville called back. "We'll tow you off."

He summoned the AVRE.

"Our hawser can reach from here, sir," the youthful NCO vehicle commander informed Andy when the Churchill halted at the water's edge.

"We'll take it from there, Sergeant," said Somerville.

With one end of the cable fixed to the AVRE, Somerville and Gilfillan waded out and fastened the other end to the raft as its crew stood by their poles. The water was chest deep.

"Back up!" Andy ordered the AVRE commander, who gave a thumbs-up sign and relayed the order to his driver.

Somerville and Gilfillan waded clear of the tautening cable and the tank slowly reversed up the bank, while the raft crew pushed hard on their poles.

A prolonged sucking sound issued forth the raft lurched free.

Cheers sounded from the wooded bluff overlooking the bank, where most of Andy's platoon waited to start work on the second raft. Andy and Sean detached the hawser from the raft and the tank men hauled it in, aided by a couple of sappers.

"Thank you, sir," said the raft sergeant, grinning broadly as his craft chugged into midstream. "We'll take soundings as we go and mark out a channel."

"Right, let's get the other one in, Sergeant," Somerville called to the AVRE commander. "Stand by, lads," he said to his men lining the bluff.

Corporal Ashbourne, Somerville's wireless operator, summoned him from the top of the causeway.

"OC's on the blower, sir," he said. "Wants to know what the hold-up is. Says he's getting earache from the tank squadron commander."

"OK, Ashy," Somerville called. He and Gilfillan plodded ashore and began trudging up the bank. "Tell him we're underway again and I'll – "

Andy never finished the sentence.

The leading infantry had overrun most of the enemy artillery positions but the odd desultory shell was still coming over, though falling some distance from Somerville's raft launchings.

Except for one.

Everyone dropped flat at the telltale shriek. It ended in an ear-battering bang. Mud and debris descended like glutinous hail.

Face down in mud, Somerville felt a kick like a mule's in his backside.

"God, I've been hit!" he exclaimed.

"Yes, sir," said Gilfillan, craning his head over his shoulder to peer at his officer's rear end. "Indeed you have."

"How bad is it?" the lieutenant asked, his voice hoarse with apprehension.

The sergeant twisted around to get a better look.

"I think I can fix you, sir," he said with confidence and reached into a trouser pocket for his jack knife.

"If you can sort of half crouch, sir," Gilfillan advised. "And drop your trousers, I'll do the necessary."

Somerville did so. Gilfillan opened the large blade of the knife and wiped it on his sleeve. "Must make sure everything's sterile, sir," he said.

With a deft movement that made Somerville wince, the sergeant dug something out of Andy's exposed flesh. Gilfillan then secured a dressing, tying it around Somerville's hips. The wound was bleeding but not copiously.

Sean handed the extracted object to his platoon commander when Andy had readjusted his trousers. Somerville gazed at the asymmetric chunk of metal about double the size of an Oxo cube and dropped it into a pocket.

"You'll have a bit of a bruise, sir," said Gilfillan.

"Feels like it," grunted Somerville. "But thanks, Sean."

"Well done, Sarge!" cried several voices from above.

"That was a near thing, sir!" exclaimed Ashbourne. White-faced and trembling, he had rushed down the causeway to assist as necessary.

"Certainly was, Ashy. You better get back and report to the OC."

"Yessir," said the corporal.

He dashed up to where Andy's jeep was parked near the second raft trailer. Andy and Sean followed.

"You should get a jab for that, sir," Sean remarked.

"Yes, Sergeant, after I've had a word with the OC," said Somerville. He was walking with a pronounced limp and his backside ached considerably.

The AVRE commander, ashen-faced as Ashbourne had been, stared down wide-eyed from his hatch as Andy and Sean trudged past.

"Good thing it was a rogue, sir," said the NCO. "We've had enough stonks lately. But we'll get on with the other raft."

"Yes, carry on, then, Sergeant," Andy rejoined, with a conscious effort to sound calm. "Right, snap to it, lads," he ordered his platoon. "We don't expect any more packages from Jerry but mind out."

"Yessir!" several voices exclaimed. The men ranged themselves beside the AVRE. They looked immensely relieved.

As the pair approached the jeep, Gilfillan handed his officer his water bottle. Andy drank gratefully and returned the container, whereupon Gilfillan took a draught himself.

"Oh, by the way, sir," said the sergeant. "Congratulations."

Somerville looked at him quizzically.

"On a most defiant gesture to the enemy while that operation was in progress."

"Hmm, thank you, Sergeant, quite[194]."

Ashbourne gave Somerville the headset. "I've told the OC I think you're OK, sir," he said.

"Thanks, Corporal," said the lieutenant. He donned the earphones and took the mike.

The major's voice sounded stridently in his ears.

"Andy! Medics are on their way. Speak to me, lad!"

A few days later, the Axis forces in Italy capitulated.

By then, Fifth Corps was converging on Venice. Somerville's platoon undertook its last job of the war in assisting with the construction of a four hundred and twenty-foot high-level Bailey bridge across the River Meduna.

"A high note to end on, Sean," Andy remarked.

"Amen to that, sir," said Gilfillan.

The squadron then went into reserve. Most of its members were looking forward to savouring the delights of the island city but Somerville made an appointment to see the OC.

He sat to attention in response to Somerville's salute, pushed aside the paperwork on his desk and placed his pipe in its bowl. The inside of the command caravan reeked of tobacco smoke.

"Suppose you want to visit your intended?" the major asked gruffly.

"Yes, sir," said Somerville. He was standing at attention, with some discomfort.

Though healing satisfactorily, his wound was still sore and continued to affect his gait. Moreover, Gilfillan had guessed right. The bruise extended from Andy's hip almost to the back of his knee.

"Well," said the OC. "You better get your third pip up. Won't be official until you're gazetted, of course but we can't have your good lady thinking the old man's a miser, can we?"

Andy departed the caravan in a state of joyful bewilderment. Ever since the major had assumed command the previous autumn, he'd kept up an almost constant refrain, to the perpetual amusement of Somerville's brother officers; "If you want to make captain under my command, Somerville…"

"I finally made it," Andy said aloud. "Should go down well in the mess."

But his first port of call, via jeep, was the vast and majestic renaissance villa near the shores of Lake Venice, set in acres of beautifully tended gardens and surrounded by extensive groves of deep green cypresses.

This was the final point reached by Halliard's hospital, since landing at Salerno in September 1943.

Andy managed to arrange his visit for when Dollie came off duty. The hospital was still busy because a fair number of wounded had been admitted from the last stages of the fighting, together with numerous liberated Allied POWs, many of them malnourished.

Resplendent in crisp grey frock, trim white head-square, polished shoes and immaculate grey cape edged with scarlet, Dollie met Somerville as arranged, on a secluded part of the verandah, shaded beneath its white stone porticos. They didn't want their moment spoiled by the bustle of the reception area.

"Oh, Livvie!" Andy exclaimed.

He swept her into his arms. Dollie clasped hers around his shoulders and they kissed passionately.

"Captain!" Dollie exclaimed afterwards, when she noticed Andy's epaulettes. "Well, let's have a cup of tea to celebrate. When did it happen?"

Somerville told her as they strolled towards the front entrance – prompting Dollie to ask another question.

"Andy, why are you walking like that?"

The future for Andy Somerville and Olivia Dale beckoned like the Promised Land. But the sudden deaths of Bronwyn and Dinah remained for them unfinished business that, together with June and Mike, Brian and Mollie, they were determined to resolve.

Other allies would join them, though in early 1945, one was preoccupied with his own particular field of battle.

February 1945, Forest of the Reichswald.

Blackstone's squadron spent most of January refitting and servicing their AVREs in the regimental workshops established near Tilburg. In company with sister units, it then laboriously journeyed fifty miles up to Nijmegen.

The drive was the most difficult the crews had experienced, with AVREs repeatedly fishtailing and slithering through snow patches and black ice.

"An absolute nightmare, sir," said Corporal Talbot.

RE field companies strove to keep the roads open and gritted for the long lines of traffic heading northeast; transporting men, guns, tanks, assault equipment, essential supplies and ammunition of all calibres for what would be the decisive campaign.

The battle for the Rhine.

Blackstone's men repeatedly stopped during the drive to assist their fellow sappers with road and bridge repair, glad once again for the protective cladding of the well-padded zoot suits in the freezing conditions.

"Always one more bridge, in Holland," their field company comrades declared.

In addition to the weather, the movement schedules themselves caused further delays. Road transport was maintained at normal levels during the day to deceive the enemy, with many mechanised units lying up camouflaged in fields or byways until nightfall, when the roads were filled to capacity.

In this way, Graham's troop took a day and a night to reach its leaguer southeast of Nijmegen, where it deployed amid woodland facing across open countryside a gloomy stretch of dark green forestry.

The Reichswald.

Steve and Mark stood in the shelter of Armadillo's hull, gazing at the two-mile-wide tree fringe through binoculars. They also scrutinised the farmland abutting the first rank of iron-dark fir trunks with their interlocking foliage.

"That's the anti-tank ditch," said Graham. He pointed to the concreted white scar slashed across the fields bordering the forest. "SBGs'll span it, though."

"Save the fascines for any craters in the tracks. Bound to be plenty," Napper said grimly.

"It'll be all hell tomorrow morning, Mark," said Graham, nodding.

Nearly eight hundred RAF heavies had already carpet-bombed the fortified towns of Cleve and Goch on the far side of the forest. More than a thousand artillery pieces would stonk the Reichswald itself, starting at 0400 hours the following day.

"Let's hope they can do for the mines, Steve," said Napper. "And take out any Jerries holed up in those cottages."

Mark rested his binoculars against his chest, clasped his arms and shivered. The afternoon was raw and drizzly. Graham, too, felt chilly and uncomfortable, despite the leather jerkins the sappers wore over their smocks and BDs. They'd packed away the zoot suits, reckoning them too bulky for the coming battle.

Now a thaw was developing, with serious implications for any armoured advance away from unsealed roads, though the weather remained bitter, with mist and stinging rainsqualls.

"Worst of both worlds," the lads had reckoned as they scrubbed the whitewash winter camouflage off the AVREs, prior to servicing the vehicles that day. "Typical."

As at Blerick and the Channel ports, the innocent-looking greensward before them would be thickly sown with deadly dragon's teeth of A/P and A/T mines. Sudden death could likewise be lurking in any of the clusters of rustic cottages to their front, in the form of the usual lethal German trio of snipers, machine gunners and *panzerfaust* operators.

The wrecks of American WACO gliders still strewn over the farmland from the abortive Market Garden operation and the burnt-out vehicles scattered along the country tracks didn't help anyone's morale, either.

Their other duties complete, the troop were setting up the tents in which they would sleep the night and breaking out compo rations for the evening meal. They would turn in as early as possible, having spent hours assembling and mounting chespale fascine bundles and SBGs now affixed to One Troop's AVREs.

Steve and Mark continued their appreciation until Hazeldene's cheery, "Brew's up, sirs," summoned them for mess.

The officers trudged back under the trees, boots crunching on pine needles, each of them experiencing the same disquiet - exacerbated by the visible reminders of last September's battles. With the Allies pressing towards the German-Dutch frontier, their enemies had recently blown dykes along the Rhine, inundating its western floodplain already saturated by the December rains and now sodden from the thaw. East of the Maas, for a thousand yards inland, the country was similarly waterlogged.

On the southern flank, the Americans were battling through fanatically defended and heavily mined forests around Aachen to capture the Roer Dams preparatory to launching their own offensive towards the Rhine, while the British and Canadians were faced with an equally gruelling task prior to securing suitable crossing places – seizing the Forest of the Reichswald.

And in doing so, they would be forced to pierce the formidable defences that had earlier prompted the abortive outflanking movement known as Market Garden.

The Siegfried Line.

"We might as well get sorted!" Steve shouted to Napper above the sudden, stupendous roar of the Allied artillery, raining salvo after salvo onto the German lines.

Graham and Napper staggered bleary-eyed from their blankets to pull on their boots and battledress trousers. The tent walls flapped in and out like a concertina and the officers felt the ground shuddering beneath their feet.

"Bofors!" yelled Napper. A brilliant red lacework of forty-mm tracer streaked overhead as he and Steve emerged from the tent into the bellowing pre-dawn darkness.

To the rear, the sky flamed and flickered with the flash and thunder of a thousand guns. The gloomy mass of forest to the officers' front was a leaping inferno of bursting shells.

A figure stumbled over to Graham. It was Hazeldene.

"We'll have a brew on, sir, soon as we can!" he yelled.

"Thanks, Corporal, carry on!" Graham yelled back. "Better spruce up," he called to Mark.

The barrage went on for six hours, augmented by rocket-firing RAF Typhoons as the sky lightened into a cold, clear morning. Finally, runnels of yellow smoke spouting from the beaten zone signified the first three hundred-yard lift.

And the start of the infantry advance.

Beneath the shrieking air, drifting smoke and bitter tang of high explosive, Graham's troop washed, shaved, breakfasted, cleaned up and set about the remaining preparations for battle.

"All dressed up and still no place to go, Steve," said Napper.

"'Fraid so," said Graham, staring to his front.

It was early afternoon. They were sitting on Armadillo's turret, gazing at the molasses-like morass left by the crabs that had flailed the mines up to the anti-tank ditch. It was all that remained of the grassy farmland.

As at Blerick, most of the crabs had become bogged, necessitating the usual laborious job for the armoured recovery vehicles.

"Rain'll slow everyone down," said Steve.

He fastened the top button of his gas cape and glanced up at the heavy cloud, for the weather had broken again. Everywhere, tracks were collapsing into quagmires, bogging tanks, vehicles and men.

Nevertheless, progress had been made.

AVREs attached to the initial assault units had gapped the A/T ditch allowing armour to provide vital support for the attacking infantry, who doggedly pressed toward their objectives.

To One Troop's front, the fortuitous capture of a bridge intact over the anti-tank ditch enabled the Scots infantry to sweep forward in their Kangaroo carriers with unexpected rapidity.

Along the way, they had mopped up numerous prisoners from the farm cottages smashed by the artillery and the fighter-bombers. The dishevelled enemy, dazed and sullen, were marched back at gunpoint past One Troop's AVREs, including walking wounded. Carriers transported other wounded POWs.

But not all the enemy were so quickly subdued.

"Trouble," said Graham tersely, a little later.

The dreaded tack-tacking of Spandaus, cough of Brens, crack of grenades, banging of mortar and shell bursts revealed that the infantry had met heavy resistance. More Kangaroo carriers motored back, this time laden with grey-faced Jocks in mud-plastered, bloodstained battledress with thick dressings around arms, legs, chests or shoulders, ministered to by alert RAMC medics holding up drip bottles for semi-conscious men on stretchers. Rain splashed on their ashen countenances.

"A/P Mines," Napper said quietly.

Steve, too, had noted the casualties with a missing foot or lower limb, stumps tied up in blood-soaked bandages.

About mid afternoon, Armadillo's radio crackled and Shoreland poked his head out of his hatch.

"OC, sir," he said to Graham and passed him the headset.

Steve listened to Blackstone's familiar, commanding tones.

"Lowland Brigade's held up at Nijmegen, Steve. Traffic jams are unbelievable. Bulldozers are going flat out to clear enough rubble for the carriers to get through but our Jocks won't be at the start line for hours. So for now, we're to dismount and help with road repair. Carriers'll take you forward."

The idea was for Blackstone's troops to pass through the forces presently engaged and help breach the defences near the town of Frasselt, where the Lowland Brigade would continue the advance. Once again, the squadron would be assisting Kinross's doughty warriors.

"Wilco, sir," said Graham and closed the mike. He glanced at Napper.

"Assemble the troop, Mark," he said. "On the double."

The carriers growled through streaming rain into a wilderness of smoking, gouged-out earth, uprooted tree trunks, shattered forest hamlets and the sharp, all-pervasive smell of HE. German corpses lay in grotesque attitudes beside silent machine guns, those not killed by the bombardment overwhelmed by the Highland Jocks' concerted assaults with Bren gun, rifle, bayonet, Sten and grenade.

The vehicles proceeded until the way was blocked by shell craters, fallen trees and collapsed former dwellings.

Incessant racket further on indicated that the infantry were still pegging away at their next objective. The slamming bangs of British seventy-five mm rounds revealed that gun tanks had kept up in support, trampling trees where they had taken a beeline through the forest to avoid the rides down which the enemy eighty-eight mm A/T guns were sighted.

But continuation of the road in this sector would help enormously with respect to re-supply, reinforcement and casualty evacuation.

"Debus!" Steve ordered when the vehicles halted. "Stay by the carriers 'til we're sorted."

Grasping the heavy pickaxes detached from the AVRE's hulls, Graham's lads leapt into black mud that almost covered their gaiters. Steve reported to the steel-helmeted, harassed-looking figure of Captain 'Hod' Stoughton, the RE field company commander. He was overseeing his sappers who were already toiling to clear debris.

"Here's the form, Steve," said Stoughton. "We fill up the craters with whatever rubble we can get from the houses – we're inside Germany so any left standing, we knock 'em down with sledgehammers or even explosives if we have to for more road ballast - except for my HQ."

"They're all clear, Hod?" Steve asked.

"Apart from where you see tapes. Avoid the places where the timber's cordoned off, too. But cut and dress anything outside of that and haul 'em across."

Steve ran his gaze over the shell-torn earth and uprooted trees.

"Corduroy road?" he asked.

"That's it. You've brought some cross-cut saws as well as your pickaxes? Good! Sooner you get cracking the better."

Steve trudged back through mud and cloying leaf mould to the rear of the carriers where his men stood shivering in the rain.

"OK, listen," he said. "Our first job is to help fill the craters, then lay a corduroy road, so you'll need your leathers."

The reference was to the leather gloves the men carried. Though their hands were tough and calloused, Graham didn't want his drivers, gunners and wireless operators risking laceration injuries. They also wore their steel tankers' narrow-brimmed helmets. Graham much preferred his beret because the helmets were bulky and uncomfortable but for the present they were a wise precaution against shrapnel.

Steve quickly briefed the troop and closed with a grim warning.

"Areas outside the tapes are swept and I guess the stonk has blown everything that can explode but watch out for pencils and anything else that looks dodgy. Don't take any chances."

The pencil mine was a fiendish new enemy innovation consisting of a metal cylinder pushed vertically into the ground with a rifle bullet inserted. It was designed to fire the round directly into the victim's crotch on detonation.

"We'll mind out, sir," said Crittenden grimly, to murmurs of agreement all round.

Graham and his sappers joined their field company colleagues in shifting heaps of rubble via tarpaulins and tipping the loads into huge shell holes where the road surface had been blown away. They also shoved in bales of straw found in the remains of woodcutters' cottages, to absorb seepage.

Then, sweating and steaming in their BDs, smocks and gas capes, they sawed, hacked and trimmed fallen pines that they hauled with rope and chain halters to be placed crossways over the filled-in pits. Other trees, somehow yet standing, were cut down, similarly dressed and transported.

The battle ahead still banged and flashed as darkness fell. The occasional incoming mortar bomb, prompting the cry, "Take cover!" sent everyone flopping to earth.

"Time and a half for this, sir," said Hazeldene, lifting his grinning face out of the mud after a mortar round had spattered everyone with muck and bark shards.

"You should write to your union rep, Ron," said Graham. Cautiously, they got up from behind the pine stump where they'd taken shelter.

In unceasing rain, the sappers continued working into the night, by the light of shaded hurricane lamps, until a wireless message was relayed from One Troop's leaguer to Stoughton's HQ. The captain picked his way along the lengthening log road to where Steve and his men were working.

"It's Mark on the blower, Steve," he said. "Looks like your party's about to start. I'll give you the gen."

They conferred inside what had been a cottage parlour, scrutinising maps by torchlight. Sheets of tarpaulin stretched between the wall frames kept off the pattering rain.

A little later, the carriers were returning Steve's troop to the leaguer.

"Hope Mr Napper and the lads've got a brew on, sir," said Talbot, wedged beside Graham in the Kangaroo's confined space.

"They'd better have," said his superior. Steve grimaced as the vehicle bumped over the newly laid logs. "Or I'll write to Mrs Vanderveer."

Steve had left Napper and his crew to guard the leaguer, aware that Mark was not happy with the decision. Graham did so partly because protocol preferred that an officer be left in charge and partly because of Napper's personal circumstances.

Similar circumstances applied, of course, to all the vehicle commanders, especially Crittenden, whose romance by correspondence with Lorraine Tyrell continued to blossom but even by One Troop standards, Katrijn Vanderveer was still very young to be an anxious fiancée – as Graham believed she soon would be, provided Napper managed to avoid Heiko's fate.

For that reason, rightly or wrongly, Graham sought to shield Mark from danger as long as possible.

But he knew – they all did – that hidden perils lurked in the sinister thickets and among their war-ravaged environs from which there might be no escape.

Like a gargantuan steel lizard clawing through primordial slime, nearly three hundred armoured vehicles and troop carriers conveying the Lowland Brigade and its support elements inched with agonising slowness through relentless downpour and near pitch darkness along the one route available to them, once a minor unsealed road, now churned into a black mud porridge.

Drivers kept to the regulation separation distance by means of the faintly luminous markers on each vehicle's rear. It required considerable concentration.

The only other illumination was the brief glare of star shells, guttering flares and flash of HE that revealed where assault brigades were still engaged, Canadian to the left, Welsh to the right, Highlanders in front.

Deep ditches bordered the track on either side, effectively mud-filled crevices. The spasms of light from the shell bursts glowed momentarily on the occasional tilted shape of an abandoned gun tank, held fast in mire and sunk up to the turret after straying from the track.

"Never get those out, sir," Shoreland remarked to Graham. "Be there 'til Doomsday."

The column edged forward, crews and passengers discomfited further by the clinging stench of exhaust fumes but they had to press on. Though hours behind schedule, the aim was for the Lowlanders to pass through their Highland comrades, negotiate another anti-tank ditch and attack two fortified villages beyond.

These were part of the Siegfried defences proper. One Troop's first job was to help bridge the A/T ditch.

Before it addressed that task, the troop had one more obstacle to surmount – trees, that also bordered the track.

With their overhanging branches.

That eventually snagged the SBG on Armadillo, as the leading bridge-carrying AVRE.

Throughout the journey, Graham had been relaying instructions to Talbot and commanders of other SBG-laden AVREs to help them avoid the densest of the foliage but in the dark, this method wasn't foolproof. And the roadway didn't allow much room for manoeuvre.

Graham heard the swishing crackle and watched in horror as the thirty-foot box girdered span reared up on its mounting.

"Get down!" he yelled to Shoreland, who like Graham was sitting with his head out of his hatch. They both ducked inside the turret.

Armadillo lurched violently as the SBG abruptly cleared the branches and whipped forward. With a crack like the snapping of a dry twig, the restraining hawser parted, the rear end with its lifting pulleys slapping down onto the turret top that Graham and Shoreland had vacated moments before. The bridge thudded ponderously into the roadway, spraying liquid mud. The eight-foot metal pipes forming the SBG's inverted V support stanchion sprung apart and the cables strung from the stanchion to the other end of the bridge fell slack.

The whole assembly lay impotent, unravelled.

"Oh," said a voice.

"Hope the winch hasn't stripped its gears," growled Steve. "Advise troop we've lost our SBG, Boff," he said to Shoreland. "And to winch SBGs to incline limit."

"Wilco, sir," said Boff. He immediately switched to the B set.

Steve had hoped to avoid the low angle option. The SBG acted like a lever, pushing down the nose of its transporting AVRE and increasing the risk of bogging in the glutinous terrain being traversed. Lowering the SBGs beyond the normal incline of sixty degrees would increase that risk even further but it was now the only way to prevent any more of the vital bridges from falling victim to the trees.

Graham climbed out his hatch, jumped down and plodded through sludge over his ankles, unmindful of the rain tinkling on his helmet and streaming off his gas cape, to inspect the hawser winch bolted to the rear engine deck. Stoker and Illingworth followed via the side doors. Talbot kept the engine idling.

To Steve's enormous relief, he found that the winch was intact.

"Bless the back room boys, lads," Graham said to his crewmen, grateful for the designers' foresight, which had ensured that the mechanism was rugged enough to withstand the shock load it had experienced.

Adamant, immediately ahead, had stopped and Hazeldene came hastening back to Armadillo.

Thanks to the strictly observed spacing of vehicles, the fallen SBG missed Adamant by several feet. Hazeldene's AVRE was loaded with a fascine and the corporal was not enjoying his wet and precarious ride on the bundle, necessary for guiding his driver.

"Everyone OK, sir?" Ronny asked anxiously. "Anything we can do?"

"We're all OK thanks, Ronny," said Graham, surveying the partly submerged SBG. "But you get on. We'll have to leave it."

"Right, sir," said Hazeldene. He returned to Adamant and in a few moments, the Churchill was disappearing into the darkness.

Armadillo's cable had fractured at the attachment to the rectangular blow plates containing a guncotton charge. Normally, the charge was set off electrically from inside the turret, parting the cables and dropping the bridge into position. Graham turned and spoke to his two crewmen.

"Right lads. We can't reassemble the beast here. Let's tidy up and get on."

"Yessir," they each said in response.

Stoker retrieved and carefully defused the charge. He passed it to Ferrarby through the side door for storage. Illingworth winched in the hind portion of the hawser and the pulleys, then he and Drac secured them. The forward lengths would have to be left with the bridge.

"OK, Boff, tell Crash to release bridge," Steve said to Shoreland, who had re-emerged through his hatch.

Shoreland relayed the instruction and Talbot reversed Armadillo to detach the SBG from its mounting affixed to the AVRE's front. The bridge dropped with a squidgy splash.

"All aboard, lads," Steve said to Stoker and Illingworth. The pair promptly scrambled back into Armadillo. "Advise rest of troop we're ready to move when they are, Boff."

"Wilco, sir," said Shoreland with a thumbs-up gesture.

The other One Troop SBG carriers, Amazon and Arrowhead, reported in turn, "SBG at incline limit, sir."

Steve acknowledged, then ordered his AVREs to advance. Armadillo accelerated with a chug and jet of exhaust smoke, clanking forward over the abandoned bridge. Vehicles to the rear resumed their crawl.

Several hours later, Graham's troop and two AVREs from Yeardley's troop arrived at the start line, an extended clearing littered around its edges with smashed trees and shorn-off stumps. Nearby, the usual melancholy sight of caved-in buildings with gaping holes in walls and roofs greeted the assault force.

Their vehicles nosed gingerly about in the gloom, fanning out to face the A/T ditch, officers and NCOs on foot guiding the drivers to avoid craters and the most sodden stretches of ground.

The rain continued without letup. Allied shellfire crashed down beyond the far side of the ditch. Tracer fired from vehicles already in position punctured the night air with glowing streaks and staccato reports.

Several officers crouched under a stretched-out tarpaulin fastened to the side of a gun Churchill belonging to the Grenadier Guards.

A broad-shouldered Grenadiers Guards major addressed his audience in a commanding voice, indicating positions on a map with a pencil torch. The listeners included Kinross for the infantry, Cavendish for the flails, Graham and a youngster named Jamie Ledbetter for the AVREs. Ledbetter was Yeardley's second-in-command and junior even to Napper. In the glow of the torch, he looked pale and anxious.

Julian was supposed to coordinate the gapping teams but he and most of his troop were still caught in traffic jams, while Blackstone's HQ Troop had a separate task. Cavendish's squadron commander was missing too. In the absence of the AVRE and flail team leaders, the Guards officer had assumed temporary command.

"This whole thing could degenerate into a Chinese fire drill, gentlemen," said the Grenadier. "But it's nearly zero five hundred and first light's in half an hour, so we've go to get on."

Curtly he issued his order of battle instructions.

"When I give the command 'Advance,' you lead with the flails, Cavendish. Then get as many SBGs across that ditch as you can, Graham. Rest of us'll provide fire support and then screen your lads in the carriers, Kinross. Any questions? None? Then, to your mounts, gentlemen. Good luck and God speed."

Loud and clear in his headset, Graham heard the order, "Advance!"

Through early morning mist and showery rain he saw Cavendish's Shermans plough noisily ahead, mud flying from their thrashing chains, interspersed with gouts of muck from exploding mines.

Several of the crabs slithered into bogs and stuck fast.

But three of them, including Cavendish's, roared at full throttle all the way to the ditch, then reversed back, turret machine gunners giving drivers direction. Sustained fire from the crabs and the Grenadiers' gun Churchills fifty to a hundred yards back from the ditch kept the enemy's heads down.

"Three lanes clear, sir," Cavendish radioed their Grenadier CO. "Ditch is a few feet wider in my sector."

"OK, Chris, well done," came the Guardsman's reply. "Your party, Steve."

Graham swallowed hard. "Wilco, sir," he said. "Going forward to reconnoitre. Amazon, Broadsword, advance," he then ordered via the B set, switching to the intercom to relay the command to Talbot.

Napper, Kinnear and Ledbetter in Two Troop's Broadsword had arrived with SBGs intact. Amazon and Broadsword pushed clumsily through slush along two of the cleared lanes.

Armadillo slithered along Cavendish's lane to the edge of the ditch. Cowering from the cacophony of covering fire, Graham surveyed the gap in front from his turret hatch. Steve then radioed the Grenadier.

"We'll use fascines here, sir."

As Talbot reversed Armadillo, Illingworth guiding him by observing from an open side door, two bangs sounded almost in unison. Napper and Ledbetter successfully exploded the charges to release their SBGs. They dropped successfully over the ditch. Covering fire continued banging away as the two AVREs crossed the ditch, followed by gun Churchills. The forward tanks kept up the fire support on the other side of the ditch.

"Adamant forward, then Arquebus, then Arrowhead," Graham ordered when Armadillo had vacated Cavendish's lane.

"Wilco, sir," his NCOs answered in turn.

Graham gave the thumbs up to Crittenden and Hazeldene, clinging to their bundles as they guided their AVREs into position.

They managed to position their loads accurately in succession, Crittenden venturing Arquebus carefully onto Adamant's fascine to release his. Kinnear then placed the SBG precisely along its chespale support. The bridge would now hold firm even with tanks crossing.

It was an awkward job and earned a hearty "Well done, lads," from both the Grenadier major and their troop commander.

Arrowhead went over, followed by Armadillo, Alligator, commanded by Corporal Briers, Bilhook, Corporal Gower's Churchill from Two Troop, then Arquebus and Adamant.

The three spare AVREs had augmented the covering fire with their Besas throughout the gaping process. These efforts expended a lot of ammunition and the logistics units had striven in atrocious conditions to replenish it, many lorries getting bogged on roads nearly two feet under water. But they succeeded magnificently and anti-tank gunners even managed to tow up some seventeen-pounders.

These were desperately needed, insofar as the weather had cancelled out Allied air cover.

Sighting reports were filtering in of German armour on the far side of the forest, not only the killer Tiger Mark Twos but also the terrifying *Jagd-panther* tank destroyer, faster and more manoeuvrable than the Tiger but still packing the same devastating eighty-eight mm high velocity weapon.

Unfortunately, one of the first attempts to get a seventeen-pounder across an SBG failed when the gun abruptly slewed, wedged itself in between the bridge's twin ramps and defied all attempts to dislodge it. The sector was thus reduced to two crossings, with a great many vehicles in need of them.

The language over the wireless was as pungent as the cordite smoke filling everyone's nostrils.

Nevertheless, after several more hours, a mixed force of infantry, armour and A/T guns were converging on the fortified villages east of the ditch.

While they waited to move forward, Graham's and other formations immediately east of the ditch suffered a deluge of enemy mortar rounds that threw up showers of muck and pine slivers. The sappers cowered inside their AVREs with jangled nerves and ringing ears.

"Trying to cut off reinforcements, sir?" Drac Stoker asked, his voice shaking. He sat hunched up on the toolbox, located behind Driver Talbot.

Graham nodded and pressed one hand to an ear stung by the bang of a near miss.

"It'll stop once the Jocks overrun the villages," he said.

"Let's hope they can get a move on, sir," said Illingworth, huddled and trembling in his seat.

Eventually, the mortaring ceased and columns of downcast POWs came marching back, chivvied along by their short-tempered Scots captors wielding Stens.

And as before, the casualty carriers came back, laden.

Graham's AVREs motored cautiously forward and leaguered for the night among an array of pines cut down by shellfire. Though still feeling disorientated by the noise of the mortar bursts, Steve and his lads helped field company sappers ensure the area was clear of mines and assisted them with extending another corduroy road.

Afterwards, the crews serviced their AVREs and snatched a quick compo meal.

By then, it was dark.

Later, in the shelter of Armadillo's hull, Graham assiduously brushed his teeth prior to carrying out other ablutions. Most of the combined troop was doing likewise.

Steve spat out a salivary mixture, rinsed his mouth with a draught from his water bottle, wiped his lips with a flannel and blew his nose softly, depositing yet another quantity of smoke-blackened mucus on a creased handkerchief.

It was still raining. Feeling damp and chilly, Graham watched the drops slide off his gas cape and felt them patter onto his beret, which he'd substituted for his helmet. He listened to the crackle of fighting ahead as the Scotsmen pushed for their next objective, a one hundred and fifty-foot high wooded knoll called Wolf's Berg. It commanded the western approach to the railhead town of Cleve. Reserves of infantry and armour had come up, to relieve those who'd made the initial assaults so that the growl and thunder of battle would continue throughout a second night.

Graham unbuttoned to empty his bladder.

Fastening his clothing afterwards, Steve hoped the relieved troops would be able to snatch some sleep before being shoved back into the firing line. Likewise, it was vital that his troops were rested, too, even though sentry duty couldn't be avoided. Together with Napper and Ledbetter, he'd set out the guard rota and would be on watch himself from midnight to zero two hundred.

"God knows, we need to get our heads down," said Graham.

They'd been on the go for nearly forty hours, a lot of it waiting and that frayed the nerves almost as much as action itself, though on the positive side, Yeardley, Blackstone and their AVREs were expected to RV with the remainder of the squadron tomorrow.

Steve climbed up to his hatch, aware of the faint hum of the wireless. He could dimly make out Shoreland's figure, head slumped to his chest, already asleep.

The lieutenant glanced at the dark shapes of the immobile AVREs and beyond to the edge of the leaguer. It surprised him how many trees were still standing out there.

To his tired brain, they seemed to be pressing in on him.

And tomorrow his troops would be fighting inside the forest itself.

One thought helped Graham to dispel his mounting fear, a whispered name.

"Kate," he said quietly, longingly.

In a farmhouse billet west of Nijmegen, Section Officer Kate Bramble wrapped herself in a rug, sat down at the wooden table in her quarters and turned up the oil lamp flame.

She listened to the rain pattering on the roof, grateful for the extra bedding and the issue of woollen pyjamas, for her sparse little room was unheated – all available fuel was allocated for cooking, lighting and water heating.

Kate yawned. She and Vicky were continuing to work extremely long hours in tracking down missing agents and following such leads as they had on the mysterious trail of Von Hollstein.

The aristocratic Nazi and his accomplice appeared to be trekking down the coast to Calais but, inexplicably, reports linked them to Northern Italy as well.

"Don't know what that is," Kate said, with a sigh, as she reflected on the dilemma once again.

She pulled the rug tighter around herself, rubbed her eyes and put pen to paper for the letter she was determined to write before turning in.

Dear Steve, she began. *Oh, how I miss you. I know where you are and I pray constantly our loving Saviour will bring you and your wonderful boys through OK.*

But even as she wrote the words, Kate feared that many thorny ways had yet to be traversed.

She was right.

Fifteen

Victors

Reichswald Forest, west of Cleve, February 1945.

Misty daylight filtered down between the great spreading canopies. Rain dripped steadily from thickly needled branches onto men and tanks striving to crash through the forest.

It was still wise to avoid the rides, if possible. Allied vehicles resorting to them where the trees grew too thickly to be pushed over had, on occasion, succumbed in sheets of flame to A/T guns and mines that menaced the tracks.

"Better to take a long way round than a short cut to disaster," Blackstone therefore advised his troop commanders.

Where the armour could carve out its own paths, trees toppled earthwards with wrenching, splintering cracks that further assailed eardrums already suffering from engines screaming in bottom gear, tank treads grinding stridently through fallen timber and the monotonous shelling.

Sometimes, answering German eighty-eight mm shells burst in treetops and white-hot fragments came hissing down among the attackers. The armoured men could avoid the menace but, as usual, their accompanying infantry suffered casualties.

Much of the forest hereabouts was still standing, the barrage of the first day having mainly mauled the western fringe of the woods.

But Allied guns kept hammering selected targets of the Siegfried defences exposed by aerial photography; pill box complexes and their interconnecting trench systems, protected by belts of wire and mines.

As on the first day, the stonk would intensify in particular spots to the so-called 'Pepper-Pot' concentration during the last few frenzied minutes before an assault, when every available gun ranged upon a specific objective to stymie the enemy occupants and obliterate wire and mines, because even where the trees were down, crab flails were too easily snagged by protruding branches.

Target map references had to be precise, to prevent friendly fire from falling short onto the attackers. Forward observation officers, sometimes from the specialised armour, ensured that they were.

Graham's troop was closing up in extended formation on a sector of the Siegfried Line, with Yeardley's following and gun tanks to either side. The sheer volume of noise from the armoured thrust made Steve cringe.

"Need a new paint job after this, sir," Shoreland remarked over the intercom.

"Can hardly wait, Boff," said Steve.

Prolonged passage through the trees was scouring the Churchills' exteriors and burnishing the metal at the same time.

But Cleve, a major objective, lay only a few miles away so the troops had to keep going.

Feeling droplets of water sliding off his beret onto his neck, Graham spoke into his mike.

"Delta One to One Troop. ETA in ten minutes. Switch to local command on arrival. Keep watching for snipers on the way in. Acknowledge, over."

One by one, the other five commanders reported back. Everyone was wary of the sniper menace.

The screen of Lowland Jocks to the troop's front, accompanied by Stoughton's sharp-eyed mine-seeking sappers on foot, had accounted for several enemy riflemen during the morning. Sustained Bren bursts into densely matted tree crowns had brought the marksmen tumbling to the forest floor or left them swaying lifeless in mid-air, still attached to the trunks by a leather strap, the corpses dripping blood that mingled with the rain.

They had voluntarily braved their own artillery fire and stayed behind to pick off select targets, especially tank commanders.

So the turret Besa gunners sprayed all the treetops they could reach on maximum elevation.

Sapper Shoreland and his colleagues added materially to the foot soldiers' score.

The complex stood among smoking shell holes, torn-up earth and scattered tree shards. A Pepper-Pot stonk had been in progress while the armour was manoeuvring into position.

Each emplacement resembled a huge circular domed cake tin, but constructed of four-inch-thick steel set in two feet of concrete, with three embrasures giving all-round traverse and sited with its neighbours for mutual support.

The pillbox to Armadillo's immediate front sported formidable field pieces though for the present, they were silent.

With good reason.

Graham's brain still felt numb from the horrendous tumult of the Pepper-Pot pounding but it had doubtless left the enemy gun crews in a much worse state of disorientation.

However, despite being repeatedly gouged by direct hits, the massive concrete structures were, as anticipated, essentially intact.

So now it was time for 'The Drill.'

"Smoke," said a calm voice in Graham's headset.

It was that of the local commander, another Grenadier Churchill officer.

Gun tanks to right and left of Armadillo lobbed smoke bombs at the neighbouring pill-boxes, effectively blinding the defenders even if they had been alert enough to retaliate.

The tactic was a suitable complement to the Pepper-Pot.

"Belt and braces," the boys called it.

"Post," said the Grenadier.

Seventy-five mm rounds slammed with banging reports and spurting smoke into the pillbox's frontal embrasures. The procedure, as indicated by the order, was called "Posting a letter."

No one moved from the pillbox.

"Dustbin," said the guardsman.

Graham switched to the intercom.

"Pillbox seventy yards direct front, fire," he ordered Ferrarby.

The stubby, two hundred and ninety mm charge arced into its target and opened up the embrasure with a shattering roar. A blizzard of concrete and steel fragments burst through the eruption of smoke from the explosion.

Graham observed movement and radioed the local commander.

"Enemy surrendering, sir," he said.

Coated in dust and shaking, the gun crew clambered out of their subterranean lair with hands up, under the watchful eyes of Scots infantry and tank machine gunners.

Had the enemy remained ensconced, the Drill entailed a fourth command.

"Flame."

Shep Tyson's crocs had followed the paths beaten out by Graham's AVREs and were on hand to do the business if needed.

They weren't.

Their foes knew 'The Drill,' too.

All the Siegfried defences in this sector were similarly dealt with, eliciting praise from the Grenadier CO.

"We've achieved a major breakthrough, lads. Excellent work," he said at a debriefing beside his Churchill when the combined force leaguered in the rainy dusk on the northeast edge of the forest.

"Wolf's Berg's been secured as well, sir," said Kinross.

"Splendid effort, Ian," the Grenadier said. "But once we leave the forest, a lot of the way to Cleve is under water, so it's going to be one hell of a party tomorrow."

"What's the latest on casualty evacuation, sir?" Kinross asked.

"Kangaroos are still getting through, though it's a slow grind," said the guardsman.

"Hard for the boys with WP burns," said Stoughton, whose sappers had joined the combined force. Some German positions had resisted attacks with phosphorus grenades.

"As usual, Hod, the lads are amazingly long-suffering," the CO said. He took out his pipe, filled and lit it. "The RAMC boys tell them that the nurses at the CCSs up near Nijmegen are the most beautiful girls in the world. I think that helps."

Graham and Kinross trudged through stodgy soil back to their respective bivouacs after the briefing. Towards Cleve and in a long arc southwards, the night sky flickered and rumbled to the sound of artillery.

"My lads are like automatons, Steve," said the Scotsman tersely. "They'll not let up, of course but they've been on the go for forty hours, on top of the fifteen we spent moving up. How're your boys doing?"

"Pretty well flayed out, Ian, especially the drivers and wireless ops," said Steve. Blinking away raindrops, he glanced up into the darkness and low cloud. "But with all this tree bashing, on top of ploughing through mud for hours on end, we're going to be needing spare parts for the AVREs pretty soon. Otherwise we'll all be packing Stens and joining your lads."

Graham felt keenly for the dogged infantry, who, as usual, were bearing the brunt of everything, often with nothing between them and death or injury than the thickness of a BD blouse. Kinross had come up by carrier with his brigade and his HQ was a muddy weapons pit with gas capes as the only protection from the elements.

But the sappers were greatly beholden to their squaddie comrades. Despite their exhaustion, the foot soldiers maintained an impenetrable barrier between would-be nighttime enemy marauders and the precious AVREs.

"We'd be glad to have you, Steve," said Ian. "Though I hope you can keep on with your speciality."

"So do I, Ian," said Graham earnestly as they parted.

Cleve, February 1945.
Graham heard Napper's voice in his ears via the B set.
"Bet Bluff Hal's missus wouldn't recognise the place, skipper."
"Right enough, Mark," said Graham into the mike. "Not exactly the setting for a Renaissance painting."

The quaint Medieval Rhineland city of Cleve had been the ancestral home of Henry the Eighth's fourth wife, Anne of Cleves.

Now, utter destruction met the eye in every direction. The desolation resulting from more than a thousand tons of bombs unleashed by the Royal Air Force had been fearfully extended during the two-day tank-infantry battle for the town's capture.

Along with many of its defenders, hundreds of Cleve's citizens lay dead.

Blackstone's and Yeardley's troops had led the way, with Graham's troop in reserve, coming up during the closing stages of the battle to petard and machine-gun the most recalcitrant of the remaining enemy positions.

"Eight hours late at the start line but Heaven knows how we got there at all," Blackstone reported over the wireless after the fall of the town. "The water came up a foot and a half on the main road. Unsealed byways just dissolved into quicksand. Swallowed everything, rubble, furniture, even civilian cars and knocked out Jerry halftracks."

Graham's troop knew only too well. They had been assisting Stoughton's field company with road maintenance again, piling stones, bricks, logs and straw bales into flooded stretches in a desperate attempt to achieve some kind of stable surface, while icy sleet driven horizontally before a gusting wind stung their faces.

Everyone's clothing was by now permanently wet and plastered with mud but tank crews could at least retreat to their vehicles.

Inside their armoured shelters, the driver or co-driver would sit with a paraffin pressure stove jammed between his knees to boil water for a brew, while the rest of the crew spread jam on biscuits and opened compo tins for the evening concoction that they heated in mess tins by the same method.

It was a procedure the crews had used since their training in England and made life a little more bearable during those bleak winter days.

Everyone was puzzled about the absence of self-warming tins of soup that had been such a boon in Holland but the mystery was never solved.

"B Echelon's probably nicked 'em," the lads reckoned, though it was more likely that with the concentration of troops in the area, these heaven-sent items were simply in short supply.

An abundance of them would definitely have benefited the infantry. Many of them had also been drafted in to help with road repair and continued to suffer in the open on returning to their sodden weapons pits.

Nevertheless, the Lowland and Highland Brigades, together with the recently arrived Wessex Division, secured Cleve after two days and a night of sustained attacks.

Graham led his troop through the town along a churned-up furrow of slimy earth littered with debris. Talbot and the other drivers negotiated difficult turns to avoid shell holes and bomb craters.

Standing half out of their hatches, the commanders and wireless operators stared at the almost continuous heaps of jagged brickwork, naked rafters, scattered timbers and twisted metal railings. Several bulldozers were at work, treads squealing as they smashed through piles of bricks to extend more routes through the town.

Any houses left standing consisted of little else but interconnected walls with the occasional remnant of roofing.

"It all looks worse in the rain, sir," said Shoreland.

"It is, Boff," his officer said.

Graham's mind was preoccupied with the squadron's next destination, where it would support the Scots and Wessex Divisions in their efforts to capture a heavily fortified town about fifteen miles south, beyond the eastern fringe of the Reichswald.

A hub of the Siegfried defences, surrounded by anti-tank ditches, the town augured another bitter, groping slog.

Even its name portended as much.

Goch.

For the best part of a week, the infantry battle for the Cleve-Goch road seethed night and day, mostly in the rain but with the blessing of one clear day that enabled fighter-bombers to strike hard at the defenders.

Having cleared the enemy from the Reichswald to the west and Cleve Forest to the east, the infantry continued its southward push, with the Wessex Division in the van for the Goch escarpment.

While Blackstone's squadron refitted its vehicles and prepared for the attack on Goch itself.

It leaguered in some abandoned farms, located on a sidetrack east of the main road and south of the ruins of Cleve. The occasion was therapeutic. Battling through the forest, breaking the Siegfried Line and supporting the capture of Cleve had been hard on crews and vehicles. Constantly mud-stained, wet and chilly, partly deafened by repeated banging of shellfire, everyone was becoming increasingly edgy and with every flick of the wireless switch, Graham could sense the tautening of nerve ends, including his own.

"It's as well we've got a breather," said Blackstone at the first briefing he held in the leaguer. "I'd rather not face another shindig without a chance to refit."

In addition to those caused by enemy action, tank losses through bogging and mechanical failure had been heavy but Blackstone's squadron was still at full strength. Now it could at least minimise the risk of breakdowns.

Vehicles were dispersed beside outbuildings or around cement quadrangles enclosed on three sides by barns and stables, where the men bivouacked and beyond which dug the latrines. Officers and senior NCOs took up residence in the farmhouses. These actually possessed flush toilets but they weren't working. Shellfire had blown in many water mains.

All livestock was gone. Even Crittenden couldn't locate any.

"Squaddies picked the area clean, sir," he told Steve.

Not a stick of furniture remained in the houses, either. Nevertheless, sufficient wood was scrounged from the forest for lighting fires on the clear day to dry out clothes, strung from manila cord fastened between the AVREs and adjacent buildings.

The wood was wet but as Hazeldene said, "Just needs a dollop of petrol to get it going, sir. Stand back, though."

Several piles of kindling were soon merrily ablaze.

"Good thing we're not likely to be visited by either of your dear ladies right now, sirs," Crittenden remarked to Graham and Napper while they stood semi-naked beside the fires for warmth, gas capes draped over their shoulders.

"I hope an event of that sort would precipitate a rush for the clotheslines, Bill," said Napper, with a mock frown.

"You can count on us to be chivalrous, sir," rejoined Crittenden cheerfully.

That day, the troop did get some visitors, who threw chivalry to the winds.

Despite the dearth of poultry and meat on the hoof, or trotter, Crittenden had unearthed a quantity of cooking apples in a hidden recess of the farm's kitchen scullery. MacGee and Tomlinson, the troop culinary experts, fired up the kitchen's wood stove that was still intact and transformed the fruit into several pies, using ground-up biscuits, bully and sausage fat and sugar.

They left two of them to cool on the sill of a kitchen window that opened onto the track by the farm.

When a platoon of Lowland Jocks trudged past, the pies went with them.

"All over in a second, sir, while I was rolling pastry and my back was turned," MacGee said plaintively to Graham, who was overseeing a vehicle maintenance check.

"I'd just nipped out for some more wood, sir," Tomlinson explained forlornly.

Bill Crittenden looked up from helping to unbolt Arquebus's engine cover plate.

"Well, lads," he said with a hint of stoicism. "They've been nicking cattle from us Sassenachs for hundreds of years. A couple of pies'd be a pushover."

However, spirits were lifted when units of the divisional Assault Park Squadron arrived. With lorries alternately towing each other out of successive bogs, they had struggled along congested roads still mired and flooded to transport the components for fascines and SBGs, together with petrol, ammunition, AVRE parts, paraffin for stoves, compo rations and jerry cans of water in abundance.

These last were particularly welcome because during the days following the capture of Cleve, the troops had possessed only sufficient water for brewing tea – and on one dismal, rain-soaked evening, not even that.

Now they could wash and shave.

Moreover, the senior logistics warrant officer even dispensed a ration of rum.

"You lads are quids in here," he informed the troop as they queued enthusiastically for their tots of the fiery liquid. "The Canadians have been island hopping further north."

So intense was the flooding nearer the Rhine, where the Canadian divisions were engaged, that DUKWs and Buffalo amphibians from Seventy-Ninth Armoured had been ferrying assault troops across open water under a screen of smoke and HE to invest enemy positions located on isolated patches of high ground.

Fighting continued to growl away to the east, where the Canadians were pushing towards Calcar, and to the south, where, several days after the fall of Cleve, a battalion from the Wessex 'Wyverns' reported triumphantly, "We're on the Goch escarpment. We can see the chimneys, on a front of four thousand yards."

The weather closed in yet again, making fighter-bomber close support impossible but bombs from a second massive RAF night raid were thudding into Goch when Blackstone's squadron debouched from its leaguers under cover of darkness.

Its AVREs were armed and readied.

Goch, February 1945.

The unprepossessing factory conurbation of sombre brickworks and bleak stone terraced tenements was becoming a magnet for several British divisions.

Highland and Lowland Scots, Wessex and Guards Armoured were all converging on the town's forbidding outskirts.

Together with units of specialised armour.

In column of route, three of Graham's AVREs lumbered cautiously along a side road leading into the northern edge of Goch, Armadillo in the lead, Arquebus and Adamant following with SBGs. Napper's half-troop would come up with fascines as soon as these were loaded and they would be accompanied by a formation of Grenadiers' gun tanks.

It was late afternoon and in addition to the effects of fading daylight and pattering rain, drifting fog marred the drivers' vision. Fortunately, however, telegraph poles lining the left side of the road helped them maintain direction. The air raids had concentrated on the town itself so that the approach roads were relatively uncratered though prolonged shelling had broken away most of the cross trees atop the poles and they hung limply down, the attached wires almost trailing on the ground.

"Getting close to the outer ditch, sir, according to the speedo," said Talbot over the intercom.

Two anti-tank ditches surrounded Goch. The Wessex Division had seized several crossing places over the outer ditch in a night attack, allowing Highland and Lowland Brigades to move through and close up on the inner ditch, while the Wyverns' divisional engineers strengthened the causeways for the passage of tanks, working throughout the night with retaliatory shells falling uncomfortably close.

"OK, Crash," said Graham. "Keep on but slow down."

He shivered. The chill of the fog seemed to be penetrating to the bone. Then a gaunt, mud-stained figure in battledress and helmet loomed out of the gloom, waving, with Sten in one hand.

Graham ordered the half-troop to halt, noting other armed and helmeted shapes dimly visible to either side of the AVREs. They were all British.

"Sergeant Deakin, sir, Wiltshire Regiment," the figure said in a tired voice with a distinct West Country accent as Armadillo drew to a stop.

"Lieutenant Graham, Sergeant, AVRE One Troop. Causeway just ahead?"

"Just ahead, sir. And it's solid. Boches haven't left any mines here, it seems. We reckon they'll have sown 'em in the town."

A nasty possibility and Graham swallowed hard. If they had reversed the mine laying strategy of Normandy, the Channel Ports and the Siegfried defences encountered earlier, the Germans had greatly exacerbated the armour's problem of supporting the infantry in the narrow thoroughfares of Goch.

"Very likely, Sergeant," Steve called down from his hatch, trying to sound casual. "Anyway, we'll push on. Another AVRE half-troop to follow, with fascines. Guards' tanks are on their way, too."

"Right you are, sir," said Deakin. "A thousand yards to the inner ditch. You'll have no trouble between here and there but the Jocks bumped Jerry as soon as they got to the ditch, as you can hear from the commotion."

The NCO pointed through the fog, in the direction of the unmistakable snarl and thump of small arms, both friend and foe.

"Boches're holed up in houses, sir," he continued. "And there's more Jerries in the brickworks further back. Like fortresses, they are. Even with the bombing, lads'll be needin' your cannon, I reckon, soon as you've dropped those bridges. Watch out for *panzerfausts*, though."

"We'll do our best, Sergeant," said Graham. "Thanks for the gen."

He ordered Talbot to advance and the other drivers to follow.

"You're welcome, sir," said the Wessex man. He tilted his helmet back with thumb and forefinger. "God speed. But while I think of it, Jerries have most likely got bazookas, too."

Graham waved and smiled as Armadillo chugged past.

"Best we get on, sir," said Shoreland. "Before he thinks of something else."

As the Churchills approached the inner ditch through clinging murk made worse by bitter tasting smoke still swirling in the aftermath of the bombing, Graham noticed another smell permeating the familiar reek of HE.

Death.

"Air raids killed loads of civilians, sir," Shoreland remarked. "Bodies from the first one have had time to decompose, I reckon."

The small arms fire was growing much louder and Graham could glimpse the pulsating glow of tracer where Jock and German were exchanging fire up ahead.

A line of trees gradually took shape ahead, cutting across that of the telegraph poles. The trees marked the near side of the second ditch. Like the poles, they too were partly shot away.

"A carrier's been hit, sir," said Shoreland grimly.

Graham nodded and ordered another halt. He had already noted the smouldering remains among the trees. About a hundred yards beyond, he could discern through the mist a line of houses. The bombing and the barrage had smashed in several of them.

"Delta One to Echo One and Fox One," said Graham into his mike. "Houses appear to be occupied by friendly forces. Will confirm."

The gunfire from the houses sounded distinctly British, directed no doubt at the erstwhile occupants who had taken out the carrier.

It had been within *panzerfaust* range, certainly within German bazooka range. Several other Kangaroos, apparently undamaged and now empty apart from their crews, had pulled back and ranged themselves by the side of the road. These would act as ambulances. Graham's troop had passed more of the carriers on the way up, heading back to collect reinforcements and ammunition.

They had also passed a number of carriers already in use as ambulances, converging onto the road from various parts of the battle front and packed with their suffering cargoes.

"Will make direct contact with infantry," Graham informed Crittenden and Hazeldene. "Stand by."

The "Wilco, sir," acknowledgements sounded in his ears.

"Push on a bit further, Crash," Graham said to his driver.

When he sensed they were nearing the infantry positions, Steve ordered Talbot to halt. Then, doffing his headset, he climbed down from Armadillo and cautiously walked forward into the rainy gloom until he heard a sentry's challenge.

Steve identified himself to the crouching figure half concealed by a hedgerow. A low whisper relayed the information and Brigade Major Kinross emerged to summon Graham into the recently-dug ditch beside the hedge that constituted his HQ. The Lowland Brigade was spread out along the inner ditch, with intense firing to right and left indicating where additional crossings were being forced.

Strictly speaking, Kinross should have been with Brigade HQ, located further back but he always stayed with the leading companies.

"Jerries in those houses caught one of the carriers with a bazooka, Steve," he explained, pointing. "And we lost some of the boys but the forward company went across the ditch on foot. They're pushing the Boche out of the houses and securing them."

Steve turned up the collar of his smock. Raindrops were spitting against his face.

"We'll drop the SBGs and go across to support your lads, Ian," said Graham. "The aerial photos show the brickworks only a couple of blocks beyond those houses."

"Aye," said the Scotsman. "The lads in the houses report they can see the chimneys. I'll show you the ditch. The ground's not too bad hereabouts, stodgy but tankable. No craters but there might be some closer to the town."

"We can fill three of them with fascines before the advance," said Graham. "Mark's bringing them up."

"Might be enough to go on with," said Ian.

The two of them crept forward through rain-soaked grass until they came upon a reserve company of Jocks lining the edges of the ditch. Graham crouched down beside a charred tree stump and stared at the obstacle's construction. He saw that it was thickly concreted for some distance either side of where it intersected the road. The enemy had not had enough time – or cement - to finish the concrete overlay and the assaulting Jocks had scaled the far wall via the earthen surface where the concrete ended – first checking for booby traps.

"Eight feet deep, less than twenty feet wide," Steve said to the major. "A Churchill's twenty-four. I'll send for my lads to drop the bridges and we'll take Armadillo straight across now."

"You can do that?" the major asked in surprise.

"Just watch us," said Graham.

"Well, Private McLaughlin and I will go over when you do," said Kinross, indicating his batman, the sentry who had challenged Graham. "I'd like to visit Battalion HQ."

"OK, Ian."

Steve glanced at the luminous dial of his watch. "The rest of the troop should be up fairly soon and the Guards."

Listening to the volume of Bren bursts and rifle fire that thumped and crackled from the houses, Graham hoped the carriers returning with ammunition wouldn't be much longer, either.

Kinross detailed McLaughlin to escort Graham back to Armadillo. The stolid rifleman was almost jaunty with the prospect of the armoured intervention.

"We'd been lying out in the rain for hours, sir," he said. "When you came, you looked like slow-moving monsters. Aye, but we'll fight our way through now."

Graham hoped his troop would vindicate his wiry companion's confidence. The Scots brigades had been in action almost continuously since joining the battle and were out on their feet but Graham knew that as long as they could stand and hold a weapon, they would fight on.

"We'll do our best to clear the way, Private McLaughlin," he said.

To the fascination of the watching infantry, Talbot drove Armadillo straight off the road into the ditch. Treads scraping and engine roaring at full throttle, the AVRE began to ascend the farther side while its rear end was still sliding down the nearer wall.

Armadillo was eventually wedged horizontally in the concrete hollow. Talbot then engaged the Churchill's 'neutral gear' that enabled one track to reverse while the other continued in the forward direction.

With its driver swinging the tiller bar violently back and forth, still maintaining full power, Armadillo lurched right and left until it climbed crabwise onto level ground[195].

A rousing Scots cheer went up. Kinross and McLaughlin joined Steve and his crew when Armadillo halted on the roadway beyond the ditch. Flashes, bangs and cracks still issued from the houses. Stray enemy rounds occasionally whipped overhead

"Your lad's a genius, Steve," said Kinross in admiration.

"No end to our talents, Ian," Steve said modestly. "You and I had better go the rest of the way on foot. Make sure there are no craters between here and the houses."

Graham ordered Crittenden and Hazeldene forward, removed his headset and leapt into the road, hoping he wouldn't have to use the Sten gun he carried.

The rain persisted but the mist had lifted sufficiently to reveal a low cloud base. Pale searchlight beams reflecting off the cloud shed a showery bluish glow over crushed and bomb-savaged buildings from which snarling tracer still spat in opposite directions across deserted, torn-up thoroughfares littered with chunks of brick and stone.

The searchlights were known as 'Monty's Moonlight,' after the army group commander. They enabled tank and infantry machine gunners to harass defenders in the enemy occupied ruins, identified by signallers in the forward positions, in touch with Battalion HQ.

This was happening all around the Goch perimeter.

Blackstone's and Yeardley's troops were in action to either flank of Graham's. Further to the right, another AVRE squadron was supporting the Highlanders' efforts to break into Goch from the west, together with elements of the Guards and the famous 'Desert Rats' Armoured Divisions.

Napper's AVREs would transport their fascines across the SBGs at first light. The remainder of Graham's troop closed up with the Jocks, now reinforced by the reserve company, and halted their Churchills in battered side streets where the rubble and remains of houses provided cover while still permitting good fields of fire.

Graham stared through his periscope, relaying instructions to his crews from Battalion HQ, established in what was left of a corner house in a cul-de-sac where Armadillo was positioned.

"Gillie to AVRE Delta One. Enemy activity, two-storey house, two hundred yards, one o'clock, Armadillo sector," said the battalion wireless operator. The target sectors were divided up according to the locations of Graham's AVREs.

Armadillo's alert gunners had seen the muzzle flashes, the bombing having enhanced the field of vision.

"Four second burst, hull and co-ax engage," said Graham to Illingworth and Shoreland, over the intercom.

Two simultaneous staccato roars sent twin tracks of blue tracer rocketing into the rain-streaked half-light. Spent cartridges rattled harshly onto the Churchill's floor, along with ejected belt links.

A pause, then Battalion HQ was on the air again.

"Thanks, AVRE Delta One. Can you order up another burst, please?"

Graham complied. Afterwards, his gunners fed fresh belts to their weapons.

Hunched as usual on the toolbox behind Talbot, Drac Stoker voiced his discontent.

"Up to our necks in brass if this goes on all night," he growled.

It did, in each sector, wherever the enemy was spotted. Occasionally, a target shot back and Spandau bullets ricocheted off the Churchills' hulls, clanging like massive gongs. Retaliation in kind was intense and invariably the other side eventually desisted.

Graham radioed the squadron's B Echelon in the early hours. It had leaguered within sight of the outer ditch.

"AVRE Delta One to Grandma's House. We are in urgent need of Besa ammunition," he said. "Over."

Steve's crewmen were collecting spent links and cartridges.

Before dawn, ammunition was replenished in abundance. It would be needed.

Morning brought chill and more drizzle. The AVRE crews again had to resort to scrounged seventy-five mm casings in which to relieve themselves. Getting rid of solid wastes meant the usual dash out the side door, spade in hand. They breakfasted lightly on hardtack, bully, and heavily sugared tea, brewed on the portable pressure stoves.

Steve gazed through his periscope and scratched the stubble on his jaw. No time for shaving or washing now. Water was dripping onto his shoulder. As usual, the turret hatches were leaking.

He heard the battalion wireless operator's voice in his ears.

"Gillie to AVRE Delta One. Large craters in streets leading to brickworks. Can you fill, over?"

"Wilco, Gillie. Bringing up fascines," said Steve. "Please confirm exact location, over."

The wireless operator did so and on Graham's orders, Napper's AVREs crept down by-roads that led to the brickworks complex, the devastated buildings on both sides now occupied by the Scots infantry. Mark leant out a side door, giving directions to his driver. Amazon cautiously surmounted piles of masonry in its path, tracks crunching the obdurate fragments.

The Churchill paused in front of the nearer of two bomb craters that obstructed the road. Napper's order came over the B set.

"Release fascine," Graham heard him say.

The guncotton charge banged, the restraining cables parted and the bundle dropped forward.

"Crater negotiable, Steve," Napper reported.

"OK, Mark, well done," said Graham.

Amazon reversed out of the way and Napper ordered up Kinnear in Arrowhead, who successfully repeated the process for the second crater. Briers in Alligator filled a third crater, discovered on a parallel approach road.

This meant that all the available fascines were used. Graham therefore dispatched Hazeldene in Adamant and Corporal Briers in Alligator to fetch two more from B Echelon. Their absence would severely stretch the remainder of his troop but Goch had received such a concentrated pounding from the RAF that the likelihood of more crater obstructions was higher than in the battle for the Channel Ports. The force commanders were forced to strike a balance.

"Sorry to have to send you back again, lads," Steve said to his NCOs via the B set.

"Never ones to hog the limelight, sir," said Briers.

"We'll second that, sir," Hazeldene added.

Steve wished that at least one armoured bulldozer and a troop of flame tanks were to hand but such as were still functioning could not be spared from other tasks. Moreover, the weather was still too inclement for air support.

And most of the flails were now out of commission, either by breakdown or bogging. The rest were deployed elsewhere.

Growling of gunfire indicated that the battle was getting underway on the flanks.

Graham advanced the troop to the start line.

This consisted of a main road that ran between the blocks of houses from which the Jocks had driven the enemy and a stone wall, now mostly broken-down, that enclosed the factory proper. The wall ran for a mile to left and right and the factory stretched southwards about the same distance to the River Niers that cut the town in two, from east to west.

Infantry scouts confirmed during the night that the arterial road, fortuitously not cratered, was free of mines.

"We don't know about the factory roads," Battalion reported tersely.

Engines muttering, AVREs and gun tanks were poised in the side streets, crews awaiting the order to advance, infantry and supporting sappers on foot crouching in the lee of the vehicles, shivering in the rain, breathing a mixture of dank air, brick dust and exhaust fumes. All reserves had now closed up for the assault.

"Let's go," said more than one exasperated foot-soldierly voice.

Via his periscope, Graham scrutinised through slanting rain several finger-like smokestacks that had somehow escaped the bombing. He noted where they abutted long, squat, sturdily constructed buildings, partially gouged out by bombing but otherwise apparently little damaged.

"Kilns," Graham said to his crews. "A lot of reinforced sections for the Boche to hide in. We'll petard the walls."

Steve saw that bomb bursts had dislocated extensive and formerly neatly-arranged stacks of manufactured bricks into ungainly heaps, creating more obstacles for vehicles and convenient niches for enemy sharpshooters. Intelligence reports indicated that civilian personnel had evacuated the factory after the fall of Nijmegen, giving the enemy several months to strengthen what Sergeant Deakin had rightly called, "fortresses."

"Armour advance," came the order from Battalion.

Graham's stomach turned over. He relayed the order to his troop.

The tanks' engines roared. The metal behemoths lurched across the road, crashed through the remnants of the stone wall and charged onto the wide forecourt of the works. Hull and co-axial machine gunners 'hosed' everything to their front, to cover the Jocks as they dashed forward to deploy. Bren gunners fired bursts at the first row of building complexes.

The gun tanks' seventy-fives and the AVREs' petards bellowed. Factory double doors and adjoining walls disintegrated in smoke, splinters and chards of brick. Infantrymen and field company sappers leapt through the cavities, covered by their mates. Automatic firing and crack of grenades sounded from the insides, followed by heavier bangs as the sappers dealt with internal fortifications by means of portable charges.

Elsewhere, the enemy hit back. From the disarranged brick stacks and narrow wall vents in kiln sets further back, Spandau bursts savaged the attackers.

Suddenly, enemy mortar bombs were crashing around the tanks and HE shells were exploding in profusion on the forecourt. The foot soldiers had fortuitously closed up on the buildings but a suspected concealed danger for tanks was quickly made manifest.

As it approached the first kiln set, now partly secured, to escape the shelling, a gun Churchill slewed to a halt with a huge bang and gout of smoke, one track torn away. The crew baled out and headed for the kiln building. Squaddies helped them drag a couple of wounded.

"Gun tank mined at access road entrance," Graham reported to his crews. "It is possible these are all mined. Drivers, keep your eyes skinned."

Steve had earlier relayed Deakin's warning to them. Asphalt dislodged and re-laid had to mean mines but the locations were not always easy to spot among the detritus of bombing and shelling.

With dire consequences for One Troop.

Steve heard Napper's voice via the B set. He had chilling news. His Churchills were travelling on a parallel axis to Graham's, against an adjacent kiln set and similar opposition.

"AVRE Able One to AVRE Delta One, AVRE Baker One mined at entrance to kiln access road. Track lost."

Beads of cold sweat broke out on Graham's forehead.

"Delta One to Able One," he said with mounting apprehension. "Casualties, over?"

"Full bale out, Delta One," said Napper. "No serious injuries, thank God but they'll have to take their chances with the squaddies."

Not an easy option under the present onslaught for men bruised and shaken but none other was to be had.

"Roger, Able One," said Graham, with relief. "Gun tank mined in similar position in this sector. Must assume all entrances to access roads mined. AVRE One Troop, stand by."

Most of the bombardment was still falling providentially to the rear, because the armour, like the infantry, had crossed the forecourt expanse. Graham ordered Shoreland to raise Battalion but the Scots' CO pre-empted him.

"Battalion, sir" said Shoreland. Graham switched to the A set.

"Gillie to AVRE Delta One, situation report, over," sounded in his earphones.

"AVRE Delta One to Gillie, under concentrated Spandau, mortar and shellfire, though most ordinance overshooting," said Graham. "First sector of kiln sets and storage buildings invested. One gun Churchill and one AVRE mined at entrances to access roads. Suspect all entrances mined. Can implement new drill. Over."

Steve was forced to shout above the clamour outside and the amplified banging of the Spandau rounds off the Armadillo's exterior. Inside, everyone's eyes were streaming from the cordite, gun oil vapour and petard propellant smoke.

The new drill had been worked out at a combined O Group during the night.

"Negative, AVRE Delta One," came the response. "Field company sappers will clear immediate sectors. Use new drill for subsequent sectors."

It was agreed that REs on foot would shift the first cluster of mines if enough could be spared from their main task of infantry support. AVRE teams would take over the job as the assault progressed and their field company comrades-in-arms became increasingly preoccupied with building clearance, especially if their own casualties mounted.

"Wilco, Gillie," said Graham. "Will provide fire support."

Steve relayed the information to Napper and Crittenden.

In between enemy salvoes and covered by heavy MG fire, sappers on the ground lifted enough mines for the AVREs to penetrate the kiln sites. Armadillo, Amazon and Arquebus petarded their foes in the rear ends of the complexes into silence, blowing out great chunks of wall on each side of their respective axes, aided by gun tanks.

The armour charged forward, their clanking treads surmounting rubble heaps, crushing masonry. Steve switched to the intercom.

Suddenly he noticed a flash from a nearby brick stack.

"*Panzerfaust!*" he yelled into the mike.

Talbot had seen it. He swerved Armadillo and the missile struck a glancing blow on the rear of the AVRE's hull, erupting in flame.

Graham shouted directions to Ferrarby and Armadillo's petard mortar boomed.

Amid the mighty shower of smoke and debris, Graham saw half a human form cartwheel into the air.

"Well done, gunner!" he said exultantly. "Hull and co-ax gunners, keep up covering fire," he ordered the troop.

The intrepid Jocks wormed their way through the brick maze under the armoured fire support. With rifle, Bren, Sten and grenade, they steadily accounted for other bazooka crews and their Spandau colleagues.

All at once, enemy mortar rounds were exploding around the kilns.

Steve contacted Battalion again.

"At least one *panzerfaust* taken out by petard, infantry have neutralised several more," He said. "Friendly artillery countering enemy shellfire but mortars now dropping in general area of advance. Over."

Shells from Allied twenty-five pounders north of Goch were whooshing overhead, ranging on German gun positions south of the town, spotted by forward observation officers attached to infantry patrols and in wireless communication with the gunners. The enemy gunners were forced to lift their fire to dual with their opposite numbers, though the Wehrmacht mortar teams had obviously altered their sights to keep harassing the attackers. Despite this impedance, the Scots infantry persevered, using all available cover. Battalion mortars retaliated against their German counterparts, approximating the range from the incoming bombs' observed trajectories.

Nevertheless, the enemy adjustments were a relief for the medics, who had established RAPs in cellars beneath the houses, amongst which the enemy shells had also been bursting. Fortunately, being of Teutonic construction, the cellars were sturdy. And thanks to the rain, the exposed timbers in the ruins would not catch fire.

B Echelon would simply have to get out of the way until the enemy guns were neutralised.

The CO's response came back.

"Well done, AVRE Delta One. We must press on to the river. Can take out the mortars on the way, own counter barrage in progress. Where are your reserves?"

"Two AVREs bringing up fascines," said Graham. "Should be here by fifteen hundred hours unless delayed by shellfire. Will use new drill from here on. Over."

"Roger, AVRE Delta One. Will inform companies. Out."

"Get Gun Baker Four," Steve said to Shoreland. "AVRE Delta One to Gun Baker Four," he said, when Boff had contacted the Grenadier Churchill leader. "Executing new drill, Derek. Keep up fire support. Over."

The measured tones of the Guards' tank commander, Captain Derek Jarren, came back over the wireless.

"Wilco, Steve. Ready when you are."

Graham breathed deeply and switched to the intercom. "Get your crowbar, Drac," he said to his explosives NCO, who constituted half of Armadillo's lifting team. Steve was the other half.

Armadillo, Arquebus and Amazon clattered past the first set of kilns onto the lateral road beyond it.

Napper, Crittenden and their explosives NCOs would also be undertaking the mine-clearing task.

To proceed to the next sector, brick stacks, kiln sets and buildings to the immediate front were gunned and petarded remorselessly, as in the initial phase of the assault. This tactic was helped by the absence of enemy A/T guns, now mostly knocked out, though as Captain Jarren remarked, "There's been enough of those blasted bazookas."

One bazooka rocket had ploughed into a gun Churchill's engine, igniting a conflagration and forcing the crew hastily to exit.

Tanks, infantry and foot sappers then advanced across the lateral road. Bren gunners, riflemen and tank machine gunners sprayed lead continuously within overlapping arcs of fire, keeping the enemies' heads down.

When the Churchills halted at the road entrances to the next block of kilns, the lifting teams leapt from the side doors and crawled forward on their bellies. First, they carefully crowbarred away the loose asphalt covering the mines and any rubble obstruction, keeping a sharp lookout for anti-personnel devices, though none were found. The mines were then lifted from their shallow cavities, disarmed and set aside.

Though hazardous, the procedure was more efficient than trying to explode the mines, because the detonators required the pressure of a tank tread to activate them.

Kinnear and his dismounted crew were keeping up with the Lowlanders and assisted the clearing teams. Their contribution speeded up the work considerably.

When the commanders returned to their vehicles and reported, "Road clear!" the combined force stormed forward, behind a steady rate of fire. AVREs and gun tanks smashed the buildings along their entire lengths and any remaining brick stacks or storage yards with petards and seventy-fives, obliterating many of the foes. The foot soldiers got the rest.

The drill was repeated for successive blocks of kiln sets.

As he ventured into the access roads, Steve kept his head down and prayed, his knees and elbows scraping uncomfortably over the harsh asphalt.

His throat had drained of saliva. His clothes were sodden with rain and perspiration, his hands greasy with grime and sweat. His temples pounded like trip hammers. All around was a howl of noise. At every instant, he cringed in mortal fear of a bullet's smashing impact. Each member of the lifting teams glanced up every couple of seconds, on the lookout for incoming mortar bombs. If necessary, he would yell a warning for the team to hasten beneath the protective bulk of the tanks.

"There has to be an easier way, Drac!" Steve shouted to Stoker on one occasion when they were forced to take cover.

"Let me know when you figure it out, sir!" the NCO shouted back. Both men were nearly deafened and visibly shaking.

As they emerged from beneath Armadillo, a dark stain suddenly materialised on Stoker's smock and he collapsed against Graham, crying, "God, sir, I've been hit!"

Graham helped him back underneath the AVRE. Steve reached over and pulled the field dressing from Drac's battledress trouser pocket. Thrusting it against the bloodied blotch on Stoker's chest, he shouted, "Medic, Medic!"

Concentrated Besa bursts from Armadillo and an adjacent gun tank and a deluge of infantry fire put paid to the sniper's audacity.

Steve could feel the sticky wetness on his fingers. They were reddened.

"They'll be here in a second, Drac!" he said vehemently.

Stoker lay with fists clenched and teeth gritted but he seemed to be breathing normally and no blood was coming out his mouth. Steve tried to reassure him.

"I don't think it's gone in, Drac," he said and shouted for the medics again.

The confined cavern where they lay on the unyielding road surface was like a furnace with the heat of the tank's engine. Graham knew with growing apprehension that they would have to move on soon, Stoker's wound notwithstanding.

To Steve's immense relief, RAMC orderlies wriggled underneath from the rear and quickly conveyed the wounded NCO to the safety of the adjacent kiln set, occupied by Scots infantry.

"I'll take over from Drac, sir, when next we have to," said Talbot when Steve scrambled back inside the Churchill.

"You're on, Crash," said Graham, fitting his headset back on.

Gradually, the drill took effect. The enemy resistance weakened. The counter fire became more intermittent; the bazooka teams were either killed or captured, likewise most of the mortar crews north of the river, constantly harried by Battalion mortars and unable to replenish ammunition. Clearing all vestiges of opposition and securing each kiln set necessitated lengthy delays between bounds but these intervals enabled B Echelon elements to re-supply the assault force with petards, shells, grenades and ball ammunition.

The thin-skinned transport bravely ran the gauntlet of the stubborn defenders' residual mortar and artillery rounds.

"You feel like a duck in a shootin' gallery, sir," the senior logistics warrant officer told Graham.

In other sectors, despite savage enemy resistance initially, Highland and Lowland infantry, bolstered by Guards, Wyverns and Desert Rats, were making good progress with their armoured support.

In Graham's area, bomb craters again barred the way.

Though as anticipated, more had been encountered in the battle through the thoroughfares, the roads were wide enough for them to be avoided.

Unfortunately, on what would be the last bound to the Niers, two large craters overlapped and could not easily be bypassed. The RAF had used the river to mark their bombing runs and the ruination was here most intense.

It was opportune, therefore, that Corporals Hazeldene and Briers should arrive with fascines.

They also brought tragic news. Hazeldene radioed Graham, his voice distraught.

"Reverend Potter's been killed, sir. Shell burst near his jeep when he was coming up to assist in the RAP. Driver got out with his legs broken but they couldn't do owt[196] for the reverend. Captain Yeardley's been killed, too, sir. Bazooka brewed his tank. Four of the boys got out."

Graham's stomach churned. He was beside himself with shock and grief but he tried to sound calm in replying to Hazeldene.

"OK, Fox One. Thanks for the report. Proceed on present course with AVRE Charlie One for fascine drop. We've lifted the mines up to here and will cover you for the drops. Over."

"Wilco, Delta One," said Hazeldene. "Over and out."

When Hazeldene and Briers approached, Besas, petards and seventy-fives blazed right and left in support, shattering brickwork and sending debris skyward enveloped in smoke and dust. Adamant and Alligator crawled noisily in bottom gear over scattered rubble to deposit their bundles in the huge pits.

They rejoined the troop. The way ahead was clear. Talbot steered Armadillo over the chespale poles that crackled beneath the AVRE's tracks.

"Coming to a scrapyard, sir," said Talbot over the intercom. "River's beyond that."

Graham gazed from his hatch. He saw an extensive enclosure, transformed by the bombing into an indescribable tangle of wreckage but which seemed to consist mainly of discarded winding house gear and engine parts, together with vast amounts of building refuse, including a pile of corrugated iron roofing.

That heap worried him. It shouldn't have been like that, not after the bombing.

"AVRE One Troop, halt," he ordered. "Get Gun Baker Four, Boff."

After the successful gapping of the craters, AVRE and Grenadier Churchills had reached the scrapyard in almost extended line, with the infantry close behind. Individual rifle shots and short automatic bursts indicated where the last of the enemy resistance to the rear was being cleaned out.

Only the occasional enemy shell now whined overhead against the supporting Allied barrage and although still a nuisance for the infantry, the mortar rain had virtually ceased. The last few admonitory rounds came from batteries south of the Niers. They received swift and abundant retribution from Battalion mortars before the armour and infantry force assaulting the southern half of Goch took them out.

The natural rain continued unabated. Everything looked smoky, grey and greasy.

Steve's Churchills drew to a stop, hugging such of the ruins as they could for cover. The accompanying Grenadier tanks followed suit. Everyone was wary, apprehensive of what might eventuate when they attempted to crash through the obstacle before them, in the final bound to the river.

"Gun Baker Four, sir," said Shoreland.

Jarren's voice spoke in Steve's earphones via the A set.

"Gun Baker Four to AVRE Delta One. What can we do for you, Steve?"

"Reference heap of tin, Derek, two o'clock from my direct front. About two-fifty yards from you. Could you please put a seventy-five through it? It's out of petard range."

"Roger, wilco, Steve," came the calm response. "Moving into position – "

Before Jarren could complete his message, Steve watched in horror as the tin heap fell apart and the unmistakable, monstrous bulk of a dreaded *Jagd-panther* lurched into view.

Its massive eighty-eight mm gun roared. A yellow-blue flash, a disintegrating wall and Amazon, to Armadillo's left, bucked on its tracks. Graham distinctly heard the mighty bang of the direct hit.

"One Troop, advance!" yelled Steve into the mike. "He can't get us all. Gunners, put down smoke. Petard when in range."

The four AVREs revved forward, grinding through the debris, firing smoke bombs from the turret mortars. To the flanks, Jarren's Grenadier Churchills manoeuvred to bring their seventy-fives to bear.

It was the best strategy. The fighting of the past few days had accounted for most of the enemy's heavy armour and reports indicated the remainder had dispersed to seek opportune targets as the Allied armour pressed forward.

Steve guessed that the *Jagd* was operating alone – no other pile of debris in the scrapyard was big enough to hide another heavy tank – and it was therefore at a disadvantage, exacerbated by its turret construction that did not allow for the same traverse as a conventional gun tank.

Engulfed in black smoke, Amazon spurted flame, then exploded. Jagged pieces whirled in all directions.

Concentrating on the *Jagd*, Graham had not observed any bale-outs. By a conscious act of the will, he forced down the hideous thoughts that battered his brain.

The monster was pivoting to range on Armadillo when the first seventy-five mm shell slammed into its hide, though ricocheting off with a blood-chilling screech.

Then another burst against its track bogies, and another.

"Petard away!"

It was Briers's voice, via the B set. Having the clearest run, Alligator had closed the range.

The powerful charge blew away part of the *Jagd's* four-feet wide track. The beast was immobilised and through the tendrils of red-brown mortar smoke, Graham could see the crew baling out. The Jocks gathered them in.

"Drivers continue advance," Steve ordered his troop. "Proceed to river line."

"Message from Battalion, sir," said Shoreland. Graham switched to the A set frequency and his blood ran cold again at the clipped tones of the Battalion signaller.

"Brigade major killed. Snipers still active in sector. AVRE and gun tank troops report when you have reached river line. Over."

"Wilco, Gillie," said Graham woodenly. "Out."

With the demise of the *Jagd*, enemy resistance virtually ended. Only a few snipers in the scrapyard remained, determined to die for the Fatherland.

The attackers ensured that they did.

At dusk, the troops leaguered on the riverside edge of the scrapyard with, as usual, a screen of infantry bivouacked around them. Across the wide stretch of sluggish, rain-pocked water, rifle and machine gun fire echoed from the southern shore, hidden in mist and deepening twilight.

Steve and Derek donned gas capes, then trudged back through the chaos of the scrapyard past the wreck of the *Jagd* to Battalion HQ, set up in what had been an office block. It lay a short distance from the fascine-filled craters and, miraculously, still possessed most of its roof.

B Echelon vehicles slowly drove through drifting smoke and haze of brick dust towards the leaguer, bringing up petrol, rations and more ammunition.

"Be glad to get my head down tonight, Steve," said Derek.

They answered a sentry's challenge and stooped to enter the block via a narrow doorway. Beyond a blackout curtain, they came to a bullet-scarred interior lit by paraffin lamps.

Dog-tired though Graham was, his fatigue dissipated at the sight before him.

Major Kinross sat on an upturned ammunition box, conversing with the battalion CO. His right arm was wrapped in a sling, the shoulder heavily bandaged. Close by sat a jaded though ever watchful Private McLaughlin, cradling his rifle.

"Ian!" exclaimed Graham. "I heard a report you were dead."

"So did I," said the Scot nonchalantly. "Bit of a mix-up, that's all. There's someone else here you should speak to."

Graham was overjoyed to see Corporal Jevons step into the lamplight, clothing burnt and one arm covered in gauze but otherwise sound.

"We all got out, sir," he said to Graham. "Wall took the sting out of the hit – feet thick, it was. Shell cut through the hull – red hot it was – flashed some Cordtex and we caught fire. But it would've been worse if you hadn't halted the troop, sir. They've taken Mr Napper back to the CCS. Hit by exploding Besa ammo and got some burns but he's in one piece. The MO said he had a good chance. Rest of us aren't too bad, sir."

The corporal glanced at his injured arm.

Fighting a constriction in his throat, Graham thanked him.

"Best get yourself back to the RAP, Corporal," said the Scots colonel gently. Another part of the office block now housed this facility.

Jevons saluted and departed, casting a grateful glance at his troop commander.

After the briefing, Graham returned to his troop as they were brewing up, having finished what maintenance they could. Steve communicated the morale-boosting news about Amazon's crew and then outlined the troop's duties.

"Each crew to provide a two-man guard for tonight, lads, two-hour shifts. We'll be helping the field companies tomorrow. Bridge repair, putting up a Bailey, or both."

Crittenden handed Graham a steaming mug.

"All one to us, sir," he said. "We'll draw straws for the guard."

Steve lapsed into an exhausted sleep an hour or so later, huddled in his seat beneath a blanket.

In the midst of slumber, his distraught brain, still reeling from the trauma of the day, picked up a voice, using the words Private McLaughlin had uttered the previous night but twisting them into what seemed like a demonic whisper.

"Lying out in the rain. Slow-moving monsters. Fight through, FIGHT THROUGH!"

Steve awoke abruptly and nearly banged his head on the periscope mounting. All was quiet inside the tank, save for the rhythmic breathing of his sleeping crew and the drumming of the rain on the turret roof.

He climbed out the side door, emptied his bladder, then resumed his seat and fell asleep. The demon had departed, for now.

After having shaved and breakfasted in the drizzly half-light of the new day, Graham's sappers joined with Hod Stoughton's field company in gathering rubble to shore up a partially destroyed arched stone bridge across the Niers.

Some infantry had in the meantime crossed the river in storm boats. Others marched over the restored bridge, weighed down with weapons and ammunition, grimy and hollow-eyed, looking like zombies but nevertheless like soldiers too.

"Canny job, boys," said a Lowland voice as the helmeted column plodded past Houghton's and Graham's men now engaged in the assembly of a pontoon Bailey to facilitate vehicle crossings.

Major Blackstone visited each segment of his spread-out command. He too was saddened by the loss of Reverend Potter and standing with Graham on the muddy shore, he confirmed Julian's death.

"All over in a second, Steve," said the OC, raising his voice above the continuous growl of transport edging across the newly completed Bailey. Tank and infantry reserves were moving up to consolidate the southern half of Goch, where the last enemy defenders were being mopped up. "Bazooka team in a three-storey house," Blackstone went on. "Gun tank nailed 'em with a seventy-five, though. Four of the boys got out through the side doors but they couldn't do anything for Julian and his wireless op."

Graham paused to digest the details. With one hand he brushed some droplets off his beret.

"Where to, now, sir?" he asked.

Blackstone pointed to the southern shore.

"We'll move through Goch and rendezvous on the approach road to Xanten," he said. "Town'll be another gapping job for us, no doubt. It's the last major stronghold west of the Rhine. River's only about a mile or so from there."

"No flooding?"

The OC shook his head.

"Ground's a bit soggy in places. But nothing like the area east of Nijmegen. In the meantime, you should know you're squadron two-IC as of now and you can put your third pip up. Congratulations, Steve."

Dutifully, they shook hands. Steve then saluted and the tall major returned to his jeep. As Graham trudged back in the rain to the troop leaguer, he felt no sense of achievement or privilege, only continuing grief and deadening fatigue.

But one had to get on. Firmly, he told himself so.

Approach to Xanten, March 1945.

At last, the weather had cleared. Blackstone's squadron harboured in a farm complex with its own amazingly intact windmill that reminded Graham of Holland. The farm's red brick buildings radiated the warmth of spring sunshine shedding its brilliant glow on fresh green fields.

The crews serviced their vehicles painstakingly in preparation for the forthcoming attack on Xanten. They even managed to re-paint them.

To Graham's great satisfaction, Sergeant Kinnear and his crew reappeared with a re-placement Arrowhead.

"Brings us up to five, sir," he said on arrival. "Congratulations, by the way."

They wouldn't receive a sixth AVRE. After months of hard usage and inevitable casualties, extra vehicles and spare crews were at a premium. Mark Napper's lads were either still convalescing or, like Jevons, would be on light duties for several weeks.

Nevertheless, the squadron had several reasons to be cheerful. Rations were good and they had time for proper rest.

And B Echelon's mobile shower unit caught up with them, enabling the men to enjoy their most thorough wash for weeks. Moreover, they received an issue of fresh clothing and underwear, to replace the mud-stained and perpetually damp uniforms they'd lived in for most of the previous month. The set-up[197] was a large tent, mounted on duckboards and partitioned by canvas screens, complete with boilers hissing steam and manifold shower rosettes dispensing magnificent hot water sprays, the runoff being collected in sumps that led to drain.

Lifebuoy soap was in plentiful supply and on emerging from the showers into the drying room, everyone collected thick woollen towels and sets of underwear that smelt freshly ironed.

"They take their job seriously, sir," said Crittenden in admiration of the unit's personnel when Steve and he moved to the next annex in the tent, where they were issued with new clothing and socks.

"No doubt about it, Sergeant," said Graham. "But of course we are the best-organised division in the entire British Army."

And the post arrived.

Steve read his letters by paraffin lamp that night, stretched out on his bedroll in the farm-house parlour that he shared with Major Blackstone, Jamie Ledbetter, now in command of Julian's troop and Lieutenant 'Dutch' Holland, second-in-command of Blackstone's troop, a tousled-headed youngster, who had coincidentally joined the squadron during its time around Eindhoven.

Two of the letters were from Mark, the handwriting shaky but legible.

Dear Steve, one of them read. *I'm at the CCS near Nijmegen. I've got some bandages on and Sister Fraser[198] is looking after me. I've just told her she is thoroughly charming and romantically Scottish (fresh!). The bit in brackets is from her, not me..."*

The second letter, dated some days later, contained poignant news.

Dear Steve,

Sent down to Eindhoven to recuperate. Katrijn came to see me. Wore that grey suit with a white blouse that she always did for church and silk stockings. Her hair was done beautifully. Wonderful perfume. She looked gorgeous. Didn't want to see her at first, what with being all trussed up, aching all over after the op at the CCS, face like a cross between Quasimodo's and an orang-a-tang's.

But she sat on the bed, leant forward and kissed me. Did my poor swollen lips a power of good, I can tell you. She whispered, "God has been kind to us, Mark." I had to agree. A lot of chaps here are badly wounded. Mama and Papa have given us their blessing so we'll be getting married as soon as I'm up and about. All the best to you and Kate. Thanks again, for halting the troop when you did.

I told Katrijn about Tubby and Julian. Mama and Papa are praying for the families and us. Marijke sends her love to Uncle Steve and Kate...

Kate had sent several letters, indicating that she and Vicky were still very busy. He'd written to her about Tubby and Julian and in reply she did her best to comfort him.

Her letters invariably concluded with, *Oh, Steve darling, I keep on praying we'll soon be together*, or words to that effect.

"So do I, sweetheart," said Graham softly.

As always, the letters from his mother indicated that he should be getting a transfer to the training wing, *or some such*, because, *surely by now, you've done your share, dear.*

"It's not that simple, Mum," he said under his breath.

And he was overjoyed to receive a hastily scribbled note from Neil.

Dear Bro, Escaped to Denmark. Quite a story, tell you when we meet up. On my way to Blighty soon. Looking forward to getting back to the squadron.

With his parents' sanity in mind, Steve replied in the sensitive and brotherly fashion that he always reserved for his beloved sibling.

Dear Clothhead. Forget the squadron. If you're not settled in a ground job and engaged to Emma by the time I get back, I'll have your guts for garters.

Neil wouldn't take a blind bit of notice, of course, except for the bit about Emma, the lovely lass from across the street back home, a bit younger than his brother and whom they'd grown up with. She had been a tremendous support to their parents, especially when Neil had gone missing.

Like as not, Graham Two, as he'd been known at school, would be trying to wangle a posting to the Far East even as he penned to Emma his heart outpourings of undying love and affection.

"Glopskull[199]," muttered Steve.

He extinguished the lamp and bade his brother officers good night.

Like Goch, Xanten was ringed by an anti-tank ditch and required, as Blackstone had predicted, "a gapping job."

Steve's troop was left in reserve, until summoned to assist with filling the segment of ditch bisecting the approach road – by hand.

"Rock-chucking again," the boys said irritably.

Armadillo's crew were slightly mollified insofar as they were ordered to bring up a fascine to replace a bundle dropped earlier that had fallen end-on, rendering it unstable for vehicle traffic.

But it was an awkward business.

With Steve on foot, issuing instructions, Talbot had to thread the AVRE and its burden past a score of rubble-carrying lorries manoeuvring in turn up to the ditch, where sweating sappers feverishly shovelled the loads off the trays, because no tippers were available.

Throttles open wide, a couple of armoured bulldozers were ponderously shoving the unloaded brick and stone into the ditch, aided by more sappers, armed with shovels and toiling non-stop.

To add to the congestion, a seventy-foot skid Bailey occupied part of the roadside, necessitating careful detours for all vehicles moving back and forth.

"We started before dawn," a perspiring, shovel-toting Jamie explained when he met Steve on the approach road. He had to speak loudly above the roar of engines and the shriek of the Allied bombardment. Traversing shells tore through morning air stained with dust and exhaust fumes.

"Towed the skid up with a couple of AVREs," said Ledbetter. "First, we got a Jumbo[200] across."

Jamie pointed at the arch over the ditch. Tanks and infantry had already crossed using the Jumbo but it would not be able to sustain the build-up of two-way traffic that would intensify during the day.

"So far so good," continued Jamie. "But then the fascine went turtle and at sun-up we found another crater beyond the ditch. Together, they're too wide for the skid, so here we are, shovelling and dozering for all we're worth. If you can get that fascine in, it'll help – "

"Take cover!"

The frantic shout cut him short. Everyone on foot dived for the embankments bordering the road. Steve hugged stony earth as an enemy shell exploded fifty yards away in a field.

"Jerry's still being a nuisance," Jamie explained. Beads of sweat dripped off his young face.

"Captain Graham, Mr Ledbetter!" called a familiar voice.

Steve recognised the tall figure of Major Blackstone. He stood next to the Jumbo with another senior officer, evidently the local commander.

Graham and Ledbetter reported briefly to their superiors and returned to their respective tasks, where Steve successfully guided the deposition of the fascine, to cheers from all and sundry.

"OK, Crash, turn her around and retire to a safe distance," Graham ordered through the side door. "Then we've all got to come back and each grab a shovel."

Amid the groans of discontent, Talbot expressed uncertainty.

"Be a bit difficult here, sir. Space is a bit narrow and it looks boggy away from the verge."

"The difficult we do immediately, Corporal," said his officer decisively. "I'll guide you and if you do screw up, rest assured it'll be my third pip that goes for a Burton[201], not your stripe."

The manoeuvre was successfully accomplished. Graham's crew returned to assist with filling the craters, taking cover from incoming shells as necessary. They caused no casualties but prompted extremely rapid turnarounds for the lorries.

The gapping task took all day but by the end of it, Xanten had fallen.

The way was open to the Rhine.

River Rhine, March 24th, 1945.

Warm spring sunlight struggled to penetrate the vast smoke screen sweeping down the east bank for seventy miles to obscure the airborne landings. Its white billows mingled with the dark smoke and dust from the artillery and bomb explosions until the scene on the banks lay half hidden under an evil-smelling shroud of dirty grey.

That scene all was feverish activity.

As anticipated, all bridges were blown but the first assault troops had gone over the previous evening in storm boats and rushed ashore against little opposition, though some of the leading infantry, outdistancing their sapper support, had stumbled into uncleared *Schuh* mines concealed in muddy soil, tragically to lose life and limb in the process.

Teams of REs were therefore now working strenuously on both banks, to locate and lift the vicious devices, stack them up for disposal and tape out cleared areas. In the meantime, the assault waves kept coming, the men crowded into a vast phalanx of DUKWs and Buffalo LVTs, supported by Sherman propeller-driven Duplex-Drive tanks, held afloat by their all-round canvas screens.

According to Major Blackstone, who stood atop the earthen dyke on the west bank, staring through binoculars, the rippling grey surface of the Rhine looked like "a regatta for outsize bath tubs."

Sudden waterspouts and the sound of explosions revealed where enemy shells were occasionally falling among the attacking fleet, threatening to capsize the craft. A handful of intrepid enemy fighter pilots broke through the huge Allied air armada in an attempt to beat up the launching and landing sites and the vessels in transit. They were invariably chased off and sometimes shot down by Allied Spitfires and Hawker Tempests that pursued the Luftwaffe with twenty-mm cannon blazing, braving the shore-based, anti-aircraft batteries firing simultaneously at the intruders. Allied fighter-bombers also hammered the enemy gun positions.

Nothing stopped the relentless tide of invasion craft.

Before the day was out, Allied ground troops made contact with men of the British Sixth Airborne Division, who had consolidated the bridgehead on the eastern shore, though at a cost of over a thousand casualties, a third of whom were killed.

Working at a raft crossing place, Steve and his troop saw Buffaloes returning across the river, loaded with casualties. They included Scots infantry and green-bereted commandos of the Special Service Brigade but most were men of the red beret, festooned in reddened dressings, trousers and smocks also stained crimson, many ashen-faced and connected to life-sustaining drips, monitored by tight-lipped orderlies.

More work for Sister Fraser, Steve reflected, and Val and Pippa.

"Would you jump out of an aeroplane, for the extra pay, Ronny?" Graham overhead MacGee ask Hazeldene, who returned the standard reply.

"Not on your life, mate."

The sappers' work continued. Across pasture land repeatedly torn up by tank treads, where unmilked cows bellowed in pain, skirting taped-off yellowing grass that betrayed the presence of mines still awaiting removal, several of Blackstone's AVREs had towed pontoon, decking and bridging sections for Class Fifty/Sixty[202] rafts to the Rhine's west bank. Others dropped fascines to fill drainage ditches cutting the line of approach.

Literally thousands more sappers were engaged on the bank in improving the approaches to the water's edge, bulldozing down the flood dykes, flattening embankments, reinforcing the soil thus laid bare with logs and layers of rubble, excavating 'seatings' for Bailey bridges, laying down causeways of giant-size chespale 'carpet' fourteen feet wide and seventy-five feet long. DD tanks and other amphibians, still queuing, would use the carpets to take the plunge.

Some of the bulldozers clanked all the way into the shallows, to gouge down sandbanks threatening to impede passage.

Further back, lines of lorries were inching along every available track and road to drop off a plethora of stores and ammunition at the forward dumps. In the meadows and polder behind the flood dykes, columns of troops were debussing from their carriers to take to the Buffaloes and DUKWs for transport over the river.

Yet other sappers were hitching armoured recovery vehicles to stranded amphibians, victims of shellfire or mechanical breakdown, and assault boats holed by bullet and shrapnel.

Aboard Armadillo as the AVRE carefully backed its trailer carrying a three-ton pontoon piece into the river, Graham heard a senior RE officer shouting to the ARV crews.

"Get those wrecks out of the way! They're blocking the traffic."

Armadillo's pontoon piece would be joined to four others to constitute one raft, to help keep the traffic going.

Three AVRE squadrons had been allocated the job of setting up the huge raft ferries at this crossing place, setting in place winches, cables and specially manufactured outsize cable drums for the three-inch thick wire rope that would be fastened to the rafts, anchored to an AVRE on the west bank and to an LVT on the eastern shore, via RAF balloon winches.

RAF technicians worked alongside the sapper crews in the operation and maintenance of the winches and the drivers on each shore kept in touch by wireless.

Although slow, this method of transport over the six-hundred-yard expanse of the Rhine was sure, and not vulnerable to the strength of the current, like the motor-powered craft. By means of the SBG sections mounted crossways on the pontoons, the rafts could carry gun tanks, AVREs laden with fascines, self-propelled guns and heavy calibre artillery pieces across in support of the troops expanding the hard-won bridgehead.

"Provided Jerry doesn't put a hole in those pontoons," said Hazeldene as he guided his driver who was nudging Adamant onto one of the rafts, complete with chespale bundle.

Filling of bomb craters and petard dislodgement of stubborn enemy were urgently needed on the other side. Graham sent Kinnear and Briers over along with Hazeldene, their Churchills also carrying fascines. Other AVREs were transported with SBGs affixed.

Enemy shellfire at other crossing places had damaged and sunk some of the rafts but they had promptly been replaced and the work of transporting the army had gone on, the places of fallen sappers immediately filled by their comrades-in-arms.

"Bully fine job all round," said one high-ranking commander.

Major Blackstone could be observed all day atop the dyke, expertly overseeing the proceedings, issuing curt instructions to his officers and occasionally assuaging the nerves of impatient senior Royal Armoured Corps officers.

"Don't worry, sir," he'd say. "My lads are honing the system to perfection. Mark my words, you'll soon be cracking about in Germany[203]."

Blackstone's sappers operated the rafts for two days and nights, ferrying across over two hundred and fifty tanks. They included Cavendish's flails and Tyson's crocodiles. The two troop leaders bestowed cheery greetings on their RE colleague.

"Hello there, Steve. Thought I'd find you here. Sappers' paradise, this."

"Hullo, Steve, mate. Place is like a bank holiday weekend. Hope you're getting overtime."

Hod Stoughton's field company arrived on the third day to construct a pontoon Bailey. Blackstone's men rendered assistance, then afterwards dismantled the rafts for return to B Echelon storage.

On a clear-skied morning at the end of March, with the rest of his squadron lined up in column of route facing the Bailey's western abutment, Blackstone issued his orders. Graham heard the crisp, commanding voice in his earphones with a sense of eager anticipation.

"By troop, drivers advance!"

Shoreland glanced across to Graham, a look of concern on his face.

"Hope the pioneers got round to milking the rest of those cows, sir," he said.

Germany, April 1945.

The squadron motored through clouds of dust along straight roads intermittently tree-lined and cutting across flat farmland that reminded Graham of the Vale of Pickering, except for the war damage to the villages the AVREs passed through.

White flags, sometimes fastened to rough wooden poles, adorned every inhabited building.

"They don't seem very pleased to see us, sir," said Shoreland, remarking on the cold stares the Churchills received from local civilians.

Organised resistance had virtually collapsed but countless minor actions were being fought as the invading columns came up against blockhouses, pillboxes and even roadblocks consisting of piled logs, where last-ditch defenders showed by means of Spandau and *panzerfaust* their willingness to die fighting for the Fuehrer.

Invariably, they did.

"More matchwood," grunted Ferrarby as Armadillo's crew watched a log roadblock disintegrate in smoke and splinters from a petard dustbin direct hit.

From time to time, Graham's troop encountered fanatical Hitler or Goering Youth, stumbling along the roadside, unarmed, in twos and threes. Some of the boys would seize bits of masonry from broken-down wayside cottages and pelt approaching tanks with them.

Steve simply ordered his gunners to "Give 'em a burst."

And more youthful blood would be staining the soil of the Fatherland.

But as the days passed, more and more of the enemy began to surrender at the first sight of the armoured columns, until they were filing past the tanks in droves towards POW cages, all weaponless, some with heads held high, others bedraggled and dejected.

Where needed, the squadron assisted with bridge laying, crater filling with fascines and other road repairs, work that was much-needed because the enemy had exercised their considerable talent for demolition to hinder the Allied advance.

The squadron was summoned on several occasions to help prepare approaches for yet more river crossings, though nothing as major as the Rhine and after advancing eighty miles to heath land near Osnabruck, Blackstone's AVREs went into corps reserve.

Drac Stoker returned during this pause, having spent some of his convalescent leave in Brussels.

He reported to Steve's Troop HQ, the tarpaulin attached to Armadillo and staked out by means of tent poles that Steve had used in Normandy. On Graham's command, Drac stood at ease in front of Steve's portable table. He then regaled his officer with vivid tales of the capital's fleshpots.

"Place is one big knocking shop[204], sir. Way things are, you could shag yourself silly, if you weren't too plastered."

Steve leant back in his foldable chair, clasped his hands behind his head and looked up at the grinning NCO.

"But no doubt you're glad to be back where the real action is, Corporal?" he asked nonchalantly.

Stoker affirmed that he was and Graham believed him.

No matter how much revelry the individual soldier might indulge in on leave, his particular troop or section remained in a very real sense, home and family. He felt isolated and vulnerable away from it.

Yet Steve knew it was a situation they would all be facing eventually, depending on how the war in the Far East went. He wondered how they would cope.

Of the war on the other side of the world, ugly rumours abounded to the effect that in Burma, Japs hid in trees and jumped on tanks passing beneath to skewer the commanders with Samurai swords.

They especially targeted troop leaders, and above.

But Graham's lads proposed a decisive counter measure.

"We'll rig up a spring-loaded harpoon next to your hatch, sir," Hazeldene explained. "Set to go off the exact second Tojo lands on the turret. Get the slit-eyed sod right up the jacksie[205]."

The idea was a good one, though it made Graham wince.

The post caught up with the unit again and one of the letters that Steve received contained unsettling news, although the writer was safe.

Hi Steve, it read. *By the time you get this, I'll be on my way home to New Brunswick. About a week ago, I had to report to the CO to brief him on company status. Quite unexpectedly, I just broke down and wept, could hardly get a single word out. The colonel called for the MO, who said my nerves were shot and I needed a rest. Not surprising, I guess. I was the last officer in the battalion from D-Day. One average, our infantry battalions have each been replaced three times over since last June...*
Yours aye,
Ben Hedges, Lt., Canadian Expeditionary Force

Steve hoped and prayed his friend would make a full recovery[206], as he continued to do for Ian Kinross and Mark, both still convalescing.

Naturally, he was overjoyed by the sheaf of envelopes addressed with Kate's neat handwriting.

So while other units of specialised armour pressed on for Bremen, Blackstone's squadron continued bivouacking on the open field with only light duties and an air of relaxation, marred solely by the necessity for washing and shaving using individual dixies, because water was rationed again.

Until a report came through of an AVRE lost with all its crew during the attack on Bremen.

"It drove over a German naval parachute sea mine, buried under rubble," Blackstone informed his command. "We are advised to take extreme care in any further motorised advance into Germany."

The squadron heeded its OC's admonition and progressed without mishap another one hundred miles, to the River Elbe. Here it supported the capture of Hamburg, with mine clearance, track laying and establishing approach and exit routes to and from the riverbanks for the attacking infantrymen. They included Kinross's old brigade.

Then Steve and his companions received a surprise that wasn't altogether welcome.

"We're having to part with our AVREs, lads," Blackstone said at a morning parade. "B Echelon will take responsibility for them and we will go by lorry to Kiel as soon as the way is cleared. There we will assist our field company colleagues with demolition work and restoration of the docks and essential services.

"Brings a lump to the throat, doesn't it, sir," said Crittenden when they were dismissed.

"Certainly does, Bill," said Steve, gazing at the troop lines of battle-scarred Churchills. "They've been good war horses."

"The best, sir," said laconic Sergeant Kinnear. "The best."

It was the end of an era.

And another one was beginning for Captain Graham. It began peaceably enough, in post-war Germany.

Sixteen

Occupiers

Schleswig Holstein, spring 1945.

A long procession of army lorries conveyed the occupying forces into northern Germany, several of them containing the men of Blackstone's squadron and their essential kit.

By the roadside, a seemingly endless column of disarmed German soldiers trudged in the opposite direction, their field-grey garb in sombre contrast to the brightness of the spring flowers in the fields bordering the road.

It was noticeable that the troops were mostly fit young men. Six years of war had clearly not exhausted Germany's manpower resources. Nevertheless, these soldiers were no doubt relieved to be spared more fighting – and that they were surrendering to the British rather than the Russians. They smiled and waved cheerfully at the truckloads of passing Tommies, many of whom waved amiably back.

"All Wehrmacht, sir, by the looks," remarked Shoreland, seated beside Graham. "No Volkssturm. Don't seem bothered they've been beaten."

"Not by us, any road," said Hazeldene, next to Shoreland.

Steve nodded.

"Yes, just glad it's over," he said.

Everyone knew that the formal surrender was only days away.

Interspersed with the soldiers were considerable numbers of refugees, mostly women with children, plodding along with bundles on their backs, pushing their worldly goods in prams, barrows or handcarts. They and the German troops with them had crossed the Baltic in overcrowded steamers, fleeing from the Russians advancing through East Prussia and Pomerania.

In contrast to the soldiers, many of the refugees appeared jaded and fearful, evidently not comprehending that the anticipated Soviet invasion of Schleswig Holstein would not now take place. The British had invaded first.

Earlier, the convoy drove through the bomb-ravaged centre of Hamburg. An easy target for the RAF, much of Hamburg had virtually been razed. Roofless, fire-gutted walls thrust starkly against the clear sky, amid the rubble of what had been city blocks.

A heavy, sour stench of death and burst sewer mains had filled everyone's nostrils.

"Enough to make you puke," said Hazeldene.

But, paradoxically, the city centre was crowded with civilians. Many were plump young *fraus* in fine clothes, unlike the refugees. Men and women alike glanced enquiringly at the trucks as they rumbled past.

"Our lasses are a lot skinnier," Shoreland remarked.

"Seems like they want us to start giving orders, sir," said Crittenden, seated opposite Graham. "Very German of them."

"Well, they're not short of nosh around here," said Graham. "So I don't suppose we will be, either."

Senior officers had expressed disquiet over the army's capacity simultaneously to feed its own personnel and to cater for the huge civilian population in the occupied area, now bereft of its erstwhile government and much of the accompanying infrastructure.

Graham reckoned that the sight of the well-fleshed women of Hamburg would have allayed some of his superiors' concerns.

Ironically, the lads were about to find themselves better fed than they had been for years.

Kiel, early May 1945.

Blackstone and Graham were standing on a bomb-pitted concrete esplanade that ran along what was left of the dockside. In one direction, the gently rippling grey-green waters of the Kiel Canal stretched away to the Baltic. In the other, mounds of shattered brick and stone sprawled chaotically towards burnt-out shells of customs houses and office blocks that had once been part of the town's thriving commercial district. Rows of empty window spaces in the building shells, darkened by dingy, derelict interiors, brooded over the scene of desolation.

All along the quayside, gangs of sombre-faced civilians were salvaging bricks and cleaning them for reuse. Like those in Hamburg, they did not seem to be undernourished. Schleswig Holstein had at least been spared famine, if not bombing.

Returned German soldiers toiled alongside the civilians.

"Conquerors turned labourers," Blackstone remarked acerbically.

The two officers gazed at the extensive concrete casements that jutted onto the esplanade, separated from each other by about a stone's throw. Their embrasures were empty, the heavy calibre anti-aircraft guns having recently been removed for scrap with the help of local contractors but the structures remained. They were huge, with built-in barracks facilities and lift wells for the magazines below ground level.

The emplacements lined both banks of the canal and Blackstone's squadron had the job of demolishing them, then redistributing the debris for crater filling and road ballast. Together with bridge repair and full restoration of essential services to the city centre; water, electricity, tram tracks, lighting and sewage, the tasks would take months to complete.

"So, we're ready to mark out the holes for drilling, then?" asked the OC.

"As you see, sir," said Graham.

He indicated to their sappers formed up beside the nearest cupola, with paintbrushes and buckets of whitewash.

"What's the latest on the air compressor sets?" Blackstone asked.

"Due tomorrow morning, sir. Along with the explosive. Tons of it. I've arranged for it to be dispersed."

Each hole pneumatically drilled in the casements would be packed with two pounds of explosive and each emplacement would require up to two hundred insertions. When detonated simultaneously by means of a wire manifold and common electrical trigger, the incremental explosives packages would break the concrete into manageable fragments.

"Than we all become barrow boys again," Hazeldene had said with distaste.

Blackstone glanced at Graham's expectant troop.

"Right, then, Steve," he said. "You better get those lads a-marking. And watch out they don't start playing noughts and crosses."

It was a relief to get back to camp after a day at the docks, in the dust and rigors of repair and demolition work, especially insofar as the mobile shower unit had arrived, followed by its laundry component.

The squadron bivouacked in and around a hamlet nestling on the edge of an extensive wood, where foxes, badgers and roe deer roamed free in considerable numbers. At night, one could hear the hooting of owls hunting for prey.

"Dead rustic, this," Illingworth remarked when they debussed from the trucks on arrival. "But I hope the snipers have all gone home," he added, nodding towards the woods. The memory of the Reichswald was still raw.

One Troop was allocated a stable block on the outskirts of the village. It had been part of a large, pre-war estate, now broken up.

"We get the doss house again," growled Hazeldene.

But the loose boxes proved to be excellent billets and fresh straw for lining them could readily be obtained from local farms in exchange for a few cigarettes. An open area immediately inside the stable entrance was easily converted into the troop's mess.

Graham occupied the groom's quarters on the first floor, a scrubbed wooden compartment overlooking the woods.

With B Echelon's water tanker providing regular supplies, ablutions and accommodation secured, latrines sited, dug and furnished, rubbish pits and combustible waste incinerator established, the lads turned to their next priority.

They put the question to Crittenden, while they were unpacking a consignment of foldable camp beds.

"What's the local grub, like, Sarge?"

"I'll find out tomorrow," Bill promised.

Promptly on return from the docks at the end of the following day's work, he borrowed a motorcycle from Squadron HQ and went on the scrounge, haversacks stuffed with cigarette packs, compo tins and chocolate draped over his shoulders.

He returned a couple of hours later. The haversacks were bulging with farm produce and a pail of fresh milk with clamped lid hung from the handlebar.

"Fresh farm eggs and butter to go with the biscuits, lads," he said triumphantly on distributing the haul. "Veg in season straight from kitchen gardens. Even got some flour for baking. Only needs a bit of yeast," he added, looking pointedly at MacGee and Tomlinson.

"Your German must be pretty good, Bill," said Kinnear in admiration.

"Language of fags, mate, and they don't mind our compo stuff, either," said Crittenden confidently. "But they speak pretty good English."

He remounted the bike and kick-started the engine.

"Better get this back before the OC finds out it's missing," he said.

The lads' resourcefulness in days to come led them to a fishing village on the east side of the canal, where world-renowned smoked Kiel sprats could be obtained in generous quantities, again in exchange for cigarettes.

The varied diet didn't end there.

"Don't forget what's on the doorstep, lads," Crittenden reminded his comrades.

Whereupon Ferrarby and Illingworth acquired Lee-Enfields from Hod Stoughton's field company lads, who were based nearby, engaged with dozers and graders in building an airstrip.

Those redoubtable chefs, MacGee and Tomlinson, agreed to "roast anything you boys bring back, provided it's not a Jerry."

Having made a success of bread baking, they were brimming with enthusiasm.

So were the huntsmen, creating something of a problem.

Several units were stationed in the vicinity and the sound of rifle shots aimed at venison on the hoof was unremitting. Bullets occasionally hummed close to the village.

"This place is getting dangerous," Blackstone told his officers at a briefing in the parlour of his billet one afternoon. The major then joined with Stoughton and other local commanders to regulate the shooting parties.

The deer steaks, nevertheless, were in the squadron's unanimous opinion, "out of this world, sir."

With the forest in such close proximity, so was the bonfire the boys kindled when they held their victory celebration on the night of the official German surrender.

Blackstone and his fellow officers stood on the fringe while the lads congregated around the fire and slaked their thirst, stimulated not only by the celebratory mood but also a particularly arduous day at the docks.

"They can probably see that blaze in Hamburg," said Blackstone. Sweet-smelling, resinous smoke swirled up into starlit skies above the roar of crackling timber.

"Where did they hide all the booze?" Dutch Holland asked in wonderment.

"Seems like there's enough to float a DD tank," said Jamie Ledbetter admiringly.

It was well-known that beer and wine had been 'liberated' in quantity for months but where the boys had cached it none of the officers knew for certain, though Blackstone remarked shrewdly, "You can bet B Echelon's involved."

"For a cut of the takings," Steve added.

Work started a little later the next day.

"It's bad enough havin' pneumatic drills in your head, sir," Hazeldene said woefully to his officer. "Without having to use one as well."

However, the discovery of gin and beer cellars, undamaged and fully stocked, rekindled the lads' enthusiasm for tippling.

"This stuff'll go well with deer meat, sir," Graham's troop assured him.

The next priority was easily satisfied. The lads simply broke the non-fraternisation rules, a misdemeanour to which the squadron's officers turned Nelsonian blind eyes.

In part, they encouraged it. As the city began to return to life, troops of all units organised football tournaments with the local young men, who were mostly discharged Wehrmacht veterans. As in Holland, the matches were well patronised and of a high standard.

But the best place for female company – and unlimited booze - was Flensberg, forty miles away by road towards Denmark and almost untouched by the war. The army had already established a salubrious nightclub in the town with a spectacular cabaret that was fast becoming the talk of the entire army group.

"Well, it's as good as ENSA, sir," Stoker told Graham on tumbling out of the liberty truck in the early a.m. after the first hectic foray into the northern fleshpot.

"And the folk are glad to see us, sir," said Jevons, who also alighted shakily. Along with the rest of Napper's lads, he was back with the squadron. "They're still comin' across the Baltic in boatloads, Jerry soldiers, loads of women and kids, scared to death of the Russians."

"They reckon we're at least human, sir," said Hazeldene, steadying himself on Jevons's shoulder. "You should take Kate there, sir," he urged.

"Yes, go on, sir," said several voices at once.

"I'll speak to Major Blackstone," Steve said quietly.

The next day, lads in some of the neighbouring units complained about the rude awakening they'd suffered following the stentorian cheer that greeted Graham's reply.

"Where is she now, Steve?" Blackstone asked during a pre-breakfast briefing in the cottage parlour early in June.

"Near Lubeck, sir," said Graham. "She's managed a posting there to check on missing agents who were helping the Danish Resistance. Reckons she'll be heading for Copenhagen soon, though right now, she's at a bit of a loose end."

Steve always sensed a tingle of excitement on recollecting Kate's recent letter containing these details – together with her congratulations on his promotion. He was wondering how to get a posting to Copenhagen himself.

Blackstone smiled considerately. Dutch and Jamie exchanged grins. Then the major leant across the polished oak table they were seated around and handed Steve a signed leave pass.

"Take a jeep and don't come back for seventy-two hours," he said.

Steve drove steadily southwards, past convoys of army lorries going in the opposite direction. He glanced from time to time at the lush farm fields that lay on each side of the road, fringed by trees spaced at regular intervals. The weather was continuing sunny and having phoned Kate to double-check that she could get time away, Steve was consumed with the thrill of anticipation.

Almost.

He couldn't shake the scripture that nagged at his brain.

I am not worthy of the least of all the mercies, and of all the truth, which thou hast shewed unto thy servant[207].

Why had he been spared?

Why not Tubby, why not Julian, or Jack Tyrell, or Don, especially Don with his young family, now without a dad?

And he'd never gotten a chance to speak with Tubby about Kate.

He rested both hands on the steering wheel, gazing down the dead straight highway. Now that hostilities were ended, Steve was also experiencing a strange remorse about his mentality in action. When friends were killed or wounded, his first thought had been, *Thank God, it wasn't me*. When enemies had died before his face, like the brick-chucking Hitler Jugend or the German blown in half at Goch, his reactions had varied from casual indifference to outright enthusiasm.

It had hardly registered that many of these young lives, either friend or foe, might have been damned straight to hell.

Steve gripped the steering wheel tighter and manoeuvred around a lumbering three-tonner. He tried desperately to focus on something more heartening – in addition to the imminent prospect of meeting up with Kate.

The wisdom of Solomon came to his rescue.

The blessing of the LORD, it maketh rich, and he addeth no sorrow with it[208].

Besides having survived, he could count further blessings. Stoughton's lads would soon have the airstrip complete, in time for Graham, Blackstone, Dutch and Jamie to fly down to Eindhoven for Mark and Katrijn's wedding.

Be a bit scarred when you see me, Mark's last letter had said. *But I'm OK.*

And Lorraine Tyrell had accepted Bill Crittenden's proposal by post.

"That shindig is going to be bigger than VE Day," Hazeldene promised.

Provided they didn't get sent to the Far East, Graham mused.

Though somehow, he sensed that wasn't going to happen.

Thoughts of Kate reasserted themselves as Steve neared his destination. With eager longing, he turned the jeep into the hedged lane that led to the manor where her unit was based.

"Oh, Steve!" exclaimed Kate, after she'd bestowed on Graham's lips the fiercest kiss she could muster. "So *wonderful* to see you!"

She could feel tears in her eyes. Skirt, semi-heels and shoulder bag notwithstanding, she'd run to meet him in the vehicle park and his embrace had lifted her off the ground.

"Oh, Kate, it's been so long," Steve whispered fervently. He pressed the side of his head against hers, still holding her close.

He let go of her and she settled herself in the jeep's front passenger seat, placing her bag on the floor.

"I've told them I'll be back when you bring me back," she said gaily.

Steve climbed into the driver's seat and started the engine.

"We're headed for Fehmarn," he said. "The boys were all for me whisking you off to Flensburg but I thought you'd prefer an island paradise instead[209].

"Capri of the Baltic, they call it," said Steve when he drove the jeep up the slipway from the vehicle ferry. "We can check in at a place along the coast here."

"Sounds like you've got it all organised," Kate enthused. She crossed her legs and adjusted her skirt, noting Steve's appreciative glance as she did so.

"The island didn't suffer much from the war," Steve explained. "And the army got it back into tourist operation pretty quickly. Priorities, you see. The boys at Squadron HQ gave me the gen. After that, it was just a phone call. Lines are all restored around here, like on the way to Lubeck."

Kate smiled winsomely.

"Sappers hard at work again, darling?"

"As usual, we're indispensable," said Graham, changing gear. "Though we did have a bit of help from Signals. They reckon it's the other way about, of course."

The road took them past grass-covered dunes adjoining pristine white beaches and quaint little cottages surrounded by neat gardens. After securing Fehmarn Island, southeast of Kiel, with its numerous inns, guesthouses and chalets, the occupation forces had made sure it continued to fulfil its pre-war – and wartime – role, as a haven for officers and their wives, or girlfriends.

Beyond the beaches, the sea sparkled in the sunlight until it blended with the shimmering horizon.

Occasionally, they drove past fields burgeoning with rapeseed, brilliant yellow beneath blue skies.

"Lovely sight, horrible name," said Kate.

Steve smiled and nodded.

"OK so long as you don't get hay fever," he said.

Kate closed her eyes and removed her cap. Holding it in her lap, she leant back in her seat. The sun felt warm on her face and the breeze ruffled her hair.

"Oh, Father, I've never been so happy in my life," she said softly.

The guest house was a two-storied thatched dwelling, elegantly constructed of pinkish-brown stone and located in a gravelled lane that meandered along the shore of a limpid green lake studded with artificial islands and home to several pairs of white swans. Turreted bedrooms, their windows projecting from the tightly interwoven grey thatch, looked out over a well-kept front lawn, enclosed by flowering shrubs that buzzed with honey bees.

Trees lining the lakeside edge of the lane were heavy with burgeoning white blossom.

"This place is lovely," said Kate when Steve parked the jeep. "How did you find out about it?"

"Brigade I Section[210] keeps up to date on everything of strategic importance, love," he said with a wink.

The innkeeper greeted them when they entered the cool confines of the exquisitely furnished front parlour. He was a jovial individual of stout build with short-cropped, fairish hair and wore a grey flannel suit with satin shirt and dark red cravat. Kate thought he looked like a Nordic version of Hermann Goering but she noted he displayed no surprise when Steve booked separate rooms. By now, he was probably accustomed to the peculiar ways of some of the English.

"Christian officer and gentleman," Kate said quietly, as Steve paid the deposit, in occupation currency.

"Thank you, Herr Hauptmann[211]," said the host courteously. He wrote Steve a receipt.

He then sounded a brass bell that stood prominently on the polished mahogany reception counter and in response, a middle-aged porter came up to carry the couple's bags to their rooms.

"The nearest beach seems like it's only a few minutes' walk?" Kate asked.

"Yes," said the innkeeper. His blue eyes twinkled. "But I should say, Fraulein, it is still very cold this time of year."

The expression on *Meinhoste's* face confirmed that he was indeed quite used to the peculiar ways of some of the English.

"I'm f-f-freezing!" wailed Kate. "And all goose pimples!"

Having taken the plunge into clear, waist-deep water, she now stood shivering violently, with chattering teeth, her arms clasped across her chest.

Kate's close-fitting, two-piece bathing suit showed off her curvaceous, long-limbed figure to perfection. Her taut cleavage and muscle-toned midriff elicited most admiring gazes from Steve.

But for Kate, they were, literally, cold comfort.

Steve stood a few feet from her, clad in a pair of khaki PT shorts, glistening droplets dripping off his lean face and wiry frame. To Kate, he seemed all chiselled muscle and impervious to the Baltic chill. She was glad he hadn't said anything about the livid scars gouged like elongated tear drops in her left thigh, showing where she'd been shot[212]. The twin blemishes would always distress her.

"Didn't you do this in SOE?" Steve asked, splashing water on his face from cupped hands.

"Th-that was b-business, not p-pleasure," Kate protested. "A-and anyway, we w-wore full kit. G-gave you a b-bit of insulation."

"You need to get acclimatised," Steve said casually. He splashed her with an armful of water.

"Ow!" yelled Kate, cringing beneath the icy shower. "Your number's up, Captain Graham," she declared and lunged at Steve with a vengeance.

They wrestled for nearly a couple of minutes, mostly submerged, until bobbing up in a swirl of foam, spluttering, embracing and kissing. Then they stroked strenuously back and forth for the better part of half an hour, each striving to outdo the other.

"C'mon," said Kate, when they splashed back through the shallows. "Race you along the beach."

She felt flushed and exhilarated. Her flesh was tingling and she loved the feel of firm sand pressing between her toes.

"Bet I can beat you up those sand hills," said Steve. The grassy, white dunes stood about a quarter of a mile away and sloped up over sixty feet from the beach.

"Bet you can't!" taunted Kate and sprinted off like Atalanta[213], with Graham in close pursuit.

They plunged up and down the sand hills for another half hour. Then, laughing, gasping and dripping perspiration, they ambled back, each with an arm about the other's waist, to where they had left their towels. Their bodies were plastered with sand.

Kate noticed that, though trying to be discreet, Steve was glancing repeatedly at her heaving breasts, conspicuous beneath her swimsuit top.

"As an officer and a gentleman, you shouldn't really be ogling my tits, Captain Graham," she admonished him. Steve looked mightily embarrassed.

"It's all right," Kate added soothingly. She rested her head against his shoulder. "I know you can't help it. I shouldn't be quite so brazen."

Looking around, she asked, "Where is everybody?"

The beach was virtually deserted.

"Wandering around town, I reckon," said Steve, evidently relieved that Kate had changed the subject. He brushed some sand from his thighs. "It isn't far. Quaint old place, I've heard, full of craft shops and Danish architecture, plus the usual amenities. Got a cinema and some good eating joints, I'm told – "

"We could go there for lunch," Kate suggested.

"Yep – after we've had another dip to wash the sand off," he said, with a mischievous grin.

They were seated beneath a coloured umbrella at one of the freshly painted tables in the forecourt of a picturesque sidewalk café. The cobbled roadway next to the pavement was a pedestrian precinct, where numerous Allied officers strolled by, arm-in-arm with their female companions. Some of the girls wore uniform but many were local *frauleins*.

Bubbling fountains, ornate statues, garden beds in full bloom, cafés doing steady business and elegant craft shop fronts of characteristically Nordic design could be seen all round the plaza. The enticing smell of cooking, the aroma of spices and the delicate fragrance of scented flowers wafted across the scene.

Steve and Kate were sipping rich black coffee. The meal had been sumptuous but the main course, consisting of succulent Baltic sprats, fresh vegetables and deliciously fried potato slices, prompted a sense of irony.

"Normandy to the Baltic," Steve said, looking amused. "A long way to come for fish and chips.

"How is Vicky?" he eventually asked. "I forgot to ask, being so overwhelmed with your breath-taking beauty."

Kate fluttered her eyelashes.

"Flatterer," she said haughtily. "But in answer to your question, she's gone to Bologna since I last wrote."

Steve paused with his cup halfway to his lips, his eyebrows knitted.

"Bologna?" he asked.

Kate nodded, dabbing the corner of her mouth with a paper napkin.

"To interview a Royal Fusilier named Briggs and his missus," she said. "ATS lassie formerly called Styles, not that either name means anything to me but evidently Briggs has come into some information via the partisans that affects the Von Hollstein case."

Steve drained his cup and replaced it in the saucer.

"In Italy?" he said in puzzlement.

"Yes, weird, I know. But it seems our Nazi aristocrat may be associated with a fifth columnist down there, posing as a chaplain attached to an MGH. Vicky plans to talk to some of its personnel, in addition to this fusilier lad."

Kate paused, sipped more coffee, then spoke again, in a subdued tone.

"Some strange things have happened, including a sudden death or two. One of Mrs Briggs's ATS friends was killed in suspicious circumstances, apparently."

The flaps of the umbrella tilted slightly in a light breeze. Steve was staring at the passers-by, clearly inwardly digesting the information.

Kate drew breath, adjusted her cap, fidgeted with the napkin for a moment and then spoke out.

"I won't be in Copenhagen for long, darling," she said quietly.

She went on quickly, trying not to notice the questioning look in his eyes as he turned to face her.

"I'll be going back to England in a few weeks. I can't tell you much more, except that I'll be getting demobbed and going to work under cover, part of this Von Hollstein business. The demob date about corresponds with my group number[214] so that shouldn't arouse suspicion."

Steve placed both hands on the white-painted tabletop. He stared at her intently.

"Can you tell me where you'll be, back home?"

Kate hesitated for a moment, then said firmly, "Derbyshire."

She mentioned a town in the area of the White Peak[215]. I owe you that much, love, she thought.

Steve's face brightened.

"Just a stone's throw from where Mum and Dad live," he said.

Kate laughed softly and rested her forearms on the table, delighted to see his face relax and the look of happiness in those endearing greyish green eyes.

"Yes, that occurred to me," she said warmly. "My mum and dad are a bit puzzled but I said I took the first position that came up – which was true, sort of."

Then she saw his face grow serious again and immediately knew why.

"But what about this Von Hollstein character and his mate, Albrecht?" Steve asked. "From what you've said, I'm guessing they're going to be somewhere in the vicinity, as impostors of some kind. Won't they recognise you?"

Kate smiled and placed a reassuring hand on his.

"I'm SOE, darling. I know how to keep my head down."

"Why can't you just have them picked up?" Steve asked, obviously perplexed.

"Well, now that we've traced them this far, we're keen to see what they're up to. So we mustn't move in too early."

Steve clasped Kate's hand.

"Are you sure?"

"Yes, don't worry," Kate whispered. She leant across and kissed him.

"I'll help you all I can," Steve said vehemently. "I probably won't be demobbed until next year but after that, I'm sure I can get work in the area."

"That'd be wonderful, darling," Kate murmured and kissed him again.

"Now," she said, sitting upright. "Will the budget stretch to another round of coffee and scones with jam and cream? Somebody must've really briefed these Krauts about the English."

Steve laughed and promptly rose to his feet.

"You bet," he said eagerly and strode off to the counter.

Kate leant against the back of her seat, closed her eyes and sighed. She had at least informed Steve of the essentials, though she couldn't bring herself to tell him about Lord Waverly, or Guillaume as was. Her emotions were still in too much of a tangle for that.

But the lines of enquiry that she and Vicky were following had borne considerable fruit in recent weeks. Von Hollstein and his accomplice had definitely reached the White Peak area.

Peter Waverly's home ground.

And if Waverly was *her* Guillaume, Kate knew that Von Hollstein's destination couldn't be coincidence, likewise his original association with Waverly on the Jed team.

Kate had already cabled this potentially crucial information to Vicky.

As yet, neither of them understood why their Nazi quarry was gravitating to that part of the country but there had to be a reason worth the obvious risk.

"I'll find out," Kate said under her breath, recalling her vow to Alain.

And she still remembered Guillaume's protective arm around her shoulders when the bridge had exploded. The strength of his presence had never left her.

She glimpsed Steve returning with the laden tray and began clearing a space on the table for it.

Once more, she pondered the gnawing questions.

If her Guillaume was Peter, how would meeting him again – assuming that she did - affect her feelings for Steve? How would Peter, alias Guillaume, react to her?

"I'll have to cross that bridge as well," Kate said to herself.

Halfway around the world, others destined to share in the trials that lay ahead were also facing changes – and thinking about home. We turn to them now.

Seventeen

Rangoon

Rangoon Road, May 1945.

"This place doesn't look like it's even seen the war," remarked Trish. Seated next to Colleen, she craned her neck to keep in view the trim colonial-style mansion they were driving past.

Colleen was preoccupied with keeping the jeep at the required distance behind Corporal Wood's lorry but she glanced at the spacious bungalows with their wide verandas set in luxuriant grounds, situated on either side of the road.

The gardens were an explosion of coloured blossom on rich green backgrounds, glistening with myriad droplets in the sun that had blazed forth during a break in the monsoon rains and the dripping vegetation steamed. The girls in their JGs sweltered in spite of the steady breeze created by the jeep's movement. Sweat oozed onto Colleen's face and trickled down her right arm each time she lowered it to change gear. A great stain of it was spread across the back of her shirt.

"Whose houses are these?" she asked. "They don't look deserted."

Rangoon had fallen soon after the capture of Pegu. Despite serious bomb damage to the port, Fourteenth Army sappers got it functioning in a few days, once Royal Navy minesweepers had cleared the harbour channel to the Gulf of Martaban and the open sea.

Now, several medical units, including Trenholme's CCS, were joining together to establish a BGH in the large, purpose-built hospital on the fringe of the town.

"Taken over by the Burmans, Coll," said Robyn from the rear. She wiped perspiration from her face with a damp handkerchief. "A lot of them were good pals with the Nips, though now of course they'd swear blind they weren't."

"They'd have moved in after our people left in forty-two," said Gwen. "Still, it's probably better than leaving the houses derelict." She too sat mopping her face.

Occasionally, Trish dabbed Colleen's eyebrows and forehead with a clean handkerchief, to save her friend the trouble while driving.

"You haven't got a fever, Coll," Trish assured her.

The remark was not mere pleasantry. Many of the casualties they were receiving continued to suffer from various tropical maladies, in addition to their wounds.

Apart from having to skirt the occasional bomb crater, the vehicles transporting Trenholme's CCS motored smoothly along the metalled highway into Rangoon. The spell of fine weather had enabled the CCS to fly out many of its patients to India and convey the rest to the recently liberated hospital in Rangoon, found to be almost intact and surprisingly well-equipped.

Trenholme explained why when he circulated the report on the hospital's condition.

"The Japs don't like looters. They cut the heads off any of their own chaps they catch doing it."

Though looting had been rife in the port area after the enemy vacated, the Japanese had held onto the hospital as long as possible before trying to escape towards the Sittang. One of Fourteenth Army's first jobs on occupying the battered city was re-establishment of law and order but great strides were also being made to restore water, sanitation and electricity - and the hospital had been the first beneficiary.

The vehicle park of hard-packed gravel formed an apron to the front and one side of the hospital building. This consisted of three storeys, each with verandas at the front and on both sides, enclosed by stone balustrades and a succession of pillars with intervening arches.

A Union Jack hung proudly, though limply, from a tall white flagpole in the centre of the front park.

"Rule Britannia," said Colleen. She dropped the jeep into low gear and turned for the gateway.

The four of them broke into the anthem as Colleen followed Wood's lorry to their allotted stand, eliciting grins, whistles and waves from the male personnel seated in the back of the three-tonner.

Colleen backed the jeep up against a grassy verge and Mostyn's driver pulled in beside them.

"C'mon, you lot," called Kiwi, jumping out. "This isn't Last Night of the Proms. Don't forget the briefing."

He hurried off to the hospital entrance, seemingly oblivious to the searing humidity. Encumbered with the captain's gear, his driver-batman followed at a more sedate pace.

Their new commanding officer, Lieutenant Colonel Partridge, would be addressing the newcomers in the hospital's conference hall at eleven hundred hours, by which time all of Trenholme's personnel were expected to have arrived. They constituted the final contingent.

Colleen and her friends alighted from the jeep and gazed at their new surroundings.

"This place is a botanical garden," said Robyn, as she shouldered her web bag. "Japs must've kept the local weed bashers hard at it."

The sight that greeted them was one of extensive cultivated beds spaced systematically across vast lawn spaces and bordering long, straight gravel walkways. Densely flowering shrubs, taller than a man and exhibiting variegated hues of colour, thrived in the rich soil. Giant trees, thickly foliaged in deep green, with moss-encrusted trunks and overspreading boughs, thrust their huge crowns up to a height of hundred feet or more.

"They've got all sorts here. Teak, paduak, neem, flame, the lot," said Trish in admiration.

"It's like a stately home," said Gwen.

Their boots crunched on the gravel as the four of them joined Vera and the other girls, also laden with personal kit. They had collected their bedrolls from Wood's lorry and the lads would bring their trunks up later, with, as usual, camp beds fastened.

"Those walkways are just the job, Trish," said Rachel with a mischievous wink at the others. "You can go meandering along them arm-in-arm with Lieutenant Calvert."

Matt Calvert and Leigh Grafton were two of the patients who had been transferred to Rangoon. Calvert's lacerations and Grafton's fracture were healing sufficiently well for Trenholme and Mostyn to agree they didn't need to be flown back to Comilla.

"Definitely!" chorused several female voices.

Everyone knew Sister Calder was overjoyed with her superiors' decision, though Colleen wondered how things would work out between Trish and Evan.

"Provided it's not tankin' it down," said Kitty Earnshaw. "Or maybe Matt will hold the umbrella for you both, with his arm around you?"

"Mmh, cosy," said Paddy Monaghan. "Kiwi would, if it was me – or any of us, come to that."

"Shut up," said Trish, laughing with embarrassment.

"Now, girls," said Vera. "We mustn't encourage idle dalliances between patients and nursing staff."

Rachel doffed her bush hat to run her fingers through wavy light brown locks damp with sweat.

"Wouldn't dream of it, Vera," she declared.

"Wouldn't you just," said Colleen, to loud agreement.

In truth, FANY Greenock would and did.

And she got away with it.

The colonel stood on a dais at the front of the hall. He was a thin-faced man of average height and slight build, with grey-black hair and a fine moustache. In hands clasped behind his back, he carried a polished, silver-tipped swagger cane and wore a jungle-green safari suit with shorts, long socks and black boots that shone like mirrors.

"Bet they keep his batman busy," Colleen whispered to Robyn as the staff filed in and stood easy. The hall had a high ceiling, with tall spaces set in bare, cream-coloured walls for ease of access. Slowly whirling ventilation fans hung from the centre line of the ceiling, evenly interspersed with electric lights.

"Probably got a bevy of Burmese for his every bidding," Robyn whispered back.

This could well have been true. The diminutive, olive-skinned local helpers assiduously undertook all tasks allocated to them. They kept the wards spotless, by means of a daily sweeping and application of whitewash and disinfectant.

"Shh," said Vera, putting a finger to her lips.

With everyone gathered, the CO began his briefing. It was clear that he was strict on discipline.

"All nursing staff to wear standard ward uniforms, with head-squares starched and shoes polished daily," he said curtly. "All patients to be dressed in hospital blues, though we will forgo the red ties until cooler weather. Likewise, the capes for the duty nursing staff. However, patients who can must black and polish boots daily, placing them at the foot of their beds with puttees wrapped in the normal manner. Orderly staff will perform this duty for any convalescents unable to do so. Duty staff will ensure that beds, together with mosquito nets, are at all times correctly in line."

He went on to explain about staff quarters, shifts and equipment and concluded his briefing by introducing Matron Wrigglesworth, a grey-haired woman of dimpled face and sturdy appearance, adorned with the scarlet cape of a regular, bearing a major's crown on each shoulder. She wore a spotless white dress with pearl buttons down the front, white buckskin shoes, matching stockings and a trim white cap – heavily starched.

Her dignified gaze swept benignly over the assemblage, clearly noting the nurses' sweat-stained field uniforms. She addressed the new arrivals separately after the CO's briefing. He had convened an additional meeting with Trenholme, Mostyn and the other MOs.

"Our local women will see to your laundry," Matron said. Her voice was resonant but not harsh.

"They'll give you each two linen bags, for used and fresh," she explained[216]. "We have electric irons available for you to press your ward uniforms. As you can see, we have lighting and ventilation fans, with our engineers having done a splendid job on our electricity generator. It'll tide us over until the mains are fully working. Water is tankered in once a day. Although it's still rationed, we've enough for cooking, drinking, sterilising, laundering and washing – the showers are canvas buckets with holes in that you've probably seen before. We anticipate the water mains will soon be back on stream but nevertheless, until further notice, you must use chlorine tablets if you drink any unboiled water, though you shouldn't have to because now that the port's operational, we can get in plenty of paraffin for heating. Mess is at thirteen hundred hours. I'll inform you of your duties afterwards. For now, we'll show you to your quarters."

"She doesn't seem like too much of a dragon," Colleen remarked after Matron had dismissed them.

A couple of Burmese orderlies were conducting Colleen and her friends to their accommodation wing on the top floor.

"True, but I think our carefree CCS-style days are over, girls," said Gwen with a sigh.

"Good thing we've only got our grey frocks and not that strait jacket Matron was wearing," declared Robyn. "Hope Pencil-moustache doesn't make us requisition any."

"You ought to show a little more respect, Sister Gray," Vera admonished her. "But, yes, those pearl buttons are brutes to fasten."

However, the showers felt luxuriant, with fresh towels being provided, though Colleen noted the wire netting over the drains.

"To keep snakes out, Sister Memsahib," said a smiling Burmese lady attendant.

And no-one could have complained about the billets, swept spotless by the Burmese cleaning ladies and white-washed, each room with its own ventilation fan and electric light – though the lights were extinguished at twenty-two hundred hours in the nurses' quarters, save for 'brown out' illumination in the corridors and wash-room annexes.

The rooms were designed like the conference hall and the wards. Open wall spaces with small glass panels above abutted the veranda, beyond which a glorious view of the gardens presented itself. A full-length woven mat could be unfurled like a Holland blind to cover the space as necessary. Above each metal-framed bed, a hook hung down from the ceiling with mosquito net attached and all the rooms, which were singles, contained, besides the bed and army mattress, a writing table, chair and wardrobe with inbuilt chest of drawers.

"Colonial extravaganza," remarked Trish.

"Waldorf Rangoon," Robyn exclaimed. She deposited her bag and bedroll with a thump on the scrubbed teak floor of her room. "Wish I could bring Jonny."

"Bed's a bit narrow," said Paddy Monaghan from across the corridor.

"All the better," said Robyn, with a cheeky grin.

The Sisters' Mess, where the Burmese women did the catering, was a further source of encouragement.

The last arrivals of nursing staff, numbering about a dozen, were grouped together for a late sitting. On this occasion, Matron was messing with them. She smiled at the expressions of amazement elicited by the immaculate table linen and the magnificent sets of cutlery and crockery.

"Yes, the Japanese kept up the décor of the colonial days." she said. "They weren't too fussy with the state of some of the wards, mind. We had to burn a lot of used straw when we first arrived."

Food was adequate, thanks to regular air drops and supplies would soon be augmented via the port. The local women also brought in substantial quantities of fresh fruit, vegetables, eggs and poultry from their villages. They were fetched by lorry in the morning for each day's work and returned in the evening.

"We reward them quite generously with cigarettes, NAAFI goods and medical care[217]," Matron explained. "They are superb cooks, as you'll no doubt agree."

The remark provoked enthusiastic agreement.

Colleen glanced at her friends as they ate. They looked strange in the uniforms that had remained in their trunks for some months. Nevertheless, all was clean, ironed and polished in accordance with the CO's requirements, though starching of head squares would have to wait – for the starch.

"I'll arrange for you to receive an issue," said Matron.

Trenholme's personnel settled smoothly into the hospital regime but a couple of days after their arrival, it was punctuated by a pleasant surprise for Colleen.

Entering the mess with Trish for a brief tea break, Colleen instantly recognised the slim brunette among the group clustered around a simmering urn.

"Mandy![218]" she exclaimed.

"Colleen!"

The two friends eagerly hugged each other, much to the delight of all.

Since the day was fine, though as usual sultry, Trish and Colleen sat with Mandy out on the veranda, after the necessary introductions had been made.

"Wasn't it wonderful about Annie's lad, Bill, after all these months?" said Mandy as they sipped their tea.

"Yes, Annie wrote to me, too," said Colleen. "We were over the moon. Still are[219]."

The pinnacle of the great Shwe Dagon glinted far off in the muggy haze.

"Wonder when they'll let us visit it?" Mandy remarked.

"Shouldn't be long, I think," said Trish. "But you must be dying to know what's happened since you last saw each other. Who's first? You've got ten minutes each."

Trish glanced at the watch fastened to her blouse and then at the others.

"Well, I'll kick off," said Colleen.

Her account of her experiences since leaving the General elicited Mandy's admiration. "You ought to write a book!" she exclaimed.

Colleen smiled, though she had not mentioned Peter Waverly, nor said much about either Hoppy's death or the attack on Naomi, who still wrote regularly from Amarillo.

"So what about you, Sister Davis?" Colleen asked eagerly. She drank a mouthful of tea and leant forward expectantly.

"Before you start, Mandy," said Trish, getting to her feet. "Anyone want another cup? I think we've got time."

Colleen drained her mug and handed it to Trish.

"Much obliged, Trish," she said. "Thirsty work, this *raconteuring*."

Mugs replenished, Mandy lit a cigarette and began her narrative.

"I came out here after a visit from Lady MountB[220]," she explained.

Crossing her legs, Mandy drew on her cigarette and exhaled smoke.

"Was at Comilla first – I can see you've been there," she said, smiling at Colleen's and Trish's simultaneous grimaces. "Then I went to Arakan until our CCS moved to Magwe[221] and now we're here."

"Where had you been before Comilla?" asked Trish.

"Normandy, then Market Garden," said Mandy. "We went up to Nijmegen in the ambulances to be on hand for the casualties while the Guards were taking the town. Hell of a traffic jam – raining of course – and we kept going past squaddies dug in on either side of the road in case the Boches counterattacked. We took over a school and got flooded with wounded almost immediately. The shelling was close enough to shake the walls. All the windows were broken, glass all over the floor. Pretty nasty."

"You must have been stuck there for quite a while," said Trish.

"Eight weeks, nearly." Mandy flicked ash off her frock. "Funny, though. I must've been coming down the line just as Annie was moving up."

"Ships passing in the night," Trish remarked.

"Yep, at least I missed the worst of the weather, there, anyway," said Mandy.

"Monty came in for some stick, didn't he, about First Airborne getting written off?" Colleen said quietly.

Mandy nodded. When she spoke, her tone was vehement, her azure eyes ablaze with indignation.

"Yes, he did, for claiming it was a ninety-percent success, since they didn't get to Arnhem. But what was he supposed to say? 'Sorry, lads, we made a balls. Your mates died in vain.' Not likely."

"They needed Nijmegen for the Rhine, didn't they?" asked Trish.

"Of course they did," Mandy rejoined. "I actually met Monty, twice, as a matter of fact."

"You were privileged," said Colleen.

"Mmh," said Trish, impressed.

"Sure was. He visited us at the CCS about a month after Market Garden. Instead of wearing BDs like we usually did, we all had to line up in ward uniform, with capes and head squares, and do the curtseying along with the saluting. When he gets to me, he says, 'Sister, I've seen you before.' He jolly well had, too. He'd come to our GH in Blighty, the one I'd been with the year before. He could name the place and the date, where we'd paraded[222]."

Her friends stared in amazement.

"And I've met Uncle Bill[223]," Mandy went on.

"At Comilla?" asked Trish. "He dropped in on us while we were there."

Mandy nodded, knocked ash off her cigarette and drank some tea.

"Our lot weren't very good with visiting brass," she said with an impish grin. "Sometimes, instead of parading us, the heads would make us all sit round in a big marquee. You remember?"

"Wasn't there long enough, fortunately," said Colleen.

"I do," said Trish, wincing. "And I'd rather have been on parade. Those benches got hard on the bum after a while."

"They sure did," Mandy affirmed. "Well, my mates and I used to twitter away on the back row until Matron told us to shut up, but when Uncle Bill came in, we all stood to attention straightaway without a word. He's got such a commanding presence, but when he was introduced to us individually, it was like talking to your dad."

"That's just what we found," said Trish. "Hey, we better get going."

She glanced at her watch and then at their companions, who were piling used mugs on the sideboard for the Burmese women to wash.

Mandy stubbed out her cigarette and after depositing their mugs, the trio joined the others filing into the corridor.

Colleen asked about Jo McCormack[218].

"Jo? Oh, you should see *her*," said Mandy with feeling. "She's a Nightingale[224]. Looks fantastic in air force blue. She was at the airfield near our CCS during Market Garden, seeing to the blokes when the Daks flew them out. Shells dropping near the runway and all sorts."

They lingered for a moment at the stairwell where they would separate en route to their different wards.

"C'mon, Mandy," said a slim, dark-haired girl who rushed past. "We haven't got all day."

"Be with you in a second, Janice," Mandy called. "Jo met a Dak pilot who'd done a couple of tours in Mosquitoes," she said to her companions. "Ship busting for Coastal Command, anywhere between Brest and Bergen. Don't fancy it. Anyway, they're engaged."

"Oh, that's wonderful!" exclaimed Colleen. "But what about *you*?"

Colleen and Trish laughed as Mandy blushed.

"I've settled one of Stedder's blokes," she said with a sigh. "You remember Captain Cosgrove? He's in Italy now."

"Oh, I *do*," said Colleen. "Lovely bloke."

"He sure is," Mandy said wistfully. "So, they did all right out of us, what with Lindy's wedding and Doreen[218] engaged to Major John's best man. She was in Bari, you know, when they had that big mustard gas explosion[225]. Bigwigs told her to keep quiet."

"Do you think she will?" asked Trish.

"Will she, hell," said Mandy firmly. "Colleen'll tell you about our Sister Doreen – "

"Mandy!" Janice called from halfway down the stairwell.

"Must dash," said Mandy. "See you later." She hurried downstairs.

"You too," said Trish as she and Colleen strode off to catch up with their companions. "They were certainly a right lot, Coll, Major John's gang."

Colleen had already entertained her friends with the story of John and Lindy's wedding.

"Ooh, they were gorgeous," she said sensuously. "Like Lieutenant Calvert."

Her companion's face almost turned crimson.

Each ward contained up to a hundred beds and most were occupied, men recovering not only from wounds sustained in action but also, as at Trenholme's CCS, jungle sores, heat stroke, malnutrition and debilitating fevers – largely the result of mosquito bites, worm infestation and the ravages of ticks and leeches. Many men suffered from skin infections aggravated by repeated insect attacks.

"Bugs think a bloke's a walking delicatessen[226], Sister," one patient said to Colleen when she came to apply lotion to his skin. It was pitted and blotched with inflammation.

Other men came in with feet like white slabs from being constantly wet.

"You could sink a knife half an inch into the soles of 'em, Sister," said one as Colleen was examining what resembled crinkled, uncooked pastry that gave off a decaying smell. "And I wouldn't feel a thing."

She'd had to peel off his socks with tongs.

"I'll dry them with alcohol," said Colleen, smiling. "Clean out all those crevices, apply the medication and give you a shot of penicillin to clear up any infection. Bet you feel that."

Sulphonamide and other constipating medication were administered to men suffering from dysentery. Fortunately, all the facilities were in proper working order and regularly disinfected.

One less than pleasant task entailed the care of Japanese wounded, too weak to resist capture.

"We treat them according to the Geneva Convention," Matron said at a briefing.

"Even though the Nips give sod all about it, Matron?" said Colleen.

"Coll," Trish murmured with a pained expression.

"Yes, in spite of that fact, Sister McGrath," Matron said stiffly.

She issued her staff with simple commands in Japanese, such as "Sit up," "Turn over," and "Put out your tongue," with which the prisoners sullenly complied. Contrary to usual hospital procedure, the CO insisted that nursing staff ministering to the Japanese always be accompanied by an armed guard.

In Colleen's case, Corporal Wood was invariably present, with his Webley revolver deliberately conspicuous.

"I must admit, I'm always glad to see the back of them, even the comfort girls," Trish remarked when a batch of prisoners was moved on for internment.

Occasionally, female Japanese camp followers were among the enemy captives. The British Sisters had to keep them apart from the Burmese women, who'd have torn them to pieces but the Japanese girls helped tend their menfolk with great devotion.

At the end of a shift on the still, humid days, after a shower and meal, Colleen and her companions were usually ready to crawl under their mosquito nets and fall blissfully asleep, semi-naked and, if it was night, partially mesmerised by the gyrating glow of fireflies buzzing in through the open window spaces. They found they only needed a blanket or to lower the matting when the monsoon rain swept along the veranda in torrents. On such nights, the air was cooler.

And always, after dark, the sound of frogs, croaking in the garden beds, was quite audible from three floors below.

"Bet they're all saying, 'Kiss me and I'll turn back into a prince,'" Robyn said to Trish and Colleen at breakfast on their first morning at the BGH.

The city was not yet considered safe for sightseeing so the girls spent their off-duty hours exploring the gardens, if it was fine, writing letters – including many for the patients – pressing uniforms, listening to the BBC World Service – Bebe Daniels[227] and ITMA[228] were the favourites - playing bridge or chess and reading, often aloud to one another.

"Or simply flaking out on your bed space," Mandy remarked, after a particularly gruelling shift.

Though they often organised PT sessions in the grounds, "to get the cobwebs out," Mandy's friend Janice remarked.

On Sundays, everyone loved listening to Gwen read the Psalms in her Welsh voice and the services, conducted by visiting padres in the conference hall, were well attended, even if one had to stand throughout.

"'Thou shalt not be afraid for the terror by night'" Colleen said to Gwen after one reading in the mess. "I sure was at the time, though."

"Well," said Gwen sympathetically. "Even the Devil himself has to get permission from Father to kill you, Coll. And where you're concerned, I don't think he ever will."

The statement proved to be prophetic.

Then Sister Jeffries received a home posting, partly because her fiancé, a senior officer, was also now back in England.

Vera had spent more than five years overseas, longer than anyone else serving at the hospital.

All the off-duty staff turned out to farewell her, on a fine but typically steamy morning. Geordie Wood was detailed to drive her to the docks, where she would embark on a hospital ship bound for Calcutta.

On arrival there, she was scheduled to return home with other long-serving personnel by Sunderland flying boat.

"I suppose I'll be back in Blighty by the end of the week, Lord willing," she said to her tearful friends when they exchanged hugs in the vehicle park. "I will be praying you all soon get home safely. Please keep in touch."

Matron described Vera's departure as "a gap we won't easily fill," but the hospital absorbed the loss, with Mandy's friend Janice Porter replacing Vera as Senior Sister. At twenty-six, she was young for the post but the routine continued.

Though it was soon to be varied by some welcome distractions.

When the army reopened the British Sports and Social Club in the town, it attracted an immediate patronage but Colonel Partridge stipulated that, "A nursing Sister may attend only if accompanied by a male officer in uniform of at least equal rank."

"No shortage of takers, I'll bet," said Robyn.

There weren't.

So the walking-out uniforms got ironed as well. Soon, a cinema was opened as part of the club.

The escorts were most chivalrous, especially to married Sisters.

"These golden bands are wonderful," said Robyn, as they waved their officer acquaintances good-bye in the vehicle park after one entertaining night out. "The blokes treat you like a duchess."

They walked across the gravel to the usual sound of croaking frogs. The night was sultry but fine. Robyn gaily held up her left hand with the third finger splayed for all to see.

"You would keep showin' it off and harping on about your Jonny," said Paddy. "Making us all jealous."

They had been out with Colleen, Trish and Rachel. Their escorts were a mixture of British officers from Fourteenth Army and the RAF.

A separate officers' club was opened in a former colonial residence, a mansion set in grounds almost as imposing as those of the hospital. It even had its own mini-theatre. Enhanced by a more intimate atmosphere than the Sports and Social Club, it was ideal for romantic tête-à-têtes and therefore preferred by Kiwi Mostyn and Paddy Monaghan, when they could get time off together.

In the meantime, other friendships begun in Trenholme's CCS were being consolidated.

"Part of recuperation," Mostyn observed dryly.

Recuperation was in fact a drawn-out process for some, not simply because of the time needed for their wounds to heal.

"I feel about ninety years old," Matt Calvert had said on the morning of the drive to Rangoon. He was walking slowly to the ambulance, watched over by Trish, who sought to reassure him.

"It's partly blood loss, Matt," she said. "Even though we transfused you, you're still recovering from the shock of that and the operation and sheer exhaustion. Also, your temperatures are up and in your present condition, even a mild fever will knock you for six."

"Walking case book, eh?" he'd said.

Again, Trish had reassured him.

"Don't worry. You'll soon be back to normal."

Corporal Grafton, whose promotion had recently come through, was similarly debilitated but after several days at the hospital, he began walking along the corridors, for exercise, or the verandas on fine days.

"Try taking a turn in the grounds," suggested Trenholme, whose patient he was. "I'll arrange for someone to be with you, just in case."

FANY Greenock promptly volunteered and Trenholme agreed. She and Grafton had already struck up an acquaintance in the CCS.

"Just let me know when you need a rest," said Rachel, the first time they strolled along the paths.

The air smelt heavy with moisture and the sun burned. Grafton felt the perspiration breaking out on his forehead and trickling down his chest.

"I think I can take a few more minutes," he said.

Gradually, he was able to go further, until one day, they walked to one of the summer-houses, situated a considerable distance from the hospital and partly hidden by shrubbery.

Rachel pushed up some fronds partly obscuring the entrance to the house. The couple went in and sat on one of the benches.

"I really appreciate these walks, Rach," Grafton said shyly. "Your company, I mean."

Rachel brushed some fallen blossoms from her skirt. She, too, spoke shyly – at first.

"So do I, Leigh. Mind you, I escort a lot of blokes around the grounds but I always look forward to our little treks."

"I'll be going back up country before too long," said Leigh. "But could we keep in touch? If I can find a dry scrap of note paper up there, I'll write."

His slim companion tucked a few loose strands of light brown hair beneath her head square and touched Grafton's arm gently.

He thrilled to the touch of Rachel's lips as she kissed him lightly on the cheek.

"Promise?" she said softly.

He nodded.

The fully-fledged kiss that followed definitely sealed the promise.

"I was holding the corporal's arm to steady him, Matron," Rachel later explained to Matron Wrigglesworth.

Along with other convalescents, Matt was also taking to the grounds on fine days. Trish went with him when she could.

Like his batman, Calvert insisted on wearing the new JGs the convalescents had been issued with, short puttees and boots that Trish knew Matt would polish regardless of the hospital regimen.

"I'm not wandering round outside in pyjamas," he said to Trish.

Eventually, Trenholme removed Matt's stitches.

"That feels much better," Calvert said to Trish when next they went walking. "But you better hang onto my arm, just in case."

Trish had held Matt's left arm during their walks, "to stop him scratching, Matron," she'd said. "He finds the stitches a bit itchy."

They came to a T intersection in the path, where a massive flame tree cast a cooling shadow on one corner. The couple paused in its shade.

"Look, Trish, there's something I must show you." Calvert said earnestly.

He reached into a trouser pocket, produced an official letter and gave it to her.

Trish instantly recognised the logo and quickly scanned the contents.

"Oh, Matt, that's wonderful!" she exclaimed. "You've been accepted."

"Arrived in yesterday's post. So, Lord willing, I'm going up to Oxford after the war."

His steely grey gaze met her calm blue eyes as he spoke again.

"There's a lot to think about," he said with considerable emotion. "But, well, I'd like you to be there, if you can be."

Trish could never explain her response to the Australian's plea, except that it was spontaneous. She leant forward, closed her eyes and kissed Matt full on the lips. He slipped both arms around Trish's waist and pulled her close, pressing his lips firmly against hers.

As they returned to the ward, Trish still holding Matt's arm, Sister Calder desperately hoped that her outward demeanour concealed her inner turmoil.

You two-timing hussy, Trish Calder, she was thinking. Oh, Mum, I wish you were here. Oh, God, what do I do?

That night, Trish lay in bed, staring upwards.

Evan Dane's letter was open on the table. It had arrived that afternoon.

Dear Trish, it read.

I hope you will understand that it is not through any loss of affection for you that I am compelled to write in this way. However, in recent months, I have come to be drawn very deeply to a senior WRN officer named Amelia who shares my vision for mission work.

After much reflection, we are firmly convinced that God would have us co-labour in the ministry as man and wife. Whilst I regret having to inform you of these devel-

opments, we both wish you every blessing for the future and trust you will be able to have confidence that the Lord's will is best.

   Yours sincerely,
   Evan

"Yes, Evan, every confidence," said Trish with a yawn. She turned on her side and nestled her head in the pillow.

Falling asleep, she reflected blissfully on Matt's battalion motto[229], from Ninth Australian Division.

What we have, we hold.

He would, she knew.

The strictures of hospital discipline notwithstanding, word of these proceedings never reached the CO, whose main activities seemed to consist of writing reports, conducting regular inspections and attending high-level conferences at Army HQ. His routine never varied.

Except in one instance, Matron, who of course knew all, maintained a sphinx-like reserve. The rest of the staff took their cue from her.

The exceptional occasion centred on none other than Sister McGrath.

Part way through a particularly humid afternoon, when the wall mats had been lowered in the wards to block the sun's intensity, a Burmese porter summoned Colleen to accompany him to the foyer.

"Colonel Sahib's order, Sister Memsahib," the little man informed her.

They descended the marble staircase into the hospital's reception area, an impressive arena of polished teak furnishings, huge potted ferns and old-style architecture dating from the days of the Raj.

For once, Colleen was oblivious to it when she caught sight of the tall officer attired in brand new JGs, who was speaking to Colonel Partridge.

"Peter!" she exclaimed.

Impulsively, she rushed into his arms and kissed him fervently.

He held her close and whispered, "I've missed you, Colleen."

But Colleen immediately noted the puckered and puffy condition of Peter's face, showing that the mosquitoes and midges had persistently preyed on him. She also noticed how yellow he looked from mepacrine, as we all do, she reflected.

Remembering that her commanding officer was present, she stepped back from Waverly when he released her from his embrace, stood to attention and smartly saluted the colonel.

"You wish to see me, sir?" she asked, trying to sound formal.

Partridge returned her salute and cleared his throat.

"Er, yes, Sister, I've arranged for Matron to cover the remainder of your shift," he explained in humility. "That will give you the opportunity to spend some time with Lord Waverly."

Colleen strove to conceal her astonishment.

"Why, thank you, sir," she said graciously. Turning to Peter, she added with affection, "Just need to change. I'll be back in a minute."

Waverly smiled and Colonel Partridge continued to look deferential.

Colleen dashed back upstairs, her ward shoes clicking rapidly on the marble steps.

Before she returned to her room, Colleen dropped in at the Sisters' Mess, desperately hoping to find some off-duty colleagues. She sighed with gratitude to see Robyn, Paddy and Janice Porter, reclining in easy chairs – for now the Mess was equipped with such – reading the latest issue of *SEAC*, imbibing tea and listening to the radio. They weren't due to come on until Colleen's shift finished.

"Look, could one of you please be a pal and help Matron with the rest of my shift?" Colleen asked while getting her breath back. "I'll do one of yours, of course. The CO's given me some time off but I must use it now."

She paused, still breathing deeply and then asked, "Can I please borrow your heels, Robbie?"

The Sisters in Trenholme's former command had greatly admired the high-heeled shoes that Robyn and Trish purchased during the Sunderbans trip. They were more *chic* than the normal, semi-heeled walking-out shoes.

The trio put their papers down, glanced at each other and then eyed Colleen with a hint of suspicion.

"Who is he?" asked Paddy.

"I'll explain later," said Colleen hastily. "I said I'd only be a minute, you see."

She looked pointedly at the watch fastened to her grey cotton blouse.

"Hmm," said Janice. "I suppose we can sort something out. As it happens, I've got a pair of heels you could have used. Maybe another time. I think they'd fit."

"Oh, thanks, Jan, on both counts!" exclaimed Colleen. "And you, too, Robbie. I owe you one."

She patted Robyn's shoulder before departing.

"You certainly do," said Robyn as Colleen hurried off. "Don't fall over and break your neck, or my heels, especially not my heels."

Janice actually possessed not one but two such pairs – one of which Colleen was destined to wear to her advantage some months later.

"I think I got most of your letters," Waverly said when he conducted Colleen to his jeep. "Sorry I didn't reply as much as I should have. Hasn't been easy keeping dry."

Colleen tightened her grip on the major's arm.

"Doesn't matter," she said. "You're here in person. But hold still for a second."

From her web bag, Colleen produced a small vial of ointment wrapped in a handkerchief and skilfully applied it to the blemishes on Waverly's face and wrists.

"Take some of the itch out of them," she said and wiped her fingers on the handkerchief.

Waverly looked pleased.

"Thank you, Sister," he said humbly.

"Don't mention it," said Colleen, kissing him lightly.

"Was able to check into the officers' club for a couple of days," Peter explained, as he climbed into the driver' seat. "I took a chance on seeing you. Very good of them to let you off."

Colleen settled back in the passenger seat and smoothed her skirt, glad that she had decided to wear a shirt only, with sleeves rolled up. It was too warm for a jacket.

"Old Pencil – I mean Colonel Partridge - would fall all over himself for the sake of a lord, milord," she said, laughing. "Which is fine with me, Peter."

She hugged him quickly as he steered the jeep towards the entrance to the grounds. On the way out, they passed a couple of ambulances coming in followed by several lorries bringing up supplies from one of the freighters berthed at the docks. Transporting wounded from the battlefront to the hospital, conveying convalescents to hospital ships for onward transfer to India and maintaining the goods and services required by the hospital was an almost round-the-clock business. Enlisted men from the unit, like Sergeant Nicholson and Corporal Wood, charged with these responsibilities, were as hard-worked as their medical and nursing officer colleagues.

Waverly parked the jeep in a tree-shaded access road beside a wide thoroughfare abutting the Shwe Dagon Pagoda's south entrance. A long flight of stone steps led up a grassy mound to the base of the pagoda, from where its huge, conical, glistening eminence rose over three hundred feet into hazy skies.

Guardian beasts of white stone, half-lion, half-dragon, painted in colours of red, blue and gold, crouched malevolently on either side of the foot of the stairs.

"Jeep should be OK here," Waverly said as he and Colleen alighted.

Fourteenth Army sentries, equipped with rifle and bayonet, policed the area. The large numbers of brown-hued Burmans who wandered along the footpaths, seemed hardly to notice them but the soldiers' presence meant that Allied servicewomen, with uniformed male escorts, could visit the area.

Peter took Colleen's hand and observing a break in the traffic, they walked briskly over the thoroughfare to the foot of steps.

Even that short effort brought them both out again in perspiration but the afternoon was continuing fine. Colleen was glad of that. Monsoon rains had bucketed down during the night and persisted until midday.

"It's taller than Saint Paul's, you know," Waverly remarked. Shading his eyes, he gazed up at the vast tapering structure before them. "Japs are supposed to have stripped off the gold leaf but stumped if I can see where."

"Can't look at it for long," said Colleen.

The surface of the pagoda radiated sheer brilliance in the sun's unrelenting glare. An onlooker couldn't stand the brightness for more than a few seconds.

"Well named, though," said Peter. "After the Philistines' idol[230]."

"Coincidence?" Colleen asked.

Though awed by the sight, she felt the same revulsion she had on having first seen the pagodas up north[231] and looking at the guardian beasts, she sensed the kind of unease Trish and Robyn had described when recollecting the excursion to Kali's temple.

Waverly shrugged.

"Same adversary. You can't go up to the base from here except in bare feet and I don't suppose we're about to oblige the Devil so let's look around elsewhere."

Her revulsion notwithstanding, Colleen found the sights fascinating.

She forgot about time as they walked - thankfully much of the way beneath shady groves - past dozens of lesser pagodas, red lacquered wooden shrines, more carved stone beasts - elephants, lions, sphinxes and hideous looking ogres, half-human, half-serpentine - and innumerable little shops or stalls, selling a seemingly infinite array of 'aids to worship;' including miniature images of Buddha, tinselled icons of him, gilt-encrusted household shrines, carvings of wood, ivory and tortoise shells, tiny marionette dolls, richly scented flowers, wax candles, joss sticks and strings of rosary beads.

"The beads are the same as the ones we had at school," said Colleen.

"Satan's the god of this world[232], Colleen," said Waverly. "You'll find the same demonic kit anywhere, more or less."

Further along, they came to an extensive bazaar where clothes, shoes, jewellery and other trinkets were on sale, together with yet more religious artefacts.

"It all looks a bit tatty," said Colleen in disappointment.

She had been hoping to find a cobbler who could make her a pair of high heels like Robyn's but the shoe stalls seemed to be manned only by retailers, mostly Chinese.

"Well, let's move on," said Waverly.

They continued threading their way through thronging, chattering crowds, occasionally exchanging greetings with other couples in uniform until they came to an array of cafés behind the bazaar, where they decided to sit for a while on one of the benches, underneath the enshrouding foliage of a full-grown neem tree.

Many locals slept on them after dark but for now, having dried off quickly in the heat after the morning rain, they served as stopping places for tourists.

Colleen removed her cap, placed it in her lap and took a small compact out of her web bag. She withdrew a comb and a mirror from it to adjust her hair. She then mopped her face with a handkerchief and dabbed on some lipstick. Replacing the compact and her cap, she removed Robyn's high heels and massaged her feet.

"You look nice," said Peter. "Really nice."

"Thank you, milord," Colleen said demurely, slipping the shoes back on.

Waverly rested his cap on his knee. He seemed unaffected by the heat.

"They can really close these stalls down fast when the rain hits," he said. "Quicker than you can say Aung San[233]."

"Not much damage here."

Colleen flicked a silver-winged insect off her arm. The aromas of brewing coffee, fragrant spices and pungent incense smoke mingled in her nostrils with the reek of packed humanity to yield the intense, unforgettable odour of the East.

"It's mainly further on, towards the docks," said Peter. "I'd offer to get you a cup of coffee," he added, gesturing towards the nearest café. "But I think it's safer not to. I've got a water bottle stashed in the jeep and of course, you are dining with me at the club this evening?"

He glanced at her, expectantly.

"Thank you, kind sir," said Colleen, smiling. "Where to, now?"

"Let's go up the west steps," Peter suggested. "You don't have to take your shoes off."

Part way up the pagoda hill, they stopped to lean against the balustrade and admire the view. In the crimson glow of late afternoon, it was magnificent, a panoramic vista ranging across tall palms ringing the pagoda precinct, extending over the sprawling expanse of the city and swinging back to the massive bulk of the pagoda, now seemingly bathed in golden fire.

Colleen rested her hands on the stone parapet and straightened up to stretch her back muscles. Her shirt still stuck to her skin but the air was cooler now and she was feeling more refreshed. She glanced at the pagoda.

"Shiniest phallus[234] in the world."

"Exactly," said Peter, with a grin.

Then he enclosed his hand on hers.

"I got a reply about your posting."

Colleen nodded, feeling a little apprehensive. One of Peter's letters had said that he had written to a friend in the War Office, enquiring about *the possibility of a home posting for a serving QA Officer interested in psychiatric work* and mentioning the hospital in Derbyshire.

In the poignant interlude outside the jungle hospital, Colleen had easily been drawn to the major's generous invitation but now she had mixed feelings because acceptance of Peter's offer could well mean a premature separation from her friends.

Colleen wasn't sure she wanted that.

She smiled and looked at him enquiringly.

"Reading between the lines, my mate put two-and-two together, of course, about us, I mean," Peter said. "But he reckons he can swing it, maybe before the end of the year. There's a catch, though."

"There always is, darling," said Colleen soothingly. She clasped both hands about his.

"Not an insurmountable one," Waverly hastened to reassure her. "It's just that you'll have to spend a bit of time at an ordinary base hospital, so they can vet you before turning you loose on the head cases. My mate suggested Catterick, since it's not far from your home address. Reckons he can fix that, too. I'd mentioned it to him. Hope that was OK."

"Of course it is," whispered Colleen. Standing on the balls of her feet, she arched her neck and kissed him.

Waverly flushed distinctly. Then, glancing at his watch and the sinking sun, he said, "Guess we better head back."

Hand-in-hand, they strolled back to the jeep, watching the trees grow black against a sky of deepening violet, listening to the drumming of cicadas. The stalls were being dismantled and cooking fires were already glowing red in the living quarters. The distinct smell of wood smoke pervaded the surroundings.

When they reached the vehicle, Colleen noted that the guard was doubled.

"Just a precaution," said Waverly. "So is this," he added and pulled up the jeep's cover.

Colleen remembered Peter's awareness of impending storms. By the time they got to the club, the skies were teeming.

Peter rummaged in the jeep for a raincoat and Colleen pulled hers out of her web bag. Together, they hurried to the club's entrance through the splashing downpour.

"I'm bustin,'" Colleen said distinctly when they entered the front parlour, now the club's reception area. "See you in a few minutes."

She strode hastily down the hall to the ladies' rest room, her heels resounding on the teak floor.

"Wonder if I should have said, 'Peter, I need to wash'?" she murmured. "Oh, well, he'll have to accept I'm a northern lass, plain-spoken."

As she pushed open the door to the Ladies' the thought occurred to her that perhaps things were moving too fast, like they had before.

But she suppressed it.

The evening nevertheless proceeded delightfully. After a splendid meal in the mansion's imposing dining room, they adjourned to the club's theatre to enjoy a recent Humphrey Bogart film, *Casablanca*[235].

An enlisted steward conducted the couple to one of the few remaining adjacent pairs of seats in the crowded rows.

"The film's got rave reviews, sir," he said to Waverly.

Despite the relaxed atmosphere – clouded with cigarette smoke – Colleen noticed how tense Peter looked when *La Marseillaise*[235] was sung, even though the rest of the audience lustily cheered and loudly echoed the more familiar lines of the chorus[236].

"Marchons! Marchons!

"Qu'un sang impur

"Abreuve nos sillons!"

She knew he was thinking about Collette. Gently, she took his hand and held it.

Rain was still pouring down when Peter brought Colleen back to the hospital. The guard had retreated onto the ground floor veranda but they snapped to attention and presented arms when Waverly and Colleen mounted the steps, wearing their raincoats as capes.

"Thank you, thank you," said the major, quickly returning the salutes.

Once inside, Colleen hugged Peter and kissed him affectionately.

"It's been wonderful, Peter," she whispered. "See you soon."

"Of course, darling. Bye for now."

When they had parted, Colleen slipped off Robyn's heels and hurried up to the Sisters' quarters in her stockinged feet, noting that all seemed subdued in the wards.

She couldn't help singing *As Time Goes By*[235] under her breath.

"You must remember this,

"A kiss is just a kiss, a sigh is just a sigh.

"The fundamental things apply,

"As time goes by."

Ironically, Colleen would discover that the movie had in a strange way portended her own future.

On reaching her room, she saw that someone had thoughtfully lowered the wall matting to keep out the rain. She placed Robyn's shoes on top of the wardrobe near the whirling fan to dry, doffed her cap, unslung her web bag, hung up her raincoat and undressed. Wrapping herself in a towel, she bagged her laundry, grabbed her toothbrush and toothpaste tube and headed for the ablutions annex.

When she came back from the shower, she changed into fresh underwear and crawled into bed.

She wasn't prepared for what happened next.

Suppressed giggles and the muffled padding of several pairs of feet sounded from the corridor.

The door to her room burst open and at the flick of the wall switch, the ceiling light shed its brownish glow – for partial light was now available in the Sisters' rooms until after midnight.

"What on earth?" Colleen exclaimed.

She sat bolt upright, threw off the mosquito netting and swung her feet onto the floor, to stare open-mouthed at the smiling faces of her friends, clad like Colleen only in bra and knickers; Gwen, Janice, Kitty, Mandy, Paddy, Rachel, Robyn and Trish.

They had brought two jugs of lime and lemon with them from the Sisters' Mess and enough glasses to go round.

Janice, being senior, reposed in Colleen's chair. Gwen and Kitty sat on Colleen's bed. The others, kneeling, arranged themselves primly on the floor. Drinks were poured and passed around.

The wry comments followed in quick succession, interspersed with giggles.

"Good thing we're all off duty," said Paddy.

"Yes, wouldn't have missed this for anything," said Gwen.

Colleen was bewildered.

"Missed what, for heaven's sake?" she asked, sipping her drink.

"Your explanation, Sister McGrath," said Janice, in her best Senior Sister's voice.

"Of how you came to be so pally with His Lordship," Kitty added.

"Word's got around, has it?" Colleen asked apprehensively.

"You bet it has," Mandy affirmed. "So we kept an eye out for you."

"He's only the most eligible bachelor in SEAC," said Robyn, topping up several glasses within reach. "After my Jonny, of course, before I got my brand on him."

"Ooh, meow, spit, hiss, what about my Gruffie?" Rachel protested.

"Let her get on with it," said Trish and rapped her knuckles on the floor. "C'mon, Coll, the floor's yours – except for the bits we're occupying."

Colleen responded with a brief account of how she had met Peter in the Karen village. Her listeners reacted with exuberance at key points.

"We've kept in touch since," said Colleen. "Though he doesn't get many chances to write."

"Hard when the heavens open every day and you're usually out in the open," said Robyn sympathetically.

Colleen nodded. "Hey, thanks for your shoes, by the way. I put them up there to dry," she said, pointing to the top of the wardrobe.

"Thanks, Coll," said Robyn. "Let me know if you want to borrow them again."

"Or mine," said Trish. "Anything we can do to further the cause."

"Same goes for me," said Janice. "Like I said."

Colleen thanked them.

"Wonder why Kiwi didn't mention anything to me," Paddy remarked. She sounded a bit miffed.

"I swore him to secrecy," Colleen explained. "Decided to keep it low key for a while, what with last time and all. Anyway, you know what the rumour mill's like around here."

"Hmm," said Paddy sceptically. "Well, I suppose I'll forgive him. Anyone like another drink?"

She reached for one of the jugs. It was about a third full.

Before anyone could respond, the door opened and Matron strode in.

"*What* is all this?" she asked sternly.

The eight Sisters immediately sprang to attention, some still holding their glasses.

"Just a bit of a get together, Matron," said Janice.

"Rather vociferous. I could hear you down the corridor."

Intent on cornering Sister McGrath, the girls had overlooked the possibility of Matron touring the nurses' quarters on her nightly rounds, as she occasionally did.

"Would you like a drink, Matron?" Robyn asked. "I'll get a clean glass."

Matron's expression softened a little.

"Thank you, Sister Gray," she said agreeably. "You're most kind."

When Robyn returned and had poured her superior a drink, Matron delivered a short homily, in between sips, on proper observance of after-hours discipline.

"And the seniors should set the example, Sister," she said in conclusion, looking keenly at Janice, who muttered, "Yes, Matron."

Colleen was desperately trying to avoid Matron's gaze. Otherwise, the twinkle in the other woman's eyes would have reduced her to hysterics. She knew her friends were likewise striving to keep straight faces.

Matron's parting shot nearly did for their composure, nonetheless.

"Imps," she said, eyeing the bevy of beautifully proportioned nubile forms paraded before her. "Just think, if the lads could see you now. Set a few pulses racing, I'll wager. Good night to you all."

"Good night, Matron," her charges chorused.

Immediately the door closed, they all collapsed, striving to stifle the peels of merriment.

"You really can laugh 'til you cry," gasped Kitty, convulsed on the floor.

Colleen managed to dine with Waverly the following night at the officer's club. Robyn, who was with her friend when the arrangements were made, generously lent Colleen her shoes again.

"Next time, they're for hire," she teased. "Bet his lordship could afford it."

Kiwi Mostyn and Paddy Monaghan would be accompanying them. Since Major the Lord Waverly had asked Colonel Partridge if he could catch up with his old friend, the CO didn't demur.

But Colleen was also pleased that Matt and Trish would be joining the party.

"Matt's going back to his battalion, tomorrow, Matron," Trish explained. "Can I spirit him away for a bit, please?"

"I'll make sure my back is turned, Sister," Matron said kindly.

Corporal Grafton was determined to return with his officer, even though his physiotherapy – conducted by FANY Greenock – wasn't complete.

"I suppose I can boot you out, though you'll have a bit of an ache for a while," Trenholme had said nonchalantly when Grafton requested to be discharged. "Got plans for this evening?"

"Yes, sir," he said eagerly.

Waverly had sent an invitation to him and Rachel, via Colleen.

"Join us if you like. I'll sign you in. No-one'll make a fuss."

No-one did.

And the couples remembered it as the most delightful evening they'd ever experienced.

Only once did anyone mention the war; Peter, who was up to date with all troop movements.

But in true gentlemanly fashion, he waited until an opportunity arose between courses, when the girls decided to go powder their noses.

"All together, so we can compare notes on you lot," Trish whispered to Matt before she departed.

"We'll be seeing each other up country," Waverly told Calvert and Grafton. "Your battalion[237] and my Karens are covering adjacent sectors."

"Japs are still trying to break through to the Sittang?" asked Calvert.

Peter nodded.

"Coming down from the Yomas like a pack of lemmings. Our job is simple."

"Intercept and destroy," said Matt.

"Correct," said Waverly. "We'll have a joint briefing tomorrow when you get there."

"Just remember," Mostyn said grimly. "I don't want to see any of you blokes in a professional capacity. Not unless I'm your local GP."

"I think we'd go along with that, sir," said Corporal Grafton. "Whether or not we plan to emigrate."

A waiter came and collected the plates from the first course.

Seeing Paddy and the other girls re-entering the restaurant, they began discussing the dessert menu that the waiter had left with them.

The four Sisters convened briefly in Trish's room after they got back to the hospital. They would be on duty when Peter, Matt and Leigh returned to their units the following day and the farewells hadn't been easy.

They knelt together in the middle of the floor.

For a little while, only the delicate whirring of the ventilation fan could be heard and the pattering of night rain against the woven mat enclosing the wall space.

Apart from the croaky frogs and they seemed strangely subdued.

Then Trish began to speak.

"Dear Father," she said. "Thank You for our menfolk. Enable us to carry out our duties in Thy strength, trusting in Thee to reunite us at the proper time. Between now and then, grant each of our men the strength to overcome the difficulties they must face. We ask also for Paddy and Kiwi to be joined together soon, as we believe it is Your will as well as theirs. We also ask for Thee to open the hearts of our friends Mandy and Janice and draw them to Thyself in lovingkindness. We ask all this in the Name of Thy Son, the Lord Jesus Christ. Amen."

"Amen," said her companions.

Eyes were moist when they had finishing praying. Paddy reached across and grasped Trish's hand.

"Thanks, Trish," she said.

Manifold duties had severely disrupted the wedding plans. Even though that was to be expected, everyone felt encouraged that a way through might soon be opened.

About a score of men from the East and West Yorkshire Regiments would be returning to their units with Calvert and Grafton.

Several had been in Colleen's particular care.

They insisted on serenading her with their own version of a familiar chorus.

"Our girl's a Yorkshire girl,
"Yorkshire through and through,
"Our girl's a Yorkshire girl,
"Eh, by gum, she's a champion,

"She's a bonny QA lass,
"In grey and scarlet dress,
"We've a sort of Yorkshire relish,
"For our Yorkshire QA rose."

Colleen was sure her face was as scarlet as the edge of her cape. She didn't trust her voice as the lads climbed into their lorry but waved to them and blew kisses until they drove out of sight.

She then took out a handkerchief and wiped her eyes.

The next day, a letter arrived from June. It reminded Colleen sharply of another prayer meeting, held on the way to the Gothic Line.

Its contents almost overwhelmed her.

Choking back tears, she sought out Trish. They went over June's letter together in Trish's room.

Dear Colleen,

Many apologies, I haven't written for a while. We moved up into Austria through the Dolomites on the way to Graz (though that's in the Russian Zone – suffice to say they are beasts; murderers and rapists mainly). However, the scenery was magnificent and we are in a wonderful location, with a fair bit of time for sight seeing, swimming and boating – some beautiful lakes close by. The weather is glorious.

I regret I have some sad news. Dinah was killed by a sniper when we left Argenta and before then, Bronwyn fell ill with cerebral malaria and died in a couple of hours, despite all we could do. Truth to tell, it was one reason for the delay in writing. I just couldn't bring myself to put pen to paper until now. None of us could and I trust we have your forgiveness. We had a lot of malaria cases from the marshes around Argenta but this was unusual. We're still getting over it and I'm sorry to be the bearer of such bad news.

Mollie was with Dinah when it happened but she's OK and, now for the good news, she and Brian are married and will be on their way home soon, with Brian's demob number coming up. What's more, Andy and Dollie have tied the knot, along with Helen and Larry and – would you believe – Mike and me! Of course, we are in the ideal place for honeymooning.

Karen got a posting to a hospital near SHAEF HQ where Barry is now and Julie got herself transferred to First Canadian Army HQ to be with Mac, who's a Warrant Officer these days. Rev Allerton kindly went up at their invitation to marry them after he'd finished with us, so he's been busy. He reckons that MGH ought to stand for 'Married – Going Home.' I should mention that owing to the lads' demob numbers, we'll also be going home and so won't see you out there – but I know you'll come visit when you get back and we all pray that won't be too long.

Just one extra thing, I can't say too much but you may be getting an official visitor soon. This person interviewed some of us recently and was very interested to learn about the near misses you've had. Sorry to keep you in the dark but you'll know when you're summoned.

In the meantime, take care and we all send our love
Remember, 'The Lord is thy keeper' Psalm 121:5
June (Halliard (!))

"That was Bronwyn's favourite Psalm," said Colleen, drying her eyes. "I think I'm here now, because of her. She finished what Annie started, and June and Dollie, got me 'accepted in the Beloved[238],' I mean."

Trish smiled and dabbed her own eyes with a handkerchief.

"Think it's time we spoke to Him again, don't you?" she said. "I wonder what that mysterious bit at the end is all about."

The mystery would take some time to unravel. But it would not be without further incident while Grandma Colleen was in the Far East.

Soon afterwards, more moves were afoot.

Kiwi Mostyn received a promotion to major and a posting to a hospital in India as senior MO for the remainder of his tenure. Sister Monaghan applied for and received a transfer to the same hospital on compassionate grounds.

"We'll be able to stop off in Calcutta for the wedding," Paddy told her friends, when she and Mostyn dropped in at the Sisters' Mess during a change of shift to convey the news. It was received with squeals of delight.

Mingaladon Airfield was now functioning and the couple would fly out by C-47 with a consignment of patients for India.

"Bit of a busman's holiday," said Kiwi nonchalantly. "Still, won't be long before we're down under."

Sarah Monaghan's family had emigrated to New Zealand pre-war. The move had fortuitously provided fertile soil for her relationship with Mostyn to develop, even in the stress of the CCS environment.

They weren't the only ones about to depart.

Major Trenholme was overdue for repatriation. He would be flying out with another batch of patients.

"If anyone deserves to go home to his missus, he does," Trish said, on hearing the news. "He looks as knackered as that poor bloke Bedser."

As promised, Trish had written to Mrs Bedser, and received a terse reply. When Trish showed the letter to Colleen, Robyn and Gwen, they thought it hilarious.

"Telling you to sling your hook, I reckon," Colleen remarked.

"And keep it slung, Calder, you gold-digger," Robyn added.

"My missive has admirably achieved its purpose," said Trish haughtily.

Everyone was glad for Major Trenholme.

His sojourn at the hospital, coming straight after the onerous responsibility for his CCS, had not been a happy one. Trenholme's pre-occupation with individual patient care had worked wonders all the way from Imphal and before but it did not always sit easily with Colonel Partridge's near-obsession with 'system' and the two were known to have had words on occasion.

"Bureaucrat," the major had been overheard to mutter on leaving the CO's office, after one such incident.

Kiwi Mostyn, who invariably backed his former CO, likewise incurred Partridge's ire but with Paddy on hand to pour out his heart to, the forthright New Zealander was able to bear the frustration more easily than Trenholme.

Others soon to go included Rachel and Kitty, recalled to their parent unit on the expiration of their stint with the Army Nursing Service, a particularly generous loan by their CO. To maintain the hospital's establishment – and Colonel Partridge's peace of mind – a replacement draft of personnel from the former European Theatre of Operations was soon to take the repatriates' places.

"Going to be quite a gang at your wedding, Paddy," said Kitty exuberantly. "My bod's a Dak pilot – based at Dum Dum, now."

"You better start writing invites for yours, Puck," said Rachel.

"We know some really good places for a honeymoon, don't we Gwennie?" said Robyn enthusiastically.

"We certainly do," said Gwen. "But, oh, it's time to go, you lot!" she added, raising her voice above the chatter.

With a clattering of cups onto the sideboard by the sink, followed by some quick hugs and heartfelt best wishes to Mostyn and Paddy, the next shift hurried off to the wards.

"Always have to get on, don't we?" Colleen remarked to Trish as they sped down the corridor.

"Yes," said her companion, adjusting her head square. "Business as usual."

It would not be long before the business would enter a new and heart-rending phase.

But at least the ordeals would soon be over for men confronting the enemy in the fighting zones.

Sittang Bend, July-August, 1945.

Another day of mist and drenching rain.

Corporal Grafton's shoulder ached, as Trenholme had predicted, though it was easing with each passing day. Nevertheless, he would have appreciated more of Rachel's physiotherapy, or simply more of Rachel.

Company HQ was established in a long bamboo *basha* with typical veranda, donated by the headman of the village that lay at the junction of the West Yorks' sector and that of Waverly's Karens. The villagers were nervous about the reputedly fierce hillmen in close proximity but Waverly tactfully allayed their fears.

"My Karens will be acting as scouts for the British battalion," he explained to the head villager. "They will be across the river a lot of the time and are not permitted to enter the village area unless ordered – and accompanied - by myself."

Thereafter, tension eased considerably.

Grafton was trudging through the gravelly stodge that constituted the village street, past dripping huts on either side, to report to Matt Calvert, now promoted Captain and having been conferred on his return from hospital by the CO as company commander.

The corporal was exhausted. Everyone was, after every patrol in the rank humidity. His section, that included his friends Stony Rockford, now a lance corporal and Signaller Terry Hogarth, was back in their thatched bungalow billet, cleaning weapons preparatory to putting on the evening brew.

But Grafton's first job was to report the outcome of the patrol to his OC.

The HQ hut lay at the end of the street, where the village perimeter merged with one of the patches of jungle that manifested itself as a dark smudge on the water-logged landscape of paddy fields extending eastwards to the Sittang.

This was the country over which the survivors of three Japanese armies were attempting to break through the Allied cordon. Almost twelve thousand of them, two-thirds their original number, were destined to die in the attempt[237] as they straggled down from the brooding mass of the Yomas.

Like all of Fourth Corps' battalions, the West Yorks had spent most of its time since the fall of Pegu on patrol; setting up ambushes astride jungle tracks, searching isolated villages or *bashas*, stumbling amid slimy morasses of meshed creepers and twisted tree roots or wading through the flooded paddies.

From time to time, the patrols encountered turgid tributaries of the Sittang that they crossed by means of canoe-like craft borrowed from the locals. Two miles an hour was good going in the conditions.

Occasionally, one of the ochre-coloured *chaungs* would reveal itself as host to swarms of dark, serpentine shapes swimming sinuously in its depths. These rivulets were too narrow for canoes but the lads never waded them.

"We'll go along the bank until we find some fallen trees where we can cross," the patrol leader invariably declared.

In the weeks since Calvert and Grafton had rejoined the battalion, its patrols had accounted for swathes of the foe, with little loss to themselves.

Although when the frenzied, emaciated Japanese had inflicted wounds, sometimes with nothing more than sharpened bamboo canes, casualty evacuation was a nightmare.

Stretcher bearers crossing the inundated fields en route for the RAPs could never lay down their burdens to rest. To do so would have drowned the casualty in two or three feet of muddy water. RAMC Corporal Stitch Kelsey and the other medics performed admirable feats of both great endurance and emergency treatment.

But of late, the West Yorks had seen no enemy, except for droves of bullet-torn and grotesquely swollen corpses floating in the twisting brown stretches of the Sittang, victims of deadly ambushes in other sectors.

However, the swarms of leeches and blizzards of mosquitoes invariably plagued the patrols with their own style of ambush. They were, as Hogarth said, "A right pain."

Grafton mounted the steps to the veranda, shook water from his bush hat and monsoon cape and entered the nearly bare room where Matt Calvert was seated at a trestle table, collating the patrols' reports by the light of a hurricane lamp.

Muted conversation sounded from an adjacent room, where the Acting CSM Fell, formerly Corporal Fell, was discussing the next day's patrolling with newly-promoted Platoon Sergeant Dymock and his section commanders. Repatriation of its longest serving members and the shortage of reinforcements had halved the battalion's effective strength, necessitating some accelerated "kicks upstairs," as Stony put it. Lieutenant Abercrombie and his colleague Lorrimer, who had recovered from his wounds, now commanded companies.

Symonds, Warwick, Howard, Moorcroft and O'Hare had all gone home, via the 'big boats' as the boys called the troop transports that they boarded at the Rangoon Docks, Howard and O'Hare after recuperating in the BGH, where the nurses were reputed to be "too beautiful for words."

But the lads were pleased to see the city as well, even if only in transit. Like all their fellow countrymen in the Black Cat Division, the West Yorks had vehemently denounced the orders sending them back up the Rangoon Road to cut off the Japs debouching from the Yomas but soon reverted to their usual stoicism, with grudging remarks like, "Ah, sod it. Charge your magazines, lads and let's get crackin'."

The corporal saluted and his officer sat upright in response. Grafton leant his rifle against a wall and looped his cape over it.

Calvert stood up and spread out a map of the sector on the table. He took a sharpened pencil and pointed to the village.

"OK, Gruffie, let's go over the route," he said.

Grafton thought his officer sounded as tired as he felt. Calvert certainly looked it, his face haggard and swollen like Grafton's with insect bites and yellow with mepacrine dosage. At least it went some way to suppressing the fevers. To combat dysentery – another source of fatigue - the MO kept everyone charged up with sulphonamide, until, as Rockford remarked, "Feels like I'm passin' bricks now."

Calvert went on as many patrols as any of his subordinates, sometimes onto the far side of the Sittang, with Waverly's Karens, to prevent any of the enemy who successfully crossed that water obstacle from reaching the Salween.

Few did.

Calvert then spent considerable time writing up his reports for Battalion HQ. Grafton reckoned his officer was probably averaging about three or fours sleep a day.

Stooped over the map, they discussed each stage of the patrol; the terrain, the conditions and the findings.

Finally, Grafton said, "We saw none but dead ones, sir and no traces of any recent passage."

Calvert straightened up and smiled thinly.

"I think we've become a no-go area for the enemy, Corporal. Well done."

Grafton rubbed his chin. Like the rest of his section, he would shave when he returned to the billet. No-one shaved before a patrol. You ran the risk of the Japs sensing your presence by the smell of soap.

"Do you think there's many more to come, sir?" he asked.

Calvert carefully refolded the map and slowly shook his head.

"I think most of those who came out of the Yomas are accounted for, Gruffie," he said.

"So we might be headed back to Rangoon, then, sir?"

The officer laughed quietly.

"The chaps deserve it. Though I guess you'd prefer Calcutta?"

Grafton flexed his shoulder, grinned and nodded. The post arrived in batches and revealed that Rachel was writing to him almost every day. He only wished that he could get dry enough to answer her letters more often.

"Very much so, sir," said Leigh. "Are you still hearing from Sister Calder?"

"Oh, yes," said Calvert with feeling. "Have a look at her latest."

Matt picked up a handwritten sheet and passed it to the corporal.

"Congratulations, sir!" Grafton exclaimed when he'd read the letter. He extended his right hand and Calvert shook it.

"Thanks, Corporal. Everything's been going splendidly of course but even so, I was a bit taken aback with an unequivocal 'Yes.' We only have to decide which side of the world we're going to live on."

As Grafton turned to go, he mentioned one further detail.

"It's still out there, isn't it, sir, that – presence - we came across in the village at Meiktila?" he said.

"Yes, Corporal," said Calvert soberly. "It is."

Twenty-four hours later, Calvert and Waverly were retracing their steps along the village street, in the rain, each officer with a carbine slung over one shoulder, muzzle down.

Together, as was customary, they had inspected the West Yorks' positions and would now check on the Karens' outposts before darkness fell.

Calvert glanced at the water streaming off his cape and dripping from the brim of his bush hat. He welcomed these inspection tours. In between checking the OPs, machine gun posts and rifle pits and commiserating with the occupants waist-deep in lukewarm runoff, he and the Englishmen conversed at length about Oxford.

"With Trish it'll be heaven, Matt," Waverly assured him. "My heartiest congratulations, by the way."

Calvert thanked him and was minded to ask about Colleen but restrained himself. Waverly seemed unaccountably diffident about her in conversation.

They paused at the edge of the jungle scrub beyond Calvert's HQ. Matt looked up at a ripple of lightning, followed by its accompanying avalanche of thunder.

"Another night at the war, Peter."

"Nearly the last, though, Matt."

"You think so?"

"I can't say too much," Waverly continued. "However, I'm informed the Yanks are about to wind it up very soon. We'll still have work to do, finding all our POWs, then kicking any leftover Japs in the direction of Tokyo. But at least the war will be over."

In the course of the next few days, two horrific man-made storms engulfed the Japanese cities of Hiroshima and Nagasaki.

And the war was over.

Though not the suffering.

Eighteen

Shadows

In mid August, the CO gathered his staff in the conference hall for another briefing.

"As you're aware, Rangoon Gaol was liberated when the city fell. Allied prisoners of war who'd been held there were taken to a hospital ship by minesweepers even while they were clearing the channel. The men were in such desperate straits. They would have been flown out had Mingaladon Airfield been operational."

The colonel glanced at a sheaf of documents on the table in front of him.

"Other POW camps are now being liberated," he said. "You'll have heard of the Burma Railway[239]?"

"Yes, sir," said several voices.

"Preliminary reports indicate that the prisoners have been kept in appalling conditions and made to work as slave labour," Partridge went on. "They will come to us very weak and malnourished, doubtless still suffering from a variety of diseases. It will be up to us to get them back to health so that they can be sent home as soon as possible."

After the briefing, Colleen and her friends sought out Sergeant Nicholson, Geordie Wood and Donny. They were in the vehicle maintenance shed, at the rear of the hospital.

"We need to get as much in the way of NAAFI goodies from the social club as we can, or anywhere else," Trish explained. "And extra eggs, fruit and veg."

"As soon as we can," Robyn added.

"We could do with a couple of lorry loads," said Gwen.

The quietly spoken Nicholson wiped his hands with an oil-stained rag. He glanced at his companions, who simply nodded.

"We'll sort it for zero nine hundred tomorrow, Sister," the sergeant said.

They did.

"Every calorie's going to be needed," said Gwen, when they unpacked the supplies the lads brought back.

She was right.

The number of patients was gradually diminishing as more and more were evacuated to India, though for several weeks, a steady stream was still being admitted. In addition to

424

scores of battle casualties sustained in patrol encounters with desperate Japanese making their final lunges for the Sittang and the Salween, men were still coming in afflicted by sores, sickness and nervous and physical exhaustion.

But in preparation for the anticipated influx of ex-POWs, ambulances conveyed as many existing patients as could be moved to the airfield and the port for transfer to India.

Finally, several wards were cleared.

"We'll be getting them in their hundreds," Matron warned. "The worst of them, too. A lot of the fitter ones have been taken straight to Comilla."

When orderlies began helping the first arrivals out of the ambulances, Colleen and Trish were watching from the first-floor veranda adjacent to their ward.

"My God," whispered Trish.

Colleen was speechless.

Most of the newcomers were almost literally walking skeletons, with knobby-jointed limbs like sticks, their muscles in threads. Ribs, collarbones and shoulders blades stuck out like herringbone ridges beneath taut skin pocked with running sores. Deep set in gaunt faces cleft with protruding cheekbones, the ex-prisoners' eyes roved blankly over their new surroundings. Only thatches of short-cropped hair showing beneath tattered headgear belied the impression of living skulls set on scrawny necks with bulging veins.

Rags of uniforms were tied around their wasted frames, though some wore no more than a loincloth.

Orderlies lifted many sufferers out of the vehicles on stretchers, or assisted amputees. Their condition was pitiful, even compared to their more able-bodied fellows.

Colleen eventually found her voice.

"Cursed Japs," she said fiercely.

All who could walk were conducted to the ground-floor showers that by now had been plumbed in to dispense hot water via oil-fired boilers in the basement. Together with the army sappers, Nicholson, Wood and other orderlies had worked hard to get this facility functioning.

Those on stretchers were brought straight to the wards and gently placed on beds, where, assisted by orderlies, the Sisters gave them sponge baths. Afterwards, they were issued with pyjamas, shorts, shirt, underwear, socks and plimsolls – for when they could walk. New bush hats replaced the frayed headgear. The rags they had worn were removed for incineration.

The wards filled rapidly as those who'd been to the showers filed in and were shown to their beds. They too had received the clothing and footwear issue.

It was found on inspection that most of the patients were suffering from a far greater incidence of malarial fevers than the battle casualties and in some cases partial blindness resulting from Vitamin B2 deficiency.

"We had no malaria suppressants at all, Sister," one ex-POW explained to Colleen as she was taking his temperature and pulse rate. "Japs kept all the medication back, until right at the end."

The speaker was a tall Australian sergeant named Manning, a sheep-farmer from a town called Inverell in northern New South Wales. He was a survivor from one of the infantry battalions of the ill-fated Australian Eighth Division, captured at the fall of Singapore.

"Sores are worse than anything I've seen," said Robyn when they were helping prepare the patients' first meal. Matron and the inspecting MOs had selected the menu with the utmost care.

"Some of them have got whole limbs ulcerated," said Gwen. "You can see inches of bone."

"Ringworm as well," Trish remarked. "And jaundice. Awful."

The girls had treated the ghastly lesions with the usual applications of gentian and sulpha powder, dressed them and, when advised by an MO, injected penicillin into the patients' buttocks, where enough flesh was in evidence.

"What the hell was that, Sister?" more than one hoarse voice asked. None of them knew of the wonder drug.

Where the individual was too emaciated for an injection, the crystals were simply sprinkled on the raw, suppurating flesh, along with the sulpha and gentian.

Some of the men suffering from beriberi or dysenteric fevers needed other specialised diets, likewise those with serious mouth ulcers, many of whom had to be fed intravenously.

Still others were diagnosed with tuberculosis.

Matron oversaw these groups personally, together with a Major Neave, who had taken over from Trenholme as second-in-command.

The first meal they served on their ward was an education for Colleen and her friends[240].

"He's got more than me, Sister!" one wraith exclaimed.

"Why can't I have the same as him, Sister?" another squeaked petulantly.

Squabbles were breaking out all over the ward.

"They're like a bunch of spoilt brats," said Gwen incredulously, poised at one end of the ward with a food trolley.

"You must have what the MO has decided," the girls kept trying to explain. "We will feed you again in a few hours. Overeating could kill you."

But the bickering continued.

"Shut up!" said a commanding voice.

Immediately, the ward fell silent.

Sergeant Manning was sitting upright in bed, glaring at all and sundry. Despite the privations of his captivity, he looked and sounded like a soldier.

"Good old Digger Manning," whispered Robyn. "Reminds me of Matt," she added with a wink at Trish.

Thanks largely to Manning's intervention, the remainder of the meal proceeded peacefully, though the men kept begging for seconds. The girls didn't have the heart to refuse them but conscious of the risk, doled out extra helpings sparingly.

Nevertheless, several patients began showing distinct signs of indigestion – in the form of sustained flatulence – and some needed basins quickly when they started to throw up.

"Might have known," Trish with a sigh. "Better tell the women to cook less next time."

She and Colleen departed to the dispensary and returned with a stack of medicine glasses and a full Winchester bottle. They poured out numerous glassfuls for Robyn and Gwen to distribute, who in the meantime cleaned up the vomit where the basins hadn't arrived in time.

"Right, you pigs," Robyn said to their charges, when the medicine was ready. "Open wide."

Two subsequent meals were conducted much more sedately and the men appreciated the NAAFI confection the girls handed around.

"Because you've been good boys - this evening, anyway," said Gwen.

But they had to ensure that each of the patients received an equal share.

Another dilemma arose when some of the men, who could walk, needed to use the facilities. Several were afraid to be accompanied individually by an orderly.

They whimpered and shrank back in their beds.

"They think they're going to be made an example of, Sister," said another Australian. "Beaten with pick handles or kicked rotten. Japs did that sometimes."

Only when one of the girls took the patient's hand and said gently, "It's all right, come with Sister," did they agree to be conducted to the toilets. Even then, Colleen or one of her companions had to wait outside the cubicle.

More bizarre behaviour occurred when it was time to settle the men down for the night.

"We can give you plenty of soap and toothpaste," the girls explained. "You don't have to hoard it under your pillow to trade for rations – or the shaving kit, either. We'll give you that tomorrow."

Some of the men had secreted scraps of bread or potato there as well and the nurses had to insist on collecting it.

"Or we'll get cockroaches and Matron will have a fit," they warned.

It transpired that their colleagues caring for the ex-POWs on other wards had experienced similar difficulties, though things were gradually settling down.

The final duty was to go round with a bottle of brandy and give each man a medicine glassful as a nightcap, something they appreciated with almost childlike glee.

"Nearly makes you cry," said Robyn while she and Colleen were returning the empty glasses to the ward sluice. With typical industry, the Burmese women had already dealt with the mountain of washing up.

Later, when most of the men were asleep, the four girls stood by John Manning's bed in the half-light of the ward and listened to his account of the fall of Singapore before Janice and Mandy came on for the night shift.

Colleen thought Manning was already looking better for the food he had ingested. With fairish hair and grey-blue eyes, he did remind her of Matt. The admissions data showed that he was twenty-eight years old. He was one of several Australians with the intake, though most of their countrymen had been flown or shipped to New Guinea in the first stage of their journey back home.

Manning wanted to talk, so the girls let him.

"Our AIF battalions were much better trained and disciplined than the Japs and a lot better at bushcraft and fire control," he began. "We beat them hands down at the Muar River[241], even though they had tanks – our A/T chaps knocked out ten of those. When we went in with the bayonet, through the rubber plantations, we killed them by the hundreds.

"Still, they outnumbered us and we hadn't any reinforcements right then, so with our wounded piling up, we had to pull back. The Japs got behind us and set up roadblocks that we had to fight through time and again, even while their air force was beating up the column – all our aircraft were destroyed by then.

"We got as far as a place called Parit Sulong, about thirty miles from the Muar. The Japs were too well dug in, so our CO ordered us to set fire to the vehicles and take to the jungle."

He paused and Gwen poured him a glass of water.

"Thank you, Sister," he said and took some careful sips.

"What happened to the wounded, John?" Robyn asked. "The ones you had to leave."

"The Japs murdered them, Sister," Manning told her. "They used bayonets, or boots. Poured petrol on some of the chaps and set them alight. There were more than a hundred."

His listeners were aghast. The sergeant took a few more sips of water and resumed speaking.

"We got to Singapore after about a week and took up positions west of the Jahore Bridge – the Causeway we called it. Lots of sub units had been cut off and caught so our battalions could only muster about two hundred men each and we were spread out through about eight miles of mangroves.

"Just before the Japs invaded, we got reinforced but these fellows had next to no training and a lot of them went to pieces when the Japs shelled us to cover their barges coming across the Jahore Straits. They shelled us for a whole day. Our CO said it was worse than Pozieres[242].

"We were outnumbered about ten to one. They just kept charging through the mangroves, screaming like banshees and we were pushed back to Tengah Airfield – about ten miles north west of the city. We held on for about a week but the Japs were all around. They'd captured the city's water supplies and their air raids were killing thousands of civilians. Your General Percival had no choice but to order the surrender, on February fifteenth, nineteen forty-two. I'll never forget the date."

He returned the empty glass to Gwen and leant back on his pillow. Colleen began to unravel the mosquito net above Manning's bed.

"Well, you better get some sleep, John," she said.

"I suppose so, Sister," he said, with a yawn. "And I'll never forget when the Japs arrived at our HQ. Drove up in a little four-door Citroen, camouflaged in palm branches. Two staff officers, their driver and a batman. They all looked pretty scruffy."

"Time to sleep, John," said Trish firmly. The four girls each tucked a corner of the net under his bed.

"I'll never forget some of our replacements, either," Manning persisted, though his voice was growing weary.

"Ran away when the Japs landed, started looting all the grog shops, drank themselves stupid and tried to fight their way aboard ships evacuating our civilians – and the nurses. Disgrace to Australia. The Divisional CO[243] gave orders to shoot them. We'd have done it, too."

His voice had sunk to a whisper. The girls crept away, reported briefly to Janice and Mandy as they came in, then retired to Trish's room, where once again, they knelt in prayer.

Prompted in part to do so by Manning's last words before he fell asleep.

"Could one of you please get me a Bible? Mine's fallen to bits."

Despite their appalling state initially, the ex-POWs' condition improved rapidly with proper food and medication.

Eye specialists caring for the partially blinded men were greatly encouraged by the restoration in vision resulting from the improved diet. It came as a relief to the sufferers, too.

The men's mouths and gums began to heal, a particular benefit insofar as dental officers inspecting the men's teeth found them in good repair.

"A few handfuls of unpolished rice a day with a bit of veg and dried meat can't do the ivories much harm, sir," the dentists were told. "Can't do much else for you, either. But the dental officers with us did a marvellous job, though."

After a week or so, many patients were evincing the kind of stoic cheerfulness typical of the British OR, provided he wasn't at death's door.

When Colleen asked one Cockney lad if he would like sugar in his tea, he said, "Stir it with your finger, Sister. It'll be sweet enough for me."

Though the absence of the BORs' Indian counterparts occasioned sadness.

"We haven't seen any sepoys, Matron," Trish observed.

"I understand most of them died, Sister," she was told.

Gradually, the survivors began to unburden about their captivity. Sometimes those who could move around did so while assisting the girls with the simpler tasks, like serving meals and collecting the plates afterwards.

"We used to have set breaks for a smoke in the camp, Sister. But now and then, the Japs would time it to the second. One time, I put my fag out just as the gong went, so to speak. My mate was still smoking when round the corner comes a guard. Sees my mate with the fag and beats the daylights out of him. Then he turns up next day and gives my mate half his lunch[244]. They were funny like that, the Japs. Hardly ever on an even keel."

"One place I was in, a lot of chaps came down with dysentery and some of 'em died. We were lowering one poor devil into the grave when his backside gave way and his bowels gushed out, all black and stinking. Horrible sound it made, too."

"Cholera was the real killer, Sister. It broke out in some of the camps along the railway. God knows how many thousands died. Us Brits and Aussies were very strict about hygiene so we could fend it off to some extent but in the Dutchies' camps and the ones for the Malays the Japs brought up as coolies, they were dropping like flies. Our MOs did a marvellous job, keeping fluids into the blokes who'd come down with it but the Japs didn't give 'em any serum until they started dying off themselves. Kept it all that time because they didn't know how to administer it. Their medics were rubbish compared to ours."

"I was on the railway when it was joined up all the way from Bangkok to Moulmein[245], where it meets the track from Mandalay. Then the Japs took us back over the railway down to a base camp. We came to an embankment and the bloke next to me starts shaking like a leaf. Says to me, 'I was on this stretch, mate. You should have seen the rubbish we piled in. I wouldn't have ridden a bicycle over it.' Still, we got back OK, praise God."

"You could get duck eggs in Thailand, Sister. We could buy 'em from the locals because the Japs paid us in *ticals* – local currency. Mostly we gave them to the boys in hospital – that was just a long bamboo hut with bamboo platforms on each side for sleeping, like the barracks we built for ourselves. I remember helping to hold a bloke down one time while the MO dug a tropical ulcer out of his leg with a sharpened spoon. Can hear him scream to this day. Eventually we got some ducks ourselves and one bloke was detailed off to catch snails for 'em. He had to sleep with the hat on his chest so the Japs'd know he was exempt some of the work details. Anyway, my mate was really glad when our troops turned up. He reckoned the snails were gettin' too fast for him."

"The Aussies always had their ANZAC Day Parades, Sister. Colonel Gallaghan[246] was our camp CO. When he was ready to start the parade, six Royal Australian Navy ratings marched up and said, 'Senior Service, sir, HMAS Perth[247].' And they led the parade."

"There was a bunch of us, Aussies and Brits, in a camp near Moulmein when we got liberated. The Japs had gone and we'd laid down in our hut out of the sun when our chaps arrived. The first into the hut was Lieutenant Gray, of the Royal Northumberland Fusiliers[248]. He's no sooner in than he's out again. I was by the entrance and I heard him say to his sergeant, 'I can't stand the smell of them,' but I smell all right now, don't I, Sister?"

"Like a rose, mate, almost," said Robyn, who was applying some calamine via a sterile cloth to a skin irritation on the man's back and chest. "My name's Gray, as it happens. Get around, don't we?"

"We fixed some of our skin rashes ourselves, Sister," the man went on. "Our aircraft started bombing the railway while we were working on it. They knocked down some telegraph poles alongside it that had those porcelain junction points on the crosstrees. We had a Sigs bloke with us and he said, 'There's sulphur in those. We can use it on our sores.' We did, and it worked a treat, for a good while."

"My Jonny's in the air force," said Robyn with a smile as she helped the patient back into his pyjama top. "I know his squadron bombed the railway earlier this year. He'd have been happy to knock those poles down for you. Very obliging lad, he is."

The patient chuckled and shared another anecdote while Robyn adjusted his pillows, then checked his condition.

"We had to unload some tins of pineapple for the Jap officers' mess one time. The Nips were hopeless at counting so we nicked about one tin in every four. They'd let us keep our bayonets so we had the tops off in no time and down it went. Perpetual motion, nearly.

"By the way, Sister," the man added with a sheepish grin. "Your Jonny's dead lucky."

"They must be getting better," Robyn told her friends at the next change of shift. "The chat-up lines are starting."

"Yes," said Mandy. "Particularly between Sergeant Manning and a certain senior Sister. You'll notice how quickly she skipped into the ward."

"Keen to continue their conversation about woolly-backs, are they?" asked Colleen. Gwen, Robyn and Trish turned toward her with puzzled looks.

"Sheep," Mandy explained. "Can tell you lot have never been to Yorkshire."

"Oh, we call them by their different breeds," said Gwen, sharing an amused nod with Robyn and Trish. "But we'll have to keep an eye on this."

Janice's parents owned a sheep farm in the Cheviot Hills of Northumberland. She and Manning began touring the wards together during the night shifts, as the sergeant gained strength.

"Since he's the senior NCO, it reassures the blokes," said Janice.

"And Sister Porter," Mandy said to the others.

During these tours, Manning described more details of his captivity. Janice subsequently relayed them to her friends.

"There's a military compound at Changi, on the eastern end of the island," the sergeant explained. "They kept thousands of us there for about three months. It's a small place and soon got pretty squalid – we had a latrine pit in one part of the enclosure and it brought swarms of flies, until we persuaded the Japs to get us some chloride of lime. The Japs gave us a daily rice ration and some pots to cook it in but we were hungry all the time and a lot of the chaps got sick. With just two pints of water a day each, we were pretty thirsty, too.

"Then they took those of us they reckoned to be fit enough up to a camp near Bangkok by rail, nine hundred miles. The journey was hell. We were in these steel boxes and they were like ovens until the guards realised they'd have to keep the doors open or we'd all be dead. They'd shut us in because they were afraid we'd try to escape but there was nowhere to go except jungle.

"Once we got to the camp we were just about mad with thirst and nearly starving. We got water but some of the boys traded all the worldly goods they had left for extra food – and then came down with dysentery because the fruit was off. Some poor beggars died of it.

"The Japs eventually got round to feeding us on a regular basis – bowl of rice and vegetable stew for each meal, occasionally with bits of meat or fish thrown in and hibiscus leaves that provided some extra vitamins. If you weren't sick, you could live on it but it wasn't enough for the kind of manual work they wanted out of us. They weren't used to feeding Europeans. But at least we had drinking water, which we boiled first, of course – we still had our pots but no KFSs. We had to fashion all our utensils from bamboo."

Janice marvelled at the matter-of-fact way in which Manning told of his ordeal. Other patients confirmed the sergeant's narrative as he and Janice spoke with them during the ward tours. John eventually related the beginning of the infamous railway.

"They took us into the Kwai Valley to set up the work camps. The lucky fellows went by Sampan, the rest of us marched through the jungle. We had to clear the scrub in whatever location we were dropped off, then build these bamboo huts, roof them over with palm leaves and set up the bamboo sleeping platforms. They housed a couple of hundred men each – two feet apart, with one hut for a hospital. It soon got pretty full, but the Japs would have a bloke back working again as soon as he could stagger, regardless of what the MO said. I suppose about half of us were sick at any one time, though it was worse at the base camps. Thousands of the boys were in a very bad way but the doctors had hardly enough medicine to fill your handbag, Sister.

"I remember the roofs of the huts leaked a lot when it rained. Still, it was a change from some of the heat. We never ran short of water, with the Kwai River close by but we always boiled it – plenty of firewood about, thank God."

As Manning gained strength, he walked with Janice in the grounds. More of his recollections emerged.

"We started on the railway by clearing a thirty-foot wide trace for the track, all by hand, with billhooks, saws and rope for pulling down the vegetation. Sometimes it took us a day to shift a big clump of bamboo.

"To build embankments, we first loosened up soil and stones with shovels, picks and crowbars, then carted it to the site in wicker baskets. It had to be packed hard so it didn't wash away in the rain but we did a lot of maintenance on embankments after the railway was finished.

"Sometimes we had explosives to blast out a cutting but as often as not, we just hacked away with chisels and hammers. If I close my eyes now, I can still conjure up the sight of a raw rock face in front of me, with nothing else except dust in the face, the sound of hammering and my mates on either side, sweat pouring off us in buckets and the insects giving us hell. That sort of work went on for days, weeks. The Japs never bypassed an obstacle. If their surveyors' plan showed the route went through some giant outcrop, that's where it went."

At this point in John's narrative, a couple of brightly coloured parrots started squawking in the top branches of a tree overhanging the path along which he and Janice were walking.

"Time was, we'd have eaten those," said John, glancing up and then smiling at Janice. He was looking much better, she thought.

The parrots flew off and the couple ambled on. John continued his story.

"To get across rivers, we first had to sink these huge timber piles. The driver was just a massive big weight looped over a wooden frame and hoisted by fifty men. We had no pulleys. Sometimes the Japs used elephants for the job. They reckoned one elephant was worth twenty prisoners – and easier to feed. I suppose they didn't mind the pounding the weight made. It jarred your head after a while.

"Once the piles were sunk, we cut and shaped the timber for the superstructure, so that the various supports dovetailed into each other. Then we hammered them fast with iron staples, big as horseshoes[249].

"The bridges were easy targets for our air force, naturally. So we had more maintenance work to do.

"The daily routine never varied. Rice and black tea for breakfast, then assemble for roll call and start work at zero eight hundred. Twelve to thirteen hundred hours was a meal break and we knocked off at sixteen hundred. Depending on how far we had to go back to camp, we sometimes could wash in the river before evening meal and roll call – we had to help the Japs with that. They couldn't count very well.

"Sundays we didn't work on the railway but the Japs always found plenty to do round the camp, so there wasn't a lot of time for rest. The worst of it was, you had no means of writing letters. Japs wouldn't allow it and it was over a year before anyone at home knew what had happened to us[250]. That was through the Red Cross and for some folk, the news wasn't good. Eventually, the Japs allowed us to receive Red Cross cards from our families – twenty-five words at a time. The folk back home got to be experts at summarising[251]."

John made this poignant revelation while he and Janice were sitting in a summerhouse. Manning needed a long rest before walking back to the ward.

"No shortage of letters now, John," said Janice warmly.

The hospital had promptly notified the families of the ex-prisoners now in its care and the letters were arriving daily, by the sackful.

He smiled at her and stared at the wooden floor, strewn with blossoms.

"Thanks so much," he said quietly. "For everything."

"Our pleasure," Janice murmured. Especially mine, she thought.

John took up his description again. He had so much to get off his chest. It seemed to Janice like a log-jam breaking.

"When we'd cleared the track and finished the bridges, we tamped down a ballast of chipped stones, anchored the sleepers in it – which we'd cut and shaped first – then put down the rails and secured them to the sleepers. A Jap locomotive carried the rails and it moved with us.

"The track was worked on from both ends, Bangkok and Moulmein and we joined the sections near the Three Pagodas Pass on the Thai-Burma frontier. The Japs even had a gilded spike for the joining ceremony but one of my battalion mates pinched it.

"The food issue was fairly regular but never sufficient. You felt worn out the whole time but somehow by the grace of God, many of us kept going, though I suppose about a third of our chaps died, on average. It was worse with the Indians, the Dutch and the Malays. They keeled over in heaps. Then we'd sometimes have to dig the mass graves and bury them.

"The MOs had one hell of a time persuading the Japs to keep up the food ration for the boys in hospital because the Japs reckoned, 'Sick men don't eat much.' But that's how they treated their own sick and in the end, our MOs were looking after them as well. Amazing

433

what they rigged up, even blood transfusion kit from stethoscope tubes and bits of bamboo. If an ulcer got so bad they had to amputate, they had a way of giving the patient a spinal injection as a local anaesthetic. The dental officers did a marvellous job, too, improvising chairs, mirrors and instruments and they could even fix a broken jaw. That happened sometimes, if a guard socked a bloke really hard – and our dentists ended up treating the Japs too.

"I have to say, the MOs did your Corps proud, Sister."

He lapsed into silence. Janice waited for him to speak again. The rustic old summerhouse, amid the humming of insects and the blaze of blossom, was so restful. John had earned this rest, Janice reflected.

"Our clothing wore out until all we had was what we stood up in when you first saw us," he said eventually. "Fortunately, we were able to make loincloths out of blankets or sacking we got from the Japs. When our boots fell to bits, we made wooden clogs, or sandals. Had to keep scrounging bits of canvas to replace the straps but they lasted until we arrived here. Just as well, because you had to watch out for scorpions in the jungle.

"As for the Japs, the engineers were from a railway regiment and very professional except that they reckoned on doing everything with limitless manpower – us. Still, we got the railway finished in about eighteen months. None of us wonders how the pyramids were built – sheer muscle power. But sometimes, the Japs would order, 'Speedo worko' for no real reason and all it did was make people collapse and cause injuries.

"Then there were the guards and their NCOs. A lot of them were morons, especially the Koreans. If even the slightest thing went wrong, they'd like as not fly into a rage and someone'd get thumped. Most of us got clobbered now and again but the Jap NCOs would beat up their own ORs as well. It was part of their system of discipline and we fell under it, too. Oftentimes, after a real bashing, an NCO might run around shouting, 'Very sorry. Alla big mistake.' Trouble was, by then some poor bloke might be dead. Even so, I don't think the guards were deliberately brutal, just stupid. You don't use your best men for guarding prisoners.

"Early this year, I was sent to a camp where they had a mixture of units, Australian and British, to act as senior Allied NCO. The other sergeants and above had all died. It's bad for morale - and health - when units were broken up, as they sometimes were for work details. Your blokes and ours always like to stay with their own mob. After I got there, I took them for Sunday services and we were allowed a midweek meeting as well. I'm a lay preacher, you see. The mercy of God did some remarkable things in the camps. A lot of fellows received the Lord[252].

"In the end, the Japs were asking us for news because they knew we'd made radios from spoons and crystals and what not. Officially, you risked a hell of a beating if you were caught but all the Japs were getting from Radio Tokyo was propaganda and we more or less did a deal. To be fair, they kept their word."

He fell silent again. Janice asked, "Are you ready to walk back, John?"

"May I take your arm, Sister?" he asked, getting to his feet.

"Indeed, you may, Sergeant," she said obligingly. Matron's bound to do her Nelson act, she told herself.

The staff encouraged all the ex-POWs to walk in the grounds. The relaxed exercise in the tranquil surroundings did much to improve the men's well-being, especially with the nurses for company. The Sisters also escorted the amputees, who persevered manfully along the gravel paths with their newly issued crutches.

"Keep this up, I'll have arms like a gorilla, Sister," one plucky, perspiring individual said to Colleen. She remembered similar scenes from the year before, at the hospital near Frosinone[253].

The nurses spent hours writing to the men's wives, parents or girlfriends. Though the patients filled out Red Cross cards that were then posted to their families, they were very keen for Colleen and her friends to send individual letters.

So the girls wrote letters by the score, addressed from Argyllshire to the Australian Alps.

"My mum and dad have got a farm in the Riverina[254], Sister," one of Manning's Australian mates explained to Colleen. "A letter from you will seem like one from the Queen[255]."

"My dad owns a fish and chip shop, Sister," said Private Harry 'Ginger' Beale, the freckled-faced Cockney lad who'd wanted his tea stirred with Colleen's finger. "Even after the Blitz, it's still standin'. If he and Mum get a letter from you, they'll frame it in the window."

Beale and others confirmed Manning's account, except in one respect.

"Sent to our camp? No, Sister, he volunteered when he heard of the state we were in but the sarge wouldn't tell you that, of course. It's because of him we're here now. Fancies that Sister Porter, doesn't he? Good luck to him, she's a stunner all right. Well, you all are."

After two or three weeks, the ex-POWs were ready to return home. Some chose to go by air, others by sea.

"We'd like to have a cruise, sir," they said to Colonel Partridge.

By now, they had all been issued with uniforms and virtually unrecognisable from when they'd first arrived. Colleen was pleased that her prediction about Sergeant Manning's appearance proved to be correct. So was Janice.

"You've done a wonderful job, Sister," the girls were told. "We'll never be able to thank you enough."

"Do you think Janice and John will keep in touch?" Colleen asked Mandy, as they watched the two of them part company. Janice gently shook John's hand as he climbed into the ambulance. With more flesh on his bones, the Australian had become a noticeably handsome man.

"Do you think the sun will rise tomorrow, Coll?" Mandy said merrily.

Sadly, deliverance from the camps for one group of ex-prisoners did not mean deliverance from captivity. These were the men whose minds were unhinged. Muttering, raving, sobbing, cursing and sometimes screaming in sudden panic, they were kept isolated from the other patients.

Several of the mental cases turned out to be some of the medical officers who had saved countless lives and earned the undying admiration of Sergeant Manning and his fellow prisoners.

Tragically, with liberation in sight, they had lost their minds.

Overall supervision of this ward constituted another onerous responsibility for Major Neave and Matron Wrigglesworth.

Together with Colonel Partridge, they stipulated that Sisters allocated to the ward always be accompanied by two male orderlies, armed.

Corporal Wood was always by Colleen's side in these circumstances.

But Colleen thought that the precautions were excessive and went to see the colonel in his office, a sparsely furnished niche on the ground floor.

"The patients are frightened by the male staff, sir," she said. "And the weapons."

The Colonel's moustache twitched.

"Perhaps, Sister," he said curtly. "But I must insist it is for your safety."

"You can't blame him, Coll," said Robyn. "That ward's like Bedlam."

The analogy was apt. Approaching the ward at night, in the brown-out and hearing the distraught cries as you got closer, was unnerving even for Sisters who had served with CCSs and despite their having dealt with many cases of battle fatigue.

Feeding, washing, shaving and accommodating the bodily functions of the mental patients was an extremely demanding task, often requiring the forcible administration of a sedative and considerable physical strength.

Some of the deranged individuals had to be tied to their beds to prevent them from thrashing wildly when the staff approached.

Nevertheless, one night, Colleen decided to test an idea she had discussed with Robyn. She produced her Bible from a skirt pocket.

"Would you go out in the corridor for a bit, please, lads?" she asked Nicholson and Wood. "I'm going to try reading to them."

"I don't like it, Sister," said the sergeant.

"Me neither, Sister," Corporal Wood affirmed. "You know the CO's orders."

"I know," said Colleen. "But Robbie's here. We'll call you back soon, I promise."

Reluctantly, the two men departed.

"Ready?" Colleen asked.

"Yep," whispered Robyn. "You read. I'll pray."

They walked slowly between the rows of beds. Colleen began reading aloud the words of the Twenty-third Psalm.

"'The Lord is my shepherd; I shall not want.

"'He maketh me to lie down in green pastures: he leadeth me beside the still waters.

"'He restoreth my soul: he leadeth me in the paths of righteousness for his name's sake.

"'Yea, though I walk through the valley of the shadow of death, I will fear no evil: for thou art with me; thy rod and thy staff they comfort me.

"'Thou preparest a table before me in the presence of mine enemies: thou anointest my head with oil; my cup runneth over.

"'Surely goodness and mercy shall follow me all the days of my life: and I will dwell in the house of the Lord for ever.'"

By the time Colleen and Robyn had walked back and forth several times, repeating the Psalm, the patients were calmer.

Unfortunately, they became agitated as soon as Nicholson and Wood reappeared.

"Seems they still think you're Japs," said Robyn with regret.

"I don't think we can leave you by yourselves anymore tonight, Sisters," said Nicholson. "You'll have to try and talk the CO round."

Encouraged by Matron, Colleen and Robyn petitioned the CO early next day but he was adamant that the orderlies remain in the wards at all times. Major Neave reluctantly supported his superior's decision.

"We can't take any chances," he explained to the girls, who were deeply disappointed.

"You did your best," said Trish sympathetically, over breakfast.

"At least you got some practice for Derbyshire, Coll," said Robyn. "If Peter wangles the transfer for you."

"Surely you can still read to them," urged Gwen. "Tell Nick and Woody to stand in a corner."

However, the mental patients were moved to a hospital in Madras, where the so-called 'head cases' were being concentrated and it wasn't possible to experiment any further.

"Pity," said Major Neave. "Could be you were onto something. They don't reckon much to those chaps' chances of recovery by the usual methods, I'm afraid[256]."

Colleen nearly cried. Nevertheless, her experiment did have one heartening outcome.

She was coming off shift one day, when Mandy spoke to her in confidence..

"Could we please join your prayer meeting, Coll, Janice and me?" she asked. "What with Sergeant Manning and your Bible cure for insanity, I think we need to."

At that, Colleen did cry.

Nineteen

Pet Rescue

Several more of Trenholme's former CCS staff were repatriated a few days later, Sergeant Nicholson, Geordie Wood and Donny among them.

Before they embussed, Colleen hugged the sinewy little collier who had saved her life and shepherded her from the day her transport had touched down in the Dry Belt all those months ago.

"You take care, Sister," he said affectionately. "Watch out for what's under your bed, like."

Then, married Sisters were notified they could rejoin their husbands.

Gwen was first to leave, by C-47 to Kandy in Ceylon, where Dai was now serving with Headquarters Allied Land Forces, South East Asia. Although monsoon rains were still deluging Rangoon, intervening drier spells were becoming longer, permitting more flights from Mingaladon Airfield.

Colleen drove her friend to the airfield. Trisha and Robyn were able to go too. They managed to squeeze Gwen's kit into the jeep along with her.

"You must come and see us," Gwen said between sobs, before emplaning. "My Dai says we'll be back in Llangollen in a few weeks but he wants us to move to Betws-y-Coed, which is all right with me except that we might be in Rhyl or Bangor for a bit, while I serve out my enlistment, you see, unless I get pregnant of course, which I suppose could happen quite soon."

"That'd be wonderful, Gwennie," said Trish, hugging her. "We'll keep in touch. Our love to Dai."

In less than a week, it was Robyn's turn.

Despite the tears, Colleen and Trish, who had taken Robyn to the airfield, were overjoyed to see Jon Gray alight from the C-47 when it came to rest.

Robyn was in his arms almost immediately.

Gray's squadron had moved back to India but having promised to meet Robyn in Rangoon, he arranged to accompany the incoming flight. Like Dai and Gwen, the couple would soon be homeward bound.

"Pulled a few strings," Jon said, while they waited in the dispersal hut over a cup of tea for the C-47 to be refuelled for the return journey to Calcutta. "You'll keep in touch? Love to see you when you get back to Blighty."

438

"Of course, Jon," Trish assured him. "But you get settled first."

Robyn sat beside her husband on a settee, holding his hand and resting her head against his. She looked so joyful – and with her walking-out uniform, she was wearing her high heels, "definitely for Jonny," she'd said.

Gazing at the lithe young airman in his immaculate JGs, with flight lieutenant's epaulettes on his shoulders, Colleen knew that Robyn had made an excellent choice.

The girls continued with their PT sessions, when they could.

Tennis outings, using the all-weather courts in either the hospital grounds or those at Government House, now re-occupied, were always popular but partly for that reason, Trish and Colleen often went for runs along the walkways, interspersed with flat-out sprints over the lawns, where it was trimmed – uncut grass could harbour snakes.

To minimise the danger, Burmese gardeners, employed on the same basis as the cleaning and catering women, regularly cut the grass with petrol-powered scythes and the steady beating of their two-stroke engines was a familiar sound on fine days.

Mandy and Janice teamed up with their two friends when their off-duty hours coincided.

"Time I chucked the fags and got in some serious training," said Mandy.

She was benefiting in every respect from the prayer meetings in Trish's room and the constant exposure to the scriptures - as were all the participants.

Patients perambulating in the grounds also derived a benefit from the sight of athletic-looking young women, loping past in plimsolls and PT gear and the girls received the usual whistles and waves.

Trish and Colleen were jogging back for a shower one morning towards mid September when a gardener waved to them from beside a plot of shrubbery.

"Sister Memsahib!" he called.

Dripping sweat, Trish and Colleen ambled over to him.

"A snake?" Trish asked.

Frogs fed off insects that populated the garden beds. Their presence in turn attracted snakes but usually by night - the reptiles were understandably averse to the gardeners' long-handled hoes.

The little man vigorously shook his head and pointed to the base of a neem tree.

Colleen crouched down and saw nestled between a pair of exposed tree roots a mottled grey creature with shaggy fur, about the size of a house cat and having cat-like whiskers but with a more pointed snout and rounded ears. It had pinkish eyes and a tail about as long as its body.

"Mongoosa!" whispered the Burman.

"It's an Indian Grey," said Trish, crouched beside Colleen. "You don't usually get them in Burma. It must have escaped from the zoo."

"I can't remember seeing one there."

"Oh, they're probably getting animals in all the time. Maybe this fellow got away in transit."

Located near the Royal Lake, Rangoon's zoological gardens remained unmolested by the war and the girls had enjoyed fascinating excursions there during their off duty hours. Trish's explanation seemed the most likely one.

"Thanks," she said to the gardener. "We'll take care of him now."

He smiled, nodded and departed to resume his tasks.

"We!" Colleen protested. She stood upright and placed her hands on her hips.

"Of course," said Trish mildly. "You're my oppo, remember?"

"How are we supposed to look after him?" Colleen asked doubtfully. "And how do you know it's a him?"

"I'm guessing. We'll sort something out."

Trish extended a coaxing hand toward the creature.

"C'mon, Monty," she said softly.

"Monty? You can't call him that, even if it is a him. And how do you know it hasn't got rabies? Matron'll go spare, not to mention old Pencil-puss."

The mongoose stretched and sniffed Trish's fingers. It then trotted forward and butted its head against her perspiring thighs. Gently, she stroked its neck and back. Colleen looked on in amazement.

"It's definitely a male," said Trish, after a cursory glance at the animal's hindquarters. "Why shouldn't we call him Monty? I don't think the field marshall would mind. Anyway, he's not going to know, is he? I'm sure we can keep him out of sight of the CO. As for Matron, we'll cross that bridge when we come to it. Oh, yes, you are handsome," she said to the mongoose, scratching its ears.

"Its fur'll get all manky with sweat. Or you'll get all manky with fur, or both."

The girls were covered in perspiration and Colleen was getting impatient. She was looking forward to showering and freshening up, with the customary draught of lemon and lime in the mess.

"Loads of folk in India have house mongooses," said Trish, standing up. "Like we did in Ranchi and like the Dalrymples I told you about."

Monty rubbed his sleek flanks on the girls' legs. Colleen thought the fur felt coarser than that of a cat.

"Shouldn't we contact the zoo?" she asked.

"Well, not just yet."

They walked back to the hospital, making for the fire escape that stood at the end of the wing housing the nurses' accommodation. They always returned that way after a PT session because it gave easier access to the shower annex and their rooms.

Too easy, as it turned out.

The girls were partly screened by garden beds so no-one noticed their four-footed companion, gambolling at their heels. Colleen was therefore a bit disconcerted that her friend's clandestine arrangements seemed already to be working.

"You won't get rabies unless he bites you," Trish explained. "And anyone who provokes him to that extent deserves it. But I never heard of anyone catching rabies from an Indian

Grey. They are diurnal, so he'll be out during the day, hunting in the early morning and late afternoon, then lying up for a sleep around midday. There'll be lots of things for him to eat. He'll even crack open a scorpion on a rock if he finds one. Of course, there's no reason we can't give him a few bits and pieces. Save some eggs and fruit from the mess. We'll just need to let the gardeners know not to disturb him – and ask the blokes in the maintenance shed to let him come in out of the rain, if he wants to."

"What if he sprays?"

"They don't spray inside. He'll only mark the grounds. No-one'll notice."

They began to ascend the fire escape. The mongoose scampered along beside them, occasionally pausing to sharpen his claws against the teak framework. Just like a cat, Colleen thought. She was still nervous about Trish's repeated use of the term, "We."

"How are you going to get him back into the grounds?" she asked.

Trish stooped to stroke Monty's flanks again. Once more, he rubbed against her legs.

"I'll entice him out here with some scraps when he's had a look at our rooms," she said. "Then we can organise a 'Monty Watch' to let him in and out as needed."

Colleen drew breath.

"You sound pretty confident."

"Oh, I'm sure the other girls won't mind," said Trish nonchalantly as she straightened up. "Or he can jump from the veranda onto that tree with those big boughs that almost touch the balustrade. He'll be quite safe. These fellows can climb like monkeys. He'll soon get used to sleeping on my bed at night and he won't go near the wards. Too many nasty smells, like antiseptic."

Colleen stared at her.

"You're going to have him on your bed?"

"Of course. We did with the one we had at Ranchi. And Tally, the Dalrymples' mongoose, slept on my bed when I stayed with them, after Jon and Robbie's wedding."

Colleen pushed ajar the door to the nurses' quarters. The mongoose nosed eagerly at the opening.

"Is he like Rikki-tikki-tavi[257]?" Colleen asked.

"The same. And he'll be just as keen to explore but if we head straight for the ablutions area, he'll hopefully follow us. That'll keep him out of the way for a bit. If anyone's in there, we can explain everything when the shrieks have died down."

Contrary to Colleen's expectations, everything worked out as Trish had forecast and Monty quickly won the affections of all the nursing and orderly staff. He also revealed an instinct for concealing himself from anyone of senior rank.

Except Matron.

On nights when Trish and Colleen were able to relax in the mess after supper, the mongoose invariably slept on Trish's lap until it was time for bed, whereupon he obediently trotted back to Trish's room with her.

It was inevitable that Matron would discover these arrangements. The bridge, about which Trish had surmised, was about to be crossed.

Entering the mess late one night, Matron stopped and stared at the recumbent, furry shape, her expression one of bewilderment.

Colleen and the other girls promptly stood up according to custom and said, "Good evening, Matron."

Apart from Trish, who looked up from her bible, smiled and then said, "Good evening, Matron."

Monty stirred, stretched, yawned and curled up again. Trish scratched his ears and stroked his neck, prompting from the creature a squeaky sound of appreciation.

Matron admirably recovered her composure.

"Good evening to you all," she said.

Deliberately looking away from Sister Calder, she asked, "Is there still some tea in that pot?"

With the end of the war and the gradual restoration of Rangoon to normality, hospital security was partly stood down.

Unfortunately, the transition resulted in a further attempt on Grandma Colleen's life, though once again, Divine Providence furnished a deliverer – in the form of Monty the mongoose.

This is how it happened.

The two shadowy figures reached the base of the fire escape undetected under cover of darkness. One of them carried a hessian sack. Partially obscured by massing clouds, a full moon gleamed whitely over the grounds. Humid and heavy, riven by lightning streaks and rumbling thunder, the air portended another bout of monsoon rain before morning.

One of the figures was a heavy-set individual in dark-coloured fatigues and plimsolls, his face blackened by burnt cork. He grimaced at his companion, who carried the sack. This individual was an Indian of spindly frame, turbaned, bare-footed and clothed in dark shorts and vest.

"Still say 'twould be better to do the job with my dirk," the first man growled, in a Clydeside burr. His calloused right hand closed on a bone-handled hilt projecting from the sheath fastened to his belt. The Scot then drew an index finger deftly across his throat. "All over in a second, after I've had my way with her, of course," he said with a malicious grin.

The Indian's eyes flashed with demonic fire. His burly companion shrank back, suddenly afraid.

"Fool!" hissed the other man. "This woman is a sacrifice to Kali-Ma. To her you owe your freedom. Would you arouse her wrath?"

Chastened, his crony fell silent. Coming from a high priest of the goddess, the threat was real.

The pair ascended the steps to the top floor. They hoisted themselves from the fire escape railing via a drainpipe onto the adjoining veranda.

Together they crept to the window space of a room.

Colleen's room.

"Are you sure it's this one?" whispered the Scot.

The Indian cast a scornful glance at his companion.

"Kali is always watching," he said malevolently. The priest squatted beside the window space, laid down the bag, untied a cord around its neck and with one hand eased the matting back. The woven covers had all been lowered during the evening, in anticipation of the approaching storm.

Using his other hand, the priest held open the bag.

"Come, my beauty," he hissed.

With forked and flicking tongue, a reptilian head emerged.

The Scot drew back, once more afraid.

He was no coward. He could face screaming banzai charges without flinching or square off against any human opponent with brick, boot, bare fists or broken bottle stub. He'd never been bested, except by that nurse bitch, who took him by surprise with her pepper trick – and he'd have her if he got the chance.

But this wasn't human. And the flint-hearted ruffian trembled at the sight of the black and yellow-banded body extending before him.

Dry scales rustled against the matting as the snake's six-foot length slid smoothly through the gap held open by its master. It disappeared into the room.

The Indian folded up the bag and the would-be assassins departed.

Colleen awoke to a particularly loud clap of thunder. She could hear the rush of rain onto the veranda's cement floor – it always seemed to come in at an angle. Drops spattered off the woven mat covering the window space.

Of heavy, coarse weave, it admitted speckled glares of illumination from the spasms of forked lightning, augmented by that from the small, glass panel above it.

Lying on her side, with her legs partly drawn up, Colleen felt something touching her thigh through the mosquito netting.

She saw what it was in the next flash of lightning and gasped in terror. Sweat prickled on her forehead.

Don't move! she screamed inwardly. God, what now?

She stared at the banded body coiled no more than two feet away.

Colleen guessed it would easily bite through the flimsy net if aroused.

God, how did it get here, she thought in desperation.

Suddenly, the snake began to uncoil. Colleen gasped again but it was slithering off her bed and making for the mat curtain. It wedged its head between the matting and the wall and began to slip through.

Colleen tore off the netting, leapt out of bed, unhooked the mat from its base and frantically pulled on the cord to raise it. If she could corner the reptile on the veranda, she'd smash the beast with her chair.

Through the opened window space, a rippling streak of lightning revealed a bizarre scene.

"Trish!" Colleen exclaimed, above the crackle of thunder.

Her friend stood dripping wet in her underwear and high heels on the veranda, her web bag around her shoulder and holding with both hands a nine-mm Browning automatic pistol, pointed downwards.

"Colleen, thank God!" said Trish with relief.

They gazed in awe at the life and death struggle before them.

The burst of thunder that woke Colleen had also woken Trish.

"Monty?" she said, sitting up in bed.

He was pawing at the wall curtain, his hair extended so that he looked twice his normal size.

Removing the mosquito net, Trish sprang to her feet, looped her web bag over her shoulder and groped in the bottom of her wardrobe for the nearest pair of shoes.

Her hand closed on her high heels. She slipped them on and hurried over to the wall curtain, unhooked its base and pulled it aside.

In a flash of lightning, she saw that Monty's eyes had turned fiery red.

He dashed onto the veranda, oblivious of the rain that gusted in beneath its arches. Trish felt the shower soak her as she followed Monty. Her hands were clasped around the grip of the pistol she had extracted from her bag and cocked.

She edged along the veranda. Monty paused, ready to spring. Trish froze.

Lightning blazed, followed by growling thunder. In horror, Trish saw the black and yellow-banded shape wriggle onto the veranda from behind the wall curtain of the next room.

Colleen's room.

"Oh, no, Colleen!" exclaimed Trish.

The snake was racing for the far end of the veranda, doubtless aware of its peril.

Monty uttered a snarling "tik-tik-tik" noise and hurtled off in pursuit.

Beset with anxiety, Trish lunged for the curtain, the web bag rasping her hip. If Colleen had been bitten, Trish knew she had seconds at best to get inside and inject Colleen with anti-venene from one of the ampoules in her bag.

If her friend wasn't already dead.

Then she saw the mat ascending and stood still with the pistol at the ready. Her heart was pounding. Would she have to deal with a human intruder as well?

"Trish!"

"Colleen, thank God!"

Trish immediately lowered the weapon, overwhelmed with relief at the sight of her friend standing poised by the window space, unharmed.

They stared at the savage combat in front of them.

Monty had seized the snake's head in his jaws. Its six-foot length was whipping and twisting in a paroxysm of panic to try and shake loose its attacker.

The snake's frenzied gyrations flung the mongoose to and fro on the veranda floor with resounding thumps until the girls feared that their pet would be knocked senseless.

But Monty's jaws clenched tighter until the snake's skull cracked and its head was crushed.

The reptile lay quivering in its death throes on the wet cement.

The mongoose trotted nonchalantly back to his grateful audience, his hair flattening, the fire subsiding in his eyes. Trish rendered her weapon safe and placed it in her bag.

Then both girls crouched down and lovingly stroked the mongoose, even as he shook water from his hair.

"Oh, Monty, you're a marvel," exclaimed Colleen, sobbing with gratitude.

Trish flung the dead snake over the balustrade.

"Anything the red ants leave, the gardeners can shovel into the incinerator," she said.

They retired to Colleen's room. She flicked on the light, lowered the wall curtain, fastened it and handed her friend a bath towel. Trish wrapped it around her shoulders and sat in Colleen's chair with Monty on her lap while Colleen removed a flask from the top drawer of her wardrobe. She poured out two medicine glassfuls of brandy, gave one to Trish and swallowed hers in single gulp.

"Monty deserves something," she said, blinking. Her eyes watered as the liquid seared down inside.

Trish fondly scratched the back of Monty's head and took a sip of brandy.

"I'll sort that. For now, we've got to decide what to do."

"What was it?" Colleen asked. She sat on the edge of her bed, shuddering.

"Banded krait," said Trish gravely. "A dozen times more deadly than a cobra."

Colleen whistled softly.

"I thought kraits were only little beggars."

"It's an exception. You mostly get them in India, especially Assam and Bengal but they range as far as the Dutch East Indies[258]."

"Well, thank God for both of you. And thanks for bringing the anti-venene, which I guess is in your bag but how come you're in your heels and where did you get that pistol from?"

"They were the nearest shoes within reach," said Trish, glancing down. "I thought a snake must have been on the veranda by the way Monty was acting – doubtless, they'd sensed each other. Charles Dalrymple gave me the Browning, after I was accosted by that drunken Jock."

Colleen nodded.

"The one you peppered?"

"That's right. I think it was a wise precaution, even though we didn't see anyone. That snake was planted."

"Planted?"

Trish took another sip of brandy and stroked Monty's back.

"Yes," she said firmly. "The banded krait's a ground snake. It would never have got here by itself. I think the Enemy's tried to get you again, Coll. As an offering to Kali-Ma. I've heard of it happening before."

"Kali's *real*[259]," Colleen said in amazement. "I still can't get over that."

"Demonic principality, in a female form[260]," said Trish with a grimace. "Makes your flesh creep, doesn't it?"

"How did they know this was my room?"

"Probably through one of our cleaning women," said Trish, with a slight shrug. "Kali's not omniscient so even her people have to rely on received information. In the meantime, we need to pray Job's hedge[261] for you, Coll. But they didn't reckon on you, did they, Monty," she added, scratching the mongoose's ears.

He made a 'tiki' sound of contentment.

"Of course not," said Colleen. She laughed at the sudden realisation. "He's out before they come and not back until well after they've left."

"Part of Father's providential care, Coll. We should be thankful the gardeners apparently didn't say anything. Either that or Kali's lot kept their enquiries to a minimum, for reasons of security."

Colleen reached over and gave Monty an affectionate pat, then placed her hands on her knees and heaved a sigh.

"I could do without this kind of notoriety, though. Do you want a top-up?"

She reached for the flask.

Trish held out her glass and unexpectedly shuddered. Monty looked up, startled, but settled down when Trish stroked him.

"Yes, please," she said. "It's starting to hit me, I think. My God, it was a near thing, Coll."

That night, the girls exchanged rooms, in case the intruders came back. Trish slept with Monty curled up beside her and the pistol under the pillow. They upended their tables against the wall mats. No-one could disturb the mats without the tables grating noisily on the floor.

The next day, Colleen and Trish took Janice and Mandy into their confidence.

Their friends were shocked but promised to help.

"Leave it with us," said Janice. "There's still a couple of our CCS blokes left. They'll fix it."

In this way, Colleen was provided with her own Browning automatic and several clips of ammunition.

"The lads said keep the safety on when it's under your pillow," said Mandy.

But soon afterwards, a longer-term solution to the problem of Colleen's personal safety presented itself.

Major-General Sir Redvers Holbrook-Smith, MC, DSO, KBE, KCMG, KCSI[262], Retired, had been installed as Governor of Burma soon after the capture of Rangoon. Towards mid-September, he hosted the official surrender of the remaining Japanese forces in Burma and Malaysia, with the Allied Supreme Commander, Admiral Lord Louis Mountbatten, presiding.

He and his wife, Lady Guinevere Holbrook-Smith, one of the most outstanding debutantes of the 1920s, had also played host and hostess to various social functions held in the Governor's residence.

But being devoted parents, they arranged outings as often as possible with their two children, Michael and Elizabeth, aged ten and seven, who had accompanied their parents from India.

The social functions, in the meantime, generated considerable enthusiasm. Many of the nurses attended, wearing gowns contrived from colourful saris and returned with high praise for their hosts.

"Sir Redvers is *so* charming. No wonder his missus had a hundred suitors in her day."

And for many of the guests.

"There's some really dashing officer blokes in this neck of the woods."

Colleen and Trish had been content to swap shifts so their colleagues could go to the functions but Matron Wrigglesworth eventually requested that, "Sisters Calder and McGrath see me in my office."

They promptly hurried downstairs to Matron's ground-floor niche. It was similar to Colonel Partridge's.

"There are a couple of spare places for a dinner party at the governor's residence tomorrow evening," Matron explained. "I've been asked to provide Sisters to fill them. You haven't been to any functions yet so would you like to go?"

"Yes, Matron," the girls chorused. Refusal wasn't an option, actually.

At the change of shift, they sought out Mandy and Janice, who had been to one of the earlier events.

"Oh, you'll love it," said Mandy. "Get one of the Burmese ladies to run you up a gown from a sari pattern. They do a marvellous job. If the do's not until tomorrow night, that'll give them plenty of time."

The local women's ability with the old-fashioned pedal sewing machines installed in their villages was by now legendary. They easily adapted their own dressmaking styles for the taller Europeans.

"And you must borrow my heels," Janice urged Colleen. "I had them done in Calcutta. Actually, I had two pairs made up, so you might as well keep one of them."

This was generosity in the extreme and Colleen hesitated but Mandy urged her to accept.

"Make the most of it, Coll. While she's on Cloud Nine. She got another letter from Down Under this morning. You know what I mean, like?"

"Shut up," said Janice, laughing with embarrassment. "But anyway, we'll look after Monty for you."

The heels fitted Colleen's feet perfectly. They were of similar elegant design to Trish's and Robyn's.

In the warmth of the early evening, with cicadas singing in the trees, Colleen and Trish awaited their escort, "dolled up, slicked up, ready to go," according to Mandy.

An ochre-coloured Oldsmobile saloon, bearing the governor's pennant on its bonnet, with a turbaned Indian driver, drew up at the bottom of the hospital's front steps.

A young, uniformed attaché emerged from the front passenger door and briskly mounted the steps.

"No traipsing about in jeeps tonight," said Colleen.

"Nineteen hundred hours, on the dot," Trish observed.

When they motored along the gravel drive of the residence, the girls gazed admiringly at the imposing, turreted red and yellow brick building with its rows of tall, arching windows showing impressively in the car's headlights.

"This place certainly missed the war," said Colleen.

Welcoming lights shone above the house's colonnaded entrance.

"Looks like Windsor Castle," said Trish.

The young attaché turned to them with a smile.

"Wait 'til you get inside, Sister," he said. "Japs looked after it quite well."

His charges were enthralled by the interior, where the main hall ascended to a huge dome ringed by skylights tapering to its centre, with the upper storeys designed as white arcades, accessed by two magnificent teak staircases. The girls' heels clicked on the ground floor that gleamed in richly patterned, tiled mosaic and they saw that the walls were decorated with exquisite Burmese wood-carvings. Beyond the foyer, a pair of arched teak doors opened into the chandeliered ballroom, of breath-taking dimensions.

"I'll take your cloaks, ladies," said their escort.

Colleen and Trish handed him the matching capes that went with their saris and the officer in turn passed them to a tall Indian servant in white uniform and red sash, a jewel-hilted dagger in his belt and fluffy feather in his turban.

The servant received the capes, bowed gracefully and carefully placed the garments in labelled compartments on one of the rows of shelves behind him.

"This way, ladies," said the attaché. He beckoned to a lighted doorway from which the buzz of conversation emanated. It lay diagonally opposite the ballroom.

The evening proved to be most enjoyable and the meal was indeed a banquet. The Holbrook-Smiths were superb hosts. Major General Sir Redvers was of average height and build, with high forehead and iron-grey hair, slightly receding but he looked most distinguished in beribboned red evening jacket and black trousers, white shirt and black bow tie.

Lady Holbrook-Smith wore a shimmering white satin ball gown and diamond tiara. Luxuriant fair tresses fell to her shoulders, though Colleen observed that her ladyship's hair was beginning to turn grey.

"I suppose it'll happen to me eventually," she said under her breath.

The other guests were mostly young officers from each of the services and their female counterparts, though since all the ladies were wearing gowns, it wasn't possible to tell whether they were WRNs, WAAFs or ATS until the introductions. Colleen and Trish were the only QAs present.

Though one of the WRNs knew Sue Lentaigne, "or Sue Embleton as she is now," the girl said. Colleen knew that because she and Sue still wrote to each other but the occasion provided a good gossip, nevertheless.

A few middle-aged couples were present, senior or retired staff officers and their wives.

After dinner, the group adjoined to the lounge, a thickly carpeted annex with full-length windows opening onto the grounds.

"One or two of the older blokes remind me of Colonel Benji," Trish warned Colleen as they left the dining hall. "Watch you don't get your bottom pinched."

But no doubt in deference to their hosts, the men appeared more eager to sample the port. They pronounced it to be excellent, along with the cigars.

"I think the coffee's the best I've ever tasted," Colleen said to Trish.

Towards the end of the evening, they conversed for several minutes with her ladyship.

"My niece is a QA," she said. "At the hospital in Poona, now. Her name's Pippa Coniston-Price[263]. If you follow show jumping, you might have heard of her."

"I certainly have," said Trish enthusiastically. "She'll be in the next Olympics, won't she?"

"If she can fit it in with being married," said Lady Holbrook-Smith. "Her man, Daveyboy, we call him, is with the Royal Marine Commando Brigade that occupied Hong Kong earlier this month[264]. They're trying to arrange their wedding by remote control."

"It can be done," said Trish.

As she and Colleen drained their cups, a Burmese steward in white and black waiter's uniform approached, offering more coffee from a silver pot.

"Oh, yes, please," the girls said eagerly.

"Well, we are praying the Lord will smooth the way for them," her ladyship continued. "They've not seen each for three years but they'd stayed faithful the whole time, to our Father in heaven as well as to each other."

"We'd be only too ready to support you in that, your ladyship," said Trish.

"Guinevere, please," said the older woman, smiling. "And thank you, ever so much. It is such a priviledge, talking to you both. I really mustn't impose but Redvers and I would very much appreciate it if you could pray for our children, too. They lost their pet mongoose a couple of weeks ago and they've been very upset. A stray dog chased him out of the grounds. One of the servants shot the dog but by then poor Teddy had disappeared and our enquiries have led nowhere. My son called him Teddy after the boy in the Kipling story, you know."

"Yes, of course," said Colleen.

She and Trish exchanged glances.

"He came with us on the flight from Lucknow," said Guinevere. "We lined a rucksack with cotton wool and he curled up inside and slept the whole way. He loved it here, until that wretched dog appeared."

"An Indian grey mongoose, nearly fully grown?" Trish asked, placing her cup in its saucer.

"Why, yes," said her ladyship in surprise.

"I think we can help you, Guinevere," said Colleen. "Are you or your husband free tomorrow?"

Naturally, the girls had to inform Colonel Partridge of the impending visit and the reason for it.

He made no comment about Monty but busied himself with arrangements to assemble an honour guard for the august visitor.

Everything depended on Monty – or Teddy – putting in an appearance at the appropriate time, because Colleen and Trish would never have confined him. The visit was set for midday, when Sir Redvers could bring the children. His wife had a prior engagement that she could not break.

"Monty – or Teddy – usually has a nap in the grounds around noon or in the vehicle maintenance shed if it's raining, sir," Trish explained. "The gardeners have told us where his other haunts are."

"Sir Redvers and Lady Guinevere were very glad to learn how the hospital staff have looked after him, sir," said Colleen. "We were going to contact the zoo, weren't we, Trish?"

"Oh, yes," said Trish emphatically. "Just needed to give the little chap time to settle down. Sir Redvers said that was the wisest thing to do."

"Hmm," said Colonel Partridge.

A short time before the governor's arrival, Trish and Colleen went to search for Monty in the grounds, because it was a fine day, though as usual warm and steamy.

"Please, Lord, help us find him, amen," said Trish.

"Amen," said Colleen.

With great relief, they located the mongoose snoozing on a patch of crumbly soil in one of the more secluded beds.

"Thank You, Father," said Trish.

Monty yawned and stretched as Trish knelt down and stroked him.

"I'll stay with him, Coll," she said. "You bring the entourage."

As Colleen retraced her steps, she couldn't help thinking, what on earth am I doing, running messages for a mongoose?

She returned several minutes later, followed by two fair-haired children in safari suits, Sir Redvers and, bringing up the rear, Colonel Partridge and Matron Wrigglesworth.

The children and their father were brimming with excitement.

The others clearly were not.

But the reunion was joyful.

"Teddy, Teddy!" the children exclaimed.

Together, they knelt down and hugged their pet in turn. Monty-Teddy seemed delighted to see them despite his rude awakening. He rubbed his head against Michael's chin and snuffed at Elizabeth's ear.

Colleen and Trish looked on benevolently, trying to avoid their superiors' gaze.

Sir Redvers vigorously shook the CO's hand.

"We can't thank you enough, Partridge," he said, with great emotion. "He's certainly come a fair trot, has our Teddy. And thank you, Matron and you too, Sisters."

He couldn't help hugging the ladies and Colleen saw tears in the eyes of this gallant and honourable man – for he was one of the best and bravest in the Empire. Charles Dalrymple had spoken of him in the highest esteem, according to Trish.

The girls and Matron got a hug from each of the children too, before the happy trio departed with the lost and found Teddy, who went with them quite willingly. When they reached the car, Teddy hopped nimbly into the rucksack Michael had brought for the journey home.

"I suppose I should have told the CO straight off," said Trish, as they waved goodbye from the hospital steps.

"You mean *we*," said Colleen. "Never mind, it's all sorted, thank God. And it was best not to tell them about the krait, wasn't it?"

"Definitely."

They stood to attention and saluted as their CO strode past into the foyer, having dismissed the guard.

"I'll see you in my office, Sisters," he said. "At thirteen hundred hours."

"Yes, sir," said the girls.

Colonel Partridge looked up from the files on his desk at Colleen and Trish, who stood before him at attention.

"As you are aware, Singapore has lately been reoccupied," he said. "And a BGH has been set up there. I have been requested to send two experienced Sisters to bring the hospital up to minimum establishment. It's not as though we are overstaffed but their need is greater than ours. I've consulted with Matron and we've decided that you should both be reassigned to Singapore. Do you have any questions?"

"No, sir," said the girls in unison.

"Very good. You'll be leaving on the first available flight tomorrow, or as soon as possible after that, weather permitting. Dismissed."

"Yes, sir," said the girls.

They saluted, about turned and marched out of the office.

"Do you reckon he meant all that palaver about experienced Sisters?" Colleen asked as they clattered back up the stairs to their ward. "Or do you think he's finally decided to get rid of us?"

"Both," said Trish.

Morning dawned humid but clear, suitable weather for flying and after an early breakfast, Colleen and Trish managed to cram all their kit into a jeep

"So long as we sit with our bedrolls in our laps," said Trish.

Their driver was a loquacious orderly corporal from London named Stan, rotund and red-faced.

"CO says to me, 'Corporal Stan, you make sure they get their flight, those two,'" said Stan as he helped the girls stow their gear. "What with lords and mongooses turnin' up out of the blue, you've made things quite hectic for the colonel sahib, you have."

His banter made the goodbyes a little easier. Quite a number of staff turned out to see the girls on their way.

"You've been such towers of strength," said Matron kindly. "Take care and God bless you both."

She hugged each of her departing Sisters in turn.

"We do so hope it works out for you and John," said Trish, hugging Janice.

"I'm sure it will, the Lord's got His hand on us," Janice reassured her. "And we'll keep praying for you and Matt."

"I suppose you'll be Lady Waverly when I see you next, Coll," said Mandy as she embraced Colleen. "The Lord's been wonderful to us, hasn't He?"

When they boarded the C-47 at Mingaladon Airfield, Trish remarked, "I feel better being back in JGs."

"Vicar's daughter turns tomboy," said Colleen.

They both laughed as they waved goodbye to the cheery little corporal who stood by the jeep on the edge of the runway.

The aircraft circled the Shwe Pagoda after take-off, before heading south. Colleen gazed at the gleaming spire projecting through wisps of morning mist and pondered the expression Mandy had used so expectantly.

Lady Waverly.

Do I really want to be Lady Waverly, Colleen wondered.

She still wasn't sure.

Twenty

Singapore

They deplaned in mid afternoon, onto the concrete apron with its Nissen huts and tented surrounds that constituted Singapore's RAF base. The airfield was situated near the notorious Changi compound, where Sergeant Manning and his comrades had been incarcerated. Now Japanese POWs resided there, under much more humane conditions than the previous incumbents.

A RASC driver met the girls and conveyed them to the Alexandra Hospital[265] in his one-and-a-half-ton lorry.

"Feels muggier than Rangoon," Colleen remarked, looking up at misty grey skies.

"Over a thousand miles closer to the equator, Coll," said Trish.

They drove past heaps of jagged brick and stone piled up on each side of the road into the city. Derelict automobiles rusted amid the wreckage beside bomb-scarred walls and the thoroughfare was crowded with civilians, who turned impassive, oriental faces towards the passing military vehicles.

"Bit of a mess here," the driver said. "And the docks. They took a while to clean up. Town centre's not too bad. Our CO reckons the Japs left it alone so they could get good photos of the victory parade they had back in forty-two."

"What's the Alexandra[266] like?" Trish asked.

The driver glanced at her with a grin.

"Better than it was, Sister," he said.

The Alexandra was an extensive, three-storeyed building of pre-war colonial style architecture, with walls of white masonry and red-tiled roofs. The girls looked up at the porticoed balconies surrounding each storey.

"Nice and airy," said Trish, while they helped the driver unload their gear from the back of the lorry. He had parked it on the concrete stand near the entrance, next to several green-painted army ambulances displaying Red Cross roundels.

Like the hospital at Rangoon, the Alexandra had a Union Jack flying from a white-painted flagpole. Colleen and the driver hoisted her trunk with camp bed attached off the tray

"Japs ransacked the hospital when the city fell," the RASC lad said. "Smashed all the equipment, even the lifts, carried off all the bedding. Left the place a tip. Bayoneted about

453

two hundred of the staff and patients. Their kind of victory celebration, I guess. Nurses had been evacuated but their ships got bombed and them as survived got taken prisoner."

"What did you do, when you got here, I mean?" asked Colleen.

She hooked her web bag and bedroll over her shoulders by their straps and grasped one of the handles on Trish's trunk to assist her lift it off the lorry. The girls were horror-struck by the driver's narrative. The Alexandra's fate, compared to that of the hospital at Rangoon, highlighted the fierce unpredictability of their oriental foes. Colleen wondered if a Japanese officer had run around after the massacre and desecration shouting, "Very sorry. Alla big mistake," to traumatised survivors.

"Herded the Jap POWs in to clean it all up, Sister," said the driver. "Worked 'em round the clock and we had everything up and running in a couple of days. Hey, give us a hand, mate."

This remark was directed to a couple of passing OR orderlies, who willingly aided in getting the girls' trunks and camp beds into the foyer.

A uniformed clerk seated behind a desk in an alcove looked up as the party entered.

"Just let that chap at Reception know you've arrived and Matron will come and meet you," said the RASC man. "Thanks for the pleasure of your company, Sisters. Hope you have an enjoyable stay."

Their service at the Alexandra would certainly prove to be interesting and for Trish, particularly enjoyable.

Matron Vivienne Leese was dark-haired, slim and vivacious. In freshly pressed grey frock and starched cap, she exuded efficiency. Colleen saw that she wore a wedding ring.

Matron returned the girls' salutes, shook hands and bade them welcome.

"We've got the wards working OK," she said. "But your quarters are bare, I'm afraid. Have you got mozzie nets?"

"Yes, Matron," said Trish. "Beds and bedrolls, as you see."

"Oh, call me Viv," said Matron. "You don't mind using your trunks for dressers?"

"We're used to that," said Colleen, smiling.

Viv nodded appreciatively.

"Our REs did a terrific job getting the facilities working, even the steriliser," she said. "But it's still perforated canvas buckets for showers in the Sisters' quarters."

"Those, too," said Trish.

"Excellent," said Viv. She asked the clerk to summon a couple of orderlies.

"I'll take you to your rooms," she said to Colleen and Trish. "It's a bit of a hike but you'll get an idea of the layout of the place. We're all in one wing at the end."

They followed her along cool corridors past wards occupied by ex-POWs, of terribly familiar skeletal appearance. Several wards contained emaciated-looking female patients.

"We've a great many former internees as patients," Viv explained, as she led the girls up a staircase. "Quite a few civilian nurses among them and our own Sisters who were captured."

"It must be hard tracking down missing civilians," Trish remarked.

"Yes," said Viv. "People were moved about quite a bit and the Japanese separated husbands from wives and children. So often, one or other didn't survive. Where the mother died, it's often been a difficult job locating any children."

Two pairs of ORs followed with the girls' trunks. At the end of a corridor on the top floor of the nurses' accommodation wing, they came to a box-shaped room, bare except for a ventilation fan and electric light bulb suspended from the ceiling. It was designed like the wards, with shuttered windows looking out onto a roofed-over balcony.

"Would you like your trunks under the windows, Sisters?" asked the senior OR, a lance corporal.

"Thank you, Corporal," said Trish. "That'll be fine."

The ORs positioned their loads and left. Viv glanced at the watch fastened to her blouse.

"You can join evening shift in one of the women's wards," she said. "See me in my office at eighteen hundred hours – it's just off the main foyer, even got my name on the door."

"Who does the laundry, Viv?" asked Trish.

She and Colleen unstrapped their beds, unpacked their mosquito nets and slung them from loops of cord that hung from the ceiling.

"We managed to recruit some local women," Viv explained. "They are mostly Chinese and they also do the washing up. See the clerk for some linen bags for your things."

"Does the WVS do all the catering?" Colleen asked, extracting her ward dress from her trunk.

"They certainly do," said Viv. "When you're sorted here, pop into the mess for tea and homemade bread and jam. They bake it every day and they'll arrange supper for you."

They had walked past the Sisters' Mess on the way to their rooms. It was a long room with several trestle tables, benches, wooden chairs, some easy chairs and the faithful tea urn situated on the work surface at one end. A couple of women in WVS dress had been at work in an adjoining kitchen, from which the rich aroma of baking bread emanated.

Viv assisted the girls in setting up their camp beds and then departed.

Colleen and Trish changed into grey ward uniform and ventured into the mess, where they introduced themselves to the other girls present and helped themselves to tea, bread and jam.

"Well, three cheers for the WVS," said Colleen.

"Amen to that," said Trish.

Their first job on the women's ward was to serve the patients' meals. Many of them had to be helped to sit up. Their wasted frames and lank hair made them look geriatric, though most were under forty years old.

Virtually all were suffering from lingering skin complaints, especially scabies. The ugly blotches would take weeks to heal. Likewise, the incidence of beriberi among the women was alarmingly high. Its effects of muscle atrophy on some parts of the body contrasted grotesquely with the swelling of the victims' feet and lower limbs resulting from waterlogged tissue.

Colleen and Trish had seen the same pitiable anomaly among men patients at Rangoon.

"As you know, it's mostly a matter of sustained good diet," Viv explained when she discussed the patients' needs with Trish and Colleen. "But the MOs will prescribe the medication as necessary. We will need to keep them on quinine, of course."

Numbers of the women had contracted tuberculosis during their captivity.

"We have an isolation ward," Matron Leese had said tersely. "They are monitored round the clock."

"I hate Japs," Colleen muttered when they collected the plates. She could feel tears in her eyes.

Trish patted her shoulder.

"At least the lassies weren't throwing up or carrying on like a flock of seagulls, the way the blokes did," said Trish. "But they sure tucked in."

"They're putting on weight too fast, though."

Most of the women had weighed less than six stone on release and many were gaining pounds disproportionately in satiating their gnawing appetites.

"Yes," said Trish with a sigh. "Too much round the middle. I suppose it can't be helped, though, like the blokes."

Some of the women could walk to the lavatories but others still needed bedpans. Colleen and Trish also provided bowls of water for them to wash their hands and brush their teeth, activities they undertook with great deliberation.

When it came time to settle the patients for the night, one hollow-eyed woman spoke gratefully to Colleen in a tired voice.

"Such a blessing, having mattresses. We only ever had bamboo to sleep on, you know, or concrete. Hard on your hipbones, when you've not got much padding there."

None of the woman wanted a brandy nightcap, though one had asked Trish for a brief change of scenery. The request caused Colleen some anxiety.

"Sister Tyndall's missing," she said. "I'm sure she's not in the loo."

The bed nearest the admin desk was empty. Its occupant, Sister Deborah Tyndall, was a QA who had been imprisoned in Sumatra for over three years.

"She wanted to go sit on the balcony for a bit," said Trish. "It was when you were at the other end of the ward. I told her I'd come and speak to her when we'd got the rest settled."

Together they went out onto the balcony. It was accessed by a pair of double doors at the end of the ward near the admin desk.

Sister Tyndall was seated in a leather armchair, looking serenely at the lights of the city. A cool breeze was wafting along the balcony.

She smiled at Colleen and Trish as they approached. Colleen noted that two of the Sister's upper teeth were missing. She had sensibly put on a long-sleeved cardigan over the blue nightdress that covered her like a sack.

Trish pulled a chair up beside her and sat down.

"Everything OK, Debs?" she asked.

"Perfect, thanks," said the other woman.

Colleen stood where she was able to see through the open shutters above Sister Tyndall's chair into the ward, partly illuminated by shaded lights at each end. Glancing at the Sister, she could see the skin tight against Deborah's cheekbones, brushed by bleached tresses that had lost all sheen. Blemishes of skin disease and the oedema of beriberi showed on her legs below the hemline of her dress.

Yet Colleen knew that Sister Tyndall had been beautiful. She was as tall as Trish or herself and it was clear that, like them, Deborah had once been strong, supple and athletic.

But her blue eyes were bright and full of sisterly affection and Colleen earnestly hoped that with the hospital's care, Deborah would soon regain her poise and beauty.

"You know," said the Sister. "When we first arrived, we thought you all had such big bosoms and big behinds. Even greyhounds like you two."

The girls laughed.

"You've had quite a time," said Colleen.

"Yes," said the Sister[267], with a sigh. "Started when I joined up, pre-war. All ready for action when the balloon went up but got posted to India. There I was, as they say, for the best part of two years, until they sent me to a hospital near the Thai border. No sooner there than we had to leave, after the Japs invaded. Got dive-bombed out of one place after another. Had lorry loads of wounded. Red crosses on the vehicles made no difference. Those of us that survived finally got here, as it happens, the Alexandra and in no time, it was full, wounded fellows lying everywhere, even in the corridors. Hardly room to walk between them. Many of the poor lads were in a terrible state, covered in dirt and grime, crying for their mothers and blood dripping through their dressings. A lot were in shellshock, sweating, white as chalk. The MOs were operating round the clock – out on their feet. Wasn't long before we were running out of dressings and morphia and so many of the boys had such awful pain. When the mains broke down, we had to carry what water we'd collected in buckets – and remove wastes the same way. I think it must have been like the Crimea."

"You must be getting tired, Debs," said Trish, hinting.

Sister Tyndall took a deep breath and leant back in the chair.

"I'm sure you'll let me witter on for a bit longer, though, Sister," she said.

Trish glanced at Colleen, who noted all was quiet in the ward and nodded.

"Please do," said Trish.

"You'd never believe I trained with Viv Leese at Tommy's[268], would you, or Viv Henley as she was then," said Deborah. "Not the way I look."

Trish gently touched the Sister's arm.

"You'll be looking much better soon," she said.

Sister Tyndall smiled wanly and picked up her narrative.

"We had to bury the patients that died in the grounds, in quicklime. Their places were soon taken. By then, it was getting bad in the city, with all the bombing. They hit the sewer mains and the mess seeped into the streets – terrible stench. Troops and locals were running around like headless chickens and being shot by Jap snipers. A lot of the soldiers looted grog shops and got drunk, so they were sitting ducks. We heard that some tried to force their way onto ships taking the evacuees, but the crewmen threw them off."

"Hang on a minute, Debs," said Colleen.

She went and fetched a blanket to cover the bare portions of Sister Tyndall's legs.

"Thanks, Coll," said Deborah. She continued with her reminiscences.

"In the end, General Percival[269] ordered all nurses to evacuate by ship. None of us wanted to leave the patients – and we didn't fancy our chances with the Jap air force all around. But those were the orders, although some civilian nurses and VADs stayed – at least they didn't get shipwrecked. Matron and I were in the last ambulance to get to the docks and all the warehouses were on fire. We found our ship by the quay with a crowd waiting to board her. It was one of the last ones to leave. Jap aircraft came in and strafed the lot. Just horrible. I remember an Australian official kneeling beside his niece, lovely girl, Australian Army nurse, blood all over her white uniform and her arm torn off. She bled to death in front of him[270]. He was nearly mad with grief. I borrowed a grey frock quick sharp when I got on board and we all changed into something darker – white dresses were too conspicuous. We tore them up for bandages, because so many folk had been wounded from the strafing. It was only a little steamer and the decks were crammed, and slippery with blood. Friday the thirteenth was the date, not a good day."

Sister Tyndall yawned. "Excuse me," she said, putting a hand over her mouth.

Again, Trish glanced at Colleen, who nodded.

"Bed time, Debs," said Trish firmly. "We'll carry on tomorrow."

The following evening, Sister Tyndall was looking more refreshed.

This time, Colleen sat beside Sister Tyndall on the balcony after lights out and Trish kept watch at the window.

"The harbour was blanketed with black smoke from the fires on shore when we weighed anchor," said Debs. "That helped hide us from the aircraft. I recall lots of other craft around; gunboats, launches, yachts, sampans and even rowing boats besides the steamers. All of them chock full with people trying to get away but I don't think many of them did.

"It was dark when we got out to sea. Us nurses were up all night trying to give first aid to the casualties but we had so little of anything that those with serious injuries, chest or abdominal wounds, just died and we had to slip them overboard."

"Would you like another blanket, Debs?" Trish asked.

Rain had begun to fall, rustling the branches of the palms in the grounds and turning the approach roads to the hospital glistening wet in the light of the street lamps. The breeze was directing the rain away from the balcony but the air was chillier than it had been the night before.

"No, thanks, Trish," said Debs with a grateful smile. "Refreshing, this rain. Now, where was I? Oh, yes. The Japs found us at daybreak. We'd come less than a hundred miles from

Singapore and dropped anchor near an island in the hope their aircraft wouldn't spot us. No such luck. They scored a direct hit. People got blown to bits, dreadful sight. That one bomb killed about thirty of the nurses, nearly a third of us and four of the five matrons aboard. The one lady that survived took shrapnel in the chest – though she lived through it, miraculously. She's one of your patients."

"Yes," said Colleen, folding her hands in her lap. "Wonderful lady."

Sister Tyndall nodded and went on.

"Well, we had to abandon ship. I remember a chap pulled my tin hat off before I dived over the side. Just as well, because it would have weighed me down. I took my shoes off, too. They were dragging me under. The water felt cool and looked so green – lovely for swimming but the current was taking me away from the island. Fortunately, one of the ship's boats came by and someone held out an oar, which I grabbed onto and they pulled me ashore.

"The Japs came in and machine-gunned us while we were helping the wounded off the beach into the scrub, so we all wormed in amongst the rocks. They seemed to machine-gun us forever.

"When they'd gone, we managed to get some lean-tos and beds made up out of branches for the casualties and we tore more strips from our dresses for bandages. Things were pretty dire, since we had a lot more injured and those of us who'd been in the water suffered from blast effects, water forced up the anal passage.

"Painful," said Trish, grimacing. "And potentially fatal."

"Yes," Deborah said vehemently. "Some folk died from internal haemorrhage later on. Others were dying there and then, of course, from GSWs and shrapnel. A lady doctor with us was doing emergency ops on the spot. She amputated one poor woman's leg, I recollect, with just enough morphia to dope her for the few minutes necessary."

Trish glanced into the ward and nodded to Colleen, indicating all was well.

"What provisions did you have?" she asked.

"Some tins of bully and biscuits," said Deborah. "But they weren't going to last long with six hundred of us, though thank God, we found a stream of fresh water. We arranged a shift system for nursing the casualties and eked out an existence for a few days until an island trader put in and took most of the sick and wounded aboard – about half the group. The lady surgeon went along to look after them. So did I, and some of the other Sisters. We were in a filthy state by then. My hair was like a bird's nest.

"It must have been about twenty-one hundred hours by the time we'd seen to the patients. Some of us went out on deck to sleep – lots of people were lying down there, because it was cooler.

"All of a sudden, we saw this glaring green light. Someone sat up and said, 'What's that?' and then everything was swallowed up in a mighty great bang. Turned out a Jap destroyer had shelled us. Blood and strips of flesh were splashed everywhere, though somehow, I wasn't hurt. I ran for the hold where a lot of the patients were but a VAD girl came struggling up the companionway, in tears with blood all over her dress. 'They're all dead,' she said. 'My own mother, too.'

"The ship then heeled right over and we virtually stepped into the water. Another QA – Gemma White[271] – and I managed to grab a couple of drifting rafts and lash them together. We swam around and eventually got together sixteen of the women and children, two of them babies."

"What about their mothers?" asked Colleen. She glanced up at Trish, whose nod indicated they should let Deborah go on for a little longer.

"Killed, or drowned," said Deborah sadly. "The youngest of the children and two of the women sat on the rafts, each holding a baby, while the rest of us clung to the lifelines. I urged them to hang on but a couple were gone by morning. And when it was light, I saw Gemma looking deathly pale, so we got her up onto the raft. I found she had this ghastly wound in the buttock and in the afternoon, she died.

"More people slipped away during that night and everyone got hideously thirsty after sunup – the heat was ferocious and we got terribly burnt by the sun, and the salt water was awful on the burns – really stung. Occasionally, though, a tropical storm came over and I tried to catch rainwater for the children in a powder compact lid I found in a pocket of the dress but I couldn't get much. One by one, the children got delirious. We pushed them onto the rafts but they thrashed about, fell off and drifted away. None of us had the strength to go after them. The babies died, too, from exposure. I went over them minutely before I let them go. I had to make sure, you see."

Deborah stopped, took out a handkerchief and dabbed her eyes. "Excuse me," she murmured.

Colleen touched the other woman's arm. She could feel tears in her own eyes.

Trish reached down and placed a comforting hand on Deborah's shoulder.

"They're with the Lord, Debs," she said, though her voice was breaking.

"I know," Deborah whispered. Regaining her composure, she resumed speaking.

"The other women disappeared, one after the other and on the third day, only two us were left, sitting back to back on the rafts, trying to paddle with bits of driftwood towards some islands but the current was against us. Then this other girl accidentally let go of her paddle and fell overboard trying to get it back. I tried to grab her dress but was too late and the current took her.

"Then came the fourth day. I was sitting on the raft, somewhere in the Java Sea, with the sun beating down, flotsam all around, and sharks swimming about, although they didn't bother me. No doubt they'd eaten their fill, with all the ships being sunk. I managed to pull in a few bits of seaweed and ate those. Tasted revolting but it was something, though I was just about dehydrated, with no water left in my little compact lid."

"You must have been getting delirious yourself by then," Colleen remarked.

"Nearly," said Deborah. She sighed and shifted in the chair. "When I saw a ship approaching in the afternoon, I thought it was a mirage but it turned out to be a Japanese destroyer. It stopped and they lowered a boat and took me on board, down to the sick bay. The doctor was a gentlemanly chap, spoke good English, gave me water to drink – not too much, or I'd have been sick. He put some lotion on my sunburn and gave me a shirt and slacks to wear, Japanese Navy issue. That's what I stood up in, for the next year and a half, until they fell apart and I got some shorts and a sun top. We were always short of clothes but after a while we stopped having periods and that helped."

"No need for sanitary towels?" Colleen asked.

Debs nodded.

"That's right. We used to make them out of bits of cloth, then wash them for reuse, until we didn't need to."

"Blessing in disguise," said Colleen gently.

"Yes, indeed," said Debs.

Trish smiled tenderly and rested her hand on Deborah's shoulder again.

"You'll be back to normal soon, Debs," she said.

"I know. Thanks, both of you," said Debs, smiling. She clasped Trish's hand briefly before going on with her recollections.

"I made myself a hat from plaited grass in the camp and some folk managed to cobble together shoes from slabs of wood and canvas strips but I never had any. That's why I don't wear them now.

"Another ship's officer questioned me about who I was and so on but after I'd said I was a QA from Singapore, he didn't bother with me any more. The doctor gave me some bread dipped in milk and then had an awning rigged up on the deck for me to sleep under, with a sack for a mattress."

Trish glanced at her watch.

"Well, it's definitely past your bedtime, Debs."

"Suppose so," said Sister Tyndall. She suppressed a yawn, rose out of her chair and strolled back to the ward arm-in-arm with the others. "Thanks for listening to me."

"It's an honour, Sister," said Colleen. Her eyes were still moist.

The following day, Deborah asked one of the duty Sisters if she could see Colleen and Trish.

"Could I please have a grey dress, like yours?" asked Sister Tyndall, when her friends arrived. "I'd like to start looking more like a QA. I mustn't impose on you but could we have a walk in the grounds some time?"

The two girls glanced at the duty Sister, who readily agreed.

"Some of the women are taking the air on the veranda," she said. "No reason you shouldn't go for a stroll."

"Then we'll sort the dress and be on our way," said Trish. "Get you a head square, too."

It would be hot in the grounds and the girls were concerned to minimise any discomfort that Deborah might experience. Sunstroke was another malady that many ex-captives had suffered from.

"Do you want to try on some shoes, Debs?" asked Colleen.

Deborah's limbs and feet were still manifesting the after effects of beriberi but Colleen thought it worth asking.

Gracefully, the Sister declined.

"Perhaps in a few days, Coll. And then I'd love to try on the heels you've both been on about."

"Our pleasure," said Colleen.

They escorted her down the stairs and out onto the lawn. It was a fine day and the grass had been newly cut.

"It feels lovely on my feet," said Debs. "Can't wait to grow into this dress."

The frock looked outsize on Deborah's angular form but Colleen noticed that the Sister's sun-browned face was gradually filling out and her hair was looking healthier.

"Tell us when you need to rest, Debs," she said.

"I will," said Deborah. "But now for the next instalment.

"The ship docked at Muntok[272], on Bangka Island, off the southeast coast of Sumatra. I found I couldn't walk, so the Japanese doctor carried me ashore and into the camp. He left me in the care of some British sailors, who gave me a mug of tea and opened a tin of fruit salad. The tea was like nectar but the fruit made me sick after about the first spoonful. I wish I'd been able to keep the tin without it being opened right then."

They came to a path. It consisted of hard-packed sand but was littered with pebbles.

"Can you manage here, Debs?" Trish asked.

"No problem," Debs rejoined. "I've got soles like elephant's hide now."

"What was the camp like?" Colleen asked.

"The place in Muntok was a gaol," said Deborah. "Designed for about two hundred coolies, to work in the fields nearby. Most of the people I'd last seen on the island were there and we were about eight hundred then, a mixture of women, children – and babies, civilian and military men, crammed into these huts with nowhere to sleep except on the concrete floor. Some of the women had taken on the job of cooks and they gave everyone a cup of rice, in half a coconut shell. I said I didn't like rice but I was told, 'You'd better like it, dear, because there's nothing else.' So I did.

"Gradually, my sunburn settled down but then these horrible red patches came up on my legs, so painful I couldn't sleep. The Japanese MO didn't know what they were but we had a fine old Scots doctor with us who said to me, 'You've got sea water boils, my dear and I'm going to have to lance them.' He only had a blunt scalpel but he got all the pus out. Just as well, because they could have killed me."

"Blood poisoning," said Trish.

"Very much so," said Deborah.

They came to an intersection in the path, where one branch led beneath some overhanging trees. The girls subtly steered Deborah towards the shaded patch as she talked.

"The discolouration took a long time to disappear, though, so take my advice and don't get shipwrecked. You two have got such good legs, you'd make Betty Grable[273] jealous. Your lads are so privileged."

Colleen and Trish were writing to Peter and Matt as often as they could and receiving replies on a similar basis. Matt and others from the West Yorks were now with the occupation forces in Thailand, helping to restore the civil administration, repatriate both Allied and Japanese prisoners and screen suspected war criminals. This task required sworn testimonies from former POWs and internees, who were being rescued in their tens of thousands from over two hundred camps, located in a vast area stretching from the Thai-Burma border to Malaya, Sumatra and the Dutch East Indies.

New camps are still being turned up, often in deep jungle, Matt had written recently to Trish. *We have to patrol areas like we did during hostilities, because the Japanese keep trying to conceal the camps' whereabouts. Gruffie – Sergeant Grafton, now - and I were on a jeep recce yesterday with a Jap officer whom we suspected of not divulging all about his former jurisdiction. We came to a village where about twenty or so women were working in the fields. I asked the Jap who they were and he said, 'Wives of local men.' They looked too tall to me and not oriental, sunburnt rather than olive-skinned. I told Gruffie to stop and went over to them. Turned out they were British women captives, including some civilian nurses. As you'd expect, they were overjoyed when they saw us. Didn't know the war had ended, only that the guards had mysteriously disappeared but they expected them back anytime and so had kept working. They'd heard nothing of their husbands and families.*

Said they'd lived the whole time in fear of rape and had tried to make themselves look as unattractive as possible to avoid it. Wasn't hard after a few months of semi-starvation but a Jap might come and take any one of them, day or night and very likely strangle or bayonet her after he'd finished. If she tried to resist, she'd get beaten to a pulp. As usual, the guards withheld medicines and food supplies and the women only found them after the Japs had gone.

They have made sworn statements and I anticipate having the satisfaction of seeing our 'guide' and his accomplices on trial for their part in this affair – of a sort all too common, I'm afraid.

Peter had written to Colleen from Japan, where he had been invited as part of the Allied delegation to witness the formal surrender signed aboard the battleship USS *Missouri*.

The delegation had been conducted around the ruins of Hiroshima and Nagasaki. Peter's letter contained details of the bomb's effects[274].

The scene is genuinely apocalyptic. Whole square miles are flattened, leaving only the odd wall and the streets that divided city blocks. The B-29 crews said that the explosion was a blue, then yellow flash as bright as the sun. It turned into a purple cloud and then became a white column of smoke shooting up 40,000 feet in the air, shaped like a mushroom. After they'd turned for home, the airmen said they could still see it from over 300 miles away.

The flash generated a fireball that vaporised thousands in an instant. We saw where their shadows were imprinted on the pavementt, even where the cement was fused - the temperatures were in thousands of degrees. We saw gravestones where the granite had melted. The blast created winds of five hundred miles an hour or more, like a volcano's breath but full of glass, wood and metal splinters. It literally shredded thousands more people or turned them into bundles of charred bones. Whole trains, full of passengers, were hurled about like toys. Lots more people choked in the dust storm the winds churned up, thick as soup.

Those who survived were found covered in fused blood, with sheets of skin flapping off, huge blisters on their bodies, some with their faces burned off and their eyeballs melted. Any hospitals still functioning had diarrhoea running down the stairs, because they were swamped with injured people unable to control themselves.

We visited one of the emergency medical centres the Allies had set up. Our medics are doing all they can but for so many of the patients, it's simply a case of keeping them doped up until they die.

The Americans estimate over a hundred thousand dead but thousands more will die, from radiation. Apparently, in between the raids, a B-29 was shot down over Hiroshima. One crewman survived, a boy of about twenty. The citizens tied him to a post with a sign on it, saying[275], 'Beat this American as you pass by.' They did so until he died. The GIs were furious when they found out and there've been reprisals – hushed up, of course. For their part, many Japanese women are getting themselves infected with VD, in order to pass it on to our soldiers. The MOs are busy with this problem as well.

Yet, if we hadn't dropped the bomb, we'd still be at war and probably most of your patients would have died in those camps.

The letter contained a brief PS.

I'm being transferred to Palestine. Not looking forward to it because we have consistently wrong-footed ourselves by reneging on the Balfour Declaration[276] and we are bound to reap the whirlwind. However, I won't be sorry to leave here. I'm going via Washington so very much regret I won't be able to drop in. However, if you haven't heard about your home posting yet, let me know and I will make enquiries. Am so much looking forward to being with you again.

Colleen wrote back and tried to comfort him. With respect to her home posting, she simply said: *We're in the Lord's hands, love.*

The trio meandered along and Deborah recounted the next stage of her Odyssey.

"After a few weeks, they moved us to Palembang, on mainland Sumatra. We were put in houses taken over from the Dutch, until they were bursting at the seams but we got enough bamboo to make some platforms for sleeping.

"I was overjoyed that some babies had been saved. They grew up to be wiry urchins of three or four when we were released. I believe the Red Cross are looking after the orphaned children now. They seemed to come through better than the adults, although a lot of them turned into very accomplished little thieves."

Deborah confirmed Matt's account of the threats of rape but also described how in her camp, they had been forestalled.

"The Japs separated us into a men's camp and one for the women and children," she said. "That made us extremely vulnerable so I asked to see the commandant. Thankfully, he agreed and I explained that the Imperial Japanese Navy had treated me with the utmost consideration and that surely the Imperial Japanese Army would extend the same courtesy to all the women in the camp. He was a sly old devil but he saw my point, so we weren't molested. It would have risked losing face, you see. Just to be on the safe side, some of us put on a hacking cough, to pretend we had tuberculosis and that helped, too – though some did get the disease before the end, sadly."

"Yes, they're here too," said Trish.

Colleen stared down at the path as they walked and reflected upon the cruel scourge she had encountered everywhere she'd nursed; Teesside, Ormeskirk, Italy, India, Burma and now here. She wondered if and when a complete cure would ever be found.

Deborah's voice made her look up again.

"For a while the Japs allowed us to have Sunday services where we sang hymns and recited any scriptures we knew. Then they stopped us. Maybe the services made them feel guilty but we were an underground church from then on.

"Of course, the guards still belted us if we didn't bow quickly enough, like we were supposed to, when one of them approached. That's how I lost my two upper teeth. The worst time was *Tenko*, or daily roll call. They'd have us standing around for hours in the sun until they got the tallies right. If the total didn't work out, they'd lose their tempers and have to start again. I don't think many of them could count past five. Someone was sure to get slapped or thumped with a rifle butt. They also resented the way that many of us 'blue-eyed English pigs' could look down on them, since we were taller. I think to show their contempt, they used to watch us, while we took our baths, stripped naked."

"You had enough water for baths?" Colleen asked.

"Just a couple of inches in the bottom of a cutaway drum you stood in," said Deborah. "With your half coconut shell to dip in and pour the water over yourself. No soap or towels or anything - not until we got here – and no privacy, either but the Japs could be very public themselves about some things. Guards overseeing our work details would often relieve themselves in full view of us.

"In Palembang, we were put to work, cultivating fields for crops – for the benefit of the Imperial Japanese Forces, of course – digging up trees and sawing them for firewood, lugging the rice sacks – they felt like bags of cement – and doing our own cooking and laundry – I spent many an hour boiling up rags in cutaway oil drums to reuse them for dressing sores. One horrible job we had was digging out the latrine pit so the refuse could be carted away and disposed of. It took weeks to persuade the Japs to empty it. They did it the first time but after that, we did. At least we had spades to shovel the waste up – into old drums that we loaded onto the cart."

They came to stretch of the grounds recently dug over. It had been the site of the burials during the days before the city's fall.

"They exhumed the graves," said Trish quietly. "And reburied the boys in the new collection cemetery. You did a good job, putting the details on the crosses."

They walked slowly past the area, conscious that many of the dead, including staff and patients massacred after the hospital's capture, could not be explicitly identified.

"We also had to fetch water, for ourselves and the Japs, from a standpipe about half a mile from the camp," said Deborah. "The guards never let us go until midday, when the sun was hottest and often we only got to keep a couple of buckets full per household, after we'd brought enough to fill the Jap officers' baths, water their gardens and provide for their cooking. In return, we always peed in their portion before we delivered it."

The others laughed.

"Who thought that up?" Colleen asked.

"The Australian Sisters," said Debs, with a grin. "They were a plucky lot. About twenty of them had been shipwrecked on Bangka Island with sixty or so men, a lot who were elderly, injured or both. When the Japs arrived, they bayoneted the men, forced the nurses out into the sea and machine-gunned them. This one girl survived[277] and stayed in the water until the Japs had gone. Then she made it to a local village where the women looked after her. When the Japs eventually caught her and brought her to us, she had to cover a bullet hole in her shirt with a water bottle. We patched it straight away. The Japs would have finished her off, if they'd seen it."

The line of trees ended and they emerged into sunshine to breathe in the fragrance of heavily scented shrubs beside the path.

"Lovely," murmured Debs, closing her eyes.

"Better than shovelling out latrines," said Trish. They all laughed at that.

"Did this Aussie girl get out OK?" Colleen asked as they ambled on.

"She did," said Debs, nodding. "Back home now, I guess. We had quite a few medical people in the camp, all told. Besides the lady doctor, who survived – and she's here too - we had forty-odd nurses, civilian and military, Australians, Brits and Dutch but we weren't allowed to nurse our menfolk, though eventually, we had our hands full looking after each other. Oftentimes, the best we could do for the sick was to wash them, try and make them more comfortable with any bedding we could scrounge from the locals and improve their diet. When they could, the local women gave us sweet potatoes, or passion fruit for the sick but our food was mostly rice with some bits of rotten vegetable. One time, we got a monkey that we shared out with six hundred of us. Tasted a bit like hare. Another time, the Japs drove fourteen pigs into the camp. We butchered them and had a real feast."

"The pigs, not the Japs?" Trish asked facetiously.

Deborah smiled at the remark.

"Well, the pigs on four legs. The guards hadn't undergone any real change of heart. You might be boiling up food for a patient too weak to help herself and a Jap would come and kick the whole lot over. Over a hundred of us died, mostly from beriberi, dysentery and malaria but some from scurvy. Their mouths got so ulcerated, they couldn't swallow, not even soup. That's what happened to one of the other QAs in the camp, but at least they got Christian burials. We had to dig the graves, naturally, though we finally got so weak it was almost impossible. A lot of the men died too but husbands and wives never knew how they were faring because the Japs never let on. When we were released, there were some sad scenes, when a husband found his wife had died or vice versa."

They came to a bench beneath a giant tree with broad-leaved foliage.

"Shall we sit here for a bit?" Trish suggested.

"Why not," said Debs, seating herself. "Wish I'd brought my cardigan to give a bit extra padding. Anyway, about May or June this year, the Japanese knew the Allies were closing in but they didn't tell us. Instead, they decided to move us to a new camp."

"To hide the evidence?" Colleen asked.

"That's it. For the first leg, we had to march – or stagger - to a river, where we got aboard this stinking ferry that took us to back to Bangka Island. It had carried coal so we were covered in coal dust when we got out onto the jetty. From there, they chivvied us aboard some lorries to the campsite, another collection of coolie huts that we filled to overflowing. The first thing we had to do was sink the posts for a perimeter fence. The ground was rock hard and using the mallet for pounding in the stakes jarred you from head to foot.

"We thought this camp was going to be healthy, since it was on high ground but cerebral malaria struck and killed more of us in three months than had died in the pervious three years. Again, we had no proper drainage or sewage; only an open tank a couple of feet across, with bamboo slats over it, like before - and again, we had to clean it out as necessary.

"One morning, the commandant assembled us, without any *Tenko* and said, 'The war is over. We are all friends now. Your soldiers will be here soon.' And to our amazement, the guards gave us a whole lot of fresh vegetables and Red Cross parcels, with powdered milk, butter, vitamin tablets, quinine and other medicines, heaps of stuff."

They were quiet for a while, relaxing in the shade. Colleen watched several huge and vividly hued butterflies circling the shrubs on the opposite side of the path. Remembering Matt's letter and recollecting that John Manning and some of the other ex-POWs had said the same, she inwardly cursed their erstwhile enemies once more. The scriptural injunction to love them was impossible outside of God's grace.

Deborah's calm voice broke the silence.

With the most shocking disclosure so far.

"Then they brought out a huge sack of letters, the ones our families had been sending us for the last three years. A lot of them were water stained. We never knew they had them."

Colleen and Trish were too stunned to say anything. Deborah spoke again.

"The next day, an entire company of our red-bereted paratroopers arrived by lorry, tall, strong, splendid-looking lads. Said they'd parachuted into Sumatra. They brought a whole lot more food for us, even bread. I ate a day's ration in one go. The lad dispensing it just laughed and said, 'Never mind, Sister. Plenty more where that came from.' And there was. In a very short time, they got us back here. I was overjoyed to meet Viv Leese. It's been like the Promised Land ever since."

"You've certainly been through the wilderness, Debs," said Trish. "Would you like to walk back for a cup of tea?"

"I think I'd like that very much, thank you," said Deborah.

They walked sedately back to the hospital. Colleen was pleased at how Deborah's hair glinted in the sunlight.

I have included the experiences of John Manning and Deborah Tyndall in the narrative because Grandma Colleen often said that they shaped her perceptions of the post war world as much as her own wartime experiences.

But for Grandma, things were moving to a terrifying climax, as we shall see.

Twenty-One

Blessings and Warnings

So many POW camps were being discovered in the hinterlands of southeast Asia and the Dutch East Indies that the occupation forces sent out repeated requests for nursing Sisters to accompany the rescue medical teams.

Colleen and Trish were among the first that Matron Leese selected to go.

"Back in JGs again, Coll," said Trish, as they made ready to depart for RAF Changi.

"Yep, more our style," said Colleen.

The teams flew by C-47s to PSP-carpeted strips the Royal Engineers had where necessary bulldozed out of virgin jungle. No natural obstacle delayed the mercy missions. The REs even blasted coral off beaches to use as ballast for local tracks ruthlessly gouged into roads for transportation overland of logistics troops, medical teams, supplies and earth-moving machinery for runway construction.

On arrival, the teams set themselves up under canvas and in *bashas*, assisted by troops already on the ground. The heat was fierce and rain squalls frequent but the monsoon had passed its peak and that aided the rescue efforts, though as usual, personnel had to smear their faces, necks, chests and arms with insect repellent to fend off black flies, midges and mosquitoes.

And they suffered anew from the inevitable sweat rashes and prickly heat.

"Like old times, this," Colleen remarked.

"Sure is," said Trish.

They were trudging through mud to a tented ward during a sudden shower, on their first rescue tour.

They and their colleagues saw for themselves the squalid huts and campsites where POWs and internees had struggled to survive.

The inmates were skeletal zombies, many in worse condition than the former captives the girls had seen in Rangoon or Singapore. Some were so desperately ill that help arrived too late. The bodies were encased in shrouds and flown to Singapore for burial, while the team set about ministering to the living; providing food and nutrition, malaria suppressants, medication for sores, ulcers and the multitude of other sicknesses encountered earlier but more prevalent here; pellagra, dengue fever, tuberculosis, stomach ulcers, scrub typhus and blindness induced by vitamin deficiency.

And many of the sufferers, civilian and military, young, old, male, female were still battling with mental trauma from their ordeals.

They appreciated Colleen and Trish reading the scriptures to them at night by hurricane lamp as they moved along the rows of camp beds.

"Could do with Geordie Wood here," said Colleen when they began their first spell of night duty.

The jungle noises shrilled around them in the warm darkness and palms on the fringes of the encampment stood out like sentinels against the night sky.

"I know," said Trish. "But at least we won't be bothered by Kali-Ma. Too far out in the sticks even for her."

It appeared the Enemy had departed for a season[278], though the girls remained vigilant.

But at a site in Thailand, they did encounter a close friend.

Captain Matt Calvert.

He was in command of the logistics force and greeted the team when it debussed. Matt promptly convened a briefing with the medical and nursing officers.

"Congratulations on your preparations, Captain," said the MO-in-charge.

"Thank you, Captain," said Matt modestly.

Trish winked at Colleen and murmured, "That's my Matt."

In addition to constructing an airstrip, the REs and logistics troops had improved or established facilities for sanitation, water supply, stores, communications, road access and accommodation, including a compound for the former guards. Many of the Japanese had been brought back well-nigh starving from jungle hideouts and then fed sufficiently to be put to work.

Matt had made sure that the enemy officers surrendered their swords in front of their men.

"They lose face and the whole lot are easier to manage," he explained at the briefing. "Give me a list of extra supplies you want and I'll get them brought in straightaway."

The MO-in-charge was an understanding man. When he completed his résumé of additional requirements, he sent Trish to Calvert's HQ with the details.

She entered through the tent flap to find Matt seated at a trestle table, making out a report. Trish saluted, removed her bush hat and handed him the list. Matt sat upright in response to her salute, received the list and got to his feet.

"I'll pass it on to my wireless operator orderly," he explained. "He's in the next tent."

When Matt returned, he and Trish embraced and kissed passionately.

"This is wonderful," he said afterwards, holding her close.

"I prayed so much Father would bring us together, when we started on these flights," said Trish. The strength in his wiry arms would have unnerved her, if she hadn't found it so pleasurable.

"You smell of insect repellent."

"Mmh, so do you."

Matt grasped her shoulders and looked her in the eyes.

"Trish," he said earnestly. "Let's get married."

"Well, we're going to, darling," she said, sounding bemused.

"I mean as soon as we can. When we can organise a few days together in Singapore, God willing."

Trish rested her head on Matt's shoulder, arms clasped about his back, feeling his cheekbone pressing into her hair. Her mind was flooded with the manifold implications of Matt's vehement request. She had to make a decision. The orderly corporal would be back any second to report his duty done and her own superior was awaiting her return.

She looked up into Matt's intense gaze, conscious now of a pervading sense of assurance.

"Yes," she said simply.

They kissed again, then went back to their duties.

Trish didn't inform Colleen of what had transpired until the return flight to Singapore, in the wake of the ex-prisoners being transferred to base hospitals.

"That's marvellous," said Colleen. "But I'm flabbergasted, nevertheless."

"So am I. It's all down to Father, now."

"It was good to see Gruffie again," Colleen said after a few moments.

"Sure was. There's another whirlwind wedding for you. Must be these tropical climes."

Away on a jeep patrol when the medical team arrived, Sergeant Grafton eagerly renewed acquaintances with Trish and Colleen the following day.

"Rachel's back home," he told them. "Making the arrangements. Says she won't mind living in Yorkshire."

"She better not," Colleen had said. "Or she'll be hearing from me."

The girls still exchanged letters with Rachel but her missives to Leigh understandably had priority.

Colleen leant back against the airframe and glanced at her companions, seated like her and Trish on the floor of the transport, their gear lashed and stowed about them. She was grateful for the smooth flying conditions that had prevailed so far. The last thing she wanted was a bout of airsickness.

"Have you decided where you're going to live yet?" Colleen asked, above the noise of the aircraft's engines. Trish paused for a moment, then smiled.

"Together," she said.

After location of the remaining camps and hospitalisation of the last ex-prisoners, the Alexandra's medical teams resumed normal duties.

Colleen and Trish returned to find that Deborah Tyndall had been repatriated, along with many of the women liberated with her, still underweight but much improved in health and spirits.

"We gave Debs some walking-out shoes with her uniform," said Viv. "She was thrilled."

But most wards remained full of those recuperating from the captivity. Between them, Trish and Colleen were responsible for well over a hundred Indian sepoys afflicted with tuberculosis and a group of civilian patients, both men and women, suffering from mental sickness, in addition to their other ailments.

They still cowered at the sight of male staff, though the quiet reading of the scriptures brought them some relief from their psychological torment. Colleen and Trish moved among these patients without trepidation. They were too weak to pose a physical threat.

Some weeks after the girls' return to Singapore, Trish received word from Matt that he would be in Singapore for a few days.

"This is it," said Trish, when she showed Colleen the dates of Matt's visit. "You are going to be my bridesmaid?"

"You bet. Are you nervous?"

"Just a bit. I better go and see Matron."

The arrangements did not pose a serious problem.

Captain Longstaff, the MO who had led the team to Thailand, agreed to act as Matt's best man. The hospital chaplain was happy to perform the ceremony and none other than Singapore's resident governor would be present to give Trish away, thanks to a request from the Holbrook-Smiths.

It is the least we can do, Guinevere replied, after Trish wrote with the news. *We're so happy for you. Davey-boy and Pippa have managed to tie the knot at last, in Kandy as it turned out, so thank you ever so much for your prayers. If you can drop in on your way back, please do so. We'd love to see you and so would Teddy, I'm sure.*

Letters from the respective in-laws were most encouraging. Comments like *Can't wait to see you* and *You'll send some photos, won't you?* permeated the family missives from each side of the globe. Colleen noticed that Matt's mother and sister and Trish's Aunt Lucy – neither her father nor her sister seemed disposed to write separately, though they appended love and best wishes to the aunt's correspondence – studiously avoided saying *Wish we could be there* – although no doubt they did - and *Will you be living here? Here* meant either Australia or England and one family was bound to suffer heartache.

Notes of congratulations poured in from men of both the West Yorkshires and Matt's original battalion, the Second-Seventeenth, AIF. Some of the compliments the Australian lads sent on viewing Trish's photo were interesting.

"'Bobby dazzler[279],'" Trish read out from Sergeant Donovan's letter. "I hope that's polite. I'd love to hug him."

"Bet he'd love it, too," said Colleen. "Not sure Matt would, though."

Matt had related how Donovan had saved his life at El Alamein.

Trish was fitted for a white satin dress and matching shoes, courtesy of the staff at Raffles Hotel, who donated the hotel's ornate conference hall for the ceremony and organised the reception. The hotel had survived the war virtually unscathed and with the Allies' return, reverted to its pre-war colonial splendour.

"Another example of the Japs respecting private property, if not private individuals," Matron Leese observed. "When they chose to."

"You're a princess," said Colleen, when she viewed Trish attired in the completed gown. "You make me ever so envious."

On the day of the wedding, Sergeant Grafton drove Matt by jeep from Selarang Barracks[280] near Changi, where the occupying forces had again taken up residence.

When Colleen saw Matt in full uniform and Sam Browne belt enter the hotel foyer, she thought he looked magnificent.

"It could have been a double wedding, if your Peter had been here, Coll," said Viv, wearing, as Colleen was, freshly pressed dress uniform.

"Sure could have," said Colleen.

So why wasn't it happening, she wondered.

Her questions would be answered, though not as she anticipated.

Matt and Trish had the option of a wedding suite at the hotel – at a price - but they chose to honeymoon elsewhere on the island.

"I think Mrs Calvert is fast becoming a colonial, Sister," Leigh said to Colleen, before she went to help Trish get changed.

"Are you going to give me any other clues about where they're going?" asked Colleen.

"No," said Gruffie, grinning mischievously.

Colleen elbowed him in the ribs and hurried upstairs in pursuit of Trish.

"She's got those heels on, Coll," said Viv after the guests assembled in front of the hotel to farewell the newlyweds. "Non regulation with QA walking-out uniform but I don't suppose anyone will mind."

"Least of all Matt," said Colleen.

She blew a kiss to her friend who was seated beside Matt in the rear of the jeep driven by Sergeant Grafton through a shower of confetti. Trish sent one in return.

A burst of rain had fallen during the ceremony but the sun had re-emerged and everything looked fresh and bright.

Ideal for the start of a marriage, Colleen decided.

She and Trish continued waving to each other until the vehicle disappeared from view.

Grafton halted the jeep at the entrance to the barracks and got out. Matt took his place behind the steering wheel and Trish climbed into the front passenger seat.

The sergeant stood to attention and saluted while the couple drove away. Trish waved affectionately to him.

For about a mile or so, they motored past green slopes covered with flowering trees, then turned right onto a minor road that led to a palm-fringed beachfront. A gentle swell lapped the shoreline, glimmering blue-green and white in the late afternoon sun.

The road ended at the foot of a large and grassy hill, where nestled several colonial style homes with verandas. The houses reminded Trish of those she had seen on the way to Rangoon.

"This is ours," said Matt, stopping the jeep at a dwelling about halfway along the row.

The beach was literally across the road.

"Water looks OK for swimming," Trish remarked.

"First thing after reveille. Zero six-thirty, followed by sprints along the sand."

"Oh," said Trish, laughing. "I'm game if you are."

Matt grinned and vaulted out of the jeep. He grasped their holdalls and Trish's web bag and strode up the path onto the veranda. Following him, Trish saw that although the garden was unkempt, excess growth was cut back and the house appeared to be in good repair, with recently restored shuttered windows and freshly painted exterior.

Matt placed the baggage on the veranda, produced a key and unlocked the glass-panelled front door.

"By your leave, milady," he said and deftly picking Trish up, carried her across the threshold.

"Thank you, kind sir."

Trish put her arms around Matt's neck and kissed him.

"My pleasure, milady," he said, lowering her carefully to her feet. "I'll secure the jeep, then bring our kit in."

"While I inspect the premises," said Trish happily.

He touched his cap, kissed her and went out.

Trish observed that the interior had recently been renovated. She could smell newly-dried paint. The sitting room contained cane chairs and leather upholstered settee, the dining room upright wooden chairs and scrubbed wooden table. The master bedroom, on the opposite side of the hall from the sitting room, was well furnished, with clean bed linen neatly folded, and mosquito netting hung ready to unravel. A stack of towels lay on the bed.

Matt returned and deposited their baggage in the bedroom. Trish took off her cap, tie and jacket and put them in the wardrobe. Rolling up her shirtsleeves, she unfastened the window shutters.

"Let in some fresh air," she said.

"It'll be getting dark fairly soon," said Matt. "I'll fire up a lamp. We've not got electricity."

Trish had noted the empty light switch sockets and the absence of bulbs. She recalled that the telegraph poles along the minor road to the house were still devoid of wires. Matt removed his cap, tie, Sam Browne belt and tunic, hung them in the wardrobe and ventured into the kitchen.

Closing the shutters, Trish followed him, her heels sounding hollowly on the bare floorboards. The kitchen windows overlooked a spacious back garden, also cut back.

Matt lit one of the paraffin lamps on the work surface and turned up the flame. It shed a golden glow over the kitchen's appurtenances.

"Table, chairs, work surface, primus stove, paraffin lamps, cupboards, drawers, sink and taps," Trish said approvingly.

She opened a drawer and saw it was stocked with cutlery and utensils. The cupboards contained mugs, crockery, cooking pots, bars of soap, matchboxes, washing powder, kitchen linen, loo rolls and paraffin cans.

"Do we have any food, my love?" asked Trish.

"We do," said Matt, opening a full-length cupboard by the door. "Gruffie sorted it first thing this morning. I made lists of everything we'd need," he added, earning an endearing smile from Trish.

The shelves were filled with compo rations that Trish immediately recognised to be of the best variety. Some fresh vegetables were stacked there as well. Several gallons of bottled water stood on the bottom shelf.

"There's no fridge of course," Matt explained. "But we can get evening meals at the barracks or the officers' club. We've enough here for meals during the day. Plumbing's OK, provided you don't mind cold showers. Bathroom, laundry and facilities are through there." He indicated an annex beyond the kitchen, adding, "We can get any washing done at the barracks, though – and there's even a regular garbage collection now. I think we'll be OK for a few days."

Trish slipped her arms around Matt's waist and leant her head against his.

"We'll be fine, darling," she murmured. "How did we come to acquire this hacienda? Are these civilian homes or married quarters?"

"Married quarters," he said, wrapping his arms about her. Once again, she thrilled to the steel-like strength in them. "There are civilian homes a bit further on but they're not refurbished yet," he continued. "They all need doing because the first of our troops who got here looted everything in sight. Since then the area's been declared Restricted and the sappers and pioneers are putting everything straight, with these houses being top priority."

"Hmm," said Trish. She gazed into Matt's eyes. "Will we be woken up by squaddies clomping in at zero six-hundred hours tomorrow to wire up the house?"

Matt kissed her.

"They'll not be back until we're gone," he said. "We've actually got neighbours on either side, senior officers and their families. This place was made available to us courtesy of the garrison commander."

"That's ever so generous. The Lord's been really good to us. Why don't you take a shower and I'll busy myself in the kitchen."

"Suits me," said Matt, kissing her again.

He returned to the bedroom to undress, hang up his clothes and collect a towel. Trish began selecting compo tins.

When Matt emerged from the shower room several minutes later, with the towel wrapped around his waist, he saw that the kitchen was deserted, though the lamp was still burning. The table was set and Trish had placed the compo tins in water-filled containers on the paraffin stove, ready for heating. She had even put a couple of candles on the table, in brass holders.

The glow of a second lamp issued from the bedroom.

Entering, Matt stared in wonderment.

Trish was hanging up her skirt and blouse in the wardrobe. Lovely and lissom in the lamplight, she stood before him in the *lingerie*, stockings and high heels purchased during the Sunderbans trip, her blonde hair unfastened and falling shining to her shoulders. Taking a small phial from her web bag, she squirted some perfume between her breasts and behind her ears. Its fragrance filled the room.

"Better than insect repellent," she said. Embracing Matt, she ran her fingers down his spine. "I'll go back to the supper in a bit, if that's OK."

It was.

"Said I'd get her back in time, didn't I, Matron?" said Matt when he and Trish met Viv and Colleen in the Alexandra's reception area.

"You certainly did, Captain," said Matron Leese, glancing at the watch attached to her blouse. "Her luggage and all."

With one arm linked in Trish's, Matt carried her holdall, her web bag looped over his shoulder.

"So, how is married life, Mrs Calvert?" asked Colleen after the exchange of hugs.

"Bliss," said Trish.

Colleen had never seen her friend looking happier.

"Have you got time for a cuppa, Matt?" Viv asked.

"Just enough, thanks Matron."

They adjoined to Viv's office, while she left the request for tea with the clerk at the reception desk.

The respite was brief. Thirty minutes later, Trish was kissing her husband goodbye in the vehicle park. Then she and her friends were waving farewell as he drove away in the jeep, en route for the barracks and after that the airfield. Matt was returning that day to Thailand. Although all former prisoners had been rescued, the work of the occupation forces would last until well into next year.

"I'll go change, Matron," said Trish huskily and dabbed her eyes with a handkerchief. "See you on the ward, Coll."

The Indian tuberculosis patients and those still suffering psychologically as well as physically from the captivity occupied Colleen and Trish's labours for the remainder of the year.

But the first Christmas after the war's end was an especially festive one. Tropical warmth notwithstanding, staff and patients alike relished the traditional fare, supplied in abundance by the military authorities.

Carol singing was addressed with alacrity.

Colleen and Trish donned their saris, nylons and high heels, then toured the wards where they sang duets as 'The Nightingale Sisters,' including in their repartee both seasonal songs and old favourites. Many patients joined in and repeatedly exclaimed, "Encore!" especially the male convalescents.

The most popular number was for many a reminder of home.
"I may be right, I may be wrong,
"But I'm perfectly willing to declare,
"That when you turned and smiled at me,
"A nightingale sang in Berkeley Square."

The renditions even heartened the suffering sepoys and brought flickers of joy to the eyes of the mentally disturbed. For these groups, recovery was agonisingly slow and in many cases might not be fully attainable.

But Colleen and Trish had problems of their own.

"I'm sorry, Coll," Trish said tearfully one night when they retired to their room. "I miss Matt so much. And he's missing me. You must be pining for Peter, too."

The exchange of letters between the couples was proceding non-stop but it couldn't make up for the separation.

Colleen knelt on the floor.

"C'mon," she said. "If the Lord can heal the broken hearted[281], He can cheer up a couple of lovesick schoolgirls like us."

Trish knelt with her. They couldn't help giggling at themselves.

By January, many of the patients from the captivity had been transferred or discharged.

New postings were therefore arranged for some of the staff, among them Colleen and Trish.

Bidding farewell to Matron Leese, they were driven to the airfield where they boarded a C-47 that would take them to Calcutta, via a stopover at Mingaladon.

The hiatus enabled them to visit the governors' residence, where the Holbrook-Smiths eagerly welcomed them. Teddy the mongoose duly appeared with Elizabeth and affectionately wove in and out between the legs of the guests, as he had done the day the girls had found him.

"I'm sure he remembers you," said Guinevere, when she conducted Colleen and Trish into the grounds, where she had requested that tea be served.

Teddy scurried around the girls as they walked along holding hands with Elizabeth.

"I'm sorry we turned up in our field kit," said Trish.

She and Colleen had donned JGs, bush hats, boots and short puttees for their journey.

"Oh, don't worry," said Guinevere. She looked charming in a floral frock and high-heeled sandals. "Redvers is in his flannels. He and Michael are practising cricket in the nets. You'll see them in a moment. They'll be delighted you've come."

"I want to be an army nurse," said Elizabeth, looking up at her escorts. "Like you and Cousin Pippa."

"She's made up her mind," said her mother.

Colleen and Trish smiled their approval.

Elizabeth Holbrook-Smith would indeed fulfil her childhood ambitions. She was destined for overseas service as a QARANC officer in Malaya, Cyprus, Borneo and Aden, where she would meet her future husband, a captain in the Royal Northumberland Fusiliers and veteran of many patrol actions in the city's notorious Crater district[282].

However, that's another story.

Unfortunately, the girls were unable to see Mandy and Janice during the stopover, because Mandy was now serving with the Indian-British General Hospital in Poona and at her own request, Janice had been reassigned to a repatriation hospital for Australian ex-POWs and other long-stay patients located near Sydney, Australia.

Nevertheless, they kept in touch by letter.

Congratulations to Trish and Matt, Janice wrote. *John and I will be getting married soon and moving to Inverell. I have family over here, as it happens, so I'm not completely deserting the fold. Come see us if you can. I'm sure Matt and John would be mates from the word go.*

Janice's prediction would soon be fulfilled.

Sheep farmer's daughter turns into sheep farmer's missus, Mandy's latest letter read. *I'm anticipating a home posting soon, to tie the knot as well. Bags of congratulations to Trish 'n Matt. Have you made up your minds about Blighty or Down Under yet?*

Circumstances were about to answer that question.

"Home sweet home," said Trish when she and Colleen deplaned at RAF Comilla.

Colleen stared at the long lines of hospital tents and *bashas* through the heat haze and swirls of dust. She hitched the strap of her web bag higher on her shoulder.

"Guess we better organise some transport and report to Matron," she said as the crewmen unloaded the rest of their baggage.

Matron Brierley was the same impressive lady who had given Colleen her orders to join Trenholme's CCS almost a year ago. She also knew Trish.

"Welcome back," she said. Matron sat upright at her desk as the two Sisters entered her tent, stood to attention and saluted. "I understand it's Sister Calvert these days." She beamed at Trish and glanced admiringly at her wedding ring.

"Yes, Matron," said Trish with due deference.

"Well, congratulations, my dear. Now, since you're both familiar with this place, we can sort you out right away."

The accommodation was a pleasant surprise. Instead of tents, nursing staff were now quartered in several recently constructed bamboo and thatched huts, clustered beneath palm trees and tall evergreens around a grassy area with shrubs in rich blossom at its centre.

"The Indian orderlies water them regularly," Matron had said.

By contrast, the grass was looking parched but the scene brought forth a sense of nostalgia for both girls.

"Laid out like a village green," said Trish.

Their duties, however, prompted harsh reminders of the war and its aftermath.

Among Trish and Colleen's patients were men still recovering from wounds received in the final battles of the Burma campaign, including the bitter engagement at Waw, near Pegu, when the Japanese had made a desperate lunge towards the southern end of Fourth Corps's area. The enemy thrust was backed up by their last remaining reserves of artillery and heavy mortars. Casualties were thus particularly heavy among the Ghurka battalion that bore the brunt of the Japanese assault.

The long drawn-out processes of repairing facial and bodily mutilation Colleen had witnessed at Frosninone the previous year seemed all the more heart-rending now. So did the sufferings of the diphtheria patients, penicillin notwithstanding and those with tuberculosis, total or partial blindness, whether through battle or captivity, or long-term kidney, cardiac, nervous or bowel complaints, often the after-effects of severe beriberi.

Many patients were continuing the struggle to come to terms with limbs lost or maimed.

Such was Lieutenant Frank Hamilton, tall, fair-haired, slender, twenty years old and a Cambridge Rugby Blue[283], who had interrupted his studies to become a subaltern of the Ghurkas.

He was a victim of the fighting near Waw.

"It was horrible black slush everywhere, Sister and pelting rain," he told Colleen. "The only dry ground was on top of railway embankments or in villages on raised patches where the Japs had dug trenches. We'd fetched up too close to the Nips for the RAF to give fire support so they made dummy runs to keep the Japs' heads down while we went in with kukri and bayonet. We sorted 'em but a Jap machine gunner cut my leg to bits."

Hamilton had kept his left foot thanks to skilled surgery and the shattered bones mended over the ensuing months but his ankle had only limited movement.

After examination of Frank's latest X-rays, his surgeon decided that the subaltern was fit for more intensive physiotherapy and assigned the task to Colleen. She was determined that by the time Hamilton went home, before the month was out, he would be walking unaided.

She placed one hand carefully on Hamilton's scarred and battered shin and the other against the sole of his foot.

"OK, Frank," she said. "I want you to extend your ankle joint and push against my hand as hard as you can. Then I want you flex it back as far as it'll go. You'll be going for a walk with me soon, without crutches."

"For that, Sister, I'll really try," he said and gritted his teeth with the effort.

Returning to the billet a few nights later, Colleen found Trish seated on her camp bed, staring intently at a telegram in the glow of a paraffin lamp.

Lips pursed, Trish handed the note to her. It was from Trish's Aunt Lucy.

Your father has been admitted to hospital, the telegram read. *It is a recurrence of the sickness he suffered in India. His condition is stable but the doctors are concerned. Ellie is staying with me. She is still a handful, I fear.*

Colleen sat on her own bed, scanned the note and handed it back.

"Seems like your dad could be in for a long stay," she said. "Be good if you could get a home posting, especially if your aunt's concerned about Ellie as well."

"I'm going to apply. After I've written to Matt."

"He'll be a tremendous encouragement," Colleen said earnestly.

"I know," said Trish. Then she added with feeling, "But I don't want to go without my oppo."

"Oh, bollocks, Trish," Colleen exclaimed. "You've got to be there."

Trish slid off her bed and knelt on the floor.

"Well, let's ask Father," she said as Colleen knelt beside her. "And about your posting, too. The War Office does seem to be taking its own sweet time, in spite of Peter's efforts."

"I don't mind being here."

Trish glanced at her and smiled.

"Now who's talking bollocks?" she said.

A couple of days passed. Then Colleen was summoned to Matron's tented office.

She went in, stood to attention and saluted. Matron sat to attention behind her desk. A slim WAAF lady of striking appearance with reddish-brown hair, dressed as Colleen was in JGs, boots and short puttees, was also present, seated on a foldable chair by Matron's desk. She too sat upright, then briskly arose, smiled and extended her right hand.

Colleen shook it briefly.

"Vicky Leonard," said the WAAF lady. "You must be Colleen."

"I am. Pleased to meet you."

Colleen noted that Vicky wore the epaulettes of a squadron officer, "a queen bee," Jon Gray would have said.

Matron got to her feet.

"I'll leave you two now and do a circuit of the wards," she said. "You can have my desk, Vicky."

Returning Colleen's second salute, she went out.

Colleen couldn't believe it. Matron had set times for her ward inspections but this wasn't one of them. And to leave her office in the care of a junior officer and a visitor, invited to use her desk of all things, was unprecedented.

Vicky moved to Matron's desk.

"Sit down, Colleen," she said.

Removing her hat, Colleen occupied the chair Vicky had vacated. She noted that her personnel file was open in front of the squadron officer. Vicky also had a pen and A5 notepad with her.

"I'll be taking notes," she said pleasantly.

"Fine."

Colleen remembered June's letter about *the official visitor* and surmised Vicky must be her, a supposition that the squadron officer confirmed.

"I believe June Halliard gave you a hint about me," Vicky said with a smile. She opened a second file.

"Yes, she did," said Colleen, returning the smile. She decided she liked Squadron Officer Leonard. "But only a hint. Not the full story."

"That's why I'm here. I'll pick up the story early in the war, with the death of a German agent. Her name was Maria Von Hollstein."

Vicky extracted a photograph from the second file, enclosed in cellophane and passed it across to Colleen.

"This is the first of a couple of remarkable coincidences in all this," she said. "I think you will recognise her."

"My God, that's Ilsa Bauer!" Colleen gasped. "I trained with her. We were told she'd been drafted into Intelligence, as a German speaker."

She handed the photograph back.

"That's what you were supposed to think," said Vicky. She gave Colleen a résumé of Ilsa's mission and violent demise[284]. The account left Colleen temporarily speechless.

"It had to be kept secret until the end of the war," Vicky explained. "Major Steadman informed your friend Anne of that at the time. Before going overseas, he helped terminate all known Nazi cells in the country but while he was serving in Italy, he had the job of identifying potential infiltrators intent on post war subversion and collaborators. Eventually, he found some, with the help of the partisans and one of his liaison men, Fusilier Brian Briggs."

"Briggsy worked with Major John?"

"He certainly did and he's no ordinary fusilier, I can tell you."

Colleen agreed with that assessment but she feared for her friends.

"Are Bill and Annie in any danger, or Brian and Mollie?" she asked apprehensively.

Vicky shook her head.

"Bill and Anne, no. The other side never learned about the circumstances of Maria's death. As for your friends who were in Italy, they're safe for now but I'll come back to the Italian connection in a while. In the meantime, the other side are persisting in their efforts, despite having lost the war. Take a look at him."

Vicky handed Colleen another photograph. It showed an officer of aristocratic appearance in the uniform of the American Office of Strategic Services and Colleen immediately saw a family resemblance with Ilsa, though the officer's hair was lighter in colour.

"Count Franz Von Hollstein, Maria's elder brother," said Vicky.

Colleen's jaw dropped.

"He's a Nazi?" she asked in disbelief.

Vicky nodded.

"We had great difficulty getting this picture. Our cousins didn't like to admit they'd been infiltrated but Von Hollstein fooled our people as well. I'll touch on that in a bit."

Colleen shook her head in amazement. She returned the photo.

"On the face of it, the Soviet menace has replaced the Nazi one but even that is part of the real enemy's grand strategy," Vicky continued. "The aim is to deceive the West and the Warsaw Pact nations into tearing each other apart until mutual devastation and loss of life force them to coalesce into a one-world regime."

Colleen was aghast. She could see where Vicky's line of argument was heading.

"Another Holy Roman Empire, only worldwide?" she asked in trepidation.

Vicky nodded solemnly.

"When the Third Reich collapsed, the Sons of Loyola[285] went into Plan B," she said. "If anything, the Allied victory opened up greater opportunities for them. We still have an empire, meaning that influential traitors in our midst could foment trouble worldwide[286]. That's where the likes of Von Hollstein come in," she added, tapping his photo with her forefinger. "He's one of their coadjutors and worked his way into SOE, where he went on a number of missions. It gave him invaluable first-hand experience of our methods - and resulted in the deaths of some French Resistance fighters. Sadly, we didn't find out until after the Normandy landings, by which time Von Hollstein had disappeared."

Colleen took a deep breath.

"I know an SOE chap. Is that the other strange coincidence?"

Vicky smiled and nodded again.

"Von Hollstein joined a Jed mission to the south of France to help the Resistance delay German reinforcements for the Normandy beachhead. Major Peter Waverly led the team. I learnt that you were friendly with him when I spoke to June and the others in Italy. Thanks to Von Hollstein, the mission was compromised with considerable losses on our side, among them the Jed French agent. One of my lasses, Section Officer Kate Bramble, was working with the Resistance there. She was captured by Von Hollstein and only narrowly escaped."

Vicky related the events of the operation. Colleen was horrified by the account of the massacre in the church.

"As I said, Von Hollstein vanished but we've located him again," said Vicky. "He smuggled himself into England by stages and is now in the White Peak area of Derbyshire."

"That's where Peter's home is!"

"Yes. And it helps explain why Von Hollstein got himself assigned to Major Waverly's team. Though we don't know exactly what he's planning or why that area is important to him. We'll have to wait and see."

"Keep him under surveillance?"

"Correct. And it's crucial we identify his contacts, which he must have. That's another reason we've got to be patient. He's been lying low for quite a while, months actually."

Vicky passed Colleen a third photograph.

"That's Kate," she said.

Colleen gazed at the likeness of the beautiful, dark-haired, young WAAF officer.

"Was her code name Collette?" she asked.

"One of them, yes."

"Peter mentioned it once, because my name sounded similar," Colleen explained as she gave the photo back to Vicky. "My God," she exclaimed, sitting upright. "He must still think she's dead. Has anyone told him she's alive?"

Vicky shook her head.

"It took us months to confirm him as the English member of the Jed team. SOE were very tight-lipped about any returned agents and Kate and I were fitting this case in with helping to trace the hundred or more that had disappeared[287]. We weren't given any information about the major's whereabouts either, though we know he's not at the ancestral home. I was going to ask if you knew anything."

Colleen relaxed back into her chair.

"His last letter said he was in Palestine. He went there from Japan via Washington and London. From what you're saying, I guess he shouldn't have told me, though it's as well he did."

Vicky laughed gently.

"It is but rest assured, the major hasn't breached any security. It's SOE who are being paranoid. So thank you. With your help, I'll contact him directly. I think it's best to do it that way."

"Sure," said Colleen, sitting upright again. "Just hang on a second."

She took out pencil and notebook from a top pocket of her shirt, wrote down Waverly's contact details and passed the note to Vicky.

"Thanks, Colleen. Has he said anything about returning home?"

"He hopes by the summer. He's been trying to arrange a posting for me to a hospital near where he lives but it's taking time to get through channels, apparently."

"If you give me the details, I'll expedite it."

Colleen did so and Vicky noted them.

"Kate is in charge of the surveillance," she said. "She's officially demobbed and she's got a backroom job at a local library, well-nigh perfect cover. That's how we discovered Peter's absence and Kate immediately recognised him from local photographs taken pre-war. I think it will be good if you can be there, too. That is, if you're prepared to help?"

"Of course."

"Thanks," said Vicky warmly. "Kate can brief you but you'll have to accept it could be dangerous."

"I understand. Though surely it's more dangerous for Kate? Won't Von Hollstein recognise her?"

"She's changed her appearance to guard against that. So she's OK for now and we have a contingency plan. She's also keeping tabs on Von Hollstein's associate, who crossed into England with him."

"His associate?"

"Character by the name of Albrecht, who turned up after Kate was nabbed," Vicky explained. "Nasty piece of work, ex-Gestapo. Here's a sketch Kate made of him."

Colleen studied the brutal countenance.

"Definitely a nasty piece of work," she said, gladly handing back the sketch. "But surely the locals will suspect them?"

"It's not that simple, Colleen. Remember, Von Hollstein originally fooled our people and Albrecht is definitely in his league. However, we've spotted them. That's the main thing."

"I suppose you want to keep all this classified for now, Vicky?" Colleen asked, after an apprehensive pause.

"I'm afraid so. It's hard on Peter but I'll brief him as soon as possible, so he'll know about Collette and what to expect when he gets home. We'll organise things from there."

The plot was getting harder to fathom. Colleen knitted her elegantly plucked eyebrows.

"Wait a minute," she said. "Whatever contacts those ex-Nazis have, they must be pretty thin on the ground. What can they hope to achieve?"

Vicky laughed again.

"You ask a lot of questions, Colleen, you'd have been good in SOE."

Then she leant forward, put her elbows on the tabletop and rested her chin on her clasped hands.

"I fear we may only be seeing the tip of a large and sinister iceberg. We mustn't underestimate them. When we move in, it has to be decisive. Until then, as I said, we need patience."

"And nerve," said Colleen slowly. "But isn't Von Hollstein taking a risk himself? Hanging around near the Waverly estate? He must know Peter will recognise him, too?"

"A calculated risk," said Vicky, nodding at Colleen's insight. "Remember, though, that Von Hollstein is cocky. Based on his past experience, he no doubt thinks he can succeed, Peter notwithstanding. That's why it's vital Kate maintains her cover. In the meantime, there's someone else you should know about."

She drew another photograph from the file.

As Vicky handed it to her, Colleen felt sure her heart skipped a beat. She was gazing into the boyish, aquiline face of a young officer wearing the insignia of the Royal Engineers. Best-looking bloke I've ever seen, Colleen said to herself. And I've seen a few.

"That's Captain Steve Graham," Vicky remarked. She explained how Graham's report had achieved a breakthrough in the hunt for Von Hollstein and his crony.

"Colossal cheek," said Colleen in amazement. "Passing off as returning SOE bods."

"I said V-H was cocky," Vicky said with a wry smile. "Our people managed to track them at various points until the trail led to the vicinity of Waverly Manor. Kate took over last summer."

"So what guises have they adopted or is that hush-hush too?"

"At present, but Kate'll put you in the picture."

"Where's Steve Graham at the moment?" Colleen asked, trying to sound objective.

"Still in Germany with the occupation forces. He's a brave and godly young man. When he gets home, he'll be working in Derbyshire too, where he can help with the operation. Also because he and Kate have become very close," Vicky added, with a smile.

"Lucky Kate," Colleen murmured, handing the photo back.

Vicky's hazel eyes twinkled.

"From where I sit, lucky Peter. However, I better bring you up to date on the Italian connection."

At that point, the tent flaps parted and Matron came in. Colleen immediately sat upright.

"Don't mind me," said Matron chattily. "Just passing by. Would you like me to send you in some tea?"

Colleen stared in astonishment. Matron's invitation meant that Vicky Leonard was a VIP and then some.

"Yes, please, Matron," said Vicky. "You'll have some, won't you, Colleen?"

"Yes, please, thank you, Matron," said Colleen, hoping her grin of gratitude wasn't too cheesy.

"This is a lot for you to take in," Vicky said considerately, when Matron had gone.

"A bit. But please go on."

Vicky spread some papers on the desk.

"As I mentioned, Major Steadman had a special job when we invaded Italy. Heaven knows how he managed it with his other duties but he reasoned that since we were on the real enemy's home patch, we might look for suspects among forces chaplains, mainly those of a particular denomination."

"Shrewd."

The tea arrived and Colleen sipped hers gratefully. It was hot, sweet and of excellent quality. Nothing but the best for Matron, she mused.

Vicky drank some tea and placed the mug on the desktop.

"Very," she said. "John was concerned to keep watch on certain individuals with roving commissions, who'd be in a position to elicit information via confessions from a wide variety of individuals, including dying men in hospital, if they were senior officers[288]."

"Callous devils," said Colleen with feeling. "I think I met one of them."

"You did. The Most Reverend Father St John Montague-Stewart. We could count that as another coincidence except that he toured most hospitals in the Italian Theatre of Operations, so it wasn't surprising you'd run into him. I take it you didn't get along?"

"Putting it mildly, no."

"John's superiors were anxious to know what M-S was up to," Vicky went on. "Unfortunately, three experienced Intelligence officers assigned to cover his movements met with sudden deaths, clearly the work of a skilled assassin, who, we believe, is now in England."

Despite the heat and humidity, Colleen shuddered.

"Where Von Hollstein is?"

"Close by. This is him. Mijo Kvaternik."

Vicky pronounced the name as "Mio Vaternick."

"Also called 'Miko.' Though that probably won't be the name he's using now. This is the only photo we have, taken pre-war, I'm afraid."

She showed it to Colleen. It depicted a square-faced man of Slavonic appearance, in jacket and tie, with dark hair brushed back. The Slav's dark eyes emanated an intense gaze and his lips were curved in a demonic smile that made Colleen shudder again.

"He must have been the swine that stabbed Naomi, in Naples, trying to get me," Colleen said in a shocked voice. "And shot Dinah. You'll know about all that?"

"Yes."

Vicky leafed through the documents in front of her.

"Why do they want to kill us?" Colleen asked tremulously.

"Your friends told me about the prayer group you had with Bronwyn Hewitt. I think that must have sent shock waves through the spiritual realm."

"You mean - ?"

Colleen stopped in mid sentence, aghast.

"I think so, Colleen," Vicky said soberly. "We wrestle not against flesh and blood but against principalities and powers[289]. That's what I meant by 'large and sinister.' Von Hollstein and his co-conspirators are hell-bent on setting up the new Dark Age. And they'll petition Death and Hell[290] to do it. That's as near as I think we'll get in this life to explaining Dinah's death. Possibly Bronwyn's and Hoppy's too and the attacks on you."

"But why were they allowed to happen?"

"I can't answer that definitely," said Vicky, shaking her head. "Maybe to alert us to how serious the situation really is. We have to believe the Lord knows what He's doing, nevertheless."

Colleen put down her mug and pressed her hands to her face. Vicky reached across and touched her arm.

"I'm sorry," said Colleen, uncovering her face.

"It's OK."

"How did you get on to Miko?" Colleen asked when she had composed herself. "And why is he still alive? I'd have thought his crowd would have topped him after he messed up in Naples?"

"Miko took out three of our best agents without a hitch. He's clearly top notch so I guess he's too valuable to lose. I'll explain later how we identified him. But I should mention that by following up Steve's report and with John Steadman's help, we discovered that M-S helped forge the documents for the count and Albrecht to get them into England[291]."

"So where's M-S?" Colleen asked, picking up her mug.

"Back home, touring parishes. We're watching him to see if he leads us to V-H's other contacts. And we also have this, which may also come as a shock, I'm afraid."

Vicky proffered a recent newspaper clipping. Colleen took it with trembling hand, astonished by the headline.

Army Psychiatrist Found Dead. Suspected Suicide

She was further shocked by the cutting's contents. They revealed that Lieutenant-Colonel Ernest Forsythe, MC, DSO, had committed suicide by self-inflicted lethal injection, brought on by severe depression in the aftermath of his divorce.

"No-one you were with in Italy wrote to you about this?" Vicky asked.

"N-no," Colleen stammered, shaking her head.

"Probably because it happened such a short time ago and our people made sure it didn't get into the national papers. However, this is the really important item."

Vicky gave Colleen an envelope containing a letter. In surprise, Colleen saw that she was the addressee and she recognised Forsythe's handwriting.

"It was murder, not suicide," said Vicky succinctly. "We created that story for the local rag, in the hope the other side would think they'd got away with it. The depression angle is a bit thin because the colonel and his wife had separated pre-war but the divorce was only last year so we hope the story will serve. In fact, he was seeing a mistress, who had a key to his flat. She called on him the night he was killed, while the assassins were still there. Not wanting to complicate matters with another murder, they decamped via the fire escape before they had time to turn the flat over."

"She must have had a fit," said Colleen, feeling dazed as she unfolded the letter.

"Nearly," Vicky said with a grimace. "But she managed to contact the police. Our people found the letter when they searched the flat. Forgive us for opening it but we had to, as part of the investigation."

"Yes, of course. God, who'd want to shack up with Eyepiece Ernie? Must be the bishop's actress[292]."

Vicky waited while Colleen read the letter.

Dear Sister McGrath, it read. *Please forgive the way I acted towards you. In part, it was because I knew there could never be anything between us, however much I wished it. But I must warn you that your life is in danger. St John has sworn to kill you. At first, he only wanted me to transfer you but now he sees you as a threat to his entire operation. And he has a terrible vision of a new world empire – genocide until the Holy Father rules supreme. Because of my position, he sought my help. At first I was persuaded until I saw the full extent of his vision, when I met his friend, whom he simply called, "The Count." I was never told his name but he is a tall man, fair-haired, well built, blue-eyed. He is Germanic but can pass of as either an American or English officer. I tell you this because you must beware of him yourself. After he boasted of duping our Intelligence, while in the Waffen SS, I told St John I wanted no part of the scheme and that is my death warrant. They are coming.*

The letter ended in an abrupt scrawl, without a signature.

"He must have made out the envelope first," said Vicky. "It seems he only had enough time to conceal it before his visitors arrived. You'll see it connects Von Hollstein and Montague-Stewart."

Colleen placed a hand to her forehead.

"Poor old pompous Ernie," she said, visibly shaken. "But no traitor, any road. It explains why M-S was worried about Bronwyn's group, with us being in Ernie's unit."

"It does. Too close for comfort, for both St John and his spiritual mentors."

Vicky got up, took a brandy bottle from the top of Matron's filing cabinet and poured some into a medicine glass.

"I'm sure Matron won't mind," said Vicky as she handed the glass to Colleen, who thanked her and took some sips.

"We confirmed our suspicions about Montague-Stewart thanks to Fusilier Briggs," said Vicky, sitting down again. "John Steadman recruited him after hearing about a soldier on a charge for flooring two Moroccan Goums, who'd made passes at Mollie, when she and Briggs were in a *trattoria* in Taranto. John reckoned a lad like that could be useful."

"I'll say."

Colleen finished the rest of the brandy and placed the glass on the table. "You'll know about his lone-wolf night patrols behind enemy lines?"

Vicky nodded, grimacing.

"He actually saw M-S in priestly garb during one of them – in a German encampment. Tailed him from your hospital on the Senio. John fixed it so Briggs could keep an eye on Montague-Stewart whenever his battalion was out of the line, which wasn't often but it was sufficient."

Colleen gaped in astonishment.

"And Briggsy must eventually have spotted Miko?" she asked shakily.

"With the help of the partisans. Fortunately for us, neither Miko nor M-S ever suspected Briggs but I reckon if Miko had tried to top him, it would have been his last waltz."

"Too right," Colleen said and sipped her tea again. "But he did for Colonel Forsythe?"

"Most likely," said Vicky gravely. "As one of the person or persons still technically unknown. You'll be glad to know Fusilier Briggs has agreed to continue helping with this case – as have all your friends I spoke to in Italy. They take it very personally and they continue praying for your safety."

"But they can't get mixed up in this," Colleen protested, gripping the arm of her chair. "They'll be starting families soon. John and Lindy have already. And Mollie's last letter said she was expecting, too."

"Major Steadman is assisting with the surveillance on St John but that won't put his family in danger," Vicky reassured her. "As for the others, they say they've prayed about it and that's that."

"I understand."

Colleen drank the remainder of her tea and placed the mug on the table beside the glass.

"In fact," Vicky continued, "Brian and Mollie are helping Kate with the surveillance. Have been for months. That's how much this investigation means to them."

"My God," Colleen whispered.

"Can you think why Montague-Stewart might regard you as a particular threat?" Vicky asked, also finishing her tea.

Colleen sat back in her chair and exhaled, recalling how she had knelt beside the dying Sergeant Prescott and held his hand. She saw again the sinister bulk of Montague-Stewart, looming predatorily out of the gloom.

"I once called his crucifix a demon magnet," she said and briefly related the circumstances, while Vicky took notes. "I must have been right," she concluded, audibly exhaling again.

"You were. Those artefacts are as dangerous as Ouija boards. The Great Enemy doesn't like being sussed[293]. He - and M-S – must see you as having a gift for spiritual discernment and great boldness[294], even before Bronwyn's prayer meeting, from which I gather you date your conversion?"

"Yes. Dangerous combination for them, I guess."

Vicky clasped her hands together.

"And it will be dangerous for you, Colleen," she warned. "We must maintain as much prayer support as we can muster. I'm working on it."

Colleen was still thinking about Sergeant Prescott. "Poor Doug," she said, drawing breath. "Thank God I was with him."

"Indeed," said Vicky sincerely.

Then Colleen realised something that had been obvious for months.

"I think we have another three, Vicky. To make up for those we've lost. Point-counter point between God and the Devil, maybe."

In a few minutes, Colleen told Vicky about Gwen, Robyn, Trish and their gallant husbands. She also related Jon Gray's experience during the Sunderbans trip and the mysterious lights, of which events the others had informed her, the intrusion of the banded krait and its spectacular demise.

Vicky précised Colleen's account.

"I'd better speak to your friend Trish," she said and turned to a fresh page in her notepad. "This adds a new dimension. And then, when I've caught up with Peter in Palestine, get back to Blighty and contact your other friends."

"I'll get Trish for you, Vicky," said Colleen. She stood up and donned her bush hat. "I trust Matron won't mind extending her inspection tour."

"I'm sure she won't," said Vicky, with her reassuring smile.

Before she departed, Colleen made a further observation, based on Vicky's remarks about Bronwyn's prayer group.

"If this thing is not simply against flesh and blood, it's a spiritual battle, not run-of-the-mill cloak and dagger. Then you need believers to fight it?"

"You're right, Colleen. Call it a combined operation."

She sat to attention as Colleen saluted.

As she walked out into the glare of the afternoon sun, bound for the long *basha* where Trish was on duty, Colleen tried to piece together the salient points of the discussion.

Though one thought emerged pre-eminent.

Steve Graham.

Twenty-Two

Homecomings

Thanks to Vicky Leonard's intervention, Colleen and Trish emplaned for Dum Dum Airfield less than a fortnight after the squadron officer's visit.

"I shall miss you, God bless," said Matron Brierley, with a benevolent smile as she bade the girls farewell on a baking hot afternoon.

According to custom, Trish and Colleen said goodbye to their patients before boarding their transport to the airstrip.

"Can we go for a short walk, Sister?" Frank Hamilton asked Colleen, when she and Trish dropped into the tented convalescent ward. "One last time."

"Of course, Frank," she said.

He put on his shoes and stood up gingerly but without help. He and Colleen strolled outside, past several wards before turning back. Hamilton's face was glistening with sweat and the young officer was breathing heavily from the effort of the walk.

"Thanks, Sister," he said.

"You're welcome, Frank. Take care, now." Colleen patted his shoulder.

"He's a good lad, Coll," Trish said when they climbed into the jeep. "He'll keep at it."

Colleen nodded. She blinked away tears as they waved to their colleagues.

Their C-47 took them the following day from Dum-Dum to Bombay, where it refuelled and flew on to the RAF station in Karachi.

Colleen gazed out of the windows at the arid brown expanse below, glad to be departing the sprawling sub-continent. She could only feel admiration for those like Trish's parents, who had voluntarily devoted their lives to ministering there.

The girls resolved not to discuss Trish's father during the return journey, resting in the Text, *Sufficient unto the day is the evil thereof*[295]. His condition was *serious but stable,* according to Aunt Lucy's latest telegram, though he was *looking forward to meeting his son-in-law.*

That heartened them both.

Colleen was further encouraged when the girls compared notes about their discussions with Vicky Leonard.

490

"It fits with what we reckoned after the krait attack, Coll but I'm gobsmacked, nevertheless," said Trish. "Still, you know Matt and I'll be with you, the whole way."

The young couple would have an essential contribution to make.

Overnighting in a Nissen hut at RAF Karachi, the girls went by RAF transport at zero five-hundred hours to the harbour side at the wide brown mouth of the Indus, where a surprise awaited them.

"Well, the station commander said a Sunderland," said Colleen. "But I didn't expect this."

She followed Trish onto the RAF launch that would ferry them to the aircraft anchored in the channel.

"Me neither," said Trish. She seated herself on the starboard bench behind the cabin. "Should be a very civilised trip."

"Maybe we should have put on walking-out uniform," Colleen remarked, glancing at the JGs they were wearing, with sleeves rolled up and top collar buttons undone. "We do look a bit downmarket."

The four-engined flying boat had been converted into a civilian airliner. Painted in gleaming white, blue and silver livery, it proudly bore the initials BOAC on its fuselage[296].

"British Overseas Airways Corporation," said Trish. "Truly posh."

"Certainly is," said Colleen. "But I suppose we better take a last look back. May not see this part of the world again."

Gazing at the receding shore, they took in the mixture of modern dock facilities and mechanised transport contrasting sharply with stately palms, mud dwellings, vociferous, ragged humanity and laden carts drawn by plodding bullocks, the sights, sounds and smells of old India, clustered beneath the intensifying heat of the morning sun.

It was a potentially volatile mixture.

Titanic forces for change were sweeping across the country.

Partition was on everyone's lips with the name Ghandi being venerated and vilified in equal measure. Strikes and race riots in Calcutta had left many dead and injured and turned streets into desolate avenues of rotting garbage, smashed furniture and decomposing animal carcasses. Colleen and Trish had nursed numerous wounded squaddies, bruised and battered with limbs broken in the line of duty trying to keep the opposing factions apart. Despite the distance, the casualties were flown to Comilla to ensure their safety.

"You've not seen strife 'til those Hindus and Muslims get stuck into each other, Sister," the girls had repeatedly been told. "Worse than Japs – at least you knew there was only one lot of them."

Even the Dalrymples were thinking of leaving. *Edith and I are getting too old for this sort of thing*, Charles wrote in his latest letter to Trish. *The days of the Raj are surely numbered.*

Aboard the Sunderland, the girls relaxed in well-padded passenger seats. The Corporation clearly had comfort in mind, appropriate insofar as besides a dozen or so service personnel, the other passengers appeared to be senior civil servants and their wives, evidently on furlough.

A liveried steward advised them to buckle their seat belts and a few minutes later, the flying boat taxied to the mouth of the river. Engines roaring, it rapidly gathered speed and lifted gracefully into the clear morning air.

Colleen leant back in her seat, ran her fingers through her hair and closed her eyes. Muted by soundproof panelling lining the inside of the fuselage, the throbbing of the engines seemed almost like a lullaby.

"Bliss," she whispered.

"Mmh," Trish murmured drowsily.

A little later the steward came by with tea and sandwiches. He obligingly explained where the aircraft's facilities were.

The Sunderland touched down in the early afternoon on the limpid waters of the Persian Gulf, near the island of Bahrain. Passengers and crew disembarked by launch to the RAF officers' tented mess, on a bluff overlooking the sea.

"Murderous, isn't it," said Colleen. She pulled her bush hat down to shield her eyes from the sun's brilliance. "Like the Dry Belt."

The civilian men were removing their jackets, loosening their ties and rolling up their sleeves. Their wives were unfurling parasols.

"Heat comes off the desert," said Trish, also adjusting her hat. "Like you would have found in Aden."

In the mess, electric fans positioned in front of soaked hessian curtains blew cool, moist air over the travellers, who tucked into a salad lunch with sliced fruit for dessert topped by condensed milk and followed by iced tea.

"Courtesy of RAF Bahrain," said their congenial squadron leader host.

The generous hospitality notwithstanding, the passengers were glad to emplane a couple of hours later, when the aircraft had been refuelled.

On the way back, the girls were startled by a plopping, hissing sound from the water as the launch nosed towards the Sunderland's gangplank.

Looking over the side, they recoiled at the sight of a tangle of writhing sea snakes.

"That's how they copulate, Sisters," said the RAF coxswain with a broad grin, as he secured the launch's steps to the gangplank. "And they squeeze all the water out between 'em, so they pop to the surface."

Colleen and Trish stepped lively to the open door in the fuselage, gripping the gangplank handrail. So did the other passengers.

"I think we've had more than enough of that species," said Colleen as they resumed their seats.

They both reached for handkerchiefs to mop their faces.

The beads of perspiration thereon were not entirely from the heat.

"Fascinating colours," said Colleen, looking out the window. "Hilly, too. Brings them all out in relief."

She leant back to let Trish see the view. The aircraft was droning over the Arabian Peninsula, an undulating landscape of red, brown and yellow.

"Not a lake in sight, though," said Trish. "Hate to cross it on camel back."

"Look," said Colleen. "The Pyramids."

Equally enthralled, Trish craned her neck to see them.

The Sunderland circled Cairo before alighting on the River Nile. The city and its famous landmarks were bathed in a vast reddish sunset. But as the aircraft glided to a halt, a strange unease struck Colleen that she couldn't identify.

Standing up after Trish to collect her web bag from the overhead luggage rack amid the bustle around her, she sharply drew breath.

You will understand tomorrow, Sister Colleen.

She shouldered her web bag and followed Trish to the exit, where crewmen were loading their holdalls into the launch.

Again, that inner Voice was warning her and Colleen wondered why.

Despite the late hour, Cairo's dockside teemed with turbaned, dark-skinned labourers noisily loading varieties of cargo into lines of Arab dhows. These were moored beside massive wooden piles supporting the long stretch of sturdy planking that constituted the docks.

As in Karachi, custom-built warehouses, cranes, lorries and European overseers blended the new world into the old. Modern freighters and motor gunboats shared berth space with the venerable dhows.

An RAF launch conveyed passengers and crew to the dockside. After they had passed through Egyptian Customs, the group boarded an RAF coach that took them some distance upriver to their overnight accommodation – a spick and span paddle steamer, fitted out as a River Nile cruise ship and moored to a small jetty, one of several in the vicinity, with similar craft alongside. Lighted lamps hung from the superstructures.

By contrast with the docks, the surroundings were tranquil. The last rays of the sun reflected off the placid waters of the Nile, lined here with tall palms instead of the trappings of trade and commerce. Bright stars twinkled in the darkening vault of the sky and the resinous smell of cooking fire smoke was diffusing through the dusk from several adobe Arab huts situated a short way off.

Colleen and Trish mounted the gangplank to the steamer with the others.

"Getting cooler," said Colleen.

The twilight was bringing respite from the heat.

"Yes, and it's walking-out uniform for this evening."

"You're right. Don't think boots and JGs will do, somehow."

The only blemish in the scene was the sight of young Egyptian males sauntering along in pairs beneath the palms, holding hands, their eyes ringed with heavily applied mascara. They were dressed in knee-length white garments that resembled nightshirts.

"Touting for tourists, you reckon?" said Colleen with distaste, as she and Trish stepped onto the deck.

"Probably. Way of life in these parts," said her friend acerbically. "According to Mum and Dad."

When everyone was aboard, white-coated native BOAC personnel, who carried the older women's overnight luggage, escorted them below decks to their cabins.

"A bit on the small side," said Trish, placing her holdall and web bag on her bunk. "Comfortable, though."

Colleen opened the shuttered doors of her cabin's wardrobe. She observed that it was scrubbed spotless and contained several hangers.

"Supper smells good," she said.

A savoury aroma was permeating the passageway.

The dining room décor vindicated the girls' decision to change into walking-out uniform. All passengers and aircrew were dressed for dinner, with service uniforms, evening frocks and white tuxedos providing a varicoloured display.

The three-course BOAC meal delightfully exceeded expectations.

In between dessert and coffee, the Sunderland captain, a tall, impressive-looking ex-RAF wing commander with dark hair and trimmed moustache, got to his feet, tapped his wine glass with a spoon, cleared his throat and called for the group's attention.

"The boat needs a bit more maintenance, ladies and gentlemen," he said in a resonant voice. "Our departure will therefore be delayed twenty-four hours. I sincerely apologise for any inconvenience but we've arranged for you to take a trip to the Pyramids and have a look at the city afterwards, so the day won't be lost. Thank you."

The captain dealt with a few questions prompted by his disclosure and sat down.

Colleen squeezed Trish's hand as the buzz of conversation resumed. She'd seen the look of anxiety in her friend's face. Then she remembered the strange experience on departing the Sunderland.

"Your dad's in the Lord's hands, Trish," she said. "Maybe Father wants us to see something tomorrow."

He did.

The civilian passengers chose to spend the day in the relative ease of Cairo's more salubrious clubs and bazaars. Younger, more adventurous types, led by ex-Wing Commander 'Kedge' Rutland, the Sunderland captain, opted for the preliminary desert excursion.

Following an early breakfast, Colleen and Trish sat behind Rutland and the RAF staff sergeant driver in the first vehicle of the convoy. A dusty jeep trip through heat and flies along unsealed thoroughfares flanked by mud-brick dwellings crowded with noisy occupants took them via dirt roads after about three quarters of an hour to the world-famous cluster of ancient massifs.

The Pyramids of Giza, and the Sphinx.

The girls alighted sweating and beating the dust out of their JGs. They stared in wonder at the huge structures, majestic in the glaring sun.

"Follow me, folks," Rutland called, waving his arm. "We can climb this one, provided you don't suffer from acrophobia."

Looking splendid in BOAC tropical uniform and peaked cap, he strode off through crusty, dun-coloured earth towards the nearest pyramid. Its sides consisted of stone ledges, the ravages of time having eroded the original limestone coating.

Colleen and Trish fell in beside Rutland, grateful for their bush hats that kept most of the sun's heat off their faces. The captain grinned at his comely companions.

"You ladies will all need hot baths tonight, along with a bit of laundering," he said. "We'll fix it for you."

"Thanks, Kedge," said Trish, smiling. "Is there likely to be any trouble?" She glanced at the weapon holstered to Rutland's belt. All the male personnel were armed.

"Just a precaution, Sister," he assured her. "Gyppos are getting a bit stirred up over who should own the Canal. They're also upset about the Kikes[297] coming back into Palestine in droves. We'll have a devil of a job there, no doubt. But I don't expect any trouble today, with us lads all armed. One shot in the air and the Wogs'll scamper off like rabbits."

He patted the holster for effect.

"How'd you get the name 'Kedge'?" Colleen asked as they mounted the first row of steps. The terraced stones were higher than normal stairs but easily negotiable, nevertheless.

"Hit a sandbar coming into Poole[298] on a filthy night in forty-three after a Biscay patrol," the Captain said, nimbly stepping from one ledge to the next. "We'd been shot up by a Junkers Eighty-eight and the controls were sloppy. Had to call for an air-sea rescue launch to kedge us off. Since I'd grounded the boat, the lads reckoned that's what they should call me, cheeky beggars, but the name stuck, like they often do."

"Aren't we landing in Poole?" Trish asked apprehensively.

"Hah, don't worry, Sister," Kedge rejoined. "Place has improved out of sight since then, with the channel having been dredged. There's hangars, jetties, cranes, slipways, workshops, customs houses, the lot. And we'll be coming in by day, so don't you fret. We'll see you right."

"All part of the corporate image, no doubt," said Trish. Kedge laughed heartily.

As they ascended, Colleen reflected on Rutland's remark about Palestine and on how closely it matched Peter's assessment. Sweating and brushing away flies, she feared for the fledgling state beyond Sinai.

"You lasses are fit, not even out of breath," said Rutland admiringly, when the group reached the summit.

"Well, that's the Army Nursing Service for you, Captain," said Trish with satisfaction. "Athletes *extraordinaire*."

"Don't forget the WAAFs," another female voice protested, joined by advocates for the WRNs and the one ATS lady present.

Owing to the number in the party, they carefully arranged themselves around a couple of the lower ledges and took it in turns to stand at the very top.

Colleen leant against the ochre-hued stone blocks of the pyramid's apex and surveyed the solemn grandeur of millennia-old history. A warm desert wind lapped her perspiring face. Apart from the faint sighing of the breeze, silence had descended over the awesome scene.

Then Colleen understood the strange warning she'd received the previous day.

"Look," she whispered to Trish, taking in with a sweep of her arm the tops of the Pyramids. "What do three pyramids look like from the top?"

"My God," said Trish. "X, X, X, or three hexs. The strongest curse in witchcraft."

"And where do you find a beast who's part cat, part man, like that monstrosity with the human head?" her friend asked, pointing to the Sphinx.

"Revelation. His number ends in X too, like 'Sphinx' and there's three of them, six, six, six. And 'Sphinx' has six letters."

"The beast has a seat, doesn't he?" Colleen whispered. "And that beast is sitting, alongside the curse[299]."

"Ex Cathedra. There's another X or two."

"So when his holiness speaks, it's a curse. Like everyone of his two-fingered blessings."

They climbed down to the next ledge, to make way for a couple of their companions.

"'The curse that goeth forth over the face of the whole earth,'" Trish said with deliberation. Colleen shared her friend's evident unease.

"We'll still have to grapple with it when we get home," she said.

At Rutland's summons, they cautiously began the descent.

"Don't look down," Kedge called cheerfully.

"You were right, Coll," said Trish. "Father did have something to show us."

Despite the warmth of the desert wind, they shivered.

Their destination the following day was the small seaport of Augusta on Sicily's southeast coast, where they stayed overnight in a white-stucco, three-storeyed hotel set amongst olive groves.

"Reminds me of Sorrento," said Colleen. After a late lunch, she and Trish were reclining in deck chairs on the balcony outside their rooms. It overlooked a beautiful expanse of white sand and sparkling sea.

Colleen also remembered they were not far from where Annie's Bill and his mates had parachuted into Sicily[300] but decided not to mention it.

"Get Peter to take you there on honeymoon, Coll," Trish suggested.

"Hmm," said Colleen. "Fancy a swim in a bit?" she asked, sitting upright.

"Why not?" Trish stretched her arms and clasped them behind her head. "Might as well make the most of this trip."

Colleen settled back to take in more of the sun. Again, she reflected how it was taken for granted that she and Peter would marry.

But she still couldn't stop thinking about Steve Graham.

"Gosh, they're as beautiful as the Himalayas," said Trish, marvelling.

"They beat the Appenines, that's for sure," Colleen said in admiration.

The girls stared at the snow-capped ranges of the Alps, gliding by the Sunderland as it droned northwest on the final leg of the journey.

After a while, Colleen glanced at her watch.

"We'll be in Poole before lunch, GMT," she said.

"Bet Kedge finds it a bit easier this time."

They both laughed and looked up expectantly at the steward who approached with tea and sandwiches.

"Home," said Trish, sipping her tea.

Colleen unwrapped her sandwiches.

"Wonder what it will feel like?"

"Different," said Trish.

The Sunderland smoothly came to rest in Poole Harbour.

"English winter's day," Trish observed.

It was almost noon but the harbour waters were grey beneath sombre skies and the low-lying foreshore appeared bleak and uninviting. A depressing first view of home, Colleen decided as they stood up to retrieve their web bags from the overhead compartments.

Nevertheless, jaunty RAF launch crews swiftly transferred passengers and their baggage to one of the new jetties Kedge had mentioned, whereupon the group went by bus to a timber and corrugated iron warehouse-like building that served as the customs house. A lorry carrying the baggage followed behind.

The girls sat relaxed on the cushioned rear seat of the coach.

"Really civilised, this," remarked Colleen.

"Chilly, though," said Trish. She folded her arms across her chest.

They had donned walking-out uniform before departing Augusta and used the Sunderland's rest room after take-off to put on woollen vests under shirt and tie. The other service personnel had done likewise. The civilians were more plentifully attired, with scarves and overcoats.

Uniformed BOAC personnel standing behind trestle tables in the customs house made sure that the girls' trunks with folded camp beds attached were checked through to their ultimate destinations. Colleen's gear was distinctly labelled for Catterick and Trish's for a private mansion between Banbury and Chipping Norton, converted into a military hospital.

"We'll sort it, ladies," said the grinning, sandy-haired clerk, clearly a local lad from his accent and probably recently demobbed. "BOAC service. I'll see to your rail warrants, now."

Colleen and Trish bade a hasty farewell to Captain Rutland and his crew, then hailed a taxi that took them to Poole Station. They each sent telegrams and headed for the platform to catch the train to Oxford.

Where a minor crisis arose.

Cumbered with holdalls and web bags, they were rapidly descending the steps from the overhead walkway, when Trish exclaimed, "Knickers!" and clutched the side of her skirt.

"Pardon?" said Colleen, surprised at her friend's uncharacteristic bluntness, at least in public.

"My knicker elastic's busted," whispered Trish, still gripping her skirt. "Haven't got time to go and change. Train'll be here any minute."

The locomotive was in fact coming into view up the track and the waiting passengers, both civilian and military, were moving to the edge of the platform.

"Get in amongst that lot," Colleen urged. "Snag your pants on your zip. I'll look after your stuff."

She pointed to a platoon of squaddies, drawn up in threes and commanded by a fierce-looking sergeant. The formation would be the last to entrain and stood motionless.

Trish slipped in between the centre and rear ranks, hitched up her skirt and made the necessary adjustment.

"Thanks, lads," said Trish as she re-emerged. "Thanks, Sergeant."

"You're welcome, Sister," said the NCO in a paternal tone.

"Disciplined lot," said Trish when she and Colleen had boarded the train and found their compartment. Because they were officers, it was in the first-class carriage.

Colleen placed her luggage on the rack above her head.

"Nearly twisted their eyeballs out of their sockets, though," she said.

Once the train was underway, Trish rummaged in her web bag for a second set of knickers and departed for the loo. Colleen stared out the window at drab-looking backyards, then glanced at the other passengers. They consisted of a pair of middle-aged senior officers and their wives, well dressed and neatly groomed. Colleen was glad of the older women's presence. She was feeling tired and ill-disposed to the certainty otherwise of being chatted up by a couple of Colonel Blimps. They for their part were occupied with the morning paper. One of the women was knitting and the other appeared engrossed in a novel with a red and yellow dust jacket.

The compartment door slid open and Trish re-entered. The others made way for her and she sat opposite Colleen. "Thank you," she said to their fellow passengers, who responded with courteous nods.

"Do you want to try the dining car, Coll?" asked Trish.

"Might as well. Long time since the last lot of BOAC sarnies[301]."

They arose, excused themselves and ventured along the corridor to the snack counter at the entrance to the dining car. Making their purchases, they occupied a vacant table inside the car, unwrapped the grease-proofing, gave thanks and set about their meal.

"Nothing like a couple of bacon butties," said Colleen with relish.

"Not bad," said Trish after the first mouthful. "Tea's as good as compo brew."

They ate watching the unfolding scenery of the New Forest, where streaks of light snow marked out rides through the dark woodlands.

"England," said Trish. "Our England."

The train journeyed over the undulating downlands of Hampshire and Berkshire, beneath a winter sun shedding its soft gleam upon farmhouses, woods and snow-mantled fields, dissected by meandering streams.

"All so peaceful out there," Colleen remarked. "Wouldn't think there'd been a war, would you?"

"Sooner it seems like a bad dream, the better," said Trish.

Though a nightmare was still to come.

By mid afternoon, the train was within sight of the spires of Oxford. Trish would detrain here and continue on to Banbury via a branch line.

Colleen helped carry her gear onto the platform.

Noise and movement were all around as departing passengers headed for the exit, incoming travellers boarded the train, porters trundled luggage, voices sounded over the PA system and bursts of steam drifted past the carriages.

In the midst of it, hugging her friend and bidding her farewell, Colleen realised things would never be the same.

She and Trish had been almost constant companions for twelve months. Even Trish's marriage hadn't affected the bond between them. Everything resumed as normal when Trish returned.

But this parting was in a sense, final. Both of them knew it and wept on each other's shoulders in the few moments they had for saying goodbye.

"Give my love to Matt and your folks," Colleen sobbed.

"And mine to yours and Peter," said Trish tearfully.

Porters' whistles were sounding and doors were slamming.

Colleen hurried back on board. Smiling through tears, the friends waved to each other as the train pulled away from the station.

Departing Oxford, the train wound through the heath and farmland of middle England, past neat little villages with their steepled parish churches residing next to well-kept greens, some still carpeted with snow. The urbanisation gradually intensified until Colleen's view from the window encompassed endless rows of dark grey terraced houses, the brooding environs of greater Birmingham, enshrouded in a smoky, rain-swept dusk, for the weather had deteriorated again.

No New Jerusalem, she thought. But it's still our England. Her eyes moistened at the thought of those who'd suffered and died to make it so.

She said goodbye to her travelling companions at Wolverhampton, alighted from the train and hastened to a neighbouring platform for the next connection. Except for numerous service personnel, conspicuous in uniform, the commuter crowds moving to and fro in transit looked pale and undernourished, dressed in drab hues of grey, faces pinched with the winter chill. The effects of six years' rationing and divers hardships would not be rectified overnight.

Colleen shared a compartment for this part of the journey with a couple of ebullient RAF officer cadets, who were delighted when the door slid back to admit the glamorous QA.

"Please, allow me, Sister," said one. He jumped up to hoist her gear onto the luggage rack.

"We're off to the dining car in a bit, Sister," said the other. "You'll let us buy you supper?"

She did. It wasn't bad, roast beef and veg, with spotted dick[302] and custard for afters.

The cadets listened agog as she related her experiences in Italy and the Far East over a pot of tea.

"You ought to write it down, Sister," they urged when she left the train at Stoke-on-Trent. "Bon voyage. Privilege to have met you. Take care."

Naturally, they carried her kit onto the platform for her. She waved fondly to them as the train drew away.

Please God, safeguard them for their mothers' sakes, she prayed, remembering the burns cases she had seen. The two lads seemed little more than schoolboys.

A branch line took her from the grimy smoke of the Potteries conurbation to a village siding about ten miles to the southeast. She was almost the only passenger. Cold night air hit her in the face as she stepped off the train and walked to the exit gate, holdall in one hand, web bag over her shoulder.

The rain had gone, so Colleen didn't bother with her monsoon mac. Bright stars glimmered in the arch of a violet sky and a frost ring encircled the moon. Patches of it glinted on the pavement.

"Better watch my step," she said.

Around her shone the street lamps and houselights gleamed invitingly as she passed by, likewise the lamp above the sign of the village pub.

No blackout now, she thought.

Her way took her to a row of slate-tiled, stone cottages in a cul-de-sac running parallel to the high street. On the opposite side of the lane and across a wide verge, a stream gurgled over its rocky bed beneath overshadowing trees.

Place must look lovely in the daytime, Colleen reflected. The Lord had provided in abundance for her friends.

She stopped at the last house on the row, leant her holdall against the wall and rapped a black iron knocker on its white-painted door.

It opened to reveal a slim young woman with light brown hair and grey eyes, wearing matching cardigan and skirt.

"Colleen, you found us!" exclaimed the girl. She threw her arms around the newcomer in a fierce embrace.

"Annie, you look great!" said Colleen vehemently, returning the hug. "Yes, your directions were perfect."

"Come in, where it's warm," her friend urged and tugged Colleen's sleeve. "I'll put the kettle on and then show you your room and everything. Have you eaten?"

"Bill's at the midweek Bible study," Anne explained as she placed the tea things on a small table. "He'll be back early though, because I told him about your telegram. Are you warm enough?"

"Yes, thanks," said Colleen.

She occupied an easy chair to one side of a log fire in the sitting room hearth. Her cap reposed on the arm of the chair and she had partly unbuttoned her tunic and loosened her tie. Extending her hands toward the blaze, Colleen wrinkled her stockinged feet on the hearth rug.

"Ooh, that feels lovely," she said. "You don't mind me taking my shoes off? I did mange to get a bath before we left Augusta."

"Make yourself at home," said Anne, with a wave of her hand. She sat in the easy chair opposite Colleen. "And help yourself to a muffin. I baked them last night. They're Bill's favourite."

Colleen bit into the blueberry cake she had selected from the tray, careful to collect the crumbs on the side plate she held.

"Mmh, they're scrumptious," she said.

Placing the muffin on the plate, she asked, "How's his new course coming along?"

"Fine. He's got several experimental trials going. A lot more satisfying than bean counting[303], he says."

"Oh, that's great. Have you heard from George and Alison lately?"

Anne shook her head and placed her cup and saucer on the table. She picked up a piece of split kindling and dropped it on the fire. Sparks flew up the chimney space.

"Not since I last wrote. But they're OK. Looking forward to parenthood."

Colleen smiled. Her and Anne's letters had kept them mutually up to date, so that Colleen knew of George Linton's marriage in the autumn to her former roommate Alison Dennis and Alison's discovery a month later that she was pregnant. Anne had also written of Bill's decision to concentrate on industrial statistics instead of accounting and had been delighted to learn of Colleen's meeting with Mandy in Rangoon. Their regular correspondence facilitated the arrangements for Colleen's overnight stay.

These days, I'm usually in before seven, one of Anne's letters had said. *Bill walks me home from the station. Just turn up when you can and take us as you find us.*

"How are things at church?" Colleen asked tentatively. She sipped her tea and broke the remainder of the muffin in half. Her friends worshipped at a local fellowship that professed to be bible-believing but Annie's letters indicated a few problems.

"OK," said Anne after a pause. "We've still got the anti-King James lobby and the ecumenical crew, though, Catholics who failed their Latin, Bill reckons, not to mention the Calvinists, who insist the Lord died only for the elect."

"Sounds like a bit of a mare's nest."

Anne nodded. "But you know what Bill's like. Stands up to the lot of them and unloads the Book every chance he gets. It's such an encouragement to the younger ones, lads and lasses who were in the forces but some of the older folk who've been there as long as the walls reckon he's divisive."

"He's a paratrooper, Annie. What do you expect?"

Anne laughed. "Do you want a top up?" she asked, reaching for the cosy-covered teapot.

"Yes, please," said Colleen. She held out her cup. "How's Mrs Royston?"

Anne poured the tea into Colleen's cup and added milk from a green and white glazed jug.

"Bearing up[304]. Bill's mum sees her a lot. Remember I wrote to you about when I met her after I first came down here, how she said to Bill, 'Why did you come back instead of my son?' I didn't say so in the letter but as God is my witness, Colleen, I nearly gave her such an earful."

"I remember. Good thing I wasn't there."

"Amen," said Anne with feeling, then added with a sigh. "It's terribly hard for so many, with loved ones who never came back, or got disabled in some way. We keep in touch with as many families as we can and the folk we served with, as you do, of course."

Colleen nodded reflectively, thinking of Hoppy and Doug. She finished her muffin and sat back, crossing her legs.

"Still enjoying your home posting[305]?" she asked.

Anne had described in her letters the work at the base hospital, located on the way to the market town of Uttoxeter. *They pronounce it 'Hutchetter' around here*, she'd written.

"Yes, I've even managed to fit in Part One Midwifery, which is a bit ironic. Though I've talked them into letting me stay on for a while."

Colleen looked her in the eye.

"You know, Annie, I *thought* so," she said joyously. "There was something about you, the moment I saw you."

Anne nodded, smiling.

"Confirmed last week."

"Oh, *Annie*, let me give you another hug."

Colleen put aside her teacup, stood up and wrapped an arm around her friend's shoulders.

"What does Bill think?" she asked, resuming her seat.

They heard the sound of the front door being unlocked.

"Ask the man himself," said Anne. "We're in here, love," she called.

As Bill came into the sitting room, Colleen realised it was the first time she'd seen him in civvies. Apart from that, he seemed the same lithe chap she remembered from when he was stationed in the northeast and used to come courting Annie by the fire escape at the General.

"Evening all," said Bill, with a welcoming smile to Colleen.

He briskly crossed the room, put an arm around Anne and lovingly kissed her.

Colleen rose to her feet again and gasped as Bill's hug forced air from her lungs.

"Hello, Colleen," he said warmly, kissing her on the cheek. "How long has it been? You look marvellous in uniform. Well, you look marvellous anyway, apart from the mepacrine tinge."

"Bill!" exclaimed Anne, laughing with embarrassment. "You shouldn't say *that*."

"It's true, though," said Colleen and smiled as she smoothed her tunic. "I still have to take the wretched pills for a few weeks, as no doubt you did, Bill."

Harris pulled the settee closer to the fire and seated himself.

"Has Annie told you our news?" he asked eagerly. Anne came and sat beside him.

"Sure has," said Colleen, sitting down again. "So what do you reckon to becoming a dad, Sergeant Harris?"

They talked until after midnight. Colleen could see that her friends regarded her testimony as an answer to prayer.

"I can't thank you enough," she said. "I'm sure that's how I met up with Bronwyn and the others."

But on retiring to the guest room, Colleen nevertheless reproached herself in the knowledge that when Bill had hugged and kissed her, she couldn't help closing her eyes and pretending he was Steve Graham.

They parted with Bill at the village station at seven a.m. the next day. His train took him to Stoke and Colleen travelled with Anne to Uttoxeter, where they said goodbye on the platform. Colleen thought her friend looked splendid in QA uniform.

"I get there by bus in plenty of time to change and start on the ward for eight," said Anne.

"You take care, Annie," said Colleen earnestly. She hugged her friend as Anne's train pulled in.

When it had gone, Colleen ascended the steps for the opposite platform. There she would connect with the train to Derby and points north.

Apart from train changes and a few time-consuming delays, the remainder of Colleen's journey proceeded steadily. She took it all in through the carriage window, first the rolling moorlands of North Staffordshire and then the crags and vales of the Derbyshire Peak.

"England, our England," she murmured, remembering Trish's remark. And as Colleen gazed at the wild beauty of the White Peak, she looked forward to her sojourn there, the sinister undertones notwithstanding.

The train chugged past the great cities of Sheffield and Leeds, where factory chimneys belched out the black smoke of forges, furnaces and mills, the throbbing, thriving heart of England's industrial north, flanked by phalanxes of soot-darkened, back-to-back tenements stretching out of sight.

"Where there's muck, there's brass[306]," said Colleen, smiling at the time-honoured Yorkshire saying. "For some, anyway."

Another train change at York and she watched the famous cathedral city with its elegant medieval Minster glide out of sight as the train rattled across the rich meadows of the North Riding. Though veiled under snow, they provided rough pasture for hardy, black-faced sheep in their shaggy coats.

"Woolly backs," Colleen whispered.

She rejoiced at the sight of the North York Moors escarpment, where stood the white horse of Kilburn, cut into the stone of the cliff face.

Colleen yawned and glanced at her watch. Nearly home, she thought. Taken a while.

In late afternoon, Colleen detrained in her hometown. She noted the repair works at the station and remembered how, almost four years ago, she and Annie had nursed casualties from the bomb blast.

Colleen had loathed the Axis powers then. On this crisp winter's day in the first year after the war, she decided that, if anything, her attitude had hardened.

The driver parked his cab outside the semi-detached on one corner of the cul-de-sac's T. Its approach road lay on the edge of the suburb. Colleen gazed across the road at frost-laden fields and tree clumps, silent in the soft glow of the setting sun, the places she had loved and explored as a child – in the boisterous company of all those ironworkers' and dockers' sons.

Home.

"Oh, no thank you, Sister," said the driver when Colleen reached for her purse. "It's because of you lassies that our lad made it home. This one's on me."

With a lump in her throat, Colleen entered by the front gate, walked to the door and rested her holdall and web bag by the step. She adjusted her cap and rapped the knocker.

The door opened. A middle-aged lady with faded auburn hair stood before her in apron, pullover and woollen skirt.

"Oh, my dear!" exclaimed the woman.

Mother and daughter embraced in the doorway and cried on each other's shoulders.

Mrs McGrath poured tea into two cups.

"You look splendid in uniform, dear," she said. "Of course, you look gorgeous in anything. I do feel sorry for that poor boy, Tony."

Oh, Mum, why do you have to bring that up, thought Colleen.

"It couldn't be helped, Mum," she said tersely.

Colleen sat at the kitchen table. The familiar backyard was dimly visible through the kitchen window in the gathering dusk. She hadn't said anything about Peter in the letters to her parents, or even to Annie and Bill. In the light of her currently uncertain feelings, she reflected that had probably been a wise decision.

Her mother placed her cup and saucer on the work surface and busied herself at the stove, where two saucepans were simmering.

"I've got some extra clothing coupons," she said. "I'm sure you're broader across the shoulders. Your tops won't fit. You should spend a day in York. They'll have the best selection."

Colleen tasted the tea. It was as good as Matron Brierley's.

"You still make the best cuppa, Mum."

Her mother smiled faintly.

"Thank you, dear."

"I'll be going to Catterick for my new posting in a few days. So the army will still be clothing me for a bit."

"Yes, of course. Like you said in your letter."

Her mother pursed her lips. Colleen braced herself, sensing what was coming.

The protestations.

"You won't have been to Mass or Confession. Or said the Rosary or prayed to the Blessed Virgin – "

Mrs McGrath broke off in mid-sentence and stared, blinking, at the contents of the saucepan that she was stirring. A savoury, meaty aroma permeated the kitchen.

"That smells delicious, Mum," said Colleen, trying to ease the tension.

"I hope you like it."

"I'm sure it'll be great. You always did have a way with the rations."

"Well, thanks to your father's kitchen garden and Oxo cubes."

Colleen's mother reached for one of the small glass containers located on a condiments rack fastened to the wall. She sprinkled some of the contents into both saucepans.

"Always better with a dash of herbs," she said tonelessly. "I hope you don't mind having supper before your bath, dear. Your father's on day shift, so he'll be in soon."

"It's OK, Mum," said Colleen. She sipped her tea.

"Your father'll be ever so glad to see you."

Her mother continued stirring, her gaze fixed on the saucepan.

Colleen took a deep breath, placed her cup in its saucer and sat upright.

"Mum, look at me," she said, gently but firmly.

Her mother laid aside the spoon, brushed her hands on her apron, sniffed and turned to face her daughter.

"Come and sit down," said Colleen. She nodded toward the chair opposite her.

Her mother did so. Colleen clasped her hand.

"Mum," she said earnestly. "I love you and Dad. You know that. I'd never do anything to hurt you. But you must understand. God sent the Lord Jesus Christ to die for us on the cross of Calvary and 'the blood of Jesus Christ His Son cleanseth us from all sin[307].' You don't need religion, so-called. All you have to do is receive the Lord's gift, of eternal forgiveness."

Mrs McGrath averted her gaze, slowly withdrew her hand from Colleen's grasp, got up and returned to the stove. She tried to smile.

"Let's not quarrel, dear, not on your first day home."

"I'll set the table," said Colleen, getting up and also attempting a smile. Well, Father, I tried, she thought.

A few minutes later, the front door opened and Colleen rushed to meet her father in the hallway.

"Oh, Dad!" she cried and threw her arms around his neck.

A hearty man with broad shoulders and a shock of hair once red, now grey, Mr McGrath seized Colleen in his brawny workman's arms with a hug that rivalled the one she'd received from Bill Harris.

"Oh, my little princess," he said, sobbing for joy. "You look wonderful, kitten."

Father and daughter wept together.

Colleen was pleased that her trunk and camp bed had arrived OK and that the silica gel and mothballs in their netting bags preserved the trunk's contents unblemished.

She unpacked her bedroll, foldable canvas bucket, basin, bath and other pieces of kit. The bulkier items she'd store in the double-doored metal locker, the bedroll she placed on her steel-framed bed, because the Nissen huts that housed the Catterick nursing staff were un-heated and cement floors didn't help, either.

Her cubicle was a single, mainly owing to the odd way this particular hut had been parti-tioned but she didn't mind. Though appreciably smaller than her room in Rangoon or the one she'd shared with Trish in Singapore, it still had sufficient extra space for a table, desk lamp and chair. The locker, equipped with shelves, was big enough to take all her kit.

She had exchanged her JGs for KDs and drawn a winter issue of ward uniform that she now wore.

"Tight-fisted lot, making me pay for the extra kit," she muttered resentfully about the QM arrangements. "Typical Yorkshire."

I'll keep quiet about the Browning for now, she decided.

The automatic pistol still reposed at the bottom of her web bag. But she knew how to look after it, thanks to Geordie Wood's weapons tuition.

Colleen hung the last of her clothes in the locker and gazed out the square window set in the hut's corrugated curving wall at the snowscape of the dales.

Then she heard a gentle voice that she instantly recognised.

"Hullo, Colleen. They said you'd arrived. Saw your name on the duty roster."

"Doreen!" exclaimed Colleen, promptly turning around.

The two friends from the General hugged each other.

"Come over to the mess for a brew," said Doreen Forrester, formerly Prentice and dressed like Colleen in winter-ward uniform, complete with white head square and grey and scarlet cape. "You'll be on duty with me but we've time for some catching up."

The Sisters' Mess was another Nissen hut, partitioned by a curtain, one half being the dining area, the other the relaxation lounge, though the hard wooden chairs and cement floor bespoke more of austerity.

However, a big iron stove with a flue poking through the corrugated roof threw out wel-coming warmth, in keeping with the friendly greetings Colleen received from several QAs occupying some of the chairs. The lasses were drinking tea, knitting and listening to a large combination radio and record player, set against the wall opposite the stove[308].

Colleen and her friend collected mugs of tea and a scone each on paper plates from the dining area and returned to the lounge. They occupied chairs sufficiently close to the stove for them to stay warm but far enough away so that their conversation didn't distract the other girls intent on the BBC broadcast.

"Yes, Mandy wrote that you'd met up in Rangoon," said Doreen. "Small world, eh?"

"Sure is. She seems to be enjoying it down south OK."

Mandy Davis, now Cosgrove, was stationed at a hospital near Hastings, where her husband was serving out his enlistment.

"Looking forward to getting demobbed though, like me," Doreen said.

Colleen bit into her scone. It was freshly baked and she hungrily consumed the fragment.

"Think you'll stay near Richmond?" she asked.

Doreen drank a mouthful of tea.

"We will. Les is from the Dales. We're also quite close to John and Lindy. They moved here after John was demobbed."

"Yes, Lindy's kept in touch. By the way, I dropped in on Bill and Annie on the way up."

Doreen raised her eyebrows.

"Oh, how are they?"

"Wonderful, Annie's expecting."

"Marvellous! Tell me more."

Colleen recounted her visit and then asked, "Mandy said you'd had some trouble at Bari?"

Doreen's expression grew serious.

"We did. Mighty big cover-up. John reckons the best thing to do is wait until I'm demobbed and then start lobbying MPs. Rest assured I intend to - "

"Hey, Dorrie, Coll," said one of the other girls. "News is about to start."

Balancing mugs and scones, they moved their chairs to listen. Colleen reflected on Doreen's words and recalled the obfuscation even Vicky Leonard had encountered in an apparently simple matter like tracing Peter Waverly.

She wondered anew about the extent of conspiracy in high places.

She was destined to learn more of it.

And of the suffering incurred, because global war was simply an outcrop of the greater evil.

Colleen's ward was housed in a long, two-storeyed brick building on the outer edge of the hospital complex.

The patients here were severely incapacitated[309]. All needed special care.

One soldier, victim of a mine blast, had lost both legs, amputated at the hip.

Another was a torso, head and buttocks, with stumps of arms and legs – and virtually moribund.

Yet another manifested a cavernous, unhealed head wound. He was semi-comatose, like the soldier so badly torn up by shrapnel he looked like a living autopsy, functioning solely by means of IV drips and drainage tubes.

Like others did, with major bodily and or facial mutilation.

Many would not live much longer but for some, the mercy of death was cruelly denied.

In a single room, one individual, who resembled a raw corpse, was kept in a hammock, partly immersed in a layer of Vaseline grease.

The man could not move himself and suffered from bedsores so Doreen and Colleen turned him from side to side several times in the course of their shift, to prevent infection. The hammock was changed regularly and steam-cleaned.

"Mustard gas?" Colleen asked softly when they left the room after the first turning session.

"Yes. He's been here since nineteen-eighteen. So you can see why I'm not about to give up about Bari. That's what they were like there. As if being half-blown to bits wasn't bad enough."

Colleen thought of the horrors wrought by the A-Bombs that Peter had described and Vicky's portent of a new Dark Age.

A chill gripped at her heart.

Besides the long-stay patients, many casualties were admitted following training accidents from the live-firing exercises regularly undertaken in the hills and dales around the camp.

These were stepped up as winter yielded to spring and better weather.

Colleen was assisting in theatre when several victims of a WP shell explosion were brought in[310]. Morphine could barely contain their pain and the RAMC orderlies ensured that the sufferers' dressings were kept soaking wet, to prevent the phosphorous from re-igniting.

Many of the wounds emitted wisps of foul-smelling smoke, nevertheless.

"OK, switch off the lights," the operating MO said when the first patient was placed on the table and anaesthetised. An orderly complied.

Colleen stared at the weird greenish glow emitted when the theatre lights were extinguished. She knew from experience in Italy and Burma this was the best way to mark out where the shell debris were embedded in the torn flesh. Then she scrutinised the patient's drips, easily but grotesquely visible in the phosphorescent glare. Maintaining the live-preserving IV fluid was critical.

"Keep everything wet," the surgeon said to his assistant orderly. "OK, Sister," he said to Colleen. "Let's get those bits out and prepare him for the *Tulle Gras*."

As a break from normal duties, Colleen undertook to obtain her driver's licence.

The benevolent staff sergeant instructor who took her out in an olive-green-painted Austin Cambridge was impressed.

"You've driven before, Sister," he said during the first lesson.

"A jeep from Meiktila to Rangoon," said his comely pupil. "Before that in Italy. And while I was training, an ex-boyfriend's MG, when he was plastered. Echoes of a misspent youth."

The NCO laughed heartily.

"Well, provided you brush up on the Highway Code, you shouldn't have any trouble, Sister. Wear your ward uniform when you go for the test. It always creates a good impression."

After a few weeks of motoring around the scenic byways of the Dales and through the winding streets of Richmond and Darlington[311], Colleen took both her test and her instructor's advice.

She passed on the first attempt.

Like Annie, Colleen then decided to enrol in Part One Midwifery. She knew that given her other duties, attainment of the qualification would be a protracted process, but the large married contingent attached to the base was yielding a local baby boom and providing many opportunities for attending deliveries.

She hoped to be allocated the Austin Cambridge for her tutorial sessions in the local general hospital, situated some distance from the base.

The army gave her a bicycle.

Apart from PT activities that were optional, drill sessions that were not – "Bit of a fag," Doreen remarked, "but good for discipline, the army reckons" – and her everyday, off-duty routine that still included copious amounts of letter-writing, Colleen was able to visit her parents fairly often, thanks to the nearby rail link.

She only wished she was closer to Bill and Annie and the friends she'd served with, particularly Trish, who wrote regularly, one of her latest letters stating that *Matt's arrived, sooner than expected, so we're overjoyed. His mum and sister hope to visit next year, God willing. Dad's still weak but convalescing at home now so we're living with him and Ellie in the Vicarage until we find a place nearer the university, for when Matt starts in September. I still won't have far to go to the hospital and Matt's really enjoying the old country – confirms the Lord's calling, he says. Everything's going OK. Must organise a get-together. Love, Trish.*

The get-together would come about sooner than expected, partly thanks to Matt's researches.

In the meantime, Colleen spent several relaxing interludes with Les and Doreen and John and Lindy.

During one of these occasions, sitting with John in the parlour of the Steadman's cottage, Colleen broached the subject of the major's investigations, while Lindy was putting to bed "the bairn," as southerner John delightfully called his baby daughter.

"Vicky told me she'd interviewed you," said John as he drew the net curtains across the parlour's front windows.

Steadman came and sat opposite her.

"Things are still quiet down there though it's only a matter of time before Von Hollstein acts," he said. "We still don't know his exact scheme, unfortunately."

Colleen gazed out a side window at the golden glow of sunset and the lengthening shadows. The sheep-dotted ridge and hollow of the Dales countryside looked green and peaceful.

She remembered Miko's evil countenance and thanked God that the Steadmans were concealed in this rustic setting, far from the murderous Slav.

"I should be on my way soon, John," she said, turning her gaze to the major. "I think I've convinced my superiors I won't be a danger to the patients. Between us, we should be able to suss out what V-H has in mind."

"I'm sure you will, Colleen," the major said with a reassuring smile. "No doubt something to do with Death and Hell, so don't take any chances. Remember Forsythe's letter. Miko's already made one attempt on you."

"I'll remember, John," said Colleen quietly.

They looked up at Lindy's slim figure, framed in the doorway to the parlour.

"She's finally off," Lindy whispered. "Now, who's for supper?"

John and Colleen each put up a hand, happy to change the subject.

In early May, Colleen received her transfer orders.

Along with a couple of letters. Their contents were startling.

One was from Kate Bramble, the other from Peter. Both were postmarked Paris.

Seated on her bed after finishing a late shift, Colleen read them by the light of her desk lamp.

Dear Colleen, said Kate's letter. *Vicky kindly forwarded me your contact details. I can appreciate this letter will come as a surprise but Vicky will brief you. I've had to pull out of the surveillance, along with Brian and Mollie. Don't worry, they're OK and no doubt they'll write soon. We've gone to safe addresses – mine's abroad, as you'll see from the postmark.*

It was a shock having to depart when we did but I'm sure your contribution will be decisive. I thank God you agreed to take part in the operation and I pray every day for your safety. I regret we won't be meeting up for a while but I look forward to when we do. I hope we'll be good friends.

Peter Waverly, 'Guillaume,' as I knew him, has diverted to my new locale. It was an emotional reunion and I trust with all my heart you will be able to understand our circumstances. We had been corresponding before he arrived and realised how deeply we felt for each other. Again, I earnestly hope you can understand.

Rest assured, you won't be alone in this last stage of the operation. Captain Steve Graham will be on the scene too. He's a splendid lad. Tough as teak, as you say in Yorkshire. Vicky's probably told you Steve's from Sheffield and I've no doubt you'll be safe and sound with him by your side.

Your sister in Christ,
Kate Bramble

Colleen's heart leapt at the sight of Steve's name. It seemed to have a habit of so doing, whenever the Captain was mentioned. Kate had kindly enclosed Steve's contact details.

She then read Peter's letter.

Dear Colleen,

I understand from Vicky that you'll be on the move soon. I hope and believe everything will work out well for you. This is certainly my continuing prayer for you and I shall always be grateful for your support and affection in the months since we met. You have indeed been a Heaven-sent comfort.

Vicky will brief you on events so I won't go into unnecessary detail, simply to let you know that I have diverted from my original course and won't be back at the old haunts for some time yet.

I am at a 'safe location' with Kate Bramble, 'Collette,' as was. You can imagine how astounded I was when Vicky told me about her and I trust you can understand what cause for rejoicing this has been, for both Kate and myself. We have exchanged several letters and in doing so confirmed the strength of our feelings for one another.

In the meantime, I have confidence that victory will be ours, with respect to the vital mission in progress. Vicky, I understand, has informed you about Captain Graham. I commend you to his care and protection, and to that of He Who said, 'I will never leave thee, nor forsake thee,' Hebrews 13:5.

Your brother in Christ,
Peter Waverly, Major

Colleen stared up at the arched roof of the hut, both letters open on her lap.

"Crumbs," she said under her breath. "Not often you get *two* DJs[312] in one go. Wonder what Steve'll say when he gets his?"

Please, Father, help me to comfort him, she prayed.

"But what if he doesn't fancy me?" she said aloud.

She leant back on her elbows and crossed her legs. The letters fluttered to the floor.

And pigs might fly, she thought. Don't be stupid, McGrath. You sure have a way of doing things, Father.

It was, Colleen realised, evidence of *the peace of God, which passeth all understanding*[313].

She now understood why Peter's letters had become so non-committal and why a letter from Vicky several days ago had contained a request for a photograph. On impulse, Colleen had two taken, both of her in walking-out uniform, one head and shoulders, the other full length, wearing her heels. She sent copies of both to Vicky.

"Gosh," said Colleen, experiencing a sudden flush of exhilaration. "Vicky's going to pass them on to Steve. I'm glad I wore the heels. Thank *you*, Janice."

Colleen picked up the letters, moved to her desk and adjusted the lamp. She then took out pen and paper to draft her replies, relishing the thought of writing to Steve.

I wonder if he'll frame it, she mused.

The Text, *He hath sent me to heal the brokenhearted*[314], promptly came to mind.

The day Colleen received her letters, Captain Graham stood staring from the window of his quarters at the familiar woodland, now green with spring growth and the adjacent fields, dappled yellow with fresh flowers. His command continued to occupy the same billets they'd been allocated a year ago and though steadily attenuated by demobilisation, had almost completed its tasks in the restoration of Kiel and its port facilities.

Steve had been heavily involved in re-installation of public utilities. He found the work challenging and extremely interesting. For that reason, the months since last summer had flown by, though he had missed not being with Kate for Christmas.

The changes taking place since the new year left Steve in command of the squadron, with Ledbetter and Holland as the rest of his officer cadre, because Blackstone had been repatriated. Many of the lads in his original troop were back home too, including Kinnear, Jevons, Stoker, Talbot and Crittenden.

Hazeldene, Ferrarby, Illingworth and Shoreland remained with the squadron, Ron promoted to sergeant and the others to corporal. Those innovative cooks, MacGee and Tomlinson, were now both corporals.

"Our girlfriends are very impressed, sir," MacGee told Graham. "Thanks for puttin' in a good word for us at Regiment."

Graham knew that if he stayed in the army, he could well be gazetted major by the end of the year. But he had decided to take the demobilisation option instead. It meant he wouldn't be stalling his parents any longer about not taking leave and also that he would be home in time for Neil and Emma's wedding. Graham Two had at least sorted his priorities in that respect, though he was still in the air force.

Mark Napper was stationed in Eindhoven, where he and Katrijn had their own flat and, according to Mark's last letter, were *looking forward to becoming a mum and dad. As you can guess, the family are ecstatic. Mama and Papa send their love. So do Jan and Marijke.*

Jan and Marijke were now engaged. Steve smiled at the thought of the various cards and letters Marijke still sent to *Dear Uncle Steve*, always appended with *love and kisses.*

Ian Kinross, back in Scotland, also wrote often. *Have decided to study for the ministry,* his last letter said. *Will be a bit of an adjustment, but I believe it to be God's calling, nevertheless.*

Steve reflected that if anyone could stand in the gap left by the death of Tubby Potter, Ian was God's man.

Bill Crittenden and Lorraine Tyrell had since married. Understandably, they'd decided on a quiet wedding, with mainly immediate family present, rather than a Hazeldene-style 'shindig.' The boys were happy for them, of course and Steve couldn't help feeling envious.

A feeling intensified by the letters that lay on his desk behind him, received that day, one from Kate, the other from Vicky.

Graham glanced at his watch, then went back to his desk and sat down. The squadron reports were nearly written up. He'd complete the job before the customary afternoon cross-country through the woods with several of the lads – an entirely safe activity now, insofar as regular and abundant food supplies obviated the need for hunting. This was good, because game had been getting scarce, with the inevitable straining of otherwise cordial relations with the local villagers.

Steve read again the letters from Kate and Vicky.

Kate's letter at least clarified why she had repeatedly fobbed him off every time he'd written proposing marriage. Her evasiveness was the reason why Steve had passed up opportunities for leave, until the brigadier was on the verge of ordering him to go home. He didn't want to set foot in Blighty without an assurance from Kate that she intended to become Mrs Steve Graham.

But that was never going to be.

Steve was still reeling from the blow, softened considerably though it was by the intriguing contents of Vicky's letter.

Dear Steve, Kate's letter read. *Vicky will explain about the investigation and she believes it will soon be successfully completed. It is vital you get there on being demobbed and Vicky's going to pull a few strings to help that along. She's marvellous at that, as you know.*

However, I won't be there.

The words had hit Steve like a punch to the solar plexus, though they explained why the letter was postmarked Paris.

Some things have happened that Vicky will explain but I and the rest of the surveillance team have been moved to safe addresses – mine being abroad as you'll see from the postmark.

One thing I must tell you, though and I pray you'll forgive me for never having mentioned it until now. I have met again an officer whom I first knew as Guillaume. He is in fact Major Peter Waverly, leader of the Jed team that Von Hollstein infiltrated.

Though Peter and I were together for only a short time during that mission, we formed a bond that endured even though Peter thought I had died in the massacre at the church and I lost track of him for many months.

We wrote to each other over the past few weeks and now that we are reunited, we find that the bond between us is stronger than ever. Dear Steve, you were such a wonderful friend and support for all those months that I earnestly hope and pray you can understand and, as I've said, find it in your heart to forgive me for not telling you everything until now.

I do pray also that our Heavenly Father will strengthen you for your part in rounding off the investigation and assure you of His best for you.

Your sister in Christ,

Kate Bramble

Steve sat back, took a couple of deep breaths and re-read Vicky's letter.

It contained details of both his occupation and accommodation in the White Peak district of Derbyshire. Kate was right. Vicky Leonard was a string-puller *par excellence*.

Steve's eyes were drawn again to the concluding paragraphs of Vicky's letter.

However it progresses, this operation is a peculiar one, in no way run-of-the-mill counter espionage. In a very real sense, it needs to be accomplished by what St Peter referred to as 'a peculiar people,' 1 Peter 2:9. You are certainly one of them. I enclose photos of someone who will be there with you. She is Nursing Officer Colleen McGrath, QAIMNS/R, originally from Teesside and with similar beliefs to yours. I met her while she was stationed in Comilla, where I informed her about you.

Colleen will be serving at a local army hospital. I trust you can be a support and encouragement to each other and I look forward to seeing both of you soon.

There followed a thumbnail sketch of Sister McGrath's war service. It was impressive. Steve read it again.

Vicky had left the most startling disclosure until last.

It happens that Colleen was friendly with a certain Major Peter Waverly, SOE, of whom Kate will no doubt inform you. However, circumstances have changed, as Kate will also explain. I enclose Colleen's contact details. You may wish to write and break the ice, so to speak.

Yours in the Lord Jesus Christ, 2 Chronicles 14:11*

Vicky Leonard, Squadron Officer, WAAF

*And Asa cried unto the LORD his God, and said, LORD, it is nothing with thee to help, whether with many, or with them that have no power: help us, O LORD our God; for we rest on thee, and in thy name we go against this multitude. O LORD, thou art our God; let not man prevail against thee.

Steve smiled.

Vicky always ended her letters with that Text. It was a good one.

Steve glanced at the address Vicky had included and took another long look at the photographs of the beautiful QA in walking-out uniform.

The state of his heart notwithstanding, he quietly whistled again.

The phone at his elbow rang stridently.

He picked up the receiver.

"Graham," he said and paused to listen. It was the brigadier, asking about the reports.

"I'll get them to the orderly room first thing tomorrow, sir," Steve told him. "They'll be on your desk typed by thirteen hundred hours."

The officer rang off, evidently satisfied.

Steve placed his elbows on the desk and rested his chin on his hands

"You sure have a way of doing things, Father," he said. Glancing down at the photos, he added, "Well, Colleen McGrath, it seems like we each have a broken heart to mend. Hope we do a good job on each other."

A Text came to mind, one that Tubby had often referred to.

This is the way, walk ye in it[315].

To explain what led up to the letters that Colleen and Steve received, we must backtrack a little, before describing the rapid culmination of sinister events that had been in preparation for several months.

Twenty-Three

Power of Darkness

This is your hour and the power of darkness Luke 22:53

Author's Note: Owing to the sensitive nature of what Squadron Officer (n) Leonard termed a 'Combined Operation,' many details must remain classified until the year 2046, i.e. for the statutory interval of one hundred years. For this reason, locations of events described in this and subsequent chapters and the industrial connection can only be given in outline. Moreover, 'Waverly Manor' and 'Deepvale House' are pseudonyms. Deepvale, the psychiatric hospital where Grandma Colleen served in 1946, has long since reverted to private ownership.

It should also be noted that some conversations and musings described are interpolations. However, they are consistent with events as Grandma Colleen and her friends managed to piece things together afterwards.

So far as we are aware, the plotters never knew explicitly of Grandma's brushes with death in the Far East.

Then, as now, the Great Enemy often acts independently of his underlings.

Sheffield, October 1945.

"Blasted rain," muttered Wilfred Houghton. "And blasted woman."
The portly executive stood in the front portico of a two-storey town house, hunched his shoulders against the rain and unfurled his umbrella.

He strode quickly down the balustraded steps to his late-model Bentley parked by the kerb.

Houghton opened the driver's door, collapsed his umbrella, slung it on the back seat and hurriedly positioned himself behind the steering wheel. He started the ignition, switched on the headlights and pulled out into the carriageway.

He was still fuming at Rita, or Rhiannon[316], as she preferred to call herself these days but reckoned nevertheless that his ultimatum would make her see sense.

"Let her stew for a couple of days," Wilfred growled, as he braked to a stop at the first set of traffic lights. "She won't want to pass up her ticket to the good life."

The windscreen wipers kept up their whirring swish, sweeping away the persistent rush of rain.

The lights changed and the high-powered vehicle sped forward. Despite the storm, the car's headlights and the streetlamps gave excellent visibility. Houghton was glad of that. Driving with dimmed lights during the blackout had been a nightmare. So easy to knock a pedestrian for six.

Leaving the city environs, he took the westward route into the Peak. This road was unlit but Houghton knew it well and the Bentley's powerful beams gave more than enough illumination. Its driver listened contentedly to the purring of the car's mighty engine. Wilfred enjoyed power, and wealth. He had plenty of both, thanks to his business enterprises. He'd done well for himself, before and during the war. Now he was doing even better, as industry geared for a post-war boom.

Disappointing though, Houghton reflected, not having Rita to spend the weekend with at the farmhouse but so what? He was a man of means and could easily find alternative female company.

But he was forced to admit Rita had made the last two years an adventure. He chuckled at the memory of his first encounter at a civic reception with this intensely emotional woman with raven black hair, piercing blue eyes and slinky figure. She'd virtually swept him off his feet. Not that he'd had any conscience about it. Things had pretty well crumbled with Judith, who was forever moaning about missing the West End. God, hadn't the woman realised there'd been a war on? He supposed he had not been much of a father, always away while the kids had been growing up but he paid for the best schools and the financial settlement at least kept his ex quiet.

Houghton dropped a gear and steadily ascended a rise, beneath the shadow of a prominent crag. The rain was easing and a pale moon was edging out from behind parting cloud.

Rita – or Rhiannon – had become good for business, too. Not only could she turn on the charm for prospective clients but her advice on seeking guidance for difficult decisions, although bizarre, had also paid handsome dividends.

He thought back to that memorable evening, a couple of months ago, when he'd been worried sick about a forthcoming venture.

"Why don't you consult a medium, darling?" Rita had said, sidling up to him in that silky nightdress and proffering a glass of wine. "I'll arrange it."

He had[317] and it worked splendidly.

Though it seemed strange that a former senior nurse would have been involved in that sort of thing. It was side to her of which he still knew little and lately, this particular eccentricity had become a nuisance.

The Bentley crested the rise and Houghton followed the ridge road as it wound serpent-like toward the valley below. He took the twists and turns with ease. His car's handling characteristics were superb.

Wilfred could not fathom why Rita wanted to get in deeper – and use his money to do it. Strange lot, too, some of her acquaintances in the weird enterprise; the tall fellow Rita introduced as "Count Franz" and his heavyset accomplice, Jozef. They claimed to be Poles.

"More like Krauts," Houghton muttered, not for the first time.

Along with them came a suspicious-looking Slav and a big, stone-faced individual who was evidently a man of the cloth. Then, to cap it all, a Gorbals ruffian turned up with a scrawny Indian who looked positively demented.

The six were a mixed group, to say the least.

Rita described the foreigners as "friends from overseas," as if there weren't enough of them in the country already.

The road flattened out toward a stretch of sycamore trees, interspersed with thickets, where the ground sloped up to the ridgeline. On the other side of the road, a steep drop fell away for two hundred feet or more.

The Bentley cruised along.

Wilfred idly switched on the car radio. He thought over Rita's repeated badgering for ready cash to support her entourage. That was how the argument had started.

"But, darling," she'd said. "You've gained so much from those consultations, surely you can plough a bit back in?"

"Not the amount *you're* asking," he'd rejoined irritably. "Either you put a sock in it or we are through, you understand?"

In the end, he had lost his temper and stormed out, leaving her spiteful and in tears, though he still reckoned they'd kiss and make up on Monday.

They wouldn't.

As the Bentley approached the line of trees, its engine spluttered and stalled. At the same time, the headlights inexplicably went out. So did the car radio.

"What the deuce?" the businessman said in exasperation.

Applying the brakes, he steered the car to a halt by the sycamores. Everything here was in shadow, the moonlight largely obscured by the ridge above.

Houghton tried to restart the engine. Nothing happened.

"Blast," he muttered and went to open the driver's door.

Suddenly he glimpsed something huge lurching out of the dark from the trees.

And two points of glowing red.

Like eyes.

His shriek of terror was cut short as the windscreen shattered and razor-sharp talons dug savagely into his throat.

Gargantuan shoves then sent the Bentley somersaulting across the road and down the cliff side. It smashed into the bottom of the ravine and exploded in flames, the driver already dead at the wheel.

Some time later, the phone rang in the town house.

517

A tall woman wearing an expensive nightgown put down her hairbrush, laid aside her cigarette and picked up the receiver.

At the sound of a man's voice, her lips curved into a malevolent smile.

"So it's done? Splendid," she said. "Oh, yes, I shall be seeing you very soon, now that the hindrance is removed. Thank you, Franz, darling."

She put the phone down and stared at herself in a full-length mirror.

"Queen Rhiannon," she declared in exultation. "High priestess of the dark powers that *I* may call forth."

Raising her masses of jet-black hair with both hands, Rita threw back her head and laughed.

The police verdict was death by accident.

The victim's immediate family reacted with understandable distress, though their grief turned to anger at the disclosure of the deceased's will.

Rita sat through the reading in black mourning attire with well-affected red-rimmed eyes and tear-stained cheeks. The abundant provision she received resulted in several months of bitter wrangling in the courts.

"That hussy won't get a penny out of us," Judith Houghton vowed.

But the terms of the will, modified by Houghton after taking up with Rita, stood nevertheless.

They enabled Rita to increase her directorships' share of Wilfred's companies – something that her fellow directors entirely favoured, in view of Rita's acknowledged acumen.

Her medium associates were still doing good business.

April 1946, a town in the White Peak.

It was a mild Sunday afternoon and the trees that overhung the walkway by the river were abundantly green with new growth.

After the morning service in the nonconformist chapel, a trio of worshippers wandered along the river path. One was a sinewy young man in a grey demob suit. With him strolled his wife, a slim lass with fair hair, in the early stages of motherhood.

Beside her walked another young woman, in a dark blue suit, with net veil attached to the brim of her hat, covering part of her face. She wore spectacles but they could not conceal her striking good looks.

"Say when you want a rest, love," said ex-Fusilier Brian Briggs. He gently held Mollie's hand.

"I'm OK, sweetheart," she said reassuringly. "So what's the latest, Kate?" she asked the third member of the trio.

They usually got together after church to review developments, then ate Sunday lunch at Kate's flat, or Brian and Mollie's. This provided further opportunity to consider the week ahead.

"Well, Vicky's confirmed that Rita has come into a considerable amount of cash," said Kate. "The court ruled in her favour and she received a sizable chunk of her late boyfriend's estate."

"That explains the flashy motor," said Brian.

Briggs was referring to Rita's brand new sports car, occasionally seen parked outside Von Hollstein's neat stone cottage. He resided there under the name of Clive Beresford. In this guise, he had recently been promoted to head of Finance at the nearby quarry site where Brian was a works clerk and Mollie served in the canteen.

"Certainly does," said Kate. "She's a good businesswoman, too, according to Vicky's note. Apparently, Wilfred introduced her to his fellow directors and she soon won them over."

They had first noticed Rita in the company of the late Wilfred socialising with Beresford-Von Hollstein at a local festival early last autumn. That event was one of the few occasions when Albrecht was seen associating with his chief. Vicky had identified Houghton from the registration number of his Bentley and in turn Rita, an ex-nurse and now a 'kept woman.'

The walkers paused to glance back at the sturdy stone bridge over the river, with its five arches and the townscape ascending beyond, dominated by the spire of the parish church.

"I love this view," said Mollie.

"Do you think Houghton's death really was an accident?" she asked as they proceeded on.

"Unlikely," said Kate. "But I'm sure the official verdict will stand. No doubt Rita's newly-acquired wealth will finance Beresford and Ainsley's enterprise in some way. It's annoying we still don't know exactly what it is."

Joe Ainsley was Albrecht's current alias. He, too, worked at the quarry, as an earthmover operator.

Kate and her friends always used the aliases in conversation as a precaution.

"He puts on a good London accent," Mollie had informed the others after she'd spoken with Albrecht the first time he appeared in the lunch queue. "Whoever trained him did a good job. He even looks jolly."

Though Ainsley didn't pass for a local man, he nevertheless fitted in because the quarry workers came from all parts of the country, with a fair-sized overseas contingent, even Germans and Austrians. The site was huge. Besides the quarry operations, it incorporated a cement works, stone size-reduction plant and a power station. Its labour force numbered in the hundreds and the canteen had to provide for staggered meal and break times.

Montague-Stewart's influence was no doubt instrumental in establishing the Nazi pair in their new identities. With Steadman's help, Vicky continued to have him shadowed. Despite his extensive travels that included visits to a number of senior politicians and civil servants – itself a matter of concern – St John had fortunately not ventured near the Peak town. Neither had Miko, but he was known to be working as a labourer less than an hour's drive away, so Vicky kept him shadowed as well.

But she reasoned the pair would not threaten the surveillance directly, while they kept apart from their Nazi accomplices.

"We believe St John will pursue his vendetta against Bronwyn's group independently – and take his time," Vicky had told the team. "'Not too much zeal,' that's his motto."

Nevertheless, if St John or Miko openly joined forces with Von Hollstein and Albrecht, Vicky stipulated that Kate and her friends must depart immediately for safe locations, according to a pre-arranged plan.

"We'll get to the bottom of it, Kate," Brian reassured her. "I managed to check out the old change room on Friday," he added, with a nodded greeting to a couple going past in the opposite direction.

The women looked at him expectantly.

"Still bare floors and rafters, apart from the benches and clothes hooks," said Briggs. "But our pair have cleaned the place up. Everything swept and scrubbed."

They came to a riverside seat, set under a willow's drooping fronds. Sitting down, they watched the water bubbling over a weir, sparkling in the spring sunshine.

"The firm's not about to re-open that section of the quarry, though?" Kate asked.

"Not that I know of," said Brian, shaking his head. "Place is overgrown, gorse and hawthorn everywhere. There are a few other buildings round about, empty storage huts and so on, plus some derelict gear; windlasses and whatnot from the open-cut operations but they closed down pre-war."

"And it borders on the Waverly estate?" Mollie asked. She raised a hand to shade her eyes from the sun.

Brian had said that with her fair skin, Mollie ought to wear a hat in the sun but she reckoned that "I wore hats at school and all through the war, including tin ones. I'll put up with a headscarf at church but that's all."

The war had definitely changed things.

"It does," said Brian. "The quarry area's still fenced off with padlocked gates where the access road dead-ends though anyone with a bit of nous[318] could pick the lock. The road forms part of the perimeter of the estate and there's a rough track near the gates that goes up the hillside onto Waverly's land proper."

"Are we any further on in finding out if his lordship forced that part of the site to close?" Mollie asked.

"'Fraid not, love," said Brian. He leant back against the crossbeams of the seat and rested his arm lightly around Mollie's shoulders. "Blokes reckon Waverly senior slipped the bosses a few backhanders[319] but that's as much as anyone knows. Strange, really. The direction of operations would only have taken in some of his waste ground and he'd have done OK from the rent."

"And the track's not used?" asked Kate. Crossing her legs, she rested her handbag on her knee.

"Not these days," said Brian. "Old man Waverly used to discourage hikers pre-war. His groundsmen had orders to warn them about trespass if they saw any and folk don't bother with the track now. That's what the blokes on site tell me. The track's actually got a branch down into the quarry. I saw that too."

Kate removed her spectacles and hat. She hated wearing them and had resented cutting and tinting her hair as well but these measures were necessary, to minimise the risk of either Von Hollstein or Albrecht recognising her.

However, Kate sensed her cover was beginning to wear thin, a state of mind not helped by the proximity of her flat to Von Hollstein's residence.

Of course, it had been deliberately chosen for its position. All credit for Kate's accommodation and Brian and Mollie's, together with their respective occupations, went to Vicky's astonishingly versatile manipulative skills, "along with Divine Intervention and various other friends," as she put it.

One of these was Vicky's fiancé, Group Captain Tom Freeman, DSO, DFC and Bar, RAF station commander where Vicky was based, an hour's drive away in Lincolnshire. Freeman had provided both Vicky and Kate with their own transport, a pair of ex-RAF Morris Eights, re-sprayed in civilian colours.

Since Kate's place of work was within walking distance, she had transferred ownership of her vehicle to Brian and Mollie, who in turn rented a garage in the lane at the rear of their flat.

"I'll pretend I don't know about it," said Tom, when Vicky informed him.

Freeman also arranged Vicky's duties so that she could visit Kate and the others at regular intervals.

Kate's flat was part of a row of semi-detached dwellings in an avenue off the high street. From her sitting room window, an observer could see everyone that went to and from Beresford's twin-gabled cottage. His house stood on a road running parallel with the high street and almost exactly opposite the intersection of the road with Kate's avenue.

Brian and Mollie were renting an upstairs flat on the other side of the road where Beresford's cottage was situated and only a short distance from it. Their flat likewise afforded an excellent view of the entrance to the subversive's house.

Albrecht lived in another part of town. His movements were also monitored but not continuously, because Vicky and Kate reasoned that all lines of investigation met in Von Hollstein.

"Keep watch on him and we keep tabs on all his accomplices," Vicky said in sum. Prompt observance of Rita's visits – beginning soon after Houghton's demise - had vindicated this supposition. "She's going to be more than just a kept woman," Vicky surmised.

After many hours of discrete monitoring spread over several months, Vicky, Kate, Brian and Mollie had built up a comprehensive picture of Von Hollstein's provincial existence.

He rode to hounds, played cricket, attended garden fetes, parish functions and invitation-only balls, even some staged at Waverly Manor.

Kate and Mollie knew this because they often voluntarily helped with the catering, thus making themselves known to Lord Waverly senior and Miss Heythorpe, Peter's former governess.

The count had clearly gleaned a considerable amount of useful local knowledge from his association with Peter and Waverly's continued absence gave Von Hollstein an added advantage that he exploited to the full.

Concerning Albrecht, Mollie deduced from her canteen observations that he was now "one of the lads."

Brian confirmed his wife's verdict. He audaciously belonged to the same football club as Albrecht and occasionally dropped in unobtrusively at the local where 'Jolly Joe' and his mates went drinking.

Albrecht never darkened the door of a church but Von Hollstein put in enough appearances at the parish church to ensure respectability with his social set. The three watchers had sometimes seen him emerge from the building after the services when they walked that way. Parish services conveniently ended about half an hour after their nonconformist equivalents.

So far, except for Mollie's canteen vigils, most of the team's efforts had focussed on the conspirators' activities during out-of-work hours and to date, allowing for the pair's settling–in phase, nothing apart from Rita's renewed appearance seemed out of the ordinary.

Something that Kate found frustrating.

But Brian's responsibilities took him to most parts of the site, whereby a couple of weeks back he had noticed Von Hollstein and Albrecht surreptitiously entering the disused area late one afternoon.

His follow-up visit now revealed that the two were preparing the long-abandoned change facility for something.

Very likely it had to do with the nearby part of Lord Waverly's land.

What though, Kate wondered, as she gazed at some white ducks paddling sedately in the shallows by the riverbank. The question vexed her more than the risk of disclosure, one that her friends valiantly agreed to continue sharing. That risk, however, told Kate that it was time for decisive action.

"I think Vicky and I should have a look around the disused area," she said. "And that bit of the Waverly estate, after dark so we don't bump into any groundsmen," she added, smiling. "Vicky's caught up in a joint service exercise right now but I'll get her to come over after that."

"OK," said Brian, "Though it seems nothing's there except bare rocks, gorse and clumps of birch."

"Well, if we have to, Vicky and I will take a couple of spades and see what's underneath them," said Kate, with a grin.

She replaced her spectacles and hat, stood up and lightly brushed the back of her skirt.

"You are coming to my place, seeing it's my turn?" she said to her friends. "I got a good joint from the butcher's yesterday."

"You're on, Kate," said her friends in unison. Brian quickly got to his feet and gently assisted Mollie to stand.

They took a side road back towards the town centre, past dignified, slate-roofed stone houses to where the memorial for local men fallen in the First War stood flanked by large tubs of spring flowers. It was located opposite the town's main hotel with its white front porch.

Kate was glad of the colour contrast the flowers and the hotel porch provided. Like Brian and Mollie, she loved the town, its beautiful surroundings and the warm-hearted folk of the Peak. But even in the sun, the buildings still looked uniformly sombre, grey or grey-brown, tinged with sooty black.

She missed the thatched wattle-and-daub[320] houses of the south where she'd grown up.

"Shall we cross here?" suggested Briggs. He paused at the edge of the cobbled-lined thoroughfare and took his wife's arm.

"Let's do," said Mollie.

Once over the high street, it was a short walk to Kate's flat. Heading towards it, past trim shop fronts with their awnings rolled up, Kate thought on her main worldly pre-occupations besides the long-drawn-out investigation.

The letters she and Steve exchanged and, more recently, the ones between her and Peter.

She knew she was being unfair to Steve. Whenever he raised the subject of marriage, she glossed over it in her reply. The evasion couldn't go on. She would have to write soon and tell him about Peter.

She *had* to meet Peter, to confirm, face-to-face, what she felt in her heart, regardless of how it defied logic.

Because Peter's first letter still quickened her pulse, whenever she thought on the words.

Dear Kate,

I was overjoyed when Vicky told me that you are alive. I have <u>*never*</u> *stopped thinking about you and indeed hoping against hope, even though we were together for only a short time - under extremely trying circumstances. Vicky gave me a copy of your photograph and I hope you will believe me when I say that you are exactly as I always imagined you.*

I am looking forward so much to meeting you again and hope and pray that you feel the same. I also hope you will feel free to write to me.

Yours sincerely,

Peter Waverly

Their letters had been going back and forth regularly since then, at least twice as many to each other as those that passed between her and Steve.

Moreover, Kate knew about Colleen and her friendship with Peter. She intended to write to Colleen, as soon as God gave her the words but the situation was delicate because by an astounding stroke of coincidence, Colleen was a friend of Brian and Mollie's. They'd served in Italy together and Colleen often wrote to Mollie.

"Amazing that Colleen's friends with Major Waverly," Mollie had once said to Kate, who responded with a tactful smile.

She unlocked the street door to her flat and ushered her companions into the narrow hall-way, permeated by the cooking aroma emanating from the downstairs flat.

"I've got our key handy," said Brian. He unlocked the inner door that led to a carpeted stairway. They each had keys to both of their respective dwellings.

"Can I use the bathroom first, please?" Mollie whispered.

"Of course you can," said Kate. "You and I'll get started with the cooking, Brian."

"As you say, ma'am," he said courteously, holding open the door. "After you, ladies."

Ascending the stairs, Kate recalled her first written words to Peter. They meant even more to her now.

Dear Peter,

You too have always been in my thoughts and I thank God we have become re-acquainted in this way.

Please write as often as you can. I so much want to see you again.

I know there are difficulties and I pray earnestly our Heavenly Father will take care of them in His wisdom.

Brian took Mollie's coat as she made for the bathroom. Removing his, he handed them both to Kate who hung them up in the coat cupboard on the landing, together with her own.

Kate's mind went back to Colleen McGrath and Steve. She prayed again, please, Father, sort us all out.

He would.

That evening, Rita's sports car drew up outside Beresford's cottage. Kate watched the tall figure with its familiar flowing hair padlock the steering wheel and gear stick, then hurry indoors.

"She's visiting more often," Mollie whispered over Kate's shoulder.

"She is," said Kate. "Something's about to happen."

Again, Kate felt apprehensive, as she had during the river walk.

She suspected Beresford had noticed her. At a recent fete, while helping as usual with the refreshments, she had seen him looking in her direction a little too often.

And not as though he was ogling her, though most of the men did – and she repeatedly had to make reference to "my bloke overseas, who'll be back home soon," when they tried to chat her up.

No, it looked more like Beresford was studying her.

He'd doubtless have done some checking on her, too.

It was worrying.

Von Hollstein and Rita embraced fiercely. When their lips parted, those of the priestess assumed a wicked smile.

"I must exercise my powers again, darling?" she asked.

Demonic passion blazed in her eyes.

"Yes. I think there's an interloper on our patch," Franz explained. "Someone I thought was dead but I think she's here."

Rita stared at him.

"She?" she asked curtly.

Von Hollstein laughed.

"Not jealous, are you, darling?" he asked. He slid his hands to the curve of her hips. She rested her head on his shoulder.

"Hardly, Franz. But what makes you think so?"

"I've seen her at a few functions, helping with the tea and buns. I didn't mind her at first. She seemed an ordinary English girl but now I'm fairly sure she's the Resistance bitch I told you about. She's changed her hair and has different clothes, of course and she wears specs that are probably fake, but I reckon it's her. What's more, she lives just down the avenue."

"Watching you, planning revenge?"

"Maybe."

"How exciting."

Rita began unbuttoning Beresford's shirt.

"You were careless, darling," she purred, placing an admonitory finger against Von Hollstein's lips. "You should have put a bullet or two through her head, or slit her pretty little throat."

"I humbly concur. But you can take care of my outstanding needs?"

"All of them, darling."

"Excellent."

They ambled towards the stairs.

Several days later, events took a sinister turn for the surveillance team.

Vicky promptly sent telegrams to the Briggses and Kate.

Miko headed your way, they read. *Decamp as planned.*

The Slav, whose alias was Radoslav Novak, had been tailed to the Peak town and observed acquiring lodgings near Joe Ainsley's digs[321].

He also had a job arranged for him as a caretaker at the local hospital. St John again, Vicky mused when she dispatched the telegrams. The hospital was some distance from the rehabilitation centre where Colleen would be based but Miko's choice of occupation worried her.

"Please, Father, help Steve protect Colleen," she prayed, knowing that Colleen could not be deterred from relocating.

But the enemy had more in store than Miko's move, though it wasn't immediately obvious.

Because in the interval between Rita's visit and Vicky's warning, Beresford and Ainsley seemed to be going about their daily routine as normal. Kate began to feel less on edge.

So she decided to follow up Brian's observations concerning the disused quarry site.

And to elucidate, if possible, the significance of its proximity to Lord Waverly's land, before contacting Vicky about a night patrol.

She felt sure that her friend, Miss Heythorpe, could enlighten her.

Kate therefore asked her superior if Lord Waverly might be approached about developing the catalogue for his own library. The manor housed a large collection of books, many of them rare.

His lordship agreed and Kate's superior happily assigned her the task.

Kate was extremely grateful to Vicky for arranging the crash course in librarianship so that she could assume her new role with competence. Her original training notwithstanding, it would have made her too conspicuous to take on a veterinary job. She had been using that occupation as cover when Von Hollstein captured her.

But the two disciplines overlapped considerably when it came to filing and accurate record keeping, so that the senior librarian was highly impressed with Kate's work.

"Play your cards right and Lord Waverly might even become our patron," she remarked enthusiastically.

In the mornings, Brian and Mollie drove Kate to a stonework bridge that spanned a stream on the edge of the estate and picked her up at the same spot in the evening. It was only about twenty minutes' walk from there to the manor, past luxuriantly green, tree-lined meadows on one side and picturesque woodland on the other, burgeoning in leaf at this time of year, the forest floor richly yellow with daffodils.

Kate enjoyed the walk in the fine weather. The morning and afternoon sunlight brought out the natural beauty of the landscape in delicately different hues.

"Door-to-door service if it's tankin' it down, though," Brian had promised.

Kate would have walked the distance in any weather. It was Peter's place.

And because she was going to Peter's home, she wore not the usual workaday attire but her best outfits, including her Sunday suit, though she dispensed with the hat - and the spectacles for the duration of the walk.

The turreted stone walls and sturdy battlements of the Waverly residence could be seen from the bridge, atop the crest of a rise that sloped gently down on the far side, encompassing wide lawns, expertly laid out garden beds, bubbling fountains and gravel walkways.

Beyond the cultivated area, the manor grounds took in undulating pasture land and woods; thick with birch, oak, larch, beech and elm, stretching to the disused quarry and sweeping back to the approach road from the bridge.

Along which Kate was walking, after Brian and Mollie had dropped her off on the morning that Vicky sent the telegrams.

The weather was continuing mild and sunny but Kate felt renewed tension.

As if she was being watched.

And she was alarmingly aware of the silence. No birds sang; no insects hummed. It was odd, distinctly odd.

Yet, the smiling Mrs Heythorpe greeted her at the front parlour as always and the governess's amiability quickly put Kate at ease.

"Tea's waiting on the patio, dear," she said affectionately and conducted Kate through open French windows to where a laden tray was set out on the gloss-painted garden table.

"Thank you, Aunt Hen," said Kate, smiling in return. They seated themselves at the table.

Kate had been working on the catalogue for the best part of a week and adored the experience – she saw it as looking after Peter's things. And she loved walking through the noble old building, with its oaken-panelled walls, sturdily beamed high ceilings, quaintly carved furniture, historic portraits, polished suits of armour, big stone fireplaces and venerable artefacts.

The library was well-lit, with full-length windows displaying a grand view of the grounds. The multiple shelves needed the customary ladders on rails to reach the top tiers and Kate realised the work would go on for some time.

Like the grounds, the manor captivated her because it was Peter's place. Miss Heythorpe had pointed out to her a portrait of the younger Lord Waverly, in uniform.

"That's Master Peter," she'd said proudly, with a wave of her arm. "After he came back from North Africa."

Kate wished she could have hung the portrait over her mantlepiece.

She also wished she could get to know Lord Waverly senior better. He was tall, grey-haired and distinctly aristocratic in his bearing. Wearing riding habit, with tweed coat and jodhpurs, he greeted her cordially on her first day, with a generous offer:

"Well, young lady, you've a job ahead of you, all right. And, yes, I'm only too happy to take up the library patronage."

But apart from the initial introduction, Kate had rarely seen him. He generally kept to his study if not out on the estate and even had his midday meal separate from Kate and Miss Heythorpe, who lunched together.

And he seemed to have a haunted look. Kate hoped that perhaps Miss Heythorpe would enlighten her in this respect as well. She had immediately been drawn to the aging governess, a cousin of his lordship, tall, like him, slightly stooped, with hair fading to white and kindly blue eyes. Henrietta Rebecca Heythorpe, or *HRH*[322] as Peter described her in one of his letters, was an aristocrat through and through.

Invariably affable, she'd said, "Call me Aunt Hen" to Kate and Mollie on first meeting them.

"Try one of these flapjacks, my dear," said Miss Heythorpe, glancing at the plate of brown oatmeal biscuits as she poured the tea. "Cook baked them yesterday. Ghastly name. So dreadfully common, I think it must be American but they are delicious."

Kate took one of the biscuits. Biting off a small piece, she had to agree but she refrained from informing Henrietta that Americans used the term to describe pancakes. At least, the ones she'd met during the war.

After a few minutes of casual conversation, one flapjack and several sips of tea, Kate broached the subject of the quarry site. She had deliberately waited until she judged that Henrietta trusted her.

"Mollie's husband Brian heard that his lordship had a bit of trouble with the quarry owners a few years back. Was that true?"

Miss Heythorpe's face stiffened into a frown. The unexpected change in the older woman's demeanour was startling.

Henrietta put down her cup and stared at the tabletop.

"I don't know all there is to know, Kate," she said, looking up anxiously. "But I believe I can trust you because you know the Saviour. You mustn't share what I'm about to tell you with anyone you wouldn't trust with your life. I mean that."

Kate replaced her teacup in its saucer. Gently, she clasped Henrietta's hand.

"You have my word, Aunt Hen."

The other woman nodded gratefully. She sat back as Kate released her hand and recounted a grim episode from the past.

"It was just after the Great War. Peter, his lordship that is, was still recovering his strength – he'd been gassed in France, you see. Young Peter was scarcely a toddler and her ladyship's health was not good. She died the following year – I'll come to that. To make matters worse, the estate was badly run-down. Then one day, a young chap I'd never seen before paid Peter a visit. Said he was from a religious order, though I never found out which one. He was in mufti, as they say. Powerfully built fellow, big, face like granite."

Kate reckoned she could hazard a guess which order. And who the visitor was.

She poured Henrietta another cup of tea. Although Miss Heythorpe did not take sugar, Kate tipped a spoonful into the liquid and stirred it before passing the cup to the governess.

"What did he want?" she asked.

Aunt Hen drank a mouthful of the sweetened concoction and murmured, "Thank you, dear.

"His order would see to all the estate's debts, the man promised," she explained. "If only they could use one of the remote corners of the grounds, for some of their rituals, a few times a year. He even showed Peter the place on a map, close to the quarry site but before those operations had started that are closed down now."

She paused, drank more tea and spoke again.

"Well, Peter agreed because that land was virtually waste and his benefactor kept his promise. Things *did* improve, until several months later, when one of our gamekeepers came to see Peter, looking white as a sheet. He'd been out checking snares, had seen a fire in the waste sector and gone to investigate."

The governess paused again. Kate saw Hen was almost trembling and squeezed her hand again.

"I gather the gamekeeper saw something pretty horrific?"

"I won't go into details," said Henrietta with a shudder. "But Peter somehow contacted the visitor and had it out with him, said he wanted them off his land, that he would have nothing more to do with them and that he'd give them back every penny, no matter what it cost him."

"But it wasn't that easy?"

Aunt Hen took another deep breath and finished her tea.

"It wasn't," she said vehemently. "That fiend laughed in Peter's face, so he told me afterwards. And threatened him. *And* made the threats good, too. First, the gamekeeper who'd broken the news died in an accident, supposedly. Then her ladyship suffered a strange relapse – she'd been on the mend, you see – and passed away. And they sent a note to Peter on the very day of his wife's funeral saying that he ought to look out for his son and heir."

Swine, thought Kate, grimacing. She was almost trembling herself, with rage. But V-H's lot must be the next generation now, she reasoned, with St John as the go-between. Allowing for the fact that Montague-Stewart was in his fifties, Aunt Hen's description fitted him.

"And part of that responsibility was to keep people away from the area?" Kate asked.

Henrietta began assembling the used crockery on the tray.

"Yes. Peter and I spoke to old Reverend Temple, our vicar at the time. The reverend advised that from what he knew of such groups, if the area in question was kept sacrosanct, so to speak, we wouldn't be bothered. 'They can be ruthless but they don't like risking publicity,' he said. And we agreed it posed too great a danger for young Peter if we went to the authorities, who would probably be powerless to help anyway."

"Or even in the order's pay?"

"That's what the reverend said, too. A most understanding man, went home to Glory just before the war, a great blow to all of us but he was ninety-seven. However, it turned out as he said, mostly."

Kate brushed a few crumbs off her lap. Aunt Hen was OK about that. "It'll feed the birds," she would say.

"The only problems arising when the quarry wanted to expand its operation and hiking became more popular around here after the Depression?" Kate suggested.

"That's right. But God has been merciful to us, Kate. Peter did manage to keep things quiet. Young Peter grew up a splendid lad, went to Oxford and came safe through the war, thank God. We never told him about this, you understand. We thought that best. But I believe he's friendly with a nursing Sister now. She'll doubtless brighten the place up if she comes to live here."

"I'm sure," murmured Kate, forcing a smile. "The estate must have improved, too, since those days?"

"It *has*," said Henrietta eagerly. "Peter's an honourable man and our Heavenly Father was kind to him. Gave him ideas on improving things. He refused to take any more money from the order and as soon as he could afford it, without going back into debt, he repaid them every penny. It's taken a toll on him, though."

Kate nodded, still enraged but concealing her feelings.

"Is the order still active around here?"

"Not so much during the war. However, I feel they're still watching us and I fear there's new evil arising."

She fell silent. Kate took off her spectacles and polished them with the hem of her skirt, gazing out over the lawns and gardens that looked so peaceful in the spring sunshine.

Then she heard Henrietta speak again and noted the other woman was looking at her with quiet assurance. Kate replaced her spectacles and smiled in return.

"But I think there's new hope for us, too," said Aunt Hen. "Shall we pray?"

They always finished teatime this way, having shared their faith with each other on the first day.

Reverently, they closed their eyes and bowed their heads.

From a distance, another pair of eyes remained open, focused on the two women.

The gaze was anything but reverent. Once more, the enemy was poised to strike.

In the late afternoon, Kate walked steadily down the approach road to the bridge, having finished for the day.

The sinking sun shone warmly in the west, its slanting rays silhouetting the limbs of the trees. Parts of the wood and meadowland were already in shadow.

Again, Kate felt tense. Again, everything around her was silent, apart from the clicking of her heels on the road.

The trees seemed to harbour some hidden menace. She fought down mounting fear.

Then she slowed to a halt.

Something was rustling the undergrowth, something big.

A stray cow, she wondered. Unlikely.

The thicket parted.

Kate's heart almost seized at the sight.

Then it began thumping as though it would burst.

Trembling, she stared in horror as a beast the size of a steer stalked in front of her.

Ten yards away, it halted and faced her.

It wasn't a steer, or even like one.

It wasn't any beast that Kate knew of on the face of the earth[323].

The beast's body resembled that of an outsize timber wolf. Its head and jaws were wolf-like but bigger than a lion's, with a mane of tangled locks. Shaggy hair straggled thickly down its flanks, chest and limbs, sticking out between its protruding claws.

Longer and thicker than a man's fingers, curved and pointed like eagles' talons, they rasped audibly on the road.

But what terrified Kate most were the creature's eyes.

They glowered like incandescent coals, black slits of pupils lancing into her very being.

Then – *it stood*, on its hind legs.

The huge jaws swung open, to reveal fangs that had not been manifested in quadrupeds since sabre-toothed tigers roamed the earth.

The beast threw back its massive head. From its throat issued a savage, hissing snarl.

Kate was petrified, gasping for breath, her heart and temples pounding. Cold beads of sweat broke out on her forehead.

The beast lowered its head and – *spoke*. In a guttural tone, charged with menace.

"You have defied our Master, you will die. I will tear out your living heart, even as it beats within your breast."

The beast began to take ponderous steps forward. Kate shuddered at the sound of its talons scraping the road. She felt her knees beginning to buckle.

She knew that if she tried to run, she was dead. Yet, in seconds, she would be dead anyway.

Ten yards became five, then three.

The beast raised a monstrous front paw, claws extended. Its growling breath enveloped her, hot, suffocating – and sulphurous.

"Lord Jesus Christ, save me," Kate prayed in desperation, out loud.

The response was so swift it shocked her, like suddenly waking from a nightmare.

Almost instantly, where she had been consumed with panic, she was now flooded with incredible calm. Her breath was returning to normal, her legs were sound.

The beast drew back its paw, as though repelled by an electric fence. Its glare of malevolence changed abruptly to staring fear. It backed away.

Another voice spoke to Kate, not audibly but sounding distinctly in her brain, comfortingly, commandingly.

Sister Kate, resist the devil and he will flee from you[324].

Sister Kate? No-one ever called her that. It was simply Kate, or Section Officer Bramble in the old days. Then she realised the Speaker was using His own special term of endearment for her.

Kate stood her ground.

She stared the creature in the eye, no longer fearful of those glowing coals and spoke out in a voice clear and calm.

"I am the daughter and servant of the Most High God and His Son the Lord Jesus Christ, bought at Calvary's cross by the shedding of His blood. You have no power over me. I command you in the Name of the Lord Jesus Christ to depart."

Again, the creature cringed visibly. With an anguished whimper, it sunk to all fours and scuttled back into the thicket. Kate heard it crashing through the brush.

She stumbled on down the road to the stone bridge, to where Brian and Mollie would be waiting. One hand gripped her shoulder bag. Her knuckles were white.

"'Yea, though I walk through the valley of the shadow of death, thou art with me,'" she kept repeating, tears running down her cheeks. "'Thy rod and thy staff, they comfort me.'"

The afternoon sun bathed her face in warmth.

"Here, love, drink this."

"Thanks, Mollie," said Kate in a whisper, as she gratefully accepted the hot cup of Horlicks. Mollie patted her shoulder and returned to the kitchen.

Kate was seated in an easy chair by Brian and Mollie's fireside, wrapped in a rug.

She had almost collapsed with relief at the sight of the red Morris and its occupants. Brian had quickly got out and helped her into the rear seat, where Mollie sat with her arm around Kate on the way home. They went in by the back way.

Kate described her ordeal between sobs during the drive. She also communicated the gist of her conversation with Henrietta.

"Well, we know what killed Houghton, then," said Brian in response, his face grim. "But we've got to go."

The telegrams they discovered on arriving home confirmed the decision. Brian had found Kate's when he had gone via back entrances to her flat to fetch her pre-packed suitcase. It stood next to his and Mollie's luggage on the sitting room floor.

Briggs had also posted the pre-written letters, informing their respective employers of *a sudden family emergency, necessitating an immediate departure.* The notes only needed dating before sealing and dispatch. If necessary, they would each send another letter, handing in their notices.

Kate was also determined to write to Aunt Hen as soon as possible, apologising for her abrupt disappearance.

Brian sat across from Kate, hands on his knees, eyeing her with concern.

"I turned off the water and electricity at your place," he said. "And double-checked for any perishables. There aren't any. Everything's locked."

Because the flats only had small iceboxes, Kate and Mollie shopped every other day for foodstuffs that could spoil.

"Thanks, Brian," said Kate, sipping the Horlicks. "Vicky'll see to the leases and all else."

"I guess it meant us to come looking for you and take us out as well."

"Then hide the bodies in the disused part of the quarry."

Kate held the mug of Horlicks in both hands and drank deeply.

"Plenty of nooks and crannies there for that," Brian said tersely. "Still, they reckoned without a daughter of the King, eh?"

Kate smiled and nodded.

Brian seemed like a panther ready to spring. If Von Hollstein or any of his cronies had tried to waylay Briggs, Kate knew it would have been the worse for them.

But she was overjoyed, like Mollie, at Brian's full acceptance of God's free grace, a fairly recent development, after he had re-read the Gospel accounts, the result of heartfelt prayers offered not only by Mollie, Vicky and Kate but "the whole gang," as Mollie put it; Rev Allerton, now a vicar near Huntingdon, Marian Lovejoy, Mike and June, Andy and Dollie and Colleen McGrath as well.

Plus their friends in Canada; Mac and Julie, Larry and Helen, Barry and Karen, all now settled in Banff, beneath the shadow of the Canadian Rockies.

"Anyone who went through what He did has to be the Man to follow," Brian had concluded.

Since then, Brian's testimony had been unequivocal and would be for all his days.

"Fusilier Briggs reporting for duty, Sir."

"But even if they are using Waverly's patch as a stamping ground for their rituals, it's hard to see how that's going to bring in a new Reich," said Brian, with a puzzled expression. "I've no doubt there's covens up and down the country. I know we had orders to keep away from parts of the Plain[325] at certain times of the year but the other side still lost the war."

Kate finished the Horlicks and placed the mug on a side table.

"This group must think they're special in some way," she remarked.

Brian shifted uneasily in his seat.

"They're prepared to kill, that's for sure," he said, with restrained anger.

They looked up as Mollie came back into the sitting room, her topcoat over one arm and in her other hand a shopping bag containing thermos flasks and several packets of sandwiches wrapped in greaseproof.

"All set," she said.

"OK, love," said Brian. "You ready, Kate?"

Kate nodded, unfolded the rug and stood up.

"I'll rinse this out," she said, glancing at the emptied mug.

"Let me," said Mollie. She placed her coat over her suitcase and the bag next to it. "You two can do the heavy work."

"Please, Father, give us journeying mercies," Kate prayed out loud as she picked up Mollie's case and coat.

"Amen," said her friends.

They would be needed.

A couple of hours' drive south took them to a quiet, leafy suburb on the outskirts of Leicester.

Brian parked the car outside a villa displaying a doctor's lantern and brass nameplate. He and his passengers got out and Brian opened the villa's front gate. Closing it after Kate and Mollie, he followed them to the front door.

It opened almost immediately when Brian rang the doorbell.

The girls each hugged the tall, dark-haired man, who admitted them.

"Good to see you all," he said enthusiastically, shaking Brian's hand. "They're here, June," Mike Halliard called over his shoulder.

"Good to see you, Mike," said Briggs. "Kate had a bit of an adventure before we set off."

"Oh?" said Halliard, frowning. "Well, let's get your cases in then you can tell us."

Mollie and Kate each hugged June when she appeared in the hallway.

"This way, Kate," she said and beckoned to the downstairs bathroom. "You'll probably be glad to get rid of that tint once and for all."

"Certainly will," said Kate as she doffed her coat.

"Can I have the specs as a souvenir, Kate?" Mollie asked.

"You sure can," said her friend.

Mike and June had kept themselves in readiness so that they could transfer responsibilities to colleagues at short notice.

The Halliards' involvement stemmed from Vicky's visit the previous year, while they were still serving in Austria.

"We'll do whatever we can," Mike had pledged.

Two principle factors influenced Vicky's decision on how the couple could assist.

The first was Mike's fluency in French and his considerable knowledge of France, beginning with cycling and mountaineering trips as a student pre-war and extending to his service with the BEF in 1940, prior to evacuation at Dunkirk.

The second was the noticeable physical resemblance between June and Kate.

The escape plan steadily unfolded.

Vicky rang Mike immediately after sending the telegrams to Kate and Brian.

Mike booked two tickets on the Dover ferry by phone and arranged for a locum to cover his practice. The replacement MD would bring his own nurse to cover for June.

Having left Kate at the Halliards, Brian and Mollie drove northwards the next day to family quarters near Vicky's base, arranged for them by Tom Freeman. With them went June, minus her wedding ring and wearing a set of Kate's clothes.

Less than an hour after Kate arrived at the Halliards, Mike was driving south with Kate towards Dover, to catch the midnight ferry for Le Havre, docking at zero eight-thirty hours the following morning.

When Reverend Allerton would pick up Mike's car from the secure enclosure at the dockside and drive back to Leicester.

"Always wanted to have a jaunt in your Rover, Mike," the jovial vicar remarked on learning of his part in the plan.

A train journey of several hours would convey Mike and Kate to a little country station near the Massif Central.

To meet Alain Hallé and his wife Yvette, so Kate could shelter in their remote hamlet, as she had done during the war.

With one difference.

Group Captain Freeman had contacted Major Waverly in Palestine, informing him of events when Vicky sent the telegrams. Peter was due to catch a flight home but acting promptly on Freeman's message, arranged a diversion to the south of France.

Freeman wired the Halliards with this news.

When she'd rinsed her hair, Kate was eager to depart.

"We should make it with about half an hour to spare," Mike said as he turned his Rover Saloon onto the open road. "The tickets are valid for a month, so if we are held up, we can always overnight in Dover."

"This is very good of you, Mike," said Kate sincerely. "And June. I'll always be grateful."

"Glad to help, Kate," said Halliard. "We should have a good run. Weather's OK and there's not much traffic this time of night. Shouldn't be too bad even getting through London. Fairly plain sailing once we're over the Thames and on the way to Dartford."

Mike was an expert driver and knew the route well. As they sped past darkened fields and through sleepy towns and villages, Kate began to relax again.

Despite her vow to kill Von Hollstein personally if she got the chance, she recognised the wisdom of deferring to Vicky's warning.

"If you have to decamp, we'll get you out of country, Kate. You're a key witness and Von Hollstein knows that."

Kate's hair, still damp, had resumed its natural colour. She was wearing a suit of June's and one of her hats. And a facsimile wedding ring. The elaborate deception was also Vicky's brainchild.

Only a most discerning observer would have noticed the difference, especially in the dark.

Unfortunately, one was ominously to hand.

St John Montague-Stewart exhaled smoke from his cigarette and idly tapped his fingers of the arm of the easy chair in the sitting room of Von Hollstein's cottage.

"Interesting the other ATS girl and her fusilier were part of it," he remarked. "I should have known."

"They fooled us," Von Hollstein admitted. "But it's only a temporary setback."

"Agreed," said St John. "Now that I've enlisted our friends in high places, I can get back to this other project."

Rita sat beside her lover on the couch, her face a mask of rage.

"That stupid Hiresh," she hissed. "I said attack without warning but he gave that bitch time to resist."

Von Hollstein placed his hand on her knee.

"It won't matter soon, my darling," he said soothingly.

"We still have complete freedom on the site," Montague-Stewart added. "Thanks in no small part to the major's prolonged absence overseas."

"A windfall from the start," said Franz. "It's also given me many more opportunities than I anticipated – and we'll put them to good use."

"I gather it's curtains for our swarthy friend?" St John asked casually.

"The Master does not tolerate a second mistake," said Rita with menace. "Hiresh confessed to me that he once failed in the Far East. This time not even Kali can save him."

St John chuckled heartlessly.

"Imagine how perplexed the local constabulary will be, wherever the body turns up," he theorised. "'Indian national, precise cause of death unknown,' the report will say, 'though possibly a sudden seizure brought on by excessive fear.' However," he added, knocking ash into a nearby tray, "we have more pressing matters at hand."

"McNabb's waiting?" Von Hollstein asked.

"He is," said St John. He placed his cigarette on the tray, sat back and steepled the tips of his fingers together. "A hefty bribe and he's now a steward, who'll board the ferry along with the doctor and his bogus wife. That bitch, as you called her," he explained, glancing at Rita.

"You're sure of all this?" she asked.

St John nodded confidently.

"Ex-Chaplain Allerton, of whom I told you, is a vicar near Huntingdon these days," he explained. "He often visits the Halliards. They're only about fifty miles away. Now, a medico of surprising eminence for his youth and a clergyman, who's virtually right-hand man to the bishop, aren't exactly inconspicuous, so it was easy for one of my novices to keep an eye on them[326]."

"We thought at first they might be the hub of resistance to our objectives, darling," Von Hollstein said, taking hold of Rita's hand.

"We were wrong," she muttered.

"Sadly, yes," said Von Hollstein. "However, if ever our birds flew the nest, we reckoned they would head for the Halliards. So Jozef drove to the vicinity as soon as we knew Hiresh had missed his target. He rang to say that Doctor Halliard had departed by car, headed south, ostensibly with his wife. They're doubtless aiming to catch the Dover ferry to Le Havre."

"But the woman is actually the Bramble hussy?" said Rita.

"Undoubtedly," St John assured her. "She bears a strong physical resemblance to Mrs Halliard, which makes the disguise feasible. They're spiriting her out of the country, as a precaution, obviously."

"To hide out with her Resistance friends," Von Hollstein added.

St John retrieved his cigarette.

"My novice says the Halliards went to the south of France recently," he said. "Rehearsing, no doubt."

"Well, at least McNabb is some use, getting more of our people into the country," Rita said reflectively. "He was no more than Hiresh's hanger-on at the séances. A complete churl."

"We knew you didn't warm to our Gorbals colleague," said Von Hollstein, chuckling. He patted Rita's hand. "But he led you to Hiresh. Look how our funds have improved thanks to our late servant of Kali."

"You've done well, Rita," St John added. He drew on his cigarette again. "It's good that we raise our own support and we certainly need your contribution. But we must make sure Bramble doesn't testify."

"McNabb may be a churl, Rita but he can do the job and dispose of Halliard, too," said Von Hollstein.

"And the rest of them?" Rita asked maliciously.

Von Hollstein rubbed her back indulgently.

"St John's other project," he said.

Inside the twin cabin, Kate slipped off her shoes, removed June's jacket and hung it in the wardrobe.

"All yours, Mike," she said, indicating the bed. "You must be knackered after that drive."

Halliard yawned and stretched.

"A bit. But can I get you something to eat? The snack bar'll be open for a couple of hours."

Kate shook her head.

"No, thanks. Mollie's sandwiches provided an elegant sufficiency and then some. You go, if you want something though."

She knelt down, took a dark-coloured sweater out of her suitcase and pulled it on over her head. It matched June's dark grey skirt – itself a perfect fit.

Mike placed his jacket on a coat hanger in the wardrobe.

"I'll follow your first suggestion, I think," he said and sat on the bed to unlace his shoes. "You'll wake me at zero four hundred?"

Kate nodded. She sat in an easy chair and wrapped a spare blanket around her legs.

"And *you'll* wake me in time for breakfast?" she asked, smiling.

Given their mutual war experiences, the arrangement was a precaution partly based on habit. Neither of them expected trouble.

They were wrong.

"Sure. There's a Webley in my suitcase, by the way. It's loaded."

"And in mine. With some other gadgets. 'Night, Mike."

"'Night. Kate," said Halliard, yawning again.

He stretched out on the bed, pulled the top blanket over himself and was asleep in minutes.

Kate adjusted the angle of the table lamp beside the chair so that she could read without disturbing Mike. She could hear the steamer's faint engine hum and sense the ship's movement as it got underway. Looking up through the porthole, she saw harbour lights glimmering past.

"So far, OK," she said quietly and glanced down at the page open on her lap.

For He shall give His angels charge over thee, to keep thee in all thy ways, she read.

"Please, Father, get us the rest of the way," she prayed.

Kate reached into her suitcase and placed the revolver under her chair.

The heavily-built bar steward cleared away the last of the glasses before lowering the bar's metal shutter. He smiled.

Zero-two hundred, the saloon clock read. Not much longer, he thought, as he wiped down the counter. We'll be well out in the Channel.

A skinny lad with brushed-back slick hair, also wearing steward's uniform, poked his head through the open door that led to the scullery behind the drinks shelves.

"Wotcha, Mac," he said. "Give you a hand with the glasses, OK?"

"Right enough, Spike. I'll bring the rest through."

When the washing up was complete, Mac said, "I'll clear out the lounge. You get some kip."

"OK, Mac," said the lad and departed for his quarters.

However, instead of tidying up, McNabb strode out of the lounge. Should be easy with a bit of luck, he thought. Everyone's bedded down. No nonsense this time.

He meant no complications, like sacrifices to Kali or beast transformations that had eventually spelt doom for his eastern companion, originally his sepoy batman.

The servant's extraordinary abilities had surfaced when he succeeded in terrifying the Indian gaolers into permitting Mac's escape after that incident with the nurse bitch.

Roles then unofficially reversed. McNabb envied the other's powers.

Though it had been horrific watching the priest being flailed by unseen fists when that other nurse somehow survived the krait attack in Rangoon. Hiresh took weeks to recover and the pair resolved via the spiritualist underground to get into Britain.

Funds from undisclosed quarters lodged in high places not only facilitated the journey but conveniently accelerated McNabb's departure from his regiment.

Back in Blighty, they eventually gravitated through the occult community to the service of a certain Queen Rhiannon and her acolytes. The employment was weird at times but paid handsomely, so McNabb asked no questions, not even when someone had to be silenced.

As now.

He stepped out of a passageway near the second-class cabins and fastened the door open, feeling the rainsquall spitting in his face. A brisk wind was whipping the sea into myriads of tossing whitecaps. With low cloud, visibility was poor and the upper deck mostly in shadow. Spray lashed the ship as it coursed through the swell.

McNabb proceeded along the deck and entered another passageway, where he descended a companionway to the first class staterooms. No screw-ups this time. Good old-fashioned lure and ambush. He knew where they were. It would simply be a case of a couple of passengers foolishly going up on deck in dangerous conditions and incurring the tragic consequences.

"Worth getting rid of two Sassenachs[327] anyhow," he muttered.

Kate looked up sharply at the knock on the door.

"Who is it?" she said. Her hand moved to her Webley.

Halliard woke immediately, removed the blanket and swung his feet onto the floor. He glanced at Kate, who put a finger to her lips.

"Steward McNabb," said a gruff voice. "Could I speak to the doctor please?"

Kate hid the Webley under the rug by her thigh. Halliard stood up, unlocked and cautiously opened the door.

They gazed at the stocky individual in steward's uniform with the mop of ginger hair, standing in the dim light of the passage.

"We have an emergency, sir," the steward said in a strong Glaswegian accent. "A passenger's been taken ill in second-class accommodation. The purser's sent me to ask you to come and help. He thinks it might be appendicitis."

"Just a minute," said Mike. He slid his shoes on and crouched down to tie the laces.

"Why didn't the purser come himself?" Kate asked.

"He didn't want to leave the woman's side," said McNabb. "He's trained as a sick berth attendant but says she needs a doctor."

Kate's eyes narrowed.

"Haven't you got one on board, as part of the crew?"

"Not for a short trip like this."

This is bollocks, Kate said to herself. She glanced at Mike, who was standing up to put on his coat.

"I'm a nurse," said Kate. "I'll help."

Her statement was partly true. Kate's wartime training included the Field Ambulance Nursing Yeomanry[328].

"Well, the purser said just to bring the doctor," the steward rejoined. "We do have a nurse. She's giving medication."

Halliard took his emergency medical bag from his suitcase.

"I'll go see what needs doing," he said to Kate. "Be back as soon as I can."

"Follow me, sir," said the steward.

Immediately Halliard closed the door, Kate threw off the rug and reached into her suitcase again.

The deck was pitching. Rain and sea-spray showered the men as they made their way along the deserted upper deck to the second-class passenger area, hanging onto various protuberances to steady themselves. Halliard was finding it difficult, having to use one hand for his bag.

"A bit wet but it's the quickest way, sir," McNabb called over his shoulder. "There's the passageway."

He pointed to the aperture in the superstructure, from which light issued.

"After you, sir," said the steward. "It's the fourth cabin on your right."

Halliard stepped in front.

McNabb deftly struck the doctor on the base of the skull with the edge of his hand. Mike slumped forward, stunned, dropping his bag.

The steward caught Halliard as he fell. McNabb jammed his hands under Mike's armpits and began dragging his victim backwards to the railing, glancing once over his shoulder at the open space between two lifeboats.

His pre-planned dropping point.

He didn't notice the slim shape concealed in the gloom by the boat at his back.

Gripping a fighting knife.

"So it's adieu to you, Doc," McNabb said out loud above the wind.

Agile as a cat, the shape leapt forward.

"No, you," hissed a female voice in McNabb's ear.

They were the last words he heard in this life.

Simultaneously, a firm hand clamped his nose and mouth. He was convulsed with shock as the six-and-a-half inch steel blade thrust savagely into his right kidney.

McNabb blacked out and let go his burden. Halliard collapsed onto the deck.

Kate wedged her body under McNabb's left shoulder. Grabbing his left arm with her left hand, she seized his trouser belt with her right. She staggered in her stockinged feet under McNabb's weight across the heaving, sea-splashed deck to the railing.

Kate left her knife in the wound, both to dispose of it and to prevent getting blood on her clothes. She'd pushed up the right sleeves of her sweater and blouse for the same reason.

Shoving McNabb's chest against the wooden upper rail, she wrapped her arms around his legs, noting the dark stain spreading in his white tunic from the spot where her knife's handle still grotesquely protruded.

Kate hoisted McNabb up and over the side.

The body toppled out of sight.

Immediately she turned around, Kate saw with vast relief Mike half-crouched on one knee, trying to stand.

"Mike, thank God!" she exclaimed and hastened over to him, grateful for the rain and spray soaking her clothes and dripping from her face and hands. It quickly removed all traces of blood from her right hand and forearm.

Mike sat in the easy chair, still groggy but recovering steadily. Kate had gently applied a damp towel to the back of his neck.

She poured him a glass of brandy, obtained from his bag that she had retrieved and handed it to him. He took it, thanked her and began to sip.

"You're going to have quite a bruise there," she said. "Cold compress notwithstanding. God, I thought he'd killed you."

"That was his plan, after which, I suppose he reckoned he'd get you," said Mike, wincing and gingerly pressing on the towel with his free hand. "June and I will be eternally grateful, Kate. Thank God for your suspicious nature – and SOE training."

Kate rearranged the pillows on the bed, trying not drip onto the blankets.

"I think Father shoved me out the door right after you'd gone, but I couldn't risk using the Webley," she said. "You better get back there as soon as you've got into some dry clothes," she insisted and gestured to the bed. "Then I'll use the bathroom to change."

Mike nodded, still feeling his wound.

"It's justifiable homicide, Kate," he said firmly when he'd finished the brandy. "You could never have overpowered him. He must have been one of Von Hollstein's lot. We slipped up somehow."

"Sure did," said Kate soberly. She rummaged in her suitcase for fresh clothing. "Father's still protecting us though, in spite of ourselves. Let's hope and pray they decide on a verdict of man overboard, death by misadventure."

"Amen," said Halliard.

Mike and Kate listened to the captain's sombre announcement at breakfast.

"Ladies and gentlemen. You may be wondering why so many members of the crew have been out and about this morning. I can confirm they have been conducting a search for Steward McNabb, who was reported missing several hours ago. I regret to announce that the search has been unsuccessful and we must conclude that our shipmate has been lost overboard."

He paused as several voices expressed dismay.

"I would ask, therefore, that we bow our heads for a minute of silence as a mark of respect," he then said.

When the time had elapsed, the captain concluded his announcement with a warning.

"As you'll recall, the weather was pretty rough last night. In such circumstances, it can be treacherous on deck even for an experienced seafarer. It's best to remain inside. Thank you, ladies and gentlemen."

The little siding nestled beside pale grey stone cottages environing the august village church with its rounded bell-tower and cone-shaped roof. Newly-born spring lambs baa-ed and frolicked on broad grassy pasture beyond the rail track. Behind the village, a long hillside covered in dark green woods formed a pleasing backdrop to the grey-pink stonework of the church tower, the crest of the ridge etched sharply against the vast blue of the sky.

Down below, it was warm in the afternoon sun and tree canopies overhanging garden walls cast speckled shadows on the gravel pathway leading from the station.

Kate saw none of it.

Immediately on alighting from the carriage, she had flung herself into the eagerly waiting arms of the tall officer in peaked cap and fresh KD uniform.

"Oh, Peter!" she exclaimed, sobbing and impulsively pressing her lips to his.

Waverly clasped Kate to his chest. When the kiss subsided, Kate rested her head on Peter's shoulder, still sobbing.

"Oh, thank God, and thank you all so much," Peter said to Alain and the others. "I'm delighted to meet you, Halliard."

Waverly unwrapped his right arm and extended his hand to Mike, who shook it firmly.

They walked to Alain's open-topped tourer. Alain, Mike and Yvette in front, carrying the suitcases, Peter and Kate bringing up the rear, arms about each other's waists.

"We will get you to Lyon tomorrow, Mike, for your flight home," said Alain.

"Thank you, Alain," said Halliard. "It's an honour to be here today," he added, glancing over his shoulder.

"*Mais oui*," said Yvette. Her husband smiled in agreement.

"We did have a bit of trouble, though, on the boat," Halliard informed them.

"Tell us about it later, *mon ami*," said Yvette. She rested Kate's suitcase on the ground and opened the tourer's boot. "Kate will be safe here, with us and Peter. We'll keep them busy on the farm, of course."

The couple stood close together a little way off, talking quietly, Kate again leaning her head on Peter's broad shoulder.

The conversation, it later transpired, concerned the letters of explanation that now had to go to Steve Graham and Colleen McGrath. Writing them would not be easy.

Alain placed Halliard's suitcase in the boot next to Kate's and winked at Yvette.

"I think Peter's father and governess will be visiting soon," she said.

"With Kate's parents, no doubt," said Alain. "We'd love to see you and June as well, Mike, and I strongly suggest that you notify your friend Reverend Allerton. I'm sure our happy couple will be eager for him to conduct the ceremony."

Mike glanced at Peter and Kate, who were kissing again.

"I'm sure you're right, Alain" he said with a broad grin.

That evening, Rita stood at the window of Von Hollstein's sitting room, glaring through the net curtains in the direction of Kate's vacated flat. Street lamps shed their yellow glow.

"That *stupid* McNabb," she snarled, clasping her arms across her chest.

St John had phoned with the grim news but added that Kate Bramble would likely remain in the south of France for some time.

Because he had further news.

"Our friends in high places inform me that Waverly has diverted on his way back from Palestine, presumably because of Miss Bramble," he'd said. "That means he is still out of the way and we can proceed as planned. It has taken years to reach this point. We cannot fail now."

Rita had flown into a rage, nevertheless.

Von Hollstein came and stood behind her. He placed his hands on her shoulders.

"Calm down, Rita," he said. "It'll be too late by the time Kate Bramble gets back - or Kate Waverly as she'll most likely be. No-one knows of our preparations."

"The site is still secure and the chamber as well? It must look spotless."

"Everything's fine."

Rita's rage gradually dissipated. She took hold of Von Hollstein's arms and slid them around her waist.

"Miko is moving to Deepvale?"

"Yes. He reckons there's a couple of possibilities at the general hospital but wants to make sure no prospects are overlooked."

Rita leant back in Von Hollstein's embrace.

"I only wish we could get one of those little sweethearts from the General up north."

"Probably all married now. And therefore disqualified."

Rita glanced at him over her shoulder.

"If we could just find one who was suitable, that would really avenge your sister."

Von Hollstein's grip around Rita's waist tightened.

"We will, my queen," he said grimly. "In good time."

Twenty-Four

Deliverance

May 1946, site engineers' extended accommodation, near the White Peak Quarry.

The engineers' Nissen huts were situated on newly-cleared ground opposite the main entrance to the site power station, about a hundred yards back from it, beside the approach road.

In one of the huts, three young men in shirtsleeves, khaki drill trousers and work boots stood around a large-scale map of the power station precinct.

The map rested on a trestle table that occupied the only available floor space. Everywhere else was taken up with desks and chairs, filing cabinets, drawing machines[329], bookshelves and glassed-in cabinets stacked to capacity with stiff cover file fasteners, blueprints and leather-bound handbooks.

Clerks, draughtsmen and engineers sat poring over their tasks or speaking on the phone. At the other end of the hut from the table, a glass-paned partition separated the section head's office space, with its niche for the departmental secretary; trim, bespectacled Mrs Jones, who clacked away at her typewriter.

The hut's windows were open for maximum comfort in the warm spring weather and through them filtered the sounds of the site; clanking, earth-moving machinery and conveyer belts, solids hoppers filling and discharging, grinding comminution plant, blasting operations and laden lorries in transit.

The three men were concentrating on an area where a new boiler and steam turbine set was to be installed. They would report their conclusions to senior management located in the main office, a three-storeyed stone block about half a mile distant, on the site proper. The block still sported its black and green wartime camouflage paint.

"We can start excavating once we're sure we won't hit any mains or power cables," said Doug Charlton. "Details are a bit sketchy in that corner."

Charlton was the section head and a rugby forward in his spare time. Sturdily built with a rugged face topped by short-cropped dark hair, he looked the part.

The second man, Geoff Jones, was senior engineer for site services. Of slighter build than Charlton, with wavy fair hair that fell onto his forehead in a twisted lock, Geoff played rugby three-quarter. He was Mrs Jones's husband.

"Best we have another look over the ground, Doug," Geoff suggested. "Bit of a dog's dinner there, I'm afraid, Steve," he said, glancing at the third man. "Map won't give all the gen. Works extended apace towards the end of the war. Growed like Topsy, as they say."

Steve Graham smiled in understanding. When old works were demolished to make way for new installations, confusion could arise. He took a pencil from behind his ear and pointed to a marking on the map.

"That sub station does look close," he remarked.

"It is," said Doug. "Access road extension'll have to be routed clear of it."

"And the new coal bunkers and the ash dumps," said Geoff.

"Who's job'll that be?" Steve asked.

"Yours, mate," said Geoff.

Steve grinned and tucked his pencil back behind his ear.

"What about condenser cooling water?" he asked.

"That's OK," said Doug. "Transfer lines and pumps well clear. Somebody definitely thought about that."

"Cooling tower capacity and treatment works?" Steve asked, scanning the map again.

"Still doing the sums on the tower," said Geoff. "Give us a hand if you like."

"Glad to," said Steve.

Doug pulled an A4 ring-bound manual off a nearby shelf and opened it.

"Cooling system's once-through," he explained to Steve. "Layout's in here. Treatment works should have enough spare capacity, even though some of the filters are knackered."

"Water goes back into the river cleaner than when it came in," said Geoff with a grin. "Still, main office is breathin' down my neck to get those filters reburbished."

"Not replaced?" Steve asked.

"Not on your life, mate," said Doug. "Bloke named Beresford's in charge of the purse strings. Head of Finance Department. Real tightwad."

"Management's white-haired boy," Geoff added. "For that reason."

Steve nodded – though his understanding went deeper than his colleagues suspected. It was his first day on the job, his first morning, in fact and everything seemed fine. He was off to an excellent start with his fellow engineers and eagerly looked forward to the challenges the job presented.

The name Beresford was nevertheless a sinister reminder of Vicky's briefing when he'd visited her in Lincolnshire soon after getting home. Likewise a reminder of Vicky's incredible string-pulling that had landed him the job. It had happened partly because the project Steve was engaged in drew heavily on government funding and in return, the government – including Vicky's contacts – could appoint some of the personnel.

As he reviewed the site investigation steps for the new access road at his desk after the meeting, Steve reflected on Geoff's evaluation of the Finance Director.

"Expert infiltrator," he murmured.

The three engineers were trudging back toward the main entrance from their site assessment tour during the afternoon. Steve asked about something that puzzled him.

"What's a couple of West Country lads doing in the Peak?"

"Well, Wessex Wyverns, weren't we?" said Geoff. "Divisional sappers. Married local girls while we were stationed around here."

"I was in special armour, First Assault Brigade," said Steve.

"Oh, aye?" said Doug with interest. "Hobo's Funnies, eh? I say, do you remember the brick stacks at Goch?"

The conversation continued enthusiastically all the way back to the hut.

At the end of the day, Steve would have taken up Doug's invitation to supper but he was forced to postpone. He'd already accepted a similar invitation, one that had emerged from an exchange of introductory letters.

"You go for your life, mate," Doug urged when Steve showed him the photo.

Of Colleen McGrath.

About the time Steve started work that morning, Colleen walked from the town's station to the street housing her flat. In uniform and carrying her holdall and web bag, she attracted appreciative stares from numerous males.

Her flat was the upstairs portion of a tall, grey stone semi-detached dwelling at the bottom of a steep cul-de-sac that ran uphill to the parish church.

Beyond it stretched broad parkland, dotted with tree copses and intersected by bridle paths.

Across the cul-de-sac stood a row of vehicle garages, extending to the stonewall abutment of the churchyard boundary.

Glancing at the garages, Colleen smiled as she unlocked the street door to her flat.

Steve Graham was now the owner of the Briggs's Morris Eight. His was the third garage from the entrance off the main road. Brian and Mollie were relocated in Huntingdon, not far from Reverend Allerton's vicarage.

"Tom reckons that 'Instead of pass the parcel, it's pass the Morris,'" Vicky told Colleen the day before. "Your accommodation's all sorted. You'll be in the top flat, I've arranged for Steve to have the ground floor one."

Vicky even provided a sketch map for Colleen to find the address.

"I think it's best to keep you away from Von Hollstein's area," she had advised. "Keep your heads down after the Sunday morning services, though. Our man sometimes attends."

Colleen entered the hallway, unlocked the inner door to the upstairs flat and ascended the stairs. On inspection, she was pleased to find cutlery, crockery, tea towels, bed linen, soap, tinned food in the pantry and various other essentials. Electric lights, water heater, gas cooker and icebox all worked OK. A full-length kitchen cupboard housed a vacuum cleaner, broom, mop, brush and shovel, dusters, household cleansers and polish. Another on the landing contained coat rail, hangers, an electric iron and ironing board.

"No traces of damp," Colleen said with approval. "Vicky's team have really done us proud here."

The bath had a shower rosette and curtain, with a twin-branched rubber hose attached to the taps. Useful if I'm in a hurry, Colleen mused. The loo, washbasin, mirror, bath, taps and towel rails all gleamed.

"We hoovered and dusted both flats," Vicky had informed her. "So everything's presentable. You've got a washroom and clothesline in the little courtyard out the back. I guess you and Steve won't mind sharing that. Garbage collection is on Thursdays."

Colleen placed her holdall and web bag in one of the bedrooms. Her tin trunk had been dispatched the day before to her new posting, the Deepvale Military Rehabilitation Centre, about fifteen minutes away by road.

Emptying her web bag, she unpacked a carefully folded ward uniform from her holdall and transferred it to the bag. She would take it with her to the hospital and change there. The remainder of her clothes she hung in the wardrobe or placed in its chest of drawers. Both smelt of camphor.

Colleen glanced at her watch.

"Better get some more food in," she said. "Then report."

The high street was only minutes away on foot, so her shopping wouldn't take long. Despite rationing, she had enough coupons for some reasonable purchases and was determined to do her best.

She would be cooking for Steve Graham that evening.

Deepvale House was a former hotel, six storeys high, of sombre brickwork and dark grey slate roof, with tall windows in groups of three on each floor. They looked to be permanently fastened. Rounded towers crowned by spires resembling witches' hats stood at the corners of one end of the imposing structure.

"Like something out of Daphne DuMaurier," said Colleen as she walked from the bus stop up the cemented flagstone drive, gazing at hotel's forbidding exterior. "Even in the sun. Must look like Wuthering Heights in the winter."

Nevertheless, the hospital's pleasant grounds considerably offset its stern appearance. Covering several acres, these contained peaceful groves of trees and carefully tended garden beds in magnificent bloom.

Colleen observed numerous patients in KDs and plimsolls seated on the grass or in deck chairs, chatting with nurses in grey and scarlet summer dress and white head squares. Several more patients were kicking a football to each other on another part of the lawn, while others played netball or croquet.

The reception area manifested old world opulence and Colleen gave her name to the orderly corporal at the desk. She noticed her trunk beneath a table beside the desk, with her camp bed attached.

"I'll arrange for a couple of the lads to drop your trunk off at your digs this afternoon, Sister," said the corporal.

"Thank you, Corporal." Colleen handed him the keys. "Can you tell me where to find Sister Bowden?"

She was the senior nursing officer to whom Colleen would report.

"First corridor on the left, Sister. Her name's on the door."

The orderly gestured in the general direction. Colleen thanked him, proceeded down the hallway and knocked at a door with J Bowden emblazoned on a brass plate.

"Come in," said a female voice.

Colleen entered, stood to attention and saluted the senior with three pips on her epaulettes, who sat upright behind her desk.

"Joan Bowden," said the Sister. She got up and extended her right hand to Colleen. "I'll show you the change room and we'll do a tour."

Sister Bowden was a slim young woman, petite, with short brown hair and a delicately boned face. Colleen noticed that Joan wore a wedding ring and judged by her accent that she was local. She gave Colleen a locker key.

"The lockers are full length," she explained. "You can easily hang a couple of ward uniforms in them."

Colleen quickly changed clothes and joined Joan in the corridor.

"I saw quite a few of the boys out in the grounds," Colleen said as they walked up the first flight of stairs. The stair carpet's distinct floral pattern provided a bright contrast to the mahogany panelled walls, teak furnishings and staircase.

"They're almost ready to be discharged," Joan explained. "We've got some others who aren't quite there yet."

The tour[330] revealed to Colleen scores of pale young men in blue hospital pyjamas and red ties, slumped on their beds, staring vacantly into space or fixedly at the floor or the ceiling, some dazed and withdrawn, others with a nervous twitch in facial muscles or hands, several muttering to themselves. Orderlies were in attendance on each ward, ready to assist the duty Sisters, should extra physical strength be required.

"Most of them aren't violent," said Joan. "But we see the occasional lapse, chaps shouting and screaming, thrashing about - that sort of thing."

She described the medication for restraint. Colleen remembered Major Elkins and the other neurosis cases at Frosinone and in the Far East.

"You give them a sedative to get them to sleep?"

"Your job when you're on nights, Colleen," Joan said with a smile. "They get up and go to the loo OK, though, even if they're like automatons. Sort of reflex action. You've probably seen that happen with similar cases?"

"Those under sedation, yes."

Colleen didn't mention how the zombie-like trance of the drugged patients unnerved her. Like Bronwyn Hewitt, she didn't trust intensive drug therapy. None of her friends did.

Sister Bowden showed Colleen various lounges where groups of patients sat in easy chairs. Many were smoking pipes or cigarettes and engaged in earnest conversation, supervised by an MO, a Sister and a couple of OR orderlies. In other rooms, patients worked at craft activities or noisily played table tennis.

"Group therapy, with a bit of activity," said Joan. "It's been found they'll talk among themselves easier than they'll talk to us. Helps them come to terms with the experience, although it can take months, even years."

Other convalescents sat in front of easels, busy with paint and brushes or charcoal markers. Some of the results were bizarre, others graphic and compelling. Colleen noticed that the MO and Sisters overseeing these sessions all wore artists' smocks. Paint splodges spattered the windows and smeared the floor, adding to the litter of crumpled paper.

Joan and Colleen paused to watch.

"Another way of getting to grips with what they've been through," Joan explained. "It's best to wear a smock if you're supervising. They clean the room thoroughly afterwards."

"So they can mess it up again?"

Before Joan could reply, one man suddenly let out an agonised groan, ripped his drawing off the easel and flung it onto the floor with a cry of exasperation in a flood of tears.

When he had recovered himself, one of the Sisters handed him another sheet from the pile on the trestle table at the front of the room and he dutifully started again.

"It takes time," said Joan as they walked up the next flight of stairs. "That chap could hardly sit still when he arrived last year. We had to keep him sedated for months. His lorry ran over a mine in North Africa. He was thrown out of the cab and suffered no more than a burst eardrum but his co-driver was killed. He blames himself, you see."

They came to a ward on the top floor where the patients sat subdued on their beds, mostly reading books or newspapers. The two Sisters paused by the vacant admin desk. Colleen saw a stack of patients' files on the desktop.

"We're looking after these fellows, Colleen," said Joan. "We hope to get some of them out into the grounds soon. One or two of them might talk to you. Next to themselves, they'll talk with us more readily than the male staff. That's why we even arrange dances sometimes, so they can meet local lasses," she added with a wink.

Colleen smiled.

"Sounds good. Shift ends at twenty hundred hours?"

"That's right. And starts at zero eight hundred. You get a couple of hours off during the day besides meal breaks, if you want to do any shopping. The town's only a few minutes away by bus. We'll swap over onto nights in three or four weeks."

The system was much the same as at Catterick.

"You can get your laundry done here and any dry cleaning," Joan added. "Arrange it with the lad at Reception. Oh, let me know whenever you want to work through, so you can get off a bit earlier. I always like to, of course but we can easily sort something out."

"Thanks, Joan. I'm sure we can."

Married QAs living at home, like Joan, Doreen or Annie, preferred to utilise the evenings, if they could, for obvious reasons.

Colleen seated herself to sift through the patients' files.

"There's the buzzer," Joan explained, pointing to an electric switch on the wall behind the desk. "If either of us has to hit the panic button, a couple of orderlies'll be here in a jiffy. While you have a gander at that lot, I'll wander along and see how the lads are doing."

Later in the shift, Colleen did speak to, or rather listened to, some of the inmates. She noted from their records that none of them was over twenty-two.

One was an ex-paratrooper, who'd suffered at Arnhem.

Colleen sat with him in the lounge, facing the doorway so she could see down the ward, while the young veteran spoke of his experience. Eyes downcast, he leant forward in his chair, puffing nervously on a cigarette, his voice repeatedly faltering.

"We were the second lift. Jerries were waitin' for us. Could hear bullets hummin' all around on the way down. Sky seemed full of them. I saw a Dak shot down. Flew into a couple of blokes, chopped 'em to bits. It's mostly a blank after that, except I remember us bein' marched off, POWs. We were in a camp in East Prussia somewhere. Winter was hell. Turnip soup and a scrap of black bread for rations mostly. I had dysentery because of it. They still have to give me a special diet. Ruskies liberated us and took us back in trucks to our side but I didn't know what day it was by then. Kept havin' flashbacks to the battle, too. That's why I'm here."

Colleen remembered how Bill Harris's brigade, in the first lift to Arnhem, had used up the element of surprise. The beleaguered First Para Brigade had not been able to support their comrades of Fourth Para Brigade arriving on the second day. Fourth Brigade flew into the teeth of intense anti-aircraft fire.

"They gave you pentathol?" Colleen asked.

She knew from his record he had been subjected to the powerful medication and also from his general demeanour. In Colleen's opinion, it did more harm than good.

The ex-para nodded, his head moving erratically up and down.

"Cheap piss-up, we called it[331]," the lad said, with a twisted smile. "Put you under for God knows how long."

Colleen looked the young man straight in the eye and smiled.

"Well, we're going to get you out from under, Eric," she said, gently but with confidence. "I want you to go for a walk with me in the grounds soon, now the weather's good."

She noted that Eric glanced out the window at the sunny skies. Even this apparently trivial reaction was progress. For months, he had been fearful of the outdoors.

"I'd like that, Sister," Eric said, displaying a more relaxed smile.

Afterwards, Colleen did walk in the grounds, with a former tank commander in Normandy, a freckly-faced corporal and sole survivor of his crew when an eighty-eight had brewed their Sherman.

Like the lorry driver, he was consumed with guilt.

"I just remember a massive bang and a sheet of flame, Sister," he said. "You've heard of 'Tommy Cookers'? That's what those Shermans were. 'Ronsons,' we called 'em, light first time[332]. Lump of molten metal took the back of my wireless op's head off. Can still see his eyes, staring like and hear him making a sort of 'quacking' noise[333]. I got out the turret, fell onto the roadside and crawled into a ditch. Could hear blokes inside screamin' until the tank exploded. I got out and they didn't, Sister."

Here he paused in his narrative and they stood by the path near some fragrant garden beds, where in the warmth of spring, insects hummed and butterflies flitted amid the splashes of colour. The corporal sobbed for a time. Colleen was glad.

This lad's emotions had effectively seized but clearly they were starting to function again.

"Half the squadron got knocked out," he said, when he had composed himself and they were walking on. "The padre and I went to get the identity discs a couple of days later, when the fires were out and the wrecks had cooled down. Had to get inside the hull, dig into what was left with a bayonet or something. Just heaps of charred flesh and bone and burnt skulls, sort of grinning, blokes I'd soldiered with. Never forget the smell."

"You've got to go on, Mitch," Colleen said softly. "For their sakes."

He looked at her as if a faint gleam of hope was diffusing into the dark recesses of his mind.

A third lad had endured jungle fighting in Burma's Chin Hills. Without warning, he got up and wandered out of the ward. Joan gave Colleen the OK and she followed him to one of the little rounded garret rooms with the spire on top that she had seen from the drive.

She found the lad sitting by himself. He smiled faintly when Colleen came in the doorway.

Though not as emaciated as the POWs she had nursed, the Burma veteran nevertheless looked gaunt, weary and hollow cheeked. His hair, dark brown in colour, was cut short, like that of the other men she'd spoken to.

"A lot of them find it too finicky to use a comb," Joan had told her.

Colleen pulled up a chair beside the man and introduced herself.

He shook her extended hand shyly.

"Bob Compton's the name, Sister," he said in a Black Country[334] accent. "Everyone calls me 'Compo'."

Gradually he began to talk.

"Monsoon rains, mud and mosquitoes, that's what I remember. Jungle growth so thick sometimes you could hardly see, even in the daytime. And leeches sucking at you the whole time. Sometimes, the ground'd give way and you'd be up to your neck in slime. Next to impossible to move guns and jeeps. Mules kept getting bogged too. Blokes were going down with malaria non-stop. Jungle noise was enough to drive you mad. Never knew when the Japs'd come screamin' in, could be on top of you in no time, especially at night and it was knives, kookers and bayonets."

Colleen knew that this patient's meat had to be pre-cut so he could eat his meals with a wooden spoon. "We can't trust him with a knife and fork," Joan said.

"If the air drops missed, the Japs got our grub," said Compton. "We ate snakes, wild fruit, birds and boar, whatever we could scrounge. Followed Japs into some tunnels once. Heard something and we opened fire. Found a lot of dead villagers. Japs had forced 'em down there as bait, you see."

Colleen remembered what Trish and the others had told her about the Chin Hills. "Some parts were really awful," Robyn recalled. "Especially during the monsoon. Where we went up to Colonel Bedser's position, it was mostly along a slope that was fairly solid ground - and cleared of Japs. Trenholme would never have let us go otherwise."

Like Frank Hamilton, Private Compton had been in some of the last battles of the campaign. He'd suffered wounds from a shellburst near Waw that had slain two of his best mates.

"Lads I'd soldiered with for a thousand miles, Sister," he said.

Later on, when it was time to serve the patients their evening meal, Colleen saw Compton standing motionless in the garret room, hands in pockets, staring into space.

"Grub's up, Compo," she said invitingly.

He didn't even seem to know she was there and only responded when she tapped him smartly on the cheek. At that, he broke down and apologised profusely for not acknowledging her.

"It's OK," Colleen whispered and guided the distraught young man back to the ward.

They were but a few of repeated conversations she and Joan would have with the men on their ward, gradually coaxing more of them to venture into the grounds.

"When they agree to go to a dance or something, that'll be a breakthrough," Joan said.

They both knew that men with severe disabilities, like those blind and limbless, had psychological traumas of their own but Deepvale's patients would not remain indefinitely in care. Purely for reasons of practicality, the army would thrust them out into civilian life in the not-too-distant future, where they would have to cope as best they could, still haunted by their deep-seated war neuroses.

"They'll probably all be gone by this time next year," said Joan sadly as she and Colleen cleaned up after supper. "We can only hope and pray they've got understanding families."

"I'd like to try reading the Bible to them at some point," said Colleen. She told Joan about her experiences with the ex-POWs.

"Worth a try," said her companion. "Especially on nights."

Colleen knew she would be seeking solace from the scriptures herself during the long hours of night duty. She was anticipating that the patients would exhibit the same kind of troubled sleep she had observed in the special wards at Frosinone, Rangoon and the Alexandra, replete with groans, cries, moans and mutterings.

That wasn't the only reason.

When she had taken Compo back to the ward, she had heard muffled footsteps from behind in the semi-gloom, going towards the garret room, like someone in the slippers the patients wore. Thinking that another convalescent was on the loose, from an adjacent ward,

Colleen had informed Joan and gone back to check, leaving Compo with an orderly. Compton hadn't heard anything.

Colleen found no-one and none of the nurses on the other ward reported any of their charges missing at the time.

When she mentioned the details to Joan, after distributing the patients' meals, her senior looked strangely tense.

"I've heard it, too, Coll, footsteps only going one way, to the garret," she said in a nervous whisper. "A lot of us have. Early last year, a patient climbed onto the roof from one of the windows and jumped to his death[335]. That's why the windows are fastened permanently on the upper floors. It's some kind of devilry, that's for sure."

Colleen had to agree.

Coming off duty later that evening, she received another shock.

The hospital employed a number of civilian caretakers. One of these was ascending the stairs as Colleen went down them into the foyer.

She glanced at him as he approached and they exchanged brief smiles of greeting.

Then Colleen had to fight to maintain her composure.

It was Miko.

She knew him instantly from the photograph.

Colleen tightened her grip on the banister. Her limbs were trembling.

I better contact Vicky, she thought in desperation as she tried to keep up casual conversation in the hallway with other nurses finishing for the day. God, he must have recognised me.

He had.

"Sister McGrath!"

Still stymied by her unexpected encounter, Colleen hadn't noticed the wiry young man standing beside the red Morris Eight parked a short distance from the entrance to the drive. She had instinctively gravitated toward the bus stop with several of her off-duty colleagues. Safety in numbers, she reckoned.

But Colleen was about to be reminded that *Safety is of the Lord*[336].

Her heart leapt again as she turned to the speaker.

"Steve!" she exclaimed. The mere sight of him was enough to reassure her.

Beaming, Colleen hastened to him and extended her right hand. Steve shook it courteously and smiled.

He had a nice smile, she thought, and a firm line of the jaw. Nicely combed brown hair, too. Dresses well. Those shoes are like mirrors. She liked the combination of light grey-brown sports jacket, dark trousers, white shirt and regimental tie.

"Decided I'd come and get you," he said. "Save you the bus fare."

She liked his voice, calm and clear, not much of a Sheffield accent but then he was an officer – and a lean and tough one at that.

Colleen saw that Steve wasn't as tall as Peter, or Tony for that matter but he was definitely the right height for her. She stood over five feet eight in her stockinged feet.

"That's very kind of you," she said. "I got some pork chops for supper and new potatoes and veg from the market."

Their arrangements had all been conducted via letters, though Colleen hadn't expected a lift from the hospital.

I'll cook supper for you if you don't mind eating a bit late, she had written.

Fine, Steve replied.

He held open the front passenger door for her.

"Sounds great," he said, with an engaging grin.

Closing the door, Steve got in the driver's side.

"Treacle duff for afters," said Colleen. She settled back against the leather-upholstered seat.

"Good old army stand by."

Steve started the engine, did a deft three-point turn and drove towards the Peak town.

"I'll whip up some custard, too."

"Better and better. Oh, I got a couple of bottles of apple juice before I set off. They're in the flat. Should go well with the pork."

"Thank you."

"My pleasure."

Colleen noticed that Steve glanced at her legs as she crossed them. Typical man, she thought, but ooh, he is gorgeous. Thank You, Father. And thank you, Kate and Peter, I guess. She purposed to write to the couple as soon as possible. Though Vicky had been taken aback at the turn of events, she'd nevertheless written encouragingly to Colleen and Steve with the words, *I think Father's still in control.*

He *is*, Colleen reflected.

She gazed at the undulating heath and fields as they drove past. The countryside looked beautiful and peaceful at the setting sun. Despite the shock of seeing Miko, she now felt completely safe with Steve at hand.

Although in a few weeks, she would have to do without his presence for a short and terrible interval of time.

The telegram on Colleen's doormat immediately caught her attention.

"What is it, Colleen?" Steve asked.

The note was from Vicky. It contained a warning about Miko's shift of location and an apology for not having discovered it sooner. It ended with the statement *Tom and I will see you both tomorrow evening*.

"Let's not talk here," Colleen said, getting out the key to her front door.

They went up into the flat. Colleen placed their coats and her cap and tie in the cupboard on the landing, where, she noted, the lads had left her trunk. She rolled up her shirtsleeves and they went into the kitchen.

Colleen explained about Miko, while tying on an apron and getting the meat out of the icebox.

"I don't like this one little bit," Steve said anxiously. "Can you avoid him?"

"Yes. It was a shock but I'm mostly with the patients. I don't think he'll try a knife attack again. This isn't Naples."

Steve still looked concerned. Colleen changed the subject.

"Did you say you had some juice?"

"I'll get it," he said, grinning.

Steve departed and returned a couple of minutes later with two slim-necked, dark glass bottles.

"I guess you know two of our other villains are at the site," he said.

Colleen had placed the chops on the grill and was putting the vegetables on to boil. She glanced anxiously at Steve.

"Yes. Would they recognise you?"

Steve started setting the table.

"I can keep out of their way. But even if they did, I'm just the gagee[337] who happened to bump into them at Boulogne and would take for granted they'd be using aliases, as SOE. Tom and Vicky are OK with that."

"That's good." Colleen adjusted the grill flame.

"I'll take you to and from the hospital every day. Whatever your shift is."

She smiled at him gratefully.

"Thanks, Steve."

Colleen wanted to hug and kiss him right there and then, though she knew that would have to wait.

But not for long.

It turned into a lovely evening, even if it had to be cut short before midnight, given the demands of the next day.

"I'll cook for both of us," Colleen said while they were washing up. "If you don't mind waiting, at least while I'm on days. I can get supper for a more sociable time when I'm on nights."

"Fine with me," Steve said amicably as he placed some dried cutlery in an open drawer. "I get off before sixteen-thirty, so I could always get extra food."

"It's a deal."

Colleen picked up a tea towel.

"Do you want to go for a run tomorrow morning?" Steve asked.

"What time?"

"What about six-fifteen? Just up the hill, round a bit of the park and back. I'll treat you to tea and toast at, say, seven-fifteen and I can easily get you to work for eight."

"You're on. And we can finish up the apple juice, too."

When Graham returned downstairs to his flat after bidding Colleen goodnight, he was mindful of Paul's exhortation to the Ephesian believers[338].

Now unto him that is able to do exceeding abundantly above all that we ask or think, according to the power that worketh in us.

Apart from that Text, his thoughts were exclusively about Colleen.

Photos nowhere did her justice. Loveliest lass he'd ever seen, beautiful green eyes, beautiful red hair, high cheekbones, gorgeous smile and those marvellous lips, perfect skin, perfect face and figure, fantastic legs. Wonderful North Riding accent. Father, You're so generous.

He knew he was being presumptuous. It was, after all, only their first meeting.

But Steve already sensed that he and Colleen had a common destiny. And he felt sure she believed it too.

Provided they got through the daunting task ahead.

Wearing PT shorts and shirts, plimsolls and army socks, Steve and Colleen strode up the hill to the parish church.

The town looked picturesque in the early morning sunshine that glinted warmly off slate roofs, where wispy smoke curled from stubby chimneys.

Colleen was unmindful of the peaceful setting, however. She was striving to keep within a respectable distance of Steve, whose muscled legs were powering like pistons. Hers were already feeling the effort.

They paused briefly at the top to enter the churchyard via its roofed wooden gateway, flanked by yew trees.

Jogging shoulder to shoulder past tombstones green with lichen, they headed for a bridleway that meandered by several copper beeches, their burnished canopies rustling in the mild breeze.

"Do you get to see your mum and dad often?" Steve asked.

"A couple of times a month," said Colleen, breathing deeply. "What about you?"

"Any weekend'll be fine from here. Sheffield's less than an hour away by car. You could come with me some time," he suggested. "Meet Neil and Emma, too."

Steve had told her about his brother and sister-in-law.

"I'd like that," said Colleen, brushing perspiration from her forehead. "I'll let you know when I've got the time."

They were so easily becoming a couple.

Tom and Vicky arrived at about eight-thirty that evening. The four of them convened in Colleen's kitchen and began tucking into the fish and chips that the visitors generously bought on the way. Colleen heated up a couple of tins of baked beans and Steve provided several more bottles of apple juice, together with a few bags of goodies purchased from the nearby bakery.

"I am sorry we didn't find out about Miko earlier," said Vicky apologetically. "It must have been a terrible shock."

"He's not bothering me," Colleen assured her. "He goes out of his way to be the model employee."

"Calls himself Radoslav, or Rad?" Vicky asked.

Colleen nodded. Inwardly, she continued to feel uneasy about Miko's true intentions and she knew Steve sensed it.

"So what are they really up to?" he asked.

"We still don't know," said Vicky, laying down her fork. "But let's recap."

She brought Steve and Colleen up to date on the details of Kate's harrowing encounter and Halliard's narrow escape, thanks to Kate.

Steve and Colleen listened in silence, though horrified by Vicky's disclosures.

Vicky also summarised Miss Heythorpe's information that Kate had passed on.

"Maybe they're planning another ceremony," said Steve. He was trying to sound calm as he topped up everyone's glass but Colleen could sense his fury. "Though I don't see how it's going to re-establish the thousand-year Reich. Even if they are petitioning Death and Hell, they don't seem to be getting any worthwhile answers."

"We still don't know why the quarry's important?" Colleen asked nervously.

"Not yet," said Vicky. "It's frustrating. And I take your point, Steve. But we have made progress with St John."

Colleen and Steve looked at her quizzically.

"Finish your supper," Tom advised. "We can give you the rest of the gen afterwards."

"And when we've helped with the washing up, we'll leave in time for you to get a good night's sleep," said Vicky kindly. "Or try to," she added with sympathy. "It's all a bit upsetting, really, coming on top of the last six years."

"We'll see it through, though, God willing," said Steve. "Like we did the last lot."

They spontaneously joined hands to pray.

As they jogged back to the flats the next morning, Steve came up with a startling proposal.

"Why don't we go out to Waverly's place this evening?"

Dripping with sweat, they paused at the front door, where Colleen unbuttoned a fob pocket in her shorts and took out the key.

"We can't just turn up unexpectedly."

She turned the key in the lock and opened the door.

Colleen knew from Vicky that Peter's emotional reunion with Kate had caused some perplexity for Lord Waverly senior and Miss Heythorpe, though it was being happily resolved. She therefore decided it was better to keep her distance for now.

"No, I mean the ground near the quarry," said Steve as they went in. "Tonight's the full moon, which is often when these rituals happen. It may or may not be on their calendar but there's no harm in checking."

"OK," said Colleen, gazing at Steve's lean and glistening face. She knew with every fibre of her being that they had embarked on a partnership for life. "Will my KDs do? They're nearly as dark as BDs."

"I'll be wearing mine," said Steve with a shrug. "Main thing is, they won't reflect. Have you got a pair of gym boots? They'll protect your ankles better than plimsolls."

"There's a Disposals in the town near the hospital. I'll get some there."

Steve reached under his shirt for a key attached to a loop of cord, pulled the loop over his head and unlocked his front door.

"Right," he said firmly. "And this evening, we'll need to burn some cork."

At about half-past eleven that night, Steve parked the Morris in a convenient lay-by.

He pointed to where the approach road to the disused site branched off, about a hundred yards up the road.

"Judging by the OS[339] map, it'll take about twenty minutes or so from here to the top of the path," said Steve. "You ready?"

Colleen moistened her lips and nodded.

Steve began quoting a verse of scripture[340].

"'Fear thou not; for I am with thee: be not dismayed; for I am thy God: I will strengthen thee; yea, I will help thee; yea, I will uphold thee with the right hand of my righteousness.'"

They finished it together.

The moon floated ghostlike above the pair as they crept along the stony, unsealed road. Colleen remembered Kate's terrible encounter and shuddered, her heart thumping. To one side of the road was open heath, silent under the moonlight. On the other, a rocky and gorse-strewn hillside, black and menacing, extended up to the border of the manor grounds.

As a precaution, Steve was carrying Colleen's nine-mm Browning in a web holster fastened to his belt.

"Where'd you get *that*?" he asked in surprise when she had shown it to him.

"You sure get into some scrapes, Sister McGrath," he said on hearing her account of the krait. "Well, I'll take care of the weapon if you want. It's not the most ladylike thing to have in your *lingerie* drawer."

Colleen was glad to let him do so. She smiled on recollecting Trish's letter in which she described showing Matt the Browning Charles had given her.

You should have seen Matt's face, Coll. "Where on earth did you get that?" he said. "You better let me take charge of it." I did.

Steve suddenly held up his hand. The pair halted.

Moonlight was glinting off some vehicles.

Graham inclined his head to Colleen's ear.

"Two Daimlers, a sports and the Bedford," he whispered. "They're here, all right."

Albrecht, or Ainsley, was known to possess a maroon-coloured Bedford Series O van. The sports car was obviously Rita's and the Daimlers no doubt provided transport for St John and his cronies.

According to Tom and Vicky, they numbered eight and occupied highly influential government posts.

Together with Rita, Beresford, Ainsley, Miko and St John himself, that made thirteen.

"A regular coven," Tom had said.

Steve whispered in Colleen's ear again.

"Wait here. I don't think they've left any sentries but I'll check. I'll also get the numbers."

Steve crept away and Colleen crouched in the ditch beside the road. Despite the warmth of the spring night, she felt herself trembling and her heart was still pounding wildly.

A couple of minutes later, Steve reappeared and beckoned her forward.

"Track's just beyond the vehicles," he said. "Follow me. You'll see better if you use the corners of your eyes and hear better if you breathe through your mouth."

The path was steep, cleft by rain runnels and studded with sharp rocks. Cautiously, they edged their way to the crest and took shelter behind some clumps of heather beneath a knot of silver birches.

Steve glanced at the luminous dial of his wristwatch and nodded to Colleen. It was almost midnight.

"God," she heard him whisper.

The moon spread its blanching glare on the scene before them, one that made Colleen cringe. She could feel sweat prickling her scalp.

The moon wasn't the only light. Six floating, phantom-like spheres marked out the points of a hexagram, the nearest about fifty yards from the watchers. They illuminated the entire arena.

"Corpse candles, like Jon and Robyn saw," Colleen whispered in Steve's ear. She had told him of the Grays' sighting during their honeymoon.

"Marking out the hex," he said softly. "Like the Pyramid curse you mentioned. No wonder Egypt's a desert."

Within the hex stood thirteen cowled figures[341], one poised over a flat, irregularly shaped boulder, about the size of an ordinary dinner table, sunk partly into the earth. It was covered with a tarpaulin and thick layers of brush, probably heather.

The upright figure held with both hands a knife upraised, its blade curved like a scimitar.

On the rock lay a tethered animal, a goat Colleen thought. Its legs were tied and two members of the group pinioned them fast. A third individual firmly held the creature's head, baring its neck to the blade above.

Uttering shrill chants, the figure plunged the knife into the creature's throat.

Then began to butcher the carcass.

A ghastly communion service followed. Colleen felt sick.

"The brush is there to soak up the blood," Steve whispered.

After further chants, a blue-green mist began to gather above the slaughtered animal.

And to assume a form, huge and sinister.

"C'mon," said Steve. "We've seen enough. Be careful on the way down."

Colleen was still sweating and trembling when they reached the car.

Not simply from what they had witnessed.

But also by the knife wielder's voice, Rita's, no doubt.

Colleen recognised it.

She told Steve when they were sipping tea in Colleen's kitchen, after having washed the cork off.

"You're sure?" he asked.

"You bet I am," Colleen said, both hands gripping her mug. "I can imagine her too, under that cowl."

"OK. I'll let Vicky know. And about the whole wretched business. It's what we've suspected. My God," he added, shaking his head.

Steve finished his tea and glanced at his watch.

"You better get some sleep, Colleen. I suggest we forgo the usual run after reveille."

Colleen shook her head.

"Not on your life. I'll be there, zero six fifteen, sharp."

"I'll see you then," said Steve, grinning.

He stood up, rinsed his mug in the sink and placed it upside down on the work surface.

Colleen saw him to the door, where he kissed her lightly on the forehead and said, "'Night Colleen."

Feeling hot and cold all over, she smiled and bade him goodnight.

Steve sent the information, including the vehicle registration numbers, and Vicky confirmed everything. Her telegram contained a further apology for not having ascertained earlier that Rita, like Rhiannon, was an alias.

We can get you out, it added.

No, Colleen replied.

A few days after the midnight reconnaissance, Colleen considered the situation over a cup of coffee during her afternoon break at the hospital.

That she and her companions were pitted against a group of devil-worshippers was clear and that they included some influential personages was also plain.

And it fitted Vicky's supposition, that she'd conveyed during the meeting in Comilla that Von Hollstein and his co-conspirators would petition Death and Hell to set up their new Dark Age.

But the question that perplexed everyone remained.

Ghastly as it was, Colleen could not see how the ritual she and Steve had witnessed would achieve that set-up. Even if, and Colleen shuddered at the thought, they could conjure up a demonic apparition, so could many a primitive Shaman and they weren't exactly in line for world domination.

She was soon to get enlightenment on that point, from two close friends.

Along with fresh terrors.

The leading conspirators met in Von Hollstein's cottage during the evening after the sacrifice. St John sat back contentedly in his armchair.

"Miko's *very* pleased," he enthused. "And so am I. Couldn't have worked out better. Though I suppose it was always a possibility, with the Brigges and their friends involved."

"I think our mutual objectives will dovetail nicely, St John," said the count. "I've spoken to Jozef. He'll have the van close by. With those two on the job, it'll go like clockwork. No-one'll suspect a thing, until it's too late."

He, too, sounded brimful of enthusiasm and extended his arm around Rita's shoulders. She sat beside him on the sofa.

Montague-Stewart nodded. He took a cigarette out of its silver case, placed it between his lips, lit it and inhaled.

"Miko's looking forward to it," he said, exhaling a shaft of smoke. "He's confirmed that the diversion is ready, thanks to a convenient suicide – and your abilities, Rita. You certainly have a way with our other - helpers."

Rita smiled cruelly and spoke with an animated voice.

"They are drawn to that sort of thing[342]. It's perfect for us. And it also means we can start taking revenge, Franz." She rubbed her head against his.

"Well, as St John said, it couldn't have worked out better," Von Hollstein acknowledged. "Especially since you already know the victim."

Rita placed her hand on his knee. Her eyes betrayed a wicked sense of anticipation.

"Oh, yes, Franz, darling. I know Sister McGrath."

But none of them remembered the words of Solomon.

Pride goeth before destruction, and an haughty spirit before a fall[343].

June 6th, 1946, 7:00 a.m.

Steve and Colleen had reached the copper beeches during their morning run. The deep red foliage, ruffled by the breeze, glinted in the sun.

Since their midnight patrol, things had been fairly quiet, almost anti-climactic. They went about their workaday routine, Steve invariably providing transport for Colleen to and from the hospital. He attended the non-conformist assembly where Brian, Mollie and Kate had been members and Colleen joined him as her schedule allowed, after which they walked by the river and she cooked Sunday lunch.

Once, they observed Beresford-Von Hollstein leaving the parish church, with Rita on his arm.

"Look quite the respectable couple, don't they?" Steve remarked dryly, while making sure he and Colleen were not noticed themselves.

They continued their briefings with Vicky and during one weekend enjoyed a day trip to Sheffield, where Colleen met Steve's family.

"We'll go see your mum and dad next time," Steve promised her. "And I'll let you drive."

Colleen drove to and from Sheffield. She liked the Morris.

"Pity I can't afford a Jag[344], though," Steve had remarked.

For almost three weeks, most of their spare time was spent in each other's company and Colleen appreciated how Steve hadn't tried to hasten the friendship unduly.

However, she sensed that early morning in June, when he halted casually beneath the copper beeches that he was about to show her more affection.

She paused beside him.

Steve glanced at his watch and gazed across the park, where several figures could be observed walking or jogging.

"Exactly two years ago," he said, "I was aboard a landing craft tank, heading in to Gold Beach at Normandy."

Colleen placed her hands on her hips and took some deep breaths. Rhythmically, her breasts rose and fell. Steve, she noted, watched out of the corner of his eye. Oh, Captain Graham, she thought admonitorily, you man, you.

"I was at a BGH in Ormeskirk."

"Peter and Kate get married soon."

"Yes. Vicky mentioned it in her latest letter to me, too."

Steve turned to face her, his countenance, like hers, streaked with perspiration, for the day was already warm. Gently, he clasped her wrists. Colleen could feel her heartbeat quickening. She drew closer to him.

"I don't feel surplus to requirements, though, do you?" Steve asked.

Smiling, she shook her head.

Then his arms were about her waist, hers were around his neck and their lips were pressing together in the most wonderful kiss either of them had ever experienced.

"Oh, Steve, Steve, I love you," Colleen whispered afterwards, resting her head against his cheek, feeling the tears of joy springing to her eyes, rejoicing at the strength of his embrace.

"I think we're very much in love, Colleen," said Steve.

He clasped her to his chest and they fervently kissed again. Colleen lightly stroked Steve's hair. Before jogging on, they stood in each other's arms for several minutes, their surroundings forgotten.

Two days later, it was Saturday[345]. Tom and Vicky convened a key briefing.

Though the group had not met as a whole before, Vicky and Tom kept everyone informed of developments. They knew of the original team's precipitate departure, the attacks on Mike and Kate and McNabb's demise.

Now was the briefing for the final showdown – to be scheduled for the end of the following week.

Having left for the south of France, along with Brian and Mollie, to attend Peter and Kate's wedding, Mike and June generously made their home available for the briefing.

"I've diverted everything to the locum again, so you won't be interrupted," Mike informed Vicky.

Steve and Colleen came down from the Peak town. Matt and Trish drove up from Banbury. Both girls secured the day off by agreeing to an extra stint on nights.

Jon and Robyn came from Lincolnshire.

Andy and Dollie Somerville were close by, at Market Harborough.

And were the last to arrive.

"Snap![346]" Robyn said happily to Dollie when Andy ushered her into the sitting room.

Robyn and Dollie had each been expecting since January.

"And looking in the bloom of health for it," Trish remarked enviously.

She vacated her place on the sofa for Dollie to sit down and perched on the arm of the piece.

"OK if I sit next to your husband?" Dollie asked, as she occupied the middle of the sofa, between Matt and Andy.

"Well, so long as you've got yours there to mind you," said Trish, with a teasing smile and putting her arm around Matt's shoulders.

Andy and Jon glanced at their expectant wives and then at Matt. Their expressions plainly said, "You're next, mate."

Colleen had explained her changed circumstances in several letters but was nevertheless relieved when she and Steve were greeted with love and understanding.

Gwen and Dai sent their apologies. *I'm due any day now*, Gwen's note said. *Dai's more nervous than I am. Quite something, being an expectant father, he says. Huh!*

But they remained wholly committed to the task, through Vicky's extensive prayer network. She had enlisted an army of supporters world-wide; Larry, Helen, Mac, Julie, Barry, Karen, Ben Hedges and his fiancée in Canada, Kiwi and Paddy in New Zealand, Irene Calvert and her family, Barney and Mrs French, John and Janice Manning in Australia, Charles, Edith and the Simpsons in India – they had decided to stay until partition, Sir Redvers and Guinevere, Nigel and Dorothy, Damian and Natalie in Burma, Brigadier General Frank and

Mrs Mildenhall, Naomi and her husband in Amarillo and of course, Peter, Kate, Alain and Yvette in France.

We are from the old Huguenots, Madame Hallé said in her letter. *And before that, our families were Albigenses*[347]. *So was Kate's family on her mother's side. It is the same war for us, for the last eight hundred years, or more.*

One wholehearted response came from a serving paratrooper in Palestine.

With you absolutely, it said, signed, *A. Chisholm, Sgt, 6ᵗʰ A/B Division*[348].

Others, like Mike and June, Brian and Mollie, came from all over the British Isles; including Matrons Brierley and Wrigglesworth, Debs (n) Tyndall, Marian Lovejoy, Val, Viv, Vera, Kitty, Mandy, Jo, Pippa, Sue and their husbands, Leigh and Rachel, John and Lindy, Les and Doreen, Sean Gilfillan and his fiancée, Bill and Anne, Anne's brother George and his wife Alison - Colleen former roommate, Jim and Jeannie Grant, Ian Kinross and his wife in Scotland, Bill and Lorraine Crittenden, Mark and Katrijn Napper, Jan and Marijke in Holland and of course, Mama and Papa Vanderveer – who would not have been left out an any price.

"Aye, count us in, me and the missus, like," Geordie Wood had said, when Vicky contacted him and mentioned Colleen. "Especially for Sister McGrath."

Additional supporters included Trish's dad and Aunt Lucy, Steve's family and Rev Allerton, who had some interesting information for Tom and Vicky.

"Never did trust Montague-Stewart," he said. "His family's Bavarian, you know. Oh, yes, came over during the Napoleonic Wars. Directly on Weishaupt's[349] orders, I shouldn't wonder. Changed their name and gradually fitted in over the generations but it's not difficult to understand where St John's allegiance lies, same place as Guido's[350]."

Vicky's explanation to her prayer warriors stated that *We covet your prayers for a special operation. Despite six years of war, the forces of evil that created Nazism are not dead. More recently, they have brought down the Iron Curtain over half of Europe. Right now, their strength is gathered in the very heart of England to unleash legions of darkness that have not stalked our land since the Middle Ages*[351]. *We are not faced with a mere handful of fifth columnists. It is principalities and powers against which we strive. We therefore earnestly ask for your prayerful support in overcoming them.*

She had kept each of them apprised of progress and her latest missive included the time and date of the next vital step in the conspirators' scheme.

Vicky had set up an easel at one end of the sitting room, with a bulldog clip and several large sheets of paper. She recounted current progress, enlarging on several bullet points listed on the top sheet, beginning with a brief recapitulation.

"As you know, four are concentrated in or around the Peak town, with a fifth, St John, on a roving commission. He has now enlisted eight more, in positions of influence. That makes thirteen. You understand the significance of that?"

Her audience did.

"They met, possibly for the first time together, on the night of the full moon, last month," Vicky said. "Steve and Colleen carried out a night reconnaissance and observed, I believe, a dress rehearsal, for the event that will take place at the next full moon."

She summarised what had happened. The others listened in shocked silence at the description of the 'communion' service.

The Daimlers' registration numbers confirmed that the vehicles belonged to two of the eight, prompting Andy to remark, "They wouldn't take the Rolls's down a dirt track."

"Shh," said Dollie and tapped him on the wrist.

Seated on a hard-backed chair next to the easel, Tom spoke with intensity.

"It's the next event we've got to stop. We know that our eight worthies have closed their diaries for that date, so that's definitely when it's happening. It *will* take place on Waverly's ground. Matt's done some vital research to demonstrate that, which we'll get to in a few minutes, after Vicky's tied up some loose ends."

He glanced at Vicky, who continued her resumé. She stood by the easel with her pointer.

"From our researches, we must conclude that some of you were shadowed in the Far East. The Great Enemy recognises *his* Enemy. As you know, one of his servants, McNabb, who tried to dispose of Mike, overplayed his hand out there." Vicky paused and glanced at Trish. Matt reached up and took his wife's hand.

"It seems McNabb gravitated into the occult via his batman," Vicky added. "A sepoy named Hiresh but in reality a high priest of Kali."

"Responsible for the lycanthrope appearances reported," said Tom. "By you, Jon and subsequently by Kate. In which guise Hiresh also killed Wilfred Houghton."

"Leaving no trace for the police to find the killer?" Gray suggested. He held Robyn's hand. She had begun to look pale.

"Exactly," said Vicky. "It was no doubt also Hiresh's aim to take out Colleen, by means of the krait. McNabb probably went with him, as a kind of bodyguard."

Trish and Colleen had informed the others of the incident.

"Maybe at least one mongoose will make it to heaven," said Andy, eliciting laughter.

"Hiresh has been eliminated," said Tom, as Vicky turned over to the next sheet on the easel. "Evidently by his Master, for failure to dispose of Kate. He was on borrowed time after missing Colleen."

"The body of an Indian national was found dumped in the East End the day after the attack on Kate," Vicky explained. "It was possible to identify him, make the connection to McNabb and in turn to those happenings in the Far East."

"Did Hiresh look like he'd died of fright?" Matt asked. Vicky nodded. "I saw a dead Jap like that," Matt went on. "During a night patrol near Meiktila. I definitely felt a presence there and later on, near the Sittang. So did some of the other blokes, Leigh Grafton especially."

"You were being shadowed too, Matt," said Vicky quietly. Trish pursed her lips and gripped Matt's hand more tightly.

"How did you find out Hiresh was a priest of Kali?" asked Andy.

"From McNabb's gaolers," said Tom. "We thought it strange they allowed themselves to be court-martialled rather than reveal exactly how he'd got away after the attack on Trish. And some of Hiresh's fellow sepoys. They were scared to talk until we showed them pictures of Hiresh dead."

"So, where are we now?" asked Dollie. Like Robyn, she was looking pale and Andy had taken hold of her hand.

Vicky turned to the next sheet on the easel. The notes thereon brought gasps of anxiety from the audience. Tom moved his chair away from the easel.

"Over to you, Matt," he said.

To put Matt Calvert's researches into context, we must briefly visit the Calder Vicarage near Banbury, shortly before the final briefing.

Reverend Simon Calder watched from his garden seat in the shade as Matt sawed through a thick bough of the May tree.

He thanked God for his first son-in-law, though he had been surprised to read of the turn of events from Trish's and Evan's letters and at first disappointed.

But no longer.

The blessing of the LORD, it maketh rich, and he addeth no sorrow with it, Solomon said[352].

It was true. Simon had never met a man more honourable than Matt, nor one that could have loved his daughter more deeply. Miranda, his late wife, would have loved Matt too.

The lad's devotion to the Saviour and command of the scriptures was unsurpassed in Simon's opinion. And he had over thirty years' experience in the ministry, dating from his position in the Chaplaincy of the original BEF that fought at Mons[353].

In the few weeks since the Australian's arrival, he had agreed with his university tutor a literature review for his researches, obtained a British driver's licence – and was teaching Trish how to drive, using Simon's Austin Seven – won the affection of both Ellie and Aunt Lucy, joined a couple of local sporting clubs, taken a part-time job as a stable hand - "My sister taught me all about horses," Matt said – and effected or arranged for numerous repairs to the vicarage including re-thatching the roof.

He had also transformed the garden, extending what Trish had begun and with her helping whenever she could.

It had become considerably overgrown. Simon's ill health prevented him from tackling it too strenuously and he didn't want anyone else working on his patch.

"You're a stubborn old coot," his sister Lucy said.

Now Matt was getting stuck into the May tree. The formidable boughs overhung the next-door neighbour's yard and the public footway that ran past the vicarage.

But on that warm Saturday evening, after some hours of Matt's tenacious sawing, most of the offending branches lay in a heap on the lawn. A lad with a cart would take them away next week.

Matt cut through the last of the branches. Simon watched the lean, muscular arms powering back and forth. His fair-haired son-in-law, stripped to the waist and wearing army boots could have outclassed any Greek god, when it came to physique.

Apart from the battle scars, though they would always be a reminder of how Trish and Matt had met.

The other lad, Matt's friend whom he had met on his return to Australia, John Manning, looked much the same from the photos his wife Janice sent to Trish, now that he had recovered from his POW experience.

John was a lay preacher and studying for the ministry.

Simon thanked God for such men. He thought on Isaiah's Text[354], *Men of stature shall come over unto thee; and they shall be thine; they shall come after thee.*

"You've done it, Father," he said prayerfully.

Having finished the task, Matt trudged perspiring back towards the house, gripping the saw in one sinewy hand. He paused by Simon's chair.

"I'll have a bath, then go get Trish," said Matt. "She's finishing early today. And could we ask you about some things later?"

"Please do," said Simon. Matt nodded his thanks and proceeded on.

Some things, thought Simon. The Enemy never let up, he reflected with a sigh. Maybe that was another reason Matt was here. He himself was too weary, and still struggling with the loss of his beloved Miranda.

And there was Ellie. Trish had been headstrong as a youngster but the Saviour's leading into the disciplines of nursing and the Army Nursing Service had matured her into the superb helpmeet she was. His elder daughter also benefited from Miranda's influence during all her formative years.

But not Ellie.

"'Hear my prayer, O Lord, and give ear unto my cry[355],'" Simon whispered.

Trish knocked on her sister's bedroom door. Minus cap and jacket she was still in her walking-out uniform, having assured her dad she would speak to her sibling as soon as she got in from the hospital.

"Matt can start supper," she'd said and kissed her husband, now bathed and casually dressed. "Almost used to the Aga, aren't you, darling?"

"We'll cope as we usually do," said Matt, glancing resignedly at Simon.

"Who is it?" asked a voice from inside.

"Me," said Trish. "Can I have a word please, Ellie?"

"You'll have to be quick, Big Sis," said Ellie as she opened the door, in a state of undress. Trish noted that Ellie's bed was covered with several outfits, some of which had spilled onto the floor among the fashion magazines and other items strewn about.

"Your room is a tip, Muffin," said Trish severely, using one of the names they had devised as children. "As usual. Two years in the army would do you good."

Trish wrinkled her nose at the smell of smoke in the room, from a lit cigarette in an ashtray. She strode across the room, threw back the curtains and opened the window.

"Do you mind!" exclaimed Ellie, clasping a red blouse to her chest. "I'm not dressed."

"You know Dad doesn't like you smoking in the house. Neither do I, for that matter."

"Oh, all right," Ellie said irritably. She stubbed the cigarette out, pulled on the blouse and reached for a matching skirt. "I suppose this is about Buzz?"

"Yes," said Trish curtly. She stood before the windowsill, hands clasped behind her back. "He's not right for you, Ellie. You're another prospective conquest. And if he scores with you, he'll move on to the next without so much as a backward glance."

Buzz was one of the airmen from the nearby American Airforce base; built like a rugby forward, fair-haired and boisterous. He was reputed to be unusually adept in "showing the gals a good time," according to the lads from the base who attended the parish church.

Perhaps too good a time, they hinted courteously.

That was rumoured to be the reason for his recent appearance as a result of a transfer from elsewhere in the country. Ellie had met him at a dance and Trish didn't like the implications at all. Neither did her dad but he was at a loss about what to do, practically. Though more exuberant than their British counterparts, the GIs who attended the parish church in considerable numbers were considerate and well-mannered but Ellie hadn't taken to any of them.

"He's fun," Ellie protested. She pulled on the skirt, zipped it, grabbed a perfume bottle and applied the spray. "And anyway, how do you know so much about him? You've not even met him."

"I've spoken to the lads at church."

"Gossip!" snapped Ellie. She reached for a hairbrush.

"And I know the type," said Trish patiently, folding her arms.

"Well, it's all right for you. *You've* got Matt."

"God can find the right man for you, Ellie, if you're prepared to trust Him."

At that moment, a jeep horn sounded. Ellie brushed past Trish and waved from the window. Trish glanced at the broad-shouldered young man in uniform behind the wheel.

Ellie gave her hair a couple of flicks with the brush, slipped her high heels on and picked up her handbag and a dark red jacket as she dashed out of the room. Tall, slender and blonde like her sister, Ellie looked good in any outfit but in Trish's opinion, this one was too low at the neck and too high at the hem.

"Gotta rush. Bye, Big Sis," Ellie called over her shoulder. She hurried downstairs and out of the house to the jeep.

Trish looked on as Ellie gave Buzz an impulsive kiss and the pair drove away.

"Please, Father, encamp around her for our sakes, as well as hers," she prayed.

Simon looked up from the open bible on his lap. Sitting together on the sofa in the parlour, Matt and Trish waited for him to frame his conclusions.

"I'm certainly pleased you found my modest library to be of some use, Matt," he said. "Though it does constitute a bit of a diversion from your main line of study."

"A necessary one, I think," said Matt.

He had been perusing some of the old works Simon possessed on the progress of the Christian Gospel in England from Roman times to the Norman Conquest. Part of his researches had disclosed a chilling account of opposition to the Gospel in the form of Satanically-inspired heathen rituals in various parts of the country.

They involved human sacrifice[341].

An old map showed some of the prime locations, including one in the White Peak, near Waverly Manor. Matt had confirmed the location on an OS map.

"I believe such practices could be invoked today," Simon said with a heavy sigh. "The English Reformation, together with the widespread circulation of the scriptures, put paid to most of these rituals but some went underground."

"To reappear as opportunity allowed?" Trish suggested.

Her father nodded gravely.

"So what would they gain?" Matt asked.

Simon glanced down at the open bible.

"The most dedicated practitioners could acquire strength like the Gadarene demoniac," he said. "Wisdom greater than our most learned intellectuals, ability to bring down the forces of nature – in addition to the demonic, capacity to inspire devotion as an angel of light, and thus power to deceive nations and set them at war [356]."

"All from cannibalistic communion services," said Matt soberly, clasping Trish's hand.

"Provided sufficient advance preparation is carried out," Simon advised. "That could take years."

"Ties in with Vicky's briefings, though," said Trish. "It's late but I'll phone her tonight."

"It's happened before," said Simon. "Remember, it took ten long centuries to bring the world out of the Dark Ages and God knows how many of our brothers and sisters in Christ died doing it. And we have seen terrible conflicts since then."

The hall clock chimed a quarter to the hour.

"We'll walk over to the church and wait for Ellie," said Matt. He and Trish stood up together. Simon glanced at them in surprise but nodded gratefully

As they went out, he returned to his bible in an attitude of prayer.

Matt and Trish hurried hand in hand in the warm darkness to the spreading yew trees by the parish church gate.

"I just felt we had to go meet her," said Matt. "I don't know why. We don't normally."

"I'm glad you did. I think Father was pushing me out the door, too."

They paused in the shadow of the yews at the sound of raised voices, coming from round the corner.

The vicarage was in a cul-de-sac, intersecting with the road through the village onto which the churchyard gate opened.

Buzz had evidently parked by the gate. He had ten minutes to get back to the base before being posted AWOL.

Ellie was drawing this fact to his attention. To Trish, she sounded scared.

Buzz, by contrast, was nonchalant.

"The top kick's[357] a buddy of mine, sugar," Trish heard him say. "We got plenty of time. I got a key to this place, see? Real nice soft bed there."

"I'm tired and I've got a headache," Ellie responded, sounding more scared.

"Say, sugar, I ain't used to takin' 'No' for an answer," was the belligerent rejoinder.

Ellie sounded panic-stricken.

"Let me go, I'll scream!"

Buzz's voice rose to a snarl.

"You do, sweetheart and I'll break your jaw!"

Matt had heard enough. In a trice, he was standing before Buzz, staring grimly down at him. The airman sharply looked up. Ellie broke free, stumbled out of the jeep and ran sobbing into Trish's arms.

"Clear off," said Matt.

Buzz began to climb out of the jeep.

"Oh, yeah, and who's gonna make me, civilian?" he growled.

Simultaneously trying to comfort her distraught sister, Trish was silently praying the men wouldn't come to blows. Buzz was huskier than Matt but Trish knew he'd be no match for her steel-sinewed veteran. She didn't relish the prospect of explaining Buzz's injuries to his CO.

"Clear off," Matt repeated, not budging. "Don't come back."

The airman paused, sized up his potential opponent and wisely departed.

"Oh, thanks, Matt," said Ellie tearfully. "And you, Big Sis."

"Deliverance, Muffin," said Trish. She kissed Matt warmly. "Thanks, love. And You, Father."

Matt put his arm around their shoulders.

"Let's go home," he said.

It was a foretaste of a greater deliverance to come. We now return to Vicky's briefing.

"Did these things really go on?" Jon asked when Matt finished speaking.

Matt glanced at his notes on the sheet.

"Something sustained the Dark Ages," he said. "More than power politics."

"And this coming Friday is a present-day revival?" said Andy. He still held Dollie's hand. She looked nauseated.

"Yes," said Matt. "It's not part of the usual occult calendar but it is the full moon. The old records give a precise method of calculation. What Steve and Colleen saw was undoubtedly a practice run."

"And next Friday's occasion will be preparation for what may be a nation-wide campaign in two years' time," said Vicky. "There's other groups in the country, many local to the various sites, but from all we can gather, this one's the spearhead."

She stood white-faced on the other side of the easel from Matt.

"The full moon and the summer solstice will coincide," said Trish. "Dad discovered that from an almanac. That's why it will be the main event."

"It's horrible," Robyn whispered. "To think of this happening, here in England, and after all we've just been through."

Jon put his arm around her.

"If the Enemy is going to grant them so much power, why didn't the other side try it during the war?" Steve asked.

"Only the real devotees go this deep into devilry," Tom explained. "The leading Nazis hardly scratched the surface[358]. This current crop represents not merely decades but possibly centuries of advanced planning. No doubt they hoped the Reich would triumph but its collapse in a way gives them their chance."

"You can see why this isn't any ordinary counter-espionage," said Vicky. "And why we need a special group, like yourselves, if we're to stop it."

"Well, that's what we signed up for," said Dollie with conviction.

Matt turned over to a new sheet on the easel.

"Another thing to consider," he said. "The victim. Ideally, a pre-pubescent virgin. But the records suggest that a young unmarried woman may also be selected, if to the best of the group's knowledge, she, too, is a virgin and as near a perfect female specimen as is possible to get."

"Dad says they anoint her first and put a white robe on her, to signify her purity," said Trish. "They drug her too, to keep her quiet. Laudanum derivative, with other opiates. Forced feeding in the old days, probably a syringe now."

"Which is why they've renovated the change shed, as a sacrifical ante-room," said Vicky. "The preparation will take about ten minutes. It'll be about a fifteen-minute walk up the track from the quarry floor to the stone altar on Waverly's land. The full moon will give good visibility but the old sketches show the corpse candles lighting the way at various sites, before they mark out the points of the hex."

"Devices of Lucifer," Matt explained. "He's the light-bearer, also transformed into an angel of light[359]. We should be in position by twenty-three thirty, no later."

Tracing out a sketch on the easel, he outlined the key part of the mission - intercepting the sacrifice.

"The priestly party of five will head for the altar where the other eight'll be assembled. The high priestess, Rita, will be in front. She'll have the sacrificial knife, so go in fast, Vicky, to be on the safe side. Two of the men, probably Franz and Albrecht, will follow with the victim. She'll be conscious but like a sleepwalker. They'll have to hold her up. The other two, that's Miko and St John, will follow, as guardians."

Methodically, they went over the rest of the operation.

"We'll check the ground as soon as we can," said Vicky. "Steve, Colleen, Tom and me. It'll be deserted until Friday."

"Have we any idea who the victim's likely to be?" Jon asked.

"Me," said Colleen. Her voice trembled.

"God, no!" exclaimed Steve. He gripped Colleen's hand. Others joined in the protest.

"Listen, all of you," Colleen said vehemently. She clasped her hand over Steve's. "Miko's their scout. That's why he's got the hospital jobs. Where else, locally, would they have a better chance of finding the person they want? We know he knows me. And St John wants me out of the way, too. Remember Ernie's note."

"You're right, Colleen," said Robyn, blinking at sudden tears. "It fits."

More than they realised. Besides Colleen, only Steve, Vicky and Tom knew about Rhiannon.

"It has to be me," Colleen said with deliberation. "Anyone else'd be out of her mind. Probably that's also why they drug the victim." She took a deep breath. "Just make sure you're on time."

"We will be, Colleen," said Steve. He held her hand more firmly.

It was the close of a beautiful day. Steve and Colleen sat together in the Morris, near where he'd called to her on the first day. She was about to go on night duty.

On Friday[360].

"Time to go," said Colleen, looking at her watch.

They had prayed and read some scriptures together, including the Twenty-third Psalm. Steve didn't want to let her go. The last week had been hell, trying to keep up appearances with their work colleagues.

And with Colleen aware that Miko always seemed to be watching.

To Steve, she had never looked so lovely. Her walking-out uniform was freshly dry-cleaned and she'd worn her best perfume.

And, though she wasn't supposed to, the high heels that made her legs look exquisite.

"I've got my ward shoes in my locker," she said.

Colleen leant over to Steve. He inclined his head to her and their lips met in fervent warmth.

"We'll go see my mum and dad tomorrow," she promised, immediately their lips parted.

"And tell them all about our wedding plans," said Steve. He'd proposed after the final briefing. Colleen accepted without hesitation.

She smiled, nodded, kissed him again, then got out of the car and began walking purposefully up the drive. Steve watched her go, an English warrior maiden, he thought.

"Father, give strength to our arm[361]," he prayed.

"Sister, could I please speak with you?"

Colleen saw Miko standing at the entrance to the ward. He looked the personification of humility.

God, Miko, thought Colleen. You could outclass Uriah Heep[362] any day. Or is it Creep?

But her stomach lurched, nevertheless. This was it. She knew.

Striving to seem nonchalant, Colleen glanced at Joan. They were seated at the admin desk at the end of ward, sipping coffee. It was ten thirty-five and despite mutterings and groanings, the patients were slumbering.

"I won't be a minute, Joan," said Colleen. She put her cup in its saucer and stood up.

"OK," said her friend. Joan suspected nothing. Vicky had left her out of the prayer chain, though with great reluctance. However, Joan was too close to the action.

"So, what is it, Rado?" Colleen asked. She tried to sound composed as she followed him along the corridor. Already, she could feel the sweat of fear on her forehead.

"The strange noises, Sister," he said, pointing. "I think I know where they are coming from."

Colleen's heart felt like a trip hammer against her rib cage. As always on nights, the area was deserted and dimly lit. Her would-be abductors had picked the time and place well. She was sure Albrecht or Von Hollstein waited up ahead.

"I don't hear anything," she said, still striving to speak casually.

As they approached the garret, she faintly smelt the sweet odour of chloroform above the normal disinfectant smell.

She had suspected it. Nevertheless, her thumping heart nearly stopped with the realisation. *They're going to do for me like Kate!*

Miko entered the garret room.

"In here, Sister," he said, beckoning.

Feigning naivety and fighting panic, Colleen stepped across the threshold.

And lost consciousness as Albrecht seized her from behind and pressed the chloroform-soaked rag against her face[363].

They placed Colleen in a wicker laundry container, descended via the service lift and drove off in Albrecht's van minutes before Joan went in search of her friend.

"So easy," said the ex-Gestapo man. He was dressed like his colleague in an orderly's uniform. Their pretence of collecting laundry had fooled everyone. Miko crouched in the back of the van, poised over the open top of the basket, ready to administer more anaesthetic as necessary, enough to keep the victim under for the journey and the preparation.

But a red Morris Eight and two jeeps followed at a distance, lights dimmed. The group had decided on pursuit, instead of waiting at the quarry, to ensure they kept the kidnappers under surveillance at all times.

In Colleen's flat, joined in spirit by many others, three young wives maintained their prayer vigil.

Colleen regained consciousness to find herself standing, arms suspended uncomfortably above her head by ropes tied to the rafters of a shed. She guessed it was the change room.

Her ankles were fastened as well, to the legs of a wooden bench set against the wall. By the light of a couple of paraffin lamps, she could make out five hooded figures.

One was Montague-Stewart. Colleen could tell that from his bulk.

Looking down, she saw her ward uniform lying on the bench and that she was clad in a full-length sleeveless white tunic tied at the throat, with splits to the thigh and a V neckline that plunged to the waist.

For the knife stroke, she realised in dismay.

She could smell a rich aromatic fragrance. Her skin felt oily and she remembered Matt's reference to the anointing. They must have sloshed it on, she thought, noticing a greasy stain on the cement floor. And Colleen knew from her semi-coherent state that she had indeed been drugged with opiates, no doubt by syringe as Trish had said, because she sensed no aftertaste. Her eyes were drifting in and out of focus. Voices seemed to come from afar off and they were distorted like in a nightmare.

Except that this nightmare was real.

But at least she had not been molested. For the sacrifice, she had to stay a virgin. Matt's briefing emphasised that.

One of the figures came near, throwing back its hood. It was Rita. Colleen instantly recognised her.

"Sister Bitch[364]," she said groggily.

The other woman's eyes narrowed.

"I'm especially pleased with our brother's choice, Sister McGrath," she hissed, glancing at another of the figures, whom Colleen realised was Miko. "You were the bane of my existence once, you and that hussy friend of yours."

Colleen felt a surge of fear for Annie, Bill and their unborn child. Dazed though she was, she promptly went on the offensive.

"Feeling was mutual," she grated. "You always did get on my tits[365]."

"So I'm going to enjoy cutting them open," Rita said maliciously[366]. She held up the wicked curved blade. Colleen almost passed out.

"Bring her!" one of the other figures commanded. Von Hollstein, Colleen guessed.

Miko and another figure, whom Colleen recognised as Albrecht, untied her hands and feet. They grabbed Colleen's arms and propelled her to the door where Von Hollstein took her right arm from Miko. She could walk with their aid.

Montague-Stewart extinguished the lamps. "We meet again, Sister," he said. "Briefly."

He sounded pleased. Colleen's head was swimming and she didn't reply.

"The lights," she heard Rita say in surprise.

Colleen experienced a strange calm. The Voice spoke within her brain.

Sister Colleen, deliverance is at hand.

"Keep going," growled Von Hollstein. "We mustn't be late."

The group progressed a few paces from the hut.

Suddenly, powerful torch beams shone in their faces, followed by a shout.

"On your knees! In the Name of the Lord Jesus Christ!"

"Tom," Colleen gasped joyfully.

Retching violently, Albrecht and Von Hollstein released Colleen and collapsed as if forced down by all-powerful, invisible hands[367]. Miko and St John were similarly pressed earthwards.

Someone dashed in and swept Colleen off her feet. It was Steve. Nimbly, he carried her from the melee.

"Oh, Steve!" Colleen exclaimed, sobbing for joy at the sight of his animated face, smeared again in burnt cork.

"You're OK now, love," Steve said. His voice was breaking with relief.

He conveyed her to the side of Albrecht's van, which she saw parked near the open entrance to the site.

Shrieking with rage, Rita tried to turn about, clutching the sacrificial knife, but Vicky had sprinted up alongside Steve. She wrested the blade from Rita's grasp, fell on top of the witch and pinned her to the ground.

While Andy, Jon, Matt and Tom pinioned the other four face down in the dirt, assisted by sturdy RAF lads in uniform, who held the torches.

The five miscreants were handcuffed.

The corpse candles flickered out.

Steve set Colleen on her feet and held her close.

Their lips pressed longingly together.

Then they heard a popping sound. A flare shot into the sky and exploded into shafts of brilliant green.

"That'll be Tom, ordering the vehicles up," said Steve. "It was good they left the gate open. We could have got in where the fence joins the hillside but Father made it easier."

As agreed during the briefing, they had reconnoitred the area a few nights back and confirmed the lie of the ground. Colleen heard engine noise and glimpsed headlights.

Behind a jeep, the faithful Morris came into sight, driven by one of the RAF lads.

An RAF van followed, requisitioned by Tom to transport the villains to a secure location. The base furnished a considerable number of believing personnel to assist the operation, led by redoubtable Flight Sergeant Ferguson, who was also a deacon in the Church of Scotland.

The convoy halted inside the quarry area, their headlamps brilliantly illuminating the scene, whereupon the five were hustled into the RAF van, under heavy guard, while the area was secured.

Vicky appeared around the side of Albrecht's vehicle. Her face was blackened, like Steve's, and she too wore dark khaki denims and gym boots. She carried Colleen's ward uniform.

"A bit crumpled and smudged, that's all," said Vicky. "We can use the robe to wipe off that oil. You'll need a bath to get it all off, though."

Steve cautiously released Colleen from his embrace.

"You OK to stand, love?" he asked, ready to support her again instantly if necessary.

Colleen leant one hand against the van's passenger door.

"Yes thanks, love, I'm coming round," she said.

Despite the drug's lingering effect, she felt steadier on her feet. Vicky placed Colleen's uniform on the bonnet of the van and began helping her off with the robe.

"I'll look the other way," said Steve.

"Thanks for everything, Vicky," said Colleen huskily. She could feel renewed sobs rising in her throat. "Thank God," she whispered. "They never knew what hit them."

Vicky smiled in a sisterly fashion and waited while Colleen composed herself.

"Well, we reckoned it might alert them when the lights backed off – scared of us," Vicky said. "But they had to get on, regardless, to be there for midnight."

Colleen slipped into her frock while Vicky helped steady her. The three of them looked up as another flare exploded overhead, red this time.

"Sergeant Ferguson," said Vicky. "He and his lads will have caught the other eight, heading back to their Daimlers."

Engine noise sounded again as the RAF van driver, guided by a couple of his mates, reversed his vehicle and drove away. He would drop Tom Freeman off to rendez-vous with Ferguson.

"You can look round, now, Steve," said Colleen. She was adjusting her head square.

"That looks fine to me," Vicky murmured.

"Those eight won't be charged with anything serious, though, will they?" Steve asked, sounding chagrined. He put his arm around Colleen.

"No," said Vicky. She folded up the sacrificial robe. "The evidence against them is entirely circumstantial, though they deserve to hang. However, I think they'll be too humiliated by tonight's turn of events to be a nuisance in the future."

Three grinning individuals in dark KDs and gym boots came sauntering up; Andy, Jon and Matt. Colleen could see their white teeth contrasting with the burnt cork on their faces.

She nestled by Steve's side. More tears of joy welled in her eyes.

"Oh, lads, thank you so much," she whispered.

"Father sure floored 'em, Coll," Andy said elatedly. "Satan bruised[368], eh, Steve?"

"Amen, mate," said Steve. Colleen sensed his voice breaking again.

Leaning on Steve's arm, she hugged and kissed Andy, Jon and Matt in turn.

"You take Colleen back to the flat, Steve," said Vicky. "Tom and I'll sort things at the hospital – they must be in quite a flap by now - and we'll collect your walking-out uniform, Colleen. I suggest if you're up to it, you and Steve go straight to your parents' place tonight. Make it a long weekend – we'll sort that with the hospital, too and the quarry."

"I am, and we will," said Colleen. "Thanks, Vicky."

She leant back against Steve's chest and he clasped both arms about her waist.

"Girls'll be over the moon to see you, Coll," said Jon with affection.

They looked up at the pale disk that still rode high in the heavens.

"'But thanks be to God, which giveth us the victory through our Lord Jesus Christ[369],'" said Vicky.

"Amen," said the others.

Twenty-Five

Desired Haven

So he bringeth them unto their desired haven - Psalm 107:30

"Yours is such a special generation: stoical, loyal, indefatigable and dutiful. You have been the bedrock of this country for all these years and it will not be the same without you. So we salute you with all our hearts."
- HRH Charles, the Prince of Wales, addressing WW2 veterans at the 60th anniversary of VJ Day, August 21st 2005

A few weeks after her ordeal, Colleen wore white again, when she and Steve exchanged marriage vows in the parish church they had passed by so often during their early morning jaunts.

They had some wedding photos taken beneath the copper beeches.

The Church of England kindly allowed them use of the venue because the non-conformist assembly hall where they usually worshipped was too small for the crowd that attended.

Reverend Allerton performed the ceremony.

"Well, I think you're the last from our MGH, Colleen," he said warmly. "I've sure had a busy time since VE Day."

Some explanation about the bride's identity was needed for Steve's army friends. He wrote to them in advance, enclosing a photograph of Colleen with each letter.

Ronny Hazeldene's reply summed up the responses.

Bookies must be glad you're not a punter, sir. You can sure the pick the winners.

Peter and Kate Waverly, back from France, were among the guests and gladly donated Waverly Manor for the reception.

Aunt Hen set about the arrangements with alacrity.

"We've had plenty of practice," she said.

"I'll supervise," said Mollie Briggs gleefully, now in an advanced stage of motherhood.

"And that's *all* you'll do," Brian insisted. "Gotta show 'em who's boss, mate," he told Steve.

Kate and Colleen met for the first time a few days before the wedding, at the manor.

It was a poignant moment and each could say the same from the heart.

578

"Thank you, dear sister, for looking after my man."

Steve and Peter amiably shook hands and began discussing the test cricket[370], along with Peter's dad. Instead of haunted, he was hearty, for the first time in many years.

"He's a changed man," Aunt Hen confided to Kate and Colleen. "Thank you both, ever so much."

Thus more lifelong friendships were formed.

Following the arrests, the Morris reverted to the RAF but Steve purchased a replacement and in it he and Colleen drove to the Lake District for a two-week honeymoon. There they visited the Grants.

Despite the huge number of casualties brought to her CCS from the Reichswald and Rhineland battles, Jeannie remembered Mark Napper.

"So wonderful about him and Katrijn," she said.

"Another undesigned coincidence," Jim remarked. "And I'm sure I caught a glimpse of you, Steve, when they brought us back across the Rhine."

"We were a bit conspicuous," said Steve.

Trish revealed to Colleen some interesting news while helping her get ready to go away.

"I got my driver's licence. And guess what, I'm expecting! But Matt says he'll drive me to the hospital when I'm due. We wanted you to be the first to know, outside immediate family. Dad's really looking forward to being a granddad and Ellie's thrilled about becoming an auntie."

Thus Colleen learned of the impending arrival of her future son-in-law.

On that note, I now turn the remainder of the narrative over to my mother, Mrs Anne Calvert, Grandma Colleen's daughter, who had first-hand experience of many of the events to be described. She also kindly wrote some of the earlier passages, like the honeymoon scenes, because I felt a bit embarrassed.

My literary son Simon has taken the reader on a long journey that now falls to me to conclude, though my beloved husband, Matt Calvert junior, is more of a writer than I. He takes after my dear departed father-in-law, Matt senior, who turned his master's studies into a most meritorious doctorate dealing with the development of the English Bible from earliest times, to the Authorised Version of 1611. His treatises on the subject continue to be much in demand among true believers.

My father-in-law's decision to settle in England was hard on Irene but she understood that her son was following God's calling and that comforted her through the years. "And wherever Matt is," she used to say, "I couldn't have wished for a more wonderful daughter-in-law."

So here is the rest of the story.

I turn first to what happened after my mother's would-be murderers were arrested.

Vicky Freeman, as she was before the summer of 1946 ended, was correct in her assessment of St John's eight accomplices.

Group Captain Freeman questioned them and they were detained for a time under the Witchcraft Act, which remained in force until 1951. However, they escaped charges of accessories to kidnapping and murder.

"We thought it would be a repeat of the earlier ritual," was their collective protestation. "We would never have countenanced such a thing as you describe."

"Not after they got caught," Dad said with feeling.

Nevertheless, as Vicky also predicted, their humiliation over the incident resulted in swift departures from public life and banishment into obscurity. It was explained as early retirement.

But the main objectives of the night ambush were achieved; to prevent the sacrifice, capture those directly responsible and forestall an occult explosion projected for the confluence of the full moon and the summer solstice, two years later.

It did not take place - then.

Yet, the case against the ringleaders never came to court, though they were placed on remand, while military and civil authorities decided on the next move.

Their deliberations came to an abrupt halt when Von Hollstein, Albrecht and Miko were found dead in their cells, of unknown causes. No further details were divulged but they probably died with expressions of horror frozen on their faces, their Master being displeased with failure.

Tom and Vicky invoked the Official Secrets Act, 1911, to cover the trio's disappearance. The quarry management, it transpired, was distressed to lose such a valued colleague as Mr Beresford.

Montague-Stewart contracted an illness that resulted in his transfer to a prison hospital. From there, he mysteriously disappeared, smuggled, it is believed, to Latin America, never to set foot in this country again. Nevertheless, he continued to exercise a malign influence from afar, to which I will allude later.

We think that St John died in 1960.

Infested with unclean spirits, Rita, Rhiannon, or Sister Bitch, as Mum and Aunt Annie called her, went insane after her arrest, was institutionalised and died in 1950. Wilfred Houghton's fellow directors were deeply sorry to lose her.

The fates of those who abducted Mum thus bore out the wisdom of Solomon, *The way of transgressors is hard*[371].

In the meantime, she and Dad were continuing to rejoice in *the way of life*[372].

Deepvale discharged the last of its patients sooner than expected, in the autumn of 1946 and my parents moved to their own cottage in a delightfully rustic village, "just inside Yorkshire," Dad said with satisfaction.

They called their home Desired Haven.

Mum left the forces and resumed her midwifery course, obtaining her qualification in 1947.

"I think I earned it," she said. "I cycled up a lot of hills for those deliveries."

Though she admitted it was partly because petrol rationing was still in force, so she couldn't use the Morris except in winter or sometimes at night. That was also why Dad travelled to and from work by public transport for several years.

I guess the next big event in their lives occurred in the summer of 1947, when they fulfilled a long-standing promise to visit Mum's friends in Canada and Naomi and her husband in Amarillo. It was quite an adventure but according to Mum, "I discovered the most exciting part was when we came back."

With me.

Before taking up the academic post that he retained until retirement in 1980, Dad remained as a site engineer at the quarry for a number of years. He worked on many projects with boon companions, Doug and Geoff and added to his wartime experience gained in Kiel, with respect to the design, installation and operation of essential services; gas, water, electricity, sewage.

So much so that in 1954, he went as part of a team that our government assembled to advise the Italian Government about the restoration of these services in various parts of the country still ravaged by the war. The quarry owners were happy for Dad to go because the payoff would come in the form of lucrative contracts for the expansion of their business into foreign markets.

Dad summed it up as, "Never do owt for nowt[373] – first rule of business."

He took the whole family. I was six years old at the time, my brother Steve nearly four. Mum and Dad had no qualms about us tagging along. Thanks to their wartime service and in Mum's words, "Our Father's leading," they knew they could cope with any eventuality.

"Chance of a lifetime," they reckoned. And so it proved to be.

On the way, we stayed for a while with Uncle Peter and Aunt Kate – as we called them – and their youngsters at their farm near the Massif in the south of France, where they often went on vacation. My brother and I were sorry to leave but we went from there to Italy and gradually worked our way south. Though Dad was often on official business, we had quite a bit of time to ourselves for touring and Steve and I will always remember the warm hospitality of the families with whom we were billeted, and the way the Italians took to us fair-haired "*Inglese* children."

We were generously provided with a car and visited many famous sites. However, what stands out in my memory is the desolation of the war, still much in evidence. We went to the place in the mountains where Mum's MGH was stationed and saw many an abandoned tank, gun or vehicle, rusting by the roadside. Our parents strictly forbade us to play on any of the wrecks near where we stopped, or even to leave their side.

"Too many things around here that might go bang, dears," said Dad.

"And if you cut yourself, you could get a nasty infection," Mum warned. "Even though you've been immunised against tetanus, we mustn't take any risks."

With a nurse for a mother, we had already been informed about the horrors of lockjaw so having due regard for Dad's warning as well, we did as we were told.

Brother Steve and I have poignant memories, too, of the Commonwealth War Graves cemeteries we visited, with all those white headstones, row on row. Bronwyn's and Dinah's graves are in a cemetery near Argenta and Hoppy and Doug still lie side by side, though re-interred, along with the others who died that night, in a collection cemetery outside Ravenna.

Mum placed a wreath on each of the graves, and shed some tears while Dad held her close. We prayed as a family and said the Twenty-third Psalm together.

Mum and Dad also took us to an elderly folk's home, situated in the fertile hills of Calabria, surrounded by green pastures filled with bleating flocks and gentle slopes of olive and vine groves in abundance.

After Mum enquired at Reception, a nurse in nun's habit conducted us across the grounds to where an old man was sitting on a bench in the shade of a fir tree. We stopped a short distance behind him.

The nurse said to Mum, "I will come back when it is time for him to go inside," and left.

"I'll go speak to him first," Mum said. "We shouldn't all descend on him at once."

He looked up as Mum approached and she said later she could read death in every line of his countenance. He was terminally ill. She thought he might not recognise her but instead, he got to his feet straightaway and embraced Mum with a cry of joy.

"My dear Sister!" he exclaimed. "How long has it been? Ten years, yes, but you have not changed, except that you are not in uniform. And this is your family?" he said enthusiastically as Mum beckoned us over. "Praise God!"

Mum introduced him as Father Alonzo. She had told us of how they had met in Naples in the summer of 1944. With the help of Uncle Peter and Major John, Mum and Dad located the retired priest's whereabouts and purposed to visit him.

While Steve and I ran around on the lawn, the three of them sat on the bench in earnest conversation. The Father was clearly distressed when Mum told him about Sister Hopgood but other things troubled him as well.

When the nun came to fetch him, he said to her, "My dear, I am sure you will not mind if Sister Graham takes my arm? We still have so much to catch up on."

I could see the nurse didn't like it but she backed off a respectable distance and my parents escorted the priest back to the home, while he leant on Mum's arm, with her stooping to listen as he continued speaking.

To Mum and Dad's amazement, Alonzo already knew of the attempt on Mum's life. When my parents described Vicky Freeman's analysis of the enemy's strategy, Alonzo not only confirmed that she was correct but that the strategy remained in place.

This is the gist of what he said:

"My friends, you have enjoyed several years of blessing but I *know* what happened to you, soon after the war. Yes, the news travelled. You helped prevent a great evil but I can assure you that the dark forces are re-gathering themselves, to assail you once more, and your allies. Your nation is strong and proud, yet that is her greatest weakness. She sees only the military threat from the Communist East but that is exactly what Mother Church *wants* her to see. Your friend Vicky was right. The real danger approaches from another quarter, to de-spoil your beloved nation. Remember, your people humiliated Mother Church *twice* in the last forty years and she will wreak revenge, not by outward show of strength but by deceit, at which she has been so adept for centuries. It will happen and I fear she has already begun."

Mum kept up regular correspondence with Alonzo until his death early in 1955. She reckoned it was probably "assisted." "I didn't like the way the nun was looking at us, love," she said to Dad as we drove away. "At all."

"Well, Alonzo's already been proved right," Dad remarked[374].

He meant that the 1735 Witchcraft Act, outlawing the kind of gatherings that would have taken my mother's life, had finally been repealed three years earlier[375]. Mum and Dad were convinced that the long arm of St John Montague-Stewart was partly to blame but as Alonzo hinted, an even greater flood of filth was about to burst forth on our nation. I'll deal with that in a moment, after concluding the narration of our Italian tour on a happier note.

When Dad finished his official business, we spent several glorious days sight-seeing Vesuvius, the Sorrentine Peninsula and Capri, where we stayed a few nights.

La Grotta Azzurra was the most spectacular sight there but Mum was noticeably keen for a swim near the Faraglioni Rocks. She even had a particular spot picked out on the rock shelf beach that fortunately turned out to be vacant, in spite of the considerable number of holidaymakers round about.

And, in keeping with local fashion, Mum wore a bikini, something she probably wouldn't have done in England though she had the perfect figure for one in those days, even after giving birth to us. For Dad's sake, she fought hard to keep it, an endeavour in which she was successful for a good many years and an inspiration to her friends.

She naturally attracted admiring stares from many other males present, particularly the Italians, but since Dad was essentially an Anglo-Saxon warrior look-alike at the time, apart from his short back-and-sides, the viewers kept their distance.

At one point, while my brother and I splashed around in the shallows, I saw Mum and Dad tenderly kissing as they reposed on the rock shelf.

Mum explained why some years later, relating the story of her wartime visit to Capri with Captain Tony.

The following summer, we went on holiday to Fehmarn Island in the Baltic, for a fascinating, fun-filled fortnight, though Steve and I were old enough to be slightly embarrassed at the sight of our normally staid parents wrestling in the sea and laughingly chasing each other up and down some sandhills, in front of sombre-faced Teutonic tourists.

Dad told us about his trip there in 1945 with Aunt Kate, when we were a bit older.

We dropped in on the Vanderveers, of course. And visited the places where Dad's friends who died in the war are buried.

Apart from those visits, our parents never spoke much about the war while we were children. Yet, we were reminded of it in other ways, sometimes humorously, especially when we visited their wartime friends or they came to see us.

I remember once when the Shorelands visited, I briefly interrupted the game we were playing with their two kids to go and ask Mum a question. She was in the kitchen with Mrs Shoreland, getting tea ready.

"Mum, why does Dad keep saying, 'Shh, shh,' whenever Uncle Boff starts talking about Monique?"

It was a put-up job, of course. Dad told Mum the story only a day or so after they first met.

Another reminder was the campaign that Doreen and other ex-QAs waged to win compensation from the government for the six hundred mustard gas victims of Bari[376]. They finally succeeded in 1986. Dorrie kept Mum informed the whole time.

To return to Alonzo's warning of impending evil, Mum and Dad made their own heartfelt protest about the downfall of our nation during the era of the so-called 'Swinging Sixties.' They did it for us, as indeed they did everything, though I didn't appreciate it then. I and my high-booted, mini-skirted friends thought the Liverpool 'Fab Four' and their contemporaries were 'cool.' It was years, and in some cases after considerable heartache, before we understood that the entertainment we idolatrously worshipped was nothing more than Voodoo jungle fertility rites of Haiti and Central Africa imported into the West via the bar and red-light districts of New Orleans's lower Basin Street.

In other words, sheer Satanic filth, as heartless as Von Hollstein's scheme.

For the corruption of the generations growing up after the war.

The strategy admirably succeeded[377].

And it was no accident that the place where it started in the West was the main stronghold of Mother Church in the strongest of the free nations.

To put Mum's protest in context, we must go back again to 1946, a few weeks after she and Dad were married, when she was invited to London to be awarded an MBE for *her gallant conduct* according to the citation, *during the night of January -[th] 1945, near the valley of the Senio in northern Italy.* She was one of a number of wartime nursing Sisters to receive decorations.

It is still edifying to contemplate the photos taken of the occasion.

One of Mum wearing her award shows this beautiful young girl in uniform with her wonderful smile and rich auburn locks, glistening QA cap badge and campaign ribbons of Italy and Burma displayed on the left breast of the immaculate tunic.

A second photo shows Mum and Dad together. Brown-haired and boyish looking, Dad has his arm around her. Still on the reserve, he is in uniform as well and reckoned it was the only time he ever condescended to wear a Sam Browne belt.

After receipt of their decorations, the wartime Sisters paraded for their distinguished patron.

They did not have much time to practise the drill but as Mum said, "It all came back." Dad's soldierly eye scrutinised the turnout, the march past in time with the massed band and the eyes-right by the royal dais with the salute from the senior nursing officer, none other than Debs (n) Tyndall.

And Dad reckoned that the performance "would have done credit to the Brigade of Guards."

Grandma and Grandad McGrath were there, too, bursting with pride. Though they never quite got free of the old religion, I think they eventually came to saving faith, largely thanks to Dad, who quickly won their hearts. That day helped, too.

It was a great occasion. If only camcorders had been around then.

Especially insofar as a formal reception was held in the evening with the medal recipients as guests of honour, attired in evening dress and at one point, everyone joined in singing Land of Hope and Glory.

The evening was preceded by an equally memorable incident – for Dad, allegedly.

According to him, the silk *lingerie* that Mum received from the generous Americans in Naples made its appearance while they were getting ready for the big do.

His story is that he walked into the bedroom of their hotel suite when Mum had slipped the garments on, with a pair of high heels and was scrutinising the effect in a full-length mirror, while applying perfume.

When he expressed his appreciation, he sat on the bed and she came and seated herself on his knee.

Following a lengthy kiss, their conversation is supposed to have gone like this.

"If I could have had a fiver for every time I've been whistled at by blokes like you in last few years, we could retire in style."

"Wearing that gear, I'm not surprised."

"It was usually field kit but that never seemed to make much difference."

"It's what's underneath that counts."

Mum neither confirmed nor denied the story.

But to continue, in 1964, the four degenerates I mentioned earlier each received the same award as Mum.

She promptly sent her MBE back, with a copy of her citation and a cover note that reads as follows:

It is with considerable regret that I am returning the enclosed decoration that I received for service as a Queen Alexandra Sister in the Italian Theatre of Operations in January 1945. I have not taken this decision lightly.

For your information, a copy of my citation is also enclosed. I would add that Nursing Officer Marjorie Hopgood, referred to therein, who died shielding a wounded soldier with her own body, was my close friend. Skilled emergency surgery, carried out by Captain James Rodwell, RAMC, subsequently saved that soldier's life.

I was deeply saddened and angered to learn that the same award as mine has recently been made to four nefarious individuals whose only real contribution to this nation has been the accelerated propagation of African sex-orgy music inextricably associated with sorcery, venereal disease and devil worship. It is a contribution that this nation could well do without.

I am not prudish. After all, I was in the British Army but for that reason, I am only too acquainted with the practice and fruits of evil. The bestowal of prominent awards on such unworthy individuals is not only the grossest insult to the memory of those who made the ultimate sacrifice, like my dear friend Sister Hopgood, but also an encouragement to the unrelenting spread of evil and a disgrace to all that is right and good, especially insofar as the recipients must have been approved at the highest level. That is why I am returning my particular award.

No good can come of your part in this dismal affair and I anticipate that quite the reverse must inevitably be the result.

As the Psalmist has said 'The wicked walk on every side, when the vilest men are exalted.'

I would wish to end this letter in the usual fashion but the action for which you must ultimately bear responsibility before God prevents me from so doing. I hope and pray that you will understand and respond to His wisdom on these matters, before His judgement falls, as it must do, in the absence of any genuine repentance on your part.

Colleen Graham, Mrs, ex QAIMNS/R

Dad appended a brief statement to the letter[378].

I fully support my wife's decision. Captain Stephen Graham, ex Royal Engineers.

Mum received an anodyne reply that expressed disappointment but not much else.

The judgement did fall, indeed was already descending. A few years later, robbed of her moral and spiritual backbone by the devil-worshipping filth of the 'Dark Continent' and the national church's spineless retreat from the Authorised 1611 Holy Bible, our nation fell helplessly into the jaws of the emerging papal Fourth Reich. Some call it a 'Union.' We call it the 'Golden Garrotte[379].'

And with our fate decided by foreigners without and traitors within, we are now *like a city that is broken down and without walls*[380], overrun by *the worst of the heathen*[381], from every corner of the globe, with many young males of the Islamic religion eager to brutalise the 'infidels' around them, after the manner of their Waffen-SS ideological forebears and in keeping with a centuries-long tradition of slavery and terror[382].

As if the legions of home-grown reprobates weren't enough.

Sadly, much Muslim-inspired violence takes place in the same area that provided an abundance of recruits for the gallant West Yorkshire Regiment, in which my father-in-law and his friend Leigh Grafton served during the Burma campaign.

And many of the tough sappers that served with Dad came from there.

To make matters worse, the area also suffered from the disastrous miners' strike of 1984 that irreparably ruptured some of the most closely-knit communities on earth.

"Scargill and Thatcher[383] between them did what Hitler never even came close to doing," Dad said.

Numerous pits had already closed and others were becoming uneconomic but as Mum said, "You don't fix a sprained wrist by amputating at the shoulder."

Mum and Dad always believed that the 1984 strike, along with the EU and Third-world immigration were yet more of the Enemy's tactics for destroying Britain[384], in addition to the corruption wrought by sixties' Beatle-mania. Its creators perfected their art in the drug dens and whorehouses of the Reeperbhan in Hamburg[385].

"Machine-gun Alley, the blokes called it in forty-five," Dad said, an allusion to the troops' method of summoning prostitutes by tapping on the barred windows of their establishments with coins. "They wouldn't have imported the devilment here, though."

That was the difference between the occupation troops, however licentious and the 'Fab Four.'

"Seems we didn't quite finish the job," said Uncle Neil, who flew on many bombing raids against Hamburg.

Obviously, the war's aftermath was a multi-headed hydra.

And it was not what Mum and Dad's generation fought and suffered for.

In hindsight, therefore, it appears that the most they achieved was a brief stay of national execution.

We don't know how long Tom and Vicky Freeman's 'Combined Operation' extended that hiatus but having blocked the occult explosion planned for the summer solstice of 1948, it was nevertheless, as my son said in his opening chapter, 'a great service.'

Even if of temporary benefit.

All Mum's ex-QA friends supported the step she took, though some in characteristically tongue-in-cheek fashion. Aunt Annie summed it up as follows:

"You were the only one of the whole gang of us to get a proper gong and you sent it back, you daft article. Mind you, we'd have all done the same."

But Mum never forgot her deliverers. She kept in touch with all those who made up Vicky Freeman's prayer army and others besides, those Mum and Dad had served with and the families of their friends who had died.

And she got replies.

Even James Rodwell, with whom Mum served in Italy, wrote back to her. Mrs Rodwell was amazed.

"He's a terrible about replying to letters," she said. "And his handwriting's even worse."

Many of that prayer army have gone home to Glory now, including Vicky herself and husband Tom. We miss them. It can truly be said that *They were a wall unto us both by night and day*[386].

And I can say with deep gratitude that when Dad and Matt senior died, it was with quiet dignity, in the presence of those they loved most, a further testimony to the Saviour's loving kindness.

Of those who remain, who were with Mum or Dad on overseas active service, Andy and Dollie still live in Market Harborough with Mollie Briggs and June Halliard in a retirement village close by.

Dai and Gwen moved to Betws-y-Coed as they'd planned, where Gwen, though widowed, is almost a matriarch in their area. She'd love to visit her friends "east of the Dyke[387]" more often but says, plausibly, "Someone has to keep an eye on the younger ones, you know."

Leigh and Rachel live in Harrogate and they kept in touch with Greg and Mrs Barraclough until Greg passed away a year or so ago. He was always grateful for my father-in-law's prompt action and Captain Mostyn's surgery that helped preserve his sight, though he needed assistance from St Dunstans[388] in later years.

Uncle Neil and Aunt Emma stayed in Yorkshire. So did Bill and Lorraine. We weren't surprised. Captain and Mandy Cosgrove settled in a moorland town about thirty minutes' drive from the General, where she and Mum trained. Mandy lives in the same town to this day.

I should mention that we still hear from the French and the Manning families in New South Wales. Janice and Mrs French kept in close touch with us all their lives and though Matt spent most of his life on the other side of the globe, he, John and Barney were living examples of the words of Solomon[389]:

Iron sharpeneth iron; so a man sharpeneth the countenance of his friend.

Jon and Robyn Gray still have their home in the Lincolnshire Wolds. In the way that our families networked, to use the modern expression, my literary son Simon, named after my grandfather-in-law, married Jon and Robyn's granddaughter. He reckons that if she donned a WW2 QA uniform and had her picture taken, it would be indistinguishable from the wartime photos of her grandmother.

Lauren has yet to take up the challenge.

"I'd feel like I was about to relive Grandma's war," she once said. "I don't think I could handle that, not after what she's told me."

So Simon doesn't push it. Sensitive lad.

Mark and Katrijn Napper live not far from Jon and Robyn. Mark says that the Wolds are probably the best compromise between Holland and the hills of Buxton. And we keep in touch with Jan and Marikje in Eindhoven. They attended Mum and Dad's funerals.

Aunt Kate finished cataloguing the books at Waverly Manor and then accepted a junior partnership with a local vet.

"Good to have an expert in situ," Uncle Peter said. "Especially at calving, foaling and lambing times."

Though it wasn't long before Kate was a mum herself, necessitating a career change.

Uncle Peter and Aunt Kate eventually retired to the south of France, leaving the manor in the care of their eldest son. They live in a lovely cottage not far from the little station where they were so joyfully reunited.

Their home is only a short walk from the cemetery where the Hallés are buried. Aunt Kate is glad of that because she often goes there to put flowers on their graves and her hip gives her "a bit of bother" these days.

From having been shot all those years ago.

But Uncle Peter says, "Apart from that, we're OK. This area seems good for health and longevity."

He could be right. Both the Hallés lived on into this century and passed away each aged over a hundred, Alain having been one of the last remaining French veterans of the Great War.

Of our overseas loved ones, Helen Jardine and Karen Congreve live within a stone's throw of each other in Banff and often write to us, as do the Hedges, also resident there. Actually, they're into email, as are a number of our extended family here, so that speeds up communication considerably.

Kitty and her husband emigrated to New Zealand, where she and Sarah Mostyn live across the street from one another in a hamlet on the west coast. *It's the quietest place on earth*, Paddy said in a letter, when I wrote to say Matt junior and I were coming to visit. She was right.

Ellie Calder never looked back after her deliverance from the oafish Buzz. She followed Trish into nursing and served for two years as an RAF Nursing Officer. Thanks to the aforementioned 'networking,' she came to know Bill Harris's younger brother Rob, whom she married while they were both stationed in Germany.

(My husband Matt junior and I grew up together by means of the same networking, though he thought I was 'a gawky kid' until I turned sixteen. Another ten years went by before we married but all that time we were a match made in Heaven, of that I've no doubt.)

Rob actually flew in the same squadron as Uncle Neil during the Berlin Airlift of 1948. He and Ellie live quite close to Trish. After Matt died, she moved from where they lived in the country to a smaller house on the outskirts of Banbury.

She is of course our 'other grandmother,' to whom my son referred in the opening chapter.

And she has kept up the ministry she shared with Matt senior. It includes giving talks to classes of school and college students. Here is an excerpt.

"As a British Army Nursing Officer during World War Two, I injected drugs in great quantities. Morphine, for example and even heroin. If a casualty has got daylight showing through his gut, he needs it. You don't. Your body is given to you as the temple of God[390]. It is not a dumping ground for toxic waste."

The local teens affectionately refer to her as Grandma T and have become her self-appointed 'minders,' fetching her shopping, doing her garden and carrying out various home maintenance jobs.

Some rough edges remain, though always in Grandma's best interests:

"Any outsiders give you hassle, Grandma T, just let us know. We'll kneecap 'em."

Lads and lasses confide in her all the time, to receive comfort and guidance from the scriptures in return.

They recognise in Grandma T one of the few links left with old England and they love her to bits, as the saying goes. She for her part is overwhelmingly grateful. "They are such a comfort," she tells us. "Like you folks have been, ever since Matt died."

Trish has experienced some health problems in the past year, which is not surprising for a woman of her age but they nearly prevented her from going to Mum's funeral. Her GP, who incidentally is June Halliard's niece, said this:

"As far as we can tell, there's no history of heart trouble in your family and you've always been as fit as a flea. I put it down to your war service in the Far East."

Those terrible years cast a long shadow.

For Mum as well. She had the added memory of her post-war ordeal and she never liked being parted from Dad for any length of time. That was another reason why we all went to Italy together.

"I depended so much on Steve, right from the day we first met outside Deepvale," she told us after Dad died. "He was God's gift, you know. I feel vulnerable now, even though I know Father's always there and you folk are so good to me."

She grew particularly wary of strangers in the last year of her life, especially if they were foreign (anyone not white Anglo-Saxon-Celtic Protestant, in Mum's estimation) and never liked going out unless one of us went with her, or our grown-up offspring. Mum said she hated being a nuisance but in truth she never was. On the contrary, we loved visiting her and having her stay with us, as she often did, or taking her to see her wartime friends.

And our youngsters were fascinated by their grandma and grandpa's reminiscences of the great World War.

Still are, as the reader will appreciate.

However, sad though we were at Mum's passing, it is a mercy that she is at rest now and rejoicing in Heaven, with Dad and the entire company of the Redeemed.

Because on earth the forces of evil never went away. Mum and Dad were in the forefront of the battle against them all their lives – and the Enemy knew it.

In other words, Mum had reason to feel vulnerable.

Yet despite her growing anxieties towards the end of her life, she and Dad never lost faith in the final victory.

To illustrate, I close with this anecdote that virtually brings us full circle.

Mum and Dad had recently moved into their new home. It was a mild autumn day.

After spending an afternoon helping Dad work on the back garden, Mum went inside to begin supper.

Dad came in a little later and said, "Come and have a look at this."

She accompanied him to the rear of the yard. It looked out over a long forested slope and growing a few feet inside the back fence was a silver birch.

Dad pointed out two raw slashes across the trunk on the side nearer the fence, about head high.

The slashes were several inches in length and appeared to have been carved by a huge cat's claw.

In the shape of an X.

"How did that get there?" Mum asked.

"I don't know," Dad said. "It wasn't there yesterday. Someone, or something, must have done it during the night."

"I guess it means the curse is still here, all the way from the Pyramids, as if I needed reminding," Mum said with a sigh.

Dad put his arm around her shoulders.

"Remember the verse Vicky quoted," he said. "'But thanks be to God, which giveth us the victory through our Lord Jesus Christ.'"

Nestling beneath Dad's arm, Mum kissed him with fervour and gazed lovingly into his eyes.

"He always will, love," she whispered. "Until we're in his presence."

Dad drew her closer. They kissed again and Dad said with assurance, "Desired haven."

Where they are now. And their testimony is that of St Paul[391], a fitting example to any believer.

I have fought a good fight, I have finished my course, I have kept the faith.

God grant that so may we. Amen.

Appendix – The Lycanthrope Plot

The assassination attempt on Kate Bramble – see Chapter 23 - required careful planning and coordination. In the absence of direct testimony or indeed any substantial corroborative evidence, the sequence of steps has nevertheless been pieced together as follows and is reckoned to be a fair representation of what happened. Hopefully, it will serve to answer any questions prompted by that part of the narrative.

We believe the lycanthrope method of attack was chosen because although Von Hollstein and Albrecht were unavoidably accessories, Franz sought to minimise the risk of suspicion, given that the conspiracy was in its final stages. As in the case of the unfortunate Wilfred Houghton, a lycanthrope murder would leave no trace to identify the killer – and in this instance, facilitate concealment of the corpses until the conspiracy was fulfilled.

Sensing Von Hollstein's continuing caution, Kate, Brian and Mollie correctly surmised that despite his apparent recognition of Kate, he would not act precipitously until his plan was on the brink of fulfilment, by which time Kate and the others believed that Tom and Vicky would have their full team on the ground, ready to intervene. The trio thus continued their surveillance.

But no-one anticipated a lycanthrope riposte.

Soon after her visit to Von Hollstein, Rita as Queen Rhiannon would have communed with Hiresh, priest of Kali and enacted the ritual by which he would assume his werebeast identity at an agreed time and place. These arrangements would have entailed occult practices that took some time to put into effect and an additional interval was needed for Hiresh to spy out his intended victim and decide on the preferred site for his attack.

This accounts for the hiatus of nearly a fortnight between Rita's meeting with Von Hollstein and the attempt on Kate's life. It is most likely that the priest carried out the counter-surveillance himself, by means of telekinesis, a Shamanistic process whereby a subject can be monitored even though the observer is many miles distant[392]. Kate and the Briggses were sure that the conspirators did not physically follow them during this time.

Kate's initiative to catalogue the library at Waverly Manor fulfilled an essential part of the surveillance but inadvertently provided the enemy with the opportunity he sought. Hiresh evidently chose his time after ensuring – telekinetically - that Kate had established a routine. He did not physically enter the grounds until the day of the projected attack, where he remained in hiding to observe Kate and Miss Heythorpe on the terrace. Later, in his werebeast guise, Hiresh confronted Kate on the road to the manor. He knew it would almost certainly be deserted at that time. In any event, he was prepared to take the risk.

His intention was to seize and dispatch Kate in the underbrush, to conceal as far as possible the signs of the murder, use his demonic power to stall the Morris - as he had done with Houghton's Bentley - when the Briggses came searching for Kate, most likely by car to save time and because Mollie was pregnant, eliminate them and remove the bodies from the scene. The second attack would be so swift the victims would have no chance to raise an alarm. In his supernatural guise, Hiresh could rapidly transport even three corpses unseen through the deserted woods, aided by the fading daylight. Under cover of darkness he would conceal them in the old quarry and obliterate his tracks. None of this would be difficult. The forest area was private land and not frequented. The abandoned quarry area was, as Brian Briggs observed, replete with ready-made places of concealment such as old excavations, spoil heaps and unused buildings – apart from the change room selected as the preparation chamber. The site was also considerably overgrown.

Hiresh could easily have been far from the area by dawn. The occult community would ensure that his movements during the time of the murders remained secret.

What of the abandoned Morris? Its disposal was key to the success of the plan and doubtless required Von Hollstein and Albrecht's assistance. The general area of the attack offered additional advantages in the form of a side road overhung with trees in deep shadow during late afternoon, with an adjacent wooded hillside. Here, from a safe distance, Albrecht could observe through binoculars the stone bridge where Brian and Mollie rendez-voused with Kate in the afternoons. On finishing work that day, he would have set out for the side road in his van after giving the Briggses a comfortable lead, intending to follow up the murders on foot[393], drive the Morris to a distant location via back roads and abandon it. It is likely he would have access to a garage to repair any damage, resulting from Hiresh's attack on the Briggses, such as a broken windscreen. A search for the Morris's missing occupants would logically start from the place where it was found abandoned. Any search of the quarry site prior to the fulfilment of the conspiracy must be considered unlikely.

Von Hollstein, in the meantime, would discreetly go by push bike to the side road and collect Albrecht's van on confirmation from Jozef of a successful attack. A time lapse of no more than an hour, probably less, would have reasonably been anticipated between the parking and retrieval of the van. The plan clearly required nerve but the plotters had plenty of that.

We think that Albrecht arrived in time to see Kate emerging from the approach road unharmed. Realising the attack had failed, he returned immediately to his van, then drove via the side road to the nearest phone box, where he put in the calls to Von Hollstein and McNabb, who of course had several hours to prepare his subterfuge.

Albrecht then drove to the vicinity of the Halliards' home to confirm the team's initial destination, on the correct assumption that even the brief time taken for Kate and the others to complete preparations for their departure would give him a satisfactory head start. From there, events continued as described.

The above suggests that the group had a contingency plan. They were probably shrewd enough to devise one. We don't know where Hiresh's Master intercepted him but deposition of the priest's body in the East End would be a simple matter for the occult underground, acting on their Master's orders.

Over sixty years later, much remains speculative but we rest in the wisdom of Solomon:

"For God shall bring every work into judgment, with every secret thing, whether it be good, or whether it be evil" Ecclesiastes 12:14

Glossary

AA	anti-aircraft
AIF	Australian Imperial Forces
alpenfestung	alpine fortress
AMC	Armed Merchant Cruiser
ANZAC	Australian and New Zealand Army Corps
A/P	anti-personnel
ark	turretless AVRE with twin twelve-foot ramps front and rear for bridging gaps. A line of arks could also bridge a shallow river.
ASC	Advanced Surgical Centre
askari	European-trained East African soldier
A/T	anti-tank
ATS	Auxiliary Territorial Service
AVRE	Assault Vehicle Royal Engineers, modified Churchill tank
B Echelon	logistic support
Bailey Bridge	pre-fabricated military bridge designed in sections for rapid assembly and dismantling. Each section consisted of ten-foot long *panels* made of steel girders connected by cross struts, I beam horizontal *transoms* for connecting the panels and elongated box-shaped *stringers* fastened between the transoms on which planking was laid. Baileys could be mounted on pontoons to bridge rivers.
Bandar-log	monkey people in Kipling's *Jungle Book*
Bangalore torpedo	metal pipe filled with explosive
Bart's	St Bartholomew's Hospital, London
basha	thatched bamboo hut
BD	battledress, made from tough, wool-based fibre
BEF	British Expeditionary Force
Bermondsey	district in London, south of the Thames
BGH	British General Hospital
bithess	tarred hessian, artificial road surface
blinder	excellent sporting performance
bobby-dazzler	WW2 Australian expression of praiseworthiness
BORs	British other ranks
box	in the CBI Theatre of Operations, a defensive perimeter. One of the best known was that established at Imphal, Assam, to stem the Japanese invasion of India, March-July 1944.
brew up	brew tea. The term was also applied to a tank hit by the enemy and set on fire.
Bridlington	Town on the Yorkshire coast.
Brummie	native of Birmingham, England
buffalo LVT	amphibious vehicle, landing vehicle, tracked
bully	tinned corned beef
burk up	be sick

bushranger	Australian highwayman, of the nineteenth century
buttoned-up	description of tanks sealed for action or crews confined to tanks
cab rank	close support aircraft for ground troops
canny	Northeast England generic term for anything good. It can also mean shrewd and in Scotland the word is confined to this meaning.
C-47	twin-engineered military transport aircraft, also called the Dakota. It has the distinction of being the only WW2 aircraft still in service. The Douglas DC-3 is its civilian counterpart
CCS	Casualty Clearing Station
chae	variation on char.
chagal	large water container
chain	twenty-two yards, an old measurement
char	tea, usually the ready-mixed British Army beverage known as 'compo' tea.
chaung	stream in Burma
chespale	interconnected chestnut palings
Chins	Burmese hill tribe loyal to the British in WW2. Others included Kachins, Karens and Nagas
Chindits	derived from chinthes. The name bestowed on Allied forces made up of British, Gurkha and West African troops who fought behind Japanese lines in Burma in WW2
chinthes	mythical beasts, supposedly temple guardians
Chokkos	diminutive of "chocolate soldiers." Militia conscripts, who served only on Australian mandated territory.
C-in-C SEAC	Commander-in-Chief, South East Asia Command, the late Lord Louis Mountbatten
CO	Commanding Officer
co-ax	machine gun mounted in tank turret, therefore co-axial with the circle of the main turret gun's traverse
conner	Maconochie's stew, available in compo rations and highly favoured by ordinary soldiers
crocodile	flame-throwing Churchill tank
CSM	company sergeant major
CWA	Country Women's Association
D plus	days after the Normandy landing of June 6th 1944. D+2 would be June 8th.
D'ye ken?	Do you know?
dah	long, double-edged, Burmese knife. A short sword, in effect.
Dak	C-47, Dakota transport aircraft
Digger	WW1, WW2 Australian infantryman
dead ground	ground out of sight in a field of fire, often a depression
dixie	rectangular metal food containers of various capacities. The smaller variety were issued to WW2 troops as part of their personal kit
DLI, Durhams	Durham Light Infantry, a famous British regiment
dolly pegs	wooden pegs used for wringing clothes
Don, Rother	rivers near Sheffield in south Yorkshire

DR	dispatch rider
DSO	Distinguished Service Order
DUKW	amphibious vehicle
Duntroon	Australia's Royal Military College
DZ	drop zone
East Anglia	counties of Norfolk and Suffolk in England
eighty-eight	German 88 mm artillery piece
ENSA	Entertainments National Service Association
ETA	estimated time of arrival
fascine	artificial roadway, constructed of interconnected wooden poles of chestnut paling, transported wrapped as a coil on the front of an AVRE. For obvious reasons, the word is from the same root as 'fascist.'
FANY	First Aid Nursing Yeomanry. The most famous member of this unit was Kay Summersby, General, later President Dwight D. Eisenhower's driver and, allegedly, mistress.
first fifteen	the premier Rugby Union football team at a school, college or university
five hundred-pounders	five hundred-pound bombs carried by ground-attack aircraft
FO	Flying Officer
FOO	Forward Observation Officer
funk hole	place of refuge
gan	Northeast England expression for "go"
gauleiter	senior German officer in an occupied district
gen	intelligence
General Wade charge	twenty-six pound explosive charge that could be placed by hand. It resembled half a doughnut in shape
Geordie	Tynesider. See below
ghat	open air crematorium
goolies	private parts
Goums	French Colonial Moroccan soldiers, expert in mountain warfare and stealth operations, but notorious for cruelty to civilians in occupied countries, e.g. Italy, especially women
Guy's	Guy's Hospital, London
gyppo	thief
Haddaway	Northeast England expression for "Don't be silly." The expression "Geddaway, " (Get away) is also used.
Halifax	four-engined WW2 heavy bomber, also used for parachuting agents and supplies into occupied territory
Harvey Nick's	Harvey Nichols. Luxury department store in London's west end. The late Princess Di used to shop there
HE	high explosive
HQ	headquarters
Hurri-bomber	ground attack version of the RAF's famous Hawker Hurricane fighter
ICI	Imperial Chemical Industries
INA	Indian National Army, allies of the Japanese in WW2. The British referred to its members as "Jiffs"

IORs	Indian other ranks
IV	intra-venous
JGs	jungle green denim fatigues
Jiff	see INA
Kachin Rangers	WW2 irregular forces drawn from Kachin hill tribe of Burma
Kali	Hindu goddess and most powerful of the Hindu deities
Karens	another Burmese hill tribe, from which irregular forces were drawn
KBE	Knight Commander of the British Empire
KCMG	Knight Commander of the Order of St Michael and St George
KCSI	Knight Commander of the Order of the Star of India
KDs	khaki drill fatigues, in shades varying from light to dark
Keighley	town in West Yorkshire. Other Yorkshire towns mentioned in Chapter 12 include Harrogate, Huddersfield and Shipley. Harrogate was – and is – largely residential. Until the 1950s, the other towns were part of the woollens and textiles industries centred on the Leeds-Bradford conurbation. The area produced a stubborn and strong-minded working class, excellent material for high quality infantry soldiers, such as those in Calvert's platoon
KFS	knife, fork, spoon
KIA	killed in action
KOYLI	Kings Own Yorkshire Light Infantry
kooker	kukri
kukri	Gurkha curved knife, blade broadening towards the point
L-5	light aircraft for delivery and evacuation of personnel
Lancaster	four-engined WW2 heavy bomber
lance-jack	lance-corporal, equivalent to private, first-class
LCI	landing craft-infantry
LCP	landing craft-personnel
LCT	landing craft-tank
Lee-Enfield	WW2 British infantry rifle
Lewes	town in southeast England
Llangollen	town in Wales
LMG	light machine gun
longyi, lungyi	wrap-around skirt
loud-hailer	megaphone
Lysander	light aircraft, like the L-5
mahout	Indian elephant driver
Maquis, Maquisards	WW2 French Resistance
marra	friend
Max Factor unit	Maxillo-Facial units, for facial and burn injuries
MC	Military Cross
MFTU	Malaria Forward Treatment Unit
MG	machine gun. Also a popular British sports car, in context.
MGH	Mobile General Hospital
MMG	medium machine gun
MO	Medical officer
moaner	moaning minnie, six-barrelled German mortar

naik	Ghurka corporal
North Riding	North Yorkshire. Until 1974, the county was divided into three "ridings" or thirds, east, west and north
Nuremberg raid	night attack by RAF Bomber Command, March 30th 1944. Of seven hundred and eighty-one aircraft that set out, ninety-four failed to return, one of the heaviest Allied loss rates of the war. See Purnell's *History of The Second World War*, Volume 4, p 1736. RAF Halifax captain and pilot, Flying Officer Cyril Barton, a committed Christian, was awarded a posthumous Victoria Cross for his part in the raid
O Group	Orders Group
OC	Officer Commanding, subordinate to the CO
OCS	Officer Candidate School
OMC	Owen Machine Carbine, similar to the British Sten and American M-3
on stag	on sentry duty
OP	observation post
OR	other rank
OSS	Office of Strategic Services, equivalent of the British SOE, Special Operations Executive
Oxford eights	eight man rowing team for Oxford University
panels	see Bailey bridge
Pathfinder	elite RAF bomber squadrons that led the raids
poilu	French infantryman of the 1914-18 War
pongo	Royal Navy slang term for soldiers
PSP	perforated steel planking
PT	physical training
PTC	preliminary training course
puggaree	thin muslin scarf worn around the crown of a hat
PX	Post Exchange, where luxury items could be bought
QA	Queen Alexandra Nursing Sister
QAIMNS	Queen Alexandra's Imperial Military Nursing Service
QARANC	Queen Alexandra's Royal Army Nursing Corps, the post war equivalent of the QAIMNS
RAAF	Royal Australian Air Force
RAEME	Royal Australian Electrical and Mechanical Engineers
RAF	Royal Air Force
RAMC	Royal Army Medical Corps
RAP	Regimental Aid Post
RASC	Royal Army Service Corps, now Royal Corps of Transport
RDF	radio direction finder
RE	Royal Engineer
Richmond, Australia	A town west of Sydney and site of a war-time Royal Australian Air Force base
RMO	regimental medical officer
RN	Royal Navy
RV	rendez-vous place
Sandhurst	Britain's Royal Military Academy, located in Hampshire

sapper	lowest rank in Corps of Royal Engineers, although term is also generic
SBGs	short box-girdered bridges
Schuh mine	German anti-personnel mine
SEAC	South East Asia Command. It directed the Burma campaign in WW2. *SEAC* was also the title of the Fourteenth Army newspaper.
Selby	Yorkshire mining town
Selfridges	luxury west end department store, like Harvey Nick's. Traditionally, one does not ask for the price in the store because "If Madame has to ask how much the garment costs, then perhaps Madame cannot afford it?"
sepoy	European-trained Indian soldier
SHAEF	Supreme Headquarters Allied Expeditionary Forces
sheila	base word for young woman. Not a proper name in the context.
SIW	self-inflicted wound
SMG	sub-machine gun
Sod's Law	like Murphy's Law
SOE	British Special Operations Executive, like the American OSS
SP gun	self-propelled gun, like a tank but with thinner armour
Star Chamber	inquisitorial court during the reign of King Charles I
stum	quiet
Stonk	Standard concentration of artillery and/or mortar fire
stringer	see Bailey Bridge
subahdar	chief Indian officer in a company of Indian soldiers
tarpaulin	canvas sheeting
SUR	Sydney University Regiment
Teller	German anti-tank mine
Tempest	Hawker Tempest, RAF fighter
terrapin	amphibious troop-carrying vehicle, similar to the American DUKW
Tiffy	Hawker Typhoon, RAF fighter-bomber
tonga	Indian horse-drawn taxi
transom	see Bailey Bridge
trig point	hilltop position for map referencing
Tulle Gras	antibiotic dressing for burns.
Tyneside	area of northeast England, around the River Tyne
UXB, UXP	unexploded bomb, projectile
VAD	Voluntary Aid Detachment, auxiliary nurses
Vale of Pickering	countryside south of the Yorkshire Moors
Vale of York	countryside south of the Yorkshire Moors
VD	venereal disease
Verey	signal flare, fired by hand-held pistol
Volkssturm	German Home Guard, composed of personnel under or over normal military age or otherwise unfit for service in the regular army
WAAF	Women's Auxiliary Air Force
WAC	Women's Army Corps

Wandsworth	district in London, south of the Thames
Wehrmacht	German Regular Army
Wellie	Wellington boots
Western Marches	Cumbria, north-west England
Westmorland	Pre-1970s county in northern England, now merged with Cumberland county to form Cumbria
wide boy	opportunist
wilco	will cooperate
WO	Warrant Officer
Woodpecker	Juki 7.7 mm machine gun. Also used as code name in Chapter 9
WP	white phosphorous. Used in artillery shells, it spontaneously combusts on contact with air.
WRNS	Women's Royal Naval Service
W/T	wireless telegraphy
Why-aye	Northeast England expression for "Why, yes" or "Well, yes."
WVS	Women's Voluntary Service

Endnotes

Chapter 1

[1] See *Sound of Battle*, by this author.

Chapter 2

[2] See *Nurses at War*, by Penny Starns, Chapter 3.

[3] Working companion, also friend. Probably from 'opposite number'

[4] Defensive perimeter. At the Imphal 'box,' March-July 1944, even medics were issued with weapons and helped to repel Japanese attacks. See *Another Brummie in Burma*, by Robert Street, Chapter 5. Female personnel had been evacuated. Here it is assumed that, with QA Sisters present and the CCS perimeter patrolled, presumably by men of a holding unit, RAMC orderlies would not be permitted to carry firearms on the wards. However, as will be seen, Lance Corporal Wood's disdain for regulations has a beneficial outcome.

[5] Troops in Burma wore short puttees in preference to gaiters because they were believed to offer better protection against leeches and other invasive vermin – although Australians in New Guinea wore calf-high gaiters. See *Quartered Safe Out Here*, by George MacDonald Fraser and Chapter 6 of this work.

Chapter 3

[6] See *Sound of Battle* by this author, Chapter 10.

[7] "English nurses?"

[8] "I'm sorry, I don't speak English."

[9] "Ah, but don't worry."

[10] "Draw a picture, yes?"

[11] "How much cost, please?"

[12] In *It Happened One Night*, released in 1934 and co-starring Clark Gable

[13] See *Children of the Sun*, by Morris West, Chapter 1, 2.

[14] See *Children of the Sun* and *Front-Line Nurse* by Eric Taylor, Chapter 7.

[15] See *Children of the Sun*, Chapter 5, *The Sharp End of War* by John Ellis, Chapter 7 and *Quiet Heroines, Nurses of the Second World War* by Brenda McBryde, Chapter 17.

[16] See *The Pink Swastika, Homosexuality in the Nazi Party* by Scott Lively and Kevin Abrams.

Chapter 4

[17] See *Sound of Battle*, Chapter 10.

[18] Based on the tune of *Lili Marlene*, this song was the 8th Army's sardonic reaction to an injudicious remark attributed to but denied by Lady Astor. See Purnell's *History of the Second World War,* Volume 5, p 2174.

[19] See *Sound of Battle*, Chapters 4, 10.

[20] See *Children of the Sun*, Chapter 8.

[21] Herculaneum was a centre of heathen philosophy at the time of eruption in AD 79. For St Paul's evaluation of such fruitless mental gymnastics, see Acts 17, AV1611.

[22] See *Sound of Battle*, Chapter 14.

Chapter 5

[23] See *A Half Acre of Hell*, by Avis D. Schorer, p 189.

[24] See discardedlies.com/entries/2005/06/sophia_fascists_and_immigrants.php and www.h-net.org/~africa/threads/moroccan.html.

[25] See *A Nurse's War*, by Brenda McBryde, Chapters 4, 12 and *Caen, Anvil of Victory*, by Alexander McKee, Chapter 11.

[26] See *Front Line Nurse*, by Eric Taylor, Chapter 9.

[27] See *A Nurse's War*, Chapter 12 and *Quiet Heroines*, Chapter 20, by Brenda McBryde.

[28] See *A Half Acre of Hell*, p 189. The British called them 'S' mines.

[29] Romans 8:28. See *Quiet Heroines*, Chapter 17. In real life, the patient did not express faith as described here but many testimonies exist of believers facing adversity. See *Living with Pain*, by evangelist Dr Sam Gipp.

[30] Ephesians 2:1

[31] See *Never Leave Your Head Uncovered, A Canadian Nursing Sister in World War Two*, by Doris V. Carter, p 77, 133.

[32] Ibid., p 78 and Google search

[33] See *Canadians in Italy, 1944*, www.bbc.co.uk/dna/ww2/A2061938.

[34] See Purnell's *History of the Second World War*, Volume 4, p 1717.

[35] A contemporary expression. See *A Nurse's War*, Chapter 8.

[36] Sister Dale's action is based on an act of outstanding bravery by Sister Anne Roberts of 63rd BGH, North Africa. See *Quiet Heroines*, p 37-38.

Chapter 6

[37] 51st Highland Division attacked on the left of the 9th Australian at El Alamein.

[38] Based on recollections of the late Reverend Reuben Baird

[39] Australian wild dog

[40] See *Sound of Battle*, Chapters 11, 13.

[41] Now a 'trendy' suburb of Sydney, Balmain was a notably tough area pre-war.

[42] See *Quiet Heroines*, Chapter 15.

[43] As told by Mr John Morris, ex AIF, deceased.

[44] See *Jesuit Plots from Elizabethan to Modern Times*, by Albert Close, Chapter 3.

[45] BBC series *The Great War*, Episode 1

[46] Adapted from *Australians in Nine Wars*, by Peter Firkins, Chapters 33, 34, *1939-1945 Australia Goes to War*, by John Robertson, Chapter 17 and *Bravery Above Blunder*, by John Coates, Chapters 3-8.

[47] From *Recollections of a Regimental Medical Officer*, by H.D. Steward, Chapter 8

[48] Based on personal account by Mr Jim Grant, ex AIF. Not to be confused with character of same name in *Sound of Battle*

[49] Motto of 2/17th Battalion, AIF, victors of Jivenaneng

[50] See *Grey Touched with Scarlet*, by Jean Bowden, Chapter 2 and *Nurses at War*, Chapter 7.

[51] 2 Peter 2:12

[52] John 1:9

[53] Based on an account by a British paratrooper of a similar experience

[54] "Very soon."

[55] "Who's there?"

[56] "Hands up!"

[57] "For France, my brave man. Let's go."

[58] A dangerous practice. The concentration required for rapid anaesthesia could prove fatal. By the grace of God, Madeleine survived. Her assailant grasped her firmly to restrain the jerky, involuntary movement that precedes loss of consciousness.

[59] No OSS operative was ever a double agent, although the Germans did penetrate some Resistance groups.

[60] "Murderer!"

[61] See *The Women who Lived for Danger*, by Marcus Binney, Chapter 3.

[62] See *Sound of Battle*, Chapter 4.

[63] Based on the massacre at Oradour-sur-Glane by the 2nd 'Das Reich' SS Panzer Division, June 10th 1944. See www.edenbridgetown.com/in_the_past/soe_story/massacre.shtml.

[64] Major-General Sir P.C.S. Hobart, KBE, CB, DSO, MC, 1885-1957

[65] 79th Armoured's insignia was the face of a bull with red-tipped horns. Sally's broadcast to the 79th is fictional.

[66] Lieutenant Graham's experiences in this and later chapters are based on:

1st Assault Brigade, RE, 1943-45

Churchill's Secret Weapons, by Patrick Delaforce

79th Armoured Division, Hobo's Funnies, by Nigel Duncan

Battle of the Reichswald, by Peter Elstob

Vanguard of Victory, The 79th Armoured Division, by David Fletcher

Mailed Fist, by John Foley

Caen, Anvil of Victory, by Alexander McKee

The History of the Corps of Royal Engineers, Volume 9

Purnell's *History of the Second World War,* Volume 5, p 1879ff

The Longest Day, by Cornelius Ryan

A British Soldier Remembers, by Ronald A Tee and Ken C Dowsett

Fighting in the Forest – Royal Tank Regiment History, www.9thrtr.com/TT/9THBAT11.htm

The Struggle for Europe, by Chester Wilmot

Flamethrower, by Andrew Wilson

The Only Way Out, by R.M. Wingfield

Lion Rampant, by Robert Woollcombe and other personal accounts, such as that by A.E. Younger, www.britannica.com/normandy/pri/Q00341.html.

[67] An AVRE squadron originally comprised 4 troops of 6 modified Churchills each. Delaforce indicates that the troops were designated zero, one, two, three, with each vehicle identified according to the wireless alphabet; Able, Baker, Charlie, Delta, Echo, Fox. Thus Graham's AVRE was Delta One. Other armoured units were organised similarly. I have assumed that each vehicle had an individual name, those in One Troop beginning with A, Two Troop, B, Three Troop C and those in Zero, or HQ Troop, beginning with H. In November 1944, the number of troops per squadron was reduced to three.

[68] See *The Struggle for Europe*, p 272.

[69] Pronounced "Avree."

[70] The Nuremberg raid of March 30th 1944 incurred some of the heaviest Allied losses of the war. Of 781 aircraft that set out, 96 were reported missing, of which 94 ultimately failed to return. See Purnell's *History of the Second World War,* Volume 4, p 1736.

Chapter 7

[71] See *Never Leave Your Head Uncovered*, p 109-111.

[72] See *In God's Name*, by David Yallop, *The Road to Rome*.

[73] See *Where it all Began, Italy 1954* by Ann Cornelisen, Chapter 10.

[74] Pius XII held many audiences with Allied service personnel during WW2.

[75] See *In God's Name*, ibid.

[76] Bermondsey, a London suburb on the south bank of the Thames, was heavily damaged by German bombing raids, 1940-41. These were known as 'the Blitz,' after *blitzkrieg*, or 'lightning war'. The Blitz would be common knowledge to the other girls, so they do not remark on it. Neither do they wish to evoke potentially painful memories for Mollie.

[77] Field-Marshall Kesselring, overall German commander in Italy

[78] Pronounced "coilies"

[79] Lieutenant Avis (n) Dagit, US Army Nurse Corps, had a similar experience at Anzio. See *A Half Acre of Hell*, Chapter 11.

[80] Based on *Front-Line Nurse*, by Eric Taylor, Chapter 12, *Combat Nurse*, by Eric Taylor, Chapter 14 and *The Function of a Field Hospital in the Chain of Evacuation in WWII*, by James K Sunshine

[81] From a recollection of Sister Dora Clements, www.spartacus.schoolnet.co.uk/2WWats.htm

[82] From *Never Leave Your Head Uncovered*, p 124

[83] The hospital where Sister Hewitt debussed

[84] Based on an incident in *Combat Nurse*, Chapter 14

[85] See *Nurses in Battledress*, by Gwladys M. Rees Aikens, p 132.

[86] Sister McGrath's attitude would seem alien today but not 60 years ago.

[87] See *Sound of Battle*, Chapters 14, 15.

Chapter 8

[88] English Baptist and pioneer missionary to India, 1761-1834

[89] The description of the Dalrymple's residence is based on an account entitled *Life in the Bungalows*, www.lib.lsu.edu/special/exhibits/india/chap3.htm.

[90] Field Marshall The Viscount Sir William Slim, K.G., G.C.B., G.C.M.G., G.C.V.O., G.B.E., D.S.O., M.C., 1891-1970, 14th Army Commander

[91] See Chapter 2.

[92] See *Another Brummie in Burma*, Chapter 6.

[93] *Mandalay*

[94] From *The Jungle Book*, by Rudyard Kipling

[95] Based on missionary accounts

[96] One Baptist minister with experience of the east has testified to the same sensation in recent decades during visitation of suburban American homes. He did not encounter it at the start of his ministry in the 1950s.

[97] See *Unexplained*, by Jerome Clark, *Reptile Men*, p 327.

[98] See *The Traitor*, by Jack Chick.

[99] Psalm 127:1. On December 3rd 1967, a UFO occupant asked essentially the same question of abductee Herb Schirmer, Nebraska patrolman.

[100] So did Judas Iscariot, John 6:70, 71

[101] Royal Navy frogmen patrolled the Irrawaddy River prior to 14th Army's crossing early in 1945. See *The Little Men*, by K.W. Cooper, Chapter 10.

[102] Nursing experiences in Burma in this and later chapters are based on accounts from:

A Detail on the Burma Front, by Winifred Beaumont

A Doctor in XIVth Army, by Charles Evans, Chapter 6

Another Brummie in Burma, Chapter 6

Defeat Into Victory, by Field Marshall the Viscount Slim, Books 4-6

Fighting Nature, Insects, Disease and Japanese, The Chindit War in Burma, by Manbahadur Rai, stickgrappler.tripod.com/bando/c26.html

Front-Line Nurse, Chapter 14

Ivy's Story, www.burmastar.org.uk/ivypric.htm

Purnell'*s History of the Second World War*, Volume 4, p 1632ff, Volume 6, p 2362ff

The Marauders, by Charlton Ogburn

Wartime Memories of a Nurse, by Kitty Calcutt, www.bbc.co.uk/dna/ww2/A1307026

[103] See Chapter 2.

[104] Tiddim fell to the 14th Army on October 17th 1944.

[105] See *Defeat Into Victory*, Book IV, Chapter 16.

[106] See Chapter 2 for Lance-Corporal Wood's timely contravention of this stricture.

Chapter 9

[107] Based on incidents described in *Caen, Anvil of Victory*, Chapter 6

[108] See *The Sharp End of War*, Chapter 7, by John Ellis.

[109] See *Caen, Anvil of Victory*, Chapter 4.

[110] The 12th SS Panzer Division, a crack unit raised from the Hitler Youth, or *Jugend*. See *Caen, Anvil of Victory*.

[111] From December 1943 until the end of the war, 48,000 Bevin Boys were directed to work in the coalmines. Bevin Boys represented 10% of male conscripts aged between 18 and 25 during the Second World War and were chosen by ballot to serve in the mining industry rather than in the armed services. They were named after the Rt Hon Ernest Bevin, the wartime Minister of Labour.

[112] See *Waffen SS*, by Martin Windrow and Michael Roffe. The 13th and 21st Waffen SS Divisions were recruited from Bosnian, Kossovan and Albanian Muslims. The units were noted for extraordinarily high rates of desertion and according to the reference, "*extreme nervousness in the face of determined opposition, accompanied by sickening cruelty to civilians.*"

[113] See *Middle East Diary 1917-1956*, by Colonel Richard Meinertzhagen, Chapter 5.

[114] See Chapter 5.

[115] A key hilltop. See *The Price of Glory, Verdun 1916*, by Alistair Horne, Chapter 14.

[116] See Delaforce, Chapter 9.

[117] Go awry. From *To a Mouse*, by Robert Burns.

[118] Japanese secret police

[119] See *Behind Japanese Lines, with the OSS in Burma*, Chapter 1, by Richard Dunlop. Much of this section has also been based on references given in Chapter 8. See notes 14, 15.

[120] After the unit's commanding officer, Brigadier Frank. D. Merrill

[121] See *OSS Detachment 101 in Burma*, history.acusd.edu/gen/WW2Timeline/detachment101.html.

[122] Contraction of "Roman candled," term for parachute that does not open. See *The Moonlight War*, by Terence O'Brien, Chapter 3. About 5% of supply parachutes failed to open but the contents of their containers could of-

ten be salvaged. For economic reasons, supply parachutes were inferior to and therefore less reliable than the X Type that Allied paratroops used and was nearly 100% successful.

Chapter 10

[123] Highly venomous snake common in South East Asia. Most species are small but the banded krait grows up to 6 feet in length. See Chapter 19.

[124] See Chapter 5.

[125] From *The Jungle Book*, by Rudyard Kipling. See Chapter 8.

[126] See *Defeat Into Victory*, Chapter 9. 14th Army Commander, Field Marshall Slim, insisted that all his formations be 95% malaria free or he would sack the formation commander. This goal was certainly achieved in the later stages of the Burma campaign, when the events described in Chapter 10 would have taken place.

[127] Based on an actual incident, recounted by Heinz Schröter in *Stalingrad*

[128] Based on an actual incident, recounted by Oliver Moxon in *The Last Monsoon*

[129] Field Marshall The Viscount Sir William Slim, K.G., G.C.B., G.C.M.G., G.C.V.O., G.B.E., D.S.O., M.C., 1891-1970, 14th Army Commander

Chapter 11

[130] Luxury 5-Star hotel in Florence.

[131] Princess Mary's Royal Air Force Nursing Service, PMRAFNS

[132] 1 Peter 2:2

[133] John 5:24

[134] John 10:28

[135] See *Babylon Mystery Religion*, by Ralph Woodrow, Chapter 5.

[136] *Christian Voice*, January 2004, reports that ex-Royal Marine Commando, Tom Roberts, was the only British soldier in WW2 to shoot down an enemy aircraft with small-arms fire. Some liberty has therefore been taken with the narrative.

[137] Based on the exploits of a WW2 German-American soldier called *"The Mad Prussian."* See *Ruckman's Battlefield Notes*, p 121.

[138] Towards the end of WW2, Lady Edwina Mountbatten, wife of Lord Louis, was instrumental in persuading nursing Sisters to volunteer for duty in the Far East. See *Front Line Nurse*, Chapter 14.

[139] German aircraft raided Bologna as late as April 1945. See *A Half Acre of Hell*, Chapter 17.

[140] Cloudy

[141] Rommel defeated the 2nd US Corps at the battle of Kasserine Pass, Tunisia, January 1943.

[142] See *Quiet Heroines*, Chapter 16.

[143] The Consolidated B-24 Liberator had a range of 2,200 miles at 215 mph. The total distance from Aden to Calcutta via Karachi is approximately 2,100 miles, so Sister McGrath could have travelled it in 15 hours flying time.

[144] Japanese American. Over 30,000 served with the American army in WW2, many in Burma.

[145] See *The Road Past Mandalay*, by John Masters and *Anyone Here Been Raped and Speaks English? A Foreign Correspondent's Life Behind the Lines* by Edward Behr.

[146] See *Sound of Battle*, Chapter 19. To clarify, Colleen would write a subsequent congratulatory letter to Anne some weeks later, on learning that her fiancé was safe. Anne did not learn this until March 1945, after the Rhine Crossing.

Chapter 12

[147] Insights into this final phase of the Burma campaign have been drawn mainly from:

Burma Star Association, extracts from *Ball of Fire*, by Anthony Brett-James, Chapters 28-30, www.burmastar.org.uk

Defeat Into Victory, Chapters 17-22

Purnell's *History of the Second World War*, Volume 6, p 2362ff, 2526ff, 2577ff

Quartered Safe Out Here, by George MacDonald Fraser

The Little Men, by K.W. Cooper

[148] A generic Yorkshire expression that can mean unusual, irritating or, as here, highly esteemed, depending on the context

[149] Any informed reader will recognise that Lieutenant Calvert is serving with the 1st Battalion of the West Yorkshire Regiment that formed part of the 48th Brigade belonging to 17th Indian 'Black Cat' Division. The 1st West Yorks served with distinction throughout the Burma campaign and I trust that my author's impression will help to commemorate the unit's excellent fighting record and not give offence.

[150] Frontline soldiers concealed surreptitious fags beneath a cupped hand, resulting in the telltale stains. See *The Little Men*, Chapter 16.

[151] Almost 4,500 Australian officers volunteered for service with the 14th Army in response to an appeal from Lord Mountbatten to AIF General Blamey late in 1944 for experienced infantry officers to replenish losses. Such was the Australian sense of commitment that unit commanders were not permitted to refuse requests for transfer. See *White Over Green, the 2/4th Infantry Battalion*, association publication.

[152] See *Quartered Safe Out Here* and *Defeat Into Victory*, Chapter 19.

[153] The description of the airdrop, which I take to be fairly typical, has been gleaned from *Quartered Safe Out Here*. I'm guessing that more than one battalion tried it on, as the saying goes.

[154] Matthew 4:4

[155] The original Shemp Howard was one of The Three Stooges, a well-known American comedy trio from the 1930s to the 1960s.

[156] 5th Indian Division. Its emblem was a red ball, provoking a ribald alternative designation from sister units – all in the best traditions of genuine camaraderie, of course.

[157] Ezekiel 39:4

[158] The ill-fated Norway campaign, April-June 1940, ended with the evacuation of British and Allied troops from Harstad. They sustained nearly 2,500 casualties.

[159] A fighting patrol, as distinct from a purely reconnaissance patrol, although tiger patrols did reconnoitre

[160] 19th Indian Division

[161] Major-General D.T. 'Punch' Cowan

[162] Flayed out. See *Quartered Safe Out Here*, p 137.

[163] Field Marshall The Viscount Sir William Slim, K.G., G.C.B., G.C.M.G., G.C.V.O., G.B.E., D.S.O., M.C., 1891-1970. The conversation here is, of course, fictional but I believe typical of Slim's military acumen. I trust, therefore, that no offence is caused.

[164] See Chapter 6.

[165] Film starring Margaret Lockwood, released in 1945. Sister Gray is, typically, engaging in what today we would call a 'wind up'.

[166] See *Quartered Safe Out Here*, p 154ff. The Border Regiment was recruited mainly from the area of northwest England now called Cumbria.

[167] Borrowed from *The Little Men*, Chapter 16, a liberty that I trust causes no offence. I found the exhortation too evocative to pass up and I hope it serves a commemorative purpose.

[168] See *Sound of Battle*, Chapter 16.

[169] 1 Corinthians 12:26

[170] Jeremiah 10:13

Chapter 13

[171] German 88-mm anti-tank weapon

[172] "We'll help, yes?"

[173] "My name is Monique. I love you, English soldier."

[174] *Forces Françaises de l'Intérieur*. Part of the French Resistance

[175] *Le Régiment de la Chaudière*. A French-Canadian unit noted for toughness and exuberance

[176] Based on the assistance that M. Louis Bertin, FFI and Boulogne taxi driver, rendered to the Allies during the battle for the town

[177] A slang term for fire support

[178] Bailey Bridge with design weight-bearing load of 40 tons

[179] See *Sound of Battle*.

[180] Navigable channels through sea minefields

[181] An all-Dutch unit serving with the British-Canadian 21st Army Group (composed of 2nd British and 1st Canadian Armies)

[182] From *God's Smuggler*, from Brother Andrew

[183] Mr Keith Bennett, a friend of my late father's, took part in these mercy flights over Holland. Along with other members of his squadron, Keith received a vivid sketch of aircraft dropping supplies, from the grateful recipients.

[184] Count Dracula's creator was novelist Bram Stoker.

[185] The tins contained a tubular central heating element.

[186] Squadron Officer Leonard's role is based loosely on that of Vera Atkins, who investigated the fate of SOE agents who failed to return from missions. See *The Women Who Lived for Danger*, by Marcus Binney.

[187] See *The Vatican Against Europe*, by Edmund Paris, Part III, Chapter III.

[188] A voice can clearly be heard shouting, *"Three cheers for Chamberlain,"* on the newsreel footage of Prime Minister Chamberlain returning from signing the infamous Munich Agreement that betrayed Czechoslovakia. It is the voice of Cardinal Hinsley. See *The Great Silence Conspiracy*, by Andrew Sinclair.

Chapter 14

[189] Notably Hugh Seagrim, of strong Christian faith, who served behind Japanese lines with the Karens between 1942-44. In an effort to stop reprisals against the hill tribesmen, Seagrim voluntarily surrendered to the Japanese in March 1944. He was subsequently executed but not before commanding the respect of his captors who referred to him as *"Big Master."* See *Undercover* by Patrick Howarth, Chapter 9.

[190] The monsoon season in Burma of 1945 broke approximately 2 weeks early.

[191] SOE teams parachuted into occupied France were called Jedburghs, or 'Jeds'.

[192] Malignant tertiary malaria, often fatal

[193] 40 tons load

[194] This incident is loosely based on an experience recorded by Peter Steadman, MC, in his book *Platoon Commander*, Chapter 6.

Chapter 15

[195] Based on an incident that Major Foley related in *Mailed Fist*

[196] Anything

[197] Based on the recollections of Andrew Wilson, *Flame thrower*

[198] See *Sound of Battle*, Chapter 16.

[199] Numbskull

[200] An arc-shaped steel bridge segment, placed by a specially modified Churchill with a frontally mounted steel arm. The Jumbo had the advantage that the arrangement was more compact than the SBG.

[201] Is relinquished, in the context

[202] 50/60 ton maximum load

[203] Delaforce, Chapter 17

[204] Whorehouse

[205] Backside

[206] Based on an incident in *The Sharp End of War*, by John Ellis, Chapter 6

Chapter 16

[207] Genesis 32:10

[208] Proverbs 10:22

[209] Fehmarn Island is a tourist destination now. I don't know if it was in mid-1945 but I am sure Captain Graham and Section Officer Bramble would have found a suitable venue for their brief break together.

[210] Intelligence Section

[211] Captain

[212] See Chapter 6.

[213] Mythological heroine, famed as the fastest runner of antiquity

[214] Group numbers referred to the post-war process of gradual demobilisation. It appears that most surviving WW2 servicemen served approximately 6 years, on average and servicewomen approximately 3, although marriage and family prematurely terminated many tenures of service for WW2 female personnel.

[215] The county of Derbyshire is divided into what is known as the White Peak, a limestone plateau to the south intersected by picturesque river valleys and the Dark, or High Peak, wilder country to the north composed of dark-coloured gritstone. The reason why the name of the town that Kate mentions has been omitted from the narrative is given in Chapter 23.

Chapter 17

[216] I adapted Matron's briefing mainly from *Ivy's Story* – see Endnote 15, Chapter 8. Sister Pritchard mentions joining the 38th BGH in May or June, 1945. She describes it as purpose-built and well-equipped. However, Jean Bowden, in *Grey Touched with Scarlet*, Chapter 4, refers to the experience of Sister Catherine Fisher, who went to a hospital in Rangoon at about the same time and found that it needed considerable cleaning up before it was in a fit state for British patients. The discrepancy may be accounted for by a few weeks' time difference or the references may be to different hospitals, because Sister Fisher's hospital received wounded Japanese patients, though Sister Pritchard does not mention this. I have opted for a middle course.

[217] See *A Doctor in XIVth Army*, by Charles Evans, Chapter 13. Money was of little use in the circumstances.

[218] See *Sound of Battle*, Chapters 4, 10.

[219] See Chapter 12.

[220] See Chapter 11, Note 3.

[221] Town on the Irrawaddy, captured by 14th Army's 33rd Corps on April 19th 1945

[222] Based on a recollection of Mr P.M. Coburn, history lecturer University of New South Wales, 1960s-70s and ex-53rd Welsh Division

[223] Field Marshall The Viscount Sir William Slim, K.G., G.C.B., G.C.M.G., G.C.V.O., G.B.E., D.S.O

[224] Princess Mary's Royal Air Force Nursing Service, PMRAFNS

[225] In December 1943, the US liberty ship, *John Harvey*, loaded with mustard gas bombs, was blown up in Bari Harbour during an air raid. American and British hospitals in the area were swamped with casualties suffering from the gas. Despite an official cover-up that lasted 40 years, Sister Anne (n) Watt, of the 98th BGH, successfully campaigned for war pensions to be granted to the survivors, by writing directly to Prime Minister, now Lady Margaret Thatcher. See *Front-Line Nurse*, Chapter 7.

[226] See *Quartered Safe Out Here*, p 268ff.

[227] The British-based American comedy duo, Bebe Daniels and Ben Lyon were a smash hit on BBC Radio during the war.

[228] *It's That Man Again*, starring comedian Tommy Handley. Another BBC smash hit during the war

[229] The actual motto of 2/17th Battalion, AIF

[230] Dagon was the fish god of the Philistines, commemorated in the cleft-shaped mitre worn by senior Catholic and High Anglican clergy. Dagon fell dismembered before the ark of the Lord in 1 Samuel 5.

[231] See Chapter 11.

[232] 2 Corinthians 4:4

[233] Burmese patriotic leader. He collaborated with the Japanese but grew disillusioned and changed sides after the British victory. Befriended by Slim, he could have been a competent post-war leader but was assassinated.

[234] See *Babylon Mystery Religion*, by Ralph Woodrow, Chapter 5.

[235] Released in 1942, also starring Ingrid Bergman, famous for the singing of *La Marsellaise* and the song *As Time Goes By*

[236] "Let's march, let's march. Let impure blood water our furrows."

[237] After the battle of Pegu, 17th Indian Division moved northwards to intercept Japanese remnants streaming eastwards from the Pegu Yomas to cross the Sittang and Salween Rivers in an effort to reach their own forces in Thailand. Arthur Swinson, in Purnell's *History of the Second World War*, Volume 6, p 2605ff, states that of the 18,000 Japanese who attempted the breakout, barely 6,000 reached the east bank of the Sittang.

On the Allied side, many British ORs in the Black Cat Division resented being deprived of the opportunity to be the first major formation into Rangoon, given that the 17th was the longest serving division in 14th Army. See *Quartered Safe Out Here*, p 235ff.

[238] Ephesians 1:6

Chapter 18

[239] The notorious Thai-Burma Railway was built by Allied forced labour during WW2, at a cost of 96,000 lives, of whom 18,000 were Allied POWs. See *Prisoner on the Kwai* by Major Basil Peacock, Purnell's *History of the Second World War*, Volume 5, p 2068ff, *The Somme to Singapore*, by Dr Charles Huxtable and *The Thai-Burma Railway and Beyond*, www.bmw.ukf.net/3pagodas/TBRandON.htm.

[240] Based on *Quiet Heroines*, by Brenda (n) McBryde, Chapter 24

[241] The battle of the Muar River, 100 miles north west of Singapore, was fought on January 16-19th 1942. It was an Australian victory, for which Lieutenant Colonel C.G.W. Anderson, CO of the Australian 2/19th Battalion was awarded the Victoria Cross.

[242] Major battle of the Somme campaign, July 1916

[243] Major-General H. Gordon Bennett. WW1 veteran of Gallipoli and the Western Front, Bennett was one of Australia's finest WW2 soldiers. With 2 of his staff officers, he escaped to Australia after the fall of Singapore in the hope that his experience would be used in later campaigns. Unfortunately, he was spurned by the high command and resigned from the army in 1944. Nevertheless, surviving veterans of the 8th Division never lost faith in their erstwhile commander.

[244] Besides the aforementioned references, the anecdotes of Sergeant Manning and the other POWs are drawn from *Australians in Nine Wars*, by Peter Firkins, Chapter 25, *Grim Glory* by Gilbert Mant and the recollections of my late Uncle, George Allan Horsburgh, who served with the 2/27th Brigade HQ, 8th Division AIF. He was a

POW in Malaya for 3 years and worked on the Burma Railway. Uncle Allan passed away in April 2004, aged 85.

[245] Situated at the mouth of the Salween, south of Rangoon

[246] Lieutenant-Colonel F.G. 'Black Jack' Gallaghan, DSO, WW1 veteran and intrepid CO of the 2/30th Battalion, AIF. His command inflicted a humiliating defeat on the Japanese near the town of Gemas, not far from the Muar River, on January 14th 1942.

[247] His Majesty's Australian Ship, the light cruiser *Perth*, was lost in the battle of the Sunda Strait, March 1st 1942, along with the American cruiser, USS *Houston*. Most of *Perth's* crew went down with her. Those that survived were taken prisoner.

[248] As reported by my late uncle

[249] One large timber bridge built to span the Mekhong River near Kanchanaburi served as the basis for the novel *The Bridge over the River Kwai* by Pierre Boule. It became unstable and was replaced by a second bridge constructed of iron and concrete, later bombed by the Allies.

[250] In my late uncle's case, 15 months

[251] My late mother was such an expert.

[252] See *Miracle on the Kwai*, by Ernest Gordon.

[253] See Chapter 5.

[254] Fruit growing area in southern New South Wales

[255] The late Queen Mother, Elizabeth (n) Bowes-Lyon, consort to His late Majesty, King George VI

[256] See *Shell Shock, The Psychological Impact of War*, by Wendy Holden, Chapter 6.

Chapter 19

[257] See *The Jungle Book*, by Rudyard Kipling.

[258] Indonesia

[259] See *The Traitor*, Chick Publications, www.chick.com/reading/tracts/0070/0070_01.asp.

[260] See Ephesians 6:12 and Revelation 17:2-6.

[261] Job 1:10

[262] Sir Redvers is a fictional character, though the king's representative was in residence in Government House in Rangoon by September 1945.

[263] See Chapter 9.

[264] See *Defeat Into Victory*, Chapter 22.

Chapter 20

[265] The Alexandra Hospital was a military hospital in Singapore pre-war. In 1945, the occupying forces found the hospital in complete disrepair but had it functioning in a couple of days, using Japanese POWs as impressed labour. See *Quiet Heroines*, Chapter 24.

Before the fall of Singapore, the Japanese massacred 200 patients and staff. See www.scholars.nus.edu.sg/landow/post/singapore/history/hospital/ah5.html.

[266] Conditions in Singapore and the related experiences of the Japanese occupation have been drawn from *From the Somme to Singapore*, by Charles Huxtable, *Grey Touched With Scarlet*, by Jean Bowden, *Quiet Heroines*, by Brenda (n) McBryde, *Queen Alexandra's Royal Army Nursing Corps*, by Juliet Piggott, *Nurses at War* by Penny Sarns, *Alexandra Hospital*, www.fepow-community.org.uk/monthly_Revue/html/alexandra_hospital.htm, www.alexhosp.com.sg/about_us/history.asp, *Raffles Hotel*, en.wikipedia.org/wiki/Raffles_Hotel, itclub.vs.moe.edu.sg/cyberfair2003/landmarks/raffleshotel.html.

[267] Sister Tyndall's reminiscences are based on those of the late Dame Margot Turner, DBE, RRC, Royal Red Cross medal and Sister Mary (n) Currie, RRC. Dame Margot became Matron-in-Chief of Queen Alexandra's Royal Army Nursing Corps after the war.

[268] St Thomas's Hospital, London

[269] The Allied commander in Singapore

[270] Based on an incident described in *Behind Japanese Lines*, by Richard Dunlop, p 221

[271] In reality, Sister Beatrice Le Blanc Smith, QAIMNS

[272] Now Mentok

[273] Hollywood actress, Betty Grable, 1917-1973, was the favourite US Forces' pin-up of WW2. Famed for her 'million dollar legs,' insured by 20th Century Fox.

[274] See Purnell's *History of the Second World War,* Volume 6, p 2649ff.

[275] As observed by Pedro Arrupe, SJ, who was a priest in Hiroshima, at the time. See *The Jesuits*, by Malachi Martin.

[276] Lord Balfour's edict of 1917, promising the Jews their national home in Israel. Successive senior ministers, notably the late Sir Winston Churchill, gradually whittled down the terms of the Declaration in order to appease the Arabs. See *Middle East Diary, 1917-1956*, by Colonel Richard Meinertzhagen.

[277] Sister Vivian (n) Bullwinkle 1915-2000, 2/13th Australian General Hospital. Her story may be found in www.angellpro.com.au/Bullwinkel.htm. Of 65 Australian Army Nursing Sisters sent to Singapore, only 24 survived.

Chapter 21

[278] Luke 4:13

[279] Wartime Australian slang for 'rare beauty,' in the context

[280] The main military barracks on Singapore, pre-war. Allied POWs like Sergeant Manning were incarcerated there before being sent to work on the Burma Railway. The barracks were restored to military use by the occupying forces in 1945.

[281] Luke 4:18

[282] See britains-smallwars.com/Aden/Happy-Valley.html.

[283] Player on the Cambridge University team, requiring a high standard of performance

[284] See *Sound of Battle*, Chapter 4.

[285] See Chapter 13.

[286] See *Vatican Assassins*, by Eric Jon Phelps.

287 See www.nationalarchives.gov.uk/releases/2003/may12/selectedagents.htm. Squadron Officer Vera Atkins, 1908-2000, accounted for the fates of all but one of the over 100 missing SOE agents.

288 See *Four Horsemen*, by Chick Publications.

289 Ephesians 6:12

290 Revelation 6:8

291 Squadron Officer Leonard's description of the ruthless conspiracy involving Von Hollstein and Montague-Stewart is drawn from several sources, including *Ravening Wolves*, by Monica Farrell, *Jesuit Plots from Elizabethan to Modern Times*, by Albert Close and *Vatican Assassins*, by Eric Jon Phelps. In Chapter 38 of his book, Mr Phelps makes reference to the *"Vatican Ratlines,"* a conspiratorial system that allowed thousands of Nazis to escape from post-war Europe.

292 Several crude jokes exist about men of the cloth and women of the stage. Sister (n) McGrath would probably have become aware of them during her unregenerate days.

293 See Matthew 16:22, 23.

294 See Acts 4:29, 31, 1 Corinthians 12:10.

Chapter 22

295 Matthew 6:34b

296 Trish and Colleen's flight home is drawn largely from the recollections of William A. Pugh, ex 358 Squadron, RAF, who described his repatriation to England in 1945 via BOAC Sunderland. See www.magweb.com/sample/ww2/wl027bp6.htm. The excursion to the Pyramids is based on Ivy Pritchard's account. See *Ivy's Story*, www.burmastar.org.uk/ivypric.htm.

297 Jews, a derogatory term

298 Ex-RAAF Sunderland pilot Ivan Southall states in his wartime narrative *They Shall Not Pass Unseen* that Poole was a notoriously difficult harbour for flying boat crews to navigate, with scarce facilities and that *"BOAC wouldn't have it at any price."* However, the corporation did use the harbour as a base soon after WW2 so considerable improvements must have been made in the latter part of the war.

299 See Zechariah 5, Revelation 13, *Mark of the Beast*, by Dr Peter S. Ruckman, Dr Ian Paisley's site, www.ianpaisley.org/article.asp?ArtKey=blessing and *Papal Blessing A Curse*, from Open Bible Publications, Belfast, www.1335.com/catalogue.html#catalogue.

300 See *Sound of Battle*, Chapter 12.

301 Sandwiches

302 A type of raisin cake and typically English dessert

303 Slang term for accountancy, Bill Harris's original occupation. See *Sound of Battle*, Chapter 1.

304 See *Sound of Battle*, Chapter 14.

305 As a married QA

306 Wealth

307 See 1 John 1:7.

[308] Sister (n) McGrath's experiences at Catterick are drawn in part from *Nurses in Battledress*, by Gwladys M. Rees Aikens.

[309] Based on accounts from Dr Peter S Ruckman's *Commentary on the Book of Job*, Chapter 6

[310] Based on Gwladys M. Rees Aikens's account

[311] The nearest large town to Catterick Camp, about ten miles distant

[312] 'Dear John' letters, in which a wife or sweetheart indicates to her husband or boyfriend she has met and fallen for another man. WW2 American servicemen originated the expression, popularised by the country singer Hank Williams, 1923-1953, who released a hit record of that title in 1951.

[313] Philippians 4:7a

[314] Luke 4:18

[315] Isaiah 30:21

Chapter 23

[316] Though a recognised forename, Rhiannon is also identified with the Nightmare Witch of Wales. See *Dancing with Demons*, by Jeff Godwin, Chick Publications, Chapter 3.

[317] During the 1960s, a businessman in New Zealand told me of this practice.

[318] Sense, also know-how

[319] Bribes or similar favours

[320] A type of construction common in the south of England, where the walls of a house appear as white squares with wooden borders painted black

[321] Accommodation

[322] A play on Miss Heythorpe's initials. HRH stands for His, or Her, Royal Highness.

[323] This incident and similar events described in this chapter are based on the true-life experiences of Rebecca Yoder-Brown, MD, a Christian doctor who ministers to victims of Satanism. See *He Came to Set the Captives Free*, Chapter 16. She describes how the werebeast she encountered had the power to stop her car engine, as in the case of the unfortunate Wilfred Houghton. Dr Yoder-Brown has her detractors, www.pfo.org/curse-th.htm, but continues her deliverance ministry together with her husband, Rev Daniel Yoder, www.harvestwarriors.com/about.htm. Well-known Christian author Josh McDowell confirms the existence of werebeasts, known as lycanthropes, in his book *Understanding the Occult*, Chapter 13. British Christian writers, Rev David Gardner, *The Trumpet Sounds for Britain*, Volume 1, Chapter 11 and Doreen Irvine, *From Witchcraft to Christ*, confirm that satanism and witchcraft are well established in this country. Doreen Irvine reveals that during the 1940s and 50s, many professional individuals, including nurses, attended satanic churches. I have no doubt that these abominations were used extensively in the last 60 years to erode the deliverance wrought by the WW2 generation.

[324] James 4:7

[325] Salisbury Plain. Doreen Irvine states that witchcraft is especially strong in the West Country.

[326] Some readers may be surprised at the involvement of Father St John Montague-Stewart, SJ, in Von Hollstein's scheme. However, as ex-Jesuit the late Dr Alberto Rivera stated, *"No group of men ever went more deeply into the occult than the Jesuits."* See *The Force*, by Chick Publications.

[327] English

[328] Female SOE operatives were trained as FANYs.

Chapter 24

[329] Large drawing board mounted on a stand with mechanical arm attached, on which a graduated T Square could be mounted. Since the 1980s, drawing machines have largely been replaced by computer draughting, with purpose built printers.

[330] Sister (n) McGrath's experiences at Deepvale are based mainly on *Combat Nurse*, by Eric Taylor, Chapter 10 and *Shell Shock*, by Wendy Holden, Chapter 6.

[331] See *Shell Shock*, p 122. Sodium pentathol was used extensively as an anti-depressant for psychiatric cases in WW2.

[332] Cigarette brand name and its motto

[333] Based on an incident in Normandy in July 1944 that Max Hastings describes in *Overlord*, Chapter 8

[334] Area between Birmingham and Wolverhampton, where coal and iron-based industries once flourished

[335] See *Combat Nurse*, Chapter 10.

[336] Proverbs 21:31

[337] Fellow

[338] Ephesians 3:20

[339] Ordinance Survey

[340] Isaiah 41:10

[341] Based on *Spellbound?* by Chick Publications

[342] All so-called hauntings are demonic and the Church of England even has an exorcism procedure for them. Mark 5:1-20 shows how demonic spirits are drawn to places of death – and the Lord's power of deliverance in such circumstances.

[343] Proverbs 16:18

[344] Jaguar, Britain's leading sports car. The first models appeared in 1932.

[345] Days, dates and phases of the moon according to month and year are all available on the web. See www.travelfurther.net/dates/datesrus.asp, home.hiwaay.net/~krcool/Astro/moon/fullmoon.htm.

[346] Children's card game, with matching suites. When two identical cards are dealt in succession, the first player to declare *"Snap!"* wins the hand. Robyn's humorous analogy is typical.

[347] 12th century Bible-believing French Christians. Persecutions instigated by Pope Innocent III almost wiped them out.

[348] See *Sound of Battle*, Chapter 19.

[349] Adam Weishaupt (1748-1830), professor of Canon law at the Jesuit University of Ingolstadt and founder of the Masonic 5th column order called the Iluminati, which derived from Ignatius Loyola's *Alumbrados*, or 'Enlightened Ones.' See *How Satan Turned America Against God*, by Dr Bill Grady, Chapter 9, *The Godfathers* and *The Force*, by Chick Publications.

[350] Guy Fawkes, of the Gunpowder Plot, November 5th 1605

[351] In 1859, Cardinal Manning (no relation to Sergeant Manning) wrote: *"I shall not say too much, if I say that we have to SUBJUGATE and SUBDUE, to CONQUER and RULE, an imperial race. Were heresy conquered in England, it would be conquered throughout the world. All its lines meet here, and therefore in England the Church of God must be gathered in its strength."* Rome will use any means to achieve her goals, including global war and the occult. Again, see *The Godfathers* and *The Force*, by Chick Publications.

[352] Proverbs 10:22

[353] The first major engagement for the British Army in WW1. The battle took place in August 1914.

[354] Isaiah 45:14

[355] Psalm 39:12

[356] The scriptures in support of Rev Calder's deductions are Mark 5, Ezekiel 28, Revelation 13, 2 Corinthians 11 and Luke 4.

[357] Senior NCO in the US military

[358] See *Satan and Swastika, The Occult and the Nazi Party*, by Francis King.

[359] 2 Corinthians 11:14

[360] June 14th 1946 was a full moon. See home.hiwaay.net/~krcool/Astro/moon/fullmoon.htm. The same source indicates a full moon at or near the summer solstice in 1948.

[361] *He hath shewed strength with his arm*, Luke 1:51.

[362] A conniving crook in David Copperfield, by Charles Dickens. Heep pretended to be 'umble, as part of his duplicity.

[363] See relevant endnote in Chapter 6. That the abduction was accomplished so efficiently indicates that the practitioners were highly skilled in the art. Time unconscious is said to be several minutes, www.ctrl-c.liu.se/~ingvar/methods/poison.html, long enough for the abductors to make their get away.

[364] See *Sound of Battle*, Chapter 4, 10.

[365] Crude female expression meaning, "You annoyed me."

[366] The macabre scene here is based on reported events. Rebecca Yoder-Brown describes a 20th century human sacrifice in *He Came to Set the Captives Free*, Chapter 8. It is estimated that 30,000 children disappear without trace each year in the USA, for occult purposes. See *Black is Beautiful*, by Dr Peter S. Ruckman, Chapter 10. The Maranatha Community's booklet *What on Earth are We Doing to Our Children?* states that nearly 100,000 young people go missing each year in Britain. While most are runaways, I believe many nevertheless become victims of satanic rituals.

[367] See *The Broken Cross*, by Chick Publications.

[368] Romans 16:20

[369] 1 Corinthians 15:57

Chapter 25

[370] The first post war England versus Australia test cricket series began in November 1946, in Australia, www.cricinfo.com/link_to_database/ARCHIVE/1940S/1946-47/ENG_IN_AUS/. An England versus India series was played in England in July-August 1946, www.cricinfo.com/link_to_database/ARCHIVE/1940S/1946/IND_IN_ENG/.

[371] Proverbs 13:15

[372] Proverbs 6:23

[373] Time-honoured Yorkshire saying meaning, "Never do anything for nothing."

[374] For deeper insight into Fr Alonzo's concerns, see the *Alberto* series, by Chick Publications.

[375] See *Britain in Sin*, available from *Christian Voice*, www.christianvoice.org.uk/resources.html.

[376] See Chapter 22 and Chapter 17, Endnote 10.

[377] See *The Truth About Rock Music*, by Dr Hugh Pyle.

[378] A number of medal winners sent their awards back in protest after the Beatles were given MBEs, www.napierchronicles.co.uk/1965.htm. See also *The Marxist Minstrels*, by David A. Noebel, Chapter 18. Noebel mentions Lieutenant Colonel Wagg, who sent back all 12 of his medals, won on active service in Afghanistan, WW1 and WW2.

[379] Allusion to the familiar symbol of the European Union, consisting of a circle of 12 yellow stars on a blue background

[380] Proverbs 25:28

[381] Ezekiel 7:24. See *The Last Days of Britain* by Lindsay Jenkins and *Overcrowded Britain* by Ashley Mote.

[382] See *Bosnian Muslims Volunteer En Masse Into Nazi SS*, www.srpska-mreza.com/library/facts/hanjar.html, *Slavery, Terrorism & Islam*, by Peter Hammond and *Fallen List*, www.drypool.net/cgi-bin/system.pl?id=nfflist for details of the hundreds of white Anglo-Saxons murdered by members of Ethnic minorities, many of whom are Muslims. Another site, www.bnp.org.uk/news_detail.php?newsId=534, highlights the plight of white girls in West Yorkshire systematically molested by Muslim adult males. The politics associated with the above sites are not the issue. The tragic and suffering victims are the issue.

[383] Arthur Scargill, President of the National Union of Miners, called his members out on strike in protest against proposed pit closures. He did so without a national ballot, thus making the strike illegal and enabling Prime Minister Margaret Thatcher to use extreme measures to crush the protest. When miners began in desperation to return to work before the official end of the strike, Yorkshire neighbourhoods noted for their strength of community spirit suffered rifts that have never healed.

[384] See *The Principality and Power of Europe*, by Adrian Hilton.

[385] See *Dancing with Demons*, by Jeff Godwin, Chapter 3.

[386] 1 Samuel 25:16a

[387] Offa's Dyke, an ancient rampart between England and Wales

[388] Charity established in 1915 for helping blind ex-servicemen and women. See www.st-dunstans.org.uk.

[389] Proverbs 27:17

[390] 1 Corinthians 3:16, 17

[391] 2 Timothy 4:7

Appendix

[392] See *He Came to Set the Captives Free*, by Rebecca Yoder-Brown, Chapter 14.

[393] The keys would be in the ignition. If not, someone of Albrecht's expertise would have no problem starting a vehicle of that make and model. The plotters would reasonably assume that Briggs would switch the engine off once it inexplicably stalled, in order not to drain the battery.

Printed in the United Kingdom
by Lightning Source UK Ltd.
111594UKS00002BA/3-4